The Maker of Universes

When Robert Wolff found a strange horn in an e͏͏͏͏͏͏͏͏͏͏ to a different universe. To blow that horn would space-time and permit entry to a cosmos whose ͏ not those known by our starry galaxy.

For that other universe was a place of tiers, world upon world piled upon each other like the landings of a sky-piercing mountain. The one to blow that horn would ascend those steps, from creation to creation, until he would come face to face with its architect. But what if that maker of universes was a madman? Or an imposter? Or a super-criminal hiding from the wrath of his own superiors ...?

To Your Scattered Bodies Go

All those who ever lived on Earth have found themselves resurrected – healthy, young, and naked as newborns – on the grassy banks of a mighty river, in a world unknown. Miraculously provided with food, but with no clues to the meaning of their strange new afterlife, billions of people from every period of Earth's history – and prehistory – must start again.

Sir Richard Francis Burton would be the first to glimpse the incredible way-station, a link between worlds. This forbidden sight would spur the renowned 19th-century explorer to uncover the truth. Along with a remarkable group of compatriots, including Alice Liddell Hargreaves (the Victorian girl who was the inspiration for *Alice in Wonderland*), an English-speaking Neanderthal, a WWII Holocaust survivor, and a wise extraterrestrial, Burton sets sail on the magnificent river. His mission: to confront humankind's mysterious bene-factors, and learn the true purpose – innocent or evil – of the Riverworld ...

Winner of the Hugo Award for best novel, 1972.

The Unreasoning Mask

It is known as the alaraf drive: instantaneous travel between two points of space. Three of special ships have been built using this technology to explore and make contact with the many sentient races inhabiting the universe.

Captain Hûd Ramstan launches his ship, *al-Buraq*, on a mind-tearing space odyssey with a planet's god in his cabin – and a planet-destroyer on the loose ...

What exactly is the vast, superpowerful, worldburning *bolg*? Can it be taken out or is it unstoppable? And who precisely is the green-cloaked mystery glimpsed by Ramstan? Can it be al-Kindhr, the Green One, mentioned in *Surat* 18 of the Qu'ran? Or is it someone older, wiser and more deadly?

Ramstan, a thoughtful and moral man, becomes a fascinated yet reluctant pawn in the hands of the strange forces which arise to fight the deadly destroyer. Ultimately, he is the one man who, in a fearful race against time, can stop the destruction. But what price must he pay for becoming the saviour of intelligent-kind?

Also by Philip José Farmer

World of Tiers
The Maker of Universes (1965)
The Gates of Creation (1966)
A Private Cosmos (1968)
Behind the Walls of Terra (1970)
The Lavalite World (1977)
Red Orc's Rage (1991)
More Than Fire (1993)

Riverworld
To Your Scattered
 Bodies Go (1971)
The Fabulous Riverboat (1971)
The Dark Design (1977)
The Magic Labyrinth (1980)
Gods of Riverworld (1983)

Herald Childe
Image of the Beast (1968)
Blown: or Sketches Among the
 Ruins of My Mind (1969)
Traitor to the Living (1973)

*Dayworld**
Dayworld (1985)*
Dayworld Rebel (1987)*
Dayworld Breakup (1990)*

*Khokarsa**
Time's Last Gift (1972)*
Hadon of Ancient
 Opar (1974)*
Flight to Opar (1976)*

*Lord Grandrith & Doc Caliban**
A Feast Unknown (1968)*
Lord of the Trees (1970)*
The Mad Goblin (1970)*

Fictional biographies
Tarzan Alive: A Definitive Biography
 of Lord Greystoke (1972)
Doc Savage: His Apocalyptic Life
 (1973)

Other novels
The Green Odyssey (1957)
Flesh (1960) (expanded 1967)*
A Woman a Day (also as The Day of
 Timestop; 1960) (expanded from
 1953 novella, 'Moth and Rust')
The Lovers (1961) (expanded from the
 1952 novella) (revised 1977)
Cache from Outer Space (1962)
Inside Outside (1964)*
Tongues of the Moon (1964)
 (expanded from the 1961 novella)
Dare (1965)
The Gate of Time (1966), revised and
 expanded as Two Hawks from
 Earth (1979)
Night of Light (1966)
Lord Tyger (1970)*
Love Song (1970)
The Stone God Awakens (1970)*
The Wind Whales of Ishmael (1971)*
The Other Log of Phileas Fogg (1973)*
Venus on the Half-Shell (1975)
 (writing as Kilgore Trout)*
Ironcastle (1976) (translation/
 expansion of work by J.-H. Rosny)
Jesus on Mars (1979)*
Dark Is the Sun (1979)
The Unreasoning Mask (1981)
Stations of the Nightmare (1982)
Greatheart Silver (1982)
A Barnstormer in Oz (1982)*
Escape From Loki (1991)

* Not available as SF Gateway eBooks

Philip José Farmer
SF GATEWAY OMNIBUS

THE MAKER OF UNIVERSES
TO YOUR SCATTERED BODIES GO
THE UNREASONING MASK

GOLLANCZ
LONDON

This omnibus copyright © The Philip José Farmer Family Trust 2014
The Maker of Universes copyright © The Philip José Farmer Family Trust 1965
To Your Scattered Bodies Go copyright © The Philip José Farmer Family Trust 1971
The Unreasoning Mask copyright © The Philip José Farmer Family Trust 1981
Introduction copyright © SFE Ltd 2014

All rights reserved

The right of Philip José Farmer to be identified as the author of this work has been asserted by him in accordance with the Copyright, Designs and Patents Act 1988.

First published in Great Britain in 2014 by
Gollancz
An imprint of the Orion Publishing Group
Orion House, 5 Upper St Martin's Lane,
London WC2H 9EA

An Hachette UK Company

A CIP catalogue record for this book
is available from the British Library

ISBN 978 0 575 11958 1

1 3 5 7 9 10 8 6 4 2

Typeset by Jouve (UK), Milton Keynes

Printed and bound by CPI Group (UK) Ltd, Croydon CR0 4YY

The Orion Publishing Group's policy is to use papers that are natural, renewable and recyclable products and made from wood grown in sustainable forests. The logging and manufacturing processes are expected to conform to the environmental regulations of the country of origin.

www.orionbooks.co.uk
www.gollancz.co.uk

CONTENTS

Introduction from The
Encyclopedia of Science Fiction   ix

The Maker of Universes   1

To Your Scattered Bodies Go   141

The Unreasoning Mask   303

ENTER THE SF GATEWAY ...

Towards the end of 2011, in conjunction with the celebration of fifty years of coherent, continuous science fiction and fantasy publishing, Gollancz launched the SF Gateway.

Over a decade after launching the landmark SF Masterworks series, we realised that the realities of commercial publishing are such that even the Masterworks could only ever scratch the surface of an author's career. Vast troves of classic SF and fantasy were almost certainly destined never again to see print. Until very recently, this meant that anyone interested in reading any of those books would have been confined to scouring second-hand bookshops. The advent of digital publishing changed that paradigm for ever.

Embracing the future even as we honour the past, Gollancz launched the SF Gateway with a view to utilising the technology that now exists to make available, for the first time, the entire backlists of an incredibly wide range of classic and modern SF and fantasy authors. Our plan, at its simplest, was – and still is! – to use this technology to build on the success of the SF and Fantasy Masterworks series and to go even further.

The SF Gateway was designed to be the new home of classic science fiction and fantasy – the most comprehensive electronic library of classic SFF titles ever assembled. The programme has been extremely well received and we've been very happy with the results. So happy, in fact, that we've decided to complete the circle and return a selection of our titles to print, in these omnibus editions.

We hope you enjoy this selection. And we hope that you'll want to explore more of the classic SF and fantasy we have available. These are wonderful books you're holding in your hand, but you'll find much, much more ... through the SF Gateway.

www.sfgateway.com

INTRODUCTION
from The Encyclopedia of Science Fiction

Philip José Farmer (1918–2009) was a US writer whose active career extended over half a century, though he was a comparatively late starter as an author, and his first story, 'O'Brien and Obrenov' for *Adventure* in March 1946, was nonfantastic and promised little. A part-time student at Bradley University, he gained a BA in English in 1950, and two years later burst onto the SF scene with his novella *The Lovers* (1952 magazine; expanded 1961). Although originally rejected by John W. Campbell Jr of *Astounding Science Fiction* and (more surprisingly) by H. L. Gold of *Galaxy Science Fiction*, it gained instant acclaim when it did appear, and won Farmer a 1953 Hugo for Most Promising New Author. It concerned Xenobiology, Parasitism and Sex, an explosive mixture, certainly for the Genre SF of that era; transgressive mixtures of this sort would feature repeatedly in Farmer's best work. After publishing such excellent short stories as 'Sail On! Sail On!' (1952) and 'Mother' (1953), Farmer became a full-time writer. His second short novel, *A Woman a Day* (1953 magazine; rev 1960), was billed as a sequel to *The Lovers* but bore little relation to the earlier story. 'Rastignac the Devil' (1954) was a further sequel. Farmer then produced two novels, both of which were accepted for publication but neither of which actually saw print at the time, the first due to the folding of *Startling Stories* (it eventually appeared as *Dare* [1965]). The second, *I Owe for the Flesh*, won a contest held by Shasta Publishers and Pocket Books, but the prize money, which came from Pocket Books, was used by Shasta founder Melvin Korshak (1923–) to pay bills, which did not keep the firm from foundering; the manuscript was lost for decades, though its premise eventually formed the basis of the Riverworld series. This double disaster forced Farmer to abandon full-time authorship for a number of years; he did not become full-time again until 1969.

Nevertheless, he produced many interesting stories for the magazines during this period, such as the Father Carmody series, published in book form as *Night of Light* (1966) and as *Father to the Stars* (1981), featuring a murderous priest who becomes ambiguously involved in various theological puzzles on several planets. The best of the sequence is *Night of Light*, the nightmarish story of a world where figments of the unconscious become tangible. Other notable stories of this period include 'The God Business' (1954), 'The Alley Man' (1959) and 'Open to Me, My Sister' (1960). The last named is the best of Farmer's biological fantasies like *The Lovers*, it was repeatedly rejected as 'disgusting' before its acceptance by *The Magazine of Fantasy and Science Fiction*.

Farmer's first novel to actually gain book publication was *The Green Odyssey* (1957), in which an Earthman escapes from captivity in an alien planet; the intricately colourful medieval culture of this planet, the high libido of its women, the mysteries buried within the sands of the desert over which the hero must flee, and the admixture of rapture and disgust with which the hero treats the venue – all go to suggest that this novel, along with Jack Vance's *Big Planet* (1957), served as a bridge between the earlier flowering of the Planetary Romance in the hands of authors like Leigh Brackett and its 1960s efflorescence in the work of Roger Zelazny and, later, Gene Wolfe. It was the first of many entertainments Farmer wrote over the years, some of which share the narrative elation of this underrated tale. Later novels in a not dissimilar vein include *The Gate of Time* (1966), *The Stone God Awakens* (1970) and *The Wind Whales of Ishmael* (1971), the last-named being an SF sequel to Herman Melville's *Moby-Dick* (1851).

In the late 1960s, Essex House, publishers of pornography, commissioned Farmer to write three erotic fantasy novels, taking full advantage of the new freedoms of the time. *The Image of the Beast* (1968), the first of the Exorcism/Herald Childe trilogy, is an effective Parody of the private eye and Gothic horror genres. It was followed by a perfunctory sequel, *Blown, or Sketches Among the Ruins of my Mind* (1969); the third Exorcism volume, *Traitor to the Living* (1973), was not published by Essex House. *Flesh* (1960) is more ambitious: a dramatization of the ideas which Robert Graves put forward in *The White Goddess* (1948), it presents a matriarchal, orgiastic society of the future; rather heavy-handed in its humour, it was considered a 'shocking' novel on first publication. *Inside Outside* (1964), a novel about a scientifically sustained afterlife, also contains some extraordinary images and grotesque ideas which resonate in the mind, though the book suffers from a lack of resolution. The novella 'Riders of the Purple Wage' (1967) – later collected in *The Purple Book* (1982) and *Riders of the Purple Wage* (1992) – won Farmer a 1968 Hugo; written in a wild and punning style, it is one of his most original works. It concerns the tribulations of a young artist in a Utopian society, and has a more explicit sexual and scatological content than anything Farmer had written before. 'The Oögenesis of Bird City' (1970) is a related story.

The novels eventually assembled as *The World of Tiers* (1981) show Farmer in a lighter vein, though the architectural elaborateness of the universe in which they are set prefigures Riverworld. The original volumes are *The Maker of Universes* (1965) (see below), *The Gates of Creation* (1966), *A Private Cosmos* (1968), *Behind the Walls of Terra* (1970) and *The Lavalite World* (1977). A much later tale, *Red Orc's Rage* (1991), recursively dramatizes the use of the previous titles in the series as tools in role-playing therapy for disturbed adolescents. In a final addition to the primary sequence, *More Than Fire: A World of Tiers Novel* (1993), some of the cosmological puzzles are resolved, and the conflict between Kickaha and Red Orc takes on an increasingly Jungian air, with each being seen as the other's shadow.

An abiding concern (or game) that would occupy much of Farmer's later career was the tying together of his own fiction (and that of many other authors) into one vast, playful mythology, with some similarities to the evolving (but never explicit) World-as-Myth overstory Robert A. Heinlein used to structure his own later tales. Much of this is worked out in the loose conglomeration of works which has been termed the Wold Newton Family series, all united under the premise that a meteorite which landed near Wold Newton in eighteenth-century Yorkshire irradiated a number of pregnant women and thus gave rise to a family of mutant Supermen. The first books to be fitted into this sequence are *A Feast Unknown: Volume IX of the Memoirs of Lord Grandrith* (1969) the first volume of the Lord Grandrith/Doc Caliban series, followed by *Lord of the Trees* (1970) and *The Mad Goblin* (1970). *A Feast Unknown* is a brilliant exploration of the sado-masochistic fantasies latent in much heroic fiction, and succeeds as Satire, as SF, and as a tribute to the creations of Edgar Rice Burroughs and Lester Dent. A narrative *tour de force*, it concerns the struggle of Lord Grandrith (i.e. Tarzan) and Doc Caliban (i.e. Doc Savage) against the Nine, a secret society of immortals. Several other texts devoted to Tarzan – though excluding *Lord Tyger* (1970), which is about a millionaire's attempt to create his own ape-man and is possibly the best written of Farmer's novels – are central to Wold Newton, in particular *Tarzan Alive: A Definitive Biography of Lord Greystoke* (1972), which includes 'Extracts from the Memoirs of "Lord Greystoke"', a spoof biography in which Farmer uses the concept of the monomyth from *The Hero With a Thousand Faces* (1949) by Joseph Campbell (1904–87) to explore the nature of the Hero's appeal. The appendices and genealogy, which link Tarzan with many other heroes of popular fiction, are at once a satire on scholarship and a serious exercise in 'creative mythography'.

Tarzan appears again in *Time's Last Gift* (1972), a preliminary novel for a subseries in the Wold Newton universe about Ancient Africa, employing settings from Burroughs and H. Rider Haggard; *Hadon of Ancient Opar* (1974) and *Flight to Opar* (1976) continue the series. Other works which contain Wold Newton material include 'Tarzan Lives: An Exclusive Interview with Lord Greystoke' (1972), 'The Obscure Life and Hard Times of Kilgore Trout' (1971), *Doc Savage: His Apocalyptic Life* (1973), *The Other Log of Phileas Fogg* (1973), 'After King Kong Fell' (1973), *The Adventure of the Peerless Peer* (1974), *Ironcastle* (1976), a liberally rewritten version of J-H Rosny aîné's *L'étonnant voyage de Hareton Ironcastle* (1922), and *Doc Savage: Escape from Loki: Doc Savage's First Adventure* (1991). Other characters incorporated into the sequence include Sherlock Holmes, Jack the Ripper, James Bond and Kilgore Trout, a Kurt Vonnegut character under whose name Farmer also published *Venus on the Half-Shell* (1975). Vonnegut later regretted allowing the use of Kilgore Trout after it was generally assumed that he himself had written *Venus on the Half-Shell* under this pseudonym. As a whole, the series parlays its conventions of 'explanation' into something close to creative chaos.

Though the fractal Wold Newton set of sequences perhaps best express his playfully serious manipulations of popular material to express a sense of the Universe as chaotically fable-like, Farmer gained greatest popular acclaim with his Riverworld series, set on a planet where a godlike race has resurrected the whole of humanity along the banks of a multi-million-mile river, the background effect being that of a Planetary Romance set within a Pocket Universe. The series is made up of *To Your Scattered Bodies Go* (1971) (see below), *The Fabulous Riverboat* (1971), *The Dark Design* (1977), *Riverworld: the Great Short Fiction of Philip José Farmer* (coll 1979), *The Magic Labyrinth* (1980), *Riverworld War: The Suppressed Fiction of Philip José Farmer* (coll 1980), *Gods of Riverworld* (1983) and *River of Eternity* (1983), the last being a rediscovered rewrite of *I Owe for the Flesh*, lost since the 1950s. As surviving characters, many of them historical figures, begin to overdose on the freedoms (or powers) they have discovered in themselves, the plots of the later volumes become increasingly chaotic, perhaps deliberately, a tendency not reversed in two late anthologies of work by other authors set in the Riverworld universe: *Tales of Riverworld* (1992) and *Quest to Riverworld* (1993), both edited by Farmer.

After *The Unreasoning Mask* (1981) (see below), Farmer embarked on the Dayworld series, whose premise derives from 'The Sliced-Crosswise Only-on-Tuesday World' (1971): in a world plagued by Overpopulation, the whole of humanity is divided into seven cohorts, each spending one day of the week awake and the rest of the time in 'stoned' immobility. In *Dayworld* (1985), *Dayworld Rebel* (1987) and *Dayworld Breakup* (1990), this premise becomes increasingly peripheral in a tale whose complications invoke A. E. Van Vogt. Here, as in all his work, Farmer is governed by an instinct for extremity, sometimes impish, sometimes flat-footed, but in its most telling enactments arousingly transgressive. It is perhaps now a moot question whether or not Farmer would have been more successful in a world which simply appreciated his flings and intuitions, and which did not recoil at his the polymorphic mutability of his depictions of Sex, which he treated as a ground-bass in the arias of human behaviour.

As it now stands, an essentially amiable (though searching) writer spent much of his career enmeshed in what now (it is hoped) seem trivial censorship disputes and strife. Two large late retrospective collections – *The Best of Philip José Farmer* (2006), a definitive assembling of his best-known stories;

INTRODUCTION

and *Pearls from Peoria* (2006), taken from the large amount of material obscurely or never-previously published – should signal an overdue assessment of his stature in the field. In 2001 he received both the SFWA Grand Master Award and the World Fantasy Award for lifetime achievement.

Out of this exceedingly prolific career, three exceptional titles have been selected here, and should give some sense of the range and vitality that so vividly characterized Farmer's career over his long prime. The first of these is *The Maker of Universes* (1965), perhaps the most elegant of the World of Tiers sequence it introduces. This tale (like its sequels) unfolds within one of a series of quasi-independent Pocket Universes, playgrounds built by the masters – who are perhaps gods, originally humanoid – whose technology is unimaginable. Access to and transport within their closed universes is provided by Matter Transmission 'gates'. The protagonist and most notable character is a present-day Earthman named Paul Janus Finnegan (his initials, PJF, reveal this ironic observer to be a stand-in for the author); but within the World of Tiers he is primarily known as Kickaha, under which significantly Native American name he acts out the role of a trickster hero indulging in merry, if bloodthirsty, exploits. The surface of the tale is exuberant, full of rapid-fire action; under the surface, however, lurk some profound depths.

This sense of skimming an alluring but dangerous surface also characterizes the second tale chosen here, *To Your Scattered Bodies Go* (1971), which is the first of the Riverworld series of Planetary Romances set within a Pocket Universe, and like *The Maker of Universes* perhaps the shapeliest of all the succeeding books in the series. It won the 1972 Hugo Award. The setting is a planet where a godlike race has resurrected the whole of humanity along the banks of a multi-million-mile river, a bit like the Afterlife setting of the Houseboat on the Styx sequence by John Kendrick Bangs, though Farmer hugely intensifies the speculative intensity of the enterprise. Both Bangs and Farmer use a device derived from the literary tradition of the Dialogue of the Dead: the use of historical personages. Farmer introduces us to characters like Sir Richard Burton (1821–90), who dominates this first tale, Mark Twain and Jack London, all of whom explore the terrain and conduct an ongoing dialogue with one another in their search to understand, in any way possible, the astonishing new universe, and the gorgeous infinite river which links them together and carries them where they will. The premise is unending; the tale itself almost seems too short. We do not want to leave.

The final tale here presented, *The Unreasoning Mask* (1981), is a singleton, and perhaps the need to tell the whole story freed Farmer to tell almost certainly the tightest tale he ever published; certainly by 1981, deep into his career, he seemed capable of anything. In this case, he gives us a Space Opera, an odyssey conducted by an odd and ambivalently winning hero named

Ramstan, in possession of the stolen idol of a God, and compelled to search for whatever deity lies within. Ramstan's ship is capable of instantaneous travel. The revelation of the nature of the God he pursues and what ensues from that discovery must be read to be believed. All in all, as these three tales demonstrate, it is a privilege to have a chance to believe in the worlds of Philip José Farmer.

For a more detailed version of the above, see Philip José Farmer's author entry in *The Encyclopedia of Science Fiction*: http://sf-encyclopedia.com/entry/farmer_philip_jose

Some terms above are capitalised when they would not normally be so rendered; this indicates that the terms represent discrete entries in *The Encyclopedia of Science Fiction*.

THE MAKER OF UNIVERSES

1

The ghost of a trumpet call wailed from the other side of the doors. The seven notes were faint and far off, ectoplasmic issue of a phantom of silver, if sound could be the stuff from which shades are formed.

Robert Wolff knew that there could be no horn or man blowing upon it behind the sliding doors. A minute ago, he had looked inside the closet. Nothing except the cement floor, the white plasterboard walls, the clothes rod and hooks, a shelf and a lightbulb was there.

Yet he had heard the trumpet notes, feeble as if singing from the other wall of the world itself. He was alone, so that he had no one with whom to check the reality of what he knew could not be real. The room in which he stood entranced was an unlikely place in which to have such an experience. But he might not be an unlikely person to have it. Lately, weird dreams had been troubling his sleep. During the day, strange thoughts and flashes of images passed through his mind, fleeting but vivid and even startling. They were unwanted, unexpected, and unresistible.

He was worried. To be ready to retire and then to suffer a mental breakdown seemed unfair. However, it could happen to him as it had to others, so the thing to do was to be examined by a doctor. But he could not bring himself to act as reason demanded. He kept waiting, and he did not say anything to anybody, least of all to his wife.

Now he stood in the recreation room of a new house in the Hohokam Homes development and stared at the closet doors. If the horn bugled again, he would slide a door back and see for himself that nothing was there. Then, knowing that his own diseased mind was generating the notes, he would forget about buying this house. He would ignore his wife's hysterical protests, and he would see a medical doctor first and then a psychotherapist.

His wife called: 'Robert! Haven't you been down there long enough? Come up here. I want to talk to you and Mr Bresson!'

'Just a minute, dear,' he said.

She called again, so close this time that he turned around. Brenda Wolff stood at the top of the steps that led down to the recreation room. She was his age, sixty-six. What beauty she had once had was now buried under fat, under heavily rouged and powdered wrinkles, thick spectacles, and steel-blue hair. He winced on seeing her, as he winced every time he looked into the mirror and saw his own bald head, deep lines from nose to mouth, and stars of grooved skin radiating from the reddened eyes. Was this his trouble? Was he unable to adjust to that which came to all men, like it or not? Or was what he disliked in his wife and himself not the physical deterioration but the knowledge that neither he nor Brenda had realized their youthful dreams? There was no way to avoid the rasps and files of time on the flesh, but time had been gracious to him in allowing him to live this long. He could not plead short duration as an excuse for not shaping his psyche into beauty. The world could not be blamed for what he was. He and he alone was responsible; at least he was strong enough to face that. He did not reproach the universe or that part of it that was his wife. He did not scream, snarl, and whine as Brenda did.

There had been times when it would have been easy to whine or weep. How many men could remember nothing before the age of twenty? He thought it was twenty, for the Wolffs, who had adopted him, had said that he'd looked that age. He had been discovered wandering in the hills of Kentucky, near the Indiana border, by old man Wolff. He had not known who he was or how he had come there. Kentucky or even the United States of America had been meaningless to him, as had all the English tongue.

The Wolffs had taken him in and notified the sheriff. An investigation by the authorities had failed to identify him. At another time, his story might have attracted nationwide attention; however, the nation had been at war with the Kaiser and had had more important things to think about. Robert, named after the Wolff's dead son, had helped work on the farm. He had also gone to school, for he had lost all memory of his education.

Worse than his lack of formal knowledge had been his ignorance of how to behave. Time and again he had embarrassed or offended others. He had suffered from the scornful or sometimes savage reaction of the hill-folk, but had learned swiftly – and his willingness to work hard, plus his great strength in defending himself, had gained respect.

In an amazingly quick time, as if he had been relearning, he had studied and passed through grade and high school. Although he had lacked by many years the full time of attendance required, he had taken and passed the entrance examinations to the university with no trouble. There he'd begun his lifelong love affair with the classical languages. Most of all he loved Greek, for it struck a chord within him; he felt at home with it.

After getting his Ph.D at the University of Chicago, he had taught at various Eastern and Midwestern universities. He had married Brenda, a beautiful girl with a lovely soul. Or so he had thought at first. Later, he had been disillusioned, but still he was fairly happy.

Always, however, the mystery of his amnesia and his origin had troubled him. For a long time it had not disturbed him, but then, on retiring ...

'Robert,' Brenda said loudly, 'come up here right now! Mr Bresson is a busy man.'

'I'm certain that Mr Bresson has had plenty of clients who like to make a leisurely surveillance,' he replied mildly. 'Or perhaps you've made up your mind that you don't want the house?'

Brenda glared at him, then waddled indignantly off. He sighed because he knew that, later, she would accuse him of deliberately making her look foolish before the real estate agent.

He turned to the closet doors again. Did he dare open them? It was absurd to freeze there, like someone in shock or in a psychotic state of indecision. But he could not move, except to give a start as the bugle again vented the seven notes, crying from behind a thick barricade but stronger in volume.

His heart thudded like an inward fist against his breast bone. He forced himself to step up to the doors and to place his hand within the brass-covered indentation at waist-level and shove the door to one side. The little rumble of the rollers drowned out the horn as the door moved to one side.

The white plaster boards of the wall had disappeared. They had become an entrance to a scene he could not possibly have imagined, although it must have originated in his mind.

Sunlight flooded in through the opening, which was large enough for him to walk through if he stooped. Vegetation that looked something like trees – but no trees of Earth – blocked part of his view. Through the branches and fronds he could see a bright green sky. He lowered his eyes to take in the scene on the ground beneath the trees. Six or seven nightmare creatures were gathered at the base of a giant boulder. It was of red, quartz-impregnated rock and shaped roughly like a toadstool. Most of the things had their black, furry, misshapen bodies turned away from him, but one presented its profile against the green sky. Its head was brutal, subhuman, and its expression was malevolent. There were knobs on its body and on its face and head, clots of flesh which gave it a half-formed appearance, as if its Maker had forgotten to smooth it out. The two short legs were like a dog's hind legs. It was stretching its long arms up toward the young man who stood on the flat top of the boulder.

This man was clothed only in a buckskin breechcloth and moccasins. He was tall, muscular, and broad-shouldered; his skin was sun-browned; his long thick hair was a reddish bronze; his face was strong and craggy with a long upper lip. He held the instrument which must have made the notes Wolff had heard.

The man kicked one of the misshapen things back down from its hold on the boulder as it crawled up toward him. He lifted the silver horn to his lips to blow again, then saw Wolff standing beyond the opening. He grinned widely, flashing white teeth. He called, 'So you finally came!'

Wolff did not move or reply. He could only think, *Now I have gone crazy! Not just auditory hallucinations, but visual! What next? Should I run screaming,* or just calmly walk away and tell Brenda that I have to see a doctor now? Now! No waiting, no explanations. Shut up, Brenda, I'm going.

He stepped back. The opening was beginning to close, the white walls were reasserting their solidity. Or rather, he was beginning to get a fresh hold on reality.

'Here!' the youth on top of the boulder shouted. 'Catch!'

He threw the horn. Turning over and over, bouncing sunlight off the silver as the light fell through the leaves, it flew straight toward the opening. Just before the walls closed in on themselves, the horn passed through the opening and struck Wolff on his knees.

He exclaimed in pain, for there was nothing ectoplasmic about the sharp impact. Through the narrow opening he could see the red-haired man holding up one hand, his thumb and index forming an O. The youth grinned and cried out, 'Good luck! Hope I see you soon! I am Kickaha!'

Like an eye slowly closing in sleep, the opening in the wall contracted. The light dimmed, and the objects began to blur. But he could see well enough to get a final glimpse, and it was then that the girl stuck her head around the trunk of a tree.

She had unhumanly large eyes, as big in proportion to her face as those of a cat. Her lips were full and crimson, her skin golden-brown. The thick wavy hair hanging loose along the side of her face was tiger-striped: slightly zigzag bands of black almost touched the ground as she leaned around the tree.

Then the walls became white as the rolled-up eye of a corpse. All was as before except for the pain in his knees and the hardness of the horn lying against his ankle.

He picked it up and turned to look at it in the light from the recreation room. Although stunned, he no longer believed that he was insane. He had seen through into another universe and something from it had been delivered to him – why or how, he did not know.

The horn was a little less than two and a half feet long and weighed less than a quarter of a pound. It was shaped like an African buffalo's horn except at the mouth, where it flared out broadly. The tip was fitted with a mouthpiece of some soft golden material; the horn itself was of silver or silver-plated metal. There were no valves, but on turning it over he saw seven little buttons in a row. A half-inch inside the mouth was a web of silvery threads. When the horn was held at an angle to the light from the bulbs overhead, the web looked as if it went deep into the horn.

It was then the light also struck the body of the horn so that he saw what he had missed during his first examination: a hieroglyph was lightly inscribed halfway down the length. It looked like nothing he had seen before, and he was an expert on all types of alphabetic writing, ideographs, and pictographs.

'Robert!' his wife said.

'Be right up, dear!' He placed the horn in the right-hand front corner of the closet and closed the door. There was nothing else he could do except to run out of the house with the horn. If he appeared with it, he would be questioned by both his wife and Bresson. Since he had not come into the house with the horn, he could not claim it was his. Bresson would want to take the instrument into his custody, since it would have been discovered on the property of his agency.

Wolff was in an agony of uncertainty. How could he get the horn out of the house? What was to prevent Bresson from bringing around other clients, perhaps today, who would see the horn as soon as they opened the closet door? A client might call it to Bresson's attention.

He walked up the steps and into the large living room. Brenda was still glaring. Bresson, a chubby, spectacled man of about thirty-five, looked uncomfortable, although he was smiling.

'Well, how do you like it?' he asked.

'Great,' Wolff replied. 'It reminds me of the type of house we have back home.'

'I like it,' Bresson said. 'I'm from the Midwest myself. I can appreciate that you might not want to live in a ranchtype home. Not that I'm knocking them. I live in one myself.'

Wolff walked to the window and looked out. The midafternoon May sun shone brightly from the blue Arizona skies. The lawn was covered with the fresh Bermuda grass, planted three weeks before, new as the houses in this just-built development of Hohokam Homes.

'Almost all the houses are ground level,' Bresson was saying. 'Excavating in this hard caliche costs a great deal, but these houses aren't expensive. Not for what you get.'

Wolff thought, *If the caliche hadn't been dug away to make room for the recreation room, what would the man on the other side have seen when the opening appeared? Would he have seen only earth and thus been denied the chance to get rid of that horn? Undoubtedly.*

'You may have read why we had to delay opening this development,' Bresson said. 'While we were digging, we uncovered a former town of the Hohokam.'

'Hohokam?' Mrs Wolff said. 'Who were they?'

'Lots of people who come into Arizona have never heard of them,' Bresson replied. 'But you can't live long in the Phoenix area without running across references to them. They were the Indians who lived a long time ago in the Valley of the Sun; they may have come here at least 1200 years ago. They dug irrigation canals, built towns here, had a swinging civilization. But something happened to them, no one knows what. They just up and disappeared several hundred years ago. Some archeologists claim the Papago and Pima Indians are their descendants.'

Mrs Wolff sniffed and said, 'I've seen them. They don't look like they could build anything except those rundown adobe shacks on the reservation.'

Wolff turned and said, almost savagely, 'The modern Maya don't look as if they could ever have built their temples or invented the concept of zero, either. But they did.'

Brenda gasped. Mr Bresson smiled even more mechanically. 'Anyway, we had to suspend digging until the archeologists were through. Held up operations about three months, but we couldn't do a thing because the state tied our hands.

'However, this may be a lucky thing for you. If we hadn't been held up, these homes might all be sold now. So everything turns out for the best, eh?'

He smiled brightly and looked from one to the other.

Wolff paused, took a deep breath, knowing what was coming from Brenda, and said, 'We'll take it. We'll sign the papers right now.'

'Robert!' Mrs Wolff shrilled. 'You didn't even ask me!'

'I'm sorry, my dear, but I've made up my mind.'

'Well, I haven't!'

'Now, now, folks, no need to rush things,' Bresson said. His smile was desperate. 'Take your time, talk it over. Even if somebody should come along and buy this particular house – and it might happen before the day's over; they're selling like hot-cakes – well, there's plenty more just like this.'

'I want *this* house.'

'Robert, are you out of your mind?' Brenda wailed. 'I've never seen you act like this before.'

'I've given in to you on almost everything,' he said. 'I wanted you to be happy. So, now, give in to me on this. It's not much to ask. Besides, you said this morning that you wanted this type of house, and Hohokam Homes are the only ones like this that we can afford.

'Let's sign the preliminary papers now. I can make out a check as an earnest.'

'I won't sign, Robert.'

'Why don't you two go home and discuss this?' Bresson said. 'I'll be available when you've reached a decision.'

'Isn't my signature good enough?' Wolff replied.

Still holding his strained smile, Bresson said, 'I'm sorry, Mrs Wolff will have to sign, too.'

Brenda smiled triumphantly.

'Promise me you won't show it to anybody else,' Wolff said. 'Not until tomorrow, anyway. If you're afraid of losing a sale, I'll make out an earnest.'

'Oh, that won't be necessary.' Bresson started toward the door with a haste that betrayed his wish to get out of an embarrassing situation. 'I won't show it to anyone until I hear from you in the morning.'

On the way back to their rooms in the Sands Motel in Tempe, neither spoke. Brenda sat rigidly and stared straight ahead through the windshield. Wolff glanced over at her now and then, noting that her nose seemed to be getting sharper and her lips thinner; if she continued, she would look exactly like a fat parrot.

And when she finally did burst loose, talking, she would sound like a fat parrot. The same old tired yet energetic torrent of reproaches and threats would issue. She would upbraid him because of his neglect of her all these years, remind him for the latest in God-knew-how-many-times that he kept his nose buried in his books or else was practicing archery or fencing, or climbing mountains, sports she could not share with him because of her arthritis, She would unreel the years of unhappiness, or claimed unhappiness, and end by weeping violently and bitterly.

Why had he stuck with her? He did not know except that he had loved her very much when they were young and also because her accusations were not entirely untrue. Moreover, he found the thought of separation painful, even more painful than the thought of staying with her.

Yet he was entitled to reap the harvests of his labors as a professor of English and classical languages. Now that he had enough money and leisure time, he could pursue studies that his duties had denied him. With this Arizona home as a base, he could even travel. Or could he? Brenda would not refuse to go with him – in fact, she would insist on accompanying him. But she would be so bored that his own life would be miserable. He could not blame her for that, for she did not have the same interests as he. But should he give up the things that made life rich for him just to make her happy? Especially since she was not going to be happy anyway?

As he expected, her tongue became quite active after supper. He listened, tried to remonstrate quietly with her and point out her lack of logic and the injustice and baselessness of her recriminations. It was no use. She ended as always, weeping and threatening to leave him or to kill herself.

This time, he did not give in.

'I want that house, and I want to enjoy life as I've planned to,' he said firmly. 'That's that.'

He put on his coat and strode to the door. 'I'll be back later. Maybe.'

She screamed and threw an ashtray at him. He ducked; the tray bounced off the door, gouging out a piece of the wood. Fortunately, she did not follow him and make a scene outside, as she had on previous occasions.

It was night now, the moon was not yet up, and the only lights came from the windows of the motel, the lamps along the streets, and numerous headlights of the cars along Apache Boulevard. He drove his car out onto the boulevard and went east, then turned south. Within a few minutes he was on the road to the Hohokam Homes. The thought of what he meant to do made his heart beat fast and turned his skin cold. This was the first time in his life that he had seriously considered committing a criminal act.

The Hohokam Homes were ablaze with lights and noisy with music over a PA system and the voices of children playing out in the street while their parents looked at the houses.

He drove on, went through Mesa, turned around and came back through Tempe and down Van Buren and into the heart of Phoenix. He cut north, then east, until he was in the town of Scottsdale. Here he stopped off for an hour and a half at a small tavern. After the luxury of four shots of Vat 69, he quit. He wanted no more – rather, feared to take more, because he did not care to be fuddled when he began his project.

When he returned to Hohokam Homes, the lights were out and silence had returned to the desert. He parked his car behind the house in which he had been that afternoon. With his gloved right fist, he smashed the window which gave him access to the recreation room.

By the time he was within the room, he was panting and his heart beat as if he had run several blocks. Though frightened, he had to smile at himself. A man who lived much in his imagination, he had often conceived of himself as a burglar – not the ordinary kind, of course, but a Raffles. Now he knew that his respect for law was too much for him ever to become a great criminal or even a minor one. His conscience was hurting him because of this small act, one that he had thought he was fully justified in carrying out. Moreover, the idea of being caught almost made him give up the horn. After living a quiet, decent and respectable life, he would be ruined if he were to be detected. Was it worth it?

He decided it was. Should he retreat now, he would wonder the rest of his life what he had missed. The greatest of all adventures waited for him, one such as no other man had experienced. If he became a coward now, he might as well shoot himself, for he would not be able to endure the loss of the horn or the self-recriminations for his lack of courage.

It was so dark in the recreation room that he had to feel his way to the closet with his fingertips. Locating the sliding doors, he moved the left-hand one, which he had pushed aside that afternoon. He nudged it slowly to avoid noise, and he stopped to listen for sounds outside the house.

Once the door was fully opened, he retreated a few steps. He placed the mouthpiece of the horn to his lips and blew softly. The blast that issued from it startled him so much that he dropped it. Groping, he finally located it in the corner of the room.

The second time, he blew hard. There was another loud note, no louder than the first. Some device in the horn, perhaps the silvery web inside its mouth, regulated the decibel level. For several minutes he stood poised with the horn raised and almost to his mouth. He was trying to reconstruct in his mind the exact sequence of the seven notes he had heard. Obviously the seven little buttons on the underside determined the various harmonies. But he could not find out which was which without experimenting and drawing attention.

He shrugged and murmured, 'What the hell.'

Again he blew, but now he pressed the buttons, operating the one closest to him first. Seven loud notes soared forth. Their values were as he remembered them but not in the sequence he recalled.

As the final blast died out, a shout came from a distance. Wolff almost panicked. He swore, lifted the horn back to his lips, and pressed the buttons in an order which he hoped would reproduce the open sesame, the musical key, to the other world.

At the same time, a flashlight beam played across the broken window of the room, then passed by. Wolff blew again. The light returned to the window. More shouts arose. Desperate, Wolff tried different combinations of buttons. The third attempt seemed to be the duplicate of that which the youth on top of the toadstool-shaped boulder had produced.

The flashlight was thrust through the broken window. A deep voice growled, 'Come on out, you in there! Come out, or I'll start shooting!'

Simultaneously, a greenish light appeared on the wall, broke through, and melted a hole. Moonlight shone through. The trees and the boulder were visible only as silhouettes against a green-silver radiating from a great globe of which the rim alone was visible.

He did not delay. He might have hesitated if he had been unnoticed, but now he knew he had to run. The other world offered uncertainty and danger, but this one had a definite, inescapable ignominy and shame. Even as the watchman repeated his demands, Wolff left him and his world behind. He had to stoop and to step high to get through the shrinking hole. When he had turned around on the other side to get a final glimpse, he saw through an opening no larger than a ship's porthole. In a few seconds, it was gone.

2

Wolff sat down on the grass to rest until he quit breathing so hard. He thought of how ironic it would be if the excitement were to be too much for his sixty-six-year-old heart. Dead on arrival. DOA. They – whoever 'they' were – would have to bury him and put above his grave: the unknown earthman.

He felt better then. He even chuckled while rising to his feet. With some courage and confidence, he looked around. The air was comfortable enough, about seventy degrees, he estimated. It bore strange and very pleasant, almost fruity, perfumes. Bird calls – he hoped they were only those – came from all around him. Somewhere far off, a low growl sounded, but he was not frightened. He was certain, with no rational ground for certainty, that it was the distance-muted crash of surf. The moon was full and enormous, two and a half times as large as Earth's.

The sky had lost the bright green it had had during the day and had become, except for the moon's radiance, as black as the night-time sky of the world he had left. A multitude of large stars moved with a speed and in directions that made him dizzy with fright and confusion. One of the stars fell toward him, became bigger and bigger, brighter and brighter, until it swooped a few feet overhead. By the orange-yellow glow from its rear, he could see four great elliptoid wings and dangling skinny legs and, briefly, the silhouette of an antennaed head.

It was a firefly of some sort with a wingspread of at least ten feet.

Wolff watched the shifting and expanding and contracting of the living constellations until he became used to them. He wondered which direction to take, and the sound of the surf finally decided him. A shoreline would give a definite point of departure, wherever he went after that. His progress was slow and cautious, with frequent stops to listen and to examine the shadows.

Something with a deep chest grunted nearby. He flattened himself on the grass under the shadow of a thick bush and tried to breathe slowly. There was a rustling noise. A twig crackled. Wolff lifted his head high enough to look out into the moonlit clearing before him. A great bulk, erect, biped, dark, and hairy, shambled by only a few yards from him.

It stopped suddenly, and Wolff's heart skipped a beat. Its head moved back and forth, permitting Wolff to get a full view of a gorilloid profile. However, it was not a gorilla – not a Terrestrial one, anyway. Its fur was not a solid black. Alternate stripes of broad black and narrow white zigzagged across its body and legs. Its arms were much shorter than those of its counterpart on Earth, and its legs were not only longer but straighter. Moreover, the forehead, although shelved with bone above the eyes, was high.

It muttered something, not an animal cry or moan but a sequence of clearly modulated syllables. The gorilla was not alone. The greenish moon exposed a patch of bare skin on the side away from Wolff. It belonged to a woman who walked by the beast's side and whose shoulders were hidden by his huge right arm.

Wolff could not see her face, but he caught enough of long slim legs, curving buttocks, a shapely arm, and long black hair to wonder if she were as beautiful from the front.

She spoke to the gorilla in a voice like the sound of silver bells. The gorilla answered her. Then the two walked out of the green moon and into the darkness of the jungle.

Wolff did not get up at once, for he was too shaken.

Finally, he rose to his feet and pushed on through the undergrowth, which was not as thick as that of an Earth jungle. Indeed, the bushes were widely separated. If the environment had not been so exotic, he would not have thought of the flora as a jungle. It was more like a park, including the soft grass, which was so short it could have been freshly mown.

Only a few paces further on, he was startled when an animal snorted and then ran in front of him. He got a glimpse of reddish antlers, a whitish nose, huge pale eyes, and a polka-dot body. It crashed by him and disappeared, but a few seconds later he heard steps behind him. He turned to see the same cervine several feet away. When it saw that it was detected, it stepped forward slowly and thrust a wet nose into his outstretched hand. Thereafter, it purred and tried to rub its flank against him. Since it weighed perhaps a quarter of a ton, it tended to push him away from it.

He leaned into it, rubbed it behind its large cupshaped ears, scratched its nose, and lightly slapped its ribs. The cervine licked him several times with a long wet tongue that rasped as roughly as that of a lion. His hopes that it would tire of its affections were soon realized. It left him with a bound as sudden as that which had brought it within his ken.

After it was gone, he felt less endangered. Would an animal be so friendly to a complete stranger if it had carnivores or hunters to fear?

The roar of the surf became louder. Within ten minutes he was at the edge of the beach. There he crouched beneath a broad and towering frond and examined the moon-brushed scene. The beach itself was white and, as his outstretched hand verified, made of very fine sand. It ran on both sides for as far as he could see, and the breadth of it, between forest and sea, was about two hundred yards. On both sides, at a distance, were fires around which capered the silhouettes of men and women. Their shouts and laughter, though muted by the distance, reinforced his impression that they must be human.

Then his gaze swept back to the beach near him. At an angle, about three hundred yards away and almost in the water, were two beings. The sight of them snatched his breath away.

It was not what they were doing that shocked him but the construction of their bodies. From the waist up the man and woman were as human as he, but at the point where their legs should have begun the body of each tapered into fins.

He was unable to restrain his curiosity. After caching the horn in a bed of feathery grasses, he crept along the edge of the jungle; when he was opposite the two, he stopped to watch. Since the male and female were now lying side by side and talking, their position allowed him to study them in more detail. He became convinced they could not pursue him with any speed on land and had no weapons. He would approach them. They might even be friendly.

When he was about twenty yards from them, he stopped to examine them again. If they were mermen, they certainly were not half-piscine. The fins at the end of their long tails were on a horizontal plane, unlike those of fish, which are vertical. And the tail did not seem to have scales. Smooth brown skin covered their hybrid bodies from top to bottom.

He coughed. They looked up, and the male shouted and the female screamed. In a motion so swift he could not comprehend the particulars but saw it as a blur, they had risen on the ends of their tails and flipped themselves upward and out into the waves. The moon flashed on a dark head rising briefly from the waves and a tail darting upward.

The surf rolled and crashed upon the white sands. The moon shone hugely and greenly. A breeze from the sea patted his sweating face and passed on to cool the jungle. A few weird cries issued from the darkness behind him, and from down the beach came the sound of human revelry.

For awhile he was webbed in thought. The speech of the two merpeople had had something familiar about it, as had that of the zebrilla (his coinage for the gorilla) and the woman. He had not recognized any individual words, but the sounds and the associated pitches had stirred something in his memory. But what? They certainly spoke no language he had ever heard before. Was it similar to one of the living languages of Earth and had he heard it on a recording or perhaps in a movie?

A hand closed on his shoulder, lifted him and whirled him around. The Gothic snout and caverned eyes of a zebrilla were thrust in his face, and an alcoholic breath struck his own nostrils. It spoke, and the woman stepped out from the bushes. She walked slowly toward him, and at any other time he would have caught his breath at the magnificent body and beautiful face. Unfortunately, he was having a hard time breathing now for a different cause. The giant ape could hurl him into the sea with even more ease and speed than that which the merpeople had shown when they had dived away. Or the huge hand could close on him and meet on crushed flesh and shattered bone.

The woman said something, and the zebrilla replied. It was then that Wolff understood several words. Their language was akin to pre-Homeric Greek, to Mycenaean.

He did not immediately burst into speech to reassure them that he was harmless and his intentions good. For one thing, he was too stunned to think clearly enough. Also, his knowledge of the Greek of that period was necessarily limited, even if it was close to the Aeolic-Ionic of the blind bard.

Finally, he managed to utter a few inappropriate phrases, but he was not so concerned with the sense as to let them know he meant no harm. Hearing him, the zebrilla grunted, said something to the girl, and lowered Wolff to the sand. He sighed with relief, but he grimaced at the pain in his shoulder. The huge hand of the monster was enormously powerful. Aside from the magnitude and hairiness, the hand was quite human.

The woman tugged at his shirt. She had a mild distaste on her face; only later was he to discover that he repulsed her. She had never seen a fat old man before. Moreover, the clothes puzzled her. She continued pulling at his shirt. Rather than have her request the zebrilla to remove it from him, he pulled it off himself. She looked at it curiously, smelled it, said, 'Ugh!' and then made some gesture.

Although he would have preferred not to understand her and was even more reluctant to obey, he decided he might as well. There was no reason to frustrate her and perhaps anger the zebrilla. He shed his clothes and waited for more orders. The woman laughed shrilly; the zebrilla barked and pounded his thigh with his huge hand so that it sounded as if an axe were chopping wood. He and the woman put their arms around each other and, laughing hysterically, staggered off down the beach.

Infuriated, humiliated, ashamed, but also thankful that he had escaped without injury, Wolff put his pants back on. Picking up his underwear, socks, and shoes, he trudged through the sand and back into the jungle. After taking the horn from its hiding place, he sat for a long while, wondering what to do. Finally, he fell asleep.

He awoke in the morning, muscle-sore, hungry, and thirsty.

The beach was alive. In addition to the merman and merwoman he had seen the night before, several large seals with bright orange coats flopped back and forth over the sand in pursuit of amber balls flung by the merpeople, and a man with ram's horns projecting from his forehead, furry legs and a short goatish tail chased by a woman who looked much like the one who had been with the zebrilla. She, however, had yellow hair. She ran until the horned man leaped upon her and bore her, laughing, to the sand. What happened thereafter showed him that these beings were as innocent of a sense of sin, and of inhibitions, as Adam and Eve must have been.

This was more than interesting, but the sight of a mermaid eating aroused him in other and more demanding directions. She held a large oval yellow fruit in one hand and a hemisphere that looked like a coconut shell in the other. The female counterpart of the man with ram's horns squatted by a fire only a few yards from him and fried a fish on the end of a stick. The odor made his mouth water and his belly rumble.

First he had to have a drink. Since the only water in sight was the ocean, he strode out upon the beach and toward the surf.

His reception was what he had expected: surprise, withdrawal, apprehension to some degree. All stopped their activities, no matter how absorbing, to stare at him. When he approached some of them he was greeted with wide eyes, open mouths, and retreat. Some of the males stood their ground, but they looked as if they were ready to run if he said boo. Not that he felt like challenging them, since the smallest had muscles that could easily overpower his tired old body.

He walked into the surf up to his waist and tasted the water. He had seen others drink from it, so he hoped that he would find it acceptable. It was pure and fresh and had a tang that he had never experienced before. After drinking his fill, he felt as if he had had a transfusion of young blood. He walked out of the ocean and back across the beach and into the jungle. The others had resumed their eating and recreations, and though they watched him with a bold direct stare they said nothing to him. He gave them a smile, but quit when it seemed to startle them. In the jungle, he searched for and found fruit and nuts such as the merwoman had been eating. The yellow fruit had a peach pie taste, and the meat inside the pseudo-coconut tasted like very tender beef mixed with small pieces of walnut.

Afterward he felt very satisfied, except for one thing: he craved his pipe. But tobacco was one thing that seemed to be missing in this paradise.

The next few days he haunted the jungle or else spent some time in or near the ocean. By then, the beach crowd had grown used to him and even began to laugh when he made his morning appearances. One day, some of the men and women jumped him and, laughing uproariously, removed his clothes. He ran after the woman with the pants, but she sped away into the jungle. When she reappeared she was emptyhanded. By now he could speak well enough to be understood if he uttered the phrases slowly. His years of teaching and study had given him a very large Greek vocabulary, and he had only to master the tones and a number of words that were not in his Autenreith.

'Why did you do that?' he asked the beautiful black-eyed nymph.

'I wanted to see what you were hiding beneath those ugly rags. Naked, you are ugly, but those things on you made you look even uglier.'

'Obscene?' he said, but she did not understand the word.

He shrugged and thought, *When in Rome* ... Only this was more like the Garden of Eden. The temperature by day or night was comfortable and varied about seven degrees. There was no problem getting a variety of food, no work demanded, no rent, no politics, no tension except an easily relieved sexual tension, no national or racial animosities. There were no bills to pay. Or were there? That you did not get something for nothing was the basic principle of the universe of Earth. Was it the same here? Somebody should have to foot the bill.

At night he slept on a pile of grass in a large hollow in a tree. This was only one of thousands of such hollows, for a particular type of tree offered this natural accommodation. Wolff did not stay in bed in the mornings, however. For some days he got up just before dawn and watched the sun arrive. Arrive was a better word than rise, for the sun certainly did not rise. On the other side of the sea was an enormous mountain range, so extensive that he could see neither end. The sun always came around the mountain and was high when it came. It proceeded straight across the green sky and did not sink but disappeared only when it went around the other end of the mountain range.

An hour later, the moon appeared. It, too, came around the mountain, sailed at the same level across the skies, and slipped around the other side of the mountain. Every other night it rained hard for an hour. Wolff usually woke then, for the air did get a little chillier. He would snuggle down in the leaves and shiver and try to get back to sleep.

He was finding it increasingly more difficult to do so with each succeeding night. He would think of his own world, the friends and the work and the fun he had there – and of his wife. What was Brenda doing now? Doubtlessly she was grieving for him. Bitter and nasty and whining though she had been too many times, she loved him. His disappearance would be a shock and a loss. However, she would be well taken care of. She had always insisted on his carrying more insurance than he could afford; this had been a quarrel between them more than once. Then it occurred to him that she would not get a cent of insurance for a long time, for proof of his death would have to be forthcoming. Still, if she had to wait until he was legally declared dead, she could survive on social security. It would mean a drastic lowering of her living standards, but it would be enough to support her.

Certainly he had no intention of going back. He was regaining his youth. Though he ate well, he was losing weight, and his muscles were getting stronger and harder. He had a spring in his legs and a sense of joy lost sometime during his early twenties. The seventh morning, he had rubbed his scalp and discovered that it was covered with little bristles. The tenth morning, he woke up with pain in his gums. He rubbed the swollen flesh and wondered if he were going to be sick. He had forgotten that there was such a thing as disease, for he had been extremely well and none of the beach crowd, as he called them, ever seemed ill.

His gums continued to hurt him for a week, after which he took to drinking the naturally fermented liquor in the 'punchnut'. This grew in great clusters high at the top of a slender tree with short, fragile, mauve branches and tobacco-pipe-shaped yellow leaves. When its leathery rind was cut open with a sharp stone, it exuded an odor as of fruity punch. It tasted like a gin tonic with a dash of cherry bitters and had a kick like a slug of tequila. It worked well in killing both the pain in his gums and the irritation the pain had generated in him.

Nine days after he first experienced the trouble with his gums, ten tiny, white, hard teeth began to shove through the flesh. Moreover, the gold fillings in the others were being pushed out by the return of the natural material. And a thick black growth covered his formerly bald pate.

This was not all. The swimming, running, and climbing had melted off the fat. The prominent veins of old age had sunk back into smooth firm flesh. He could run for long stretches without being winded or feel as if his heart would burst. All this he delighted in, but not without wondering why and how it had come about.

He asked several among the beach-crowd about their seemingly universal youth. They had one reply: 'It's the Lord's will.'

At first he thought they were speaking of the Creator, which seemed strange to him. As far as he could tell, they had no religion. Certainly they did not have one with any organized approach, rituals, or sacraments.

'Who is the Lord?' he asked. He thought that perhaps he had mistranslated their word *wanaks*, that it might have a slightly different meaning than that found in Homer.

Ipsewas, the zebrilla, the most intelligent of all he had so far met, answered, 'He lives on top of the world, beyond Okeanos.' Ipsewas pointed up and over the sea, toward the mountain range at its other side. 'The Lord lives in a beautiful and impregnable palace on top of the world. He it was who made this world and who made us. He used to come down often to make merry with us. We do as the Lord says and play with him. But we are always frightened. If he becomes angry or is displeased, he is likely to kill us. Or worse.'

Wolff smiled and nodded his head. So Ipsewas and the others had no more rational explanation of the origins or workings of their world than the people of his. But the beach-crowd did have one thing lacking on Earth. They had uniformity of opinion. Everyone he asked gave him the same answer as the zebrilla.

'It is the will of the Lord. He made the world, he made us.'

'How do you know?' Wolff asked. He did not expect any more than he had gotten on Earth when he asked the question. But he was surprised.

'Oh,' replied a mermaid, Paiawa, 'the Lord told us so. Besides, my mother told me, too. She ought to know. The Lord made her body; she remembers when he did it, although that was so long, long ago.'

'Indeed?' Wolff said, wondering whether or not she were pulling his leg, and thinking also that it would be difficult to retaliate by doing the same to her. 'And where is your mother? I'd like to talk to her.'

Paiawa waved a hand toward the west. 'Somewhere along there.'

'Somewhere' could be thousands of miles away, for he had no idea how far the beach extended.

'I haven't seen her for a long time,' Paiawa added.

'How long?' Wolff said.

Paiawa wrinkled her lovely brow and pursed her lips. Very kissable, Wolff thought. And that body! The return of his youth was bringing back a strong awareness of sex.

Paiawa smiled at him and said, 'You *are* showing some interest in me, aren't you?'

He flushed and would have walked away, but he wanted an answer to his question. 'How many years since you saw your mother?' he asked again.

Paiawa could not answer. The word for 'year' was not in her vocabulary.

He shrugged and walked swiftly away, to disappear behind the savagely colored foliage by the beach. She called after him, archly at first, then angrily when it became evident he was not going to turn back. She made a few disparaging remarks about him as compared to the other males. He did not argue with her – it would have been beneath his dignity, and besides, what she said was true. Even though his body was rapidly regaining its youth and strength, it still suffered in comparison with the near-perfect specimens all around him.

He dropped this line of thought, and considered Paiawa's story. If he could locate her mother or one of her mother's contemporaries in age, he might be able to find out more about the Lord. He did not discredit Paiawa's story, which would have been incredible on Earth. These people just did not lie. Fiction was a stranger to them. Such truthfulness had its advantages, but it also meant that they were decidedly limited in imagination and had little humor or wit. They laughed often enough, but it was over rather obvious and petty things. Slapstick was as high as their comedy went – and crude practical jokes.

He cursed because he was having difficulty in staying on his intended track of thought. His trouble with concentration seemed to get stronger every day. Now, what had he been thinking about when he'd strayed off to his unhappiness over his maladjustment with the local society? Oh, yes, Paiawa's mother! Some of the oldsters might be able to enlighten him – if he could locate any. How could he identify any when all adults looked the same age? There were only a very few youngsters, perhaps three in the several hundred beings he had encountered so far. Moreover, among the many animals and birds here (some rather weird ones, too), only a half-dozen had not been adults.

If there were few births, the scale was balanced by the absence of death. He had seen three dead animals, two killed by accident and the third during a battle with another over a female. Even that had been an accident, for the defeated male, a lemon-colored antelope with four horns curved into figure-eights, had turned to run away and broken his neck while jumping over a log.

The flesh of the dead animal had not had a chance to rot and stink. Several omnipresent creatures that looked like small bipedal foxes with white noses, floppy basset-hound ears, and monkey paws had eaten the corpse within a matter of an hour. The foxes scoured the jungle and scavenged everything – fruit, nuts, berries, corpses. They had a taste for the rotten; they would ignore fresh fruits for bruised. But they were not sour notes in the symphony of beauty and life. Even in the Garden of Eden, garbage collectors were necessary.

At times Wolff would look across the blue, white-capped Okeanos at the mountain range, called Thayaphayawoed. Perhaps the Lord did live up there. It might be worthwhile to cross the sea and climb up the formidable steps on the chance that some of the mystery of this universe would be revealed. But the more he tried to estimate the height of Thayaphayawoed, the less he thought of the idea. The black cliffs soared up and up and up until the eye wearied and the mind staggered. No man could live on its top, because there would be no air to breathe.

3

One day Robert Wolff removed the silver horn from its hiding place in the hollow of a tree. Setting off through the forest, he walked toward the boulder from which the man who called himself Kickaha had thrown the horn. Kickaha and the bumpy creatures had dropped out of sight as if they never existed and no one to whom he had talked had ever seen or heard of them. He would re-enter his native world and give it another chance. If he thought its advantages outweighed those of the Garden planet, he would remain there. Or, perhaps, he could travel back and forth and so get the best of both. When tired of one, he would vacation in the other.

On the way, he stopped for a moment at an invitation from Elikopis to have a drink and to talk. Elikopis, whose name meant 'Bright-eyed,' was a beautiful, magnificently rounded dryad. She was closer to being 'normal' than anyone he had so far met. If her hair had not been a deep purple, she would, properly clothed, have attracted no more attention on Earth than was usually bestowed on a woman of surpassing fairness.

In addition, she was one of the very few who could carry on a worthwhile conversation. She did not think that conversation consisted of chattering away or laughing loudly without cause and ignoring the words of those who were supposed to be communicating with her. Wolff had been disgusted and depressed to find that most of the beach-crowd or the forest-crowd were monologists, however intensely they seemed to be speaking or however gregarious they were.

Elikopis was different, perhaps because she was not a member of any 'crowd,' although it was more likely that the reverse was the cause. In this world along the sea, the natives, lacking even the technology of the Australian aborigine (and not needing even that) had developed an extremely complex social relationship. Each group had definite beach and forest territories with internal prestige levels. Each was able to recite to detail (and loved to) his/her horizontal/vertical position in comparison with each person of the group, which usually numbered about thirty. They could and would recite the arguments, reconciliations, character faults and virtues, athletic prowess or lack thereof, skill in their many childish games, and evaluate the sexual ability of each.

Elikopis had a sense of humor as bright as her eyes, but she also had some sensitivity. Today, she had an extra attraction, a mirror of glass set in a golden circle encrusted with diamonds. It was one of the few artifacts he had seen.

'Where did you get that?' he asked.

'Oh, the Lord gave it to me,' Elikopis replied. 'Once, a long time ago, I was one of his favorites. Whenever he came down from the top of the world to visit here, he would spend much time with me. Chryseis and I were the ones he loved the most. Would you believe it, the others still hate us for that? That's why I'm so lonely – not that being with the others is much help.'

'And what did the Lord look like?'

She laughed and said, 'From the neck down, he looked much like any tall, well-built man such as you.'

She put her arm around his neck and began kissing him on his cheek, her lips slowly traveling toward his ear.

'His face?' Wolff said.

'I do not know. I could feel it, but I could not see it. A radiance from it blinded me. When he got close to me, I had to close my eyes, it was so bright.'

She shut his mouth with her kisses, and presently he forgot his questions. But when she was lying half-asleep on the soft grass by his side, he picked up the mirror and looked into it. His heart opened with delight. He looked like he had when he had been twenty-five. This he had known but had not been able to fully realize until now.

'And if I return to Earth, will I age as swiftly as I have regained my youth?'

He rose and stood for awhile in thought. Then he said, 'Who do I think I'm kidding? I'm not going back.'

'If you're leaving me now,' Elikopis said drowsily, 'look for Chryseis.

Something has happened to her; she runs away every time anybody gets close. Even I, her only friend, can't approach her. Something dreadful has occurred, something she won't talk about. You'll love her. She's not like the others; she's like me.'

'All right,' Wolff replied absently. 'I will.'

He walked until he was alone. Even if he did not intend to use the gate through which he had come, he did want to experiment with the horn. Perhaps there were other gates. It was possible that at any place where the horn was blown, a gate would open.

The tree under which he had stopped was one of the numerous cornucopias. It was two hundred feet tall, thirty feet thick, had a smooth, almost oily, azure bark, and branches as thick as his thigh and about sixty feet long. The branches were twigless and leafless. At the end of each was a hard-shelled flower, eight feet long and shaped exactly like a cornucopia.

Out of the cornucopias intermittent trickles of chocolatey stuff fell to the ground. The product tasted like honey with a very slight flavor of tobacco – a curious mixture, yet one he liked. Every creature of the forest ate it.

Under the cornucopia tree, he blew the horn. No 'gate' appeared. He tried again a hundred yards away but without success. So, he decided, the horn worked only in certain areas, perhaps only in that place by the toadstool-shaped boulder.

Then he glimpsed the head of the girl who had come from around the tree that first time the gate had opened. She had the same heart-shaped face, enormous eyes, full crimson lips, and long tiger-stripes of black and auburn hair.

He greeted her, but she fled. Her body was beautiful; her legs were the longest, in proportion to her body, that he had ever seen in a woman. Moreover, she was slimmer than the other too-curved and great-busted females of this world.

Wolff ran after her. The girl cast a look over her shoulder, gave a cry of despair, and continued to run. He almost stopped then, for he had not gotten such a reaction from any of the natives. An initial withdrawal, yes, but not sheer panic and utter fright.

The girl ran until she could go no more. Sobbing for breath, she leaned against a moss-covered boulder near a small cataract. Ankle-high yellow flowers in the form of question-marks surrounded her. An owl-eyed bird with corkscrew feathers and long forward-bending legs stood on top of the boulder and blinked down at them. It uttered soft *wee-wee-wee!* cries.

Approaching slowly and smiling, Wolff said, 'Don't be afraid of me. I won't harm you. I just want to talk to you.'

The girl pointed a shaking finger at the horn. In a quavery voice she said, 'Where did you get that?'

'I got it from a man who called himself Kickaha. You saw him. Do you know him?'

The girl's huge eyes were dark green; he thought them the most beautiful he had ever seen. This despite, or maybe because of, the catlike pupils.

She shook her head. 'No. I did not know him. I first saw him when those' – she swallowed and turned pale and looked as if she were going to vomit – 'things chased him to the boulder. And I saw them drag him off the boulder and take him away.'

'Then he wasn't ended?' Wolff asked. He did not say *killed* or *slain* or *dead*, for these were taboo words.

'No. Perhaps those things meant to do something even worse than ... ending him?'

'Why run from me?' Wolff said. 'I am not one of those things.'

'I ... I can't talk about it.'

Wolff considered her reluctance to speak of unpleasantness. These people had so few repulsive or dangerous phenomena in their lives, yet they could not face even these. They were overly conditioned to the easy and the beautiful.

'I don't care whether or not you want to talk about it,' he said. 'You must. It's very important.'

She turned her face away. 'I won't.'

'Which way did they go?'

'Who?'

'Those monsters. And Kickaha.'

'I heard him call them *gworl*,' she said. 'I never heard that word before. They ... the gworl ... must come from somewhere else.' She pointed seawards and up. 'They must come from the mountain. Up there, somewhere.'

Suddenly she turned to him and came close to him. Her huge eyes were raised to his, and even at this moment he could not help thinking how exquisite her features were and how smooth and creamy her skin was.

'Let's get away from here!' she cried. 'Far away! Those things are still here. Some of them may have taken Kickaha away, but all of them didn't leave! I saw a couple a few days ago. They were hiding in the hollow of a tree. Their eyes shone like those of animals, and they have a horrible odor, like rotten fungus-covered fruit!'

She put her hand on the horn. 'I think they want this!'

Wolff said, 'And I blew the horn. If they're anywhere near, they must have heard it!'

He looked around through the trees. Something glittered behind a bush about a hundred yards away.

He kept his eyes on the bush, and presently he saw the bush tremble and the flash of sunlight again. He took the girl's slender hand in his and said, 'Let's get going. But walk as if we'd seen nothing. Be nonchalant.'

She pulled back on his hand and said, 'What's wrong?'

'Don't get hysterical. I think I saw something behind a bush. It might be nothing, then again it could be the gworl. Don't look over there! You'll give us away!'

He spoke too late, for she had jerked her head around. She gasped and moved close to him. 'They ... they!'

He looked in the direction of her pointing finger and saw two dark, squat figures shamble from behind the bush. Each carried a long, wide, curved blade of steel in its hand. They waved the knives and shouted something in hoarse rasping voices. They wore no clothes over their dark furry bodies, but broad belts around their waists supported scabbards from which protruded knife-handles.

Wolff said, 'Don't panic. I don't think they can run very fast on those short bent legs. Where's a good place to get away from them, someplace they can't follow us?'

'Across the sea,' she said in a shaking voice. 'I don't think they could find us if we got far enough ahead of them. We can go on a *histoikhthys*.'

She was referring to one of the huge molluscs that abounded in the sea. These had bodies covered with paper-thin but tough shells shaped like a racing yacht's hull. A slender but strong rod of cartilage projected vertically from the back of each, and a triangular sail of flesh, so thin it was transparent, grew from the cartilage mast. The angle of the sail was controlled by muscular movement, and the force of the wind on the sail, plus expulsion of a jet of water, enabled the creature to move slightly in a wind or a calm. The merpeople and the sentients who lived on the beach often hitched rides on these creatures, steering them by pressure on exposed nerve centers.

'You think the gworl will have to use a boat?' he said. 'If so, they'll be out of luck unless they make one. I've never seen any kind of sea craft here.'

Wolff looked behind him frequently. The gworl were coming at a faster pace, their bodies rolling like those of drunken sailors at every step. Wolff and the girl came to a stream which was about seventy feet broad and, at the deepest, rose to their waists. The water was cool but not chilling, clear, with silvery fish darting back and forth in it. When they reached the other side, they hid behind a large cornucopia tree. The girl urged him to continue, but he said, 'They'll be at a disadvantage when they're in the middle of the stream.'

'What do you mean?' she asked.

He did not reply. After placing the horn behind the tree, he looked around until he found a stone. It was half the size of his head, round, and rough enough to be held firmly in his hand. He hefted one of the fallen cornucopias. Though huge, it was hollow and weighed no more than twenty pounds. By then, the two gworl were on the bank of the opposite side of the stream. It was then that he discovered a weakness of the hideous creatures. They walked back and forth along the bank, shook their knives in fury, and growled so loudly in their throaty language that he could hear them from his hiding place. Finally, one of them stuck a broad splayed foot in the water. He withdrew it almost immediately, shook it as a cat shakes a wet paw, and said something to the other gworl. That one rasped back, then screamed at him.

The gworl with the wet foot shouted back, but he stepped into the water and reluctantly waded through it. Wolff watched him and also noted that the other was going to hang back until the creature had passed the middle of the stream; then he picked up the cornucopia in one hand, the stone in the other, and ran toward the stream. Behind him, the girl screamed. Wolff cursed because it gave the gworl notice that he was coming.

The gworl paused, the water up to its waist, yelled at Wolff and brandished the knife. Wolff reserved his breath, for he did not want to waste his wind. He sped toward the edge of the water, while the gworl resumed his progress to the same bank. The gworl on the opposite edge had frozen at Wolff's appearance; now he had plunged into the stream to help the other. This action fell in with Wolff's plans. He only hoped that he could deal with the first before the second reached the middle.

The nearest gworl flipped his knife; Wolff lifted the cornucopia before him. The knife thudded into its thin but tough shell with a force that almost tore it from his grasp. The gworl began to draw another knife from its scabbard. Wolff did not stop to pull the first knife from the cornucopia; he kept on running. Just as the gworl raised the knife to slash at Wolff, Wolff dropped the stone, lifted the great bell-shape high, and slammed it over the gworl.

A muffled squawk came from within the shell. The cornucopia tilted over, the gworl with it, and both began floating downstream. Wolff ran into the water, picked up the stone, and grabbed the gworl by one of its thrashing feet. He took a hurried glance at the other and saw it was raising its knife for a throw. Wolff grabbed the handle of the knife that was sticking in the shell, tore it out, and then threw himself down behind the shelter of the bell-shape. He was forced to release his hold on the gworl's hairy foot, but he escaped the knife. It flew over the rim of the shell and buried itself to the hilt in the mud of the bank.

At the same time, the gworl within the cornucopia slid out, sputtering. Wolff stabbed at its side; the knife slid off one of the cartilaginous bumps. The gworl screamed and turned toward him. Wolff rose and thrust with all his strength at its belly. The knife went in to the hilt. The gworl grabbed at it; Wolff stepped back; the gworl fell into the water. The cornucopia floated away, leaving Wolff exposed, the knife gone, and only the stone in his hand. The remaining gworl was advancing on him, holding its knife across its breast. Evidently it did not intend to try for a second throw. It meant to close in on Wolff.

Wolff forced himself to delay until the thing was only ten feet from him. Meanwhile, he crouched down so that the water came to his chest and hid the stone, which he had shifted from his left to his right hand. Now he could see the gworl's face clearly. It had a very low forehead, a double ridge of bone above the eyes, thick mossy eyebrows, close-set lemon-yellow eyes, a flat, single-nostriled nose, thin black animal lips, a prognathous jaw which curved far out and gave the mouth a froglike appearance, no chin, and the sharp, widely separated teeth of a carnivore. The head, face, and body were covered with long, thick, dark fur. The neck was very thick, and the shoulders were stooped. Its wet fur stank like rotten fungus-diseased fruit.

Wolff was scared at the thing's hideousness, but he held his ground. If he broke and ran, he would go down with a knife in his back.

When the gworl, alternately hissing and rasping in its ugly speech, had come within six feet, Wolff stood up. He raised his stone, and the gworl, seeing his intention, raised his knife to throw it. The stone flew straight and thudded into a bump on the forehead. The creature staggered backward, dropped the knife, and fell on its back in the water. Wolff waded toward it, groped in the water for the stone, found it, and came up from the water in time to face the gworl. Although it had a dazed expression and its eyes were slightly crossed, it was not out of the fight. And it held another knife.

Wolff raised the stone high and brought it down on top of the skull. There was a loud crack. The gworl fell back again, disappearing in the water, and appeared several yards away floating on its face.

Reaction took him. His heart was hammering so hard he thought it would rupture, he was shaking all over, and he was sick. But he remembered the knife stuck in the mud and retrieved it.

The girl was still behind the tree. She looked too horror-struck to speak. Wolff picked up the horn, took the girl's arm with one hand, and shook her roughly.

'Snap out of it! Think how lucky you are! You could be dead instead of them!'

She burst into a long wailing, then began weeping. He waited until she seemed to have no more grief in her before speaking. 'I don't even know your name.'

Her enormous eyes were reddened, and her face looked older. Even so, he thought, he had not seen an Earthwoman who could compare with her. Her beauty made the terror of the fight thin away.

'I'm Chryseis,' she said. As if she were proud of it but at the same time shy of her proudness, she said, 'I'm the only woman here who is allowed that name. The Lord forbade others to take it.'

He growled, 'The Lord again. Always the Lord. Who in hell is the Lord?'

'You really don't know?' she replied as if she could not believe him.

'No, I don't.' He was silent for a moment, then said her name as if he were tasting it. 'Chryseis, heh? It's not unknown on Earth, although I fear that the university at which I was teaching is full of illiterates who've never heard the name. They know that Homer composed the Iliad, and that's about it.

'Chryseis, the daughter of Chryses, a priest of Apollo. She was captured by the Greeks during the siege of Troy and given to Agamemnon. But Agamemnon was forced to restore her to her father because of the pestilence sent by Apollo.'

Chryseis was silent for so long that Wolff became impatient. He decided that they should move away from this area, but he was not certain which direction to take or how far to go.

Chryseis, frowning, said, 'That was a long time ago. I can barely remember it. It's all so vague now.'

'What are you talking about?'

'Me. My father. Agamemnon. The war.'

'Well, what about it?' He was thinking that he would like to go to the base of the mountains. There, he could get some idea of what a climb entailed.

'I am Chryseis,' she said. 'The one you were talking about. You sound as if you had just come from Earth. Oh, tell me, is it true?'

He sighed. These people did not lie, but there was nothing to keep them from believing that their stories were true. He had heard enough incredible things to know that they were not only badly misinformed but likely to reconstruct the past to suit themselves. They did so in all sincerity, of course.

'I don't want to shatter your little dream-world,' he said, 'but this Chryseis, if she even existed, died at least 3000 years ago. Moreover, she was a human being. She did not have tiger-striped hair and eyes with feline pupils.'

'Nor did I ... then. It was the Lord who abducted me, brought me to this universe, and changed my body. Just as it was he who abducted the others, changed them, or else inserted their brains in bodies he created.'

She gestured seaward and upward. 'He lives up there now, and we don't see him very often. Some say that he disappeared a long time ago, and a new Lord has taken his place.'

'Let's get away from here,' he said. 'We can talk about this later.'

They had gone only a quarter of a mile when Chryseis gestured at him to hide with her behind a thick purple-branched, gold-leaved bush. He crouched by her and, parting the branches a little, saw what had disturbed her. Several yards away was a hairy-legged man with heavy ram's horns on top of his head. Sitting on a low branch at a level with the man's eyes was a giant raven. It was as large as a golden eagle and had a high forehead. The skull looked as if it could house a brain the size of a fox terrier's.

Wolff was not surprised at the bulk of the raven, for he had seen some rather enormous creatures. But he was shocked to find the bird and the man carrying on a conversation.

'The Eye of the Lord,' Chryseis whispered. She stabbed a finger at the raven in answer to his puzzled look. 'That's one of the Lord's spies. They fly over the world and see what's going on and then carry the news back to the Lord.'

Wolff thought of Chryseis' apparently sincere remark about the insertion of brains into bodies by the Lord. To his question, she replied, 'Yes, but I do not know if he put human brains into the ravens' heads. He may have grown small brains with the larger human brains as models, then educated the ravens. Or he could have used just part of a human brain.'

Unfortunately, though they strained their ears, they could only catch a few words here and there. Several minutes passed. The raven, loudly croaking a goodbye in distorted but understandable Greek, launched himself from the branch. He dropped heavily, but his great wings beat fast, and they carried him upward before he touched ground. In a minute he was lost behind the heavy foliage of the trees. A little later, Wolff caught a glimpse of him through a break in the vegetation. The giant black bird was gaining altitude slowly, his point of flight the mountain across the sea.

He noticed that Chryseis was trembling. He said, 'What could the raven tell the Lord that would scare you so?'

'I am not frightened so much for myself as I am for you. If the Lord discovers you are here, he will want to kill you. He does not like uninvited guests in his world.'

She placed her hand on the horn and shivered again. 'I know that it was Kickaha who gave you this, and that you can't help it that you have it. But the Lord might not know it isn't your fault. Or, even if he did, he might not care. He would be terribly angry if he thought you'd had anything to do with stealing it. He would do awful things to you; you would be better off if you ended yourself now rather than have the Lord get his hands on you.'

'Kickaha stole the horn? How do you know?'

'Oh, believe me, I know. It is the Lord's. And Kickaha must have stolen it, for the Lord would never give it to anyone.'

'I'm confused,' Wolff said. 'But maybe we can straighten it all out someday. The thing that bothers me right now is, where's Kickaha?'

Chryseis pointed toward the mountain and said, 'The gworl took him there. But before they did ...'

She covered her face with her hands; tears seeped through the fingers.

'They did something to him?' Wolff said.

She shook her head. 'No. They did something to ... to ...'

Wolff took her hands from her face. 'If you can't talk about it, would you show it to me?'

'I can't. It's ... too horrible. I get sick.'

'Show me anyway.'

'I'll take you near there. But don't ask me to look at ... her ... again.'

She began walking, and he followed her. Every now and then she would stop, but he would gently urge her on. After a zigzag course of over half a mile, she stopped. Ahead of them was a small forest of bushes twice as high as Wolff's head. The leaves of the branches of one bush interlaced with those of its neighbors. The leaves were broad and elephant-ear-shaped, light green with broad red veins, and tipped with a rusty fleur-de-lys.

'She's in there,' Chryseis said. 'I saw the gworl ... catch her and drag her into the bushes. I followed ... I ...' She could talk no more.

Wolff, knife in one hand, pushed the branches of the bushes aside. He found himself in a natural clearing. In the middle, on the short green grass, lay the scattered bones of a human female. The bones were gray and devoid of flesh, and bore little toothmarks, by which he knew that the bipedal vulpine scavengers had gotten to her.

He was not horrified, but he could imagine how Chryseis must have felt. She must have seen part of what had taken place, probably a rape, then murder in some gruesome fashion. She would have reacted like the other dwellers in the Garden. Death was something so horrible that the word for it had long ago become taboo and then dropped out of the language. Here, nothing but pleasant thoughts and acts were to be contemplated, and anything else was to be shut out.

He returned to Chryseis, who looked with her enormous eyes at him as if she wanted him to tell her that there was nothing within the clearing. He said, 'She's only bones now, and far past any suffering.'

'The gworl will pay for this!' she said savagely. 'The Lord does not allow his creatures to be hurt! This Garden is his, and any intruders are punished!'

'Good for you,' he said. 'I was beginning to think that you may have become frozen by the shock. Hate the gworl all you want; they deserve it. And you need to break loose.'

She screamed and leaped at him and beat on his chest with her fists. Then she began weeping, and presently he took her in his arms. He raised her face and kissed her. She kissed him back passionately, though the tears were still flowing.

Afterward, she said, 'I ran to the beach to tell my people what I'd seen. But they wouldn't listen. They turned their backs on me and pretended they hadn't heard me. I kept trying to make them listen, but Owisandros' – the ram-horned man who had been talking with the raven – 'Owisandros hit me with his fist and told me to go away. After that, none of them would have anything to do with me. And I ... I needed friends and love.'

'You don't get friends or love by telling people what they don't want to hear,' he said. 'Here or on Earth. But you have me, Chryseis, and I have you. I think I'm beginning to fall in love with you, although I may just be reacting to loneliness and to the most strange beauty I've ever seen. And to my new youth.'

He sat up and gestured at the mountain. 'If the gworl are intruders here, where did they come from? Why were they after the horn? Why did they take Kickaha with them? And who is Kickaha?'

'He comes from up there, too. But I think he's an Earthman.'

'What do you mean, Earthman? You say you're from Earth.'

'I mean he's a newcomer. I don't know. I just had a feeling he was.'

He stood up and lifted her up by her hands. 'Let's go after him.'

Chryseis sucked in her breath and, one hand on her breast, backed away from him. 'No!'

'Chryseis, I could stay here with you and be very happy. For awhile. But I'd always be wondering what all this is about the Lord and what happened to Kickaha. I only saw him for a few seconds, but I think I'd like him very much. Besides, he didn't throw the horn to me just because I happened to be there. I have a hunch that he did it for a good reason, and that I should find out why. And I can't rest while he's in the hands of those things, the gworl.'

He took her hand from her breast and kissed the hand. 'It's about time you left this Paradise that is no Paradise. You can't stay here forever, a child forever.'

She shook her head. 'I wouldn't be any help to you. I'd just get in your way. And ... leaving ... leaving I'd, well, I'd just end.'

'You're going to have to learn a new vocabulary,' he said. 'Death will be just one of the many new words you'll be able to speak without a second thought or a shiver. You will be a better woman for it. Refusing to say it doesn't stop it from happening, you know. Your friend's bones are there whether or not you can talk about them.'

'That's horrible!'

'The truth often is.'

He turned away from her and started toward the beach. After a hundred yards, he stopped to look back. She had just started running after him. He waited for her, took her in his arms, kissed her, and said, 'You may find it hard going, Chryseis, but you won't be bored, won't have to drink yourself into a stupor to endure life.'

'I hope so,' she said in a low voice. 'But I'm scared.'

'So am I, but we're going.'

4

He took her hand in his as they walked side by side toward the roar of the surf. They had traveled not more than a hundred yards when Wolff saw the first gworl. It stepped out from behind a tree and seemed to be as surprised as they. It shouted, snatched its knife out, then turned to yell at others behind it. In a few seconds, a party of seven had formed, each gworl with a long curved knife.

Wolff and Chryseis had a fifty-yard headstart. Still holding Chryseis' hand, the horn in his other hand, Robert Wolff ran as fast as he could.

'I don't know!' she said despairingly. 'We could hide in a tree hollow, but we'd be trapped if they found us.'

They ran on. Now and then he looked back: the brush was thick hereabouts and hid some of the gworl, but there were always one or two in evidence.

'The boulder!' he said. 'It's just ahead. We'll take that way out!'

Suddenly he knew how much he did not want to return to his native world. Even if it meant a route of escape and a temporary hiding place, he did not want to go back. The prospect of being trapped there and being unable to return here was so appalling that he almost decided not to blow the horn. But he had to do so. Where else could he go?

The decision was taken away from him a few seconds later. As he and Chryseis sped toward the boulder, he saw several dark figures hunched at its base. These rose and became gworl with flashing knives and long white canines.

Wolff and the girl angled away while the three at the boulder joined the chase. These were nearer than the others, only twenty yards behind the fugitives.

'Don't you know any place?' he panted.

'Over the edge,' she said. 'That's the only place they might not follow us. I've been down the face of the rim; there're caves there. But it's dangerous.'

He did not reply, saving his breath for the run. His legs felt heavy and his lungs and throat burned. Chryseis seemed to be in better shape than he: she ran easily, her long legs pumping, breathing deeply but not agonizingly.

'Another two minutes, we'll be there,' she said.

The two minutes seemed much longer, but every time he felt he had to stop, he took another look behind him and renewed his strength. The gworl, although even further behind, were in sight. They rolled along on their short, crooked legs, their bumpy faces set with determination.

'Maybe if you gave them the horn,' Chryseis said, 'they'd go away. I think they want the horn, not us.'

'I'll do it if I have to,' he gasped. 'But only as a last resort.'

Suddenly, they were going up a steep slope. Now his legs did feel burdened, but he had caught his second wind and thought that he could go awhile longer. Then they were on top of the hill and at the edge of a cliff.

Chryseis stopped him from walking on. She advanced ahead of him to the edge, halted, looked over, and beckoned him. When he was by her side, he, too, gazed down. His stomach clenched like a fist.

Composed of hard black shiny rock, the cliff went straight down for several miles. Then, nothing.

Nothing but the green sky.

'So … it is the edge … of the world!' he said.

Chryseis did not answer him. She trotted ahead of him, looking over the side of the cliff, halting briefly now and then to examine the rim.

'About sixty yards more,' she said. 'Beyond those trees that grow right up to the edge.'

She started running swiftly with him close behind her. At the same time, a gworl burst out of the bushes growing on the inner edge of the hill. He turned once to yell, obviously notifying his fellows that he had found the quarry. Then he attacked without waiting for them.

Wolff ran toward the gworl. When he saw the creature lift its knife to throw, he hurled the horn at it. This took the gworl by surprise – or perhaps the turning horn reflected sunlight into his eyes. Whatever the cause, his hesitation was enough for Wolff to get the advantage. He sped in as the gworl both ducked and reached a hand out for the horn. The huge hairy fingers curled around the horn, a cry of grating delight came from the creature, and Wolff was on him. He thrust at the protruding belly; the gworl brought his own knife up; the two blades clanged.

Having missed the first stroke, Wolff wanted to run again. This thing was undoubtedly skilled at knife-fighting. Wolff knew fencing quite well and had never given up its practice. But there was a big difference between dueling with the rapier and dirty in-close knivery, and he knew it. Yet he could not leave. In the first place, the gworl would down him with a thrown blade in his back before he could take four steps. Also, there was the horn, clenched in the gnarled left fist of the gworl. Wolff could not leave that.

The gworl, realizing that Wolff was in a very bad situation, grinned. His upper canines shone long and wet and yellow and sharp. With those, thought Wolff, the thing did not need a knife.

Something golden-brown, trailing long black-and-auburn-striped hair, flashed by Wolff. The gworl's eyes opened, and he started to turn to his left. The butt end of a pole, a long stick stripped of its leaves and part of its bark, drove into the gworl's chest. At the other end was Chryseis. She had run at top speed with the dead branch held like a vaulter's pole, but just before impact she had lowered it and it hit the creature with enough speed and weight behind it to bowl him over backward. The horn dropped from his fist, but the knife remained in the other.

Wolff jumped forward and thrust the end of his blade between two cartilaginous bosses and into the gworl's thick neck. The muscles were thick and tough there, but not enough to stop the blade. Only when the steel severed the windpipe did it halt.

Wolff handed Chryseis the gworl's knife. 'Here, take it!'

She accepted it, but she seemed to be in shock. Wolff slapped her savagely until the glaze went from her eyes. 'You did fine!' he said. 'Which would you rather see dead, me or him?'

He removed the belt from the corpse and fastened it on himself. Now he had three knives. He scabbarded the bloody weapon, took the horn in one hand, Chryseis' hand in the other, and began running again. Behind them, a howl arose as the first of the gworl came over the edge of the hill. However, Wolff and Chryseis had about thirty yards' start, which they maintained until they reached the group of trees growing on the rim. Chryseis took the lead. She let herself face down on the rim and rolled over. Wolff looked over once before blindly following and saw a small ledge about six feet down from the rim. She had already let herself down the ledge and now was hanging by her hands. She dropped again, this time to a much more narrow ledge. But it did not end; it ran at a forty-five degree angle down the face of the cliff. They could use it if they faced inward against the stone cliff-wall and moved sideways, their hands spread to gain friction against the wall.

Wolff used both hands also; he had stuck the horn through the belt.

There was a howl from above. He looked up to see the first of the gworl dropping onto the ledge. Then he glanced back at Chryseis and almost fell off from shock. She was gone.

Slowly, he turned his head to see over his shoulder and down below. He fully expected to find her falling down the face of the cliff, if not already past it and plunging into the green abyss.

'Wolff!' she said. Her head was sticking out from the cliff itself. 'There's a cave here. Hurry.'

Trembling, sweating, he inched along the ledge to her and presently was inside an opening. The ceiling of the cave was several feet higher than his head; he could almost touch the walls on both sides when he stretched out his arms; the interior ran into the darkness.

'How far back does it go?'

'Not very far. But there's a natural shaft, a fault in the rock, that leads down. It opens on the bottom of the world; there's nothing below, nothing but air and sky.'

'This can't be,' he said slowly. 'But it is. A universe founded on physical principles completely different than those of my universe. A flat planet with edges. But I don't understand how gravity works here. Where is its center?'

She shrugged and said, 'The Lord may have told me a long time ago. But I've forgotten. I'd even forgotten he told me that Earth was round.'

Wolff took the leather belt off, slid the scabbards off it, and picked up an oval black rock weighing about ten pounds. He slipped the belt through the buckle and then placed the stone within the loop. After piercing a hole near the buckle with the point of his knife, he tightened the loop. He had only to buckle the belt, and he was armed with a thong at the end of which was a heavy stone.

'You get behind and to one side of me,' he said. 'If I miss any, if one gets in past me, you push while he's off-balance. But don't go over yourself. Do you think you can do it?'

She nodded her head but evidently did not trust herself to speak.

'This is asking a lot of you. I'd understand if you cracked up completely. But, basically, you're made of sturdy ancient-Hellenic stock. They were a pretty tough lot in those days; you can't have lost your strength, even in this deadening pseudo-Paradise.'

'I wasn't Achaean,' she said. 'I was Sminthean. But you are, in a way, right. I don't feel as badly as I thought I would. Only ...'

'Only it takes getting used to,' he said. He was encouraged, for he had expected a different reaction. If she could keep it up, the two of them might make it through this. But if she fell apart and he had a hysterical woman to control, both might fall under the attack of the gworl.

'Speaking of which,' he muttered as he saw black, hairy, gnarled fingers slide around the corner of the cave. He swung the belt hard so that the stone at its end smashed the hand. There was a bellow of surprise and pain, then a long ululating scream as the gworl fell. Wolff did not wait for the next one to appear. He got as close to the lip of the cave ledge as he dared and swung the stone again. It whipped around the corner and thudded against something soft. Another scream came, and it, too, faded away into the nothingness of the green sky.

'Three down, seven to go! Provided that no more have joined them.'

He said to Chryseis, 'They may not be able to get in here. But they can starve us out.'

'The horn?'

He laughed. 'They wouldn't let us go now even if I did hand them the horn. And I don't intend for them to get it. I'll throw the horn into the sky rather than do that.'

A figure was silhouetted against the mouth of the cave as it dropped from above. The gworl, swinging in, landed on his feet and teetered for a second. But he threw himself forward, rolled in a hairy ball, and was up on his feet again. Wolff was so surprised that he failed to react immediately. He had not expected them to be able to climb above the cave and let themselves down, for the rock above the cave had looked smooth. Somehow, one had done it, and now he was inside, on his feet, a knife in hand.

Wolff whirled the stone at the belt-end and loosed it at the gworl. The creature flipped its knife at him; Wolff dodged but spoiled his aim of the stone. It flew over the furry bumpy head; the thrown knife brushed him lightly on his shoulder. He jumped for his own knife on the floor of the cave, saw another dark shape drop into the cave from above, and a third come around the corner of the mouth.

Something hit his head. His vision blurred, his senses grew dim, his knees buckled.

When he awoke, a pain in the side of his head, he had a frightening sensation. He seemed to be upside down and floating above a vast polished black disc. A rope was tied around his neck, and his hands were tied behind his back. He was hanging with his feet up in the empty air, yet there was only a slight tension of rope around his neck.

Bending his head back, he could see that the rope led upward into a shaft in the disc and that at the far end of the shaft was a pale light.

He groaned and closed his eyes, but opened them again. The world seemed to spin. Suddenly he was reoriented. Now he knew that he was not suspended upside down against all the laws of gravity. He was hanging by a rope from the bottom underside of the planet. The green below him was the sky.

He thought, *I should have strangled before now. But there is no gravity pulling me downward.*

He kicked his feet, and the reaction drove him upward. The mouth of the shaft came closer. His head entered it, but something resisted him. His motion slowed, stopped, and, as if there were an invisible and compressed spring against his head, he began to move back down. Not until the rope tightened again did he stop his flight.

The gworl had done this to him. After knocking him out, they had let him down the shaft, or more probably, had carried him down. The shaft was narrow enough for a man to get down it with his back to one wall and his feet braced against the other. The descent would scrape the skin off a man, but the hairy hide of the gworl had looked tough enough to withstand descent and ascent without injury. Then a rope had been lowered, placed around his neck, and he had been dropped through the hole in the bottom of the world.

There was no way of getting himself back up. He would starve to death. His body would dangle in the winds of space until the rope rotted. He would not then fall, but would drift about in the shadow cast by the disc. The gworl he had knocked off the ledge had fallen, but their acceleration had kept them going.

Though despairing because of his situation, he could not help speculating about the gravitational configuration of the flat planet. The center must be at the very bottom; all attraction was upward through the mass of the planet. On this side, there was none.

What had the gworl done to Chryseis? Had they killed her as they had her friend?

He knew then that however they had dealt with her, they had purposely not hung her with him. They had planned that part of his agony would be that of not knowing her fate. As long as he could live at the end of this rope, he would wonder what had happened to her. He would conjure a multitude of possibilities, all horrible.

For a long time he hung suspended at a slight degree from the perpendicular, since the wind held him steady. Here, where there was no gravity, he could not swing like a pendulum.

Although he remained in the shadow of the black disc, he could see the progress of the sun. The sun itself was invisible, hidden by the disc, but the light from it fell on the rim of the great curve and slowly marched along it. The green sky beneath the sun glowed brightly, while the unlit portions before and after became dark. Then a paler lighting along the edge of the disc came into his sight, and he knew that the moon was following the sun.

It must be midnight, he thought. *If the gworl are taking her someplace, they could be some distance out on the sea. If they've been torturing her, she could be dead. If they've hurt her, I hope she's dead.*

Abruptly, while he hung in the gloom beneath the bottom of the world, he felt the rope at his neck jerk. The noose tightened, although not enough to choke him, and he was being drawn upward toward the shaft. He craned his neck to see who was hauling him up, but he could not penetrate the darkness of the mouth of the shaft. Then his head broke through the web of gravity – like surface tension on water, he thought – and he was hoisted clear of the abyss. Great strong hands and arms came around him to hug him against a hard, warm, furry chest. An alcoholic breath blew into his face. A leathery mouth scraped his cheek as the creature hugged him closer and began inching up the shaft with Wolff in its arms. Fur scraped on rock as the thing pushed with its legs. There was a jerk as the legs came up suddenly and took a new hold, followed by another scrape and lunge upward.

'Ipsewas?' Wolff said.

The zebrilla replied, 'Ipsewas. Don't talk now. I have to save my wind. This isn't easy.'

Wolff obeyed, although he had a difficult time in not asking about

Chryseis. When they reached the top of the shaft, Ipsewas removed the rope from his neck and tossed him onto the floor of the cave.

Now at last he dared to speak. 'Where is Chryseis?'

Ipsewas landed on the cave floor softly, turned Wolff over, and began to untie the knots around his wrists. He was breathing heavily from the trip up the shaft, but he said, 'The gworl took her with them to a big dugout and began to sail across the sea toward the mountain. She shouted at me, begged me to help her. Then a gworl hit her, knocked her unconscious, I suppose. I was sitting there, drunk as the Lord, half-unconscious myself with nut juice, having a good time with Autonoe – you know, the *akowile* with the big mouth.

'Before Chryseis was knocked out, she screamed something about you hanging from the Hole in the Bottom of the World. I didn't know what she was talking about, because it's been a long time since I was here. How long ago I hate to say. Matter of fact, I don't really know. Everything's pretty much of a haze anymore, you know.'

'No, I don't,' Wolff said. He rose and rubbed his wrists. 'But I'm afraid that if I stay here much longer, I might end up in an alcoholic fog, too.'

'I was thinking about going after her,' Ipsewas said. 'But the gworl flashed those long knives at me and said they'd kill me. I watched them drag their boat out of the bushes, and about then I decided, what the hell, if they killed me, so what? I wasn't going to let them get away with threatening me or taking poor little Chryseis off to only the Lord knows what. Chryseis and I were friends in the old days, in the Troad, you know, although we haven't had too much to do with each other here for some time. I think it's been a long time. Anyway, I suddenly craved some real adventure, some genuine excitement – and I loathed those monstrous bumpy creatures.

'I ran after them, but by then they'd launched the boat, with Chryseis in it. I looked around for a *histoikhthys*, thinking I could ram their boat with it. Once I had them in the water, they'd be mine, knives or not. The way they acted in the boat showed me that they felt far from confident on the sea. I doubt they can even swim.'

'I doubt it, too.' Wolff said.

'But there wasn't a *histoikhthys* in reaching distance. And the wind was taking the boat away; it had a large lateen sail. I went back to Autonoe and took another drink. I might have forgotten about you, just as I was trying to forget about Chryseis. I was sure she was going to get hurt, and I couldn't bear to think about it, so I wanted to drink myself into oblivion. But Autonoe, bless her poor boozed-up brain, reminded me of what Chryseis had said about you.

'I took off fast, and looked around for awhile, because I couldn't remember just where the ledges were that led to the cave. I almost gave up and started drinking again. But something kept me going. Maybe I wanted to do just one good thing in this eternity of doing nothing, good or evil.'

'If you hadn't come, I'd have hung there until I died of thirst. Now, Chryseis has a chance, if I can find her. I'm going after her. Do you want to come along?'

Wolff expected Ipsewas to say yes, but he did not think that Ipsewas would stick to his determination once the trip across the sea faced him. He was surprised, however.

The zebrilla swam out, seized a projection of shell as a *histoikhthys* sailed by, and swung himself upon the back of the creature. He guided it back to the beach by pressing upon the great nerve spots, dark purple blotches visible on the exposed skin just back of the cone-shaped shell that formed the prow of the creature.

Wolff, under Ipsewas' guidance, maintained pressure on a spot to hold the sailfish (for that was the literal translation of *histoikhthys*) on the beach. The zebrilla gathered several armloads of fruit and nuts and a large collection of the punchnuts.

'We have to eat and drink, especially drink,' Ipsewas muttered. 'It may be a long way across Okeanos to the foot of the mountain. I don't remember.'

A few minutes after the supplies had been stored in one of the natural receptacles on the sailfish's shell, they left. The wind caught the thin cartilage sail, and the great mollusc gulped in water through its mouth and ejected it through a fleshy valve in its rear.

'The gworl have a headstart,' Ipsewas said, 'but they can't match our speed. They won't get to the other side long before we do.' He broke open a punchnut and offered Wolff a drink. Wolff accepted. He was exhausted but nerve-strung. He needed something to knock him out and let him sleep. A curve of the shell afforded a cavelike ledge for him to crawl within. He lay hugged against the bare skin of the sailfish, which was warm. In a short time he was asleep, but his last glimpse was of the shouldering bulk of Ipsewas, his stripes blurred in the moonlight, crouching by the nerve spots. Ipsewas was lifting another punchnut above his head and pouring the liquid contents into his outthrust gorilloid lips.

When Wolff awoke, he found the sun was just coming around the curve of the mountain. The full moon (it was always full, for the shadow of the planet never fell on it) was just slipping around the other side of the mountain.

Refreshed but hungry, he ate some of the fruit and the protein-rich nuts. Ipsewas showed him how he could vary his diet with the 'bloodberries.' These were shiny maroon balls that grew in clusters at the tips of fleshy stalks that sprouted out of the shell. Each was large as a baseball and had a thin, easily torn skin that exuded a liquid that looked and tasted like blood. The meat within tasted like raw beef with a soupcon of shrimp.

'They fall off when they're ripe, and the fish get most of them,' Ipsewas said. 'But some float in to the beach. They're best when you get them right off the stalk.'

Wolff crouched down by Ipsewas. Between mouthfuls, he said, 'The *histoikhthys* is handy. They seem almost too much of a good thing.'

'The Lord designed and made them for our pleasure and his,' Ipsewas replied.

'The Lord made this universe?' Wolff said, no longer sure that the story was a myth.

'You better believe it,' Ipsewas replied, and took another drink. 'Because if you don't, the Lord will end you. As it is, I doubt that he'll let you continue, anyway. He doesn't like uninvited guests.'

Ipsewas lifted the nut and said, 'Here's to your escaping his notice. And a sudden end and damnation to the Lord.'

He dropped the nut and leaped at Wolff. Wolff was so taken by surprise he had no chance to defend himself. He went sprawling into the hollow of shell in which he had slept, with Ipsewas' bulk on him.

'Quiet!' Ipsewas said. 'Stay curled up inside here until I tell you it's all right. It's an Eye of the Lord.'

Wolff shrank back against the hard shell and tried to make himself one with the shadow of the interior. However, he did look out with one eye and thus he saw the ragged shadow of the raven scud across, followed by the creature itself. The dour bird flashed over once, wheeled, and began to glide in for a landing on the stern of the sailfish.

'Damn him! He can't help seeing me,' Wolff muttered to himself.

'Don't panic,' Ipsewas called. 'Ahhh!'

There was a thud, a splash, and a scream that made Wolff start up and bump his head hard against the shell above him. Through the flashes of light and darkness, he saw the raven hanging limply within two giant claws. If the raven was eagle-sized, the killer that had dropped like a bolt from the green sky seemed, in that first second of shock, to be as huge as a roc. Wolff's vision straightened and cleared, and he saw an eagle with a light-green body, a pale red head, and a pale yellow beak. It was six times the bulk of the raven, and its wings, each at least thirty feet long, were flapping heavily as it strove to lift higher from the sea into which its missile thrust had carried both it and its prey. With each powerful downpush, it rose a few inches higher. Presently it began climbing higher, but before it got too far away, it turned its head and allowed Wolff to see its eyes. They were black shields mirroring the flames of death. Wolff shuddered; he had never seen such naked lust for killing.

'Well may you shudder,' Ipsewas said. His grinning head was thrust into the cave of the shell. 'That was one of Podarge's pets. Podarge hates the Lord and would attack him herself if she got the chance, even if she knew it would be her end. Which it would. She knows she can't get near the Lord, but she can tell her pets to eat up the Eyes of the Lord. Which they do, as you have seen.'

Wolff left the cavern of the shell and stood for awhile, watching the shrinking figure of the eagle and its kill.

'Who is Podarge?'

'She is, like me, one of the Lord's monsters. She, too, once lived on the shores of the Aegean; she was a beautiful young girl. That was when the great king Priamos and the godlike Achilles and crafty Odysseus lived. I knew them all; they would spit on the Kretan Ipsewas, the once-brave sailor and spear-fighter, if they could see me now. But I was talking of Podarge. The Lord took her to this world and fashioned a monstrous body and placed her brain within it.

'She lives up there someplace, in a cave on the very face of the mountain. She hates the Lord; she also hates every normal human being and will eat them, if her pets don't get them first. But most of all she hates the Lord.'

That seemed to be all that Ipsewas knew about her, except that Podarge had not been her name before the Lord had taken her. Also, he remembered having been well acquainted with her. Wolff questioned him further, for he was interested in what Ipsewas could tell him about Agamemnon and Achilles and Odysseus and the other heroes of Homer's epic. He told the zebrilla that Agamemnon was supposed to be a historical character. But what about Achilles and Odysseus? Had they really existed?

'Of course they did,' Ipsewas said. He grunted, then continued, 'I suppose you're curious about those days. But there is little I can tell you. It's been too long ago. Too many idle days. Days? – centuries, millenia! – the Lord alone knows. Too much alcohol, too.'

During the rest of the day and part of the night, Wolff tried to pump Ipsewas, but he got little for his trouble. Ipsewas, bored, drank half his supply of nuts and finally passed out snoring. Dawn came green and golden around the mountain. Wolff stared down into the waters, so clear that he could see the hundreds of thousands of fish, of fantastic configurations and splendors of colors. A bright-orange seal rose from the depths, a creature like a living diamond in its mouth. A purple-veined octopus, shooting backward, jetted by the seal. Far, far down, something enormous and white appeared for a second, then dived back toward the bottom.

Presently the roar of the surf came to him, and a thin white line frothed at the base of Thayaphayawoed. The mountain, so smooth at a distance, was now broken by fissures, by juts and spires, by rearing scarps and frozen fountains of stone. Thayaphayawoed went up and up and up; it seemed to hang over the world.

Wolff shook Ipsewas until, moaning and muttering, the zebrilla rose to his feet. He blinked reddened eyes, scratched, coughed, then reached for another punchnut. Finally, at Wolff's urging, he steered the sailfish so that its course paralleled the base of the mountain.

'I used to be familiar with this area,' he said. 'Once I thought about climbing the mountain, finding the Lord, and trying to …' He paused, scratched his head, winced, and said, 'Kill him! There! I knew I could remember the word. But it was no use. I didn't have the guts to try it alone.'

'You're with me now,' Wolff said.

Ipsewas shook his head and took another drink. 'Now isn't then. If you'd been with me then … Well, what's the use of talking? You weren't even born then. Your great-great-great-great-grandfather wasn't born then. No, it's too late.'

He was silent while he busied himself with guiding the sailfish through an opening in the mountain. The great creature abruptly swerved; the cartilage sail folded up against the mast of stiff bone-braced cartilage; the body rose on a huge wave. And then they were within the calm waters of a narrow, steep, and dark fjord.

Ipsewas pointed at a series of rough ledges.

'Take that. You can get far. How far I don't know. I got tired and scared and I went back to the Garden. Never to return, I thought.'

Wolff pleaded with Ipsewas. He said that he needed Ipsewas' strength very much and that Chryseis needed him. But the zebrilla shook his massive somber head.

'I'll give you my blessing, for what it's worth.'

'And I thank you for what you've done,' Wolff said. 'If you hadn't cared enough to come after me, I'd still be swinging at the end of a rope. Maybe I'll see you again. With Chryseis.'

'The Lord is too powerful,' Ipsewas replied. 'Do you think you have a chance against a being who can create his own private universe?'

'I have a chance,' Wolff said. 'As long as I fight and use my wits and have some luck, I have a chance.'

He jumped off the decklike shell and almost slipped on the wet rock. Ipsewas called, 'A bad omen, my friend!'

Wolff turned and smiled at him and shouted, 'I don't believe in omens, my superstitious Greek friend! So long!'

5

He began climbing and did not stop to look down until about an hour had passed. The great white body of the *histoikhthys* was a slim, pale thread by then, and Ipsewas was only a black dot on its axis. Although he knew he could not be seen, he waved at Ipsewas and resumed climbing.

Another hour's scrambling and clinging on the rocks brought him out of the fjord and onto a broad ledge on the face of the cliff. Here it was bright sunshine again. The mountain seemed as high as ever, and the way was as hard. On the other hand, it seemed no more difficult, although that was nothing over which to exult. His hands and knees were bleeding and the ascent had made him tired. At first he was going to spend the night there, but he changed his mind. As long as the light lasted, he should take advantage of it.

Again he wondered if Ipsewas was correct about the gworl probably having taken just this route. Ipsewas claimed that there were other passages along the mountain where the sea rammed against it, but these were far away. He had looked for signs that the gworl had come this way and had found none. This did not mean that they had taken another path – if you could call this ragged verticality a path.

A few minutes later he came to one of the many trees that grew out of the rock itself. Beneath its twisted gray branches and mottled brown and green leaves were broken and empty nutshells and the cores of fruit. They were fresh. Somebody had paused for lunch not too long ago. The sight gave him new strength. Also, there was enough meat left in the nutshells for him to half-satisfy the pangs in his belly. The remnants of the fruits gave him moisture to put in his dry mouth.

Six days he climbed, and six nights rested. There was life on the face of the perpendicular, small trees and large bushes grew on the ledges, from the caves, and from the cracks. Birds of all sorts abounded, and many little animals. These fed off the berries and nuts or on each other. He killed birds with stones and ate their flesh raw. He discovered flint and chipped out a crude but sharp knife. With this, he made a short spear with a wooden shaft and another flint for the tip. He grew lean and hard with thick callouses on his hands and feet and knees. His beard lengthened.

On the morning of the seventh day, he looked out from a ledge and estimated that he must be at least twelve thousand feet above the sea. Yet the air was no thinner or colder than when he had begun climbing. The sea, which must have been at least two hundred miles across, looked like a broad river. Beyond was the rim of the world's edge, the Garden from which he had set out in pursuit of Chryseis and the gworl. It was as narrow as a cat's whisker. Beyond it, only the green sky.

At midnoon on the eighth day, he came across a snake feeding upon a dead gworl. Forty feet long, it was covered with black diamond spots and crimson seals of Solomon. The feet that arrayed both sides grew out of the body without the blessing of legs and were distressingly human-shaped. Its jaws were lined with three rows of sharkish teeth.

Wolff attacked it boldly, because he saw that a knife was sticking from its middle part and fresh blood was still oozing out. The snake hissed, uncoiled, and began to back away. Wolff stabbed at it a few times, and it lunged at him. Wolff drove the point of the flint into one of the large dull-green eyes. The snake hissed loudly and reared, its two-score of five-toed feet kicking. Wolff tore the spear loose from the bloodied eye and thrust it into the dead white area just below the snake's jaw The flint went in deeply; the snake jerked so violently that it tore the shaft loose from Wolff's grip. But the creature fell over on its side, breathing deeply, and after awhile it died.

There was a scream above him, followed by a shadow. Wolff had heard that scream before, when he had been on the sailfish. He dived to one side and rolled across the ledge. Coming to a fissure, he crawled within it and turned to see what had threatened him. It was one of the enormous, wide-winged, green-bodied, red-headed, yellow-beaked eagles. It was crouched on the snake and tearing out gobbets with a beak as sharp as the teeth in the snake's jaws. Between gulps it glared at Wolff, who tried to shrink even further within the protection of the fissure.

Wolff had to stay within his crevice until the bird had filled its crop. Since this took all the rest of the day and the eagle did not leave the two corpses that night, Wolff became hungry, thirsty, and more than uncomfortable. By morning, he was also getting angry. The eagle was sitting by the two corpses, its wings folded around its body and its head drooping. Wolff thought that, if it were asleep, now would be the time to make a break. He stepped out of the crevice, wincing with the pain of stiff muscles. As he did so, the eagle jerked its head up, half-spread its wings, and screamed at him. Wolff retreated to the crevice.

By noon, the eagle still showed no intention of leaving. It ate little and seemed to be fighting drowsiness. Occasionally it belched. The sun beat down upon the bird and the two corpses. All three stank. Wolff began to despair. For all he knew, the eagle would remain until it had picked both reptile and gworl bare to the bone. By that time, he, Wolff, would be half-dead of starvation and thirst.

He left the fissure and picked up the spear. This had fallen out when the bird had ripped out the flesh around it. He jabbed threateningly at the eagle, which glared, hissed, and then screamed at him. Wolff shouted back and slowly backed away from the bird. It advanced with short slow steps, rolling slightly. Wolff stopped, yelled again, and jumped at the eagle. Startled, it leaped back and screamed again.

Wolff resumed his cautious retreat, but this time the eagle did not go after him. Only when the curve of the mountain took the predator out of view did Wolff resume climbing. He made sure that there was always a place to dodge into if the bird should come after him. However, no shadow fell on him. Apparently the eagle had wanted only to protect its food.

The middle of the next morning, he came across another gworl. This one had a smashed leg and was sitting with its back against the trunk of a small tree. It brandished a knife at a dozen red and rangy hoglike beasts with hooves like those of mountain goats. These paced back and forth before the crippled gworl and grunted in their throats. Now and then one made a short charge, but stopped a few feet away from the waving knife.

Wolff climbed a boulder and began throwing rocks at the hooved carnivores. A minute later, he wished he had not drawn attention to himself. The beasts clambered up the steep boulder as if stairs had been built for them. Only by rapid thrusting with the spear did he manage to push them back down on the ledge below. The flint tip dug into their tough hides a little but not enough to seriously hurt them.

Squealing, they landed on the rock below, only to scramble back up toward him. Their boar-tusks slashed close to him; a pair almost snipped one of his feet. He was busy trying to keep them from swarming over him when a moment came when all were on the ledge and none on the boulder. He dropped his spear, lifted a rock twice the size of his head, and hurled it down on the back of a boar. The beast screamed and tried to crawl away on its two undamaged front legs. The pack closed in on his paralyzed rear legs and began eating them. When the wounded beast turned to defend himself, he was seized by the throat. In a moment he was dead and being torn apart.

Wolff picked up his spear, climbed down the other side of the rock, and walked to the gworl. He kept an eye upon the feeders, but they did no more than raise their heads briefly to check on him before resuming their tearing at the carcass.

The gworl snarled at Wolff and held its knife ready. Wolff stopped far enough away so that he could dodge if the knife were thrown. A splinter of bone stuck out from the ravaged leg below the knee. The eyes of the gworl, sunk under the pads of cartilage on its low forehead, looked glassy.

Wolff had an unexpected reaction. He had thought that he would at once and savagely kill any gworl he came across. But now he wanted to talk to him.

So lonely had he become during the days and nights of climbing that he was glad to speak even to this loathsome creature.

He said, in Greek, 'Is there any way in which I can help you?'

The gworl spoke in the back-of-the-throat syllables of its kind and raised the knife. Wolff started walking toward it, then hurled himself to one side as the knife whished by his head. He retrieved the knife, then walked up to the gworl and spoke to him again. The thing grated back, but in a weaker voice. Wolff, bending over to repeat his question, was struck in the face with a mass of saliva.

That triggered off his hate and fear. He rammed the knife into the thick neck; the gworl kicked violently several times and died. Wolff wiped the knife on the dark fur and looked through the leather bag attached to the gworl's belt. It contained dried meat, dried fruit, some dark, hard bread, and a canteen with a fiery liquor. Wolff was not sure about where the meat came from, but he told himself that he was too hungry to be picky. Biting into the bread was an experience; it was almost as hard as stone but, when softened with saliva, tasted like graham crackers.

Wolff kept on climbing. The days and nights passed with no more signs of the gworl. The air was as thick and warm as at sea level, yet he estimated that he must be at least 30,000 feet up. The sea below was a thin silver girdle around the waist of the world.

That night he awakened to feel dozens of small furry hands on his body. He struggled, only to find that the many hands were too strong. They gripped him fast while others tied his hands and feet together with a rope that had a grassy texture. Presently he was lifted high and carried out onto the stone apron before the small cave in which he had slept. The moonlight showed several score bipeds, each about two and a half feet high. They were covered with sleek gray fur, mouselike, but had a white ruff around their necks. The faces were black and pushed in and resembled a bat's. Their ears were enormous and pointed.

Silently, they rushed him over the apron and into another fissure. This opened to reveal a large chamber about thirty feet wide and twenty high. Moonlight bored through a crack in the ceiling and revealed what his nose had already detected, a pile of bones with some rotting flesh. He was set down near the bones while his captors retreated to one corner of the cave. They began talking, or at least twittering, among themselves. One walked over to Wolff, looked at him a moment, and sank onto his knees by Wolff's throat. A second later, he was gnawing at the throat with tiny but very sharp teeth. Others followed him; teeth began chewing all over his body.

It was all done in a literally deadly silence. Even Wolff made no noise beyond his harsh breathing as he struggled. The sharp little pains of the teeth quickly passed, as if some mild anaesthetic were being released into his blood.

He began to feel drowsy. Despite himself, he quit fighting. A pleasant numbness spread through him. It did not seem worthwhile to battle for his life; why not go out pleasantly? At least his death would not be useless. There was something noble in giving his body so that these little beings could fill their bellies and be well-fed and happy for a few days.

A light burst into the cave. Through the warm haze, he saw the bat-faces leap away from him and run to the extreme end of the cave, where they cowered together. The light became stronger and was revealed as a torch of burning pine. An old man's face followed the light and bent over him. He had a long white beard, a sunken mouth, a curved sharp nose, and huge supraorbital ridges with bristling eyebrows. A dirty white robe covered his shrunken body. His big-veined hand held a staff on the end of which was a sapphire, large as Wolff's fist, carved in the image of a harpy.

Wolff tried to speak but could only mutter a tangled speech, as if he were coming up out of ether after an operation. The old man gestured with the staff, and several of the batfaces detached themselves from the mass of fur. They scurried sideways across the floor, their slanted eyes turned fearfully toward the old man. Quickly, they untied Wolff. He managed to rise to his feet, but he was so wobbly that the old man had to support him out of the cave.

The ancient spoke in Mycenaean Greek. 'You'll feel better soon. The venom does not last long.'

'Who are you? Where are you taking me?'

'Out of this danger,' the old man said. Wolff pondered the enigmatic answer. By the time that his mind and body were functioning well again, they had come to another entrance to a cave. They went through a complex of chambers that gradually led them upward. When they had covered about two miles, the old man stopped before a cave with an iron door. He handed the torch to Wolff, pulled the door open, and waved him on in. Wolff entered into a large cavern bright with torches. The door clanged behind him, succeeded by the thud of a bolt shooting fast.

The first thing that struck him was the choking odor. The next, the two green red-headed eagles that closed in on him. One spoke in a voice like a giant parrot and ordered him to march on ahead. He did so, noting at the same time that the batfaces must have removed his knife. The weapon would not have done him much good. The cave was thronged with the birds, each of which towered above him.

Against one wall were two cages made of thin iron bars. In one was a group of six gworl. In the other was a tall well-built youth wearing a deerskin breechcloth. He grinned at Wolff and said, 'So you made it! How you've changed!'

Only then did the reddish-bronze hair, long upper lip, and craggy but merry face become familiar. Wolff recognized the man who had thrown the horn from the gworl-besieged boulder and who called himself Kickaha.

6

Wolff did not have time to reply, for the cage door was opened by one of the eagles, who used his foot as effectively as a hand. A powerful head and hard beak shoved him into the cage; the door ground shut behind him.

'So, here you are,' Kickaha said in a rich baritone voice. 'The question is, what do we do now? Our stay here may be short and unpleasant.'

Wolff, looking through the bars, saw a throne carved out of rock, and on it a woman. A half-woman, rather, for she had wings instead of arms and the lower part of her body was that of a bird. The legs, however, were much thicker in proportion than those of a normal-sized Earth eagle. They had to support more weight, Wolff thought, and he knew that here was another of the Lord's laboratory-produced monsters. She must be the Podarge of whom Ipsewas had spoken.

From the waist up she was such a woman as few men are privileged to see. Her skin was white as a milky opal, her breasts superb, the throat a column of beauty. The hair was long and black and straight and fell on both sides of a face that was even more beautiful than Chryseis', an admission that he had not thought it possible to evoke from him.

However, there was something horrible in the beauty: a madness. The eyes were fierce as those of a caged falcon teased beyond endurance.

Wolff tore his eyes from hers and looked about the cave. 'Where is Chryseis?' he whispered.

'Who?' Kickaha whispered back.

With a few quick sentences, Wolff described her and what had happened to him.

Kickaha shook his head. 'I've never seen her.'

'But the gworl?'

'There were two bands of them. The other must have Chryseis and the horn. Don't worry about them. If we don't talk our way out of this, we're done for. And in a very hideous way.'

Wolff asked about the old man. Kickaha replied that he had once been Podarge's lover. He was an aborigine, one of those who had been brought into this universe shortly after the Lord had fashioned it. The harpy now kept him to do the menial work which required human hands. The old man had come at Podarge's order to rescue Wolff from the batfaces, undoubtedly because she had long ago heard from her pets of Wolff's presence in her domain.

Podarge stirred restlessly on her throne and unfolded her wings. They came together before her with a splitting noise like distant lightning.

'You two there!' she shouted. 'Quit your whispering! Kickaha, what more do you have to say for yourself before I loose my pets?'

'I can only repeat, at the risk of seeming tiresome, what I said before!' Kickaha replied loudly. 'I am as much the enemy of the Lord as you, and he hates me, he would kill me! He knows I stole his horn and that I'm a danger to him. His Eyes rove the four levels of the world and fly up and down the mountains to find me. And ...'

'Where is this horn you said you stole from the Lord? Why don't you have it now? I think you are lying to save your worthless carcass!'

'I told you that I opened a gate to the next world and that I threw it to a man who appeared at the gate. He stands before you now.'

Podarge turned her head as an eagle swivels hers, and she glared at Wolff. 'I see no horn. I see only some tough stringy meat behind a black beard!'

'He says that another band of gworl stole it from him,' Kickaha replied. 'He was chasing after them to get it back when the batfaces captured him and you so magnanimously rescued him. Release us, gracious and beautiful Podarge, and we will get the horn back. With it, we will be in a position to fight the Lord. He can be beaten! He may be the powerful Lord, but he is not all-powerful! If he were, he would have found us and the horn long ago!'

Podarge stood up, preened her wings, and walked down the steps from the throne and across the floor to the cage. She did not bob as a bird does when walking, but strode stiff-legged.

'I wish that I could believe you,' she said in a lower but just as intense voice. 'If only I could! I have waited through the years and the centuries and the millenia, oh, so long that my heart aches to think of the time! If I thought that the weapons for striking back at him had finally come within my hands ...'

She stared at them, held her wings out before her, and said, 'See! "My hands," I said. But I do not have hands, nor the body that was once mine. That ...' And she burst into a raging invective that made Wolff shrink. It was not the words but the fury, bordering on divinity or mindlessness, that made him grow cold.

'If the Lord can be overthrown – and I believe he can – you will be given back your human body,' Kickaha said when she had finished.

She panted with a clench of her anger and stared at them with the lust of murder. Wolff felt that all was lost, but her next words showed that the passion was not for them.

'The old Lord has been gone for a long time, so the rumor says. I sent one of my pets to investigate, and she came back with a strange tale. She said that there is a new Lord there, but she did not know whether or not it was the same Lord in a new body. I sent her back to the Lord, who refused my pleas to be given my rightful body again. So it does not matter whether or not there is another Lord. He is just as evil and hateful as the old one, if he is indeed not the old one. But I must know!

'First, whoever now is the Lord must die. Then I will find out if he had a new body or not. If the old Lord has left this universe, I will track him through the worlds and find him!'

'You can't do that without the horn,' Kickaha said. 'It and it alone opens the gate without a counter-device in the other world.'

'What have I to lose?' Podarge said. 'If you are lying and betray me, I will have you in the end, and the hunt might be fun. If you mean what you say, then we will see what happens.'

She spoke to the eagle beside her, and it opened the gate. Kickaha and Wolff followed the harpy across the cave to a great table with chairs around it. Only then did Wolff see that the chamber was a treasure house; the loot of a world was piled up in it. There were large open chests crammed with gleaming jewels, pearl necklaces, and golden and silver cups of exquisite shape. There were small figurines of ivory and of some shining hard-grained black wood. There were magnificent paintings. Armor and weapons of all kinds, except firearms, were piled carelessly at various places.

Podarge commanded them to sit down in ornately wrought chairs with carved lion's feet. She beckoned with a wing, and out of the shadows stepped a young man. He carried a heavy golden tray on which were three finely chiseled cups of crystal-quartz. These were fashioned as leaping fish with wide open mouths; the mouths were filled with a rich dark red wine.

'One of her lovers,' Kickaha whispered in answer to Wolff's curious stare at the handsome blond youth. 'Carried by her eagles from the level known as Dracheland or Teutonia. Poor fellow! But it's better than being eaten alive by her pets, and he always has the hope of escaping to make his life bearable.'

Kickaha drank and breathed out satisfaction at the heavy but blood-brightening taste. Wolff felt the wine writhe as if alive. Podarge gripped the cup between the tips of her two wings and lifted it to her lips.

'To the death and damnation of the Lord. Therefore, to your success!'

The two drank again. Podarge put her cup down and flicked Wolff lightly across the face with the ends of the feathers of one wing. 'Tell me your story.'

Wolff talked for a long while. He ate from slices of a roast goat-pig, a light brown bread, and fruit, and he drank the wine. His head began reeling, but he talked on and on, stopping only when Podarge questioned him about something. Fresh torches replaced the old and still he talked.

Abruptly, he awoke. Sunshine was coming in from another cave, lighting the empty cup and the table on which his head had lain while he had slept. Kickaha, grinning, stood by him.

'Let's go,' he said. 'Podarge wants us to get started early. She's eager for revenge. And I want to get out before she changes her mind. You don't know how lucky we are. We're the only prisoners she's ever given freedom.'

Wolff sat up and groaned with the ache in his shoulders and neck. His head felt fuzzy and a little heavy, but he had had worse hangovers.

'What did you do after I fell asleep?' he said.

Kickaha smiled broadly. 'I paid the final price. But it wasn't bad, not bad at all. Rather peculiar at first, but I'm an adaptable fellow.'

They walked out of the cave into the next one and from thence onto the wide lip of stone jutting from the cliff. Wolff turned for one last look and saw several eagles, green monoliths, standing by the entrance to the inner cave. There was a flash of white skin and black wings as Podarge crossed stiff-legged before the giant birds.

'Come on,' Kickaha said. 'Podarge and her pets are hungry. You didn't see her try to get the gworl to plead for mercy. I'll say one thing for them, they didn't whine or cry. They spat at her.'

Wolff jumped as a ripsaw scream came from the cave mouth. Kickaha took Wolff's arm and urged him into a fast walk. More jagged cries tore from eagle beaks, mingled with the ululations from beings in fear and pain of death.

'That'd be us, too,' Kickaha said, 'if we hadn't had something to trade for our lives.'

They began climbing and by nightfall were three thousand feet higher. Kickaha untied the knapsack of leather from his back and produced various articles. Among these was a box of matches, with one of which he started a fire. Meat and bread and a small bottle of the Rhadamanthean wine followed. The bag and the contents were gifts from Podarge.

'We've got about four days of climbing before we get to the next level,' the youth said. 'Then, the fabulous world of Amerindia.'

Wolff started to ask questions, but Kickaha said the he ought to explain the physical structure of the planet. Wolff listened patiently, and when he had heard Kickaha out, he did not scoff. Moreover, Kickaha's explanation corresponded with what he had so far seen. Wolff's intentions to ask how Kickaha, obviously a native of Earth, had come here were frustrated. The youth, complaining that he had not slept for a long time and had had an especially exhausting night, fell asleep.

Wolff stared for awhile into the flames of the dying fire. He had seen and experienced much in a short time, but he had much more to go through. That is, he would if he lived. A whooping cry rose from the depths, and a great green eagle screamed somewhere in the air along the mountain-face.

He wondered where Chryseis was tonight. Was she alive and if so, how was she faring? And where was the horn? Kickaha had said that they had to find the horn if they were to have any success at all. Without it, they would inevitably lose.

So thinking, he too fell asleep.

Four days later, when the sun was in the midpoint of its course around the planet, they pulled themselves over the rim. Before them was a plain that rolled for at least 160 miles before the horizon dropped it out of sight. To both sides, perhaps a hundred miles away, were mountain ranges. These might be large enough to cause comparison with the Himalayas. But they were mice beside the monolith, Abharhploonta, that dominated this section of the multilevel planet. Abharhploonta was, so Kickaha claimed, fifteen hundred miles from the rim, yet it looked no more than fifty miles away. It towered fully as high as the mountain up which they had just climbed.

'Now you get the idea,' Kickaha said. 'This world is not pear-shaped. It's a planetary Tower of Babylon. A series of staggered columns, each smaller than the one beneath it. On the very apex of this Earth-sized tower is the palace of the Lord. As you can see, we have a long way to go.

'But it's a great life while it lasts! I've had a wild and wonderful time! If the Lord struck me at this moment, I couldn't complain. Although, of course, I would, being human and therefore bitter about being cut off in my prime! And believe me, my friend, I'm prime!'

Wolff could not help smiling at the youth. He looked so gay and buoyant, like a bronze statue suddenly touched into animation and overflowingly joyous because he was alive.

'Okay!' Kickaha cried. 'The first thing we have to do is get some fitting clothes for you! Nakedness is chic in the level below, but not on this one. You have to wear at least a breechcloth and a feather in your hair; otherwise the natives will have contempt for you. And contempt here means slavery or death for the contemptible.'

He began walking along the rim, Wolff with him.

'Observe how green and lush the grass is and how it is as high as our knees, Bob. It affords pasture for browsers and grazers. But it is also high enough to conceal the beasts that feed on the grass-eaters. So beware! The plains puma and the dire wolf and the striped hunting dog and the giant weasel prowl through the grasses. Then there is Felis Atrox, whom I call the atrocious lion. He once roamed the plains of the North American Southwest, became extinct there about 10,000 years ago. He's very much alive here, one-third larger than the African lion and twice as nasty.

'Hey, look there! Mammoths!'

Wolff wanted to stop to watch the huge gray beasts, which were about a quarter of a mile away. But Kickaha urged him on. 'There're plenty more around, and there'll be times when you wish there weren't. Spend your time watching the grass. If it moves contrary to the wind, tell me.'

They walked swiftly for two miles. During this time, they came close to a band of wild horses. The stallions whickered and raced up to investigate them, then stood their ground, pawing and snorting, until the two had passed. They were magnificent animals, tall, sleek, and black or glossy red or spotted white and black.

'Nothing of your Indian pony there,' Kickaha said. 'I think the Lord imported nothing but the best stock.'

Presently, Kickaha stopped by a pile of rocks. 'My marker,' he said. He walked straight inward across the plain from the cairn. After a mile they came to a tall tree. The youth leaped up, grabbed the lowest branch, and began climbing. Halfway up, he reached a hollow and brought out a large bag. On returning, Kickaha took out of the bag two bows, two quivers of arrows, a deerskin breechcloth, and a belt with a skin scabbard in which was a long steel knife.

Wolff put on the loincloth and belt and took the bow and quiver.

'You know how to use these?' Kickaha said.

'I've practised all my life.'

'Good. You'll get more than one chance to put your skill to the test. Let's go. We've many a mile to cover.'

They began wolf-trotting: run a hundred steps, walk a hundred steps. Kickaha pointed to the range of mountains to their right.

'There is where my tribe, the Hrowakas, the Bear People, live. Eighty miles away. Once we get there, we can take it easy for awhile, and make preparations for the long journey ahead of us.'

'You don't look like an Indian,' Wolff said.

'And you, my friend, don't look like a sixty-six-year-old man, either. But here we are. Okay. I've put off telling my story because I wanted to hear yours first. Tonight I'll talk.'

They did not speak much more that day. Wolff exclaimed now and then at the animals he saw. There were great herds of bison, dark, shaggy, bearded, and far larger than their cousins of Earth. There were other herds of horses and a creature that looked like the prototype of the camel. More mammoths and then a family of steppe mastodons. A pack of six dire wolves raced alongside the two for awhile at a distance of a hundred yards. These stood almost as high as Wolff's shoulder.

Kickaha, seeing Wolff's alarm, laughed and said, 'They won't attack us unless they're hungry. That isn't very likely with all the game around here. They're just curious.'

Presently, the giant wolves curved away, their speed increasing as they flushed some striped antelopes out of a grove of trees.

'This is North America as it was a long time before the white man,' Kickaha said, 'Fresh, spacious, with a multitude of animals and a few tribes roaming around.'

A flock of a hundred ducks flew overhead, honking. Out of the green sky, a hawk fell, struck with a thud, and the flock was minus one comrade. 'The Happy Hunting Ground!' Kickaha cried. 'Only it's not so happy sometimes.'

Several hours before the sun went around the mountain, they stopped by a small lake. Kickaha found the tree in which he had built a platform.

'We'll sleep here tonight, taking turns on watch. About the only animal that might attack us in the tree is the giant weasel, but he's enough to worry about. Besides, and worse, there could be war parties.'

Kickaha left with his bow in hand and returned in fifteen minutes with a large buck rabbit. Wolff had started a small fire with little smoke; over this they roasted the rabbit. While they ate, Kickaha explained the topography of the country.

'Whatever else you can say about the Lord, you can't deny he did a good job of designing this world. You take this level, Amerindia. It's not really flat. It has a series of slight curves each about 160 miles long. These allow the water to run off, creeks and rivers and lakes to form. There's no snow anywhere on the planet – can't be, with no seasons and a fairly uniform climate. But it rains every day – the clouds come in from space somewhere.'

They finished eating the rabbit and covered the fire. Wolff took first watch. Kickaha talked all through Wolff's turn at guard. And Wolff stayed awake through Kickaha's watch to listen.

In the beginning, a long time ago, more than 20,000 years, the Lords had dwelt in a universe parallel to Earth's. They were not known as the Lords then. There were not very many of them at that time, for they were the survivors of a millenia-long struggle with another species. They numbered perhaps ten thousand in all.

'But what they lacked in quantity they more than possessed in quality,' Kickaha said. 'They had a science and technology that makes ours, Earth's, look like the wisdom of Tasmanian aborigines. They were able to construct these private universes. And they did.

'At first each universe was a sort of playground, a microcosmic country club for small groups. Then, as was inevitable, since these people were human beings no matter how godlike in their powers, they quarreled. The feeling of property was, is, as strong in them as in us. There was a struggle among them. I suppose there were also deaths from accident and suicide. Also, the isolation and loneliness of the Lords made them megalomaniacs, natural when you consider that each played the part of a little god and came to believe in his role.

'To compress an eons-long story into a few words, the Lord who built this particular universe eventually found himself alone. Jadawin was his name, and he did not even have a mate of his own kind. He did not want one. Why should he share this world with an equal, when he could be a Zeus with a million Europas, with the loveliest of Ledas?

'He had populated this world with beings abducted from other universes, mainly Earth's, or created in the laboratories in the palace on top of the highest tier. He had created divine beauties and exotic monsters as he wished.

'The only trouble was, the Lords were not content to rule over just one universe. They began to covet the worlds of the others. And so the struggle was continued. They erected nearly impregnable defenses and conceived almost invincible offenses. The battle became a deadly game. This fatal play was inevitable, when you consider that boredom and ennui were enemies the Lords could not keep away. When you are near-omnipotent, and your creatures are too lowly and weak to interest you forever, what thrill is there besides risking your immortality against another immortal?'

'But how did you come into this?' Wolff said.

'I? My name on Earth was Paul Janus Finnegan. My middle name was my mother's family name. As you know, it also happens to be that of the Latin god of gates and of the old and new year, the god with two faces, one looking ahead and one looking behind.'

Kickaha grinned and said, 'Janus is very appropriate, don't you think? I am a man of two worlds, and I came through the gate between. Not that I have ever returned to Earth or want to. I've had adventures and I've gained a stature here I never could have had on that grimy old globe. Kickaha isn't my only name, and I'm a chief on this tier and a big shot of sorts on other tiers. As you will find out.'

Wolff was beginning to wonder about him. He had been so evasive that Wolff suspected Kickaha had another identity about which he did not intend to talk.

'I know what you're thinking, but don't you believe it,' Kickaha said. 'I'm a trickster, but I'm leveling with you. By the way, did you know how I came by my name among the Bear People? In their language, a *kickaha* is a mythological character, a semidivine trickster. Something like the Old Man Coyote of the Plains or Nanabozho of the Ojibway or Wakdjunkaga of the Winnebago. Some day I'll tell you how I earned that name and how I became a councilor of the Hrowakas. But I've more important things to tell you now.'

7

In 1941, at the age of twenty-three, Paul Finnegan had volunteered for the U.S. Cavalry because he loved horses. A short time later, he found himself driving a tank. He was with the Eighth Army and so eventually crossed the Rhine. One day, after having helped take a small town, he discovered an extraordinary object in the ruins of the local museum. It was a crescent of silvery metal, so hard that hammer blows did not dent it nor an acetylene torch melt it.

'I asked some of the citizens about it. All they knew was that it had been in the museum a long time. A professor of chemistry, after making some tests on it, had tried to interest the University of Munich in it but had failed.

'I took it home with me after the war, along with other souvenirs. Then I went back to the University of Indiana. My father had left me enough money to see me through for a few years, so I had a nice little apartment, a sports car, and so on.

'A friend of mine was a newspaper reporter. I told him about the crescent and its peculiar properties and unknown composition. He wrote a story about it which was printed in Bloomington, and the story was picked up by a syndicate. It didn't create much interest among scientists – in fact, they wanted nothing to do with it.

'Three days later, a man calling himself Mr Vannax appeared at my apartment. I thought he was Dutch because of his name and his foreign accent. He wanted to see the crescent. I obliged. He got very excited, although he tried to to appear calm. He said he'd like to buy it from me. I asked how much he'd pay, and he said he'd give ten thousand dollars, but no more.

'"Sure you can go higher," I said,' Kickaha continued. '"Because if you don't, you'll get nowhere."

'"Twenty thousand?" Vannax said.

'"Let's pump it up a bit," I said.

'"Thirty thousand?"'

Finnegan decided to plunge. He asked Vannax if he would pay $100,000. Vannax became even redder in the face and swelled up 'like a hoppy toad,' as Finnegan-Kickaha said. But he replied that he would have the sum in twenty-four hours.

'Then I knew I really had something,' Kickaha said to Wolff. 'The question was, what? Also, why did this Vannax character so desperately want it? And what kind of a nut was he? No one with good sense, no normal human being, would rise so fast to the bait. He'd be cagier.'

'What did Vannax look like?' Wolff asked.

'Oh, he was a big guy, a well-preserved sixty-five. He had an eagle beak and eagle eyes. He was dressed in expensive conservative clothes. He had a powerful personality, but he was trying to restrain it, to be real nice. And having a hell of a time doing it. He seemed to be a man who wasn't used to being balked in any thing.'

'"Make it $300,000, and it's yours" I said. I never dreamed he'd say yes. I thought he'd get mad and take off. Because I wasn't going to sell the crescent, not if he offered me a million.'

Vannax, although furious, said that he would pay $300,000 but Finnegan would have to give him an additional twenty-four hours.

'"You have to tell me why you want the crescent and what good it is first," I said.

'"Nothing doing!" he shouted. "It is enough for you to rob me, you pig of a merchant, you, you earth … worm!"'

'"Get out before I throw you out. Or before I call the police," I said.'

Vannax began shouting in a foreign tongue. Finnegan went into his bedroom and came out with a .45 automatic. Vannax did not know it was not loaded. He left, although he was cursing and talking to himself all the way to his 1940 Rolls-Royce.

That night Finnegan had trouble getting to sleep. It was after 2:00 A.M. before he succeeded, and even then he kept waking up. During one of his rousings he heard a noise in the front room. Quietly, he rolled out of bed and took the .45, now loaded, from under his pillow. On the way to the bedroom door he picked up his flashlight from the bureau.

Its beam caught Vannax stooping over in the middle of the living room. The silvery crescent was in his hand.

'Then I saw the second crescent on the floor. Vannax had brought another with him. I'd caught him in the act of placing the two together to form a complete circle. I didn't know why he was doing it, but I found out a moment later.

'I told him to put his hands up. He did so, but he lifted his foot to step into the circle. I told him not to move even a trifle, or I'd shoot. He put one foot inside the circle, anyway. So I fired. I shot over his head, and the slug went into a corner of the room. I just wanted to scare him, figuring if he got shaken up enough he might start talking. He was scared all right; he jumped back.

'I walked across the room while he backed up toward the door. He was babbling like a maniac, threatening me in one breath and offering me half a million in the next. I thought I'd back him up against the door and jam the .45 in his belly. He'd really talk then, spill his guts out about the crescent.

'But as I followed him across the room I stepped into the circle formed by the two crescents. He saw what I was doing and screamed at me not to. Too late then. He and the apartment disappeared, and I found myself still in the circle – only it wasn't quite the same – and in this world. In the palace of the Lord, on top of the world.'

Kickaha said he might have gone into shock then. But he had avidly read fantasy and science-fiction since the fourth grade of grammar school. The idea of parallel universes and devices for transition between them was familiar. He had been conditioned to accept such concepts. In fact, he half-believed in them. Thus he was flexible-minded enough to bend without breaking and then bounce back. Although frightened, he was at the same time excited and curious.

'I figured out why Vannax hadn't followed me through the gate. The two crescents, placed together, formed a "circuit". But they weren't activated until a living being stepped within whatever sort of "field" they radiated. Then one semicircle remained behind on Earth while the other was gated through to this universe, where it latched onto a semicircle waiting for it. In other words, it takes three crescents to make a circuit. One in the world to which you're going, and two in the one you're leaving. You step in; one crescent transfers over to the single one in the next universe, leaving only one crescent in the world you just left.

'Vannax must have come to Earth by means of these crescents. And he would not, could not, do so unless there had been a crescent already on Earth. Somehow, maybe we'll never know, he lost one of them on Earth. Maybe it was stolen by someone who didn't know its true value. Anyway, he must've been searching for it, and when that news story went out about the one I had found in Germany, he knew what it was. After talking to me, he concluded I might not sell it. So he got into my apartment with the crescent he did have. He was just about to complete the circle and pass on over when I stopped him.

'He must be stranded on Earth and unable to get here unless he finds another crescent. For all I know, there may be others on Earth. The one I got in Germany might not even be the one he lost.'

Finnegan wandered about the 'palace' for a long while. It was immense, staggeringly beautiful and exotic and filled with treasure, jewels and artifacts. There were also laboratories, or perhaps bioprocess chambers was a better title. In these, Finnegan saw strange creatures slowly forming within huge transparent cylinders. There were many consoles with many operating devices, but he had no idea what they did. The symbols beneath the buttons and levers were unfamiliar.

'I was lucky. The palace is filled with traps to snare or kill the uninvited. But they were not set – why, I don't know, any more than I knew then why the place was untenanted. But it was a break for me.'

Finnegan left the palace for awhile to go through the exquisite garden that surrounded it. He came to the edge of the monolith on which the palace and garden were.

'You've seen enough to imagine how I felt when I looked over the edge. The monolith must be at least thirty thousand feet high. Below it is the tier that the Lord named Atlantis. I don't know whether the Earth myth of Atlantis was founded on this Atlantis or whether the Lord got the name from the myth.

'Below Atlantis is the tier called Dracheland. Then, Amerindia. One sweep of my eye took it in, just as you can see one side of the Earth from a rocket. No details, of course, just big clouds, large lakes, seas, and outlines of continents. And a good part of each successively lower tier was obscured by the one just above it.

'But I could make out the Tower of Babylon structure of this world, even though I didn't, at that time, understand what I was seeing. It was just too unexpected and alien for me to apprehend any sort of *gestalt*. It didn't mean anything.'

Finnegan could, however, understand that he was in a desperate situation. He had no means of leaving the top of this world except by trying to return to Earth through the crescents. Unlike the sides of the other monoliths, the face of this one was smooth as a bearing ball. Nor was he going to use the crescents again, not with Vannax undoubtedly waiting for him.

Although he was in no danger of starving – there was food and water enough to last for years – he could not and did not want to stay there. He dreaded the return of the owner, for he might have a very nasty temper. There were some things in the palace which made Kickaha feel uneasy.

'But the gworl came,' Kickaha said. 'I suppose – I know – they came from another universe through a gate similar to that which had opened the way for me. At the time, I had no way of knowing how or why they were in the palace. But I was glad I'd gotten there first. If I'd fallen into their hands …! Later, I figured out they were agents for another Lord. He's sent them to steal the horn. Now, I'd seen the horn during my wandering about the palace, and had even blown it. But I didn't know how to press the combinations of buttons on it to make it work. As a matter of fact, I didn't know its real purpose.

'The gworl came into the palace. A hundred or so of them. Fortunately, I saw them first. Right away, they let their lust for murder get them into trouble. They tried to kill some of the Eyes of the Lord, the eagle-sized ravens in the garden. These hadn't bothered me, perhaps because they thought I was a guest or didn't look dangerous.

'The gworl tried to slit a raven's throat, and the ravens attacked them. The gworl retreated into the palace, where the big birds followed them. There were blood and feathers and pieces of bumpy hairy hide and a few corpses of both sides all over that end of the palace. During the battle, I noticed a gworl coming out of a room with the horn. He went through the corridors as if looking for something.'

Finnegan followed the gworl into another room, about the size of two dirigible hangars. This held a swimming pool and a number of interesting but enigmatic devices. On a marble pedestal was a large golden model of the planet. On each of its levels were several jewels. As Finnegan was to discover, the diamonds, rubies, and sapphires were arranged to form symbols. These indicated various points of resonance.'

'Points of resonance?'

'Yes. The symbols were coded mnemonics of the combination of notes required to open gates at certain places. Some gates open to other universes, but others are simply gates between the tiers on this world. These enabled the Lord to travel instantaneously from one level to the next. Associated with the symbols were tiny models of outstanding characteristics of the resonant points on the various tiers.'

The gworl with the horn must have been told by the Lord how to read the symbols. Apparently, he was testing for the Lord to make sure he had the correct horn. He blew seven notes toward the pool, and the waters parted to reveal a piece of dry land with scarlet trees around it and a green sky beyond.

'It was the conceit of the original Lord to enter into the Atlantean tier through the pool itself. I didn't know at that time where the gate led to. But I saw my only chance to escape from the trap of the palace, and I took it. Coming up from behind the gworl, I snatched the horn from his hand and pushed him sideways into the pool – not into the gate, but into the water.

'You never heard such squawks and screams and such thrashings around. All the fear they don't have for other things is packed into a dread of water. This gworl went down, came up sputtering and yelling, and then managed to grab hold of the side of the gate. A gate has definite edges, you know, tangible if changing.

'I heard roars and shouts behind me. A dozen gworl with big and bloody knives were entering the room. I dived into the hole, which had started shrinking. It was so small I scraped the skin off my knees going through. But I got through, and the hole closed. It took off both the arms of the gworl who was trying to get out of the water and follow me. I had the horn in my hand, and I was out of their reach for the time being.'

Kickaha grinned as if relishing the memory. Wolff said, 'The Lord who sent the gworl ahead is the present Lord, right? Who is he?'

'Arwoor. The Lord who's missing was known as Jadawin. He must be the man who called himself Vannax. Arwoor moved in, and ever since he's been trying to find me and the horn.'

Kickaha outlined what had happened to him since he had found himself on the Atlantean tier. During the twenty years (of Earth time), he had been living on one tier or another, always in disguise. The gworl and the ravens, now serving the Lord Arwoor, had never stopped looking for him. But there were long periods of time, sometimes two or three years on end, when Kickaha had not been disturbed.

'Wait a minute,' Wolff said. 'If the gates between the tiers were closed, how did the gworl get down off the monolith to chase you?'

Kickaha had not been able to understand that either. However, when captured by the gworl in the Garden level, he had questioned them. Although surly, they had given him some answers. They had been lowered to the Atlantean tier by cords.

'Thirty thousand feet?' Wolff said.

'Sure, why not? The palace is a fabulous many-chambered storehouse. If I'd had a chance to look long enough, I'd have found the cords myself. Anyway, the gworl told me they were charged by the Lord Arwoor not to kill me. Even if it meant having to let me escape at the time. He wants me to enjoy a series of exquisite tortures. The gworl said that Arwoor had been working on new and subtle techniques, plus refining some of the well established methods. You can imagine how I was sweating it out on the journey back.'

After his capture in the Garden, Kickaha was taken across Okeanos to the base of the monolith. While they were climbing up it, a raven Eye stopped them. He had carried the news of Kickaha's capture to the Lord, who sent him back with orders. The gworl were to split into two bands. One was to continue with Kickaha. The other was to return to the Garden rim. If the man who now had the horn were to return through the gate with it, he was to be captured. The horn would be brought back to the Lord.

Kickaha said, 'I imagine Arwoor wanted you brought back, too. He probably forgot to relay such an order to the gworl through the raven. Or else he assumed you'd be taken to him, forgetting that the gworl are very literal-minded and unimaginative.

'I don't know why the gworl captured Chryseis. Perhaps they intend to use her as a peace-offering to the Lord. The gworl know he is displeased with them because I've led them such a long and sometimes merry chase. They may mean to placate him with the former Lord's most beautiful masterpiece.'

Wolff said, 'Then the present Lord can't travel between tiers via the resonance points?'

'Not without the horn. And I'll bet he's in a hot-and-cold running sweat right now. There's nothing to prevent the gworl from using the horn to go to another universe and present it to another Lord. Nothing except their ignorance of where the resonance points are. If they should find one ... However, they didn't use it by the boulder, so I imagine they won't try it elsewhere. They're vicious but not bright.'

Wolff said, 'If the Lords are such masters of super-science, why doesn't Arwoor use aircraft to travel?'

Kickaha laughed for a long time. Then he said, 'That's the joker. The Lords are heirs to a science and power far surpassing Earth's. But the scientists and technicians of their people are dead. The ones now living know how to operate their devices, but they are incapable of explaining the principles behind them or of repairing them.

'The millenia-long power struggle killed off all but a few. These few, despite their vast powers, are ignoramuses. They're sybarites, megalomaniacs, paranoiacs, you name it. Anything but scientists.

'It's possible that Arwoor may be a dispossessed Lord. He had to run for his life, and it was only because Jadawin was gone for some reason from this world that Arwoor was able to gain possession of it. He came empty-handed into the palace; he has no access to any powers except those in the palace, many of which he may not know how to control. He's one up in this Lordly game of musical universes, but he's still handicapped.'

Kickaha fell asleep. Wolff stared into the night, for he was on first watch. He did not find the story incredible, but he did think that there were holes in it. Kickaha had much more explaining to do. Then there was Chryseis. He thought of an achingly beautiful face with delicate bone structure and great cat-pupiled eyes. Where was Chryseis, how was she faring, and would he ever see her again?

8

During Wolff's second watch, something black and long and swift slipped through the moonlight between two bushes. Wolff sent an arrow into the predator, which gave a whistling scream and reared up on its hind legs, towering twice as high as a horse. Wolff fitted another arrow to the string and fired it into the white belly. Still the animal did not die, but went whistling and crashing away through the brush.

By then Kickaha, knife in hand, was beside him. 'You were lucky,' he said. 'You don't always see them, and then, pffft! They go for the throat.'

'I could have used an elephant gun,' Wolff said, 'and I'm not sure that would have stopped it. By the way, why don't the gworl – or the Indians, from what you've told me – use firearms?'

'It's strictly forbidden by the Lord. You see, the Lord doesn't like some things. He wants to keep his people at a certain population level, at a certain technological level, and within certain social structures. The Lord runs a tight planet.

'For instance, he likes cleanliness. You may have noticed that the folk of Okeanos are a lazy, happy-go-lucky lot. Yet they always clean up their messes. No litter anywhere. The same goes on this level, on every level. The Amerindians are also personally clean, and so are the Drachelanders and Atlanteans. The Lord wants it that way, and the penalty for disobedience is death.'

'How does he enforce his rules?' Wolff asked.

'Mostly by having implanted them in the mores of the inhabitants. Originally, he had a close contact with the priests and medicine men, and by using religion – with himself as the deity – he formed and hardened the ways of the populace. He liked neatness, disliked firearms or any form of advanced technology. Maybe he was a romantic; I don't know. But the various societies on this world are mainly conformist and static.

'So what? Is progress necessarily desirable or a static society undesirable? Personally, though I detest the Lord's arrogance, his cruelty and lack of humanity, I approve of some of the things he's done. With some exceptions, I like this world, far prefer it to Earth.'

'You're a romantic, too!'

'Maybe. This world is real and grim enough, as you already know. But it's free of grit and grime, of diseases of any land, of flies and mosquitoes and lice. Youth lasts as long as you live. All in all, its not such a bad place to live in. Not for me, anyway.'

Wolff was on the last watch when the sun rounded the corner of the world. The starflies paled, and the sky was green wine. The air passed cool fingers over the two men and washed their lungs with invigorating currents. They stretched and then went down from the platform to hunt for breakfast. Later, full of roast rabbit and juicy berries, they renewed their journey.

The evening of the third day after, while the sun was a hand's breadth from slipping around the monolith, they were out on the plain. Ahead of them was a tall hill beyond which, so Kickaha said, was a small woods. One of the high trees there would give them refuge for the night.

Suddenly a party of about forty men rode around the hill. They were dark-skinned and wore their hair in two long braids. Their faces were painted with white and red streaks and black X's. Their lower arms bore small round shields, and they held lances or bows in their hands. Some wore bear-heads as helmets; others had feathers stuck into caps or wore bonnets with sweeping bird feathers.

Seeing the two men on foot before them, the riders yelled and urged their horses into a gallop. Lances tipped with steel points were leveled. Bows were fitted with arrows, and heavy steel axes or blade-studded clubs were lifted.

'Stand firm!' Kickaha said. He was grinning. 'They are the Hrowakas, the Bear People. My people.'

He stepped forward and lifted his bow above him with both hands. He shouted at the charging men in their own tongue, a speech with many glottalized stops, nasalized vowels, and a swift-rising but slow-descending intonation.

Recognizing him, they shouted, *'AngKungawas TreKickaha!'* They galloped by, their spears stabbing as closely as possible without touching him, the clubs and axes whistling across his face or above his head, and arrows plunging near his feet or even between them.

Wolff was given the same treatment, which he bore without flinching. Like Kickaha, he showed a smile, but he did not think that it was relaxed.

The Hrowakas wheeled their horses and charged back. This time they pulled their beasts up short, rearing, kicking, and whinnying. Kickaha leaped up and dragged a feather-bonneted youth from his animal. Laughing and panting, the two wrestled on the ground until Kickaha had pinned the Hrowaka. Then Kickaha arose and introduced the loser to Wolff.

'NgashuTangis, one of my brothers-in-law.'

Two Amerinds dismounted and greeted Kickaha with much embracing and excited speech. Kickaha waited until they were calmed down and then began to speak long and earnestly. He frequently jabbed his finger toward Wolff. After a fifteen-minute discourse, interrupted now and then by a brief question, he turned smiling to Wolff.

'We're in luck. They're on their way to raid the Tsenakwa, who live fairly close to the Trees of Many Shadows. I explained what we were doing here, though not all of it by any means. They don't know we're bucking the Lord himself, and I'm not about to tell them. But they do know we're on the trail of Chryseis and the gworl and that you're a friend of mine. They also know that Podarge is helping us. They've got a great respect for her and her eagles and would like to do her a favor if they could.

'They've got plenty of spare horses, so take your choice. Only thing I hate about this is that you won't get to visit the lodges of the Bear People and I'll miss seeing my two wives, Giushowei and Angwanat. But you can't have everything.'

The war party rode hard that day and the next, changing horses every half-hour. Wolff became saddle-sore – blanket-sore, rather. By the third morning he was in as good a shape as any of the Bear People and could stay on a horse all day without feeling that he had lockjaw in every muscle of his body and even in some of the bones.

The fourth day, the party was held up for eight hours. A herd of the giant bearded bison marched across their path; the beasts formed a column two miles across and ten miles long, a barrier that no one, man or animal, could cross. Wolff chafed, but the others were not too unhappy, because riders and horses alike needed a rest. Then, at the end of the column, a hundred Shanikotsa hunters rode by, intent on driving their lances and arrows into the bison on the fringes. The Hrowakas wanted to swoop down upon them and slay the entire group and only an impassioned speech by Kickaha kept them back. Afterwards, Kickaha told Wolff that the Bear People thought one of them was equal to ten of any other tribe.

'They're great fighters, but a little bit overconfident and arrogant. If you know how many times I've had to talk them out of getting into situations where they would have been wiped out!'

They rode on, but were halted at the end of an hour by NgashuTangis, one of the scouts for that day. He charged in yelling and gesturing. Kickaha questioned him, then said to Wolff, 'One of Podarge's pets is a couple of miles from here. She landed in a tree and requested NgashuTangis to bring me to her. She can't make it herself; she's been ripped up by a flock of ravens and is in a bad way. Hurry!'

The eagle was sitting on the lowest branch of a lone tree, her talons clutched about the narrow limb, which bent under her weight. Dried red-black blood covered her green feathers, and one eye had been torn out. With the other, she glared at the Bear People, who kept a respectful distance. She spoke in Mycenaean to Kickaha and Wolff.

'I am Aglaia. I know you of old, Kickaha – Kickaha the trickster. And I saw you, O Wolff, when you were a guest of great-winged Podarge, my sister and queen. She it was who sent many of us out to search for the dryad Chryseis and the gworl and the horn of the Lord. But I, I alone, saw them enter the Trees of Many Shadows on the other side of the plain.

'I swooped down on them, hoping to surprise them and seize the horn. But they saw me and formed a wall of knives against which I could only impale myself. So I flew back up, so high they could not see me. But I, farsighted treader of the skies, could see them.'

'They're arrogant even while dying,' Kickaha said softly in English to Wolff. 'Rightly so.'

The eagle drank water offered by Kickaha, and continued. 'When night fell, they camped at the edge of a copse of trees. I landed on the tree below which the dryad slept under a deerskin robe. It had dried blood on it, I suppose from the man who had been killed by the gworl. They were butchering him, getting ready to cook him over their fires.

'I came down to the ground on the opposite side of the tree. I had hoped to talk to the dryad, perhaps even enable her to escape. But a gworl sitting near her heard the flutter of my wings. He looked around the tree, and that was his mistake, for my claws took him in his eyes. He dropped his knife and tried to tear me loose from his face. And so he did, but much of his face and both eyes came along with my talons. I told the dryad to run then, but she stood up and the robe fell off. I could see then that her hands and her legs were bound.

'I went into the brush, leaving the gworl to wail for his eyes. For his death, too, because his fellows would not be burdened with a blind warrior. I escaped through the woods and back to the plains. There I was able to fly off again. I flew toward the nest of the Bear People to tell you, O Kickaha and O Wolff, beloved of the dryad. I flew all night and on into the day.

'But a hunting pack of the Eyes of the Lord saw me first. They were above and ahead of me, in the glare of the sun. They plummeted down, those playhawks, and took me by surprise. I fell, driven by their impact and by the weight of a dozen with their talons clamped upon me. I fell, turning over and over and bleeding under the thrusts of flint-sharp beaks.

'Then, I, Aglaia, sister of Podarge, righted myself and also gathered my senses. I seized the shrieking ravens and bit their heads off or tore their wings or legs off. I killed the dozen on me, only to be attacked by the rest of the pack. These I fought, and the story was the same. They died, but in their dying they caused my death. Only because they were so many.'

There was a silence. She glared at them with her remaining eye, but the life was swiftly unraveling from it to reveal the blank spool of death. The Bear People had fallen quiet; even the horses ceased snorting. The wind whispering in from the skies was the loudest noise.

Abruptly, Aglaia spoke in a weak but still arrogantly harsh voice.

'Tell Podarge she need not be ashamed of me. And promise me, O Kickaha – no trickster words to me – promise me that Podarge will be told.'

'I promise, O Aglaia,' Kickaha said. 'Your sisters will come here and carry your body far out from the rims of the tiers, out in the green skies, and you will be launched to float through the abyss, free in death as in life, until you fall into the sun or find your resting place upon the moon.'

'I hold you to it, manling,' she said.

Her head drooped, and she fell forward. But the iron talons were locked in on the branch so that she swung back and forth, upside down. The wings sagged and spread out, the tips brushing the ends of the grass.

Kickaha exploded into orders. Two men were dispatched to look for eagles to be informed of Aglaia's report and of her death. He said nothing, of course, about the horn, and he had to spend some time in teaching the two a short speech in Mycenaean. After being satisfied that they had memorized it satisfactorily, he sent them on their way. Then the party was delayed further in getting Aglaia's body to a higher position in the tree, where she would be beyond the reach of any carnivore except the puma and the carrion birds.

It was necessary to chop off the limb to which she clung and to hoist the heavy body up to another limb. Here she was tied with rawhide to the trunk and in an upright position.

'There!' Kickaha said when the work was done. 'No creature will come near her as long as she seems to be alive. All fear the eagles of Podarge.'

The afternoon of the sixth day after Aglaia the party made a long stop at a waterhole. The horses were given a chance to rest and to fill their bellies with the long green grass. Kickaha and Wolff squatted side by side on top of a small hill and chewed on an antelope steak. Wolff was gazing interestedly at a small herd of mastodons only four hundred yards away. Near them, crouched in the grass, was a striped male lion, a 900-pound specimen of Felix Atrox. The lion had some slight hopes of getting a chance at one of the calves.

Kickaha said, 'The gworl were damn lucky to make the forest in one piece, especially since they're on foot. Between here and the Trees of Many Shadows are the Tsenakwa and other tribes. And the KhingGatawriT.'

'The Half-Horses?' Wolff said. In the few days with the Hrowakas, he had picked up an amazing amount of vocabulary items and was even beginning to grasp some of the complicated syntax.

'The Half-Horses. *Hoi Kentauroi*. Centaurs. The Lord made them, just as he's made the other monsters of this world. There are many tribes of them on the Amerindian plains. Some are Scythian or Sarmatian speakers, since the Lord snatched part of his centaur material from those ancient steppe-dwellers. But others have adopted the tongues of their human neighbors. All have adopted the Plains tribal culture – with some variations.'

The war party came to the Great Trade Path. This was distinguisable from the rest of the plain only by posts driven into the ground at mile-intervals and topped by carved ebony images of the Tishquetmoac god of commerce, Ishquettlammu. Kickaha urged the party into a gallop as they came near it and it did not slow until the Path was far behind.

'If the Great Trade Path ran to the forest, instead of parallel with it,' he told Wolff, 'we'd have it made. As long as we stayed on it, we'd be undisturbed. The Path is sacrosanct; even the wild Half-Horses respect it. All the tribes get their steel weapons, cloth blankets, jewelry, chocolate, fine tobacco, and so on from the Tishquetmoac, the only civilized people on this tier. I hurried us across the Path because I wouldn't be able to stop the Hrowakas from tarrying for a few days' trade if we came across a merchant caravan. You'll notice our braves have more furs than they need on their horses. That's just in case. But we're okay now.'

Six days went by with no sign of enemy tribes except the black-and-red striped tepees of the Irennussoik at a distance. No warriors rode out to challenge them, but Kickaha did not relax until many miles had fallen behind them. The next day the plain began to change: the knee-high and bright green grass was interspersed with a bluish grass only several inches high. Soon the party was riding over a rolling land of blue.

'The stamping ground of the Half-Horse,' Kickaha said. He sent the scouts to a greater distance from the main party.

'Don't let yourself be taken alive,' he reminded Wolff.

'Especially by the Half-Horse. A human plains tribe might decide to adopt you instead of killing you if you had guts enough to sing merrily and spit in their faces while they roasted you over a low fire. But the Half-Horses don't even have human slaves. They'd keep you alive and screaming for weeks.'

On the fourth day after Kickaha's warning, they topped a rise and saw a black band ahead.

'Trees growing along the Winnkaknaw River,' Kickaha said. 'We're almost halfway to the Trees of Many Shadows. Let's push the horses until we get to the river. I've got a hunch we've eaten up most of our luck.'

He fell silent as he and the others saw a flash of sun on white several miles to their right. Then the white horse of Wicked Knife, a scout, disappeared into a shallow between rises. A few seconds later, a dark mass appeared on the rise behind him.

'The Half-Horse!' Kickaha yelled. 'Let's go! Make for the river! We can make a stand in the trees along it, if we can get there!'

9

With a single lurch, the entire war party broke into a gallop. Wolff crouched over his horse, a magnificent roan stallion, urging it on although it needed no encouragement. The plain sped by as the roan stretched his heart to drive his legs. Despite his intensity on speed, Wolff kept glancing to his right. Wicked Knife's white mare was visible now and then as she came over a swell of the plain. The scout was directing her at an angle toward his people. Less than a quarter of a mile behind, and gaining, was the horde of Half-Horse. They numbered at least a hundred and fifty, maybe more.

Kickaha brought his stallion, a golden animal with a pale silvery mane and tail, alongside Wolff. 'When they catch up with us – which they will – stay by my side! I'm organizing a column of twos, a classic maneuver, tried and true! That way, each man can guard the other's side!'

He dropped back to give orders to the rest. Wolff guided his roan to follow in line behind Wolverine Paws and Sleeps Standing Up. Behind him, White Nose Bear and Big Blanket were trying to maintain an even distance from him. The rest of the party was strung out in a disorder which Kickaha and a councillor, Spider Legs, were trying to break up.

Presently, the forty were arranged in a ragged column. Kickaha rode up beside Wolff and shouted above the pound of hooves and whistling of wind: 'They're stupid as porcupines! They wanted to turn and charge the centaurs! But I talked some sense into them!'

Two more scouts, Drunken Bear and Too Many Wives, were riding in from the left to join them. Kickaha gestured at them to fall in at the rear. Instead, the two continued their 90-degree approach and rode on past the tail of the column.

'The fools are going to rescue Wicked Knife – they think!'

The two scouts and Wicked Knife approached toward a converging point. Wicked Knife was only four hundred yards away from the Hrowakas with the Half-Horses several hundred yards behind him. They were lessening the gap with every second, traveling at a speed no horse burdened with a rider could match. As they came closer, they could be seen in enough detail for Wolff to understand just what they were.

They were indeed centaurs, although not quite as the painters of Earth had depicted. This was not surprising. The Lord, when forming them in his biolabs, had had to make certain concessions to reality. The main adjustment had been regulated by the need for oxygen. The large animal part of a centaur had to breathe, a fact ignored by the conventional Terrestrial representations. Air had to be supplied not only to the upper and human torso but to the lower and theriomorphic body. The relatively small lungs of the upper part could not handle the air requirements.

Moreover, the belly of the human trunk would have stopped all supply of nourishment to the large body beneath it. Or, if the small belly was attached to the greater equine digestive organs to transmit the food, diet was still a problem. Human teeth would quickly wear out under the abrasion of grass.

Thus the hybrid beings coming so swiftly and threateningly toward the men did not quite match the mythical creatures that had served as their models. The mouths and necks were proportionately large to allow intake of enough oxygen. In place of the human lungs was a bellowslike organ which drove the air through a throatlike opening and thence into the great lungs of the hippoid body. These lungs were larger than a horse's, for the vertical part increased the oxygen demands. Space for the bigger lungs was made by removal of the larger herbivore digestive organs and substitution of a smaller carnivore stomach. The centaur ate meat, including the flesh of his Amerind victims.

The equine part was about the size of an Indian pony of Earth. The hides were red, black, white, palomino, and pinto. The horsehair covered all but the face. This was almost twice as large as a normal-sized man's and was broad, high-cheekboned, and big-nosed. They were, on a larger scale, the features of the Plains Indians of Earth, the faces of Roman Nose, Sitting Bull, and Crazy Horse. Warpaint streaked their features and feathered bonnets and helmets of buffalo hides with projecting horns were on their heads.

Their weapons were the same as those of the Hrowakas, except for one item. This was the bola: two round stones, each secured to the end of a strip of rawhide. Even as Wolff wondered what he would do if a bola were cast at him, he saw them put into action. Wicked Knife and Drunken Bear and Too Many Wives had met and were racing beside each other about twenty yards ahead of their pursuers. Drunken Bear turned and shot an arrow. The missile plunged into the swelling bellows-organ beneath the human-chest of a Half-Horse. The Half-Horse went down and turned over and over and then lay still. The upper torso was bent at an angle that could result only from a broken spine. This despite the fact that a universal joint of bone and cartilage at the juncture of the human and equine permitted extreme flexibility of the upper torso.

Drunken Bear shouted and waved his bow. He had made the first kill, and his exploit would be sung for many years in the Hrowakas Council House.

If there's anybody left to tell about it, Wolff thought.

A number of bolas, whirled around and around till the stones were barely visible, were released. Rotating like airplane propellers that had spun off from their shafts, the bolas flew through the air. The stone at the end of one struck Drunken Bear on the neck and hurled him from his horse, cutting off his victory chant in the middle. Another bola wrapped itself around the hind leg of his horse to send it crashing into the ground.

Wolff, at the same time as some of the Hrowakas, released an arrow. He could not tell if it went home, for it was difficult to get a good aim and release from a position on a galloping horse. But four arrows did strike, and four Half-Horses fell. Wolff at once drew another arrow from the quiver on his back, noting at the same time that Too Many Wives and his horse were on the ground. Too Many Wives had an arrow sticking from his back.

Now, Wicked Knife was overtaken. Instead of spearing him, the Half-Horses split up to come in on either side of him.

'No!' Wolff cried. 'Don't let them do it!'

Wicked Knife, however, had not earned his public name for no good reason. If the Half-Horse passed up the chance to kill him so they could take him alive for torture, they would have to pay for their mistake. He flipped his long Tishquetmoac knife through the air into the equine body of the

Half-Horse closest to him. The centaur cartwheeled. Wicked Knife drew another blade from his scabbard and, even as a spear was driven into his horse, he launched himself onto the centaur who had thrust the spear.

Wolff caught a glimpse of him through the massed bodies. He had landed on the back of the centaur, which almost collapsed at the impact of his weight but managed to recover and bear him along. Wicked Knife drove his knife into the back of the human torso. Hooves flashed; the centaur's tail rose into the air above the mob, followed by the rump and the hindlegs.

Wolff thought that Wicked Knife was finished. But no, there he was, miraculously on his feet and then, suddenly, on the horse-barrel of another centaur. This time Wicked Knife held the edge of his blade against his enemy's throat. Apparently he was threatening to cut the jugular vein if the Half-Horse did not carry him out and away from the others.

But a lance, thrust from behind, plunged into Wicked Knife's back. Not, however, before he had carried out his threat and slashed open the neck of the Half-Horse he rode.

'I saw that!' Kickaha shouted. 'What a man, that Wicked Knife! After what he did, not even the savage Half-Horse would dare mutilate his body! They honor a foe who gives them a great fight, although they'll eat him, of course.'

Now the KhingGatawriT came up closely behind the end of the Hrowakas train. They split up into parts and increased their speed to overtake them on both sides. Kickaha told Wolff that the Half-Horses would not, at first, close in on the Hrowakas in a mass charge. They would try to have some fun with their enemies and would also give their untried young warriors a chance to show their skill and courage.

A black-and-white-spotted Half-Horse, wearing a single hawk's feather in a band around his head, detached himself from the main group on the left. Whirling a bola in his right hand, holding a feathered lance in his left, he charged at an angle toward Kickaha. The stones at the rawhide ends circled to become a blur, then darted from his hand. Their path of flight was downward, toward the legs of his enemy's horse.

Kickaha leaned out and deftly stuck the tip of his lance at the bola. The lancehead was so timed that it met the rawhide in the middle. Kickaha raised the lance, the bola whirled around and around it, and wrapped itself shut. A good part of the energy of the bola was absorbed by the length of the lance. Also, the lance was brought over in an arc to Kickaha's right side nearly striking Wolff, who had to duck. Even so, Kickaha almost lost the lance, for it slid from his hand, carried by the inertia of the bola. But he kept his grip and shook the lance with the bola at its upper end.

The frustrated Half-Horse shook his fist in fury and would have charged Kickaha with his lance. A roar of acclamation and admiration arose from the two columns of centaurs. A chief raced out to forestall the youngster. He spoke a few words to send him in shame back to the main body. The chief was a large roan with a many-feathered bonnet and a number of black chevrons, crossed with a bar, painted on his equine ribs.

'Charging Lion!' Kickaha shouted in English. 'He thinks I'm worthy of his attention!'

He yelled something in the chief's language and then whooped with laughter as the dark skin became even darker. Charging Lion shouted back and spurted forward to bring him even with his insulter. The lance in his right hand stabbed at Kickaha, who countered with his own. The two shafts bounced off each other. Kickaha immediately detached his small mammoth-hide shield from his left arm. He blocked another thrust from the centaur's lance with his lance, then spun the shield like a disc. It sailed out and struck Charging Lion's right foreleg.

The centaur slipped and fell on his front legs and skidded upright through the grass. When he attempted to rise, he found that his right front leg was lamed. A yell broke loose from his group; a dozen bonneted chiefs ran with leveled lances at Charging Lion. He bore himself bravely and waited for his death with folded arms as a great, but now defeated and crippled, Half-Horse should.

'Pass the word along to slow down!' Kickaha said. 'The horses can't keep this pace up much longer; their lungs are foaming out now. Maybe we can spare them and gain some time if the Half-Horses want to blood some more of their untrieds. If they don't, well, what's the difference?'

'It's been fun,' Wolff said. 'If we don't make it, we can at least say we weren't bored.'

Kickaha rode close enough to clap Wolff on the shoulder. 'You're a man after my own heart! I'm happy to have known you. Oh oh! Here comes an unblooded now! But he's going to pick on Wolverine Paws!'

Wolverine Paws, one of Kickaha's fathers-in-law, was at the head of the Hrowakas column and just in front of Wolff. He screamed insults at the Half-Horse charging in with circling bola, and then threw his lance. The Half-Horse, seeing the weapon flying toward him, loosed the bola before he had intended. The lance pierced his shoulder; the bola went true anyway and wrapped itself around Wolverine Paws. Unconscious from a blow by one of the stones, he fell off his horse.

The horses of both Wolff and Kickaha leaped over his body, which was lying before them. Kickaha leaned down to his right and stabbed Wolverine Paws with his lance.

'They won't take delight in torturing you, Wolverine Paws!' Kickaha said. 'And you have made them pay for a life with a life.'

A period of individual combat followed. Again and again a young untried charged out of the main group to challenge one of the human beings. Sometimes the man won, sometimes the centaur. At the end of a nightmare thirty minutes, the forty Hrowakas had become twenty-eight. Wolff's turn was with a large warrior armed with a club tipped with steel points. He also carried a small round shield with which he tried to duplicate Kickaha's trick. It did not work, for Wolff deflected the shield with the point of his lance. However, his guard was open for a moment, during which the centaur took his advantage. He galloped in so close that Wolff could not turn to draw far back enough to use the lance.

The club was raised high; the sun glittered on the sharp tips of its spike. The huge broad painted face was split with a grin of triumph. Wolff had no time to dodge and if he tried to grab the club he would end with a smashed and mangled hand. Without thinking, he did a thing that surprised both himself and the centaur. Perhaps he was inspired by Wicked Knife's feat. He launched himself from his horse, came in under the club, and grappled the Half-Horse around the neck. His foe squawked with dismay. Then they went down to the ground with a shock that knocked the wind from both.

Wolff leaped up, hoping that Kickaha had grabbed his horse so he could remount. Kickaha was holding it, but he was making no move to bring it back. Indeed, both the Hrowakas and Half-Horse had stopped.

'Rules of war!' Kickaha shouted. 'Whoever gets the club first should win!'

Wolff and the centaur, now on his hooves, made a dash for the club, which was about thirty feet behind them. Four-legged speed was too much for two-legged. The centaur reached the club ten feet ahead of him. Without checking his pace, the centaur leaned his human trunk down and scooped up the club. Then he slowed and whirled, so swiftly that he had to rear up on his hind legs.

Wolff had not stopped running. He came in and then up at the Half-Horse even as it reared. A hoof flashed out at him, but he was by it, though the leg brushed against him. He crashed into the upper part, carried it back a little with him, and both fell again.

Despite the impact, Wolff kept his right arm around the centaur's neck. He hung on while the creature struggled to his hooves. The centaur had lost the club and now strove to overcome the human with sheer strength. Again he grinned, for he outweighed Wolff by at least seven hundred pounds. His torso, chest, and arms were also far bulkier than Wolff's.

Wolff braced his feet against the shoving weight of the centaur and would not move back. The grip around the huge neck tightened, and suddenly the Half-Horse could not breathe.

Then the Half-Horse tried to get his knife out, but Wolff grabbed the wrist with his other hand and twisted. The centaur screamed with the pain and dropped the knife.

A roar of surprise came from the watching Half-Horses. They had never seen such power in a mere man before.

Wolff strained, jerked, and brought the struggling warrior to his foreknees. His left fist punched into the heaving bellows beneath the ribs and sank in. The Half-Horse gave a loud whoosh. Wolff released his hold, stepped back, and used his right fist against the thick jaw of the half-unconscious centaur. The head snapped back, and the centaur fell over. Before he could regain consciousness, his skull was smashed by his own club.

Wolff remounted, and the three columns rode on at a canter. For awhile, the Half-Horse made no move against their enemies. Their chiefs seemed to be discussing something. Whatever it was they intended to do, they lost their chance a moment later.

The cavalcades went over a slight rise and down into a broad hollow. This was just enough to conceal from them the pride of lions that had been lying there. Apparently the twenty or so of Felis Atrox had fed off a protocamel the night before and had been too drowsy to pay any attention to the noise of the approaching hooves. But now that the intruders were suddenly among them, the great cats sprang into action. Their fury was aggravated even more by their desire to protect the cubs among them.

Wolff and Kickaha were lucky. Although there were huge shapes bounding on every side, none came at them. But Wolff did get close enough to a male to view every awe-inspiring detail, and that was as close as he ever cared to be. The cat was almost as large as a horse and, though he lacked the mane of the African lion, he did not lack for majesty and ferocity. He bounded by Wolff and hurled himself upon the nearest centaur, which went down screaming. The jaws closed on the centaur's throat, and it was dead. Instead of worrying the corpse, as he might normally have done, the male sprang upon another Half-Horse, and this one went down as easily.

All was a chaos of roaring cats and screaming horses, men, and Half-Horse. It was everyone for himself; to hell with the battle that had been going on.

It took only thirty seconds for Wolff and Kickaha and those Hrowakas who had been fortunate enough not to be attacked to ride out of the hollow. They did not need to urge their horses to speed, but they did have trouble keeping them from running themselves to death.

Behind them, but at a distance now, the centaurs who had evaded the lions streamed out of the hollow. Instead of pursuing the Hrowakas at once, they rode to a safe distance from the lions and then paused to evaluate their losses. Actually, they had not suffered more than a dozen casualties, but they had been severely shaken up.

'A break for us!' Kickaha shouted. 'However, unless we can get to the woods before they catch up again, we're done for! They aren't going to continue the individual combats anymore. They'll make a concerted charge!'

The woods that they longed for still looked as far off as ever. Wolff did not think that his horse, magnificent beast though it was, could make it. Its coat was dark with sweat, and it was breathing heavily. Yet it pounded on, an engine of finely tempered flesh and spirit that would run until its heart ruptured.

Now the Half-Horse were in full gallop and slowly catching up with them. In a few minutes they were within arrow range. A few shafts came flying by the pursued and plunged into the grass. Thereafter, the centaurs held their fire, for they saw that bows were too inaccurate with the speed and unevenness at which both archer and target were traveling.

Suddenly Kickaha gave a whoop of delight. 'Keep going!' he shouted at them all. 'May the Spirit of AkjawDimis favor you!'

Wolff did not understand him until he looked at where Kickaha's finger was pointing. Before them, half-hidden by the tall grass, were thousands of little mounds of earth. Before these sat creatures that looked like striped prairie dogs.

The next moment, the Hrowakas had ridden into the colony with the Half-Horse immediately behind them. Shouts and screams arose as horses and centaurs, stepping into holes, went crashing down. The beasts and the Half-Horses that had fallen down kicked and screamed with the pain of broken legs. The centaurs just behind the first wave reared to halt themselves, and those following rammed into them. For a minute, a pile of tangled and kicking four-legged bodies was spread across the border of the prairie-dog field. The Half-Horses lucky enough to be far enough behind halted and watched their stricken comrades. Then they trotted cautiously, intent on where they placed their hooves. They cut the throats of those with broken legs and arms.

The Hrowakas, though aware of what was taking place behind them, had not stayed to watch. They pushed on but at a reduced pace. Now, they had ten horses and twelve men; Hums Like A Bee and Tall Grass were riding double with two whose horses had not broken their legs.

Kickaha, looking at them, shook his head. Wolff knew what he was thinking. He would have to order Hums Like A Bee and Tall Grass to get off and go on foot. Otherwise, not only they but the men who had picked them up would inevitably be overtaken. Then Kickaha, saying, 'To hell with it, I won't abandon them!' dropped back. He spoke briefly to the tandem riders and brought his horse back up alongside Wolff. 'If they go, we all go,' he said. 'But you don't have to stay with us, Bob. Your loyalty lies elsewhere. No reason for you to sacrifice yourself for us and lose Chryseis and the horn.'

'I'll stay,' Wolff said.

Kickaha grinned and slapped him on the shoulder. 'I'd hoped we could get to the woods, but we won't make it. Almost but not quite. By the time we get to that big hill just half a mile ahead, we'll be caught up with. Too bad. The woods are only another half-mile away.'

The prairie-dog colony was as suddenly behind them as it had been before them. The Hrowakas urged their beasts to a gallop. A minute later, the centaurs had passed safely through the field, and they, too, were at full speed. Up the hill went the pursued and at the top they halted to form a circle.

Wolff pointed down the side of the hill and across the plain at a small river. There were woods along it, but it was not that which caused his excitement. At the river's edge, partially blocked by the trees, white tepees shone.

Kickaha looked long before saying, 'The Tsenakwa. The mortal enemy of the Bear People, as who isn't?'

'Here they come,' Wolff said. 'They must have been notified by sentinels.'

He gestured at a disorganized body of horsemen riding out of the woods, the sun striking off white horses, white shields, and white feathers and sparking the tips of lance.

One of the Hrowakas, seeing them, began a high-pitched wailing song. Kickaha shouted at him, and Wolff understood enough to know that Kickaha was telling him to shut up. Now was no time for a death-song; they would cheat the Half-Horse and the Tsenakwa yet.

'I was going to order our last stand here,' Kickaha said. 'But not now. We'll ride toward the Tsenakwa, then cut away from them and toward the woods along the river. How we come out depends on whether or not both our enemies decide to fight. If one refuses, the other will get us. If not ... Let's go!'

Haiyeeing, they pounded their heels against the ribs of their beasts. Down the hill, straight toward the Tsenakwa, they rode. Wolff glanced back over his shoulder and saw that the Half-Horse were speeding down the side of the hill after them. Kickaha yelled, 'I didn't think they'd pass this up. There'll be a lot of women wailing in the lodges tonight, but it won't be only among the Bear People!'

Now the Hrowakas were close enough to discern the devices on the shields of the Tsenakwa. These were black swastikas, a symbol Wolff was not surprised to see. The crooked cross was ancient and widespread on Earth; it was known by the Trojans, Cretans, Romans, Celts, Norse, Indian Buddhists and Brahmans, the Chinese, and throughout pre-Columbian North America. Nor was he surprised to see that the oncoming Indians were red-haired. Kickaha had told him that the Tsenakwa dyed their black locks.

Still in an unordered mass but now bunched more closely together, the Tsenakwa leveled their lances and gave their charge-cry, an imitation of the scream of a hawk. Kickaha, in the lead, raised his hand, held it for a moment, then chopped it downward. His horse veered to the left and away, the line of the Bear people following him, he the head and the others the body of the snake.

Kickaha had cut it close, but he had used correct and exact timing. As the

Half-Horse and Tsenakwa plunged with a crash and flurry into each other and were embroiled in a melee, the Hrowakas pulled away. They gained the woods, slowed to go through the trees and underbrush, and then were crossing the river. Even so, Kickaha had to argue with several of the braves. These wanted to sneak back across the river and raid the tepees of the Tsenakwa while their warriors were occupied with the Half-Horse.

'Makes sense to me,' Wolff said, 'if we stay there only long enough to pick up horses. Hums Like A Bee and Tall Grass can't keep on riding double.'

Kickaha shrugged and gave the order. The raid took five minutes. The Hrowakas recrossed the river and burst from the trees and among the tepees with wild shouts. The women and children screamed and took refuge in the trees or lodges. Some of the Hrowakas wanted not only the horses but loot. Kickaha said that he would kill the first man he caught stealing anything besides bows and arrows. But he did reach down off his horse and give a pretty but battling woman a long kiss.

'Tell your men I would have taken you to bed and made you forever after dissatisfied with the puny ones of your tribe!' Kickaha said to her. 'But we have more important things to do!' Laughing, he released the woman, who ran into her lodge. He did pause long enough to make water into the big cooking pot in the middle of the camp, a deadly insult, and then he ordered the party to ride off.

10

They rode on for two weeks and then were at the edge of the Trees of Many Shadows. Here Kickaha took a long farewell of the Hrowakas. These also each came to Wolff and, laying their hands upon his shoulders, made a farewell speech. He was one of them now. When he returned, he should take a house and wife among them and ride out on hunts and war with them. He was *KwashingDa*, the Strong One; he had made his kill side by side with them; he had outwrestled a Half-Horse; he would be given a bear cub to raise as his own; he would be blessed by the Lord and have sons and daughters, and so forth and so on.

Gravely, Wolff replied that he could think of no greater honor than to be accepted by the Bear People. He meant it.

Many days later, they had passed through the Many Shadows. They lost both horses one night to something that left footprints ten times as large as a man's, and four-toed. Wolff was both saddened and enraged, for he had a great affection for his animal. He wanted to pursue the WaGanassit and take vengeance. Kickaha threw his hands up in horror at the suggestion.

'Be happy you weren't carried off, too!' he said. 'The WaGanassit is covered with scales that are half-silicon. Your arrows would bounce off. Forget about the horses. We can come back someday and hunt it down. They can be trapped and then roasted in a fire, which I'd like to do, but we have to be practical. Let's go.'

On the other side of the Many Shadows, they built a canoe and went down a broad river that passed through many large and small lakes. The country was hilly here, with steep cliffs at many places. It reminded Wolff of the dells of Wisconsin.

'Beautiful land, but the Chacopewachi and the Enwaddit live here.'

Thirteen days later, during which they had had to paddle furiously three times to escape pursuing canoes of warriors, they left the canoe. Having crossed a broad and high range of hills, mostly at night, they came to a great lake. Again they built a canoe and set out across the waters. Five days of paddling brought them to the base of the monolith, Abharhploonta. They began their slow ascent, as dangerous as that up the first monolith. By the time they reached the top, they had expended their supply of arrows and were suffering several nasty wounds.

'You can see why traffic between the tiers is limited,' Kickaha said. 'In the first place, the Lord has forbidden it. However, that doesn't keep the irreverent and adventurous, nor the trader, from attempting it.

'Between the rim and Dracheland is several thousand miles of jungle with large plateaus interspersed here and there. The Guzirit River is only a hundred miles away. We'll go there and look for passage on a riverboat.'

They prepared flint tips and shafts for arrows. Wolff killed a tapirlike animal. Its flesh was a little rank, but it filled their bellies with strength. He wanted then to push on, finding Kickaha's reluctance aggravating.

Kickaha looked up into the green sky and said, 'I was hoping one of Podarge's pets would find us and have news for us. After all, we don't know which direction the gworl are taking. They have to go toward the mountain, but they could take two paths. They could go all the way through the jungle, a route not recommended for safety. Or they could take a boat down the Guzirit. That has its dangers, too, especially for rather outstanding creatures like the gworl. And Chryseis would bring a high price in the slave market.'

'We can't wait forever for an eagle,' Wolff said.

'No, nor will we have to,' Kickaha said. He pointed up, and Wolff, following the direction of his fingertip, saw a flash of yellow. It disappeared, only to come into view a moment later. The eagle was dropping swiftly, wings folded. Shortly, it checked its drop and glided in.

Phthie introduced herself and immediately thereafter said that she carried good news. She had spotted the gworl and the woman, Chryseis, only four hundred miles ahead of them. They had taken passage on a merchant boat and were traveling down the Guzirit toward the Land of Armored Men.

'Did you see the horn?' Kickaha said.

'No,' Phthie replied. 'But they doubtless have it concealed in one of the skin bags they were carrying. I snatched one of the bags away from a gworl on the chance it might contain the horn. For my troubles, I got a bag full of junk and almost received an arrow through my wing.'

'The gworl have bows?' Wolff asked, surprised.

'No. The rivermen shot at me.'

Wolff, asking about the ravens, was told that there were many. Apparently the Lord must have ordered a number to keep watch on the gworl.

'That's bad,' Kickaha said. 'If they spot us, we're in real trouble.'

'They don't know what you look like,' Phthie said. 'I've eavesdropped on the ravens when they were talking, hiding when I longed to seize them and tear them apart. But I have orders from my mistress, and I obey. The gworl have tried to describe you to the Eyes of the Lord. The ravens are looking for two traveling together, both tall, one black-haired, the other bronze-haired. But that is all they know, and many men conform to that description. The ravens, however, will be watching for two men on the trail of the gworl.'

'I'll dye my beard, and we'll get Khamshem clothes,' Kickaha said.

Phthie said that she must be getting on. She had been on her way to report to Podarge, having left another sister to continue the surveillance of the gworl, when she had spied the two. Kickaha thanked her and made sure that she would carry his regards to Podarge. After the giant bird had launched herself from the rim of the monolith, the men went into the jungle.

'Walk softly, speak quietly,' Kickaha said. 'Here be tigers. In fact, the jungle's lousy with them. Here also be the great axebeak. Its a wingless bird so big and fierce even one of Podarge's pets would skedaddle away from it. I saw two tigers and an axebeak tangle once, and the tigers didn't hang around long before they caught on it'd be a good idea to take off fast.'

Despite Kickaha's warnings, they saw very little life except for a vast number of many-colored birds, monkeys, and mouse-sized antlered beetles. For the beetles, Kickaha had one word: 'poisonous.' Thereafter, Wolff took care before bedding down that none were about.

Before reaching their immediate destination, Kickaha looked for a plant, the *ghubharash*. Locating a group after a half-day's search, he pounded the fibers, cooked them, and extracted a blackish liquid. With this he stained his hair, beard, and his skin from top to bottom.

'I'll explain my green eyes with a tale of having a slave-mother from Teutonia,' he said. 'Here. Use some yourself. You could stand being a little darker.'

They came to a half-ruined city of stone and wide-mouthed squatting idols.

The citizens were a short, thin, and dark people who dressed in maroon capes and black loincloths. Men and women wore their hair long and plastered with butter, which they derived from the milk of piebald goats that leaped from ruin to ruin and fed on the grasses between the cracks in the stone. These people, the Kaidushang, kept cobras in little cages and often took their pets out to fondle. They chewed dhiz, a plant which turned their teeth black and gave their eyes a smoldering look and their motions a slowness.

Kickaha, using H'vaizhum, the pidgin rivertalk, bartered with the elders. He traded a leg of a hippopotamuslike beast he and Wolff had killed for Khamshem garments. The two donned the red and green turbans adorned with *kigglibash* feathers, sleeveless white shirts, baggy pantaloons of purple, sashes that wound around and around their waists many times, and the black, curling-toed slippers.

Despite their dhiz-stupored minds, the elders were shrewd in their trading. Not until Kickaha brought a very small sapphire from his bag – one of the jewels given him by Podarge – would they sell the pearl-encrusted scabbards and the scimitars in their hidden stock.

'I hope a boat comes along soon,' Kickaha said. 'Now that they know I have stones, they might try to slit our throats. Sorry, Bob, but we're going to have to keep watch at night. They also like to send in their snakes to do their dirty work for them.'

That very day, a merchantman sailed around the bend of the river. At sight of the two standing on the rotting pier and waving long white handkerchiefs, the captain ordered the anchor dropped and sails lowered.

Wolff and Kickaha got into the small boat lowered for them and were rowed out to the *Khrillquz*. This was about forty feet long, low amidships but with towering decks fore and aft, and one fore-and-aft sail and jib. The sailors were mainly of that branch of Khamshem folk called the Shibacub. They spoke a tongue the phonology and structure of which had been described by Kickaha to Wolff. He was sure that it was an archaic form of Semitic influenced by the aboriginal tongues.

The captain, Arkhyurel, greeted them politely on the poop deck. He sat cross-legged on a pile of cushions and rich rugs and sipped on a tiny cup of thick wine.

Kickaha, calling himself Ishnaqrubel, gave his carefully prepared story. He and his companion, a man under a vow not to speak again until he returned to his wife in the far off land of Shiashtu, had been in the jungle for several years. They had been searching for the fabled lost city of Ziqooant.

The captain's black and tangled eyebrows rose, and he stroked the dark-brown beard that fell to his waist. He asked them to sit down and to accept a cup of the Akhashtum wine while they told their tale. Kickaha's eyes shone and he grinned as he plunged into his narration. Wolff did not understand him, yet he was sure that his friend was in raptures with his long, richly detailed, and adventurous lies. He only hoped Kickaha would not get too carried away and arouse the captain's incredulity.

The hours passed while the caravel sailed down the river. A sailor clad only in a scarlet loincloth, bangs hanging down below his eyes, played softly on a flute on the foredeck. Food was carried to them on silver and gold platters: roasted monkey, stuffed bird, a black hard bread, and a tart jelly. Wolff found the meat too highly spiced, but he ate.

The sun neared its nightly turn around the mountain, and the captain arose. He led them to a little shrine behind the wheel; here was an idol of green jade, Tartartar. The captain chanted a prayer, the prime prayer to the Lord. Then Arkhyurel got down on his knees before the minor god of his own nation and made obeisance. A sailor sprinkled a little incense on the tiny fire glowing in the hollow in Tartartar's lap. While the fumes spread over the ship, those of the captain's faith prayed also. Later, the mariners of other gods made their private devotions.

That night, the two lay on the mid-deck on a pile of furs which the captain had furnished them.

'I don't know about this guy Arkhyurel,' Kickaha said. 'I told him we failed to locate the city of Ziqooant but that we did find a small treasure cache. Nothing to brag about but enough to let us live modestly without worry when we return to Shiashtu. He didn't ask to see the jewels, even though I said I'd give him a big ruby for our passage. These people take their time in their dealings; it's an insult to rush business. But his greed may overrule his sense of hospitality and business ethics if he thinks he can get a big haul just by cutting our throats and dumping our bodies into the river.'

He stopped for a moment. Cries of many birds came from the branches along the river; now and then a great saurian bellowed from the bank or from the river itself.

'If he's going to do anything dishonorable, he'll do it in the next thousand miles. This is a lonely stretch of river; after that, the towns and cities begin to get more numerous.'

The next afternoon, sitting under a canopy erected for their comfort, Kickaha presented the captain with the ruby, enormous and beautifully cut. With it, Kickaha could have purchased the boat itself and the crew from the captain. He hoped that Arkhyurel would be more than satisfied with it; the captain himself could retire on its sale if he wished. Kickaha then did what he had wanted to avoid but knew that he could not. He brought out the rest of the jewels: diamonds, sapphires, rubies, garnets, tourmalines and topazes. Arkhyurel smiled and licked his lips and fondled the stones for three hours. Finally he forced himself to give them back.

That night, while lying on their beds on the deck, Kickaha brought out a parchment map which he had borrowed from the captain. He indicated a great bend of the river and tapped a circle marked with the curlicue syllabary symbols of Khamshem writing.

'The city of Khotsiqsh. Abandoned by the people who built it, like the one from which we boarded this boat, and inhabited by a half-savage tribe, the Weezwart. We'll quietly leave the ship the night we drop anchor there and cut across the thin neck of land to the river. We may be able to pick up enough time to intercept the boat that's carrying the gworl. If we don't, we'll still be way ahead of this boat. We'll take another merchant. Or, if none is available, we'll hire a Weezwart dugout and crew.'

Twelve days later the *Khrillquz* tied up alongside a massive but cracked pier. The Weezwart crowded the stone tongue and shouted at the sailors and showed them jars of dhiz, and of laburnum, singing birds in wooden cages, monkeys and servals on the end of leashes, artifacts from hidden and ruined cities in the jungle, bags and purses made from the pebbly hides of the river saurians, and cloaks from tigers and leopards. They even had a baby axeback, which they knew the captain would pay a price for and would sell to the Bashishub, the king, of Shibacub. Their main wares, however, were their women. These, clad from head to foot in cheap cotton robes of scarlet and green, paraded back and forth on the pier. They would flash open their robes and then quickly close them, all the while screaming the price of a night's rent to the women-starved sailors. The men, wearing only white turbans and fantastic codpieces, stood to one side, chewed dhiz, and grinned. All carried six-foot-long blow-guns and long, thin, crooked knives stuck into the tangled knots of hair on top of their heads.

During the trading between the captain and Weezwart, Kickaha and Wolff prowled through the cyclopean stands and falls of the city. Abruptly, Wolff said, 'You have the jewels with you. Why don't we get a Weezwart guide and take off now? Why wait until nightfall?'

'I like your style, friend,' Kickaha said. 'Okay. Let's go.'

They found a tall thin man, Wiwhin, who eagerly accepted their offer when Kickaha showed him a topaz. At their insistence, he did not tell his wife where he was going but straightway led them into the jungle. He knew the paths well and, as promised, delivered them to the city of Qirruqshak within two days. Here he demanded another jewel, saying that he would not tell anybody at all about them if he was given a bonus.

'I did not promise you a bonus,' Kickaha said. 'But I like the fine spirit of free enterprise you show, my friend. So here's another. But if you try for a third, I shall kill you.'

Wiwhin smiled and bowed and took the second topaz and trotted off into the jungle. Kickaha, staring after him, said, 'Maybe I should've killed him anyway. The Weezwart don't even have the word *honor* in their vocabulary.'

They walked into the ruins. After a half-hour of climbing and threading their way between collapsed buildings and piles of dirt, they found themselves on the river-side of the city. Here were gathered the Dholinz, a folk of the same language family as the Weezwart. But the men had long, drooping moustaches and the women painted their upper lips black and wore nose-rings. With them was a group of merchants from the land which had given all the Khamshem-speakers their name. There was no river-caravel by the pier. Kickaha, seeing this, halted and started to turn back into the ruins. He was too late, for the Khamshem saw him and called out to them.

'Might as well brave it out,' Kickaha muttered to Wolff. 'If I holler, run like hell! Those birds are slave-dealers.'

There were about thirty of the Khamshem, all armed with scimitars and daggers. In addition, they had about fifty soldiers, tall broad-shouldered men, lighter than the Khamshem, with swirling patterns tattooed on their faces and shoulders. These, Kickaha said, were the Sholkin mercenaries often used by the Khamshem. They were famous spearmen, mountain people, herders of goats, scorners of women as good for nothing but housework, fieldwork, and bearers of children.

'Don't let them take you alive,' was Kickaha's final warning before he smiled and greeted the leader of the Khamshem. This was a very tall and thickly muscled man named Abiru. He had a face that would have been handsome if his nose had not been a little too large and curved like a scimitar. He answered Kickaha politely enough, but his large black eyes weighed them as if they were so many pounds of merchandisable flesh.

Kickaha gave him the story he had told Arkhyurel but shortened it considerably and left out the jewels. He said that they would wait until a merchant boat came along and would take it back to Shiashtu. And how was the great Abiru doing?

(By now, Wolff's quickness at picking up languages enabled him to understand the Khamshem tongue when it was on a simple conversational basis.)

Abiru replied that, thanks to the Lord and Tartartar, this business venture had been very rewarding. Besides the usual type of slave-material picked up, he had captured a group of very strange creatures. Also, a woman of surpassing beauty, the like of which had never been seen before. Not, at least, on this tier.

Wolff's heart began to beat hard. Was it possible?

Abiru asked if they would care to take a peek at his captives.

Kickaha flicked a look of warning at Wolff but replied that he would very much like to see both the curious beings and the fabulously beautiful woman. Abiru beckoned to the captain of the mercenaries and ordered him and ten of his men to come along. Then Wolff scented the danger of which Kickaha had been aware from the beginning. He knew that they should run, though this was not likely to be successful. The Sholkin seemed accustomed to bringing down fugitives with their spears. But he wanted desperately to see Chryseis again. Since Kickaha made no move, Wolff decided not to do so on his own. Kickaha, having more experience, presumably knew how best to act.

Abiru, chatting pleasantly of the attractions of the capital city of Khamshem, led them down the underbrush-grown street and to a great stepped building with broken statues on the levels. He halted before an entrance by which stood ten more Sholkin. Even before they went in, Wolff knew that the gworl were there. Riding over the stink of unwashed human bodies was the rotten-fruit odor of the bumpy people.

The chamber within was huge and cool and twilighty. Against the far wall, squatting on the dirt piled on the stone floor, was a line of about a hundred men and women and thirty gworl. All were connected by long, thin iron chains around iron collars about their necks.

Wolff looked for Chryseis. She was not there.

Abiru, answering the unspoken question, said, 'I keep the cat-eyed one apart. She has a woman attendant and a special guard. She gets all the attention and care that a precious jewel should.'

Wolff could not restrain himself. He said, 'I would like to see her.'

Abiru stared and said, 'You have a strange accent. Didn't your companion say you were from the land of Shiashtu, also?'

He waved a hand at the soldiers, who moved forward, their spears leveled. 'Never mind. If you see the woman, you will see her from the end of a chain.'

Kickaha sputtered indignantly. 'We are subjects of the king of Khamshem and free men! You cannot do this to us! It will cost you your head, after certain legal tortures, of course!'

Abiru smiled. 'I do not intend to take you back to Khamshem, friend. We are going to Teutonia, where you will bring a good price, being a strong man, albeit too talkative. However, we can take care of that by slicing off your tongue.'

The scimitars of the two men were removed along with the bag. Herded by the spears, they moved to the end of the line, immediately behind the gworl, and were secured with iron collars. Abiru, dumping the contents of the bag on the floor, swore as he saw the pile of jewels.

'So, you did find something in the lost cities? How fortunate for us. I'm almost – but not quite – tempted to release you for having enriched me so.'

'How corny can you get?' Kickaha muttered in English. 'He talks like a grade-B movie villain. Damn him! If I get the chance, I'll cut out more than his tongue.'

Abiru, happy with his riches, left. Wolff examined the chain attached to the collar. It was made of small links. He might be able to break it if the iron was not too high a quality. On Earth, he had amused himself, secretly of course, by snapping just such chains. But he could not try until nightfall.

Behind Wolff, Kickaha whispered, 'The gworl won't recognize us in this get-up, so let's leave it that way.'

'What about the horn?' Wolff said.

Kickaha, speaking the early Middle High German form of Teutonic, tried to engage the gworl in conversation. After narrowly missing getting hit in the face with a gob of saliva, he quit. He did manage to talk to one of the Sholkin soldiers and some of the human slaves. From them he gleaned much information.

The gworl had been passengers on the *Qaqiirzhub*, captained by one Rakhamen. Putting in at this city, the captain had met Abiru and invited him aboard for a cup of wine. That night – in fact, the night before Wolff had entered the city – Abiru and his men had seized the boat. During the struggle, the captain and several of his sailors had been slain. The rest were now in the chain-line. The boat had been sent on down the river and up a tributary with a crew to be sold to a river-pirate of whom Abiru had heard.

As for the horn, none of the crew of the *Qaqiirzhub* had heard of it. Nor would the soldiers supply any news. Kickaha told Wolff that he did not think that Abiru was likely to let anybody else learn about it. He must recognize it, for everybody had heard of the horn of the Lord. It was part of the universal religion and described in the various sacred literatures.

Night came. Soldiers entered with torches and food for the slaves. After meal time, two Sholkin remained within the chamber and an unknown number stood guard outside. The sanitary arrangements were abominable; the odor became stifling. Apparently Abiru did not care about observing the proprieties as laid down by the Lord. However, some of the more religious Sholkin must have complained, for several Dholinz entered and cleaned up. Water in buckets was dashed over each slave, and several buckets were left for drinking. The gworl howled when the water struck them and complained and cursed for a long time afterwards. Kickaha added to Wolff's store of information by telling him that the gworl, like the kangaroo rat and other desert animals of Earth, did not have to drink water. They had a biological device, similar to the arid-dwellers, which oxidized their fat into the hydrogen oxide required.

The moon came up. The slaves lay on the floor or leaned against the wall and slept. Kickaha and Wolff pretended to do likewise. When the moon had come around into position so that it could be seen through the doorway, Wolff said, 'I'm going to try to break the chains. If I don't have time to break yours, we'll have to do a Siamese twin act.'

'Let's go,' Kickaha whispered back.

The length of the chain between each collar was about six feet. Wolff slowly inched his way toward the nearest gworl to give himself enough slack. Kickaha crept along with him. The journey took about fifteen minutes, for they did not want the two sentinels in the chamber to become aware of their progress. Then Wolff, his back turned to the guards, took the chain in his two hands. He pulled and felt the links hold fast. Slow tension would not do the job. So, a quick jerk. The links broke with a noise.

The two Sholkin, who had been talking loudly and laughing to keep each other awake, stopped. Wolff did not dare to turn over to look at them. He waited while the Sholkin discussed the possible origin of the sound. Apparently it did not occur to them that it could be the chain parting. They spent some time holding the torches high and peering up toward the ceiling. One made a joke, the other laughed, and they resumed their conversation.

'Want to try for two?' Kickaha said.

'I hate to, but we'll be handicapped if I don't,' Wolff said.

He had to wait a awhile, for the gworl to whom he had been attached had been awakened by the breaking. He lifted his head and muttered something in his file-against-steel speech. Wolff began sweating even more heavily. If the gworl sat up or tried to stand up, his motion would reveal the damage.

After a heart-piercing minute, the gworl settled back down and soon was snoring again. Wolff relaxed a little. He even grinned tightly, for the gworl's actions had given him an idea.

'Crawl up toward me as if you wanted to warm yourself against me,' Wolff said softly.

'You kidding?' Kickaha whispered back. 'I feel as if I'm in a steam bath. But okay. Here goes.'

He inched forward until his head was opposite Wolff's knees.

'When I snap the chain, don't go into action,' Wolff said. 'I have an idea for bringing the guards over here without alarming those outside.'

'I hope they don't change guards just as we're starting to operate,' Kickaha said.

'Pray to the Lord,' Wolff replied. 'Earth's.'

'He helps him who helps himself,' Kickaha said.

Wolff jerked with all his strength; the links parted with a noise. This time, the guards stopped talking and the gworl rose up abruptly. Wolff bit down hard on the toe of the gworl. The creature did not cry out but grunted and started to rise. One of the guards ordered him to remain seated, and both started toward him. The gworl did not understand the language. He did understand the tone of voice, and the spear waved at him. He lifted his foot and began to rub it, meanwhile grating curses at Wolff.

The torches became brighter as the feet of the guards scraped against the stone exposed beneath the loose dirt. Wolff said, 'Now!'

He and Kickaha arose simultaneously, whirled, and were facing the surprised Sholkin. A spearhead was within Wolff's reach. His hand slid along it, grasped the shaft just behind the point, and jerked. The guard opened his mouth to yell, but it snapped shut as the lifted butt of the spear cracked against his jaw.

Kickaha had not been so fortunate. The Sholkin stepped back and raised his spear to throw it. Kickaha went at him as a tackler after the man with the ball; he came in low, rolled, and the spear clanged against the wall.

By then, the silence was gone. One guard started to yell. The gworl picked up the weapon that had fallen by his side and threw it. The head drove into the exposed neck of the guard, and the point came out through the back of the neck.

Kickaha jerked the spearhead loose, drew the dead guard's knife from his scabbard, and flipped it. The first Sholkin to enter from outside received it to the hilt in his solar plexus. Seeing him go down, others who had been so eager to follow him withdrew. Wolff took the knife from the other corpse, shoved it into his sash, and said, 'Where do we go from here?'

Kickaha slid the knife from the solar plexus and wiped it on the corpse's hair. 'Not through that door. Too many.'

Wolff pointed at a doorway at the far end and started to run toward it. On the way, he scooped up the torch dropped by the guard. Kickaha did the same. The doorway was partly choked up by dirt, forcing them to get down on their hands and knees and crawl through. Presently they were at the place through which the dirt had dropped. The moon revealed an empty place in the stone slabs of the ceiling.

'They must know about this,' Wolff said. 'They can't be that careless. We'd better go further back in.'

They had scarcely moved past the point below the break in the roof when torches flared above. The two scuttled ahead as fast as they could while Sholkin voices came excitedly through the opening. A second later, a spear slammed into the dirt, narrowly missing Wolff's leg.

'They'll be coming in after us, now that they know we've left the main chamber,' Kickaha said.

They went on, taking branches which seemed to offer access to the rear. Suddenly the floor sank beneath Kickaha. He tried to scramble on across before the stone on which he was would drop, but he did not make it. One side of a large slab came up, and that side which had dropped propelled Kickaha into a hole. Kickaha yelled, at the same time releasing the hold on his torch. Both fell.

Wolff was left staring at the tipped slab and the gap beside it. No light came from the hole, so the torch had either gone out or the hole was so deep that the flare was out of sight. Moaning in his anxiety, he crawled forward and held the torch over the edge while he looked below. The shaft was at least ten feet wide and fifty deep. It had been dug out of the dirt. But there was no Kickaha nor even a depression to indicate where he had landed.

Wolff called his name, at the same time hearing the shouts of the Sholkin as they crawled through the corridors in pursuit.

Receiving no answer, he extended his body as far as he dared over the lip of the shaft and examined the depth more closely. All his waving about of the torch to illuminate the dark places showed nothing but the fallen extinguished torch.

Some of the edges of the bottom remained black as if there were holes in the sides. He could only conclude that Kickaha had gone into one of these.

Now the sound of voices became louder and the first flickerings of a torch came from around the corner at the end of the hall. He could do nothing but continue. He rose as far as possible, threw his torch ahead of him to the other side, and leaped with all the strength of his legs. He shot in an almost horizontal position, hit the lip, which was wet soft earth, and slid forward on his face. He was safe, although his legs were sticking out over the edge.

Picking up the torch, which was still burning, he crawled on. At the end of the corridor he found one branch completely blocked by fallen earth. The other was partially stopped up by a great slab of smoothly cut stone lying at a forty-five degree angle to horizontal. By the sacrifice of some skin on his chest and back, he squeezed through between the earth and the stone. Beyond was an enormous chamber, even larger than the one in which the slaves had been kept.

There was a series of rough terraces formed by slippage of stone at the opposite end. He made his way up these toward the corner of the ceiling and the wall. A patch of moonlight shone through this, his only means of exit. He put his torch out. If the Sholkin were roaming around the top of the building, they would see the light from it coming through the small hole. At the cavity, he crouched for awhile on the narrow ledge beneath it and listened carefully. If his torch had been seen, he would be caught as he slid out of the hole, helpless to defend himself. Finally, hearing only distant shouts, and knowing that he must use this only exit, he pulled himself through it.

He was near the top of the mound of dirt which covered the rear part of the building. Below him were torches. Abiru was standing in their light, shaking his fist at a soldier and yelling.

Wolff looked down at the earth beneath his feet, imagined the stone and the hollows they contained, and the shaft down which Kickaha had hurtled to his death.

He raised his spear and murmured, 'Ave atque vale, Kickaha!'

He wished he could take some more Sholkin lives – especially that of Abiru – in payment for Kickaha's. But he had to be practical. There was Chryseis, and there was the horn. But he felt empty and weak, as if part of his soul had left him.

11

That night he hid in the branches of a tall tree some distance from the city. His plan was to follow the slavers and rescue Chryseis and the horn at the first chance. The slavers would have to take the trail near which he waited; it was the only one leading inward to Teutonia. Dawn came while he waited, hungry and thirsty. By noon he became impatient. Surely they would not still be looking for him. At evening, he decided that he had to have at least a drink of water. He climbed down and headed for a nearby stream. A growl sent him up another tree. Presently a family of leopards slipped through the bush and lapped at the water. By the time they were through and had slid back into the bush, the sun was close to the corner of the monolith.

He returned to the trail, confident that he had been too close to it for a large train of human beings to walk by unheard. Yet no one came. That night he sneaked into the ruins and close to the building from which he had escaped. No one was in evidence. Sure now that they had left, he prowled through the bush-grown lanes and streets until he came upon a man sitting against a tree. The man was half-unconscious from dhiz, but Wolff woke him by slapping him hard against his cheeks. Holding his knife against his throat, he questioned him. Despite his limited Khamshem and the Dholinz's even lesser mastery, they managed to communicate. Abiru and his party had left that morning on three large war-canoes with hired Dholinz paddlers.

Wolff knocked the man unconscious and went down to the pier. It was deserted, thus giving him a choice of any craft there he wanted. He took a narrow light boat with a sail and set off down the river.

Two thousand miles later, he was on the borders of Teutonia and the civilized Khamshem. The trail had led him down the Guzirit River for three hundred miles, then across country. Although he should have caught up with the slow-moving train long before, he had lost them three times and been detained at other times by tigers and axebeaks.

Gradually the land sloped upward. Suddenly a plateau rose from the jungle. A climb of a mere six thousand feet was nothing to a man who had twice scaled thirty thousand. Once over the rim, he found himself in a different country. Though the air was no cooler, it bred oak, sycamore, yew, box elder, walnut, cottonwood and linden. However, the animals differed. He had walked no more than two miles through the twilight of an oak forest before he was forced to hide.

A dragon slowly paced by him, looked at him once, hissed, and went on. It resembled the conventional Western representations, was about forty feet long, ten feet high, and was covered with large scaly plates. It did not breathe fire. In fact, it stopped a hundred feet from Wolff's tree-branch refuge and began to eat upon a tall patch of grass. So, Wolff thought, there was more than one type of dragon. Wondering how he would be able to tell the carnivous type from the herbivorous without first assuring a safe observation post, Wolff climbed down from the tree. The dragon continued to munch while its belly, or bellies, emitted a weak thunder of digestion.

More cautiously than before, Wolff passed beneath the giant limbs of the trees and the moss, cataracts of green that hung from the limbs. Dawn of the next day found him leaving the edge of the forest. Before him the land dipped gently. He could see for many miles. To his right, at the bottom of a valley, was a river. On the opposite side, topping a column of shaggy rock, was a tiny castle. At the foot of the rock was a minute village. Smoke rose from the chimneys to bring a lump in his throat. It seemed to him that he would like nothing better than to sit down at a breakfast table over a cup of coffee with friends, after a good night's sleep in a soft bed, and chatter away about nothing in particular. God! How he missed the faces and the voices of genuine human beings, of a place where every hand was not against him!

A few tears trickled down his cheek. He dried them and went on his way. He had made his choice and must take the bad with the good, just as he would have in the Earth he had renounced. And this world, at this moment, anyway, was not so bad. It was fresh and green with no telephone lines, billboards, paper and cans strewn along the countryside, no smog or threat of bomb. There was much to be said for it, no matter how bad his present situation might be. And he had that for which many men would have sold their souls: youth combined with the experience of age.

Only an hour later, he wondered if he would be able to retain the gift. He had come to a narrow dirt road and was striding along it when a knight rode around the bend in the road, followed by two men-at-arms. His horse was huge and black and accoutered partly in armor. The knight was clad in black plate-and-mail armor which, to Wolff, looked like the type worn in Germany of the thirteenth century. His visor was up, revealing a grim hawk's face with bright blue eyes.

The knight reined in his horse. He called to Wolff in the Middle High German speech with which Wolff had become acquainted through Kickaha and also through his studies on Earth. The language had, of course, changed somewhat and was loaded with Khamshem and aboriginal loan-words. But Wolff could make out most of what his accoster said.

'Stand still, oaf!' the man cried. 'What are you doing with a bow?'

'May it please your august self,' Wolff replied sarcastically, 'I am a hunter and so bear the king's license to carry a bow.'

'You are a liar! I know every lawful hunter for miles hereabouts. You look like a Saracen to me or even a Yidshe, you are so dark. Throw down your bow and surrender, or I will cut you down like the swine you are!'

'Come and take it,' Wolff said, his rage swelling.

The knight couched his lance, and his steed broke into a gallop.

Wolff resisted the impulse to hurl himself to either side or back from the glittering tip of the lance. At what he hoped was the exact split-second, he threw himself forward. The lance dipped to run him through, slid less than an inch over him, and then drove into the ground. Like a pole-vaulter, the knight rose from the saddle and, still clutching the lance, described an arc. His helmet struck the ground first at the end of the arc, the impact of which must have knocked him out or broken his neck or back, for he did not move.

Wolff did not waste his time. He removed the scabbarded sword of the knight and placed the belt around his waist. The dead man's horse, a magnificent roan, had come back to stand by his ex-master. Wolff mounted him and rode off.

Teutonia was so named because of its conquest by a group of The Teutonic Order or Teutonic Knights of St Mary's Hospital at Jerusalem. This order originated during the Third Crusade but later deviated from its original purpose. In 1229 *der Deutsche Orden* began the conquest of Prussia to convert the Baltic pagans and to prepare for colonization by Germans. A group had entered the Lord's planet on this tier, either through accident, which did not seem likely, or because the Lord had deliberately opened a gate for them or forcibly caused them to enter.

Whatever the cause, the Ritters of the Teutonic Knights had conquered the aborigines and established a society based on that which they had left on Earth. This, of course, had changed both because of natural evolution and the Lord's desire to model it to his own wishes. The original single kingdom or Grand Marshalry had degenerated into a number of independent kingdoms. These, in turn, consisted of loosely bound baronetcies and a host of outlaw or robber baronetcies.

Another aspect of the plateau was the state of Yidshe. The founders of this had entered through a gate coevally with the Teutonic Knights. Again, whether they had entered accidentally or through design of the Lord was unknown. But a number of Yiddish-speaking Germans had established themselves at the eastern end of the plateau. Though originally merchants, they had become masters of the native population. Also, they had adopted the feudal-chivalry setup of the Teutonic Order – probably had had to do so to survive. It was this state that the first knight had referred to when he had accused Wolff of being a Yidshe.

Thinking of this, Wolff had to chuckle. Again, it might have been accident that the Germans had entered into a level where the archaic-Semitic

Khamshem already existed and where their contemporaries were the despised Jews. But Wolff thought he could see the ironic face of the Lord smiling behind the situation.

Actually, there were not any Christians or Jews in Dracheland. Although the two faiths still used their original titles, both had become perverted. The Lord had taken the place of Yahweh and Gott, but he was addressed by these names. Other changes in theology had followed: ceremonies, rituals, sacraments, and the literature had subtly become twisted. The parent faiths of both would have rejected their descendants in this world as heretics.

Wolff made his way toward von Elgers'. He could not do so as swiftly as he wished, because he had to avoid the roads and the villages along the way. After being forced to kill the knight, he did not even dare cut through the baronetcy of von Laurentius, as he had at first planned. The entire country would be searching for him; men and dogs would be everywhere. The rough hills marking the boundary were his most immediate form of passage, which he took.

Two days later, he came to a point where he could descend without being within the suzerainty of von Laurentius. As he was clambering down a steep but not especially difficult hill, he came around a corner. Below him was a broad meadow by a riverlet. Two camps were pitched at opposite ends. Around the brave flag-and-pennon draped pavilions in the center of each were a number of smaller tents, cooking fires, and horses. Most of the men were in two groups. They were watching their champion and his antagonist, who were charging each other with couched lances. Even as Wolff saw them, they met together in the middle of the field with a fearful clang. One knight went sailing backward with the lance of the other jammed into his shield. The other, however, lost his balance and fell with a clang several seconds later.

Wolff studied the tableau. It was no ordinary jousting tourney. The peasants and the townspeople who should have thronged the sides and the jerrybuilt stadium with its flowerbed of brilliantly dressed nobility and ladies were absent. This was a lonely place beside the road where champions had pitched their tents and were taking on all qualified passersby.

Wolff worked his way down the hill. Although exposed to the sight of those below, he did not think that they would take much interest in a lone traveler at this time. He was right. No one hastened from either camp to question him. He was able to walk up to the edge of the meadow and make a leisurely inspection.

The flag above the pavilion to his left bore a yellow field with a Solomon's seal. By this he knew that a Yidshe champion had pitched his tent here. Below the national flag was a green banner with a silver fish and hawk. The other camp had several state and personal pennons. One of them leaped out into Wolff's gaze and caused him to cry out with surprise. On a white field was a red ass's head with a hand below it, all fingers clenched but the middle. Kickaha had once told him of it, and Wolff had gotten a big laugh out of it. It was just like Kickaha to pick such a coat of arms.

Wolff sobered then, knowing that, more likely, it was borne by the man who took care of Kickaha's territory while he was gone.

He changed his decision to pass on by the field. He had to determine for himself that the man using that banner was not Kickaha, even though he knew that his friend's bones must be rotting under a pile of dirt at the bottom of a shaft in a ruined city of the jungle.

Unchallenged, he made his way across the field and into the camp at the western end. Men-at-arms and retainers stared, only to turn away from his glare. Somebody muttered, 'Yidshe dog!' but none owned to the comment when he turned. He went on around a line of horses tethered to a post and up to the knight who was his goal. This one was clad in shining red armor, visor down, and held a huge lance upright while he waited his turn. The lance bore near its tip a pennon on which were the red ass's head and human hand.

Wolff placed himself near the prancing horse, making it even more nervous. He cried out in German, 'Baron von Horstmann?'

There was a muffled exclamation, a pause, and the knight's hand raised his visor. Wolff almost wept with joy. The merry long-lipped face of Finnegan-Kickaha-von Horstmann was inside the helmet.

'Don't say anything,' Kickaha cautioned. 'I don't know how in hell you found me, but I'm sure happy about it. I'll see you in a moment. That is, if I come back alive. This funem Laksfalk is one tough hombre.'

12

Trumpets flared. Kickaha rode out to a spot indicated by the marshals. A shaven-headed, long-robed priest blessed him while, at the other end of the field, a rabbi was saying something to Baron funem Laksfalk. The Yidshe champion was a large man in a silver armor, his helmet shaped like a fish's head. His steed was a huge powerful black. The trumpets blew again. The two contenders dipped their lances in salute. Kickaha briefly gripped his lance with his left hand while he crossed himself with his right. (He was a stickler for observing the religious rules of the people among whom he happened to be at the moment.)

Another blast of long-shafted, big-mouthed trumpets was followed by the thunder of the hooves of the knight's horses and the cheers of the onlookers.

The two met exactly in the middle of the field, as did the lance of each in the middle of the other's shield. Both fell with a clangor that startled the birds from the nearby trees, as they had been startled many times that day. The horses rolled on the ground.

The men of each knight ran out onto the field to pick up their chief and to drag away the horses, both of which had broken their necks. For a moment, Wolff thought that the Yidshe and Kickaha were also dead, for neither stirred. After being carried back, however, Kickaha came to. He grinned feebly, and said, 'You ought to see the other guy.'

'He's okay,' Wolff said after a glance at the other camp.

'Too bad,' Kickaha replied. 'I was hoping he wouldn't give us any more trouble. He's held me up too long as it is.'

Kickaha ordered all but Wolff to leave the tent. His men seemed reluctant to leave him but they obeyed, though not without warning looks at Wolff. Kickaha said, 'I was on my way from my castle to von Elgers' when I passed funem Laksfalk's pavilion. If I'd been alone, I would have thumbed my nose at his challenge and ridden on. But there were also Teutoniacs there, and I had my own men to consider. I couldn't afford to get a reputation of cowardice; my own men would've pelted me with rotten cabbage and I'd have had to fight every knight in the land to prove my courage. I figured that it wouldn't take me long to straighten out the Yidshe on who the best man was, and then I could take off.

'It didn't work out that way. The marshals had me listed in the Number Three position. That meant I had to joust with three men for three days before I'd get to the big time. I protested; no use. So I swore to myself and sweated it out. You saw my second encounter with funem Laksfalk. We both knocked each other off the saddle the first time, too. Even so, that's more than the others have done. They're burned up because a Yidshe has defeated every Teuton except me. Besides, he's killed two already and crippled another for life.'

While listening to Kickaha, Wolff had been taking the armor off. Kickaha sat up suddenly, groaning and wincing, and said, 'Hey, how in hell did you get here?'

'I walked mostly. But I thought you were dead.'

'The report wasn't too grossly exaggerated. When I fell down that shaft I landed halfway up on a ledge of dirt. It broke off and started a little cave-in that buried me after I landed on the bottom. But I wasn't knocked out long, and the dirt only lightly covered my face, so I wasn't asphyxiated. I lay quiet for a while because the Sholkin were looking down the hole then. They even threw a spear down, but it missed me by a mole's hair.

'After a couple of hours, I dug myself out. I had a time getting out, I can tell you. The dirt kept breaking off, and I kept falling back. It must've taken me ten hours, but I was lucky at that. Now, how did *you* get here, you big lunk?'

Wolff told him. Kickaha frowned and said, 'So I was right in figuring that Abiru would come to von Elgers' on his way. Listen, we got to get out of here and fast. How would you like to take a swing at the big Yid?'

Wolff protested that he knew nothing of the fine points of jousting, that it took a lifetime to learn. Kickaha said, 'If you were going to break a lance with him, you'd be right. But we'll challenge him to a contest with swords, no shields. Broadswording isn't exactly duelling with a rapier or saber; it's main strength and that's what you've got!'

'I'm not a knight. The others saw me enter as a common vagrant.'

'Nonsense! You think these chevaliers don't go around in disguise all the time? I'll tell them you're a Saracen, pagan Khamshem, but you're a real good friend of mine, I rescued you from a dragon or some cock-and-bull story like that. They'll eat it up. I got it! You're the Saracen Wolf – there's a famous knight by that name. You've been journeying in disguise, hoping to find me and pay me back for saving you from the dragon. I'm too hurt to break another lance with funem Laksfalk – that's no lie; I'm so stiff and sore I can hardly move – and you're taking up the gauntlet for me.'

Wolff asked what excuse he would give for not using the lance.

Kickaha said, 'I'll give them some story. Say a thieving knight stole your lance and you've sworn never to use one until you get the stolen one back. They'll accept that. They're always making some goofy vow or other. They act just like a bunch of knights from King Arthur's Round Table. No such knights ever existed on Earth, but it must have pleased the Lord to make these act as if they just rode out of Camelot. He was a romantic, whatever else you can say about him.'

Wolff said he was reluctant, but if it would help speed them to von Elgers', he would do anything. Kickaha's own armor was not large enough for Wolff, so the armor of a Yidshe knight Kickaha had killed the day before was brought in. The retainers clad him in blue plates and chain-mail and then led him out to his horse. This was a beautiful palomino mare that had also belonged to the knight Kickaha had slain, the Ritter oyf Roytfeldz. With only a little difficulty, Wolff mounted the charger. He had expected that the armor would be so heavy a crane would have to lift him upon the saddle. Kickaha told him that that might have once been true here, but the knights had long since gone back to lighter plates and more chain-mail.

The Yidshe go-between came to announce that funem Laksfalk had accepted the challenge despite the Saracen Wolf's lack of credentials. If the valiant and honorable robber Baron Horst von Horstmann vouched for the Wolf, that was good enough for funem Laksfalk. The speech was a formality. The Yidshe champion would not for one moment have thought of turning down a challenge.

'Face is the big thing here,' Kickaha said to Wolff. Having managed to limp out of his tent, he was giving his friend last-minute instructions. 'Man, am I glad you came along. I couldn't have taken one more fall, and I didn't dare back out.'

Again, the trumpets flourished. The palomino and the black broke into a headlong gallop. They passed each other going at full speed, during which time both men swung their swords. They clanged together; a paralyzing shock ran down Wolff's hand and arm. However, when he turned his charger, he saw that his antagonist's sword was on the ground. The Yidshe was dismounting swiftly to get to the blade before Wolff. He was in such a hurry he slipped and fell headlong onto the ground.

Wolff rode his horse up slowly and took his time dismounting to allow the other to recover. At this chivalrous move, both camps broke into cheers. By the rules, Wolff could have stayed in the saddle and cut funem Laksfalk down without permitting him to pick up his weapon.

On the ground, they faced each other. The Yidshe knight raised his visor, revealing a handsome face. He had a thick moustache and pale blue eyes. He said, 'I pray you let me see your face, noble one. You are a true knight for not striking me down while helpless.'

Wolff lifted his visor for a few seconds. Both then advanced and brought their blades together again. Once more, Wolff's stroke was so powerful that it tore the blade of the other from his grip.

Funem Laksfalk raised his visor, this time with his left arm. He said, 'I cannot use my right arm. If you will permit me to use my left?'

Wolff saluted and stepped back. His opponent gripped the long hilt of his sword and, stepping close, brought it around from the side with all his force. Once more, the shock of Wolff's stroke broke the Yidshe's grasp.

Funem Laksfalk lifted his visor for the third time. 'You are such a champion as I have never met. I am loath to admit it, but you have defeated me. And that is something I have never said nor thought to say. You have the strength of the Lord himself.'

'You may keep your life, your honor, and your armor and horse,' Wolff replied. 'I want only that my friend von Horstmann and I be allowed to go on without further challenges. We have an appointment.'

The Yidshe answered that it would be so. Wolff returned to his camp, there to be greeted joyously, even by those who had thought of him as a Khamshem dog.

Chortling, Kickaha ordered camp struck. Wolff asked him if he did not think they could make far better time unencumbered with a train.

'Sure, but it's not done very often,' Kickaha replied. 'Oh, well, you're right. I'll send them on home. And we'll get these damn locomotive plates off.'

They had not ridden far before they heard the drum of hooves. Coming up the road behind them was funem Laksfalk, also minus his armor. They halted until he had overtaken them.

'Noble knights,' he said, smiling, 'I know that you are on a quest. Would it be too much to ask for me to ask to join? I would feel honored. I also feel that only by assisting you can I redeem my defeat.'

Kickaha looked at Wolff and said, 'It's up to you. But I like his style.'

'Would you bind yourself to aid us in whatever we do? As long as it is not dishonorable, of course. You may release yourself from your oath at any time, but you must swear by all that's holy that you will never aid our enemies.'

'By God's blood and the beard of Moses, I swear.'

That night, while they made camp in a brake alongside a brook, Kickaha said, 'There's one problem that having funem Laksfalk along might complicate. We have to get the stain off your skin, and that beard has to go, too. Otherwise, if we run into Abiru, he might identify you.'

'One lie always leads to another,' Wolff said. 'Well, tell him that I'm the younger son of a baron who kicked me out because my jealous brother falsely accused me. I've been traveling around since then, disguised as a Saracen. But I intend to return to my fathers castle – he's dead now – and challenge my brother to a duel.'

'Fabulous! You're a second Kickaha! But what about when he learns of Chryseis and the horn?'

'We'll think of something. Maybe the truth. He can always back out when he finds he's bucking the Lord.'

The next morning they rode until they came to the village of Etzelbrand. Here Kickaha purchased some chemicals from the local white-wizard and made a preparation to remove the stain. Once past the village, they stopped off at the brook. Funem Laksfalk watched with interest, then amazement, then suspicion as the beard came off, followed by the stain.

'God's eyes! You were a Khamshem, now you could be a Yidshe!'

Kickaha thereupon launched into a three-hour, much-detailed story in which Wolff was the bastard son of a Yidshe maiden lady and a Teutoniac knight on a quest. The knight, a Robert von Wolfram, had stayed at a Yidshe castle after covering himself with glory during a tournament. He and the maiden had fallen in love, too much so. When the knight had ridden out, vowing to return after completing his quest he had left Rivke pregnant. But von Wolfram had been killed and the girl had had to bear young Robert in shame. Her father had kicked her out and sent her to a little village in Khamshem to live there forever. The girl had died when giving birth to Robert, but a faithful old servant had revealed the secret of his birth to Robert. The young bastard had sworn that when he gained manhood, he would go to the castle of his father's people and claim his rightful inheritance. Rivke's father was dead now but his brother, a wicked old man, held the castle. Robert intended to wrest the baronetcy from him if he would not give it up.

Funem Laksfalk had tears in his eyes at the end of the story. He said, 'I will ride with you, Robert, and help you against your wicked uncle. Thus may I redeem my defeat.'

Later, Wolff reproached Kickaha for making up such a fantastic story, so detailed that he might easily be tripped up. Moreover, he did not like to deceive such a man as the Yidshe knight.

'Nonsense! You couldn't tell him the whole truth, and it's easier to make up a whole lie than a half-truth! Besides, look at how much he enjoyed his little cry! And, I am Kickaha, the *kickaha*, the tricky one, the maker of fantasies and of realities. I am the man whom boundaries cannot hold. I slip from one to another, in-again-out-again Finnegan. I seem to be killed, yet I pop up again, alive, grinning, and kicking! I am quicker than men who are stronger than me, and stronger than those who are quicker! I have few loyalties, but those are unshakable! I am the ladies' darling wherever I go, and many are the tears shed after I slip through the night like a red-headed ghost! But tears cannot hold me any more than chains! Off I go, and where I will appear or what my name will be, few know! I am the Lord's gadfly; he cannot sleep at nights because I elude his Eyes, the ravens, and his hunters, the gworl!'

Kickaha stopped and began laughing uproariously. Wolff had to grin back. Kickaha's manner made it plain that he was poking fun at himself. However, he did half-believe it, and why should he not? What he said was not actually exaggeration.

This thought opened the way to a train of speculation that brought a frown to Wolff. Was it possible that Kickaha was the Lord himself in disguise? He could be amusing himself by running with hare and hound both. What better entertainment for a Lord, a man who has to look far and deep for something new with which to stave off ennui? There were many unexplained things about him.

Wolff, searching Kickaha's face for some clue to the mystery, felt his doubts evaporate. Surely that merry face was not the mask for a hideously cold being who toyed with lives. And then there was Kickaha's undeniably Hoosier accent and idioms. Could a Lord master these?

Well, why not? Kickaha had evidently mastered other languages and dialects as well.

So it went in Wolff's mind that long afternoon as they rode. But dinner and drink and good fellowship dispelled them so that, at bedtime, he had forgotten his doubts. The three had stopped at a tavern in the village of Gnazelschist and eaten heartily. Wolff and Kickaha devoured a roast suckling pig between them. Funem Laksfalk, although he shaved and had other liberal views of his religion, refused the taboo pork. He ate beef – although he knew it had not been slaughtered a la kosher. All three downed many steins of the excellent local dark beer, and during the drink-conversation Wolff told funem Laksfalk a somewhat edited story about their search for Chryseis – a noble quest indeed, they agreed, and then they all staggered off to bed.

In the morning, they took a shortcut through the hills which would save them three days' time – if they got through. The road was rarely traveled, and with good reason, for outlaws and dragons frequented the area. They made good speed, saw no men-of-the-woods and only one dragon. The scaly monster scrambled up from a ditch a hundred yards ahead of them. It snorted and disappeared into the trees on the other side of the road, as eager as they to avoid a fight.

Coming down out of the hills to the main highway, Wolff said, 'A raven's following us.'

'Yeah, I know it, but don't get your neck hot. They're all over the place. I doubt that it knows who we are. I sincerely hope it doesn't.'

At noon of the following day, they entered the territory of the Komtur of Tregyln. More than twenty-four hours later, they arrived within sight of the castle of Tregyln, the Baron von Elgers' seat of power. This was the largest castle Wolff had so far seen. It was built of black stone and was situated on top of a high hill a mile from the town of Tregyln.

In full armor, pennoned lances held upright, the three rode boldly to the moat that surrounded the castle. A warder came out of a small blockhouse by the moat and politely inquired of them their business.

'Take word to the noble lord that three knights of good fame would be his guests,' Kickaha said. 'The Barons von Horstmann and von Wolfram and the far-famed Yidshe baron, funem Laksfalk. We look for a noble to hire us for fighting or to send us on a quest.'

The sergeant shouted at a corporal, who ran off across the drawbridge. A few minutes afterwards, one of von Elgers' sons, a youth splendidly dressed, rode out to welcome them. Inside the huge courtyard, Wolff saw something that disturbed him. Several Khamshem and Sholkin were lounging around or playing dice.

'They won't recognize either one of us,' Kickaha said. 'Cheer up. If they're here, then so are Chryseis and the horn.'

After making sure that their horses were well taken care of, the three went to the quarters given them. They bathed and put on the brilliantly colored new clothes sent up to them by von Elgers. Wolff observed that these differed little from the garments worn during the thirteenth century. The only innovations, Kickaha said, were traceable to aboriginal influence.

By the time they entered the vast dining-hall, the supper was in full blast. Blast was the right word, for the uproar was deafening. Half the guests were reeling, and the others did not move much because they had passed the reeling stage. Von Elgers managed to rise to greet his guests. Graciously, he apologized for being found in such a condition at such an early hour.

'We have been entertaining our Khamshem guest for several days. He has brought unexpected wealth to us, and we've been spending a little of it on a celebration.'

He turned to introduce Abiru, did so too swiftly, and almost fell. Abiru rose to return their bow. His black eyes flickered like a sword point over them; his smile was broad but mechanical. Unlike the others, he appeared sober. The three took their seats, which were close to the Khamshem because the previous occupants had passed out under the table. Abiru seemed eager to talk to them.

'If you are looking for service, you have found your man. I am paying the baron to conduct me to the hinterland, but I can always use more swords. The road to my destination is long and hard and beset with many perils.'

'And where is your destination?' Kickaha asked. No one looking at him would have thought him any more than idly interested in Abiru for he was hotly scanning the blonde beauty across the table from him.

'There is no secret about that,' Abiru said. 'The lord of Kranzelkracht is said to be a very strange man, but it is also said that he has more wealth even than the Grand Marshal of Teutonia.'

'I know that for a fact,' Kickaha replied. 'I have been there, and I have seen his treasures. Many years ago, so it is said, he dared the displeasure of the Lord and climbed the great mountain to the tier of Atlantis. He robbed the treasure house of the Rhadamanthus himself and got away with a bagful of jewels. Since then, von Kranzelkracht has increased his wealth by conquering the states around his. It is said that the Grand Marshal is worried by this and is thinking of organizing a crusade against him. The Marshal claims that the man is a heretic. But if he were, would not the Lord have blasted him with lightning long ago?'

Abiru bowed his head and touched his forehead with his fingertips.

'The Lord works in mysterious ways. Besides, who but the Lord knows the truth? In any event, I am taking my slaves and certain possessions to Kranzelkracht. I expect to make an enormous profit from my venture, and those knights bold enough to share it will gain much gold – not to mention fame.'

Abiru paused to drink from a glass of wine. Kickaha, aside to Wolff, said, 'The man's as big a liar as I am. He intends to use us to get him as far as Kranzelkracht, which is near the foot of the monolith. Then he will take Chryseis and the horn up to Atlantis, where he should be paid with a houseful of jewels and gold for the two.'

'That is, unless his game is even deeper than I think at this moment.'

He lifted his stein and drank for a long time, or appeared to. Setting the stein down with a crash, he said, 'I'll be damned if there isn't something familiar about Abiru! I had a funny feeling the first time I saw him, but I was too busy thereafter to think much about it. Now, I know I've seen him before.'

Wolff replied that that was not amazing. How many faces had he seen during his twenty-year wanderings?

'Maybe you're right,' Kickaha muttered. 'But I don't think it was any slight acquaintance I had with him. I'd sure like to scrape off his beard.'

Abiru arose and excused himself, saying that it was the hour of prayer to the Lord and his personal deity, Tartartar. He would be back after his devotions. At this, von Elgers beckoned to two men-at-arms and ordered them to accompany him to his quarters and make sure that he was safe. Abiru bowed and thanked him for his consideration. Wolff did not miss the intent behind the baron's polite words. He did not trust the Khamshem, and Abiru knew it. Von Elgers, despite his drunkenness, was aware of what was going on and would detect anything out of the way.

'Yeah, you're right about him,' Kickaha said. 'He didn't get to where he is by turning his back on his enemies. And try to conceal your impatience, Bob. We've got a long wait ahead of us. Act drunk, make a few passes at the ladies – they'll think you're queer if you don't. But don't go off with any. We got to keep each other in sight so we can take off together when the right time comes.'

13

Wolff drank enough to loosen the wires that seemed to be wound around him. He even began to talk with the Lady Alison, wife of the baron of the Wenzelbricht March. A dark-haired and blue-eyed woman of statuesque beauty, she wore a clinging white samite gown. It was so low cut that she should have been satisfied with its exhilarating effect on the men, but she kept dropping her fan and picking it up herself. At any time other than this, Wolff would have been happy to break his woman-fast with her. It was obvious he would have no trouble doing so, for she was flattered that the great von Wolfram was interested in her. She had heard of his victory over funem Laksfalk. But he could think only of Chryseis, who must be somewhere in the castle. Nobody had mentioned her, and he dared not. Yet he was aching to do so and several times found that he had to bite the question off the tip of his tongue.

Presently, and just at the right time for him – since he could not any longer refuse the Lady Alison's bold hints without offending her – Kickaha was at his side. Kickaha had brought Alison's husband along to give Wolff a reasonable excuse for leaving. Later, Kickaha revealed that he had dragged von Wenzelbricht away from another woman on the pretext that his wife demanded he come to her. Both Kickaha and Wolff walked away, leaving the beer-stupored baron to explain just what he wanted of her. Since neither he nor his wife knew, they must have had an interesting, if mystifying conversation.

Wolff gestured at funem Laksfalk to join them. Together, the three pretended to stagger off to the toilet. Once out of sight of those in the dining-hall, they hurried down a hall away from their supposed destination. Unhindered, they climbed four flights of steps. They were armed only with daggers, for it would have been an insult to wear armor or swords to dinner. Wolff, however, had managed to untie a long cord from the draperies in his apartment. He wore this coiled around his waist under his shirt.

The Yidshe knight said, 'I overheard Abiru talk with his lieutenant, Rhamnish. They spoke in the trade language of H'vaizhum, little knowing that I have traveled on the Guzirit River in the jungle area. Abiru asked Rhamnish if he had found out yet where von Elgers had taken Chryseis. Rhamnish said that he had spent some gold and time in talking to servants and guards. All he could find out was that she is on the east side of the castle. The gworl, by the way, are in the dungeon.'

'Why should von Elgers keep Chryseis from Abiru?' Wolff said. 'Isn't she Abiru's property?'

'Maybe the baron has some designs on her,' Kickaha said. 'If she's as extraordinary and beautiful as you say …'

'We've got to find her!'

'Don't get your neck hot. We will. Oh, oh, there's a guard at the end of the hall. Keep walking toward him – stagger a little more.'

The guard raised his spear as they reeled in front of him. In a polite but firm voice, he told them they must go back. The baron had forbidden anybody, under pain of death, to proceed further.

'All right,' Wolff said, slurring the words. He started to turn, then suddenly leaped and grabbed the spear. Before the startled sentry could loose the yell from his open mouth, he was slammed against the door and the shaft of the spear was brought up hard against his throat. Wolff continued to press it. The sentry's eyes goggled, his face became red, then blue. A minute later, he slumped forward, dead.

The Yidshe dragged the body down the hall and into a side-room. When he returned, he reported that he had hidden the corpse behind a large chest.

'Too bad,' Kickaha said cheerfully. 'He may have been a nice kid. But if we have to fight our way out, we'll have one less in our way.'

However, the dead man had had no key to unlock the door.

'Von Elgers is probably the only man who has one, and we'd play hell getting it off him,' Kickaha said. 'Okay. We'll go around.'

He led them back down the hall to another room. They climbed through its tall pointed window. Beyond its ledge was a series of projections, stones carved in the shape of dragon heads, fiends, boars. The adornments had not been spaced to provide for easy climbing, but a brave or desperate man could ascend them. Fifty feet below them, the surface of the moat glittered dully in the light of torches on the drawbridge. Fortunately, thick black clouds covered the moon and would prevent those below from seeing the climbers.

Kickaha looked down at Wolff, who was clinging to a stone gargoyle, one foot on a snake-head. 'Hey, did I forget to tell you that the baron keeps the moat stocked with water-dragons? They're not very big, only about twenty feet long, and they don't have any legs. But they're usually underfed.'

'There are times when I find your humor in bad taste,' Wolff said fiercely. 'Get going.'

Kickaha gave a low laugh and continued climbing. Wolff followed, after glancing down to make sure that the Yidshe was doing all right. Kickaha stopped and said, 'There's a window here, but it's barred. I don't think there's anyone inside. It's dark.'

Kickaha continued climbing. Wolff paused to look inside the window. It was black as the inside of a cave fish's eye. He reached through the bars and groped around until his fingers closed on a candle. Lifting it carefully so that it would come out of its holder, he passed it through the bars. With one arm hooked around a steel rod, he hung while he fished a match from the little bag on his belt with the other hand.

From above, Kickaha said, 'What are you doing?'

Wolff told him, and Kickaha said, 'I spoke Chryseis' name a couple of times. There's no one in there. Quit wasting time.'

'I want to make sure.'

'You're too thorough; you pay too much attention to detail. You got to take big cuts if you want to chop down a tree. Come on.'

Not bothering to reply, Wolff struck the match. It flared up and almost went out in the breeze, but he managed to stick it inside the window quickly enough. The flare of light showed a bedroom with no occupant.

'You satisfied?' Kickaha's voice came, weaker because he was climbing upward. 'We got one more chance, the bartizan. If there's no one ... Anyway, I don't know how – *ugh!*'

Afterwards, Wolff was thankful that he had been so reluctant to give up his hopes that Chryseis would be in the room. He had let the match burn out until it threatened his fingers and only then let go of it. Immediately after that and Kickaha's muffled exclamation, he was struck by a falling body. The impact felt as if it had almost torn his arm loose from its socket. He gave a grunt that echoed the one from above and hung on with one arm. Kickaha clung to him for several seconds, shivered, then breathed deeply and resumed his climb. Neither said a word about it, but both knew that if it had not been for Wolff's stubbornness, Kickaha's fall would also have knocked Wolff from a precarious hold on a gargoyle. Possibly funem Laksfalk would have been dislodged also, for he was directly below Wolff.

The bartizan was a large one. It was about one third of the way up the wall, projected far outward from the wall, and a light fell from its cross-shaped window. The wall a little distance above it was bare of decoration.

An uproar broke loose below and a fainter one within the castle. Wolff stopped to look down toward the drawbridge, thinking that they must have been seen. However, although there were a number of men-at-arms and guests on the drawbridge and the grounds outside, many with torches, not a single one was looking up toward the climbers. They seemed to be searching for someone in the bushes and trees.

He thought that their absence and the body of the guard had been noted. They would have to fight their way out. But let them find Chryseis first and get her loose; then would be time to think of battle.

Kickaha, ahead of him, said, 'Come on, Bob!' His voice was so excited that Wolff knew he must have located Chryseis. He climbed swiftly, more swiftly than good sense permitted. It was necessary to climb to one side of the projection, for its underside angled outward. Kickaha was lying on the flat top of the bartizan and just in the act of pulling himself back from its edge. 'You have to hang upside down to look in the window, Bob. She's there, and she's alone. But the window's too narrow for either of you to go through.'

Wolff slid out over the edge of the projection while Kickaha grabbed his legs. He went out and over, the black moat below, and bent down until he would have fallen if his legs had not been held. The slit in the stone showed him the face of Chryseis, inverted. She was smiling but tears were rolling down her cheeks.

Afterward, he did not exactly remember what they said to each other, for he was in a fever of exaltation, succeeded by a chill of frustration and despair, then followed by another fever. He felt as if he could talk forever, and he reached his hand out to touch hers. She strained against the opening in the rock in vain to reach him.

'Never mind, Chryseis,' he said. 'You know we're here. We're not going to leave until we take you away, I swear it.'

'Ask her where the horn is!' Kickaha said.

Hearing him, Chryseis said, 'I do not know, but I think that von Elgers has it.'

'Has he bothered you?' Wolff asked savagely.

'Not so far, but I do not know how long it will be before he takes me to bed,' she replied. 'He's restrained himself only because he does not want to lower the price he'll get for me. He says he's never seen a woman like me.'

Wolff swore, then laughed. It was like her to talk thus frankly, for in the Garden world self-admiration was an accepted attitude.

'Cut out the unnecessary chatter,' Kickaha said. 'There'll be time for that if we get her out.'

Chryseis answered Wolff's questions as concisely and clearly as possible. She described the route to this room. She did not know how many guards were stationed outside her door or on the way up.

'I do know one thing that the baron does not,' she said. 'He thinks that Abiru is taking me to von Kranzelkracht. I know better. Abiru means to ascend the Doozvillnava to Atlantis. There he will sell me to the Rhadamanthus.'

'He won't sell you to anybody, because I'm going to kill him,' Wolff said. 'I have to go now, Chryseis, but I'll be back as soon as possible. And I won't be coming this way. Until then, I love you.'

Chryseis cried, 'I have not heard a man tell me that for a thousand years! Oh, Robert Wolff, I love you! But I am afraid! I ...'

'You don't have to be afraid of anything,' he said. 'Not while I am alive, and I don't intend to die.'

He gave the word for Kickaha to drag him back onto the rooftop of the bartizan. He rose and almost fell over from dizziness, for his head was gorged with blood.

'The Yidshe has already started down,' Kickaha said. 'I sent him to find out if we can get back the way we came and also to see what's causing the uproar.'

'Us?'

'I don't think so. The first thing they'd do, they'd check on Chryseis. Which they haven't done.'

The descent was even slower and more dangerous than the climb up, but they made it without mishap. Funem Laksfalk was waiting for them by the window which had given them access to the outside.

'They've found the guard you killed,' he said. 'But they don't think we had anything to do with it. The gworl broke loose from the dungeon and killed a number of men. They also seized their own weapons. Some got outside but not all.'

The three left the room and merged quickly with the searchers. They had no chance to go up the flight of steps at the end of which was the room where Chryseis was imprisoned. Without a doubt, von Elgers would have made sure that the guards were increased.

They wandered around the castle for several hours, acquainting themselves with its layout. They noted that, though the shock of the gworl's escape had sobered the Teutons somewhat, they were still very drunk. Wolff suggested that they go to their room, and talk about possible plans. Perhaps they could think of something reasonably workable.

Their room was on the fifth story and by a window at an angle below the window of Chryseis' bartizan. To get to it, they had to pass many men and women, all stinking of beer and wine, reeling, babbling away, and accomplishing very little. Their room could not have been entered and searched, for only they and the chief warder had the keys. He had been too busy elsewhere to get to their room. Besides, how could the gworl enter through a locked door?

The moment Wolff stepped into his room, he knew that they had somehow entered. The musty rotten-fruit stench hit him in the nostrils. He pulled the other two inside and swiftly shut and locked the door behind them. Then he turned with his dagger in his hand. Kickaha also, his nostrils dilating and his eyes stabbing, had his blade out. Only funem Laksfalk was unaware that anything was wrong except for an unpleasant odor.

Wolff whispered to him; the Yidshe walked toward the wall to get their swords, then stopped. The racks were empty.

Silently and slowly, Wolff went into the other room. Kickaha, behind him, held a torch. The flame flickered and cast humped shadows that made Wolff start. He had been sure that they were the gworl.

The light advanced; the shadows fled or changed into harmless shapes.

'They're here,' Wolff said softly. 'Or they've just left. But where could they go?'

Kickaha pointed at the high drapes that were drawn over the window. Wolff strode up to them and began thrusting through the red-purple velvet cloth. His blade met only air and the stone of the wall. Kickaha pulled the drapes back to reveal what the dagger had told him. There were no gworl.

'They came in through the window,' the Yidshe said. 'But why?'

Wolff lifted his eyes at the moment, and he swore. He stepped back to warn his friends, but they were already looking upward. There, hanging upside down by their knees from the heavy iron drapery rod, were two gworl. Both had long, bloody knives in their hands. One, in addition, clutched the silver horn.

The two creatures stiffened their legs the second they realized they were discovered. Both managed to flip over and come down heads-up. The one to the right kicked out with his feet. Wolff rolled and then was up, but Kickaha had missed with his knife and the gworl had not. It slid from his palm through a short distance into Kickaha's arm.

The other threw his knife at funem Laksfalk. It struck the Yidshe in the solar plexus with a force that made him bend over and stagger back. A few seconds later, he straightened up to reveal why the knife had failed to enter his flesh. Through the tear in his shirt gleamed the steel of light chain-mail.

By then, the gworl with the horn had gone through the window. The others could not rush to the window because the gworl left behind was putting up a savage battle. He knocked down Wolff again, but with his fist this time. He threw himself like a whirlwind at Kickaha, his fists flailing, and drove him back. The Yidshe, his knife in hand, jumped at him and thrust for his belly, only to have his wrist seized and turned until he cried out with the pain and the knife fell from his fist.

Kickaha, lying on the floor, raised one leg and then drove the heel of his foot against the gworl's ankle. He fell, although he did not hit the floor because Wolff seized him. Around and around, their arms locked around each other, they circled. Each was trying to break the other's back and also trying to trip the other. Wolff succeeded in throwing him over. They toppled against the wall with the gworl receiving the most damage when the back of his head struck the wall.

For a flicker of an eyelid, he was stunned. This gave Wolff enough time to pull the stinking, hairy, bumpy creature hard against him and pull with all his strength against the gworl's spine. Too heavily muscled and too heavily boned, the gworl resisted the spine-snapping. By then, the other two men were upon him with their knives. They thrust several times and would have continued to try for a fatal spot in the tough cartilage-roughened hide had Wolff not told them to stop.

Stepping back, he released the gworl, who fell bleeding and glaze-eyed to the floor. Wolff ignored him for a moment to look out the window after the gworl who had escaped with the horn. A party of horsemen, holding torches, was thundering over the drawbridge and out into the country. The light showed only the smooth black waters of the moat; there was no gworl climbing down the wall. Wolff turned back to the gworl who had remained behind.

'His name is Diskibibol, and the other is Smeel,' Kickaha said.

'Smeel must have drowned,' Wolff said. 'Even if he could swim, the water-dragons might have gotten him. But he can't swim.'

Wolff thought of the horn lying in the muck at the bottom of the moat. 'Apparently no one saw Smeel fall. So the horn's safe there, for the time being.'

The gworl spoke. Although he used German, he could not master the sounds accurately. His words grated deep in the back of his throat. 'You will die, humans. The Lord will win; Arwoor is the Lord; he cannot be defeated by filth such as you. But before you die, you will suffer the most … the … the most …'

He began coughing, threw up blood, and continued to do so until he was dead.

'We'd better get rid of his body,' Wolff said. 'We might have a hard time explaining what he was doing here. And von Elgers might connect the missing horn with their presence here.'

A look out of the window showed him that the search party was far down the trail road leading to the town. For the moment, at least, no one was on the bridge. He lifted the heavy corpse up and shoved it out the window. After Kickaha's wound was bandaged, Wolff and the Yidshe wiped up the evidences of the struggle.

Only after they were through did funem Laksfalk speak. His face pale and grim. 'That was the horn of the Lord. I insist that you tell me how it got here and what your part is in this ... this seeming blasphemy.'

'Now's the time for the whole truth,' Kickaha said. 'You tell him, Bob. For once, I don't feel like hogging the conversation.'

Wolff was concerned for Kickaha, for his face, too, was pale, and the blood was oozing out through the thick bandages. Nevertheless, he told the Yidshe what he could as swiftly as possible.

The knight listened well, although he could not help interjecting questions frequently or swearing when Wolff told him something particularly amazing.

'By God,' he said when Wolff seemed to be finished, 'this tale of another world would make me call you a liar if the rabbis had not already told me that my ancestors, and those of the Teutons, had come from just such a place. Then there is the Book of the Second Exodus, which says the same thing and also claims that the Lord came from a different world.

'Still, I had always thought these tales the stuff that holy men, who are a trifle mad, dream up. I would never have dreamed of saying so aloud, of course, for I did not want to be stoned for heresy. Also, there's always the doubt that these could be true. And the Lord punishes those who deny him; there's no doubt of that.

'Now, you put me in a situation no man could envy. I know you two for the most redoubtable knights it has ever been my fortune to encounter. You are such men as would not lie; I would stake my life on that. And your story rings true as the armor of the great dragon-slayer, fun Zilberbergl. Yet, I do not know.'

He shook his head. 'To seek to enter the citadel of the Lord himself, to strike against the Lord! That frightens me. For the first time in my life, I, Leyb funem Laksfalk, admit that I am afraid.'

Wolff said, 'You gave your oath to us. We release you but ask that you do as you swore. That is, you tell no one of us or our quest.'

Angrily, the Yidshe said, 'I did not say I would quit you! I will not, at least not yet. There is this that makes me think you might be telling the truth. The Lord is omnipotent, yet his holy horn has been in your hands and those of the gworl, and the Lord has done nothing. Perhaps ...'

Wolff replied that he did not have time to wait for him to make up his mind. The horn must be recovered now, while there was the opportunity.

And Chryseis must be freed at the first chance. He led them from the room and into another, unoccupied at the moment. There they took three swords to replace theirs, which the gworl must have cast out of the window into the moat. Within a few minutes, they were outside the castle and pretending to search through the woods for the gworl.

By then most of the Teutons outside had returned to the castle. The three waited until the stragglers decided that no gworl were around. When the last of these had gone across the drawbridge, Wolff and his friends put out their torches. Two sentries remained at the guardhouse by the end of the bridge. These, however, were a hundred yards distant and could not see into the shadows where the three crouched. Moreover, they were too busy discussing the events of the night and looking into the darkness of the woods. They were not the original sentries, for these had been killed by the gworl when they had made their dash for freedom across the bridge.

'The point just below our window should be where the horn is,' Wolff said. 'Only ...'

'The water-dragons,' Kickaha said. 'They'll have dragged off Smeel and Diskibibol's bodies to their lairs, wherever those are. But there might be some others cruising around. I'd go, but this wound of mine would draw them at once.'

'I was just talking to myself,' Wolff said. He began to take off his clothes. 'How deep's the moat?'

'You'll find out,' Kickaha said.

Wolff saw something gleam redly in the reflected light from the distant bridge torches. An animal's eyes, he thought. The next moment, he and the others were caught within something sticky and binding. The stuff, whatever it was, covered his eyes and blinded him.

He fought savagely but silently. Though he did not know who his assailants were, he did not intend to arouse the castle people. However the struggle came out, the issue did not concern them; he knew that.

The more he thrashed, the tighter the webs clung to him and bound him. Eventually, raging, breathing hard, he was helpless. Only then did a voice speak, low and rasping. A knife cut the web to leave his face exposed. In the dim light of the distant torches, he could see two other figures wrapped in the stuff and a dozen crooked shapes. The rotten-fruit stench was powerful.

'I am Ghaghrill, the Zdrrikh'agh of Abbkmung. You are Robert Wolff and our great enemy Kickaha, and the third one I do not know.'

'The Baron funem Laksfalk!' the Yidshe said. 'Release me, and you will soon find out whether I am a good man to know or not, you stinking swine!'

'Quiet! We know you have somehow slain two of my best killers, Smeel and Diskibibol, though they could not have been so fierce if they allowed themselves to be defeated by such as you. We saw Diskibibol fall from where we hid in the woods. And we saw Smeel jump with the horn.'

Ghaghrill paused, then said, 'You, Wolff, will go after the horn into the waters and bring it back to us. If you do, I swear by the honor of the Lord that we will release all three of you. The Lord wants Kickaha, too, but not as badly as the horn, and he said that we were not to kill him, even if we had to let him go to keep from killing him. We obey the Lord, for he is the greatest killer of all.'

'And if I refuse?' Wolff said. 'It is almost certain death for me with the water-dragons in the moat.'

'It will be certain death for you if you don't.'

Wolff considered. He was the logical choice, he had to admit. The quality and relationship of the Yidshe was unknown to the gworl, so they could not let him go after the horn; he might fail to return. Kickaha was a prize second only to the horn. Besides, he was wounded, and the blood from the wound would attract the water-monsters. Wolff, if he cared for Kickaha, would return. They could not, of course, be sure of the depth of his feelings for Kickaha. That was a chance they would have to take.

One thing was certain. No gworl was about to venture into such deep water if he had someone else to do it for him.

'Very well,' Wolff said. 'Let me loose, and I will go after the horn. But at least give me a knife to defend myself against the dragons.'

'No,' Ghaghrill said.

Wolff shrugged. After he was cut loose of the web-net, he removed all of his clothes except his shirt. This covered the cord wound around his waist.

'Don't do it, Bob,' Kickaha said. 'You can't trust a gworl any more than his master. They will take the horn from you and then do to us what they wish. And laugh at us for being their tools.'

'I don't have any choice,' Wolff said. 'If I find the horn, I'll be back. If I don't return, you'll know I died trying.'

'You'll die anyway,' Kickaha replied. There was a smack of a fist against flesh. Kickaha cursed but did so softly.

'Speak any more, Kickaha,' Ghaghrill said, 'and I will cut out your tongue. The Lord did not forbid that.'

14

Wolff looked up at the window, from which a torch light still shone. He walked into the water, which was chilly but not cold. His feet sank into thick gluey mud which evoked images of the many corpses whose rotting flesh must form part of this mud. And he could not keep from thinking of the saurians swimming out there. If he was lucky, they would not be in the immediate neighborhood. If they had dragged off the bodies of Smeel and Diskibibol ... Better quit dwelling on them and start swimming.

The moat was at least two hundred yards wide at this point. He even stopped at the midway point to tread water and turn around to look at the shore. From this distance he could see nothing of the group.

On the other hand, they could not see him either. And Ghaghrill had given him no time limit to return. However, he knew that if he were not back before dawn, he would not find them there.

At a spot immediately below the light from the window, he dived. Down he went, the water becoming colder almost with every stroke. His ears began to ache, then to hurt intensely. He blew some bubbles of air out to relieve the pressure, but he was not helped much by this. Just as it seemed that he could go no deeper without his ears bursting, his hand plunged into soft mud. Restraining the desire to turn at once and swim upwards for the blessed relief from pressure and the absolutely needed air, he groped around on the floor of the moat. He found nothing but mud and, once, a bone. He drove himself until he knew he had to have air.

Twice he rose to the surface and then dived again. By now, he knew that even if the horn were lying on the bottom, he might not ever find it. Blind in the murky waters, he could pass within an inch of the horn and never know it. Moreover, it was possible that Smeel had thrown the horn far away from him when he had fallen. Or a water-dragon could have carried it off with Smeel's corpse, even swallowed the horn.

The third time, he swam a few strokes to the right from his previous dives before plunging under. He dived down at what he hoped was a ninety-degree angle from the bottom. In the blackness, he had no way of determining direction. His hand plowed into the mud; he settled close to it to feel around, and his fingers closed upon cold metal. A quick slide of them along the object passed over seven little buttons.

When he reached the surface, he trod water and gasped for wind. Now to make the trip back, which he hoped he could do. The water-dragons could still show up.

Then he forgot the dragons, for he could see nothing. The torchlight from the drawbridge, the feeble moonglow through the clouds, the light from the window overhead, all these were gone.

Wolff forced himself to keep on treading water while he thought his situation through. For one thing, there was no breeze. The air was stale. Thus, he could only be in one place, and it was his fortune that such a place happened to be just where he had dived. Also, it was his luck that he had come up from the bottom at an oblique angle.

Still, he could not see which way was shoreward and which way was castleward. To find out took only a few strokes. His hand contacted stone – stone bricks. He groped along it until it began to curve inward. Following the curve, he finally came to that which he had hoped for. It was a flight of stone steps that rose out of the water and led upward.

He climbed up it, slowly, his hand out for a sudden obstacle. His feet slid over each step, ready to pause if an opening appeared or a step seemed loose. After twenty steps upward, he came to their end. He was in a corridor cut out of stone.

Von Elgers, or whoever had built the castle, had constructed a means for secret entrance and exit. An opening below water level in the walls led to a chamber, a little port, and from thence into the castle. Now, Wolff had the horn and a way to get unnoticed into the castle. But he did not know what to do. Should he return the horn to the gworl first? Afterward, he and the two others could return this way and search for Chryseis.

He doubted that Ghaghrill would keep his word. However, even if the gworl were to release their captives, if they swam to this place, Kickaha's wound would draw the saurians and all three would be lost. Chryseis would have no chance of getting free. Kickaha could not be left behind while the other two went back to the castle. He would be exposed as soon as dawn came. He could hide in the woods, but the chances were that another hunting party would be searching that area then. Especially after it was discovered that the three stranger knights were gone.

He decided to go on down the hall. This was too good a chance to pass up. He would do his best before daylight. If he failed, then he would go back with the horn.

The horn! No use taking that with him. Should he be captured without it, his knowledge of its location might help him.

He returned to where the steps came to an end below the water. He dived down to a depth of about ten feet and left the horn on the mud.

Back in the corridor, he shuffled until he came to more steps at its end. The flight led upward on a tight spiraling course. A count of steps led him to think that he had ascended at least five stories. At every estimated story he felt around the narrow walls for doors or releases to open doors. He found none.

At what could have been the seventh story, he saw a tiny beam of light from a hole in the wall. Bending down, he peered through it. By the far end of the room, seated at a table, a bottle of wine before him, was Baron von Elgers. The man seated across the table from the baron was Abiru.

The baron's face was flushed by more than drink. He snarled at Abiru, 'That's all I intend to say, Khamshem! You will get the horn back from the gworl, or I'll have your head! Only first you'll be taken to the dungeon! I have some curious iron devices there that you will be interested in!'

Abiru rose. His face was as pale beneath its dark pigment as the baron's was crimson.

'Believe me, sire, if the horn has been taken by the gworl, it will be recovered. They can't have gone far with it – if they have it – and they can easily be tracked down. They can't pass themselves off as human beings, you know. Besides, they're stupid.'

The baron roared, stood up, and crashed his fist against the top of the table.

'Stupid! They were clever enough to break out of my dungeon, and I would would have sworn that no one could do that! And they found my room and took the horn! You call that stupid!'

'At least,' Abiru said, 'they didn't steal the girl, too. I'll get something out of this. She should fetch a fabulous price.'

'She'll fetch nothing for you! She is mine!'

Abiru glared and said, 'She is my property. I obtained her at great peril and brought her all this way at much expense. I am entitled to her. What are you, a man of honor or a thief?'

Von Elgers struck him and knocked him down. Abiru, rubbing his cheek, got to his feet at once. Looking steadily at the baron, his voice tight, he said, 'And what about my jewels?'

'They are in my castle!' the baron shouted. 'And what is in my castle is the von Elgers'!'

He strode away out of Wolff's sight but apparently opened a door. He bellowed for the guard, and when they had come they took Abiru away between them.

'You are fortunate I do not kill you!' the baron raged. 'I am allowing you to keep your life, you miserable dog! You should get down on your knees and thank me for that! Now get out of the castle at once. If I hear that you are not making all possible speed to another state, I will have you hung on the nearest tree!' Abiru did not reply. The door closed. The baron paced back and forth for awhile, then abruptly came toward the wall behind which Wolff was crouched. Wolff left the peephole and retreated far down the steps. He hoped he had chosen the right direction in which to go. If the baron came down the staircase, he could force Wolff into the water and perhaps back out into the moat. But he did not think the baron intended to come that way.

For a second the light was cut off. A section of wall swung out with the baron's finger thrust through the hole. The torch held by von Elgers lit the well. Wolff crouched down behind the shadow cast by a turn of the corkscrew case. Presently, the light became weaker as the baron carried it up the steps. Wolff followed.

He could not keep his eyes on von Elgers all the time, for he had to dodge down behind various turns to keep from being detected if the baron should look downward. So it was that he did not see von Elgers leave the stairs nor know it until the light suddenly went out.

He went swiftly after the baron, although he did pause by the peephole. He stuck his finger in it and lifted upward. A small section gave way, a click sounded, and a door swung open for him. The inner side of the door formed part of the wall of the baron's quarters. Wolff stepped into the room, chose a thin eight-inch dagger from a rack in the wall, and went back out to the stairs. After shutting the door, he climbed upward.

This time he had no light from a hole to guide him. Nor was he even sure that he had stopped at the same place as the baron. He had made a rough estimate of the height from himself to the baron when the baron had disappeared. There was nothing else to do but feel around for the device which the baron must have used to open another door. When he placed his ear against the wall to listen for voices, he heard nothing.

His fingers slid over bricks and moisture-crumbled mortar until they met wood. That was all he could find: stone and a wooden frame in which a broad and high panel of wood was smoothly inset. There was nothing to indicate an open-sesame.

He climbed a few steps more and continued to probe. The bricks were innocent of any trigger or catch. He returned to the spot opposite the door and felt the wall there. Nothing.

Now he was frantic. He was sure that von Elgers had gone to Chryseis' room, and not just to talk. He went back down the steps and fingered the walls. Still nothing.

Again he tried the area around the door with no success. He pushed on one side of the door, only to find it would not budge. For a moment he thought of hammering on the wood and attracting von Elgers. If the baron were to come through to investigate, he would be helpless for a moment to an attack from above.

He rejected the idea. The baron was too canny to fall for such a trick. While he was unlikely to go for help, because he would not want to reveal the passageway to others, he could leave Chryseis' room through the regular door. The guard posted outside might wonder where he came from, although he would probably think that the baron had been inside before the watch had been changed. In any case, the baron could permanently shut the mouth of a suspicious guard. Wolff pushed in on the other side of the door, and it swung inward. It had not been locked; all it needed was pressure on the correct side.

He groaned softly at missing the obvious so long and stepped through. It was dark beyond the door; he was in a small room, almost a closet. This was composed of mortared bricks, except at one side. Here a metal rod poked from the wooden wall. Before working it, Wolff placed his ear against the wall. Muffled voices came through, too faint for him to recognize.

The metal rod had to be pulled out to activate the release on the door. Dagger in hand, Wolff stepped through it. He was in a large chamber of great stone blocks. There was a large bed with four ornately carved posters of glossy black wood and a bright-pink tassled canopy. Beyond it was the narrow cross-shaped window through which he had looked earlier that night.

Von Elgers' back was to him. The baron had Chryseis in his arms and was forcing her toward the bed. Her eyes were closed, and her head was turned away to avoid von Elgers' kisses. Both of them were still fully clothed.

Wolff bounded across the room, seized the baron by the shoulder, and pulled him backward. The baron let loose of Chryseis to reach for the dagger in his scabbard, then remembered that he had brought none. Apparently he had not intended to give Chryseis a chance to stab him.

His face, so flaming before, was gray now. His mouth worked, the cry for help to the guards outside the door frozen by surprise and fear.

Wolff gave him no chance to summon help. He dropped the dagger to strike the baron on the chin with his fist. Von Elgers, unconscious, slumped. Wolff did not want to waste any time, so he brushed by Chryseis, huge-eyed and pale. He cut off two strips of cloth from the bedsheets. The smaller he placed inside the baron's mouth, the larger he used as a gag. Then he removed a piece of the cord around his waist and tied von Elgers' hands in front of him. Hoisting the limp body over his shoulder, he said to Chryseis, 'Come on. We can talk later.'

He did pause to give instructions to Chryseis to close the wall-door behind them. There was no sense in letting others find the passageway when they finally came to investigate the baron's long absence. Chryseis held the torch behind him as they went down the steps. When they had come to the water, Wolff told her what they must do to escape. First, he had to retrieve the horn. Having done so, he scooped up water with his hands and threw it on the baron's face. When he saw his eyes open, he informed him of what he must do.

Von Elgers shook his head no. Wolff said, 'Either you go with us as hostage and take your chances with the water-dragons or you die right now. So which is it?'

The baron nodded. Wolff cut his bonds but attached the end of the cord to his ankle. All three went into the water. Immediately, von Elgers swam out to the wall and dived. The others followed under the wall, which only went about four feet below the surface. Coming up on the other side, Wolff saw that the clouds were beginning to break. The moon would soon be bearing down in all her green brightness.

As directed, the baron and Chryseis swam at an angle toward the other side of the moat. Wolff followed with the end of the cord in one hand. With its burden, they could not go swiftly. In fifteen minutes the moon would be rounding the monolith, with the sun not far behind at the other corner. There was not much time for Wolff to carry out his plan, but it was impossible to keep control of the baron unless they took their time.

Their point of arrival at the bank of the moat was a hundred yards beyond where the gworl and their captives waited. Within a few minutes they were around the curve of the castle and out of sight of the gworl and the guards on the bridge even if the moon became unclouded. This path was a necessary evil – evil because every second in the water meant more chance for the dragons to discover them.

When they were within twenty yards of their goal, Wolff felt rather than saw the roil of water. He turned to see the surface lift a little and a small wave coming toward him. He drew up his feet and kicked. They struck something hard and solid enough to allow him to spring away. He shot backward, dropping the end of the cord at the same time. The bulk passed between him and Chryseis, struck von Elgers, and was gone.

So was Wolff's hostage.

They abandoned any attempt to keep from making splashing noises. They swam as hard as they could. Only when they reached the bank and scrambled up onto it and ran to a tree did they stop. Sobbing for breath, they clung to the trunk.

Wolff did not wait until he had fully regained his breath. The sun would be around Doozvillnavava within a few minutes. He told Chryseis to wait for him. If he did not return shortly after sunaround, he would not be coming for a long time – if ever. She would have to leave and hide in the woods and then do whatever she could.

She begged him not to go, for she could not stand the idea of being all alone there.

'I have to,' he said, handing her an extra dagger which he had stuck through his shirt and secured by knotting the shirttail about it.

'I will use it on myself if you are killed,' she said.

He was in agony at the thought of her being so helpless, but there was nothing he could do about it.

'Kill me now before you leave me,' she said. 'I've gone through too much; I can't stand any more.'

He kissed her lightly on the lips and said, 'Sure you can. You're tougher than you used to be and always were tougher than you thought. Look at you now. You can say *kill* and *death* without so much as flinching.'

He was gone, running crouched over toward the spot where he had left his friends and the gworl. When he estimated he was about twenty yards from them, he stopped to listen. He heard nothing except the cry of a night-bird and a muffled shout from somewhere in the castle. On his hands and knees, the dagger in his teeth, he crawled toward the place opposite the light from the window of his quarters. At any moment he expected to smell the musty odor and to see a clump of blackness against the lesser dark.

But there was nobody there. Only the glimmer-gray remnants of the webnets remained to show that the gworl had actually been there.

He prowled around the area. When it became evident that there was no clue and that the sun would shortly expose him to the bridge guards, he returned to Chryseis. She clung to him and cried a little.

'See! I'm here after all,' he said. 'But we have to get out of here now.'

'We're going back to Okeanos?'

'No, we're going after my friends.'

They trotted away, past the castle and toward the monolith. The absence of the baron would soon be noticed. For miles around, no ordinary hiding place would be safe. And the gworl, knowing this, must also be making speed toward Doozvillnavava. No matter how badly they wanted the horn, they could not hang around now. Moreover, they must think that Wolff had drowned or been taken by a dragon. To them, the horn might be out of reach just now, but they could return when it was safe to do so.

Wolff pushed hard. Except for brief rests, they did not stop until they had reached the thick forest of the Rauhwald. There they crawled beneath the tangled thorns and through the intertwined bushes until their knees bled and their joints ached. Chryseis collapsed. Wolff gathered many of the plentiful berries for them to feed upon. They slept all night, and in the morning resumed their all-fours progress. By the time they had reached the other side of the Rauhwald, they were covered with thorn-wounds. There was no one waiting for them on the other side, as he had feared there would be.

This and another thing made him happy. He had come across evidence that the gworl had also passed his way. There were bits of coarse gworl hair on thorns and pieces of cloth. No doubt Kickaha had managed to drop these to mark the way if Wolff should be following.

15

After a month, they finally arrived at the foot of the monolith, Doozvillnavava. They knew they were on the right trail, since they had heard rumors of the gworl and even talked with those who had sighted them from a distance.

'I don't know why they've gone so far from the horn,' he said. 'Perhaps they mean to hole up in a cave in the face of the mountain and will come back down after the cry for them has died out.'

'Or it could be,' Chryseis said, 'that they have orders from the Lord to bring Kickaha back first. He has been like an insect on the Lord's eardrum so long that the Lord must be crazed even by the thought of him. Maybe he wants to make sure that Kickaha is out of the way before he sends the gworl again for the horn.'

Wolff agreed that she could be right. It was even possible that the Lord was going to come down from the palace via the same cords by which he had lowered the gworl. That did not seem likely, however, for the Lord would not want to be stranded. Could he trust the gworl to hoist him back up?

Wolff looked at the eye-staggering heights of the continent-broad tower of Doozvillnavava. It was, according to Kickaha, at least twice as high as the monolith of Abharhploonta, which supported the tier of Dracheland. It soared 60,000 feet or more, and the creatures that lived on the ledges and recesses and in the caves were fully as dreadful and hungry as those on the other monoliths. Doozvillnavava was gnarled and scoured and slashed and bristly; its ravaged face had an enormous recession that gave it a dark and gaping mouth; the giant seemed ready to eat all who dared to annoy it.

Chryseis, also examining the savage cliffs and their incredible height, shivered. But she said nothing; she had quit voicing her fears some time ago.

It could be that she was no longer concerned with herself, Wolff thought, but was intent upon the life within her. She was sure that she was pregnant.

He put his arm around her, kissed her, and said, 'I'd like to start at once, but we'll have to make preparations for several days. We can't attack that monster without resting or without enough food.'

Three days later, dressed in tough buckskin garments and carrying ropes, weapons, climbing tools, and bags of food and water, they began the ascent. Wolff bore the horn in a soft leather bag tied to his back.

Ninety-one days later, they were at an estimated half-way point. And at least every other step had been a battle against smooth verticality, rotten and treacherous rock, or against the predators. These included the many-footed snake he had encountered on Thayaphayawoed, wolves with great rock-gripping paws, the boulder ape, ostrich-sized axebeaks, and the small but deadly downdropper.

When the two climbed over the edge of the top of Doozvillnavava, they had been 186 days on the journey. Neither was the same, physically or mentally, as at the start. Wolff weighed less but he had far more endurance and wiriness to his strength. He bore the scars of downdroppers, boulder apes, and axebeaks on his face and body. His hatred for the Lord was even more intense, for Chryseis had lost the foetus before they had gotten 10,000 feet up. Such was to be expected, but he could not forget that they would not have had to make the climb if it had not been for the Lord.

Chryseis had been toughened in body and spirit by her experiences before she had started up Doozvillnavava. Yet the things and situations on this monolith had been far worse than anything previously, and she might have broken. That she did not vindicated Wolff's original feeling that she was basically of strong fiber. The effect of the millenia of sapping life in the Garden had been sloughed off. The Chryseis who conquered this monolith was much like the woman who had been abducted from the savage and demanding life of the ancient Aegean. Only she was far wiser.

Wolff waited for several days to rest and hunt and repair the bows and make new arrows. He also kept a watch for an eagle. He had not been in contact with any since he had talked to Phthie in the ruined city by the river of Guzirit. No green-bodied yellow-headed bird appeared, so he reluctantly decided to enter the jungle. As on Dracheland, a thousand-mile thick belt of jungle circled the entire rim. Within the belt was the land of Atlantis. This, exclusive of the monolith in its center, covered an area the size of France and Germany combined.

Wolff had looked for the pillar on top of which was the Lord's palace, since Kickaha had said that it could be seen from the rim even though it was much more slender than any of the other monoliths. He could see only a vast and dark continent of clouds, jagged and coiled with lightning. Idaquizzoorhruz was hidden. Nor, whenever Wolff ascended a high hill or climbed a tall tree, could he see it. A week later, the stormclouds continued to shroud the pillar of stone. This worried him, for he had not seen such a storm in the three and a half years he had been on this planet.

Fifteen days passed. On the sixteenth, they found on the narrow green-fraught path a headless corpse. A yard away in the bush was the turbaned head of a Khamshem.

'Abiru could be trailing the gworl, too,' he said. 'Maybe the gworl took his jewels when they left von Elgers' castle. Or, more likely, he thinks they have the horn.'

A mile and a half further on, they came across another Khamshem, his stomach ripped open and his entrails hanging out. Wolff tried to get information out of him until he found that the man was too far gone. Wolff put him out of his pain, noting that Chryseis did not even look away while he did so. Afterward, he put his knife in his belt and held the Khamshem's scimitar in his right hand. He felt that he would soon need it.

A half-hour later, he heard shouts and whoops down the trail. He and Chryseis concealed themselves in the foilage beside the path. Abiru and two Khamshem came running with death loping after them in the form of three squat Negroids with painted faces and long kinky scarlet-dyed beards. One threw his spear; it sailed through the air to end in the back of a Khamshem. He plunged forward without a sound and slid on the soft damp earth like a sailboat launched into eternity, the spear as the mast. The other two Khamshem turned to make a stand.

Wolff had to admire Abiru, who fought with great skill and courage. Although his companion went down with a spear in his solar plexus, Abiru continued to slash with his scimitar. Presently two of the savages were dead, and the third turned tail. After the Negroid had disappeared, Wolff came up silently behind Abiru. He struck with the edge of his palm to paralyze the man's arm and cause the scimitar to drop.

Abiru was so startled and scared he could not talk. On seeing Chryseis step out from the bushes, his eyes bulged even more. Wolff asked him what the situation was. After a struggle, Abiru regained his tongue and began to talk. As Wolff had guessed, he had pursued the gworl with his men and a number of Sholkin. Some miles from here, he had caught up with them. Rather, they had caught him. The ambush had been half-successful, for it had slain or incapacitated a good third of the Khamshem. All this had been done without loss to the gworl, who had cast knives from trees or from the bushes.

The Khamshem had broken away and fled, hoping to make a stand in a better place down the trail – if they could find one. Then both hunted and hunter had run into a horde of black savages.

'And there'll be more of them soon looking for you,' Wolff said. 'What about Kickaha and funem Laksfalk?'

'I do not know about Kickaha. He was not with the gworl. But the Yidshe knight was.'

For a moment, Wolff thought of killing Abiru. However, he disliked doing it in cold blood and he also wanted to ask him more questions. He believed that there was more to him than he pretended to be. Shoving Abiru on ahead with the point of the scimitar, he went down the trail. Abiru protested that they would be killed; Wolff told him to shut up. In a few minutes they heard the shouts and screams of men in battle. They crossed a shallow stream and were at the bottom of a steep, high hill.

This was so rocky that comparatively little vegetation covered it. Along a line up the hill was the wake of the fight – dead and wounded gworl, Khamshem, Sholkin, and savages. Near the top of the hill, their backs against a V-shaped wall and under an overhang formed by two huge boulders, three held off the blacks. These were a gworl, a Khamshem, and the Yidshe baron. Even as Wolff and Chryseis started to go up, the Khamshem fell, pierced by several of the shovel-sized spearheads. Wolff told Chryseis to go back. For answer, she fitted an arrow to her bow and shot. A savage in the rear of the mob fell backward, the shaft sticking from his back.

Wolff smiled grimly and began to work his own bow. He and Chryseis chose only those at the extreme rear, hoping to shoot down a number before those at the front noticed. They were successful until the twelfth fell. A savage happened to glance back and see the man behind him crumple. He yelled and pulled at the arms of those nearest him. These immediately brandished their spears and began running down the hill toward the two, leaving most of their party to attack the gworl and the Yidshe. Before they had reached the bottom half of the hill, four more were down.

Three more tumbled headlong and rolled down with shafts in them. The remaining six lost their zeal to come at close quarters. Halting, they threw their spears, which were launched at such a distance that the archers had no trouble dodging them. Wolff and Chryseis, operating coolly and skillfully from much practice and experience, then shot four more. The two survivors, screaming, ran back up to their fellows. Neither made it, although one was only wounded in the leg.

By then, the gworl had fallen. Funem Laksfalk was left alone against forty. He did have a slight advantage, which was that they could get to him only two at a time. The walls of the boulders and the barricade of corpses prevented the others from swarming over him. Funem Laksfalk, his scimitar bloody and swinging, sang loudly some Yiddish fighting song.

Wolff and Chryseis took partial cover behind two boulders and renewed their rear attack. Five more fell, but the quivers of both were empty. Wolff said, 'Pull some from the corpses and use them again. I'm going to help him.'

He picked up a spear and ran at an angle across and up the hill, hoping that the savages would be too occupied to see him. When he had come around the hill, he saw two savages crouched on top of the boulder. These were kept from jumping down upon the Yidshe's rear by the overhang of the roughly shaped boulders. But they were waiting for a moment when he would venture too far out from its protection.

Wolff hurled his spear and caught one in the buttocks. The savage cried out and pitched forward from the rock and, presumably, on his fellows below. The other stood up and whirled around in time to get Wolff's knife in his belly. He fell backwards off the rock.

Wolff lifted a small boulder and heaved it on top of one of the great boulders and climbed up after it. Then he lifted the small boulder again, raised it above his head, and walked to the front of the great boulder. He yelled and threw it down into the crowd. They looked up in time to see the rock descending on them. It smashed at least three and rolled down the hill. At that, the survivors fled in a panic. Perhaps they thought that there must be others than Wolff. Or because they were undisciplined savages, they had been unnerved by too many losses already. The sight of so many of their dead shot down behind them must also have added to their panic.

Wolff hoped they would not return. To add fuel to their fright, he leaped down and picked up the boulder again and sent it crashing down the hill after them. It leaped and bounded as if it were a wolf after a rabbit and actually struck one more before it reached bottom.

Chryseis, from behind her boulder, put two more arrows into the savages.

He turned to the baron and found him lying on the ground. His face was gray, and blood was welling from around the spearhead driven into his chest.

'You!' he said faintly. 'The man from the other world. You saw me fight?'

Wolff stepped down by him to examine the wound. 'I saw. You fought like one of Joshua's warriors, my friend. You fought as I have never seen a man fight. You must have slain at least twenty.'

Funem Laksfalk managed to smile a trifle. 'It was twenty-five. I counted them.'

Then he smiled broadly and said, 'We are both stretching the truth a trifle, as our friend Kickaha would say. But not too much. It was a great fight. I only regret that I had to fight unfriended and unarmored and in a lonely place where none will ever know that a funem Laksfalk added honor to the name. Even if it was against a bunch of howling and naked savages.'

'They will know,' Wolff said. 'I will tell them some day.'

He did not give false words of comfort. He and the Yidshe both knew that death was around the corner, sniffing eagerly at the end of the track. 'Do you know what happened to Kickaha?' he said.

'Ah, that trickster? He slipped his chains one night. He tried to loosen mine, too, but he could not. Then he left, with the promise that he would return to free me. And so he will, but he will be too late.'

Wolff looked down the hill. Chryseis was climbing toward him with several arrows which she had recovered from corpses. The blacks had regrouped at the foot and were talking animatedly among themselves. Others came out of the jungle to join them. The fresh ones swelled the number to forty. These were led by a man garbed in feathers and wearing a hideous wooden mask. He whirled a bull-roarer, leaped up and down, and seemed to be haranguing them.

The Yidshe asked Wolff what was happening. Wolff told him. The Yidshe spoke so weakly that Wolff had to put his ear close to the knight's mouth.

'It was my fondest dream, Baron Wolff, that I would some day fight by your side. Ah, what a noble pair of knights we would have made, in armor and swinging our ... S'iz kalt.'

The lips became silent and blue. Wolff rose to look down the hill again. The savages were moving up and also spreading out to prevent flight. Wolff set to work dragging bodies and piling them to form a rampart. The only hope, a weak one, was to permit passage for only one or two to attack at a time. If they lost enough men, they might get discouraged and leave. He did not really think so, for these savages showed a remarkable persistence despite what must be to them staggering losses. Also, they could always retreat just far enough to wait for Wolff and Chryseis to be driven from their refuge by thirst and hunger.

The savages stopped halfway up to give those who had gone around the hill time to establish their stations. Then, at a cry from the man in the wooden mask, they climbed up as swiftly as possible. The two defenders made no move until the thrown spears rattled against the sides of the boulders or plunged into the barricade of dead. Wolff shot twice, Chryseis three times. Not one arrow missed.

Wolff loosed his final shaft. It struck the mask of the leader and knocked him back down the hill. A moment later he threw off the mask. Although his face was bleeding, he led the second charge.

A weird ululation arose from the jungle. The savages stopped, spun, and became silent as they stared at the green around the hill. Again, the swelling-falling cry came from somewhere in the trees.

Abruptly, a bronze-haired man clad only in a leopard loincloth raced from the jungle. He carried a spear in one hand and a long knife in the other. Coiled around his shoulder was a lariat, and a quiver and bow were hung from a belt over the other shoulder. Behind him, a mass of hulking, long-armed, mound-chested, and long-fanged apes poured from the trees.

At sight of these, the savages cried out aloud and tried to run around the hill. Other apes appeared from the other side; like hairy jaws, the two columns closed on the blacks.

There was a brief fight. Some apes fell with spears in their bellies, but most of the blacks threw down their weapons and tried to run or else crouched, trembling and paralyzed. Only twelve escaped.

Wolff, smiling and laughing in his relief, said to the man in the leopard-skin, 'And how are you named on this tier?'

Kickaha grinned back. 'I'll give you one guess.'

His smile died when he saw the baron. 'Damn it! It took me too much time to find the apes and then to find you! He was a good man, the Yidshe; I liked his style. Damn it! Anyway, I promised him that if he died I'd take his bones back to his ancestral castle, and that's one promise I'll keep. Not just now, though. We have some business to attend to.'

Kickaha called some of the apes to be introduced. 'As you'll notice,' he said to Wolff, 'they're built more like your friend Ipsewas than true apes. Their legs are too long and their arms too short. Like Ipsewas and unlike the great apes of my favorite childhood author, they have the brains of men. They hate the Lord for what he has done to them; they not only want revenge, they want a chance to walk around in human bodies again.'

Not until then did Wolff remember Abiru. He was nowhere to be seen. Apparently he had slipped off when Wolff had gone to funem Laksfalk's aid.

That night, around a fire and eating roast deer, Wolff and Chryseis heard about the cataclysm taking place in Atlantis. It had started with the new temple that the Rhadamanthus of Atlantis had started to build. Ostensibly the tower was for the greater glory of the Lord. It was to reach higher than any building ever known on the planet. The Rhadamanthus recruited his entire state to erect the temple. He kept on adding story to story until it looked as if he wanted to reach the sky itself.

Men asked each other when there would be an end to the work. All were slaves with but one purpose in mind: build. Yet they dared not speak openly, for the soldiers of the Rhadamanthus killed all who objected or who failed to labor. Then it became obvious that the Rhadamanthus had something else besides a temple in his crazed mind. The Rhadamanthus intended to erect a means to storm the heavens themselves, the palace of the Lord.

'A thirty-thousand-foot building?' said Wolff.

'Yeah. It couldn't be done, of course, not with the technology available in Atlantis. But the Rhadamanthus was mad; he really thought he could do it. Maybe he was encouraged because the Lord hadn't appeared for so many years, and he thought that maybe the rumors were true that the Lord was gone. Of course, the ravens must have told him different, but he could have figured they were lying to protect themselves.'

Kickaha said that the devastating phenomena now destroying Atlantis were proof of more than that the Lord was revenging himself against the hubris of Rhadamanthus. The Lord must have finally unlocked the secrets of how to operate some of the devices in the palace.

'The Lord who disappeared would have taken precautions against a new occupant manipulating his powers. But the new Lord has at last succeeded in learning where the controls of the storm-makers are.'

Proof: the gigantic hurricanes, tornados, and continual rain sweeping the land. The Lord must be out to rid this tier of all life.

Before reaching the edge of the jungle, they met the tidal wave of refugees. These had stories of horses and great buildings blown down, of men picked up and carried off and smashed by the winds, of the floods that were stripping the earth of trees and all life and even washing away the hills.

By then, Kickaha's party had to lean to walk against the wind. The clouds closed around them; rain struck them; lightning blinded and crashed on all sides.

Even so, there were periods when the rain and lightning ceased. The energies loosed by Arwoor had to spend themselves, and new forces had to be built up before being released again. In these comparative lulls, the party made progress, although slowly. They crossed swollen rivers bearing the wreck of a civilization: houses, trees, furniture, chariots, the corpses of men, women, children, dogs, horses, birds and wild animals. The forests were uprooted or smashed by the strokes of electrical bolts. Every valley was running with water; every depression was filled. And a choking stench filled the air.

When their journey was little more than half-completed, the clouds began to thin away. They were in the sunshine again, but in a land silent with death. Only the roar of water or the cry of a bird that had somehow survived broke the stone of quiet. Sometimes the howl of a demented human being sent chills through them, but these were few.

The last cloud was carried off. And the white monolith of Idaquizzoorhruz shone before them, three hundred miles away on the horizonless plain. The city of Atlantis – or what was left of it – was a hundred miles distant. It took them twenty days to reach its outskirts through flood and debris.

'Can the Lord see us now?' Wolff asked.

Kickaha said, 'I suppose he could with some sort of telescope. I'm glad you asked, though, because we'd better start traveling by night. Even so, we'll be spotted by them.'

He pointed at a raven flying over.

Passing through the ruins of the capital city, they came near the imperial zoo of Rhadamanthus. There were some strong cages left standing, and one of these contained an eagle. On the muddy bottom were a number of bones, feathers, and beaks. The caged eagles had evaded starvation by eating each other. The lone survivor sat emaciated, weak and miserable on the highest perch.

Wolff opened the cage, and he and Kickaha talked to the eagle, Armonide. At first, Armonide wanted nothing but to attack them, enfeebled though she was. Wolff threw her several pieces of meat, then the two men continued their story. Armonide said that they were liars and had some human, and therefore evil, purpose in mind. When she had heard Wolff's story through and his pointing out that they did not have to release her, she began to believe. When Wolff explained that he had a plan in mind to gain revenge upon the Lord, the dullness in her eyes was replaced by a sharp light. The idea of actually assaulting the Lord, perhaps successfully, was more food than meat itself. She stayed with them for three days, eating, gaining strength, and memorizing exactly what she was to tell Podarge.

'You will see the Lord's death yet, and new and youthful and lovely maiden bodies will be yours,' Wolff said. 'But only if Podarge does as I ask her.'

Armonide launched herself from a cliff, swooped down, flapped her spreading wings, and began to climb. Presently the green feathers of her body were absorbed by the green sky. Her red head became a black dot, and then it too was gone.

Wolff and his party remained in the tangle of fallen trees until night before going on. By now, through some subtle process, Wolff had become the nominal leader. Before, Kickaha had had the reins in his hands with the approval of all. Something had happened to give Wolff the power of decision-making. He did not know what, for Kickaha was as boisterous and vigorous as before. And the passing of captainship had not been caused by a deliberate effort on Wolff's part. It was as if Kickaha had been waiting until Wolff had learned all he could from him. Then Kickaha had handed over the baton.

They traveled strictly within the night-hours, during which time they saw very few ravens. Apparently there was no need for them in this area since it was under the close surveillance of the Lord himself. Besides, who would dare intrude here after the anger of the Lord had been so catastrophically wrought?

On arriving at the great tumbled mass of Rhadamanthus' tower, they took refuge within the ruins. There was more than enough metal for Wolff's plan. Their only two problems were getting enough food and trying to conceal the noise of their sawing and hammering and the glare of their little smithies. The first was solved when they discovered a storehouse of grain and dried meat. Much of the supplies had been destroyed by fire and then by water, but there was enough left to see them through several weeks. The second was dealt with by working deep within the underground chambers. The tunneling took five days, a period which did not concern Wolff because he knew that it would be some time before Armonide would reach Podarge – if she got to her destination at all. Many things could happen to her on the way, especially an attack by the ravens.

'What if she doesn't make it?' Chryseis asked.

'Then we'll have to think of something else,' Wolff replied. He fondled the horn and pressed its seven buttons. 'Kickaha knows the gate through which he came when he left the palace. We could go back through it. But it would be folly. The present Lord would not be so stupid as not to leave a heavy guard there.'

Three weeks passed. The supply of food was so low that hunters would have to be sent out. This was dangerous even at night, for there was no telling when a raven might be around. Moreover, for all Wolff knew the Lord could have devices for seeing as easily at night as at day.

At the end of the fourth week, Wolff had to give up his dependence on Podarge. Either Armonide had not reached her or Podarge had refused to listen.

That very night, as he sat under cover of a huge plate of bent steel and stared at the moon, he heard the rustle of wings. He peered into the darkness. Suddenly, moonlight shone on something black and pale, and Podarge was before him. Behind her were many winged shapes and the gleam of moon on yellow beaks and redly shining eyes.

Wolff led them down through the tunnels and into a large chamber. By the small fires, he looked again into the tragically beautiful face of the harpy. But now that she thought she could strike back at the Lord, she actually looked happy. Her flock had carried food along, so, while all ate, Wolff explained his plan to her. Even as they were discussing the details, one of the apes, a guard, brought in a man he had caught skulking about the ruins. He was Abiru the Khamshem.

'This is unfortunate for you and a sorry thing for me,' Wolff said. 'I can't just tie you up and leave you here. If you escaped and contacted a raven, the Lord would be forewarned. So, you must die. Unless you can convince me otherwise.'

Abiru looked about him and saw only death.

'Very well,' he said. 'I had not wanted to speak nor will I speak before everyone, if I can avoid it. Believe me, I must talk to you alone. It is as much for your life as for mine.'

'There is nothing you can say that could not be said before all,' Wolff replied. 'Speak up.'

Kickaha placed his mouth close to Wolff's ear and whispered, 'Better do as he says.'

Wolff was astonished. The doubts about Kickaha's true identity came back to him. Both requests were so strange and unexpected that he had a momentary feeling of disassociation. He seemed to be floating away from them all.

'If no one objects, I will hear him alone,' he said. Podarge frowned and opened her mouth, but before she could say anything she was interrupted by Kickaha. 'Great One, now is the time for trust. You must believe in us, have confidence. Would you lose your only chance for revenge and for getting your human body back? You must go along with us on this. If you interfere, all is lost.'

Podarge said, 'I do not know what this is all about, and I feel that I am somehow being betrayed. But I will do as you say, Kickaha, for I know of you and know that you are a bitter enemy of the Lord. But do not try my patience too far.'

Then Kickaha whispered an even stranger thing to Wolff. 'Now I recognize Abiru. The beard and the stain on his skin fooled me, plus not having heard his voice for twenty years.'

Wolff's heart beat fast with an undefined apprehension. He took his scimitar and conducted Abiru, whose hands were bound behind him, into a small room. And here he listened.

16

An hour later, he returned to the others. He looked stunned.

'Abiru will go with us,' he said. 'He could be very valuable. We need every hand we can get and every man with knowledge.'

'Would you care to explain that?' Podarge said. She was narrow-eyed, the mask of madness forming over her face.

'No, I will not and cannot,' he replied. 'But I feel more strongly than ever that we have a good chance for victory. Now, Podarge, how strong are your eagles? Have they flown so far tonight that we must wait until tomorrow night for them to rest?'

Podarge answered that they were ready for the task ahead of them. She wanted to delay no longer.

Wolff gave his orders, which were relayed by Kickaha to the apes, since they obeyed only him. They carried out the large crossbars and the ropes to the outside, and the others followed them.

In the bright light of the moon, they lifted the thin but strong crossbars. The human beings and the fifty apes then fitted themselves into the weblike cradles beneath the crossbars and tied straps to secure themselves. Eagles gripped the ropes attached to each of the four ends of the bars and another gripped the rope tied to the center of the cross. Wolff gave the signal. Though there had been no chance to train, each bird jumped simultaneously into the air, flapped her wings, and slowly rose upward. The ropes were paid out to over fifty feet to give the eagles a chance to gain altitude before the cross-bars and the human attached to each had to be lifted.

Wolff felt a sudden jerk, and he uncoiled his bent legs to give an extra push upward. The bar tilted to one side, almost swinging him over against one of the bars. Podarge, flying over the others, gave an order. The eagles pulled up more rope or released more length to adjust for balance. In a few seconds, the cross-bars were at the correct level.

On Earth this plan would not have been workable. A bird the size of the eagle probably could not have gotten into the air without launching herself from a high cliff. Even then, her flight would have been very slow, maybe too slow to keep from stalling or sinking back to Earth. However, the Lord had given the eagles muscles with strength to match their weight.

They rose up and up. The pale sides of the monolith, a mile away, glimmered in the moonlight. Wolff clutched the straps of his cradle and looked at the others. Chryseis and Kickaha waved back. Abiru was motionless. The shattered and prone wreck of Rhadamanthus' tower became smaller. No ravens flew by to be startled and to wing upward to warn the Lord. Those eagles not serving as carriers spread wide to forestall such a possibility. The air was filled with an armada; the beat of their wings drummed loudly in Wolff's ears, so loudly that he could not imagine the noise not traveling for miles.

The time came when this side of ravaged Atlantis was spread out in the moonlight for him to scan in one sweep of the eye. Then the rim appeared, and part of the tier below it. Dracheland became visible as a great half-disc of darkness. The hours crept by. The mass of Amerindia appeared, grew and was suddenly chopped off at the rim. The garden of Okeanos, so far below Amerindia and so narrow, could not be seen.

Both the moon and the sun were visible now because of the comparative slenderness of this monolith. Nevertheless, the eagles and their burdens were still in darkness, in the shadow of Idaquizzoorhruz. It would not last for long. Soon this side would be under the full glare of the daytime luninary. Any ravens would be able to see them from miles away. The party had, however, drifted close to the monolith, so that anyone on top would have to be on the edge to detect them.

At last, after over four hours, just as the sun touched them, they were level with the top. Beside them was the garden of the Lord, a place of flaming beauty. Beyond rose the towers and minarets and flying buttresses and spiderweb architectures of the palace of the Lord. It soared up for two hundred feet and covered, according to Kickaha, more than three hundred acres.

They did not have time to appreciate its wonder, for the ravens in the garden were screaming. Already the hundreds of Podarge's pets had swooped down upon them and were killing them. Others were winging toward the many windows to enter and seek out the Lord.

Wolff saw a number get inside before the traps of the Lord could be activated. Shortly thereafter, those attempting to climb in through the openings disappeared in a clap of thunder and a flash of lighting. Charred to the bone, they fell off the ledges and onto the ground below or on the rooftops or buttresses.

The human beings and the apes settled to the ground just outside a diamond-shaped door of rose stone set with rubies. The eagles released the ropes and gathered by Podarge to wait for her orders.

Wolff untied the ropes from the metal rings on the cross-bars. Then he lifted the bars above his head. After running to a point just a few feet from the diamond-shaped doorway, he cast the steel cross into it. One bar went through the entrance; the two at right angles to it jammed against the sides of the door.

Flame exploded again and again. Thunder deafened him. Tongues of searing voltage leaped out at him. Suddenly, smoke poured from within the palace, and the lightning ceased. The ravaging device had either burned out from the load or was temporarily discharged.

Wolff took one glance around him. Other entrances were also spurting blasts of flame or else their defenses had burned out. Eagles had taken many of the cross-bars and were dropping them at an angle into the windows above. He leaped over the white-hot liquid of his cross-bar and through the door. Chryseis and Kickaha joined him from another entrance. Behind Kickaha came the horde of giant apes. Each carried a sword or battle-axe in his hand.

Kickaha asked, 'Is it coming back to you?'

Wolff nodded. 'Not all, but enough, I hope. Where's Abiru?'

'Podarge and a couple of the apes are keeping an eye on him. He could try something for his own purposes.'

Wolff in the lead, they walked down a hall the walls of which were painted with murals that would have delighted and awed the most critical of Terrestrials. At the far end was a low gate of delicate and intricate tracery and of a shimmering bluish metal. They proceeded toward it but stopped as a raven, fleeing for its life, sped over them. Behind it came an eagle.

The raven passed over the gate, and as it did so it flew headlong into an invisible screen. Abruptly, the raven was a scatter of thin slices of flesh, bones and feathers. The pursuing eagle screamed as it saw this and tried to check her flight, but too late. She too was cut into strips.

Wolff pulled the left section of the gate toward him instead of pushing in on it as he would naturally have done. He said, 'It should be okay now. But I'm glad the raven triggered the screen first. I hadn't remembered it.'

Still, he stuck his sword forward to test, then it came back to him that only living matter activated the trap. There was nothing to do but to trust that he could remember correctly. He walked forward without feeling anything but the air, and the others followed.

'The Lord will be holed up in the center of the palace, where the defense control room is,' he said. 'Some of the defenses are automatic, but there are others he can operate himself. That is, if he's found out how to operate them, and he's certainly had enough time to learn.'

They padded through a mile of corridors and rooms, each one of which could have detained anyone with a sense of beauty for days. Every now and then a boom or a scream announced a trap set off somewhere in the palace.

A dozen times, they were halted by Wolff. He stood frowning for awhile until he suddenly smiled. Then he would move a picture at an angle or touch a spot on the murals: the eye of a painted man, the horn of a buffalo in a scene of the Amerindian plains, the hilt of a sword in the scabbard of a knight in a Teutoniac tableau. Then he would walk forward.

Finally, he summoned an eagle. 'Go bring Podarge and the others,' he said. 'There is no use their sacrificing themselves any more. I will show the way.'

He said to Kickaha, 'The sense of *déjà vu* is getting stronger every minute. But I don't remember all. Just certain details.'

'As long as they're the significant details, that's all that matters at this moment,' Kickaha said. His grin was broad, and his face was lit with the delight of conflict. 'Now you can see why I didn't dare to try re-entry by myself. I got the guts but I lack the knowledge.'

Chryseis said, 'I don't understand.'

Wolff pulled her to him and squeezed her. 'You will soon. That is, if we make it. I've much to tell you, and you have much to forgive.'

A door ahead of them slid into the wall, and a man in armor clanked toward them. He held a huge axe in one hand, swinging it as if it were a feather.

'It's no man,' Wolff said. 'It's one of the Lord's taloses.'

'A robot!' Kickaha said.

Wolff thought, *Not quite in the sense Kickaha means*. It was not all steel and plastic and electrical wires. Half of it was protein, formed in the biobanks of the Lord. It had a will for survival that no machine of all-inanimate parts could have. This was a strength and also a weakness.

He spoke to Kickaha, who ordered the apes behind him to obey Wolff. A dozen stepped forward, side by side, and hurled their axes simultaneously. The talos dodged but could not evade all. It was struck with a force and precision that would have chopped it apart if it had not been armor-plated. It fell backward and rolled, then rose to its feet. While it was down, Wolff ran at it. He struck at it with his scimitar at the juncture of shoulder and neck. The blade broke without cutting into the metal. However, the force of the blow did knock the talos down again.

Wolff dropped his weapons, seized the talos around its waist, and lifted it. Silently, for it had no voice-chords, the armored thing kicked and reached down to grip Wolff. He hurled it against the wall, and it crashed down on the floor. As it began to get to its feet once more, Wolff drew his dagger and drove it into one of the eye-holes. There was a crack as the plastic over the eye gave way and was dislodged. The tip of the knife broke off, and Wolff was hurled back by a blow from the mailed fist. He came back quickly, grabbed the extended fist again, turned, and flopped it over his back. Before it could arise, it found itself gripped and hoisted high again. Wolff ran to the window and threw it headlong out.

It turned over and over and smashed against the ground four stories below. For a moment it lay as if broken, then it began to rise again. Wolff shouted at some eagles outside on a buttress. They launched themselves, soared down, and a pair grabbed the talos' arms. Up they rose, found it too heavy, and sank back. But they were able to keep it aloft a few inches from the ground. Over the surface, between buttresses and curiously carved columns, they flew. Their destination was the edge of the monolith, from which they would drop the talos. Not even its armor could withstand the force at the end of the 30,000-foot fall.

Wherever the Lord was hidden, he must have seen the fate of the single talos he had released. Now, a panel in the wall slid back, and twenty taloses came out, each with an axe in his hand. Wolff spoke to the apes. These hurled their axes again, knocking down many of the things. The gorilla-sized anthropoids charged in and several seized each talos. Although the mechanical strength of each android was more than that of a single ape, the talos was outmatched by two. While one ape wrestled with an android, the other gripped the helmet-head and twisted. Metal creaked under the strain; suddenly, neck-mechanisms broke with a snap. Helmets rolled on the floor with an ichorish liquid flowing out. Other taloses were lifted up and passed from hand to hand and dumped out of the window. Eagles carried each one off to the rim.

Even so, seven apes died, cut down by axes or with their own heads twisted off. The quick-to-learn protein brains of the semiautomatons imitated the actions of their antagonists, if it was to their advantage.

A little further on in the hall, thick sheets of metal slid down before and behind them to block off advance or retreat. Wolff had forgotten this until just a second before the plates were lowered. They descended swiftly but not so swiftly that he did not have time to topple a marble stone pedestal with a statue on it. The end of the fallen column lay under the plate and prevented its complete closure. The forces driving the plate were, however, so strong that the edge of the plate began to drive into the stone. The party slid on their backs through the decreasing space. At the same time, water flooded into the area. If it had not been for the delay in closing the plate, they would have been drowned.

Sloshing ankle deep in water, they went down the hall and up another flight of steps. Wolff stopped them by a window, through which he cast an axe. No thunder and lightning resulted, so he leaned out and called Podarge and her eagles in to him. Having been blocked off by the plates, they had gone outside to find another route.

'We are close to the heart of the palace, to the room in which the Lord must be,' he said. 'Every corridor from here on in has walls which hold dozens of laser beam-projectors. The beams can form a network through which no one could penetrate alive.'

He paused, then said, 'The Lord could sit in there forever. The fuel for his projectors will not give out, and he has food and drink enough to last for any siege. But there's an old military axiom which states that any defense, no matter how formidable, can be broken if the right offense is found.'

He said to Kickaha, 'When you took the gate through the Atlantean tier, you left the crescent behind you. Do you remember where?'

Kickaha grinned and said, 'Yeah! I stuck it behind a statue in a room near the swimming pool. But what if it was found by the gworl?'

'Then I'll have to think of something else. Let's see if we can find the crescent.'

'What's the idea?' Kickaha said in a low voice.

Wolff explained that Arwoor must have an escape route from the control room. As Wolff remembered it, there was a crescent set in the floor and several loose ones available. Each of these, when placed in contact with the immobile crescent, would open a gate to the universe for which the loose one had a resonance. None of them gave access to other levels of the planet in this universe. Only the horn could effect a gate between tiers.

'Sure,' Kickaha said. 'But what good will the crescent do us even if we find it? It has to be matched up against another, and where's the other? Anyway, anyone using it would only be taken through to Earth.'

Wolff pointed over his back to indicate the long leather box slung there by a strap. 'I have the horn.'

They started down a corridor. Podarge strode after them. 'What are you up to?' she asked fiercely.

Wolff answered that they were looking for means to get within the control room. Podarge should stay behind to handle any emergency. She refused, saying that she wanted them in her sight now that they were so close to the Lord. Besides, if they could get through to the Lord, they would have to take her along. She reminded Wolff of his promise that the Lord would be hers to do with as she wished. He shrugged and walked on.

They located the room in which was the statue behind which Kickaha had concealed the crescent. But it had been overturned in the struggle between apes and gworl. Their bodies lay sprawled around the room. Wolff stopped in surprise. He had seen no gworl since entering the palace and had taken it for granted that all had perished during the fight with the savages. The Lord had not sent all of them after Kickaha.

Kickaha cried, 'The crescent's gone!'

'Either it was found some time ago or someone just found it after the statue was knocked over,' Wolff said. 'I have an idea of who did take it. Have you seen Abiru?'

Neither of the others had seen him since shortly after the invasion of the palace had started. The harpy, who was supposed to keep an eye on him, had lost him.

Wolff ran toward the labs with Kickaha and Podarge, wings half-opened, behind him. By the time he had covered the 3000 feet to it, Wolff was winded. Breathing hard, he stopped at the entrance.

'Vannax may be gone already and within the control room,' he said. 'But if he's still in there working on the crescent, we'd better enter quietly and hope to surprise him.'

'Vannax?' Podarge said.

Wolff swore mentally. He and Kickaha had not wanted to reveal the identity of Abiru until later, Podarge hated the Lord so much that she would have killed him at once. Wolff wanted to keep him alive because Vannax, if he did not try to betray them, could be valuable in the taking of the palace. Wolff had promised Vannax that he could go into another world to try his luck there if he helped them against Arwoor. And Vannax had explained how he had managed to get back to this universe. After Kickaha (born Finnegan) had accidentally come here, taking a crescent with him, Vannax had continued his search for another. He had been successful in, of all places, a pawn shop in Peoria, Illinois. How it had gotten there and what Lord had lost it on Earth would never be known. Doubtless there were other crescents in obscure places on Earth. However, the crescent he had found had passed him through a gate located on the Amerindian tier. Vannax had climbed Thayaphayawoed to Khamshem, where he had been lucky enough to capture the gworl, Chryseis, and the horn. Thereafter, he had made his way toward the palace hoping to get within.

Wolff muttered, 'The old saying goes that you can't trust a Lord.'

'What did you say?' Podarge asked. 'And I repeat, who is Vannax?'

Wolff was relieved that she did not know the name. He answered that Abiru had sometimes disguised himself under that name. Not wanting to reply to any more questions, and feeling that time was vital, he entered the laboratory. It was a room broad enough and high-ceilinged enough to house a dozen jet airliners. Cabinets and consoles and various apparatuses, however, gave it a crowded appearance. A hundred yards away, Vannax was bent over a huge console, working with the buttons and levers.

Silently, the three advanced on him. They were soon close enough to see that two crescents were locked down on the console. On the broad screen above Vannax was the ghostly image of a third semicircle. Wavy lines of light ran across it.

Vannax suddenly gave an *ah!* of delight as another crescent appeared by the first on the screen. He manipulated several dials to make the two images move toward each other and then merge into a single one again.

Wolff knew that the machine was sending out a frequency-tracer and had located that of the crescent set into the floor of the control room. Next, Vannax would subject the crescents clamped to the console to a treatment which would change their resonance to match that of the control room. Where Vannax had gotten the two semicircles was a mystery until Wolff thought of that crescent which must have accompanied him when he passed through the gate to the Amerindian tier. Somehow, during the time between his capture and the flight, he had gotten hold of this crescent. He must have hidden it in the ruins before the ape had captured him.

Vannax looked up from his work, saw the three, glanced at the screen, and snatched the two crescents from the spring-type clamps on the console. The three ran toward him as he placed one crescent on the floor and then the other. He laughed, made an obscene gesture, and stepped into the circle, a dagger in his hand.

Wolff gave a cry of despair, for they were too far away to stop him. Then he stopped and threw a hand over his eyes, but too late to shut out the blinding flash. He heard Kickaha and Podarge, also blinded, shouting. He heard Vannax's scream and smelled the burned flesh and clothes.

Sightlessly, he advanced until his feet touched the hot corpse.

'What the hell happened?' Kickaha said. 'God, I hope we're not permanently blinded!'

'Vannax thought he was slipping in through Arwoor's gate in the control room,' Wolff said. 'But Arwoor had set a trap. He could have been satisfied with wrecking the matcher, but it must have amused him to kill the man who would try it.'

He stood and waited, knowing that time was getting short and that he was not serving his cause or anyone else's by his patience with his blindness. But there was nothing else he could do. And, after what seemed like an unbearably long time, sight began to come back.

Vannax was lying on his back, charred and unrecognizable. The two crescents were still on the floor and undamaged. These were separated a moment later by Wolff with a scribe from a console.

'He was a traitor,' Wolff said in a low voice to Kickaha. 'But he did us a service. I meant to try the same trick, only I was going to use the horn to activate the crescent you hid after I'd changed its resonance.'

Pretending to inspect other consoles for boobytraps, he managed to get Kickaha and himself out of ear-range of Podarge.

'I didn't want to do it,' he whispered. 'But I'm going to have to. The horn must be used if we're to drive Arwoor out of the control room or get him before he can use his crescents to escape.'

'I don't get you,' Kickaha said.

'When I had the palace built, I incorporated a thermitic substance in the plastic shell of the control room. It can be triggered only by a certain sequence of notes from the horn, combined with another little trick. I don't want to set the stuff off because the control room will then also be lost. And this place will be indefensible later against any other Lords.'

'You better do it,' Kickaha said. 'Only thing is, what's to keep Arwoor from getting away through the crescents?'

Wolff smiled and pointed at the console. 'Arwoor should have destroyed that instead of indulging his sadistic imagination. Like all weapons, it's two-edged.'

He activated the control, and, again, an image of the crescent shone on the screen. Curving lines of light ran across the plate. Wolff went to another console and opened a little door on the top to reveal a panel with unmarked controls. After flipping two, he pressed a button. The screen went blank.

'The resonance of his crescent has been changed,' Wolff said. 'When he goes to use it with any of the others he has, he'll get a hell of a shock. Not the kind Vannax got. He just won't have a gate through which to escape.'

'You Lords are a mean, crafty, sneaky bunch,' Kickaha said. 'But I like your style, anyway.'

He left the room. A moment later, his shouts came down the corridor. Podarge started to leave the room, then stopped to glare suspiciously at Wolff. He broke into a run. Podarge, satisfied he was coming, raced ahead. Wolff stopped and removed the horn from the case. He reached a finger into its mouth, hooked it through the only opening in the weblike structure therein large enough to accept his finger. A pull drew the web out. He turned it around and inserted it with its front now toward the inside of the horn. Then he put the horn back into the case and ran after the harpy.

She was with Kickaha, who was explaining that he thought he had seen a gworl but it was just a prowling eagle. Wolff said they must go back to the others. He did not explain that it was necessary that the horn be within a certain distance of the control room walls. When they had returned to the hall outside the control room, Wolff opened the case. Kickaha stood behind Podarge, ready to knock her unconscious if she started any trouble. What they could do with the eagles, besides sicking the apes on them, was another matter.

Podarge exclaimed when she saw the horn but made no hostile move. Wolff lifted the horn to his lips and hoped he could remember the correct sequence of notes. Much had come back to him since he had talked with Vannax; much was yet lost.

He had just placed the mouthpiece to his lips when a voice roared out. It seemed to come from ceiling and walls and floor, from everywhere. It spoke in the language of the Lords, for which Wolff was glad. Podarge would not know the tongue.

'Jadawin! I did not recognize you until I saw you with the horn! I thought you looked familiar – I should have known. But it's been such a long time! How long?'

'It's been many centuries, or millenia, depending upon the time scale. So, we two old enemies face each other again. But this time you have no way out. You will die as Vannax died.'

'How so?' roared Arwoor's voice.

'I will cause the walls of your seemingly impregnable fortress to melt. You will either stay inside and roast or come out and die another way. I don't think you'll stay in.'

Suddenly he was seized with a concern and a sense of injustice. If Podarge should kill Arwoor, she would not be killing the man who was responsible for her present state. It did not matter that Arwoor would have done the same thing if he had been the Lord of this world at that time.

On the other hand, he, Wolff, was not to blame, either. He was not the Lord Jadawin who had constructed this universe and then manipulated it so foully for so many of its creatures and abducted Terrestrials. The attack of amnesia had been complete; it had wiped all of Jadawin from him and made him a blank page. Out of the blankness had emerged a new man, Wolff, one incapable of acting like Jadawin or any of the other Lords.

And he was still Wolff, except that he remembered what he had been. The thought made him sick and contrite and eager to make amends as best he could. Was this the way to start, by allowing Arwoor to die horribly for a crime he had not commited?

'Jadawin!' boomed Arwoor. 'You may think you have won this move! But I have topped you again! I have one more coin to put on the table, and its value is far more than what your horn will do to me!'

'And what is that?' Wolff asked. He had a black feeling that Arwoor was not bluffing.

'I've planted one of the bombs I brought with me when I was dispossessed of Chiffaenir. It's under the palace, and when I so desire, it will go off and blow the whole top of this monolith off. It's true I'll die, too, but I'll take my old enemy with me! And your woman and friends will die, too! Think of them!'

Wolff was thinking of them. He was in agony.

'What are your terms?' he asked. 'I know that you don't want to die. You're so miserable you *should* want to die, but you've clung to your worthless life for ten thousand years.'

'Enough of your insults! Will you or won't you? My finger is an inch above the button.' Arwoor chuckled and continued, 'Even if I'm bluffing, which I'm not, you can't afford to take the chance.'

Wolff spoke to the others, who had been listening without understanding but knew something drastic had happened. He explained as much as he dared, omitting any connection of himself with the Lords.

Podarge, her face a study in combined frustration and madness, said, 'Ask him what his terms are.'

She added, 'After this is all over, you have much to explain to me, O Wolff.'

Arwoor replied, 'You must give me the silver horn, the all-precious and unique work of the master, Ilmarwolkin. I will use it to open the gate in the pool and pass through to the Atlantian tier. That is all I want, except your promise that none will come after me until the gate is closed.'

Wolff considered for a few seconds. Then he said, 'Very well. You may come out now. I swear to you on my honor as Wolff and by the Hand of Detiuw that I will give you the horn and I will send no one after you until the gate is closed.'

Arwoor laughed and said, 'I'm coming out.'

Wolff waited until the door at the end of the hall was swinging out. Knowing that he could not be overheard by Arwoor then, he said to Podarge, 'Arwoor thinks he has us, and he may well be confident. He will emerge through the gate at a place forty miles from here, near Ikwekwa, a suburb of the city of Atlantis. He would still be at the mercy of you and your eagles if there were not another resonant point only ten miles from there. This point will open when the horn is blown and admit him to another universe. I will show you where it is after Arwoor goes through the pool.'

Arwoor advanced confidently. He was a tall, broad-shouldered and good-looking man with wavy blond hair and blue eyes. He took the horn from Wolff, bowed ironically, and walked on down the hall. Podarge stared at him so madly that Wolff was afraid that she would leap upon him. But he had told her that he must keep his promises: the one to her and the one to Arwoor.

Arwoor strode past the silent and menacing files as if they were no more than statues of marble. Wolff did not wait for him to get to the pool, but went at once into the control room. A quick examination showed him that Arwoor had left a device which would depress the button to set off the bomb. Doubtless he had given himself plenty of time to get away. Nevertheless, Wolff sweated until he had removed the device. By then, Kickaha had returned from watching Arwoor go through the gate in the pool.

'He got away, all right,' he said, 'but it wasn't as easy as he had thought. The place of emergence was under water, caused by the flood he himself had created. He had to drop into the water and swim for it. He was still swimming when the gate closed.'

Wolff took Podarge into a huge map room, and indicated the town near which the gate was. Then, in the visual-room, he showed her the gate at close range on a screen. Podarge studied the map and the screen for a minute. She gave an order to her eagles, and they trooped out after her. Even the apes were awed by the glare of death in their eyes.

Arwoor was forty miles from the monolith, but he had ten miles to travel. Moreover, Podarge and her pets were launching themselves from a point 30,000 feet up. They would descend at such an angle and for such a distance that they could build up great speed. It would be a close race between Podarge and her quarry.

While he waited before the screen, Wolff had time to do much thinking. Eventually, he would tell Chryseis who he was and how he had come to be Wolff. She would know that he had been to another universe to visit one of the rare friendly Lords. The Vaernirn became lonely, despite their great powers, and wanted to socialize now and then with their peers. On his return to this universe, he had fallen into a trap set by Vannax, another dispossessed Lord. Jadawin had been hurled into the universe of Earth, but he had taken the surprised Vannax with him. Vannax had escaped with a crescent after the savage tussle on the hill slope. What had happened to the other crescent, Wolff did not know. But Vannax had not had it, that was sure.

Amnesia had struck then, and Jadawin had lost all memory – had become, in effect, a baby, a *tabula rasa*. Then the Wolffs had taken him in, and his education as an Earthman had begun.

Wolff did not know the reason for the amnesia. It might have been caused by a blow on the head during his struggle with Vannax. Or it might have resulted from the terror of being marooned and helpless on an alien planet. Lords had depended upon their inherited sciences so long that, stripped of them, they became less than men.

Or his loss of memory might have come from the long struggle with his conscience. For years before being thrust willynilly into another world, he had been dissatisfied with himself, disgusted with his ways and saddened by his loneliness and insecurity. No being was more powerful than a Lord, yet none was lonelier or more conscious that any minute might be his last. Other Lords were plotting against him; all had to be on guard every minute.

Whatever the reason, he had become Wolff. But, as Kickaha pointed out, there was an affinity between him and the horn and the points of resonance. It had been no accident that he had happened to be in the basement of that house in Arizona when Kickaha had blown the horn. Kickaha had had his suspicions that Wolff was a dispossessed Lord deprived of his memory.

Wolff knew now why he had learned the languages here so extraordinarily quickly. He was remembering them. And he had had such a swift and powerful attraction to Chryseis because she had been his favorite of all the women of his domain. He had even been thinking of bringing her to the palace and making her his Lady.

She did not know who he was on meeting him as Wolff because she had never seen his face. That cheap trick of the dazzling radiance had concealed his features. As for his voice, he had used a device to magnify and distort it, merely to further awe his worshippers. Nor was his great strength natural, for he had used the bioprocesses to equip himself with superior muscles.

He would make such amends as he could for the cruelty and arrogance of Jadawin, a being now so little a part of him. He would make new human bodies in the biocylinders and insert in them the brains of Podarge and her sisters, Kickaha's apes, Ipsewas, and any others who so desired. He would allow the people of Atlantis to rebuild, and he would not be a tyrant. He was not going to interfere in the affairs of the world of tiers unless it was absolutely necessary.

Kickaha called him to the screen. Arwoor had somehow found a horse in that land of the dead and was riding him furiously.

'The luck of the devil!' Kickaha said, and he groaned.

'I think the devil's after him,' Wolff said. Arwoor had looked behind and above him and then begun to beat his horse with a stick.

'He's going to make it!' Kickaha said. 'There's a Temple of the Lord only a half-mile ahead!'

Wolff looked at the great white stone structure on top of a high hill. Within it was the secret chamber which he himself had used when he had been Jadawin.

He shook his head and said, 'No!'

Podarge swooped within the field of vision. She was coming at great speed, her wings flapping, her face thrust forward, white against the green sky. Behind her came her eagles.

Arwoor rode the horse as far up the hill as he could. Then the mare's legs gave out, and she collapsed. Arwoor hit the ground running. Podarge dived at him. Arwoor dodged like a rabbit fleeing from a hawk. The harpy followed him in his zigzags, guessed which way he would go during one of his side-leaps, and was on him. Her claws struck his back. He threw his hands in the air and his mouth became an O through which soared a scream, voiceless to the watchers of the screen.

Arwoor fell with Podarge upon him. The other eagles landed and gathered to watch.

TO YOUR SCATTERED BODIES GO

1

His wife had held him in her arms as if she could keep death away from him.

He had cried out, 'My God, I am a dead man!'

The door to the room had opened, and he had seen a giant, black, one-humped camel outside and had heard the tinkle of the bells on its harness as the hot desert wind touched them. Then a huge black face topped by a great black turban had appeared in the doorway. The black eunuch had come in through the door, moving like a cloud, with a gigantic scimitar in his hand. Death, the Destroyer of Delights and the Sunderer of Society, had arrived at last.

Blackness. Nothingness. He did not even know that his heart had given out forever. Nothingness.

Then his eyes opened. His heart was beating strongly. He was strong, very strong! All the pain of the gout in his feet, the agony in his liver, the torture in his heart, all were gone.

It was so quiet he could hear the blood moving in his head. He was alone in a world of soundlessness.

A bright light of equal intensity was everywhere. He could see, yet he did not understand what he was seeing. What were these things above, beside, below him? Where was he?

He tried to sit up and felt, numbly, a panic. There was nothing to sit up upon because he was hanging in nothingness. The attempt sent him forward and over, very slowly, as if he were in a bath of thin treacle. A foot from his fingertips was a rod of bright red metal. The rod came from above, from infinity, and went on down to infinity. He tried to grasp it because it was the nearest solid object, but something invisible was resisting him. It was as if lines of some force were pushing against him, repelling him.

Slowly, he turned over in a somersault. Then the resistance halted him with his fingertips about six inches from the rod. He straightened his body out and moved forward a fraction of an inch. At the same time, his body began to rotate on its longitudinal axis. He sucked in air with a loud sawing noise. Though he knew no hold existed for him, he could not help flailing his arms in panic to try to seize onto something.

Now he was face 'down,' or was it 'up'? Whatever the direction, it was opposite to that toward which he had been looking when he had awakened. Not that this matttered. 'Above' him and 'below' him the view was the same.

He was suspended in space, kept from falling by an invisible and unfelt cocoon. Six feet 'below' him was the body of a woman with a very pale skin. She was naked and completely hairless. She seemed to be asleep. Her eyes were closed, and her breasts rose and fell gently. Her legs were together and straight out, and her arms were by her side. She turned slowly like a chicken on a spit.

The same force that was rotating her was also rotating him. He spun slowly away from her, saw other naked and hairless bodies, men, women, and children, opposite him in silent spinning rows. Above him was the rotating naked and hairless body of a Negro.

He lowered his head so that he could see along his own body. He was naked and hairless, too. His skin was smooth, and the muscles of his belly were ridged, and his thighs were packed with strong young muscles. The veins that had stood out like blue mole-ridges were gone. He no longer had the body of the enfeebled and sick sixty-nine-year-old man who had been dying only a moment ago. And the hundred or so scars were gone.

He realized then that there were no old men or women among the bodies surrounding him. All seemed to be about twenty-five years old, though it was difficult to determine the exact age, since the hairless heads and pubes made them seem older and younger at the same time.

He had boasted that he knew no fear. Now fear ripped away the cry forming in this throat. His fear pressed down on him and squeezed the new life from him.

He had been stunned at first because he was still living. Then his position in space and the arrangement of his new environment had frozen his senses. He was seeing and feeling through a thick semi-opaque window. After a few seconds something snapped inside him. He could almost hear it, as if a window had suddenly been raised.

The world took a shape which he could grasp, though he could not comprehend it. Above him, on both sides, below him, as far as he could see, bodies floated. They were arranged in vertical and horizontal rows. The up-and-down ranks were separated by red rods, slender as broomsticks, one of which was twelve inches from the feet of the sleepers and the other twelve inches from their heads. Each body was spaced about six feet from the body above and below and on each side.

The rods came up from an abyss without bottom and soared into an abyss without ceiling. That grayness into which the rods and the bodies, up and down, right and left, disappeared was neither the sky nor the earth. There was nothing in the distance except the lackluster of infinity.

On one side was a dark man with Tuscan features. On his other side was an Asiatic Indian and beyond her a large Nordic-looking man. Not until the third revolution was he able to determine what was so odd about the man.

The right arm, from a point just below the elbow, was red. It seemed to lack the outer layer of skin.

A few seconds later, several rows away, he saw a male adult body lacking the skin and all the muscles of the face.

There were other bodies that were not quite complete. Far away, glimpsed unclearly, was a skeleton and a jumble of organs inside it.

He continued turning and observing while his heart slammed against his chest with terror. By then he understood that he was in some colossal chamber and that the metal rods were radiating some force that somehow supported and revolved millions – maybe billions – of human beings.

Where was this place?

Certainly, it was not the city of Trieste of the Austro-Hungarian Empire of 1890.

It was like no hell or heaven of which he had ever heard or read, and he had thought that he was acquainted with every theory of the afterlife.

He had died. Now he was alive. He had scoffed all his life at a life-after-death. For once, he could not deny that he had been wrong. But there was no one present to say, 'I told you so, you damned infidel!'

Of all the millions, he alone was awake.

As he turned at an estimated rate of one complete revolution per ten seconds, he saw something else that caused him to gasp with amazement. Five rows away was a body that seemed, at first glance, to be human. But no member of *Homo sapiens* had three fingers and a thumb on each hand and four toes on each foot. Nor a nose and thin black leathery lips like a dog's. Nor a scrotum with many small knobs. Nor ears with such strange convolutions.

Terror faded away. His heart quit beating so swiftly, though it did not return to normal. His brain unfroze. He must get out of this situation where he was as helpless as a hog on a turnspit. He would get to somebody who could tell him what he was doing here, how he had come here, why he was here.

To decide was to act.

He drew up his legs and kicked and found that the action, the reaction, rather, drove him forward a half-inch. Again, he kicked and moved against the resistance. But, as he paused, he was slowly moved back toward his original location. And his legs and arms were gently pushed toward their original rigid position.

In a frenzy, kicking his legs and moving his arms in a swimmer's breast stroke, he managed to fight toward the rod. The closer he got to it, the stronger the web of force became. He did not give up. If he did, he would be back where he had been and without enough strength to begin fighting again. It was not his nature to give up until all his strength had been expended.

He was breathing hoarsely, his body was coated with sweat, his arms and legs moved as if in a thick jelly, and his progress was imperceptible. Then, the fingertips of his left hand touched the rod. It felt warm and hard.

Suddenly, he knew which way was 'down.' He fell.

The touch had broken the spell. The webs of air around him snapped soundlessly, and he was plunging.

He was close enough to the rod to seize it with one hand. The sudden checking of his fall brought his hip up against the rod with a painful impact. The skin of his hand burned as he slid down the rod, and then his other hand clutched the rod, and he had stopped.

In front of him, on the other side of the rod, the bodies had started to fall. They descended with the velocity of a falling body on Earth, and each maintained its stretched-out position and the original distance between the body above and below. They even continued to revolve.

It was then that the puffs of air on his naked sweating back made him twist around on the rod. Behind him, in the vertical row of bodies that he had just occupied, the sleepers were also falling. One after the other, as if methodically dropped through a trapdoor, spinning slowly, they hurtled by him. Their heads missed him by a few inches. He was fortunate not to have been knocked off the rod and sent plunging into the abyss along with them.

In stately procession, they fell. Body after body shooting down on both sides of the rod, while the other rows of millions upon millions slept on.

For a while, he stared. Then he began counting bodies; he had always been a devoted enumerator. But when he had counted 3,001, he quit. After that he gazed at the cataract of flesh. How far up, how immeasurably far up, were they stacked? And how far down could they fall? Unwittingly, he had precipitated them when his touch had disrupted the force emanating from the rod.

He could not climb up the rod, but he could climb down it. He began to let himself down, and then he looked upward and he forgot about the bodies hurtling by him. Somewhere overhead, a humming was overriding the whooshing sound of the falling bodies.

A narrow craft, of some bright green substance and shaped like a canoe, was sinking between the column of the fallers and the neighboring column of suspended. The aerial canoe had no visible means of support, he thought, and it was a measure of his terror that he did not even think about his pun. No visible means of support. Like a magical vessel out of *The Thousand and One Nights*.

A face appeared over the edge of the vessel. The craft stopped, and the humming noise ceased. Another face was by the first. Both had long, dark, and straight hair. Presently, the faces withdrew, the humming was renewed, and the canoe again descended toward him. When it was about five feet above him it halted. There was a single small symbol on the green bow: a white spiral that exploded to the right. One of the canoe's occupants spoke in a language with many vowels and a distinct and frequently recurring glottal stop. It sounded like Polynesian.

Abruptly, the invisible cocoon around him reasserted itself. The falling bodies began to slow in their rate of descent and then stopped. The man on the rod felt the retaining force close in on him and lift him up. Though he clung desperately to the rod, his legs were moved up and then away and his body followed it. Soon he was looking downward. His hands were torn loose; he felt as if his grip on life, on sanity, on the world, had also been torn away. He began to drift upward and to revolve. He went by the aerial canoe and rose above it. The two men in the canoe were naked, dark-skinned as Yemenite Arabs, and handsome. Their features were Nordic, resembling those of some Icelanders he had known.

One of them lifted a hand which held a pencil-sized metal object. The man sighted along it as if he were going to shoot something from it.

The man floating in the air shouted with rage and hate and frustration and flailed his arms to swim toward the machine.

'I'll kill!' he screamed. 'Kill! Kill!'

Oblivion came again.

2

God was standing over him as he lay on the grass by the waters and the weeping willows. He lay wide-eyed and as weak as a baby just born. God was poking him in the ribs with the end of an iron cane. God was a tall man of middle age. He had a long black forked beard, and He was wearing the Sunday best of an English gentleman of the 53rd year of Queen Victoria's reign.

'You're late,' God said. 'Long past due for the payment of your debt, you know.'

'What debt?' Richard Francis Burton said. He passed his fingertips over his ribs to make sure that all were still there.

'You owe for the flesh,' replied God, poking him again with the cane. 'Not to mention the spirit. You owe for the flesh and the spirit, which are one and the same thing.'

Burton struggled to get up onto his feet. Nobody, not even God, was going to punch Richard Burton in the ribs and get away without a battle.

God, ignoring the futile efforts, pulled a large gold watch from His vest pocket, unsnapped its heavy enscrolled gold lid, looked at the hands, and said, 'Long past due.'

God held out His other hand, its palm turned up.

'Pay up, sir. Otherwise, I'll be forced to foreclose.'

'Foreclose on what?'

Darkness fell. God began to dissolve into the darkness. It was then that Burton saw that God resembled himself. He had the same black straight hair, the same Arabic face with the dark stabbing eyes, high cheekbones, heavy lips, and the thrust-out, deeply cleft chin. The same long deep scars, witnesses of the Somali javelin which pierced his jaws in that fight at Berbera, were on His cheeks. His hands and feet were small, contrasting with His broad shoulders and massive chest. And He had the long thick mustachios and the long forked beard that had caused the Bedouin to name Burton 'the Father of mustachios.'

'You look like the Devil,' Burton said, but God had become just another shadow in the darkness.

3

Burton was still sleeping, but he was so close to the surface of consciousness that he was aware that he had been dreaming. Light was replacing the night.

Then his eyes did open. And he did not know where he was.

A blue sky was above. A gentle breeze flowed over his naked body. His hairless head and his back and legs and the palms of his hands were against grass. He turned his head to the right and saw a plain covered with very short, very green, very thick grass. The plain sloped gently upward for a mile. Beyond the plain was a range of hills that started out mildly, then became steeper and higher and very irregular in shape as they climbed toward the mountains. The hills seemed to run for about two and a half miles. All were covered with trees, some of which blazed with scarlets, azures, bright greens, flaming yellows, and deep pinks. The mountains beyond the hills rose suddenly, perpendicularly, and unbelievably high. They were black and bluish-green, looking like a glassy igneous rock with huge splotches of lichen covering at least a quarter of the surface.

Between him and the hills were many human bodies. The closest one, only a few feet away, was that of the white woman who had been below him in that vertical row.

He wanted to rise up, but he was sluggish and numb. All he could do for the moment, and that required a strong effort, was to turn his head to the left. There were more naked bodies there on a plain that sloped down to a river perhaps 10 yards away. The river was about a mile wide, and on its other side was another plain, probably about a mile broad and sloping upward to foothills covered with more of the trees and then the towering precipitous black and bluish-green mountains. That was the east, he thought frozenly. The sun had just risen over the top of the mountain there.

Almost by the river's edge was a strange structure. It was a gray red-flecked granite and was shaped like a mushroom. Its broad base could not be more than five feet high, and the mushroom top had a diameter of about fifty feet.

He managed to rise far enough to support himself on one elbow.

There were more mushroom-shaped granites along both sides of the river.

Everywhere on the plain were unclothed bald-headed human beings, spaced about six feet apart. Most were still on their backs and gazing into the sky. Others were beginning to stir, to look around, or even sitting up.

He sat up also and felt his head and face with both hands. They were smooth.

His body was not that wrinkled, ridged, bumpy, withered body of the sixty-nine-year-old which had lain on his deathbed. It was the smooth-skinned and powerfully muscled body he had when he was twenty-five years old. The same body he had when he was floating between those rods in that dream. Dream? It had seemed too vivid to be a dream. It was *not* a dream.

Around his wrist was a thin band of transparent material. It was connected to a six-inch-long strap of the same material. The other end was clenched about a metallic arc, the handle of a grayish metal cylinder with a closed cover.

Idly, not concentrating because his mind was too sluggish, he lifted the cylinder. It weighed less than a pound, so it could not be of iron even if it was hollow. Its diameter was a foot and a half and it was over two and a half feet tall.

Everyone had a similar object strapped to his wrist.

Unsteadily, his heart beginning to pick up speed as his senses became unnumbed, he got to his feet.

Others were rising, too. Many had faces which were slack or congealed with an icy wonder. Some looked fearful. Their eyes were wide and rolling; their chests rose and fell swiftly; their breaths hissed out. Some were shaking as if an icy wind had swept over them, though the air was pleasantly warm.

The strange thing, the really alien and frightening thing, was the almost complete silence. Nobody said a word; there was only the hissing of breaths of those near him, a tiny slap as a man smacked himself on his leg; a low whistling from a woman.

Their mouths hung open, as if they were about to say something.

They began moving about, looking into each other's faces, sometimes reaching out to lightly touch another. They shuffled their bare feet, turned this way, turned back the other way, gazed at the hills, the trees covered with the huge vividly colored blooms, the lichenous and soaring mountains, the sparkling and green river, the mushroom-shaped stones, the straps and the gray metallic containers.

Some felt their naked skulls and their faces.

Everybody was encased in a mindless motion and in silence.

Suddenly, a woman began moaning. She sank to her knees, threw her head and her shoulders back, and she howled. At the same time, far down the riverbank, somebody else howled.

It was as if these two cries were signals. Or as if the two were double keys to the human voice and had unlocked it.

The men and women and children began screaming or sobbing or tearing at their faces with their nails or beating themselves on their breasts or falling on their knees and lifting their hands in prayer or throwing themselves down and trying to bury their faces in the grass as if, ostrich-like, to avoid being seen, or rolling back and forth, barking like dogs or howling like wolves.

The terror and the hysteria gripped Burton. He wanted to go to his knees and pray for salvation from judgment. He wanted mercy. He did not want to see the blinding face of God appear over the mountains, a face brighter than the sun. He was not as brave and as guiltless as he had thought. Judgment would be so terrifying, so utterly *final*, that he could not bear to think about it.

Once, he had had a fantasy about standing before God after he had died. He had been little and naked and in the middle of a vast plain, like this, but he had been all alone. Then God, great as a mountain, had strode toward him. And he, Burton, had stood his ground and defied God.

There was no God here, but he fled anyway. He ran across the plain, pushing men and women out of the way, running around some, leaping over others as they rolled on the ground. As he ran, he howled, 'No! No! No!' His arms windmilled to fend off unseen terrors. The cylinder strapped to his wrist whirled around and around.

When he was panting so that he could no longer howl, and his legs and arms were hung with weights, and his lungs burned, and his heart boomed, he threw himself down under the first of the trees.

After a while, he sat up and faced toward the plain. The mob noise had changed from screams and howls to a gigantic chattering. The majority were talking to each other, though it did not seem that anybody was listening. Burton could not hear any of the individual words. Some men and women were embracing and kissing as if they had been acquainted in their previous lives and now were holding each other to reassure each other of their identities and of their reality.

There were a number of children in the great crowd. Not one was under five years of age, however. Like their elders, their heads were hairless. Half of them were weeping, rooted to one spot. Others, also crying out, were running back and forth, looking into the faces above them, obviously seeking their parents.

He was beginning to breathe more easily. He stood up and turned around. The tree under which he was standing was a red pine (sometimes wrongly called a Norway pine) about two hundred feet tall. Beside it was a tree of a type he had never seen. He doubted that it had existed on Earth. (He was sure that he was not on Earth, though he could not have given any specific reasons at that moment.) It had a thick, gnarled blackish trunk and many thick branches bearing triangular six-feet-long leaves, green with scarlet lacings. It was about three hundred feet high. There were also trees that looked like white and black oaks, firs, Western yew, and lodgepole pine.

Here and there were clumps of tall bamboo-like plants, and everywhere that there were no trees or bamboo was a grass about three feet high. There were no animals in sight. No insects and no birds.

He looked around for a stick or a club. He did not have the slightest idea what was on the agenda for humanity, but if it was left unsupervised or uncontrolled it would soon be reverting to its normal state. Once the shock was over, the people would be looking out for themselves, and that meant that some would be bullying others.

He found nothing useful as a weapon. Then it occurred to him that the metal cylinder could be used as a weapon. He banged it against a tree. Though it had little weight, it was extremely hard.

He raised the lid, which was hinged inside at one end. The hollow interior had six snap-down rings of metal, three on each side and spaced so that each could hold a deep cup or dish or rectangular container of gray metal. All the containers were empty. He closed the lid. Doubtless he would find out in time what the function of the cylinder was.

Whatever else had happened, resurrection had not resulted in bodies of fragile misty ectoplasm. He was all bone and blood and flesh.

Though he still felt somewhat detached from reality, as if he had been disengaged from the gears of the world, he was emerging from his shock.

He was thirsty. He would have to go down and drink from the river and hope that it would not be poisoned. At this thought, he grinned wryly, and stroked his upper lip. His finger felt disappointed. That was a curious reaction, he thought, and then he remembered that his thick moustache was gone. Oh, yes, he had hoped that the river water would not be poisoned. What a strange thought! Why should the dead be brought back to life only to be killed again? But he stood for a long while under the tree. He hated to go back through that madly talking, hysterically sobbing crowd to reach the river. Here, away from the mob, he was free from much of the terror and the panic and the shock that covered them like a sea. If he ventured back, he would be caught up in their emotions again.

Presently, he saw a figure detach itself from the naked throng and walk toward him. He saw that it was not human.

It was then that Burton was sure that this Resurrection Day was not the one which any religion had stated would occur. Burton had not believed in the God portrayed by the Christians, Moslems, Hindus, or any faith. In fact, he was not sure that he believed in any Creator whatsoever. He had believed in Richard Francis Burton and a few friends. He was sure that when he died, the world would cease to exist.

4

Waking up after death, in this valley by this river, he had been powerless to defend himself against the doubts that existed in *every* man exposed to an early religious conditioning and to an adult society which preached its convictions at every chance.

Now, seeing the alien approach, he was sure that there was some other explanation for this event than a supernatural one. There was a physical, a scientific, reason for his being here; he did not have to resort to Judeo-Christian-Moslem myths for cause.

The creature, it, he – it undoubtedly was a male – was a biped about six feet eight inches tall. The pink-skinned body was very thin; there were three fingers and a thumb on each hand and four very long and thin toes on each foot. There were two dark red spots below the male nipples on the chest. The face was semi-human. Thick black eyebrows swept down to the protruding cheekbones and flared out to cover them with a brownish down. The sides of his nostrils were fringed with a thin membrane about a sixteenth of an inch long. The thick pad of cartilage on the end of his nose was deeply cleft. The lips were thin, leathery, and black. The ears were lobeless and the convolutions within were nonhuman. His scrotum looked as if it contained many small testes.

He had seen this creature floating in the ranks a few rows away in that nightmare place.

The creature stopped a few feet away, smiled, and revealed quite human teeth. He said, 'I hope you speak English. However, I can speak with some fluency in Russian, Mandarin Chinese, or Hindustani.'

Burton felt a slight shock, as if a dog or an ape had spoken to him.

'You speak Midwestern American English,' he replied. 'Quite well, too. Although too precisely.'

'Thank you,' the creature said. 'I followed you because you seemed the only person with enough sense to get away from that chaos. Perhaps you have some explanation for this ... what do you call it? ... resurrection?'

'No more than you,' Burton said. 'In fact, I don't have any explanation for your existence, before or after resurrection.'

The thick eyebrows of the alien twitched, a gesture which Burton was to find indicated surprise or puzzlement.

'No? That is strange. I would have sworn that not one of the six billion of Earth's inhabitants had not heard of or seen me on TV.'

'TV?'

The creature's brows twitched again.

'You don't know what TV ...'

His voice trailed, then he smiled again.

'Of course, how stupid of me! You must have died before I came to Earth!'

'When was that?'

The alien's eyebrows rose (equivalent to a human frown as Burton would find), and he said slowly, 'Let's see. I believe it was, in your chronology, AD 2002. When did you die?'

'It must have been in AD 1890,' Burton said. The creature had brought back his sense that all this was not real. He ran his tongue around his mouth; the back teeth he had lost when the Somali spear ran through his cheeks were now replaced. But he was still circumcised, and the men on the riverbank – most of whom had been crying out in the Austrian-German, Italian, or the Slovenian of Trieste – were also circumcised. Yet, in his time, most of the males in that area would have been uncircumcised.

'At least,' Burton added, 'I remember nothing after 20 October 1890.'

'*Aah*,' the creature said. 'So, I left my native planet approximately 200 years before you died. My planet? It was a satellite of that star you Terrestrials call Tau Ceti. We placed ourselves in suspended animation, and, when our ship approached your sun, we were automatically thawed out, and ... but you do not know what I am talking about?'

'Not quite. Things are happening too fast. I would like to get details later. What is your name?'

'Monat Grrautut. Yours?'

'Richard Francis Burton at your service.'

He bowed slightly and smiled. Despite the strangeness of the creature and some repulsive physical aspects, Burton found himself warming to him.

'The late Captain Sir Richard Francis Burton,' he added. 'Most recently Her Majesty's Consul in the Austro-Hungarian port of Trieste.'

'Elizabeth?'

'I lived in the nineteenth century, not the sixteenth.'

'A Queen Elizabeth reigned over Great Britain in the twentieth century,' Monat said.

He turned to look toward the riverbank.

'Why are they so afraid? All the human beings I met were either sure that there would be no afterlife or else that they would get preferential treatment in the hereafter.'

Burton grinned and said, 'Those who denied the hereafter are sure they're in Hell because they denied it. Those who knew they would go to Heaven are shocked, I would imagine, to find themselves naked. You see, most of the illustrations of our afterlives showed those in Hell as naked and those in Heaven as being clothed. So, if you're resurrected bare-ass naked, you must be in Hell.'

'You seem amused,' Monat said.

'I wasn't so amused a few minutes ago,' Burton said. 'And I'm shaken. Very shaken. But seeing you here makes me think that things are not what people thought they would be. They seldom are. And God, if He's going to make an appearance, does not seem to be in a hurry about it. I think there's an explanation for this, but it won't match any of the conjectures I knew on Earth.'

'I doubt we're on Earth,' Monat said. He pointed upward with long slim fingers which bore thick cartilage pads instead of nails.

He said, 'If you look steadily there, with your eyes shielded, you can see another celestial body near the sun. It is not the moon.'

Burton cupped his hands over his eyes, the metal cylinder on his shoulder, and stared at the point indicated. He saw a faintly glowing body which seemed to be an eighth of the size of a full moon. When he put his hands down, he said, 'A star?'

Monat said, 'I believe so. I thought I saw several other very faint bodies elsewhere in the sky, but I'm not sure. We will know when night comes.'

'Where do you think we are?'

'I would not know.'

Monat gestured at the sun.

'It is rising and so it will descend, and then night should come. I think that it would be best to prepare for the night. And for other events. It is warm and getting warmer, but the night may be cold and it might rain. We should build a shelter of some sort. And we should also think about finding food. Though I imagine that this device' – he indicated the cylinder – 'will feed us.'

Burton said, 'What makes you think that?'

'I looked inside mine. It contains dishes and cups, all empty now, but obviously made to be filled.'

Burton felt less unreal. The being – the Tau Cetan! – talked so pragmatically, so sensibly, that he provided an anchor to which Burton could tie his senses before they drifted away again. And, despite the repulsive alienness of the creature, he exuded a friendliness and an openness that warmed Burton. Moreover, any creature that came from a civilization which could span many trillions of miles of interstellar space must have very valuable knowledge and resources.

Others were beginning to separate themselves from the crowd. A group of about ten men and women walked slowly toward him. Some were talking, but others were silent and wide-eyed. They did not seem to have a definite goal in mind; they just floated along like a cloud driven by a wind. When they got near Burton and Monat, they stopped walking.

A man trailing the group especially attracted Burton's scrutiny. Monat was obviously nonhuman, but this fellow was sub-human or pre-human. He stood about five feet tall. He was squat and powerfully muscled. His head was thrust forward on a bowed and very thick neck. The forehead was low and slanting. The skull was long and narrow. Enormous supraorbital ridges shadowed dark brown eyes. The nose was a smear of flesh with arching nostrils, and the bulging bones of his jaws pushed his thin lips out. He may have been covered with as much hair as an ape at one time, but now, like everybody else, he was stripped of hair.

The huge hands looked as if they could squeeze water from a stone.

He kept looking behind him as if he feared that someone was sneaking up on him. The human beings moved away from him when he approached them.

But then another man walked up to him and said something to the sub-human in English. It was evident that the man did not expect to be understood but that he was trying to be friendly. His voice, however, was almost hoarse. The newcomer was a muscular youth about six feet tall. He had a face that looked handsome when he faced Burton but was comically craggy in profile. His eyes were green.

The sub-human jumped a little when he was addressed. He peered at the grinning youth from under the bars of bone. Then he smiled, revealing large thick teeth, and spoke in a language Burton did not recognize. He pointed to himself and said something that sounded like *Kazzintuitruaabemss*. Later, Burton would find out that it was his name and it meant Man-Who-Slew-The-Long-White-Tooth.

The others consisted of five men and four women. Two of the men had known each other in Earthlife, and one of them had been married to one of the women. All were Italians or Slovenes who had died in Trieste, apparently about 1890, though he knew none of them.

'You there,' Burton said, pointing to the man who had spoken in English. 'Step forward. What is your name?'

The man approached him hesitantly. He said, 'You're English, right?'

The man spoke with an American Midwest flatness.

Burton held out his hand and said, 'I am. Burton here.'

The fellow raised hairless eyebrows and said, 'Burton?' He leaned forward and peered at Burton's face. 'It's hard to say it couldn't be …'

He straightened up. 'Name's Peter Frigate. F-R-I-G-A-T-E.'

He looked around him and then said in a voice even more strained, 'It's hard to talk coherently. Everybody's in such a state of shock, you know. I feel as if I'm coming apart. But … here we are … alive again … young again … no hellfire … not yet, anyway. Born in 1918, died 2008 … because of what this extra-Terrestrial did … don't hold it against him … only defending himself, you know.'

Frigate's voice died away to a whisper. He grinned nervously at Monat.

Burton said, 'You know this … Monat Grrautut?'

'Not exactly,' Frigate said. 'I saw enough of him on TV, of course, and heard enough and read enough about him.'

He held out his hand as if he expected it to be rejected. Monat smiled, and they shook hands.

Frigate said, 'I think it'd be a good idea if we banded together. We may need protection.'

'Why?' Burton said, though he knew well enough.

'You know how rotten most humans are,' Frigate said. 'Once people get used to being resurrected, they'll be fighting for women and food and anything that takes their fancy. And I think we ought to be buddies with this Neanderthal or whatever he is. Anyway, he'll be a good man in a fight.'

Kazz, as he was named later on, seemed pathetically eager to be accepted. At the same time, he was suspicious of anyone who got too close.

A woman walked by then, muttering over and over in German, 'My God! What have I done to offend Thee?'

A man, both fists clenched and raised to shoulder height, was shouting in Yiddish, 'My beard! My beard!'

Another man was pointing at his genitals and saying in Slovenian, 'They've made a Jew of me! A Jew! Do you think that …? No, it couldn't be!'

Burton grinned savagely and said, 'It doesn't occur to him that maybe they have made a Mohammedan out of him or an Australian aborigine or an ancient Egyptian, all of whom practiced circumcision.'

'What did he say?' asked Frigate. Burton translated; Frigate laughed.

A woman hurried by; she was making a pathetic attempt to cover her breasts and her pubic regions with her hands. She was muttering, 'What will they think, what will they think?' And she disappeared behind the trees.

A man and a woman passed them; they were talking loudly in Italian as if they were separated by a broad highway.

'We can't be in Heaven ... I know, oh my God, I know! ... There was Giuseppe Zomzini and you know what a wicked man he was ... he ought to burn in hellfire! I know, I know ... he stole from the treasury, he frequented whorehouses, he drank himself to death ... yet ... he's here! ... I know, I know ...'

Another woman was running and screaming in German, 'Daddy! Daddy! Where are you? It's your own darling Hilda!'

A man scowled at them and said repeatedly, in Hungarian, 'I'm as good as anyone and better than some. To hell with them.'

A woman said, 'I wasted my whole life, my whole life. I did everything for them, and now ...'

A man, swinging the metal cylinder before him as if it were a censer, called out, 'Follow me to the mountains! Follow me! I know the truth, good people! Follow me! We'll be safe in the bosom of the Lord! Don't believe this illusion around you; follow me! I'll open your eyes!'

Others spoke gibberish or were silent, their lips tight as if they feared to utter what was within them.

'It'll take some time before they straighten out,' Burton said. He felt that it would take a long time before the world became mundane for him, too.

'They may never know the truth,' Frigate said.

'What do you mean?'

'They didn't know the Truth – capital T – on Earth, so why should they here? What makes you think we're going to get a revelation?'

Burton shrugged and said, 'I don't. But I do think we ought to determine just what our environment is and how we can survive in it. The fortune of a man who sits, sits also.'

He pointed toward the riverbank. 'See those stone mushrooms? They seem to be spaced out at intervals of a mile. I wonder what their purpose is?'

Monat said, 'If you had taken a close look at that one, you would have seen that its surface contains about 700 round indentations. These are just the right size for the base of a cylinder to fit in. In fact, there is a cylinder in the center of the top surface. I think that if we examine that cylinder we may be able to determine their purpose. I suspect that it was placed there so we'd do just that.'

5

A woman approached them. She was of medium height, had a superb shape, and a face that would have been beautiful if it had been framed by hair. Her eyes were large and dark. She made no attempt to cover herself with her hands. Burton was not the least bit aroused looking at her or any of the women. He was too deeply numbed.

The woman spoke in a well-modulated voice and an Oxford accent. 'I beg your pardon, gentlemen. I couldn't help overhearing you. You're the only English voices I've heard since I woke up ... here, wherever here is. I am an Englishwoman, and I am looking for protection. I throw myself on your mercy.'

'Fortunately for you, Madame,' Burton said, 'you come to the right men. At least, speaking for myself, I can assure you that you will get all the protection I can afford. Though, if I were like some of the English gentlemen I've known, you might not have fared so well. By the way, this gentleman is not English. He's Yankee.'

It seemed strange to be speaking so formally this day of all days, with all the wailing and shouting up and down the valley and everybody birth-naked and as hairless as eels.

The woman held out her hand to Burton. 'I'm Mrs Hargreaves,' she said.

Burton took the hand, and, bowing, kissed it lightly. He felt foolish, but, at the same time, the gesture strengthened his hold on sanity. If the forms of polite society could be preserved perhaps the 'rightness' of things might also be restored.

'The late Captain Sir Richard Francis Burton,' he said, grinning slightly at the *late*. 'Perhaps you've heard of me?'

She snatched her hand away and then extended it again.

'Yes, I've heard of you, Sir Richard.'

Somebody said, 'It can't be!'

Burton looked at Frigate, who had spoken in such a low tone.

'And why not?' he said.

'Richard Burton!' Frigate said. 'Yes. I wondered, but without any hair? ...'

'Yaas?' Burton drawled.

'Yaas!' Frigate said. 'Just as the books said!'

'What are you talking about?'

Frigate breathed in deeply and then said, 'Never mind now, Mr Burton. I'll explain later. Just take it that I'm very shaken up. Not in my right mind. You understand that, of course.'

He looked intently at Mrs Hargreaves, shook his head, and said, 'Is your name Alice?'

'Why, yes!' she said, smiling and becoming beautiful, hair or no hair. 'How did you know? Have I met you? No, I don't think so.'

'Alice Pleasance Liddell Hargreaves?'

'Yes!'

'I have to go sit down,' the American said. He walked under the tree and sat down with his back to the trunk. His eyes looked a little glazed.

'Aftershock,' Burton said.

He could expect such erratic behavior and speech from the others for some time. He could expect a certain amount of non-rational behavior from himself, too. The important thing was to get shelter and food and some plan for common defense.

Burton spoke in Italian and Slovenian to the others and then made the introductions. They did not protest when he suggested that they should follow him down to the river's edge.

'I'm sure we're all thirsty,' he said. 'And we should investigate that stone mushroom.'

They walked back to the plain behind them. The people were sitting on the grass or milling about. They passed one couple arguing loudly and red-facedly. Apparently, they had been husband and wife and were continuing a lifelong dispute. Suddenly, the man turned and walked away. The wife looked unbelievingly at him and then ran after him. He thrust her away so violently that she fell on the grass. He quickly lost himself in the crowd, but the woman wandered around, calling his name and threatening to make a scandal if he did not come out of hiding.

Burton thought briefly of his own wife, Isabel. He had not seen her in this crowd, though that did not mean that she was not in it. But she would have been looking for him. She would not stop until she found him.

He pushed through the crowd to the river's edge and then got down on his knees and scooped up water with his hands. It was cool and clear and refreshing. His stomach felt as if it were absolutely empty. After he had satisfied his thirst, he became hungry.

'The waters of the River of Life,' Burton said. 'The Styx? Lethe? No, not Lethe. I remember everything about my Earthly existence.'

'I wish I could forget mine,' Frigate said.

Alice Hargreaves was kneeling by the edge and dipping water with one hand while she leaned on the other arm. Her figure was certainly lovely, Burton thought. He wondered if she would be blonde when her hair grew out, if it grew out. Perhaps Whoever had put them here intended they should all be bald, forever, for some reason of Theirs.

They climbed upon the top of the nearest mushroom structure. The granite was a dense-grained gray flecked heavily with red. On its flat surface were seven hundred indentations, forming fifty concentric circles. The depression in the center held a metal cylinder. A little dark-skinned man with a big nose and receding chin was examining the cylinder. As they approached, he looked up and smiled.

'This one won't open,' he said in German. 'Perhaps it will later. I'm sure it's there as an example of what to do with our own containers.'

He introduced himself as Lev Ruach and switched to a heavily accented English when Burton, Frigate, and Hargreaves gave their names.

'I was an atheist,' he said, seeming to speak to himself more than to them. 'Now, I don't know! This place is as big a shock to an atheist, you know, as to those devout believers who had pictured an afterlife quite different from this. Well, so I was wrong. It wouldn't be the first time.'

He chuckled, and said to Monat, 'I recognized you at once. It's a good thing for you that you were resurrected in a group mainly consisting of people who died in the nineteenth century. Otherwise, you'd be lynched.'

'Why is that?' Burton asked.

'He killed Earth,' Frigate said. 'At least, I *think* he did.'

'The scanner,' Monat said dolefully, 'was adjusted to kill only human beings. And it would not have exterminated all of mankind. It would have ceased operating after a predetermined number – unfortunately, a large number – had lost their lives. Believe me, my friends, I did not want to do that. You do not know what an agony it cost me to make the decision to press the button. But I had to protect my people. You forced my hand.'

'It started when Monat was on a live show,' Frigate said. 'Monat made an unfortunate remark. He said that his scientists had the knowledge and ability to keep people from getting old. Theoretically, using Tau Cetan techniques, a man could live forever. But the knowledge was not used on his planet; it was forbidden. The interviewer asked him if these techniques could be applied to Terrestrials. Monat replied that there was no reason why not. But rejuvenation was denied to his own kind for a very good reason, and this also applied to Terrestrials. By then, the government censor realized what was happening and cut off the audio. But it was too late.'

'Later,' Lev Ruach said, 'the American government reported that Monat had misunderstood the question, that his knowledge of English had led him to make a misstatement. But it was too late. The people of America, and of the world, demanded that Monat reveal the secret of eternal youth.'

'Which I did not have,' said Monat. 'Not a single one of our expedition had the knowledge. In fact, very few people on my planet had it. But it did no good to tell the people this. They thought I was lying. There was a riot, and a mob stormed the guards around our ship and broke into it. I saw my friends torn to pieces while they tried to reason with the mob. *Reason!*'

'But I did what I did, not for revenge, but for a very different motive. I knew that, after we were killed, or even if we weren't, the U.S. government would restore order. And it would have the ship in its possession. It wouldn't be long before Terrestrial scientists would know how to duplicate it. Inevitably, the Terrestrials would launch an invasion fleet against our world. So, to make sure that Earth would be set back many centuries, maybe thousands of years, knowing that I must do the dreadful thing to save my own world, I sent the signal to the scanner to orbit. I would not have had to do that if I could have gotten to the destruct-button and blown up the ship. But I could not get to the control room. So, I pressed the scanner-activation button. A short time later, the mob blew off the door of the room in which I had taken refuge. I remember nothing after that.'

Frigate said, 'I was in a hospital in Western Samoa, dying of cancer, wondering if I would be buried next to Robert Louis Stevenson. Not much chance, I was thinking. Still, I had translated the *Iliad* and the *Odyssey* into Samoan ... Then, the news came. People all over the world were falling dead. The pattern of fatality was obvious. The Tau Cetan satellite was radiating something that dropped human beings in their tracks. The last I heard was that the U.S., England, Russia, China, France, and Israel were all sending up rockets to intercept it, blow it up. And the scanner was on a path which would take it over Samoa within a few hours. The excitement must have been too much for me in my weakened condition. I became unconscious. That is all I remember.'

'The interceptors failed,' Ruach said. 'The scanner blew them up before they even got close.'

Burton thought he had a lot to learn about post-1890, but now was not the time to talk about it. 'I suggest we go up into the hills,' he said. 'We should learn what type of vegetation grows there and if it can be useful. Also, if there is any flint we can work into weapons. This Old Stone Age fellow must be familiar with stone-working. He can show us how.'

They walked across the mile-broad plain and into the hills. On the way, several others joined their group. One was a little girl, about seven years old, with dark blue eyes and a beautiful face. She looked pathetically at Burton, who asked her in twelve languages if any of her parents or relatives were nearby. She replied in a language none of them knew. The linguists among them tried every tongue at their disposal, most of the European speeches and many of the African or Asiatic: Hebrew, Hindustani, Arabic, a Berber dialect, Romany, Turkish, Persian, Latin, Greek, Pushtu.

Frigate, who knew a little Welsh and Gaelic, spoke to her. Her eyes widened, and then she frowned. The words seemed to have a certain familiarity or similarity to her speech, but they were not close enough to be intelligible.

'For all we know,' Frigate said, 'she could be an ancient Gaul. She keeps using the word Gwenafra. Could that be her name?'

'We'll teach her English,' Burton said. 'And we'll call her Gwenafra.' He picked up the child in his arms and started to walk with her. She burst into tears, but she made no effort to free herself. The weeping was a release from what must have been almost unbearable tension and a joy at finding a guardian. Burton bent his neck to place his face against her body. He did not want the others to see the tears in his eyes.

Where the plain met the hills, as if a line had been drawn, the short grass ceased and the thick, coarse esparto-like grass, waist-high, began. Here, too, the towering pines, red pines and lodgepole pines, the oaks, the yew, the gnarled giants with scarlet and green leaves, and the bamboo grew thickly. The bamboo consisted of many varieties, from slender stalks only a few feet high to plants over fifty feet high. Many of the trees were overgrown with the vines bearing huge green, red, yellow, and blue flowers.

'Bamboo is the material for spear-shafts,' Burton said, 'pipes for conducting water, containers, the basic stuff for building houses, furniture, boats, charcoal, even for making gunpowder. And the young stalks of some may be good for eating. But we need stone for tools to cut down and shape the wood.'

They climbed over hills whose height increased as they neared the mountain. After they had walked about two miles as the crow flies, eight miles as the caterpillar crawls, they were stopped by the mountain. This rose in a sheer cliff-face of some blue-black igneous rock on which grew huge patches of a blue-green lichen. There was no way of determining how high it was, but Burton did not think that he was wrong in estimating it as at least 20,000 feet high. As far as they could see up and down the valley, it presented a solid front.

'Have you noticed the complete absence of animal life?' Frigate said. 'Not even an insect.'

Burton exclaimed. He strode to a pile of broken rock and picked up a fist-sized chunk of greenish stone. 'Chert,' he said. 'If there's enough, we can make knives, spearheads, adzes, axes. And with them build houses, boats, and many other things.'

'Tools and weapons must be bound to wooden shafts,' Frigate said. 'What do we use as binding material?'

'Perhaps human skin,' Burton said.

The others looked shocked. Burton gave a strange chirruping laugh, incongruous in so masculine-looking a man. He said, 'If we're forced to kill in self-defense or lucky enough to stumble over a corpse some assassin has been kind enough to prepare for us, we'd be fools not to use what we need. However, if any of you feel self-sacrificing enough to offer your own epidermises for the good of the group, step forward! We'll remember you in our wills.'

'Surely, you're joking,' Alice Hargreaves said. 'I can't say I particularly care for such talk.'

Frigate said, 'Hang around him, and you'll hear lots worse,' but he did not explain what he meant.

6

Burton examined the rock along the base of the mountain. The blue-black densely grained stone of the mountain itself was some kind of basalt. But there were pieces of chert scattered on the surface of the earth or sticking out of the surface at the base. These looked as if they might have fallen down from a projection above, so it was possible that the mountain was not a solid mass of basalt. Using a piece of chert which had a thin edge, he scraped away a patch of the lichenous growth. The stone beneath it seemed to be a greenish dolomite. Apparently, the pieces of chert had come from the dolomite, though there was no evidence of decay or fracture of the vein.

The lichen could be *Parmelia saxitilis*, which also grew on old bones, including skulls, and hence, according to The Doctrine of Signatures, was a cure for epilepsy and a healing salve for wounds.

Hearing stone banging away on stone, he returned to the group. All were standing around the sub-human and the American, who were squatting back to back and working on the chert. Both had knocked out rough hand axes. While the others watched, they produced six more. Then each took a large chert nodule and broke it into two with a hammerstone. Using one piece of the nodule, they began to knock long thin flakes from the outside rim of the nodule. They rotated the nodule and banged away until each had about a dozen blades.

They continued to work, one a type of man who had lived a hundred thousand years or more before Christ, the other the refined end of human evolution, a product of the highest civilization (technologically speaking) of Earth, and, indeed, one of the last men on Earth – if he was to be believed.

Suddenly, Frigate howled, jumped up, and hopped around holding his left thumb. One of his strokes had missed its target. Kazz grinned, exposing huge teeth like tombstones. He got up, too, and walked into the grass with his curious rolling gait. He returned a few minutes later with six bamboo sticks with sharpened ends and several with straight ends. He sat down and worked on one stick until he had split the end and inserted the triangular chipped-down point of an axe head into the split end. This he bound with some long grasses.

Within half an hour, the group was armed with hand axes, axes with bamboo hafts, daggers, and spears with wooden points and with stone tips.

By then Frigate's hand had quit hurting so much and the bleeding had stopped. Burton asked him how he happened to be so proficient in stoneworking.

'I was an amateur anthropologist,' he said. 'A lot of people – a lot relatively speaking – learned how to make tools and weapons from stone as a hobby. Some of us got pretty good at it, though I don't think any modern ever got as skillful and as swift as a Neolithic specialist. Those guys did it all their lives, you know.

'Also, I just happen to know a lot about working bamboo, too, so I can be of some value to you.'

They began walking back to the river. They paused a moment on top of a tall hill. The sun was almost directly overhead. They could see for many miles along the river and also across the river. Although they were too far away to make out any figures on the other side of the mile-wide stream, they could see the mushroom-shaped structures there. The terrain on the other side was the same as that on theirs. A mile-wide plain, perhaps two and a half miles of foothills covered with trees. Beyond, the straight-up face of an insurmountable black and bluish-green mountain.

North and south, the valley ran straight for about ten miles. Then it curved, and the river was lost to sight.

'Sunrise must come late and sunset early,' Burton said. 'Well, we must make the most of the bright hours.'

At that moment, everybody jumped and many cried out. A blue flame arose from the top of each stone structure, soared up at least twenty feet, then disappeared. A few seconds later, a sound of distant thunder passed them. The boom struck the mountain behind them and echoed.

Burton scooped up the little girl in his arms and began to trot down the hill. Though they maintained a good pace, they were forced to walk from time to time to regain their breaths. Nevertheless, Burton felt wonderful. It had been so many years since he could use his muscles so profligately that he did not want to stop enjoying the sensation. He could scarcely believe that, only a short time ago, his right foot had been swollen with gout, and his heart had beaten wildly if he climbed a few steps.

They came to the plain and continued trotting, for they could see that there was much excitement around one of the structures. Burton swore at those in his way and pushed them aside. He got black looks but no one tried to push back. Abruptly, he was in the space cleared around the base. And he saw what had attracted them. He also smelled it.

Frigate, behind him, said, 'Oh, my God!' and tried to retch on his empty stomach.

Burton had seen too much in his lifetime to be easily affected by grisly sights. Moreover, he could take himself to one remove from reality when things became too grim or too painful. Sometimes he made the move, the sidestepping of things-as-they-were, with an effort of will. Usually, it occurred automatically. In this case, the displacement was done automatically.

The corpse lay on its side and half under the edge of the mushroom top. Its skin was completely burned off, and the naked muscles were charred. The nose and ears, fingers, toes, and the genitals had been burned away or were only shapeless stubs.

Near it, on her knees, was a woman mumbling a prayer in Italian. She had huge black eyes which would have been beautiful if they had not been reddened and puffy with tears. She had a magnificent figure which would have caught all his attention under different circumstances.

'What happened?' he said.

The woman stopped praying and looked at him. She got to her feet and whispered, 'Father Giuseppe was leaning against the rock; he said he was hungry. He said he didn't see much sense in being brought back to life only to starve to death. I said that we wouldn't die, how could we? We'd been raised from the dead, and we'd be provided for. He said maybe we were in hell. We'd go hungry and naked forever. I told him not to blaspheme, of all people he should be the last to blaspheme. But he said that this was not what he'd been telling everybody for forty years would happen and then ... and then ...'

Burton waited a few seconds, and then said, 'And then?'

'Father Giuseppe said that at least there wasn't any hellfire, but that that would be better than starving for eternity. And then the flames reached out and wrapped him inside them, and there was a noise like a bomb exploding, and then he was dead, burned to death. It was horrible, horrible.'

Burton moved north of the corpse to get the wind behind him, but even here the stench was sickening. It was not the odor as much as the idea of death that upset him. The first day of the Resurrection was only half over and a man was dead. Did this mean that the resurrected were just as vulnerable to death as in Earthlife? If so, what sense was there to it?

Frigate had quit trying to heave on an empty stomach. Pale and shaking, he got to his feet and approached Burton. He kept his back turned to the dead man.

'Hadn't we better get rid of that?' he said, jerking his thumb over his shoulder.

'I suppose so,' Burton said coolly. 'It's too bad his skin is ruined, though.'

He grinned at the American. Frigate looked even more shocked.

'Here,' Burton said. 'Grab hold of his feet, I'll take the other end. We'll toss him into the river.'

'The river?' Frigate said.

'Yaas. Unless you want to carry him into the hills and chop out a hole for him there.'

'I can't,' Frigate said, and walked away. Burton looked disgustedly after him and then signaled to the sub-human. Kazz grunted and shuffled forward to the body with that peculiar walking-on-the-side-of-his-feet gait. He stooped over and, before Burton could get hold of the blackened stumps of the feet, Kazz had lifted the body above his head, walked a few steps to the edge of the river, and tossed the corpse into the water. It sank immediately and was moved by the current along the shore. Kazz decided that this was not good enough. He waded out after it up to his waist and stooped down, submerging himself for a minute. Evidently he was shoving the body out into the deeper part.

Alice Hargreaves had watched with horror. Now she said, 'But that's the water we'll be drinking!'

'The river looks big enough to purify itself,' Burton said. 'At any rate, we have more things to worry about than proper sanitation procedures.'

Burton turned when Monat touched his shoulder and said, 'Look at that!' The water was boiling about where the body should be. Abruptly, a silvery white-finned back broke the surface.

'It looks as if your worry about the water being contaminated is in vain,' Burton said to Alice Hargreaves. 'The river has scavengers. I wonder ... I wonder if it's safe to swim.'

At least, the sub-human had gotten out without being attacked. He was standing before Burton, brushing the water off his hairless body, and grinning with those huge teeth. He was frighteningly ugly. But he had the knowledge of a primitive man, knowledge which had already been handy in a world of primitive conditions. And he would be a damned good man to have at your back in a fight. Short though he was, he was immensely powerful. Those heavy bones afforded a broad base for heavy muscles. It was evident that he had, for some reason, become attached to Burton. Burton liked to think the savage, with a savage's instincts, 'knew' that Burton was the man to follow if he would survive. Moreover, a sub-human or pre-human, being closer to the animals, would also be more psychic. So he would detect Burton's own well-developed psychic powers and would feel an affinity to Burton, even though he was *Homo sapiens*.

Then Burton reminded himself that his reputation for psychism had been built up by himself and that he was half-charlatan. He had talked about his powers so much, and had listened to his wife so much, that he had come to believe in them himself. But there were moments when he remembered that his 'powers' were at least half-fake.

Nevertheless, he was a capable hypnotist, and he did believe that his eyes radiated a peculiar extrasensory power, when he wished them to do so. It may have been this that attracted the half-man.

'The rock discharged a tremendous energy,' Lev Ruach said. 'It must have been electrical. But why? I can't believe that the discharge was purposeless.'

Burton looked across the mushroom-shape of the rock. The gray cylinder in the center depression seemed to be undamaged by the discharge. He touched the stone. It was no warmer than might have been expected from its exposure to the sun.

Lev Ruach said, 'Don't touch it. There might be another ...' and he stopped when he saw his warning was too late.

'Another discharge?' Burton said. 'I don't think so. Not for some time yet, anyway. That cylinder was left here so we could learn something from it.'

He put his hands on the top of the mushroom structure and jumped forward. He came up and onto the top with an ease that gladdened him. It had been so many years since he had felt so young and so powerful. Or so hungry.

A few in the crowd cried out to him to get down off the rock before the blue flames came again. Others looked as if they hoped that another discharge would occur. The majority were content to let him take the risks.

Nothing happened, although he had not been too sure he would not be incinerated. The stone felt only pleasantly warm on his bare feet.

He walked over the depressions to the cylinder and put his fingers under the rim of the cover. It rose easily. His heart beating with excitement, he looked inside it. He had expected the miracle, and there it was. The racks within held six containers, each of which was full.

He signaled to his group to come up. Kazz vaulted up easily. Frigate, who had recovered from his sickness, got onto the top with an athlete's ease. If the fellow did not have such a queasy stomach, he might be an asset, Burton thought. Frigate turned and pulled up Alice, who came over the edge at the ends of his hands.

When they crowded around him, their heads bent over the interior of the cylinder, Burton said, 'It's a veritable grail! Look! Steak, a thick juicy steak! Bread and butter! Jam! Salad! And what's that? A package of cigarettes? Yaas! And a cigar! And a cup of bourbon, very good stuff by its odor! Something ... what is it?'

'Looks like sticks of gum,' Frigate said. 'Unwrapped. And that must be a ... what? A lighter for the smokes?'

'Food!' a man shouted. He was a large man, not a member of what Burton thought of as 'his group.' He had followed them, and others were scrambling up on the rock. Burton reached down past the containers into the cylinder and gripped the small silvery rectangular object on the bottom. Frigate had said this might be a lighter. Burton did not know what a 'lighter' was, but he suspected that it provided flame for the cigarettes. He kept the object in the palm of his hand and with the other he closed the lid. His mouth was watering, and his belly was rumbling. The others were just as eager as he; their expressions showed that they could not understand why he was not removing the food.

The large man said, in a loud blustery Triestan Italian, 'I'm hungry, and I'll kill anybody who tries to stop me. Open that!'

The others said nothing, but it was evident that they expected Burton to take the lead in the defense. Instead, he said, 'Open it yourself,' and turned away. The others hesitated. They had seen and smelled the food. Kazz was drooling. But Burton said, 'Look at that mob. There'll be a fight here in a minute. I say, let them fight over their morsels. Not that I'm avoiding a battle, you understand,' he added, looking fiercely at them. 'But I'm certain that we'll all have our own cylinders full of food by supper time. These cylinders, call them grails, if you please, just need to be left on the rock to be filled. That is obvious, that's why this grail was placed here.'

He walked to the edge of the stone near the water and got off. By then the top was jammed with people and more were trying to get on. The large man had seized a steak and bitten into it, but someone had tried to snatch it away from him. He yelled with fury and, suddenly, rammed through those between him and the river. He went over the edge and into the water, emerging a moment later. In the meantime, men and women were screaming and striking each other over the rest of the food and goods in the cylinder.

The man who had jumped into the river floated off on his back while he ate the rest of the steak. Burton watched him closely, half-expecting him to be seized by fish. But he drifted on down the stream, undisturbed.

The rocks to the north and south, on both sides of the river, were crowded with struggling humans.

Burton walked until he was free of the crowd and sat down. His group squatted by him or stood up and watched the writhing and noisy mass. The grailstone looked like a toadstool engulfed in pale maggots. Very noisy maggots. Some of them were now also red, because blood had been spilled.

The most depressing aspect of the scene was the reaction of the children. The younger ones had stayed back from the rock, but they knew that there was food in the grail. They were crying from hunger and from terror caused by the screaming and fighting of the adults on the stone. The little girl with Burton was dry-eyed, but she was shaking. She stood by Burton and put her arms around his neck. He patted her on the back and murmured encouraging words which she could not understand but the tone of which helped to quiet her.

The sun was on its descent. Within about two hours it would be hidden by the towering western mountain, though a genuine dusk presumably would not happen for many hours. There was no way to determine how long the day was here. The temperature had gone up, but sitting in the sun was not by any means unbearable, and the steady breeze helped cool them off.

Kazz made signs indicating that he would like a fire and also pointed at the tip of a bamboo spear. No doubt he wanted to fire-harden the tip.

Burton had inspected the metal object taken from the grail. It was of a hard silvery metal, rectangular, flat, about two inches long and three-tenths across. It had a small hole in one end and a slide on the other. Burton put his thumbnail against the projection at the end of the slide and pushed. The slide moved downward about two-sixteenths of an inch, and a wire about one-tenth of an inch in diameter and a half-inch long slid out of the hole in the end. Even in the bright sunlight, it glowed whitely. He touched the tip of the wire to a blade of grass; the blade shriveled up at once. Applied to the tip of the bamboo spear, it burned a tiny hole. Burton pushed the slide back into its original position, and the wire withdrew, like the hot head of a brazen turtle, into the silvery shell.

Both Frigate and Ruach wondered aloud at the power contained in the tiny pack. To make the wire that hot required much voltage. How many charges would the battery or the radioactive pile that must be in it give? How could the lighter's power pack be renewed?

There were many questions that could not be immediately answered or, perhaps, never. The greatest was how they could have been brought back to life in rejuvenated bodies. Whoever had done it possessed a science that was godlike. But speculation about it, though it would give them something to talk about, would solve nothing.

After a while, the crowd dispersed. The cylinder was left on its side on top of the grailstone. Several bodies were sprawled there, and a number of men and women who got off the rock were hurt. Burton went through the crowd. One woman's face had been clawed, especially around her right eye. She was sobbing with no one to pay attention to her. Another man was sitting on the ground and holding his groin, which had been raked with sharp fingernails.

Of the four lying on top of the stone, three were unconscious. These recovered with water dashed into their faces from the grail. The fourth, a short slender man, was dead. Someone had twisted his head until his neck had broken.

Burton looked up at the sun again and said, 'I don't know exactly when supper time will occur. I suggest we return not too long after the sun goes down behind the mountain. We will set our grails, or glory buckets, or lunch-pails, or whatever you wish to call them, in these depressions. And then we'll wait. In the meantime ...'

He could have tossed this body into the river, too, but he had now thought of a use, perhaps uses, for it. He told the others what he wanted, and they got the corpse down off the stone and started to carry it across the plain. Frigate and Galeazzi, a former importer of Trieste, took the first turn. Frigate had evidently not cared for the job, but when Burton asked him if he would, he nodded. He picked up the man's feet and led with Galeazzi holding the dead man under the armpits. Alice walked behind Burton with the child's hand in hers. Some in the crowd looked curiously or called out comments or questions, but Burton ignored them. After half a mile, Kazz and Monat took over the corpse. The child did not seem too disturbed by the dead man. She had been curious about the first corpse, instead of being horrified by its burned appearance.

'If she really is an ancient Gaul,' Frigate said, 'she may be used to seeing charred bodies. If I remember correctly, the Gauls burned sacrifices alive in big wicker baskets at religious ceremonies. I don't remember what god or goddess the ceremonies were in honor of. I wish I had a library to refer to. Do you think we'll ever have one here? I think I would go nuts if I didn't have books to read.'

'That remains to be seen,' Burton said. 'If we're not provided with a library, we'll make our own. If it's possible to do so.'

He thought that Frigate's question was a silly one, but then not everybody was quite in their right minds at this time.

At the foothills, two men, Rocco and Brontich, succeeded Kazz and Monat. Burton led them past the trees through the waist-high grass. The saw-edged grass scraped their legs. Burton cut off a stalk with his knife and tested the stalk for toughness and flexibility. Frigate kept close to his elbow and seemed unable to stop chattering. Probably, Burton thought, he talked to keep from thinking about the two deaths.

'If everyone who has ever lived has been resurrected here, think of the research to be done! Think of the historical mysteries and questions you could clear up! You could talk to John Wilkes Booth and find out if Secretary of War Stanton really was behind the Lincoln assassination. You might ferret out the identity of Jack the Ripper. Find out if Joan of Arc actually did belong to a witch cult. Talk to Napoleon's Marshal Ney; see if he did escape the firing squad and become a schoolteacher in America. Get the true story on Pearl Harbor. See the face of the Man in the Iron Mask, if there ever was such a person. Interview Lucrezia Borgia and those who knew her and determine if she was the poisoning bitch most people think she was. Learn the identity of the assassin of the two little princes in the Tower. Maybe Richard III did kill them.

'And you, Richard Francis Burton, there are many questions about your own life that your biographers would like to have answered. Did you really have a Persian love you were going to marry and for whom you were going to renounce your true identity and become a native? Did she die before you could marry her, and did her death really embitter you, and did you carry a torch for her the rest of your life?'

Burton glared at him. He had just met the man and here he was, asking the most personal and prying questions. Nothing excused this.

Frigate backed away, saying, 'And … and … well, it'll all have to wait, I can see that. But did you know that your wife had extreme unction administered to you shortly after you died and that you were buried in a Catholic cemetery – you, the infidel?'

Lev Ruach, whose eyes had been widening while Frigate was rattling on, said. 'You're Burton, the explorer and linguist? The discoverer of Lake Tanganyika? The one who made a pilgrimage to Mecca while disguised as a Moslem? The translator of *The Thousand and One Nights*?'

'I have no desire to lie nor need to. I am he.'

Lev Ruach spat at Burton, but the wind carried it away. 'You son of a bitch!' he cried. 'You foul Nazi bastard! I read about you! You were, in many ways, an admirable person, I suppose! But you were an anti-Semite!'

7

Burton was startled. He said, 'My enemies spread that baseless and vicious rumor. But anybody acquainted with the facts and with me would know better. And now, I think you'd …'

'I suppose you didn't write *The Jew, The Gypsy, and El Islam*?' Ruach said, sneering.

'I did,' Burton replied. His face was red, and when he looked down, he saw that his body was also flushed. 'And now, as I started to say before you so boorishly interrupted me, I think you had better go. Ordinarily, I would be at your throat by now. A man who talks to me like that has to defend his words with deeds. But this is a strange situation, and perhaps you are overwrought. I do not know. But if you do not apologize now, or walk off, I am going to make another corpse.'

Ruach clenched his fists and glared at Burton; then he spun around and stalked off.

'What is a Nazi?' Burton said to Frigate.

The American explained as best he could. Burton said, 'I have much to learn about what happened after I died. That man is mistaken about me. I'm no Nazi. England, you say, became a second-class power? Only fifty years after my death? I find that difficult to believe.'

'Why would I lie to you?' Frigate said. 'Don't feel bad about it. Before the end of the twentieth century, she had risen again, and in a most curious way, though it was too late ...'

Listening to the Yankee, Burton felt pride for his country. Although England had treated him more than shabbily during his lifetime, and although he had always wanted to get out of the island whenever he had been on it, he would defend it to the death. And he had been devoted to the Queen.

Abruptly, he said, 'If you guessed my identity, why didn't you say something about it?'

'I wanted to be sure. Besides, we've not had much time for social intercourse,' Frigate said. 'Or any other kind, either,' he added, looking sidewise at Alice Hargreaves's magnificent figure.

'I know about *her*, too,' he said, 'if she's the woman I think she is.'

'That's more than I do,' Burton replied. He stopped. They had gone up the slope of the first hill and were on its top. They lowered the body to the ground beneath a giant red pine.

Immediately, Kazz, chert knife in his hand, squatted down by the charred corpse. He raised his head upward and uttered a few phrases in what must have been a religious chant. Then, before the others could object, he had cut into the body and removed the liver.

Most of the group cried out in horror. Burton grunted. Monat stared.

Kazz's big teeth bit into the bloody organ and tore off a large chunk. His massively muscled and thickly boned jaws began chewing, and he half-closed his eyes in ecstasy. Burton stepped up to him and held out his hand, intending to remonstrate. Kazz grinned broadly and cut off a piece and offered it to Burton. He was very surprised at Burton's refusal.

'A cannibal!' Alice Hargreaves said. 'Oh, my God, a bloody, stinking cannibal! And this is the promised afterlife!'

'He's no worse than our own ancestors,' Burton said. He had recovered from the shock, and was even enjoying – a little – the reaction of the others. 'In a land where there seems to be precious little food, his action is eminently practical. Well, our problem of burying a corpse without proper digging tools is solved. Furthermore, if we're wrong about the grails being a source of food, we may be emulating Kazz before long!'

'Never!' Alice said. 'I'd die first!'

'That is exactly what you would do,' Burton replied, coolly. 'I suggest we retire and leave him to his meal. It doesn't do anything for my own appetite, and I find his table manners as abominable as those of a Yankee frontiersman's. Or a country prelate's,' he added for Alice's benefit.

They walked out of sight of Kazz and behind one of the great gnarled trees. Alice said, 'I don't want him around. He's an animal, an abomination! Why, I wouldn't feel safe for a second with him around!'

'You asked me for protection,' Burton said. 'I'll give it to you as long as you are a member of this party. But you'll also have to accept my decisions. One of which is that the apeman remains with us. We need his strength and his skills, which seem to be very appropriate for this type of country. We've become primitives; therefore, we can learn from a primitive. He stays.'

Alice looked at the others with silent appeal. Monat twitched his eyebrows. Frigate shrugged his shoulders and said, 'Mrs Hargreaves, if you can possibly do it, forget your mores, your conventions. We're not in a proper upper-class Victorian heaven. Or, indeed, in any sort of heaven ever dreamed of. You can't think and behave as you did on Earth. For one thing, you come from a society where women covered themselves from neck to foot in heavy garments, and the sight of a woman's knee was a stirring sexual event. Yet, you seem to suffer no embarrassment because you're nude. You are as poised and dignified as if you wore a nun's habit.'

Alice said, 'I don't like it. But why should I be embarrassed? Where all are nude, none are nude. It's the thing to do, in fact, the only thing that can be done. If some angel were to give me a complete outfit, I wouldn't wear it. I'd be out of style. And my figure is good. If it weren't I might be suffering more.'

The two men laughed, and Frigate said, 'You're fabulous, Alice. Absolutely. I may call you Alice? Mrs Hargreaves seems so formal when you're nude.'

She did not reply but walked away and disappeared behind a large tree. Burton said, 'Something will have to be done about sanitation in the near future. Which means that somebody will have to decide the health policies and have the power to make regulations and enforce them. How does one form legislative, judicial, and executive bodies from the present state of anarchy?'

'To get to more immediate problems,' Frigate said, 'what do we do about the dead man?'

He was only a little less pale than a moment ago when Kazz had made his incisions with his chert knife.

Burton said, 'I'm sure that human skin, properly tanned, or human gut, properly treated, will be far superior to grass for making ropes or bindings. I intend to cut off some strips. Do you want to help me?'

Only the wind rustling the leaves and the tops of the grass broke the silence. The sun beat down and brought out sweat which dried rapidly in the wind. No bird cried, no insect buzzed. And then the shrill voice of the little girl shattered the quiet. Alice's voice answered her, and the little girl ran to her behind the tree.

'I'll try,' the American said. 'But I don't know. I've gone through more than enough for one day.'

'You do as you please then,' Burton said. 'But anybody who helps me gets first call on the use of the skin. You may wish you could have some in order to bind an axe head to a haft.'

Frigate gulped audibly and then said, 'I'll come.'

Kazz was still squatting in the grass by the body, holding the bloody liver with one hand and the bloody stone knife with the other. Seeing Burton, he grinned with stained lips and cut off a piece of liver. Burton shook his head. The others, Galeazzi, Brontich, Maria Tucci, Filipo Rocco, Rosa Nalini, Caterina Capone, Fiorenza Fiorri, Babich, and Giunta, had retreated from the grisly scene. They were on the other side of a thick-trunked pine and talking subduedly in Italian.

Burton squatted down by the body and applied the point of the knife, beginning just above the right knee and continuing to the collarbone. Frigate stood by him and stared. He became even more pale, and his trembling increased. But he stood firm until two long strips had been lifted from the body.

'Care to try your hand at it?' Burton said. He rolled the body over on its side so that other, even longer, strips could be taken. Frigate took the bloody-tipped knife and set to work, his teeth gritted.

'Not so deep,' Burton said and, a moment later, 'Now you're not cutting deeply enough. Here, give me the knife. Watch!'

'I had a neighbor who used to hang up his rabbits behind his garage and cut their throats right after breaking their necks,' Frigate said. 'I watched once. That was enough.'

'You can't afford to be fastidious or weak-stomached,' Burton said. 'You're living in the most primitive of conditions. You have to be a primitive to survive, like it or not.'

Brontich, the tall skinny Slovene who had once been an innkeeper, ran up to them. He said, 'We just found another of those big mushroom-shaped stones. About forty yards from here. It was hidden behind some trees down in a hollow.'

Burton's first delight in hectoring Frigate had passed. He was beginning to feel sorry for the fellow. He said, 'Look, Peter, why don't you go investigate the stone? If there is one here, we can save ourselves a trip back to the river.'

He handed Frigate his grail. 'Put this in a hole on the stone, but remember exactly which hole you put it in. Have the others do that, too. Make sure that they know where they put their own grails. Wouldn't want to have any quarrels about that, you know.'

Strangely, Frigate was reluctant to go. He seemed to feel that he had disgraced himself by his weakness. He stood there for a moment, shifting his weight from one leg to another and sighing several times. Then, as Burton continued to scrape away at the underside of the skin strips, he walked away. He carried the two grails in one hand and his stone axe head in the other.

Burton stopped working after the American was out of sight. He had been interested in finding out how to cut off strips, and he might dissect the body's trunk to remove the entrails. But he could do nothing at this time about preserving the skin or guts. It was possible that the bark of the oak-like trees might contain tannin which could be used with other materials to convert human skin into leather. By the time that was done, however, these strips would have rotted. Still, he had not wasted his time. The efficiency of the stone knives was proven, and he had reinforced his weak memory of human anatomy. When they were juveniles in Pisa, Richard Burton and his brother Edward had associated with the Italian medical students of the university. Both of the Burton youths had learned much from the students and neither had abandoned their interest in anatomy. Edward became a surgeon, and Richard had attended a number of lectures and public and private dissections in London. But he had forgotten much of what he had learned.

Abruptly, the sun went past the shoulder of the mountain. A pale shadow fell over him, and, within a few minutes, the entire valley was in the dusk. But the sky was a bright blue for a long time. The breeze continued to flow at the same rate. The moisture-laden air became a little cooler. Burton and the Neanderthal left the body and followed the sounds of the others' voices. These were by the grailstone of which Brontich had spoken. Burton wondered if there were others near the base of the mountain, strung out at approximate distances of a mile. This one lacked the grail in the center depression, however. Perhaps this meant that it was not ready to operate. He did not think so. It could be assumed that Whoever had made the grailstones had placed the grails in the center holes of those on the river's edge because the resurrectees would be using these first. By the time they found the inland stones, they would know how to use them.

The grails were set on the depressions of the outmost circle. Their owners stood or sat around, talking but with their minds on the grails. All were wondering when – or perhaps if – the next blue flames would come. Much of their conversation was about how hungry they were. The rest was mainly surmise about how they had come here, Who had put them here, where They were, and what was being planned for them. A few spoke of their lives on Earth.

Burton sat down beneath the wide-flung and densely leaved branches of the gnarled black-trunked Irontree. He felt tired, as all, except Kazz, obviously did. His empty belly and his stretched-out nerves kept him from dozing off, although the quiet voices and the rustle of leaves conduced to sleep. The hollow in which the group waited was formed by a level space at the junction of four hills and was surrounded by trees. Though it was darker than on top of the hills, it also seemed to be a little warmer. After a while, as the dusk and the chill increased, Burton organized a firewood-collecting party. Using the knives and hand axes, they cut down many mature bamboo plants and gathered piles of grass. With the white-hot wire of the lighter, Burton started a fire of leaves and grass. These were green, and so the fire was smoky and unsatisfactory until the bamboo was put on.

Suddenly, an explosion made them jump. Some of the women screamed. They had forgotten about watching the grailstone. Burton turned just in time to see the blue flames soar up about twenty feet. The heat from the discharge could be felt by Brontich, who was about twenty feet from it.

Then the noise was gone, and they stared at the grails. Burton was the first upon the stone again; most of them did not care to venture on the stone too soon after the flames. He lifted the lid of his grail, looked within, and whooped with delight. The others climbed up and opened their own grails. Within a minute, they were seated near the fire eating rapidly, exclaiming with ecstasy, pointing out to each other what they'd found, laughing, and joking. Things were not so bad after all. Whoever was responsible for this was taking care of them.

There was food in plenty, even after fasting all day, or, as Frigate put it, 'probably fasting for half of eternity.' He meant by this, as he explained to Monat, that there was no telling how much time had elapsed between AD 2008 and today. This world wasn't built in a day, and preparing humanity for resurrection would take more than seven days. That is, if all of this had been brought about by scientific means, not by supernatural.

Burton's grail had yielded a four-inch cube of steak; a small ball of dark bread; butter; potatoes and gravy; lettuce with salad dressing of an unfamiliar but delicious taste. In addition, there was a five-ounce cup containing an excellent bourbon and another small cup with four ice cubes in it.

There was more, all the better because unexpected. A small briar pipe. A sack of pipe tobacco. Three panatela-shaped cigars. A plastic package with ten cigarettes.

'Unfiltered!' Frigate said.

There was also one small brown cigarette which Burton and Frigate smelled and said, at the same time, 'Marihuana!'

Alice, holding up a pair of small metallic scissors and a black comb, said, 'Evidently we're going to get our hair back. Otherwise, there'd be no need for these. I'm so glad! But do ... They ... really expect me to use this?'

She held out a tube of bright red lipstick.

'Or me?' Frigate said, also looking at a similar tube.

'They're eminently practical,' Monat said, turning over a packet of what was obviously toilet paper. Then he pulled out a sphere of green soap.

Burton's steak was very tender, although he would have preferred it rare. On the other hand, Frigate complained because it was not cooked enough.

'Evidently, these grails do not contain menus tailored for the individual owner,' Frigate said. 'Which may be why we men also get lipstick and the women got pipes. It's a mass production.'

'Two miracles in one day,' Burton said. 'That is, if they are such. I prefer a rational explanation and intend to get it. I don't think anyone can, as yet, tell me how we were resurrected. But perhaps you twentieth-centurians have a reasonable theory for the seemingly magical appearance of these articles in a previously empty container?'

'If you compare the exterior and interior of the grail,' Monat said, 'you will observe an approximate five-centimeter difference in depth. The false bottom must conceal a molar circuitry which is able to convert energy to matter. The energy, obviously, comes during the discharge from the rocks. In addition to the e-m converter, the grail must hold molar templates ...? molds ...? which form the matter into various combinations of elements and compounds.

'I'm safe in my speculations, for we had a similar converter on my native planet. But nothing as miniature as this, I assure you.'

'Same on Earth,' Frigate said. 'They were making iron out of pure energy before AD 2002, but it was a very cumbersome and expensive process with an almost microscopic yield.'

'Good,' Burton said. 'All this has cost us nothing. So far ...'

He fell silent for a while, thinking of the dream he had when awakening.

'Pay up,' God had said. *'You owe for the flesh.'*

What had that meant? On Earth, at Trieste, in 1890, he had been dying in his wife's arms and asking for ... what? Chloroform? Something. He could not remember. Then, oblivion. And he had awakened in that nightmare place and had seen things that were not on Earth nor, as far as he knew, on this planet. But that experience had been no dream.

8

They finished eating and replaced the containers in the racks within the grails. Since there was no water nearby, they would have to wait until morning to wash the containers. Frigate and Kazz, however, had made several buckets out of sections of the giant bamboo. The American volunteered to walk back to the river, if some of them would go with him, and fill the sections with water. Burton wondered why the fellow volunteered. Then, looking at Alice, he knew why. Frigate must be hoping to find some congenial female companionship. Evidently he took it for granted that Alice Hargreaves preferred Burton. And the other women, Tucci, Malini, Capone, and Fiorri, had made their choices of, respectively, Galeazzi, Brontich, Rocco, and Giunta. Babich had wandered off, possibly for the same reason that Frigate had for wishing to leave.

Monat and Kazz went with Frigate. The sky was suddenly crowded with gigantic sparks and great luminous gas clouds. The glitter of jam-packed stars, some so large they seemed to be broken-off pieces of Earth's moon, and the shine of the clouds, awed them and made them feel pitifully microscopic and ill-made.

Burton lay on his back on a pile of tree leaves and puffed on a cigar. It was excellent, and in the London of his day would have cost at least a shilling. He did not feel so minute and unworthy now. The stars were inanimate matter, and he was alive. No star could ever know the delicious taste of an expensive cigar. Nor could it know the ecstasy of holding a warm well-curved woman next to it.

On the other side of the fire, half or wholly lost in the grasses and the shadows, were the Triestans. The liquor had uninhibited them, though part of their sense of freedom may have come from joy at being alive and young again. They giggled and laughed and rolled back and forth in the grass and made loud noises while kissing. And then, couple by couple, they retreated into the darkness. Or at least, made no more loud noises.

The little girl had fallen asleep by Alice. The firelight flickered over Alice's handsome aristocratic face and bald head and on the magnificent body and long legs. Burton suddenly knew that all of him had been resurrected. He definitely was not the old man who, during the last sixteen years of his life, had paid so heavily for the many fevers and sicknesses that had squeezed him dry in the tropics. Now he was young again, healthy, and possessed by the old clamoring demon.

Yet he had given his promise to protect her. He could make no move, say no word which she could interpret as seductive.

Well, she was not the only woman in the world. As a matter of fact, he had the whole world of women, if not at his disposal, at least available to be asked. That is, he did if everybody who had died on Earth was on this planet. She would be only one among many billions (possibly thirty-six billion, if Frigate's estimate was correct). But there was, of course, no such evidence that this was the case.

The hell of it was that Alice might as well be the only one in the world, at this moment, anyway. He could not get up and walk off into the darkness looking for another woman, because that would leave her and the child unprotected. She certainly would not feel safe with Monat and Kazz, nor could he blame her. They were so terrifyingly ugly. Nor could he entrust her to Frigate – if Frigate returned tonight, which Burton doubted – because the fellow was an unknown quantity.

Burton suddenly laughed loudly at his situation. He had decided that he might as well stick it out for tonight. This thought set him laughing again, and he did not stop until Alice asked him if he was all right.

'More right than you will ever know,' he said, turning his back to her. He reached into his grail and extracted the last item. This was a small flat stick of chicle-like substance. Frigate, before leaving, had remarked that their unknown benefactors must be American. Otherwise, they would not have thought of providing chewing gum.

After stubbing out his cigar on the ground, Burton popped the stick into his mouth. He said, 'This has a strange but rather delicious taste. Have you tried yours?'

'I am tempted, but I imagine I'd look like a cow chewing her cud.'

'Forget about being a lady,' Burton said. 'Do you think that beings with the power to resurrect you would have vulgar tastes?'

Alice smiled slightly, said, 'I really wouldn't know,' and placed the stick in her mouth. For a moment, they chewed idly, looking across the fire at each other. She was unable to look him full in the eyes for more than a few seconds at a time.

Burton said, 'Frigate mentioned that he knew you. *Of* you, rather. Just who are you, if you will pardon my unseemly curiosity?'

'There are no secrets among the dead,' she replied lightly. 'Or among the ex-dead, either.'

She had been born Alice Pleasance Liddell on 25 April 1852. (Burton was thirty then.) She was the direct descendant of King Edward III and his son, John of Gaunt. Her father was dean of Christ Church College of Oxford and co-author of a famous Greek-English lexicon. (Liddell and Scott! Burton thought.) She had had a happy childhood, an excellent education, and had met many famous people of her times: Gladstone, Matthew Arnold, the Prince of Wales, who was placed under her father's care while he was at

Oxford. Her husband had been Reginald Gervis Hargreaves, and she had loved him very much. He had been a 'country gentleman,' liked to hunt, fish, play cricket, raise trees, and read French literature. She had three sons, all captains, two of whom died in the Great War of 1914–18. (This was the second time that day that Burton had heard of the Great War.)

She talked on and on as if drink had loosened her tongue. Or as if she wanted to place a barrier of conversation between her and Burton.

She talked of Dinah, the tabby kitten she had loved when she was a child, the great trees of her husband's arboretum, how her father, when working on his lexicon, would always sneeze at twelve o'clock in the afternoon, no one knew why … at the age of eighty, she was given an honorary Doctor of Letters by the American university, Columbia, because of the vital part she had played in the genesis of Mr Dodgson's famous book. (She neglected to mention the title and Burton, though a voracious reader, did not recall any works by a Mr Dodgson.)

'That was a golden afternoon indeed,' she said, 'despite the official meteorological report. On 4 July, 1862, I was ten … my sisters and I were wearing black shoes, white openwork socks, white cotton dresses, and hats with large brims.'

Her eyes were wide, and she shook now and then as if she were struggling inside herself, and she began to talk even faster.

'Mr Dodgson and Mr Duckworth carried the picnic baskets … we set off in our boat from Folly Bridge up the Isis, upstream for a change. Mr Duckworth rowed stroke; the drops fell off his paddle like tears of glass on the smooth mirror of the Isis, and …'

Burton heard the last words as if they had been roared at him. Astonished, he gazed at Alice, whose lips seemed to be moving as if she were conversing at a normal speech level. Her eyes were now fixed on him, but they seemed to be boring through him into a space and a time beyond. Her hands were half-raised as if she were surprised at something and could not move them.

Every sound was magnified. He could hear the breathing of the little girl, the pounding of her heart and Alice's, the gurgle of the workings of Alice's intestines and of the breeze as it slipped across the branches of the trees. From far away, a cry came.

He rose and listened. What was happening? Why the heightening of senses? Why could he hear their hearts but not his? He was also aware of the shape and texture of the grass under his feet. Almost, he could feel the individual molecules of the air as they bumped into his body.

Alice, too, had risen. She said, 'What is happening?' and her voice fell against him like a heavy gust of wind.

He did not reply, for he was staring at her. Now, it seemed to him, he could really *see* her body for the first time. And he could see *her*, too. The entire Alice.

Alice came toward him with her arms held out, her eyes half-shut, her mouth moist. She swayed, and she crooned, 'Richard! Richard!'

Then she stopped; her eyes widened. He stepped toward her, his arms out. She cried, 'No!' and turned and ran into the darkness among the trees.

For a second, he stood still. It did not seem possible that she, whom he loved as he had never loved anybody, could not love him back.

She must be teasing him. That was it. He ran after her, and called her name over and over.

It must have been hours later when the rain fell against them. Either the effect of the drug had worn off or the cold water helped dispel it, for both seemed to emerge from the ecstasy and the dreamlike state at the same time. She looked up at him as lightning lit their features, and she screamed and pushed him violently.

He fell on the grass, but reached out a hand and grabbed her ankle as she scrambled away from him on all fours.

'What's the matter with you?' he shouted.

Alice quit struggling. She sat down, hid her face against her knees, and her body shook with sobs. Burton rose and placed his hands under her chin and forced her to look upward. Lightning hit nearby again and showed him her tortured face.

'You promised to protect me!' she cried out.

'You didn't act as if you wanted to be protected,' he said. 'I didn't promise to protect you against a natural human impulse.'

'Impulse!' she said. 'Impulse! My God, I've never done anything like this in my life! I've always been good! I was a virgin when I married, and I stayed faithful to my husband all my life! And now ... a total stranger! Just like that! I don't know what got into me!'

'Then I've been a failure,' Burton said, and laughed. But he was beginning to feel regret and sorrow. If only it had been her own will, her own wish, then he would not now be having the slightest bite of conscience. But that gum had contained some powerful drug, and it had made them behave as lovers whose passion knew no limits. She had certainly cooperated as enthusiastically as any experienced woman in a Turkish harem.

'You needn't feel the least bit contrite or self-reproachful,' he said gently. 'You were possessed. Blame the drug.'

'I did it!' she said. 'I ... I! I wanted to! Oh, what a vile low whore I am!'

'I don't remember offering you any money.'

He did not mean to be heartless. He wanted to make her so angry that she would forget her self-abasement. And he succeeded. She jumped up and attacked his chest and face with her nails. She called him names that a highbred and gentle lady of Victoria's day should never have known.

Burton caught her wrists to prevent further damage and held her while she spewed more filth at him. Finally, when she had fallen silent and had begun weeping again, he led her toward the camp site. The fire was wet ashes. He scraped off the top layer and dropped a handful of grass, which had been protected from the rain by the tree, onto the embers. By its light, he saw the little girl sleeping huddled between Kazz and Monat under a pile of grass beneath the irontree. He returned to Alice, who was sitting under another tree.

'Stay away,' she said. 'I never want to see you again! You have dishonored me, dirtied me! And after you gave your word to protect me!'

'You can freeze if you wish,' he said. 'I was merely going to suggest that we huddle together to keep warm. But, if you wish discomfort, so be it. I'll tell you again that what we did was generated by the drug. No, not generated. Drugs don't generate desires or actions; they merely allow them to be released. Our normal inhibitions were dissolved, and neither one of us can blame ourself or the other.

'However, I'd be a liar if I said I didn't enjoy it, and you'd be a liar if you claimed you didn't. So, why gash yourself with the knives of conscience?'

'I'm not a beast like you! I'm a good Christian God-fearing virtuous woman!'

'No doubt,' Burton said dryly. 'However, let me stress again one thing. I doubt if you would have done what you did if you had not wished in your heart to do so. The drug suppressed your inhibitions, but it certainly did not put in your mind the idea of what to do. The idea was already there. Any action that resulted from taking the drug came from you, from what you wanted to do.'

'I know that!' she screamed. 'Do you think I'm some stupid simple serving girl? I have a brain! I know what I did and why! It's just that I never dreamed that I could be such … such a *person!* But I must have been! Must *be!*'

Burton tried to console her, to show her that everyone had certain unwished-for elements in their nature. He pointed out that the dogma of original sin surely covered this; she was human; therefore, she had dark desires in her. And so forth. The more he tried to make her feel better, the worse she felt. Then, shivering with cold, and tired of the useless arguments, he gave up. He crawled in between Monat and Kazz and took the little girl in his arms. The warmth of the three bodies and the cover of the grass pile and the feel of the naked bodies soothed him. He went to sleep with Alice's weeping coming to him faintly through the grass cover.

9

When he awoke, he was in the gray light of the false dawn, which the Arabs called the *wolf's tail*. Monat, Kazz, and the child were still sleeping. He scratched for a while at the itchy spots caused by the rough-edged grass and then crawled out. The fire was out; water drops hung from the leaves of the trees and the tips of the grass blades. He shivered with the cold. But he did not feel tired nor have any ill effects from the drug, as he had expected. He found a pile of comparatively dry bamboo under some grass beneath a tree. He rebuilt the fire with this and in a short time was comfortable. Then he saw the bamboo containers, and he drank water from one. Alice was sitting up in a mound of grass and staring sullenly at him. Her skin was ridged with goosebumps.

'Come and get warm!' he said.

She crawled out, stood up, walked over to the bamboo bucket, bent down, scooped up water, and splashed it over her face. Then she squatted down by the fire, warming her hands over a small flame. If everybody is naked, how quickly even the most modest lose their modesty, he thought.

A moment later, Burton heard the rustle of grass to the east. A naked head, Peter Frigate's, appeared. He strode from the grass, and was followed by the naked head of a woman. Emerging from the grass, she revealed a wet but beautiful body. Her eyes were large and a dark green, and her lips were a little too thick for beauty. But her other features were exquisite.

Frigate was smiling broadly. He turned and pulled her into the warmth of the fire with his hand.

'You look like the cat who ate the canary,' Burton said. 'What happened to your hand?'

Peter Frigate looked at the knuckles of his right hand. They were swelled, and there were scratches on the back of the hand.

'I got into a fight,' he said He pointed a finger at the woman, who was squatting near Alice and warming herself. 'It was a madhouse down by the river last night. That gum must contain a drug of some sort. You wouldn't believe what people were doing. Or would you? After all, you're Richard Francis Burton. Anyway, all women, including the ugly ones, were occupied, one way or another. I got scared at what was going on and then I got mad. I hit two men with my grail, knocked them out. They were attacking a ten-year-old girl. I may have killed them; I hope I did. I tried to get the girl to come with me, but she ran away into the night.

'I decided to come back here. I was beginning to react pretty badly from what I'd done to those two men even if they deserved it. The drug was responsible; it must have released a lifetime of rage and frustration. So I started back here and then I came across two more men, only these were attacking a woman, this one. I think she wasn't resisting the idea of intercourse so much as she was their idea of simultaneous attack, if you know what I mean. Anyway, she was screaming, or trying to, and struggling, and they had just started to hit her. So I hit them with my fist and kicked them and then banged away on them with my grail.

'Then I took the woman, her name's Loghu, by the way, that's all I know about her since I can't understand a word of her language, and she went with me.'

He grinned again. 'But we never got there.'

He quit grinning, and shuddered.

'Then we woke up with the rain and lightning and thunder coming down like the wrath of God. I thought that maybe, don't laugh, that it was Judgment Day, that God had given us free rein for a day so He could let us judge ourselves. And now we were going to be cast into the pit.'

He laughed tightly and said, 'I've been an agnostic since I was fourteen years old, and I died one at the age of ninety, although I was thinking about calling in a priest then. But the little child that's scared of the Old Father God and Hellfire and Damnation, he's still down there, even in the old man. Or in the young man raised from the dead.'

'What happened?' Burton said. 'Did the world end in a crack of thunder and a stroke of lightning? You're still here, I see, and you've not renounced the delights of sin in the person of this woman.'

'We found a grailstone near the mountains. About a mile west of here. We got lost, wandered around, cold, wet, jumping every time the lightning struck nearby. Then we found the grailstone. It was jammed with people, but they were exceptionally friendly, and there were so many bodies it was very warm, even if some rain did leak down through the grass. We finally went to sleep, long after the rain quit. When I woke up, I searched through the grass until I found Loghu. She got lost during the night, somehow. She seemed pleased to see me, though, and I like her. There's an affinity between us. Maybe I'll find out why when she learns to speak English. I tried that and French and German and tags of Russian, Lithuanian, Gaelic, all the Scandinavian tongues, including Finnish, classical Nahuatl, Arabic, Hebrew, Onondaga Iroquois, Ojibway, Italian, Spanish, Latin, modern and Homeric Greek, and a dozen others. Result: a blank look.'

'You must be quite a linguist,' Burton said.

'I'm not fluent in any of those,' Frigate said. 'I can read most of them but can speak only everyday phrases. Unlike you, I am not master of thirty-nine languages – including pornography.'

The fellow seemed to know much about himself, Burton thought. He would find out just how much at a later time.

'I'll be frank with you, Peter,' Burton said. 'Your account of your aggressiveness amazed me. I had not thought you capable of attacking and beating that many men. Your queasiness ...'

'It was the gum, of course. It opened the door of the cage.'

Frigate squatted down by Loghu and rubbed his shoulder against hers. She looked at him out of slightly slanted eyes. The woman would be beautiful once her hair grew out.

Frigate continued, 'I'm so timorous and queasy because I am afraid of the anger, the desire to do violence, that lies not too deeply within me. I fear violence because I am violent. I fear what will happen if I am not afraid. Hell, I've known that for forty years. Much good the knowledge has done me!'

He looked at Alice and said, 'Good morning!'

Alice replied cheerily enough, and she even smiled at Loghu when she was introduced. She would look at Burton, and she would answer his direct questions. But she would not chat with him or give him anything but a stern face.

Monat, Razz, and the little girl, all yawning, came to the fireside. Burton prowled around the edges of the camp and found that the Triestans were gone. Some had left their grails behind. He cursed them for their carelessness and thought about leaving the grails in the grass to teach them a lesson. But he eventually placed the cylinders in depressions on the gallstone.

If their owners did not return, they would go hungry unless someone shared their food with them. In the meantime, the food in their grails would have to be untouched. He would be unable to open them. They had discovered yesterday that only the owner of a grail could open it. Experimentation with a long stick had determined also that the owner had to touch the grail with his fingers or some part of his body before the lid would open. It was Frigate's theory that a mechanism in the grail was keyed to the peculiar configuration of skin voltage of the owner. Or perhaps the grail contained a very sensitive detector of the individual's brain waves.

The sky had become bright by then. The sun was still on the other side of the 20,000-foot high eastern mountain. Approximately a half hour later, the grailrock spurted blue flame with a roll of thunder. Thunder from the stones along the river echoed against the mountain.

The grails yielded bacon and eggs, ham, toast, butter, jam, milk, a quarter of a cantaloupe, cigarettes, and a cupful of dark brown crystals which Frigate said was instant coffee. He drank the milk in one cup, rinsed it out in water in a bamboo container, filled the cup with water, and set it by the fire. When the water was boiling, he put a teaspoonful of the crystals into the water and stirred it. The coffee was delicious, and there were enough crystals to provide six cups. Then Alice put the crystals into the water before heating it over the fire and found that it was not necessary to use the fire. The water boiled within three seconds after the crystals were placed into the cold water.

After eating, they washed out the containers and replaced them in the grails. Burton strapped his grail onto his wrist. He intended to explore, and he certainly was not going to leave the grail on the stone. Though it could do no one but himself any good, vicious people might take it just for the pleasure of seeing him starve.

Burton started his language lessons with the little girl and Kazz, and Frigate got Loghu to sit in on them. Frigate suggested that a universal language should be adopted because of the many many languages and dialects, perhaps fifty to sixty thousand, that mankind had used in his several million years of existence and which he was using along the river. That is, provided that all of mankind had been resurrected. After all, all he knew about was the few square miles he had seen. But it would be a good idea to start propagating Esperanto, the synthetic language invented by the Polish oculist, Doctor Zamenhof, in 1887. Its grammar was very simple and absolutely regular, and its sound combinations, though not as easy for everybody to pronounce as claimed, were still relatively easy. And the basis of the vocabulary was Latin with many words from English and German and other West European languages.

'I had heard about it before I died,' Burton said. 'But I never saw any samples of it. Perhaps it may become useful. But, in the meantime, I'll teach these two English.'

'But most of the people here speak Italian or Slovenian!' Frigate said.

'That may be true, though we haven't any survey as yet. However, I don't intend to stay here, you can be sure of that.'

'I could have predicted that,' Frigate muttered. 'You always did get restless; you had to move on.'

Burton glared at Frigate and then started the lessons. For about fifteen minutes, he drilled them in the identification and pronunciation of nineteen nouns and a few verbs: fire, bamboo, grail, man, woman, girl, hand, feet, eye, teeth, eat, walk, run, talk, danger, I, you, they, us. He intended that he should learn as much from them as they from him. In time, he would be able to speak their tongues, whatever they were.

The sun cleared the top of the eastern range. The air became warmer, and they let the fire die. They were well into the second day of resurrection. And they knew almost nothing about this world or what their eventual fate was supposed to be or Who was determining their fate.

Lev Ruach stuck his big-nosed face through the grass and said, 'May I join you?'

Burton nodded, and Frigate said, 'Sure, why not?'

Ruach stepped out of the grass. A short pale-skinned woman with great brown eyes and lovely delicate features followed him. Ruach introduced her as Tanya Kauwitz. He had met her last night, and they had stayed together, since they had a number of things in common. She was of Russian-Jewish descent, was born in 1958 in the Bronx, New York City, had become an English schoolteacher, married a businessman who made a million and dropped dead when she was forty-five, leaving her free to marry a wonderful man with whom she had been in love for fifteen years. Six months later, she was dead of cancer. Tanya, not Lev, gave this information and in one sentence.

'It was hell down on the plains last night,' Lev said. 'Tanya and I had to run for our lives into the woods. So I decided that I would find you and ask if we could stay with you. I apologize for my hasty remarks of yesterday, Mr Burton. I think that my observations were valid, but the attitudes I was speaking of should be considered in the context of your other attitudes.'

'We'll go into that some other time,' Burton said. 'At the time I wrote that book, I was suffering from the vile and malicious lies of the money lenders of Damascus, and they ...'

'Certainly, Mr Burton,' Ruach said. 'As you say, later. I just wanted to make the point that I consider you to be a very capable and strong person, and I would like to join your group. We're in a state of anarchy, if you can call anarchy a state, and many of us need protection.'

Burton did not like to be interrupted. He scowled and said, 'Please permit me to explain myself. I ...'

Frigate stood up and said, 'Here come the others. Wonder where they've been?'

Only four of the original nine had come back, however. Maria Tucci explained that they had wandered away together after chewing the gum, and eventually ended up by one of the big bonfires on the plains. Then many things had happened; there had been fights and attacks by men on women, men on men, women on men, women on women, and even attacks on children. The group had split up in the chaos, she had met the other three only an hour ago while she was searching in the hills for the grailstone.

Lev added some details. The results of chewing the narcotic gum had been tragic, amusing, or gratifying, depending, apparently, upon individual reaction. The gum had had an aphrodisiac effect upon many, but it also had many other effects. Consider the husband and wife, who had died in Opcina, a suburb of Trieste, in 1899. They had been resurrected within six feet of each other. They had wept with joy at being reunited when so many couples had not been. They thanked God for their good luck, though they also had made some loud comments that this world was not what they had been promised.

But they had had fifty years of married bliss and now looked forward to being together for eternity.

Only a few minutes after both had chewed the gum, the man had strangled his wife, heaved her body into the river, picked up another woman in his arms, and run off into the darkness of the woods with her.

Another man had leaped upon a grailstone and delivered a speech that lasted all night, even through the rain. To the few who could hear, and the even fewer who listened, he had demonstrated the principles of a perfect society and how these could be carried out in practice. By dawn, he was so hoarse he could only croak a few words. On Earth, he had seldom bothered to vote.

A man and a woman, outraged at the public display of carnality, had forcefully tried to separate couples. The results: bruises, bloody noses, split lips, and two concussions, all theirs. Some men and women had spent the night on their knees praying and confessing their sins.

Some children had been badly beaten, raped, or murdered, or all three. But not everybody had succumbed to the madness. A number of adults had protected the children, or tried to.

Ruach described the despair and disgust of a Croat Moslem and an Austrian Jew because their grails contained pork. A Hindu screamed obscenities because his grail offered him meat.

A fourth man, crying out that they were in the hands of devils, had hurled his cigarettes into the river.

Several had said to him, 'Why didn't you give us the cigarettes if you didn't want them?'

'Tobacco is the invention of the devil; it was the weed created by Satan in the Garden of Eden!'

A man said, 'At least you could have shared the cigarettes with us. It wouldn't hurt you.'

'I would like to throw all the evil stuff into the river!' he had shouted.

'You're an insufferable bigot and crazy to boot,' another had replied, and struck him in the mouth. Before the tobacco-hater could get up off the ground, he was hit and kicked by four others.

Later, the tobacco-hater had staggered up and, weeping with rage, cried, 'What have I done to deserve this, O Lord, my God! I have always been a good man. I gave thousands of pounds to charities, I worshipped in Thy temple three times a week, I waged a lifelong war against sin and corruption, I …'

'I know you!' a woman had shouted. She was a tall blue-eyed girl with a handsome face and well-curved figure. 'I know you! Sir Robert Smithson!'

He had stopped talking and had blinked at her. 'I don't know you!'

'You wouldn't! But you should! I'm one of the thousands of girls who had to work sixteen hours a day, six and a half days a week, so you could live in your big house on the hill and dress in fine clothes and so your horses and dogs could eat far better than I could! I was one of your factory girls! My father slaved for you, my mother slaved for you, my brothers and sisters, those who weren't too sick or who didn't die because of too little or too bad food, dirty beds, drafty windows, and rat bites, slaved for you. My father lost a hand in one of your machines, and you kicked him out without a penny. My mother died of the white plague. I was coughing out my life, too, my fine baronet, while you stuffed yourself with rich foods and sat in easy chairs and dozed off in your big expensive church pew and gave thousands to feed the poor unfortunates in Asia and to send missionaries to convert the poor heathens in Africa. I coughed out my lungs, and I had to go a-whoring to make enough money to feed my kid sisters and brothers. And I caught syphilis, you bloody pious bastard, because you wanted to wring out every drop of sweat and blood I had and those poor devils like me had! I died in prison because you told the police they should deal harshly with prostitution. You ... you ...!'

Smithson had gone red at first, then pale. Then he had drawn himself up straight, scowling at the woman, and said, 'You whores always have somebody to blame for your unbridled lusts, your evil ways. God knows that I followed His ways.'

He had turned and had walked off, but the woman ran after him and swung her grail at him. It came around swiftly; somebody shouted; he spun and ducked. The grail almost grazed the top of his head.

Smithson ran past the woman before she could recover and quickly lost himself in the crowd. Unfortunately, Ruach said, very few understood what was going on because they couldn't speak English.

'Sir Robert Smithson,' Burton said. 'If I remember correctly, he owned cotton mills and steelworks in Manchester. He was noted for his philanthropies and his good works among the heathens. Died in 1870 or thereabouts at the age of eighty.'

'And probably convinced that he would be rewarded in Heaven,' Lev Ruach said. 'Of course, it would never have occurred to him that he was a murderer many times over.'

'If he hadn't exploited the poor, someone else would have done so.'

'That is an excuse used by many throughout men's history,' Lev said. 'Besides, there *were* industrialists in your country who saw to it that wages and conditions in their factories were improved. Robert Owen was one, I believe.'

10

'I don't see much sense in arguing about what went on in the past,' Frigate said. 'I think we should do something about our present situation.'

Burton stood up. 'You're right, Yank! We need roofs over our heads, tools, God knows what else! But first, I think we should take a look at the cities of the plains and see what the citizens are doing there.'

At that moment, Alice came through the trees on the hill above them. Frigate saw her first. He burst out laughing. 'The latest in ladies' wear!'

She had cut lengths of the grass with her scissors and plaited them into a two-piece garment. One was a sort of poncho which covered her breasts and the other a skirt which fell to her calves.

The effect was strange, though one that she should have expected. When she was naked, the hairless head still did not detract too much from her femaleness and her beauty. But with the green, bulky, and shapeless garments, her face suddenly became masculine and ugly.

The other women crowded around her and examined the weaving of the grass lengths and the grass belt that secured the skirt.

'It's very itchy, very uncomfortable,' Alice said. 'But it's decent. That's all I can say for it.'

'Apparently you did not mean what you said about your unconcern with nudity in a land where all are nude,' Burton said.

Alice stared coolly and said, 'I expect that everybody will be wearing these. Every decent man and woman, that is.'

'I supposed that Mrs Grundy would rear her ugly head here,' Burton replied.

'It was a shock to be among so many naked people,' Frigate said. 'Even though nudity on the beach and in the private home became commonplace in the late '80's. But it didn't take long for everyone to get used to it. Everyone except the hopelessly neurotic, I suppose.'

Burton swung around and spoke to the other women. 'What about you ladies? Are you going to wear these ugly and scratchy haycocks because one of your sex suddenly decides that she has private parts again? Can something that has been so public become private?'

Loghu, Tanya, and Alice did not understand him because he spoke in Italian. He repeated in English for the benefit of the last two.

Alice flushed and said, 'What I wear is my business. If anybody else cares to go naked when I'm decently covered, well ...!'

Loghu had not understood a word, but she understood what was going on.

She laughed and turned away. The other women seemed to be trying to guess what each one intended to do. The ugliness and the uncomfortableness of the clothing were not the issues.

'While you females are trying to make up your minds,' Burton said, 'it would be nice if you would take a bamboo pail and go with us to the river. We can bathe, fill the pails with water, find out the situation in the plains, and then return here. We may be able to build several houses – or temporary shelters – before nightfall.'

They started down the hills, pushing through the grass and carrying their grails, chert weapons, bamboo spears and buckets. They had not gone far before they encountered a number of people. Apparently, many plains dwellers had decided to move out. Not only that, some had also found chert and had made tools and weapons. These had learned the technique of working with stone from somebody, possibly from other primitives in the area. So far, Burton had seen only two specimens of non-*Homo sapiens*, and these were with him. But wherever the techniques had been learned, they had been put to good use. They passed two half-completed bamboo huts. These were round, one-roomed, and would have conical roofs thatched with the huge triangular leaves from the irontrees and with the long hill grass. One man, using a chert adze and axe, was building a short-legged bamboo bed.

Except for a number erecting rather crude huts or lean-tos without stone tools at the edge of the plains, and for a number swimming in the river, the plain was deserted. The bodies from last night's madness had been removed. So far, no one had put on a grass skirt, and many stared at Alice or even laughed and made raucous comments. Alice turned red, but she made no move to get rid of her clothes. The sun was getting hot, however, and she was scratching under her breast garment and under her skirt. It was a measure of the intensity of the irritation that she, raised by strict Victorian upper-class standards, would scratch in public.

However, when they got to the river, they saw a dozen heaps of stuff that turned out to be grass dresses. These had been left on the edge of the river by the men and women now laughing, splashing, and swimming in the river.

It was certainly a contrast to the beaches he knew. These were the same people who had accepted the bathing machines, the suits that covered them from ankle to neck, and all the other modest devices, as absolutely moral and vital to the continuation of the proper society – theirs. Yet, only one day after finding themselves here, they were swimming in the nude. And enjoying it.

Part of the acceptance of their unclothed state came from the shock of the resurrection. In addition, there was not much they could do about it that first day. And there had been a leavening of the civilized with savage peoples, or tropical civilized peoples, who were not particularly shocked by nudity.

He called out to a woman who was standing to her waist in the water. She had a coarsely pretty face and sparkling blue eyes.

'That is the woman who attacked Sir Robert Smithson,' Lev, Ruach said. 'I believe her name is Wilfreda Allport.'

Burton looked at her curiously and with appreciation of her splendid bust. He called out, 'How's the water?'

'Very nice!' she said, smiling.

He unstrapped his grail, put down the container, which held his chert knife and hand axe, and waded in with his cake of green soap. The water felt as if it was about ten degrees below his body temperature. He soaped himself while he struck up a conversation with Wilfreda. If she still harbored any resentment about Smithson, she did not show it. Her accent was heavily North Country, perhaps Cumberland.

Burton said to her, 'I heard about your little to-do with the late great hypocrite, the baronet. You should be happy now, though. You're healthy and young and beautiful again, and you don't have to toil for your bread. Also, you can do for love what you had to do for money.'

There was no use beating around the bush with a factory girl. Not that she had any.

Wilfreda gave him a stare as cool as any he had received from Alice Hargreaves. She said, 'Now, haven't you the ruddy nerve? English, aren't you? I can't place your accent, London, I'd say, with a touch of something foreign.'

'You're close,' he said, laughing. 'I'm Richard Burton, by the way. How would you like to join our group? We've banded together for protection, we're going to build some houses this afternoon. We've got a grailstone all to ourselves up in the hills.'

Wilfreda looked at the Tau Cetan and the Neanderthal. 'They're part of your mob, now? I heard about 'em; they say the monster's a man from the stars, come along in AD 2000, they do say.'

'He won't hurt you,' Burton said. 'Neither will the sub-human. What do you say?'

'I'm only a woman,' she said. 'What do I have to offer?'

'All a woman has to offer,' Burton said, grinning.

Surprisingly, she burst out laughing. She touched his chest and said, 'Now ain't you the clever one? What's the matter, you can't get no girl of your own?'

'I had one and lost her,' Burton said. That was not entirely true. He was not sure what Alice intended to do. He could not understand why she continued to stay with his group if she was so horrified and disgusted. Perhaps it was because she preferred the evil she knew to the evil she did not know. At the moment, he himself felt only disgust at her stupidity, but he did not want her to go. That love he had experienced last night may have been caused by the drug, but he still felt a residue of it. Then why was he asking this woman to join them? Perhaps it was to make Alice jealous. Perhaps it was to have a woman to fall back upon if Alice refused him tonight. Perhaps ... he did not know why.

Alice stood upon the bank, her toes almost touching the water. The bank was, at this point, only an inch above the water. The short grass continued from the plain to form a solid mat that grew down on the river bed. Burton could feel the grass under his feet as far as he could wade. He threw his soap onto the bank and swam out for about forty feet and dived down. Here the current suddenly became stronger and the depth much greater. He swam down, his eyes open, until the light failed and his ears hurt. He continued on down and then his fingers touched bottom. There was grass there, too.

When he swam back to where the water was up to his waist, he saw that Alice had shed her clothes. She was in closer to the shore, but squatting so that the water was up to her neck. She was soaping her head and face.

He called to Frigate, 'Why don't you come in?'

'I'm guarding the grails,' Frigate said.

'Very good!'

Burton swore under his breath. He should have thought of that and appointed somebody as a guard. He wasn't in actuality a good leader, he tended to let things go to pot, to permit them to disintegrate. Admit it. On Earth he had been the head of many expeditions, none of which had been distinguished by efficiency or strong management. Yet, during the Crimean War, when he was head of Beatson's Irregulars, training the wild Turkish cavalry, the Bashi-Bazouks, he had done quite well, far better than most. So he should not be reprimanding himself ...

Lev Ruach climbed out of the water and ran his hands over his skinny body to take off the drops. Burton got out, too, and sat down beside him. Alice turned her back on him, whether on purpose or not he had no way of knowing, of course.

'It's not just being young again that delights me,' Lev said in his heavily accented English. 'It's having this leg back.'

He tapped his right knee.

'I lost it in a traffic accident on the New Jersey Turnpike when I was fifty years old.'

He laughed and said, 'There was an irony to the situation that some might call fate. I had been captured by Arabs two years before when I was looking for minerals in the desert, in the state of Israel, you understand ...'

'You mean Palestine?' Burton said.

'The Jews founded an independent state in 1948,' Lev said. 'You wouldn't know about that, of course. I'll tell you all about it some time. Anyway, I was captured and tortured by Arab guerrillas. I won't go into the details; it makes me sick to recall it. But I escaped that night, though not before bashing in the heads of two with a rock and shooting two more with a rifle. The others fled, and I got away. I was lucky. An army patrol picked me up. However, two years later, when I was in the States, driving down the Turnpike, a truck, a big semi, I'll describe that later, too, cut in front of me and jackknifed and I crashed into it. I was badly hurt, and my right leg was amputated below the knee. But the point of this story is that the truck driver had been born in Syria. So, you see the Arabs were out to get me, and they did, though they did not kill me. That job was done by our friend from Tau Ceti. Though I can't say he did anything to humanity except hurry up its doom.'

'What do you mean by that?' Burton said.

'There were millions dying from famine, even the States were on a strictly rationed diet, and pollution of our water, land, and air was killing other millions. The scientists said that half of Earth's oxygen supply would be cut off in ten years because the phytoplankton of the oceans – they furnished half the world's oxygen, you know – were dying. The oceans were polluted.'

'The *oceans?*'

'You don't believe it? Well, you died in 1890, so you find it hard to credit. But some people were predicting in 1968 exactly what did happen in 2008. I believed them, I was a biochemist. But most of the population, especially those who counted, the masses and the politicians, refused to believe until it was too late. Measures were taken as the situation got worse, but they were always too weak and too late and fought against by groups that stood to lose money, if effective measures were taken. But it's a long sad story, and if we're to build houses, we'd best start immediately after lunch.'

Alice came out of the river and ran her hands over her body. The sun and the breeze dried her off quickly. She picked up her grass clothes but did not put them back on. Wilfreda asked her about them. Alice replied that they made her itch too much, but she would keep them to wear at night if it got cold. Alice was polite to Wilfreda but obviously aloof. She had overheard much of the conversation and so knew that Wilfreda had been a factory girl who had become a whore and then had died of syphilis. Or at least Wilfreda thought that the disease had killed her. She did not remember dying. Undoubtedly, as she had said cheerily, she had lost her mind first.

Alice, hearing this, moved even further away. Burton grinned, wondering what she would do if she knew that he had suffered from the same disease, caught from a slave girl in Cairo when he had been disguised as a Moslem during his trip to Mecca in 1853. He had been 'cured' and his mind had not been physically affected, though his mental suffering had been intense. But the point was that resurrection had given everybody a fresh, young, and undiseased body, and what a person had been on Earth should not influence another's attitude toward them.

Should not was not, however, *would* not.

He could not really blame Alice Hargreaves. She was the product of her society – like all women, she was what men had made her – and she had strength of character and flexibility of mind to lift herself above some of the prejudices of her time and her class. She had adapted to the nudity well enough, and she was not openly hostile or contemptuous of the girl. She had performed an act with Burton that went against a lifetime of overt and covert indoctrination. And that was on the night of the first day of her life after death, when she should have been on her knees singing hosannas because she had 'sinned' and promising that she would never 'sin' again as long as she was not put in hellfire.

As they walked across the plain, he thought about her, turning his head now and then to look back at her. That hairless head made her face look so much older but the hairlessness made her look so childlike below the navel. They all bore this contradiction, old man or woman above the neck, young child below the bellybutton.

He dropped back until he was by her side. This put him behind Frigate and Loghu. The view of Loghu would yield some profit even if his attempt to talk to Alice resulted in nothing. Loghu had a beautifully rounded posterior; her buttocks were like two eggs. And she swayed as enchantingly as Alice.

He spoke in a low voice, 'If last night distressed you so much, why do you stay with me?'

Her beautiful face became twisted and ugly.

'I am not staying with *you*! I am staying with the *group*! Moreover, I've *been* thinking about last night, though it pains me to do so. I must be fair. It was the narcotic in that hideous gum that made both of us behave the … way we did. At least, I know it was responsible for my behavior. And I'm giving you the benefit of the doubt.'

'Then there's no hope of repetition?'

'How can you ask that! Certainly not! How dare you?'

'I did not force you,' he said. 'As I have pointed out, you did what you would do if you were not restrained by your inhibitions. Those inhibitions are good things – under certain circumstances, such as being the lawful wedded wife of a man you love in the England of Earth. But Earth no longer exists, not as we knew it. Neither does England. Neither does English society. And if all of mankind has been resurrected and is scattered along this river, you still may never see your husband again. You are no longer married.

Remember ... *til death do us part*? You have died, and, therefore, parted. Moreover, *there is no giving into marriage in heaven.*'

'You are a blasphemer, Mr Burton. I read about you in the newspapers, and I read some of your books about Africa and India and that one about the Mormons in the States. I also heard stories, most of which I found hard to believe, they made you out to be so wicked. Reginald was very indignant when he read your *Kasidah*. He said he'd have no such foul atheistic literature in his house, and he threw all your books into the furnace.'

'If I'm so wicked, and you feel you're a *fallen* woman, why don't you leave?'

'Must I repeat everything? The next group might have even worse men in it. And, as you have been so kind to point out, you did not force me. Anyway, I'm sure that you have some kind of heart beneath that cynical and mocking air. I saw you weeping when you were carrying Gwenafra and she was crying.'

'You have found me out,' he said, grinning. 'Very well. So be it. I will be chivalrous, I will not attempt to seduce you or to molest you in any way. But the next time you see me chewing the gum, you would do well to hide. Meanwhile, I give my word of honor; you have nothing to fear from me as long as I am not under the influence of the gum.'

Her eyes widened, and she stopped. 'You plan to use it again?'

'Why not? It apparently turned some people into violent beasts, but it had no such effect on me. I feel no craving for it, so I doubt it's habit-forming. I used to smoke a pipe of opium now and then, you know, and I did not become addicted to it, so I don't suppose I have a psychological weakness for drugs.'

'I understood that you were very often deep in your cups, Mister Burton. You and that nauseating creature, Mr Swinburne ...'

She stopped talking. A man had called out to her, and, though she did not understand Italian, she understood his obscene gesture. She blushed all over but walked briskly on. Burton glared at the man. He was a well-built brown-skinned youth with a big nose, a weak chin, and close-set eyes. His speech was that of the criminal class of the city of Bologna, where Burton had spent much time while investigating Etruscan relics and graves. Behind him were ten men, most of them as unprepossessing and as wicked-looking as their leader, and five women. It was evident that the men wanted to add more women to the group. It was also evident that they would like to get their hands on the stone weapons of Burton's group. They were armed only with their grails or with bamboo sticks.

11

Burton spoke sharply, and his people closed up. Kazz did not understand his words, but he sensed at once what was happening. He dropped back to form the rearguard with Burton. His brutish appearance and the hand axe in his huge fist checked the Bolognese somewhat. They followed the group, making loud comments and threats, but they did not get much closer. When they reached the hills, however, the leader of the gang shouted a command, and it attacked.

The youth with the close-set eyes, yelling, swinging his grail at the end of the strap, ran at Burton. Burton gauged the swing of the cylinder and then launched his bamboo spear just as the grail was arcing outward. The stone tip went into the man's solar plexus, and he fell on his side with the spear sticking in him. The sub-human struck a swinging grail with a stick, which was knocked out of his hand. He leaped inward and brought the edge of the hand axe against the top of the head of his attacker, and that man went down with a bloody skull.

Little Lev Ruach threw his grail into the chest of a man and ran up and jumped on him. His feet drove into the face of the man, who was getting up again. The man went backward; Ruach bounded up and gashed the man's shoulder with his chert knife. The man, screaming, got to his feet and raced away.

Frigate did better than Burton had expected him to, since he had turned pale and begun shaking when the gang had first challenged them. His grail was strapped to his left wrist while his right held a hand axe. He charged into the group, was hit on the shoulder with a grail, the impact of which was lessened when he partially blocked it with his grail, and he fell on his side. A man lifted a bamboo stick with both hands to bring it down on Frigate, but he rolled away, bringing his grail up and blocking the stick as it came down. Then he was up, his head butting into the man and carrying him back. Both went down, Frigate on top, and his stone axe struck the man twice on the temple.

Alice had thrown her grail into the face of a man and then stabbed at him with the fire-sharpened end of her bamboo spear. Loghu ran around to the side of the man and hit him across the head with her stick so hard that he dropped to his knees.

The fight was over in sixty seconds. The other men fled with their women behind them. Burton turned the screaming leader onto his back and pulled his spear out of the pit of his stomach. The tip had not gone in more than half an inch.

The man got to his feet and, clutching the streaming wound, staggered off across the plains. Two of the gang were unconscious but would probably survive. The man Frigate had attacked was dead.

The American had turned from pale to red and then back to pale. But he did not look contrite or sickened. If his expression held anything, it was elation. And relief.

He said, 'That was the first man I've ever killed! The first!'

'I doubt that it'll be the last,' Burton said. 'Unless you're killed first.'

Ruach, looking at the corpse, said, 'A dead man looks just as dead here as on Earth. I wonder where those who are killed in the afterlife go?'

'If we live long enough, we might find out. You two women gave a very fine account of yourselves.'

Alice said, 'I did what had to be done,' and walked away. She was pale and shaking. Loghu, on the other hand, seemed exhilarated.

They got to the grailstone about a half hour before noon. Things had changed. Their quiet little hollow contained about sixty people, many of whom were working on pieces of chert. One man was holding a bloody eye into which a chip of stone had flown. Several more were bleeding from the face or holding smashed fingers.

Burton was upset but he could do nothing about it. The only hope for regaining the quiet retreat was that the lack of water would drive the intruders away. That hope went quickly. A woman told him that there was a small cataract about a mile and a half to the west. It fell from the top of the mountain down the tip of an arrowhead-shaped canyon and into a large hole which it had only half-filled. Eventually, it should spill out and take a course through the hills and spread out on the plain. Unless, of course, stone from the mountain base was brought down to make a channel for the stream.

'Or we make water pipes out of the big bamboo,' Frigate said.

They put their grails on the rock, each carefully noting the exact location of his, and they waited. He intended to move on after the grails were filled. A location halfway between the cataract and the grailstone would be advantageous, and they might not be so crowded.

The blue flames roared out above the stone just as the sun reached its zenith. This time, the grails yielded an antipasto salad, Italian black bread with melted garlic butter, spaghetti and meatballs, a cupful of dry red wine, grapes, more coffee crystals, ten cigarettes, a marihuana stick, a cigar, more toilet paper and a cake of soap, and four chocolate creams. Some people complained that they did not like Italian food, but no one refused to eat.

The group, smoking their cigarettes, walked along the base of the mountain to the cataract. This was at the end of the triangular canyon, where a number of men and women had set up camp around the hole. The water was icy cold. After washing out their containers, drying them, and refilling the buckets, they went back in the direction of the grailstone. After a half mile, they chose a hill covered by pines except for the apex, on which a great irontree grew. There was plenty of bamboo of all sizes growing around them. Under the direction of Kazz and of Frigate, who had spent a few years in Malaysia, they cut down bamboo and built their huts. These were round buildings with a single door and a window in the rear and a conical thatched roof. They worked swiftly and did not try for nicety, so that by dinnertime everything except the roofs was finished. Frigate and Monat were picked to stay behind as guards while the others took the grails to the stone. Here they found about 300 people constructing lean-tos and huts. Burton had expected this. Most people would not want to walk a half mile every day three times a day for their meals. They would prefer to cluster around the grailstones. The huts here were arranged haphazardly and closer than necessary. There was still the problem of getting fresh water, which was why he was surprised that there were so many here. But he was informed by a pretty Slovene that a source of water had been found close by only this afternoon. A spring ran from a cave almost in a straight line up from the rock. Burton investigated. Water had broken out from a cave and was trickling down the face of the cliff into a basin about fifty feet wide and eight deep.

He wondered if this was an afterthought on the part of Whoever had created this place.

He returned just as the blue flames thundered.

Kazz suddenly stopped to relieve himself. He did not bother to turn away; Loghu giggled; Tanya turned red; the Italian women were used to seeing men leaning against buildings wherever the fancy took them; Wilfreda was used to anything; Alice, surprisingly, ignored him as if he were a dog. And that might explain her attitude. To her, Kazz was not human and so could not be expected to act as humans were expected to act.

There was no reason to reprimand Kazz for this just now, especially when Kazz did not understand his language. But he would have to use sign language the next time Kazz proceeded to relieve himself while they were sitting around and eating. Everybody had to learn certain limits, and anything that upset others while they were eating should be forbidden. And that, he thought, included quarreling during mealtimes. To be fair, he would have to admit that he had participated in more than his share of dinner disputes in his lifetime.

He patted Kazz on top of the bread loaf-shaped skull as he passed him. Kazz looked at him and Burton shook his head, figuring that Kazz would find out why when he learned to speak English. But he forgot his intention, and he stopped and rubbed the top of his own head. Yes, there was a very fine fuzz there.

He felt his face, which was as smooth as ever. But his armpits were fuzzy.

The pubic area was, however, smooth. That might be a slower growth than scalp hair, though. He told the others, and they inspected themselves and each other. It was true. Their hair was returning, at least, on their heads and their armpits. Kazz was the exception. His hair was growing out all over him except on his face.

The discovery made them jubilant. Laughing, joking, they walked along the base of the mountain in the shadow. They turned east then and waded through the grass of four hills before coming up the slope of the hill they were beginning to think of as home. Halfway up it, they stopped, silent. Frigate and Monat had not returned their calls.

After telling them to spread out and to proceed slowly, Burton led them up the hill. The huts were deserted, and several of the little huts had been kicked or trampled. He felt a chill, as if a cold wind had blown on him. The silence, the damaged huts, the complete absence of the two, was foreboding.

A minute later, they heard a halloo and turned to look down the hill. The skin-heads of Monat and Frigate appeared in the grasses and then they were coming up the hill. Monat looked grave, but the American was grinning. His face was bruised over the cheek, and the knuckles of both hands were torn and bloody.

'We just got back from chasing off four men and three women who wanted to take over our huts,' he said. 'I told them they could build their own, and that you'd be back right away and beat hell out of them if they didn't take off. They understood me all right, they spoke English. They had been resurrected at the grailstone a mile north of ours along the river. Most of the people there were Triestans of your time, but about ten, all together, were Chicagoans who'd died about 1985. The distribution of the dead sure is funny, isn't it? There's a random choice operating along here, I'd say.

'Anyway, I told them what Mark Twain said the devil said. *You Chicagoans think you're the best people here whereas the truth is you're just the most numerous.* That didn't go over very well, they seemed to think that I should be buddy-buddies with them because I was an American. One of the women offered herself to me if I'd change sides and take their part in appropriating the huts. She was the one who was living with two of the men. I said no. They said they'd take the huts anyway, and over my dead body if they had to.

'But they talked more brave than they were. Monat scared them just by looking at them. And we did have the stone weapons and spears. Still, their leader was whipping them up into rushing us, when I took a good hard look at one of them.

'His head was bald so he didn't have that thick straight black hair, and he was about thirty-five when I first knew him, and he wore thick shell-rimmed glasses then, and I hadn't seen him for fifty-four years. But I stepped up closer, and I looked into his face, which was grinning just like I remembered it, like the proverbial skunk, and I said, "*Lem? Lem Sharkko! It* is *Lem Sharkko*, isn't it?"

'His eyes opened then, and he grinned even more, and he took my hand, *my hand*, after *all* he'd done to me, and he cried out as if we were long-lost brothers, "It is, it is I. It's Pete Frigate! My God, Pete Frigate!"

'I was almost glad to see him and for the same reason he said he was glad to see me. But then I told myself, "This is the crooked publisher that cheated you out of $4,000 when you were just getting started as a writer and ruined your career for years. This is the slimy schlock dealer who cheated you and at least four other writers out of a lot of money and then declared bankruptcy and skipped. And then he inherited a lot of money from an uncle and lived very well indeed, thus proving that crime *did* pay. This is the man you have not forgotten, not only because of what he did to you and others but because of so many other crooked publishers you ran into later on."'

Burton grinned and said, 'I once said that priests, politicians, and publishers would never get past the gates of heaven. But I was wrong, that is, if this is heaven.'

'Yeah, I know,' Frigate said. 'I've never forgotten that you said that. Anyway, I put down my natural joy at seeing a familiar face again, and I said, "Sharkko ..."'

'With a name like that, he got you to trust him?' Alice said.

'He told me it was a Czech name that meant *trustworthy*. Like everything else he told me, it was a lie. Anyway, I had just about convinced myself that Monat and I should let them take over. We'd retire and then we'd run them out when you came back from the grailstone. That was the smart thing to do. But when I recognized Sharkko, I got so *mad!* I said, grinning, "Gee, it's really great to see your face after all these years. Especially here where there are no cops or courts!"

'And I hit him right in the nose! He went over flat on his back, with his nose spouting blood. Monat and I rushed the others, and I kicked one, and then another hit me on the cheek with his grail. I was knocked silly, but Monat knocked one out with the butt of his spear and cracked the ribs of another; he's skinny but he's awful *fast*, and what *he* doesn't know about self-defense – or offense! Sharkko got up then and I hit with my other fist but only a glancing blow along his jaw. It hurt my fist more than it hurt his jaw. He spun around and took off, and I went after him. The others took off, too, with Monat beating them on the tail with his spear. I chased Sharkko up the next hill and caught him on the downslope and punched him but good! He crawled away, begging for *mercy*, which I gave him with a kick in the rear that rolled him howling all the way down the hill.'

Frigate was still shaking with reaction, but he was pleased.

'I was afraid I was going to turn chicken there for a while,' he said. 'After all, all that had been so long ago and in another world, and maybe we're here to forgive our enemies – and some of our friends – and be forgiven. But on the other hand, I thought, maybe we're here so we can give a little back of what we had to take on Earth. What about it, Lev? Wouldn't you like a chance to turn Hitler over a fire? Very slowly over a fire?'

'I don't think you could compare a crooked publisher to Hitler,' Ruach said. 'No, I wouldn't want to turn him over a fire. I might want to starve him to death, or feed him just enough to keep him alive. But I wouldn't do that. What good would it do? Would it make him change his mind about anything, would he then believe that Jews were human beings? No, I would do nothing to him if he were in my power except kill him so he couldn't hurt others. But I'm not so sure that killing him would mean he'd stay dead. Not here.'

'You're a real Christian,' Frigate said, grinning.

'I thought you were my friend!' Ruach said.

12

This was the second time that Burton had heard the name Hitler. He intended to find out all about him, but at the moment everybody would have to put off talking to finish the roofs on the huts. They all pitched in, cutting off more grass with the little scissors they had found in their grails, or climbing the irontrees and tearing off the huge triangular green and scarlet-laced leaves. The roofs left much to be desired. Burton meant to search around for a professional thatcher and learn the proper techniques. The beds would have to be, for the time being, piles of grass on top of which were piles of the softer irontree leaves. The blankets would be another pile of the same leaves.

'Thank God, or Whoever, that there is no insect life,' Burton said.

He lifted the gray metal cup which still held two ounces of the best scotch he had ever tasted.

'Here's to Whoever. If he had raised us just to live on an exact duplicate of Earth, we'd be sharing our beds with ten thousands kinds of biting, scratching, stinging, scraping, tickling, bloodsucking vermin.'

They drank, and then they sat around the fire for a while and smoked and talked. The shadow darkened, the sky lost its blue, and the gigantic stars and great sheets, which had been dimly seen ghosts just before dusk, blossomed out. The sky was indeed a blaze of glory.

'Like a Sime illustration,' Frigate said.

Burton did not know what a Sime was. Half of the conversation with the non-nineteenth centurians consisted of them explaining their references and he explaining his.

Burton rose and went over to the other side of the fire and squatted by Alice. She had just returned from putting the little girl, Gwenafra, to bed in a hut.

Burton held out a stick of gum to Alice and said, 'I just had half a piece. Would you care for the other half?'

She looked at him without expression and said, 'No, thanks.'

'There are eight huts,' he said. 'There isn't any doubt about who is sharing which hut with whom, except for Wilfreda, you, and me.'

'I don't think there's any doubt about that,' she said.

'Then you're sleeping with Gwenafra?'

She kept her face turned away from him. He squatted for a few seconds and then got up and went back to the other side and sat down by Wilfreda.

'You can move on, Sir Richard,' she said. Her lip was curled. 'Lord grab me, I don't like being second choice. You could of asked 'er where nobody could of seen you. I got some pride, too.'

He was silent for a minute. His first impulse had been to lash out at her with a sharp-pointed insult. But she was right. He had been too contemptuous of her. Even if she had been a whore, she had a right to be treated as a human being. Especially since she maintained that it was hunger that had driven her to prostitution, though he had been skeptical about that. Too many prostitutes had to rationalize their profession; too many had justifying fantasies about their entrance into the business. Yet, her rage at Smithson and her behavior toward him indicated that she was sincere.

He stood up and said, 'I didn't mean to hurt your feelings.'

'Are you in love with her?' Wilfreda said, looking up at him.

'I've only told one woman that I ever loved her,' he said.

'Your wife?'

'No. The girl died before I could marry her.'

'And how long was you married?'

'Twenty-nine years, though it's none of your business.'

'Lord grab me! All that time, and you never once told her you loved her!'

'It wasn't necessary,' he said, and walked away. The hut he chose was occupied by Monat and Kazz. Kazz was snoring away; Monat was leaning on his elbow and smoking a marihuana stick. Monat preferred that to tobacco, because it tasted more like his native tobacco. However, he got little effect from it. On the other hand, tobacco sometimes gave him fleeting but vividly colored visions.

Burton decided to save the rest of his dreamgum, as he called it. He lit up a cigarette, knowing that marihuana would probably make his rage and frustration even darker. He asked Monat questions about his home, Ghuurrkh. He was intensely interested, but the marihuana betrayed him, and he drifted away while the Cetan's voice became fainter and fainter.

'... cover your eyes now, boys!' Gilchrist said in his broad Scots speech.

Richard looked at Edward; Edward grinned and put his hands over his eyes, but he was surely peeking through the spaces between his fingers. Richard placed his own hands over his eyes and continued to stand on tiptoe. Although he and his brother were standing on boxes, they still had to stretch to see over the heads of the adults in front of them.

The woman's head was in the stock by now; her long brown hair had fallen over her face. He wished he could see her expression as she stared down at the basket waiting for her, or for her head, rather.

'Don't peek now, boys!' Gilchrist said again.

There was a roll of drums, a single shout, and the blade raced downward, and then a concerted shout from the crowd, mingled with some screams and moans, and the head fell down. The neck spurted out blood and would never stop. It kept spurting and spurting while the sun gleamed on it, it spurted out and covered the crowd and, though he was at least fifty yards from her, the blood struck him in the hands and seeped down between his fingers and over his face, filling his eyes and blinding him and making his lips sticky and salty. He screamed ...

'Wake up, Dick!' Monat was saying. He was shaking Burton by the shoulder. 'Wake up! You must have been having a nightmare!'

Burton, sobbing and shivering, sat up. He rubbed his hands and then felt his face. Both were wet. But with perspiration, not with blood.

'I was dreaming,' he said. 'I was just six years old and in the city of Tours. In France, where we were living then. My tutor, John Gilchrist, took me and my brother Edward to see the execution of a woman who had poisoned her family. It was a treat, Gilchrist said.

'I was excited, and I peeked through my fingers when he told us not to watch the final seconds, when the blade of the guillotine came down. But I did; I had to. I remember getting a little sick at my stomach but that was the only effect the gruesome scene had on me. I seemed to have dislocated myself while I was watching it; it was as if I saw the whole thing through a thick glass, as if it were unreal. Or I was unreal. So I wasn't really horrified.'

Monat had lit another marihuana. Its light was enough so that Burton could see him shaking his head. 'How savage! You mean that you not only killed your criminals, you cut their heads off! In public. And you allowed children to see it!'

'They were a little more humane in England,' Burton said. 'They hung the criminals!'

'At least the French permitted the people to be fully aware that they were spilling the blood of their criminals,' Monat said. 'The blood was on their hands. But apparently this aspect did not occur to anyone. Not consciously, anyway. So now, after how many years – sixty-three? – you smoke some marihuana and you relive an incident which you had always believed did not harm you. But, this time, you recoil with horror. You screamed like a frightened child. You reacted as you should have reacted when you were a child. I would say that the marihuana dug away some deep layers of repression and uncovered the horror that had been buried there for sixty-three years.'

'Perhaps,' Burton said.

He stopped. There was thunder and lightning in the distance. A minute later, a rushing sound came, and then the patter of drops on the roof. It had rained about this time last night, about three in the morning, he would guess. And this second night, it was raining about the same time. The downpour became heavy, but the roof had been packed tightly, and no water dripped down through it. Some water did, however, come under the back wall, which was uphill. It spread out over the floor but did not wet them, since the grass and leaves under them formed a mat about ten inches thick.

Burton talked with Monat until the rain ceased approximately half an hour later. Monat fell asleep; Kazz had never awakened. Burton tried to get back to sleep but could not. He had never felt so alone, and he was afraid that he might slip back into the nightmare. After a while, he left the hut and walked to the one which Wilfreda had chosen. He smelled the tobacco before he got to the doorway. The tip of her cigarette glowed in the dark. She was a dim figure sitting upright in the pile of grass and leaves.

'Hello,' she said. 'I was hoping you would come.'

'It's the instinct to own property,' Burton said.

'I doubt that it's an instinct in man,' Frigate said. 'Some people in the '60's – 1960's, that is – tried to demonstrate that man had an instinct which they called the *territorial imperative*. But …'

'I like that phrase. It has a fine ring to it,' Burton said.

'I knew you'd like it,' Frigate said. 'But Ardrey and others tried to prove that man not only had an instinct to claim a certain area of land as his own, he also was descended from a killer ape. And the instinct to kill was still strong in his heritage from the killer ape. Which explained national boundaries, patriotism both national and local, capitalism, war, murder, crime, and so forth. But the other school of thought, or of the temperamental inclination, maintained that all these are the results of culture, of the cultural continuity of societies dedicated from earliest times to tribal hostilities, to war, to murder, to crime, and so forth. Change the culture, and the killer ape is missing. Missing because he was never there, like the little man on the stairs. The killer was the society, and society bred the new killers out of every batch of babies. But there were some societies, composed of pre-literates, it is true, but still societies, that did not breed killers. And they were proof that man was not descended from a killer ape. Or I should say, he was perhaps descended from the ape but he did not carry the killing genes any longer, any more than he carried the genes for a heavy supraorbital ridge of hairy skin or thick bones or a skull with only 650 cubic centimeters capacity.'

'That is all very interesting,' Burton said. 'We'll go into the theory more deeply at another time. Let me point out to you, however, that almost every member of resurrected humanity comes from a culture which encouraged war and murder and crime and rape and robbery and madness. It is these people among whom we are living and with whom we have to deal. There may be a new generation some day. I don't know. It's too early to say, since we've only been here for seven days. But, like it or not, we are in a world populated by beings who quite often act as *if* they were killer apes.

'In the meantime, let's get back to our model.'

They were sitting on bamboo stools before Burton's hut. On a little bamboo table in front of them was a model of a boat made from pine and bamboo. It had a double hull across the top of which was a platform with a low railing in the center. It had a single mast, very tall, with a fore-and-aft rig, a balloon jib sail, and a slightly raised bridge with a wheel. Burton and Frigate had used chert knives and the edge of the scissors to carve the model of the catamaran. Burton had decided to name the boat, when it was built, *The Hadji*. It would be going on a pilgrimage, though its goal was not Mecca. He intended to sail it up The River as far as it would go. (By now, the river had become The River.)

The two had been talking about the *territorial imperative* because of some anticipated difficulties in getting the boat built. By now the people in this area were somewhat settled. They had staked out their property and constructed their dwellings or were still working on them. These ranged all the way from lean-tos to relatively grandiose buildings that would be made of bamboo logs and stone, have four rooms, and be two stories high. Most of them were near the grailstones along The River and at the base of the mountain. Burton's survey, completed two days before, resulted in an estimate of about 260 to 261 people per square mile. For every square mile of flat plain on each side of The River, there were approximately 2.4 square miles of hills. But the hills were so high and irregular that their actual inhabitable area was about nine square miles. In the three areas that he had studied, he found that about one-third had built their dwellings close to the Riverside grailstone and one-third around the inland grailstones. Two hundred and sixty-one persons per square mile seemed like a heavy population, but the hills were so heavily wooded and convoluted in topography that a small group living there could feel isolated. And the plain was seldom crowded except at mealtimes, because the plains people were in the woods or fishing along the edge of The River. Many were working on dugouts or bamboo boats with the idea of fishing in the middle of The River. Or, like Burton, of going exploring.

The stands of bamboo had disappeared, although it was evident that they would be quickly replaced. The bamboo had a phenomenal growth. Burton estimated that a fifty-foot high plant could grow from start to finish in ten days.

His gang had worked hard and cut down all they thought they would need for the boat. But they wanted to keep thieves away, so they used more wood to erect a high fence. This was being finished the same day that the model was completed. The trouble was that they would have to build the boat on the plain. It could never be gotten through the woods and down the various hills if it were built on this site.

'Yeah, but if we move out and set up a new base, we'll run into opposition,' Frigate had said. 'There isn't a square inch of the high-grass border that isn't claimed. As it is, you have to trespass to get to the plain. So far, nobody has tried to be hard-nosed about their property rights, but this can change any day. And if you build the ship a little back from the high-grass border, you can get it out of the woods okay and between the huts. But you'd have to set up a guard night and day, otherwise your stuff will be stolen. Or destroyed. You know these barbarians.'

He was referring to the huts wrecked while their owners were away and to the fouling of the pools below the cataract and the spring. He was also referring to the highly unsanitary habits of many of the locals. These would not use the little outhouses put up by various people for the public.

'We'll erect new houses and a boatyard as close to the border as we can get,' Burton said. 'Then we'll chop down any tree that gets in our way and we'll ram our way past anybody who refuses us right-of-way.'

It was Alice who went down to some people who had huts on the border between the plain and the hills and talked them into making a trade. She did not tell anybody what she intended. She had known of three couples who were unhappy with their location because of lack of privacy. These made an agreement and moved into the huts of Burton's gang on the twelfth day after Resurrection, on a Thursday. By a generally agreed upon convention, Sunday, the first, was Resurrection Day. Ruach said he would prefer that the first day be called Saturday, or even better, just First Day. But he was in an area predominately Gentile – or ex-Gentile (but once a Gentile always a Gentile) – so he would go along with the others. Ruach had a bamboo stick on which he kept count of the days by notching it each morning. The stick was driven into the ground before his hut.

Transferring the lumber for the boat took four days of heavy work. By then, the Italian couples decided that they had had enough of *working their fingers to the bone*. After all, why get on a boat and go some place else when every place was probably just like this? They had obviously been raised from the dead so they could enjoy themselves. Otherwise, why the liquor, the cigarettes, the marihuana, the dreamgum, and the nudity?

They left without ill feelings on the part of anybody; in fact, they were given a going-away party. The next day, the twentieth of Year 1, A.R., two events occurred, one of which solved one puzzle and the other of which added one, though it was not very important.

The group went across the plain to the grailstone at dawn. They found two new people near the grailstone, both of them sleeping. They were easily aroused, but they seemed alarmed and confused. One was a tall brown-skinned man who spoke an unknown language. The other was a tall, handsome, well-muscled man with gray eyes and black hair. His speech was unintelligible until Burton suddenly understood that he was speaking English. It was the Cumberland dialect of the English spoken during the reign of King Edward I, sometimes called *Longshanks*. Once Burton and Frigate had mastered the sounds and made certain transpositions, they were able to carry on a halting conversation with him. Frigate had an extensive reading vocabulary of Early Middle English, but he had never encountered many of the words or certain grammatical usages.

John de Greystock was born in the manor of Greystoke in the Cumberland country. He had accompanied Edward I into France when the king invaded Gascony. There he had distinguished himself in arms, if he was to be believed. Later, he was summoned to Parliament as Baron Greystoke and then again went to the wars in Gascony. He was in the retinue of Bishop Anthony Bec, Patriarch of Jerusalem. In the 28th and 29th years of Edward's reign, he fought against the Scots. He died in 1305, without children, but he settled his manor and barony on his cousin, Ralph, son of Lord Grimthorpe in Yorkshire.

He had been resurrected somewhere along The River among a people about ninety percent early fourteenth-century English and Scottish and ten percent ancient Sybarites. The peoples across The River were a mixture of Mongols of the time of Kubla Khan and some dark people the identity of which Greystoke did not know. His description fitted North American Indians.

The nineteenth day after Resurrection, the savages across The River had attacked. Apparently they did so for no other reason than they wanted a good fight, which they got. The weapons were mostly sticks and grails, because there was little stone in the area. John de Greystock put ten Mongols out of commission with his grail and then was hit on the head with a rock and stabbed with the fire-hardened tip of a bamboo spear. He awoke, naked, with only his grail – or a grail – by this grailstone.

The other man told his story with signs and pantomime. He had been fishing when his hook was taken by something so powerful that it pulled him into the water. Coming back up, he had struck his head on the bottom of the boat and drowned.

The question of what happened to those who were killed in the afterlife was answered. Why they were not raised in the same area as in which they died was another question.

The second event was the failure of the grails to deliver the noonday meal. Instead, crammed inside the cylinders were six cloths. These were of various sizes and of many different colors, hues, and patterns. Four were obviously designed to be worn as kilts. They could be fastened around the body with magnetic tabs inside the cloth. Two were of thinner almost transparent material and obviously made as brassieres, though they could be used for other purposes. Though the cloth was soft and absorbent, it stood up under the roughest treatment and could not be cut by the sharpest chert or bamboo knife.

Mankind gave a collective whoop of delight on finding these 'towels.' Though men and women had by then become accustomed, or at least resigned, to nudity, the more aesthetic and the less adaptable had found the universal spectacle of human genitalia unbeautiful or even repulsive. Now, they had kilts and bras and turbans. The latter were used to cover up their heads while their hair was growing back in. Later, turbans became a customary headgear.

Hair was returning everywhere except on the face.

Burton was bitter about this. He had always taken pride in his long mustachios and forked beard; he claimed that their absence made him feel more naked than the lack of trousers.

Wilfreda had laughed and said, 'I'm glad they're gone. I've always hated hair on men's faces. Kissing a man with a beard was like sticking my face in a bunch of broken bedsprings.'

13

Sixty days had passed. The boat had been pushed across the plain on big bamboo rollers. The day of the launching had arrived. *The Hadji* was about forty feet long and essentially consisted of two sharp-prowed bamboo hulls fastened together with a platform, a bowsprit with a balloon sail and a single mast, fore-and-aft rigged, with sails of woven bamboo fibers. It was steered by a great oar of pine, since a rudder and steering wheel were not practicable. Their only material for ropes at this time was the grass, though it would not be long before leather ropes would be made from the tanned skin and entrails of some of the larger river fish. A dugout fashioned by Kazz from a pine log was tied down to the foredeck.

Before they could get it into the water, Kazz made some difficulties. By now, he could speak a very broken and limited English and some oaths in Arabic, Baluchi, Swahili, and Italian, all learned from Burton.

'Must need ... wacha call it? ... *wallah!* ... what it word? ... kill somebody before place boat on river ... you know ... *merda* ... need word, Burton-naq ... you give, Burton-naq word ... word ... kill man so god, *Kabburganagruebemss* water god ... no sink boat ... get angry ... drown us ... eat us:

'Sacrifice?' Burton said.

'Many bloody thanks, Burton-naq. Sacrifice! Cut throat ... put on boat ... rub it on wood ... then water god not mad at us ...'

'We don't do that,' Burton said.

Kazz argued but finally agreed to get on the boat. His face was long, and he looked very nervous. Burton, to ease him, told him that this was not Earth. It was a different world, as he could see at a quick glance around him and especially at the stars. The gods did not live in this valley. Kazz listened and smiled, but he still looked as if he expected to see the hideous green-bearded face and bulging fishy eyes of *Kabburganagruebemss* rising from the depths.

The plain was crowded around the boat that morning. Everybody was there for many miles around, since anything out of the usual was entertainment. They shouted and laughed and joked. Though some of the comments were derisive, all were in good humor. Before the boat was rolled off the bank into The River, Burton stood up on its 'bridge,' a slightly raised platform, and held up his hand for silence. The crowd's chatter died away, and he spoke in Italian.

'Fellow lazari, friends, dwellers in the valley of the Promised Land! We leave you in a few minutes ...'

'If the boat doesn't capsize!' Frigate muttered.

'... to go up The River, against the wind and the current. We take the difficult route because the difficult always yields the greatest reward, if you believe what the moralists on Earth told us, and you know now how much to believe them!'

Laughter. With scowls here and there from diehard religionists.

'On Earth, as some of you may know, I once led an expedition into deepest and darkest Africa to find the headwaters of the Nile. I did not find them, though I came close, and I was cheated out of the rewards by a man who owed everything to me, a Mister John Hanning Speke. If I should encounter him on my journey upRiver, I will know how to deal with him ...'

'Good God!' Frigate said. 'Would you have him kill himself again with remorse and shame?'

'... but the point is that this River may be one far far greater than any Nile, which as you may or may not know, was the longest river on Earth, despite the erroneous claims of Americans for their Amazon and Missouri-Mississippi complexes. Some of you have asked why we should set out for a goal that lies we know not how far away or that might not even exist. I will tell you that we are setting sail because the Unknown exists and we would make it the Known. That's all! And here, contrary to our sad and frustrating experience on Earth, money is not required to outfit us or to keep us going. King Cash is dead, and good riddance to him! Nor do we have to fill out hundreds of petitions and forms and beg audiences of influential people and minor bureaucrats to get permission to pass up The River. There are no national borders ...'

'... as yet,' Frigate said.

'... nor passports required nor officials to bribe. We just build a boat without having to obtain a license, and we sail off without a by-your-leave from any muckamuck, high, middle, or low. We are free for the first time in man's history. Free! And so we bid you adieu, for I will not say goodbye ...'

'... you never would,' Frigate muttered.

'... because we may be back a thousand years or so from now! So I say adieu, the crew says adieu, we thank you for your help in building the boat and for your help in launching us. I hereby hand over my position as Her British Majesty's Consul at Trieste to whomever wishes to accept it and declare myself to be a free citizen of the world of The River! I will pay tribute to none, owe fealty to none; to myself only will I be true!'

'Do what thy manhood bids thee do, from none but self expect applause;
'He noblest lives and noblest dies who makes and keeps his self-made laws,'
Frigate chanted.

Burton glanced at the American but did not stop his speech. Frigate was quoting lines from Burton's poem, *The Kasidah of Haji Abdu Al-Yazdi*. It was not the first time that he had quoted from Burton's prose or poetry. And though Burton sometimes found the American to be irritating, he could not become too angry at a man who had admired him enough to memorize his words.

A few minutes later, when the boat was pushed into The River by some men and women and the crowd was cheering, Frigate quoted him again. He looked at the thousands of handsome youths by the waters, their skins bronzed by the sun, their kilts and bras and turbans wind-moved and colorful, and he said,

*'Ah! gay the day with shine of sun, and bright the breeze, and blithe the throng
'Met on the Riverbank to play, when I was young, when I was young.'*

The boat slid out, and its prow was turned by the wind and the current downstream, but Burton shouted orders, and the sails were pulled up, and he turned the great handle of the paddle so that the nose swung around and then they were beating to windward. *The Hadji* rose and fell in the waves, the water hissing as it was cut by the twin prows. The sun was bright and warm, the breeze cooled them off, they felt happy but also a little anxious as the familiar banks and faces faded away. They had no maps nor travelers' tales to guide them; the world would be created with every mile forward.

That evening, as they made their first beaching, an incident occurred that puzzled Burton. Kazz had just stepped ashore among a group of curious people, when he became very excited. He began to jabber in his native tongue and tried to seize a man standing near. The man fled and was quickly lost in the crowd.

When asked by Burton what he was doing, Kazz said, 'He not got ... uh whacha call it? ... it ...' and he pointed at his forehead. Then he traced several unfamiliar symbols in the air. Burton meant to pursue the matter, but Alice, suddenly wailing, ran up to a man. Evidently, she had thought he was a son who had been killed in World War I. There was some confusion. Alice admitted that she had made a mistake. By then, other business came up. Kazz did not mention the matter again, and Burton forgot about it. But he was to remember.

Exactly 415 days later, they had passed 24,900 grailrocks on the right bank of The River. Tacking, running against wind and current, averaging sixty miles a day, stopping during the day to charge their grails and at night to sleep, sometimes stopping all day so they could stretch their legs and talk to others besides the crew, they had journeyed 24,900 miles. On Earth, that distance would have been about once around the equator. If the Mississippi-Missouri, Nile, Congo, Amazon, Yangtze, Volga, Amur, Hwang, Lena, and Zambezi had been put end to end to make one great river, it still would not have been as long as that stretch of The River they had passed. Yet The River went on and on, making great bends, winding back and forth. Everywhere were the plains along the stream, the tree-covered hills behind, and, towering, impassable, unbroken, the mountain range.

Occasionally, the plains narrowed, and the hills advanced to The Riveredge. Sometimes, The River widened and became a lake, three miles, five miles, six miles across. Now and then, the line of the mountains curved in toward each other, and the boat shot through canyons where the narrow passage forced the current to boil through and the sky was a blue thread far far above and the black walls pressed in on them.

And, always, there was humankind. Day and night, men, women, and children thronged the banks of The River and in the hills were more.

By then, the sailors recognized a pattern. Humanity had been resurrected along The River in a rough chronological and national sequence. The boat had passed by the area that held Slovenes, Italians, and Austrians who had died in the last decade of the nineteenth century, had passed by Hungarians, Norwegians, Finns, Greeks, Albanians, and Irish. Occasionally, they put in at areas which held peoples from other times and places. One was a twenty-mile stretch containing Australian aborigines who had never seen a European while on Earth. Another hundred-mile length was populated by Tocharians (Loghu's people). These had lived around the time of Christ in what later became Chinese Turkestan. They represented the easternmost extension of Indo-European speakers in ancient times; their culture had flourished for a while, then died before the encroachment of the desert and invasions of barbarians.

Through admittedly hasty and uncertain surveys, Burton had determined that each area was, in general, comprised of about 60 per cent of a particular nationality and century, 30 percent of some other people, usually from a different time, and 10 per cent from any time and place.

All men had awakened from death circumcised. All women had been resurrected as virgins. For most women, Burton commented, this state had not lasted beyond the first night on this planet.

So far, they had neither seen nor heard of a pregnant woman. Whoever had placed them here must have sterilized them, and with good reason. If mankind could reproduce, the Rivervalley would be jammed solid with bodies within a century.

At first, there had seemed to be no animal life but man. Now it was known that several species of worms emerged from the soil at night. And The River contained at least a hundred species of fish, ranging from creatures six inches long to the sperm whale-sized fish, the 'riverdragon,' which lived on the bottom of The River a thousand feet down. Frigate said that the animals were there for a good purpose. The fish scavenged to keep The River waters clean. Some types of worm ate waste matter and corpses. Other types served the normal function of earthworms.

Gwenafra was a little taller. All the children were growing up. Within twelve years, there would not be an infant or adolescent within the valley, if conditions everywhere conformed to what the voyagers had so far seen.

Burton, thinking of this, said to Alice, 'This Reverend Dodgson friend of yours, the fellow who loved only little girls. He'll be in a frustrating situation then, won't he?'

'Dodgson was no pervert,' Frigate said. 'But what about those whose only sexual objects are children? What will they do when there are no more children? And what will those who got their kicks by mistreating or torturing animals do? You know, I've regretted the absence of animals. I love cats and dogs, bears, elephants, most animals. Not monkeys, they're too much like humans. But I'm glad they're not here. They can't be abused now. All the poor helpless animals who were in pain or going hungry or thirsty because of some thoughtless or vicious human being. Not now.'

He patted Gwenafra's blonde hair which was almost six inches long.

'I felt much the same about the helpless and abused little ones, too.'

'What kind of a world is it that doesn't have children,' Alice said. 'For that matter, what kind without animals? If they can't be mistreated or abused any more, they can't be petted and loved.'

'One thing balances out another in this world,' Burton said. 'You can't have love without hate, kindness without malice, peace without war. In any event, we don't have a choice in the matter. The invisible Lords of this world have decreed that we do not have animals and that women no longer bear children. So be it.'

The morning of the 416th day of their journey was like every morning. The sun had risen above the top of the range on their left. The wind from upRiver was an estimated fifteen miles per hour, as always. The warmth rose steadily with the sun and would reach the estimated 85 degrees Fahrenheit at approximately 2 in the afternoon. The catamaran, *The Hadji*, tacked back and forth. Burton stood on the 'bridge' with both hands on the long thick pine tiller on his right, while the wind and the sun beat on his darkly tanned skin. He wore a scarlet and black checked kilt reaching almost to his knees and a necklace made of the convoluted shiny-black vertebrae of the hornfish. This was a six-foot long fish with a six-inch long horn that projected unicorn-like from its forehead. The hornfish lived about a hundred feet below the surface and was brought in on a line with difficulty. But its vertebrae made beautiful necklaces, its skin, properly tanned, made sandals and armor and shields or could be worked into tough pliable ropes and belts. Its flesh was delicious. But the horn was the most valuable item. It tipped spears or arrows or went into a wood handle to make a stiletto.

On a stand near him, encased in the transparent bladder of a fish, was a bow. It was made of the curved bones protruding from the sides of the mouth of the whale-sized dragonfish. When the ends of each had been cut so that one fitted into the other, a double recurved bow was the result. Fitted with a string from the gut of the dragonfish, this made a bow that only a very powerful man could fully draw. Burton had run across one forty days ago and offered its owner forty cigarettes, ten cigars, and thirty ounces of whiskey for it. The offer was turned down. So Burton and Kazz came back late that night and stole the bow. Or, rather, made a trade, since Burton felt compelled to leave his yew bow in exchange.

Since then, he had rationalized that he had every right to steal the bow. The owner had boasted that he had murdered a man to get the bow. So taking it from him was taking it from a thief and a killer. Nevertheless, Burton suffered from thrusts of conscience when he thought about it, which was not often.

Burton took *The Hadji* back and forth across the narrowing channel. For about five miles, The River had widened out to a three and a half mile broad lake, and now it was forming into a narrow channel less than half a mile across. The channel curved and disappeared between the walls of a canyon.

There the boat would creep along because it would be bucking an accelerated current and the space allowed for tacking was so limited. But he had been through similar straits many times and so was not apprehensive about this. Still, every time it happened, he could not help thinking of the boat as being reborn. It passed from a lake, a womb, through a tight opening and out into another lake. It was a bursting of waters in many ways, and there was always the chance of a fabulous adventure, of a revelation, on the other side.

The catamaran turned away from a grailstone, only twenty yards off. There were many people on the right-side plain, which was only half a mile across here. They shouted at the boat or waved or shook their fists or shouted obscenities, unheard but understood by Burton because of so many experiences. But they did not seem hostile; it was just that strangers were always greeted by the locals in a varied manner. The locals here were a short, dark-skinned, dark-haired, thin-bodied people. They spoke a language that Ruach said was probably proto-Hamite-Semitic. They had lived on Earth somewhere in North Africa or Mesopotamia when those countries had been much more fertile. They wore the towels as kilts but the women went bare-breasted and used the 'bras' as neckscarfs or turbans. They occupied the right bank for sixty grailstones, that is, sixty miles. The people before them had been strung out for eighty grailstones and had been tenth-century AD Ceylonese with a minority of pre-Columbian Mayans.

'The mixing bowl of Time,' Frigate called the distribution of humanity. 'The greatest anthropological and social experiment ever.'

His statements were not too farfetched. It did look as if the various peoples had been mixed up so that they might learn something from each other. In some cases, the alien groups had managed to create various social lubricants and lived in relative amity. In other cases, there was a slaughter of one side by the other, or a mutual near-extermination, or slavery, of the defeated.

For some time after the resurrection, anarchy had been the usual rule.

People had 'milled around' and formed little groups for defense in very small areas. Then the natural leaders and power seekers had come to the front, and the natural followers had lined up behind the leaders of their choice – or the leaders' choice, in many cases.

One of the several political systems that had resulted was that of 'grail slavery.' A dominant group in an area held the weaker prisoners. They gave the slave enough to eat because the grail of a dead slave became useless. But they took the cigarettes, the cigars, the marihuana, the dreamgum, the liquor, and the tastier food.

At least thirty times, *The Hadji* had started to put into a grailstone and had come close to being seized by grail slavers. But Burton and the others were on the alert for signs of slave states. Neighboring states often warned them. Twenty times, boats had put out to intercept them instead of trying to lure them ashore, and *The Hadji* had narrowly escaped being run down or boarded. Five times, Burton had been forced to turn back and sail downstream. His catamaran had always outrun the pursuers, who were reluctant to chase him outside their borders. Then *The Hadji* had sneaked back at night and sailed past the slavers.

A number of times, *The Hadji* had been unable to put into shore because the slave states occupied both banks for very long stretches. Then the crew went on half-rations, or, if they were lucky, caught enough fish to fill their bellies.

The proto-Hamite-Semites of this area had been friendly enough after they were assured that the crew of *The Hadji* had no evil intentions. An eighteenth-century Muscovite had warned them that there were slave states on the other side of the channel. He did not know too much about them because of the precipitous mountains. A few boats had sailed through the channel and almost none had returned. Those that did brought news of evil men on the other side.

So *The Hadji* was loaded with bamboo shoots, dried fish, and supplies saved over a period of two weeks from the grails.

There was still about half an hour before the strait would be entered. Burton kept half his mind on his sailing and half on the crew. They were sprawled on the foredeck, taking in the sun or else sitting with their backs against the roofed coaming which they called the 'fo'c'sle.'

John de Greystock was affixing the thin carved bones of a hornfish to the butt of an arrow. The bones served quite well as feathers in a world where birds did not exist. Greystock, or Lord Greystoke, as Frigate insisted on calling him for some private self-amusing reason, was a good man in a fight or when hard work was needed. He was an interesting, if almost unbelievably vulgar, talker, full of anecdotes of the campaigns in Gascony and on the border, of his conquests of women, of gossip about Edward Longshanks, and of course, of information about his times. But he was also very hardheaded and narrow-minded in many things – from the viewpoint of a later age – and not overly clean. He claimed to have been very devout in Earthlife, and he probably told the truth, otherwise, he would not have been honored by being attached to the retinue of the Patriarch of Jerusalem. But, now that his faith had been discredited, he hated priests. And he was apt to drive any he met into a fury with his scorn, hoping that they would attack him. Some did, and he came close to killing them. Burton had cautiously reprimanded him for this (you did not speak harshly to de Greystock unless you wished to fight to the death with him), pointing out that when they were guests in a strange land, and immensely outnumbered by their hosts, they should act as guests. De Greystock admitted that Burton was right, but he could not keep from baiting every priest he met. Fortunately, they were not often in areas where there were Christian priests. Moreover, there were very few of these who admitted that they had been such.

Beside him, talking earnestly, was his current woman, born Mary Rutherfurd in 1637, died Lady Warwickshire in 1674. She was English but of an age 300 years later than his, so there were many differences in their attitudes and actions. Burton did not give them much longer to stay together.

Kazz was sprawled out on the deck with his head in the lap of Fatima, a Turkish woman whom the Neanderthal had met forty days ago during a lunch stop. Fatima, as Frigate had said, seemed to be 'hung up on hair.' That was his explanation for the obsession of the seventeenth-century wife of a baker of Ankara for Kazz. She found everything about him stimulating but it was the hairiness that sent her into ecstasies. Everybody was pleased about this, most of all Kazz. He had not seen a single female of his own species during their long trip, though he had heard about some. Most women shied away from him because of his hairy and brutish appearance. He had had no permanent female companionship until he met Fatima.

Little Lev Ruach was leaning against the forward bulkhead of the fo'c'sle, where he was making a slingshot from the leather of a hornfish. A bag by his side contained about thirty stones picked up during the last twenty days. By his side, talking swiftly, incessantly exposing her long white teeth, was Esther Rodriguez. She had replaced Tanya, who had been henpecking Lev before *The Hadji* set off. Tanya was a very attractive and petite woman but she seemed unable to keep from 'remodeling' her men; Lev found out that she had 'remodeled' her father and uncle and two brothers and two husbands. She tried to do the same for, or to, Lev, usually in a loud voice so that other males in the neighborhood could benefit by her advice. One day, just as *The Hadji* was about to sail, Lev had jumped aboard, turned, and said, 'Goodbye, Tanya. I can't stand any more reforming from The Bigmouth from The Bronx. Find somebody else; somebody that's perfect.'

Tanya had gasped, turned white, and then started screaming at Lev. She still was screaming, judging by her mouth, long after *The Hadji* had sailed out of earshot. The others laughed and congratulated Lev, but he only smiled sadly. Two weeks later, in an area predominantly ancient Libyan, he met Esther, a fifteenth-century Sephardic Jewess.

'Why don't you try your luck with a Gentile?' Frigate had said.

Lev had shrugged his narrow shoulders. 'I have. But sooner or later you get into a big fight, and they lose their temper and call you a goddam kike. The same thing also happens with my Jewish women, but from them I can take it.'

'Listen, friend,' the American said. 'There are billions of Gentiles along this river who've never heard of a Jew. They can't be prejudiced. Try one of them.'

'I'll stick to the evil I know.'

'You mean you're stuck to it,' Frigate said.

Burton sometimes wondered why Ruach stayed with the boat. He had never made any more references to *The Jew, The Gypsy, and El Islam*, though he often questioned Burton about other aspects of his past. He was friendly enough but had a certain indefinable reserve. Though small, he was a good man in a fight and he had been invaluable in teaching Burton judo, karate, and jukado. His sadness, which hung about him like a thin mist even when he was laughing, or making love, according to Tanya, came from mental scars. These resulted from his terrible experiences in concentration camps in Germany and Russia, or so he claimed. Tanya had said that Lev was born sad; he inherited all the genes of sorrow from the time when his ancestors sat down by the willows of Babylon.

Monat was another case of sadness, though he could come out of it fully at times. The Tau Cetan kept looking for one of his own kind, for one of the thirty males and females who had been torn apart by the lynch mob. He did not give himself much chance. Thirty in an estimated thirty-five to thirty-six billion strung out along a river that could be ten million miles long made it improbable that he would ever see even one. But there was hope.

Alice Hargreaves was sitting forward of the fo'c'sle, only the top of her head in his view, and looking at the people on the banks whenever the boat got close enough for her to make out individual faces. She was searching for her husband, Reginald, and also for her three sons and for her mother and father and her sisters and brothers. For any dear familiar face. The implications were that she would leave the boat as soon as this happened. Burton had not commented on this. But he felt a pain in his chest when he thought of it. He wished that she would leave and yet he did not wish it. To get her out of sight would eventually be to get her out of his mind. It was inevitable. But he did not want the inevitable. He felt for her as he had for his Persian love, and to lose her, too, would be to suffer the same long-lived torture.

Yet he had never said a word about how he felt to her. He talked to her, jested with her, showed her a concern that he found galling because she did not return it, and, in the end, got her to relax when with him. That is, she would relax if there were others around. When they were alone, she tightened up.

She had never used the dreamgum since that first night. He had used it for a third time and then hoarded his share and traded it for other items. The last time he had chewed it, with the hope of an unusually ecstatic lovemaking with Wilfreda, he had been plunged back into the horrible sickness of the 'little irons,' the sickness that had almost killed him during his expedition to Lake Tanganyika. Speke had been in the nightmare, and he had killed Speke. Speke had died in a hunting 'accident' which everybody had thought was a suicide even if they had not said so. Speke, tormented by remorse because he had betrayed Burton, had shot himself. But in the nightmare, he had strangled Speke when Speke bent over to ask him how he was. Then, just as the vision faded, he had kissed Speke's dead lips.

14

Well, he had known that he had loved Speke at the same time that he hated him, justifiably hated him. But the knowledge of his love had been very fleeting and infrequent and it had not affected him. During the dreamgum nightmare, he had felt so horrified at the realization that love lay far beneath his hate that he had screamed. He awakened to find Wilfreda shaking him, demanding to know what had happened. Wilfreda had smoked opium or drunk it in her beer when on Earth, but here, after one session with dreamgum, she had been afraid to chew any more. Her horror came from seeing again the death of a younger sister from tuberculosis and, at the same time, reliving her first experience as a whore.

'It's a strange psychedelic,' Ruach had told Burton. He had explained what the word meant. The discussion about that had gone on for a long time. 'It seems to bring up traumatic incidents in a mixture of reality and symbolism. Not always. Sometimes it's an aphrodisiac. Sometimes, as they said, it takes you on a beautiful trip. But I would guess that dreamgum has been provided us for therapeutic, if not cathartic, reasons. It's up to us to find out just how to use it.'

'Why don't you chew it more often?' Frigate had said.

'For the same reason that some people refused to go into psychotherapy or quit before they were through; I'm afraid.'

'Yeah, me, too,' Frigate said. 'But some day, when we stop off some place for a long time, I'm going to chew a stick every night, so help me. Even if it scares hell out of me. Of course, that's easy to say now.'

Peter Jairus Frigate had been born only twenty-eight years after Burton had died, yet the world between them was wide. They saw so many things so differently; they would have argued violently if Frigate was able to argue violently. Not on matters of discipline in the group or in running the boat. But on so many matters of looking at the world. Yet, in many ways, Frigate was much like Burton, and it may have been this that had caused him to be so fascinated by Burton on Earth. Frigate had picked up in 1938 a soft-cover book by Fairfax Downey titled *Burton: Arabian Nights' Adventurer*. The front page illustration was of Burton at the age of fifty. The savage face, the high brow and prominent supraorbital ridges, the heavy black brows, the straight but harsh nose, the great scar on his cheek, the thick 'sensual' lips, the heavy down-drooping moustache, the heavy forked beard, the essential broodingness and aggressiveness of the face, had caused him to buy the book.

'I'd never heard of you before, Dick,' Frigate said. 'But I read the book at once and was fascinated. There was something about you, aside from the obvious derring-do of your life, your swordsmanship, mastery of many languages, disguises as a native doctor, native merchantman, as a pilgrim to Mecca, the first European to get out of the sacred city of Harar alive, discoverer of Lake Tanganyika and near-discoverer of the source of the Nile, co-founder of the Royal Anthropological Society, inventor of the term ESP, translator of the Arabian Nights, student of the sexual practices of the East, and so forth ...

'Aside from all this, fascinating enough in itself, you had a special affinity for me. I went to the public library – Peoria was a small city but had many books on you and about you, donated by some admirer of yours who'd passed on – and I read these. Then I started to collect first editions by you and about you. I became a fiction writer eventually, but I planned to write a huge definitive biography of you, travel everywhere you had been, take photographs and notes of these places, found a society to collect funds for the preservation of your tomb ...'

This was the first time Frigate had mentioned his tomb. Burton, startled, said, 'Where?' Then, 'Oh, of course! Mortlake! I'd forgotten! Was the tomb really in the form of an Arab tent, as Isabel and I had planned?'

'Sure. But the cemetery was swallowed up in a slum, the tomb was defaced by vandals, there were weeds up to your tokus and talk of moving the bodies to a more remote section of England, though by then it was hard to find a really remote section.'

'And did you found your society and preserve my tomb?' Burton said.

He had gotten used to the idea by then of having been dead, but to talk with someone who had seen his tomb made his skin chill for a moment.

Frigate took a deep breath. Apologetically, he said, 'No. By the time I was in a position to do that, I would have felt guilty spending time and money on the dead. The world was in too much of a mess. The living needed all the attention they could get. Pollution, poverty, oppression, and so forth. These were the important things.'

'And that giant definitive biography?'

Again, Frigate spoke apologetically. 'When I first read about you, I thought I was the only one deeply interested in you or even aware of you. But there was an upsurge of interest in you in the '60's. Quite a few books were written about you and even one about your wife.'

'Isabel? Someone wrote a book about her? Why?'

Frigate had grinned. 'She was a pretty interesting woman. Very aggravating, I'll admit, pitifully superstitious and schizophrenic and self-fooling. Very few would ever forgive her for burning your manuscripts and your journals ...'

'What?' Burton had roared. 'Burn ...?'

Frigate nodded and said, 'What your doctor, Grenfell Baker, described as "the ruthless holocaust that followed his lamented death." She burned your translation of *The Perfumed Garden*, claiming you would not have wanted to publish it unless you needed the money for it, and you didn't need it, of course, because you were now dead.'

Burton was speechless for one of the few times in his life.

Frigate looked out of the corner of his eyes at Burton and grinned. He seemed to be enjoying Burton's distress.

'Burning *The Perfumed Garden* wasn't so bad, though bad enough. But to burn both sets of your journals, the private ones in which, supposedly, you let loose all your deepest thoughts and most burning hates, and even the public ones, the diary of daily events, well, I never forgave her! Neither did a lot of people. That was a great loss; only one of your notebooks, a small one, escaped, and that was burned during the bombing of London in World War II.'

He paused and said, 'Is it true that you converted to the Catholic Church on your deathbed, as your wife claimed?'

'I may have,' Burton said. 'Isabel had been after me for years to convert, though she never dared urge me directly. When I was so sick there, at the last, I may have told her I would do so in order to make her happy. She was so grief-stricken, so distressed, so afraid my soul would burn in Hell.'

'Then you did love her?' Frigate had said.

'I would have done the same for a dog,' Burton replied.

'For somebody who can be so upsettingly frank and direct, you can be very ambiguous at times.'

This conversation had taken place about two months after First Day, A.R. 1. The result had been something like that which Doctor Johnson would have felt on encountering another Boswell.

This had been the second stage of their curious relationship. Frigate became closer but, at the same time, more of an annoyance. The American had always been restrained in his comments on Burton's attitudes, undoubtedly because he did not want to anger him. Frigate made a very conscious effort not to anger anybody. But he also made unconscious efforts to antagonize them. His hostilities came out in many subtle, and some not so subtle, actions and words. Burton did not like this. He was direct, not at all afraid of anger. Perhaps, as Frigate pointed out, he was too eager for hostile confrontations.

One evening, as they were sitting around a fire under a grailstone, Frigate had spoken about Karachi. This village, which later became the capital of Pakistan, the nation created in 1947, had only 2,000 population in Burton's time. By 1970, its population was approximately 2,000,000. That led to Frigate's asking, rather indirectly, about the report Burton had made to his general, Sir Robert Napier, on houses of male prostitution in Karachi. The report was supposed to be kept in the secret files of the East India Army, but it was found by one of the many enemies of Burton. Though the report was never mentioned publicly, it had been used against him throughout his life. Burton had disguised himself as a native in order to get into the house and make observations that no European would have been allowed to make. He had been proud that he had escaped detection, and he had taken the unsavory job because he was the only one who could do it and because his beloved leader, Napier, had asked him to.

Burton had replied to Frigate's questions somewhat surlily. Alice had angered him earlier that day – she seemed to be able to do so very easily lately – and he was thinking of a way to anger her. Now he seized upon the opportunity given him by Frigate. He launched into an uninhibited account of what went on in the Karachi houses. Ruach finally got up and walked away. Frigate looked as if he were sick, but he stayed. Wilfreda laughed until she rolled on the ground. Kazz and Monat kept stolid expressions. Gwenafra was sleeping on the boat, so Burton did not have to take her into account. Loghu seemed to be fascinated but also slightly repulsed.

Alice, his main target, turned pale and then, later, red. Finally, she rose and said, 'Really, Mr Burton, I had thought you were low before. But to brag of this … this … you are utterly contemptible, degenerate, and repulsive. Not that I believe a word of what you've been telling me. I can't believe that anybody would behave as you claim you did and then boast about it. You are living up to your reputation as a man who likes to shock others no matter what damage it does to his own reputation.'

She had walked off into the darkness.

Frigate had said, 'Sometime, maybe, you will tell me how much of that is true. I used to think as she did. But when I got older, more evidence about you was turned up, and one biographer made a psychoanalysis of you based on your own writing and various documentary sources.'

'And the conclusions?' Burton said mockingly.

'Later, Dick,' Frigate said. 'Ruffian Dick,' he added, and he, too, left.

Now, standing at the tiller, watching the sun beat down on the group, listening to the hissing of water cut by the two sharp prows, and the creaking of rigging, he wondered what lay ahead on the other side of the canyon-like channel. Not the end of The River, surely. That would probably go on forever. But the end of the group might be near. They had been cooped up too long together. Too many days had been spent on the narrow deck with too little to do except talk or help sail the ship. They were rubbing each other raw and had been doing it for a long time. Even Wilfreda had been quiet and unresponsive lately. Not that he had been too stimulating. Frankly, he was tired of her. He did not hate her or wish her any ill. He was just tired of her, and the fact that he could have her and not have Alice Hargreaves made him even more tired of her.

Lev Ruach was staying away from him or speaking as little as possible, and Lev was arguing even more with Esther about his dietary habits and his daydreaming and why didn't he ever talk to her?

Frigate was mad at him about something. But Frigate would never come out and say anything, the coward, until he was driven into a corner and tormented into a mindless rage. Loghu was angry and scornful of Frigate because he was as sullen with her as with the others. Loghu was also angry with him, Burton, because he had turned her down when they had been alone gathering bamboo in the hills several weeks ago. He had told her no, adding that he had no moral scruples against making love to her, but that he would not betray Frigate or any other member of the crew. Loghu said that it was not that she did not love Frigate; it was just that she needed a change now and then. Just as Frigate did.

Alice had said that she was about to give up hope of ever seeing anybody she knew again. They must have passed an estimated 44,370,000 people, at least, and not once had she seen anybody she had known on Earth. She had seen some that she had mistaken for old acquaintances. And she admitted that she had only seen a small percentage of the 44,370,000 at close range or even at far range. But that did not matter. She was getting abysmally depressed and weary of sitting on this cramped foredeck all day with her only exercise handling the tiller or the rigging or opening and closing her lips with conversation, most of it inane.

Burton did not want to admit it, but he was afraid that she might leave. She might just get off at the next stop, walk off onto the shore with her grail and few belongings, and say good-bye. See you in a hundred years or so. Perhaps. The chief thing keeping her on the boat so far had been Gwenafra. She was raising the little ancient Briton as a Victorian-lady-cum-post-Ressurrection-mores-child. This was a most curious mixture, but not any more curious than anything else along The River.

Burton himself was weary of the eternal voyaging on the little vessel. He wanted to find some hospitable area and settle down there to rest, then to study, to engage in local activities, to get his land legs back, and allow the drive to get out and away to build up again. But he wanted to do it with Alice as his hut-mate.

'The fortune of the man who sits also sits,' he muttered. He would have to take action with Alice; he had been a gentleman long enough. He would woo her; he would take her by storm. He had been an aggressive lover when a young man, then he had gotten used to being the loved, not the lover, after he got married. And his old habit patterns, old neural circuits, were still with him. He was an old person in a new body.

The Hadji entered the dark and turbulent channel. The blue-black rock walls rose on both sides and the boat went down a curve and the broad lake behind was lost. Everybody was busy then, jumping to handle the sails as Burton took *The Hadji* back and forth in the quarter-mile wide stream and against a current that raised high waves. The boat rose and dipped sharply and heeled far over when they changed course abruptly. It often came within a few feet of the canyon walls, where the waves slapped massively against the rock. But he had been sailing the boat so long that he had become a part of it, and his crew had worked with him so long that they could anticipate his orders, though they never acted ahead of them.

The passage took about thirty minutes. It caused anxiety in some – no doubt of Frigate and Ruach being worried – but it also exhilarated all of them. The boredom and the sullenness were, temporarily, at least, gone.

The Hadji came out into the sunshine of another lake. This was about four miles wide and stretched northward as far as they could see. The mountains abruptly fell away; the plains on both sides resumed the usual mile width.

There were fifty or so craft in view, ranging from pine dugouts to two-masted bamboo boats. Most of them seemed to be engaged in fishing. To the left, a mile away, was the ubiquitous grailstone, and along the shore were dark figures. Behind them, on the plain and hills, were bamboo huts in the usual style of what Frigate called Neo-Polynesian or, sometimes, Post-Mortem Riparian Architecture.

On the right, about half a mile from the exit of the canyon, was a large log fort. Before it were ten massive log docks with a variety of large and small boats. A few minutes after *The Hadji* appeared, drums began beating. These could be hollow logs or drums made with tanned fish skin or human skin. There was already a crowd in front of the fort, but a large number swarmed out of it and from a collection of huts behind it. They piled into the boats, and these cast off.

On the left bank, the dark figures were launching dugouts, canoes, and single-masted boats.

It looked as if both shores were sending boats out in a competition to seize *The Hadji* first.

Burton took the boat back and forth as required, cutting in between the other boats several times. The men on the right were closer; they were white and well-armed, but they made no effort to use their bows. A man standing in the prow of a war-canoe with thirty paddlers shouted at them, in German, to surrender.

'You will not be harmed!'

'We come in peace!' Frigate bawled at him.

'He knows that!' Burton said. 'It's evident that we few aren't going to attack them!'

Drums were beating on both sides of The River now. It sounded as if the lake shores were alive with drums. And the shores were certainly alive with men, all armed. Other boats were being put out to intercept them. Behind them, the boats that had first gone out were pursuing but losing distance.

Burton hesitated. Should he bring *The Hadji* on around and go back through the channel and then return at night? It would be a dangerous maneuver, because the 20,000-foot high walls would block out the light from the blazing stars and gas sheets. They would be almost blind.

And this craft did seem to be faster than anything the enemy had. So far, that is. Far in the distance, tall sails were coming swiftly toward him. Still, they had the wind and current behind them, and if he avoided them, could they outstrip him when they, too, had to tack?

All the vessels he had seen so far had been loaded with men, thus slowing them down. Even a boat that had the same potentialities as *The Hadji* would not keep up with her if she were loaded with warriors.

He decided to keep on running upRiver.

Ten minutes later, as he was running close-hauled, another large war canoe cut across his path. This held sixteen paddlers on each side and supported a small deck in the bow and the stern. Two men stood on each deck beside a catapult mounted on a wooden pedestal. The two in the bow placed a round object which sputtered smoke in the pocket of the catapult. One pulled the catch, and the arm of the machine banged against the crossbeam. The canoe shuddered, and there was a slight halt in the deep rhythmic grunting of the paddlers. The smoking object flew in a high arc until it was about twenty feet in front of *The Hadji* and ten feet above the water. It exploded with a loud noise and much black smoke, quickly cleared away by the breeze.

Some of the women screamed, and a man shouted. He thought, there is sulfur in this area. Otherwise, they would not have been able to make gunpowder.

He called to Loghu and Esther Rodriguez to take over at the tiller. Both women were pale, but they seemed calm enough, although neither woman had ever experienced a bomb.

Gwenafra had been put inside the fo'c'sle. Alice had a yew bow in her hand and a quiver of arrows strapped to her back. Her pale skin contrasted shockingly with the red lipstick and the green eyelid-makeup. But she had been through at least ten running battles on the water, and her nerves were as steady as the chalk cliffs of Dover. Moreover, she was the best archer of the lot. Burton was a superb marksman with a firearm but he lacked practice with the bow. Kazz could draw the riverdragon-horn bow even deeper than Burton, but his marksmanship was abominable. Frigate claimed it would never be very good; like most pre-literates, he lacked a development of the sense of perspective.

The catapult men did not fit another bomb to the machine. Evidently, the bomb had been a warning to stop. Burton intended to stop for nothing. Their pursuers could have shot them full of arrows several times. That they had refrained meant that they wanted *The Hadji* crew alive.

The canoe, water boiling from its prow, paddles flashing in the sun, paddlers grunting in unison, passed closely to the stern of *The Hadji*. The two men on the foredeck leaped outward, and the canoe rocked. One man splashed into the water, his fingertips striking the edge of the deck. The other landed on his knees on the edge. He gripped a bamboo knife between his teeth; his belt held two sheaths, one with a small stone axe and the other with a hornfish stiletto. For a second, as he tried to grab onto the wet planking and pull himself up, he stared upward into Burton's eyes. His hair was a rich yellow, his eyes were a pale blue, and his face was classically handsome. His intention was probably to wound one or two of the crew and then to dive off, maybe with a woman in his arms. While he kept *The Hadji* crew busy, his fellows would sail up and engage *The Hadji* and pour aboard, and that would be that.

He did not have much chance of carrying out his plan, probably knew it, and did not care. Most men still feared death because the fear was in the cells of their bodies, and they reacted instinctively. A few had overcome their fear, and others had never really felt it.

Burton stepped up and banged the man on the side of the head with his axe. The man's mouth opened; the bamboo knife fell out; he collapsed face down on the deck. Burton picked up the knife, untied the man's belt, and shoved him off into the water with his foot. At that, a roar came from the men in the war canoe, which was turning around. Burton saw that the shore was coming up fast, and he gave orders to tack. The vessel swung around, and the boom swung by. Then they were beating across The River, with a dozen boats speeding toward them. Three were four-man dugouts, four were big war canoes, and five were two-masted schooners. The latter held a number of catapults and many men on the decks.

Halfway across The River, Burton ordered *The Hadji* swung around again. The maneuver allowed the sail ships to get much closer, but he had calculated for that. Now, sailing close-hauled again, *The Hadji* cut water between the two schooners. They were so close that he could clearly see the features of all aboard both craft. They were mostly Caucasian, though they ranged from very dark to Nordic pale. The captain of the boat on the portside shouted in German at Burton, demanding that he surrender.

'We will not harm you if you give up, but we will torture you if you continue to fight!'

He spoke German with an accent that sounded Hungarian.

For reply, Burton and Alice shot arrows. Alice's shaft missed the captain but hit the helmsman, and he staggered back and fell over the railing. The craft immediately veered. The captain sprang to the wheel, and Burton's second shaft went through the back of his knee.

Both schooners struck slantingly with a great crash and shot off with much tearing up of timbers, men screaming and falling onto the decks or falling overboard. Even if the boats did not sink, they would be out of action.

But just before they hit, their archers had put a dozen flaming arrows into the bamboo sails of *The Hadji*. The shafts carried dry grass which had been soaked with turpentine made from pine resin, and these, fanned by the wind, spread the flames quickly.

Burton took the tiller back from the women and shouted orders. The crew dipped fired-clay vessels and their open grails into The River and then threw the water on the flames. Loghu, who could climb like a monkey, went up the mast with a rope around her shoulder. She let the rope down and pulled up the containers of water.

This permitted the other schooners and several canoes to draw close. One on a course which would put it directly in the path of *The Hadji*. Burton swung the boat around again, but it was sluggish because of Loghu's weight on the mast. It wheeled around, the boom swung wildly as the men failed to keep control of its ropes, and more arrows struck the sail and spread more fire. Several arrows thunked into the deck. For a moment, Burton thought that the enemy had changed his mind and was trying to down them. But the arrows were just misdirected.

Again, *The Hadji* sliced between two schooners. The captains and the crew of both were grinning. Perhaps they had been bored for a long time and were enjoying the pursuit. Even so, the crews ducked behind the railings, leaving the officers, helmsmen, and the archers to receive the fire from *The Hadji*. There was a strumming, and dark streaks with red heads and blue tails went halfway through the sails in two dozen places, a number drove into the mast or the boom, a dozen hissed into the water, one shot by Burton a few inches from his head.

Alice, Ruach, Kazz, de Greystock, Wilfreda, and he had shot while Esther handled the tiller. Loghu was frozen halfway up the mast, waiting until the arrow fire quit. The five arrows found three targets of flesh, a captain, a helmsman, and a sailor who stuck his head up at the wrong time for him.

Esther screamed, and Burton spun. The war canoe had come out from behind the schooner and was a few feet in front of *The Hadji*'s bow. There was no way to avoid a collision. The two men on the platform were diving off the side, and the paddlers were standing up or trying to stand up so they could get overboard. Then *The Hadji* smashed into its port near the bow, cracking it open, turning it over, and spilling its crew into The River. Those on *The Hadji* were thrown forward, and de Greystock went into the water. Burton slid on his face and chest and knees, burning off the skin.

Esther had been torn from the tiller and rolled across the deck until she thumped against the edge of the fo'c'sle coaming. She lay there without moving.

Burton looked upward. The sail was blazing away beyond hope of being saved. Loghu was gone, so she must have been hurled off at the moment of impact. Then, getting up, he saw her and de Greystock swimming back to *The Hadji*. The water around them was boiling with the splashing of the dispossessed canoemen, many of whom, judging by their cries, could not swim.

Burton called to the men to help the two aboard while he inspected the damage. Both prows of the very thin twin hulls had been smashed open by the crash. Water was pouring inside. And the smoke from the burning sail and mast was curling around them, causing Alice and Gwenafra to cough.

Another war canoe was approaching swiftly from the north; the two schooners were sailing close-hauled toward them.

They could fight and draw some blood from their enemies, who would be holding themselves back to keep from killing them. Or they could swim for it. Either way, they would be captured.

Loghu and de Greystock were pulled aboard. Frigate reported that Esther could not be brought back to consciousness. Ruach felt her pulse and opened her eyes and then walked back to Burton.

'She's not dead, but she's totally out.'

Burton said, 'You women know what will happen to you. It's up to you, of course, but I suggest you swim down as deeply as you can and draw in a good breath of water. You'll wake up tomorrow, good as new.'

Gwenafra had come out from the fo'c'sle. She wrapped her arms round his waist and looked up, dry-eyed but scared. He hugged her with one arm and then said, 'Alice! Take her with you!'

'Where?' Alice said. She looked at the canoe and back at him. She coughed again as more smoke wrapped around her and then she moved forward, upwind.

'When you go down.'

He gestured at The River.

'I can't do that,' she said.

'You wouldn't want those men to get her, too. She's only a little girl but they'll not stop for that.'

Alice looked as if her face was going to crumple and wash away with tears. But she did not weep.

She said, 'Very well. It's no sin now, killing yourself. I just hope …'

He said, 'Yes.'

He did not drawl the word; there was no time to drawl anything out. The canoe was within forty feet of them.

'The next place might be just as bad or worse than this one,' Alice said. 'And Gwenafra will wake up all alone. You know that the chances of us being resurrected at the same place are slight.'

'That can't be helped,' he said.

She clamped her lips, then opened them and said, 'I'll fight until the last moment. Then …'

'It may be too late,' he said. He picked up his bow and drew an arrow from his quiver. De Greystock had lost his bow, so he took Kazz's. The Neanderthal placed a stone in a sling and began whirling it. Lev picked up his sling and chose a stone for its pocket. Monat used Esther's bow, since he had lost his, also.

The captain of the canoe shouted in German, 'Lay down your arms! You won't be harmed!'

He fell off the platform onto a paddler a second later as Alice's arrow went through his chest. Another arrow, probably de Greystock's, spun the second man off the platform and into the water. A stone hit a paddler in the shoulder, and he collapsed with a cry. Another stone struck glancingly off another paddler's head, and he lost his paddle.

The canoe kept on coming. The two men on the aft platform urged the crew to continue driving toward *The Hadji*. Then they fell with arrows in them.

Burton looked behind him. The two schooners were letting their sails drop now. Evidently they would slide on up to *The Hadji* where the sailors would throw their grappling hooks into it. But if they got too close, the flames might spread to them.

The canoe rammed into *The Hadji* with fourteen of the original complement dead or too wounded to fight. Just before the canoe's prow hit, the survivors dropped their paddles and raised small round leather shields. Even so, two arrows went through two shields and into the arms of the men holding them. That still left twenty men against six men, five women, and a child.

But one was a five-foot high hairy man with tremendous strength and a big stone axe. Kazz jumped into the air just before the canoe rammed the starboard hull and came down in it a second after it had halted. His axe crushed two skulls and then drove through the bottom of the canoe. Water poured in, and de Greystock, shouting something in his Cumberland Middle English, leaped down beside Kazz. He held a stiletto in one hand and a big oak club with flint spikes in the other.

The others on *The Hadji* continued to shoot their arrows. Suddenly, Kazz and de Greystock were scrambling back onto the catamaran and the canoe was sinking with its dead, dying, and its scared survivors. A number drowned; the others either swam away or tried to get aboard *The Hadji*. These fell back with their fingers chopped off or stamped flat.

Something struck on the deck near him and then something else coiled around him. Burton spun and slashed at the leather rope which had settled around his neck. He leaped to one side to avoid another and yanked savagely at a third rope and pulled the man on the other end over the railing. The man, screaming, pitched out and struck the deck of *The Hadji* with his shoulder. Burton smashed in his face with his axe.

By now men were dropping from the decks of both schooners and ropes were falling everywhere. The smoke and the flames added to the confusion, though they may have helped *The Hadji*'s crew more than the boarders.

Burton shouted at Alice to get Gwenafra and jump into The River. He could not find her and then had to parry the thrust of a big black with a spear. The man seemed to have forgotten any orders to capture Burton; he looked as if he meant to kill. Burton knocked the short spear aside and whirled, lashing out as he went by with the axe and smashed its edge against the black's neck. Burton continued to whirl, felt a sharp pain in his ribs, another in his shoulder, but knocked two men down and then was in the water. He fell between the schooner and *The Hadji*, went down, released the axe and pulled the stiletto from its sheath. When he came up, he was looking up at a tall, rawboned, redheaded man who was lifting the screaming Gwenafra above him with both hands. The man pitched her far out into the water.

Burton dived again and coming up saw Gwenafra's face only a few feet before him. It was gray, and her eyes were dull. Then he saw the blood darkening the water around her. She disappeared before he could get to her. He dived down after her, caught her and pulled her back up. A hornfish tip was stuck into her back.

He let her body go. He did not know why the man had killed her when he could have easily taken her prisoner. Perhaps Alice had stabbed her and the man had figured that she was as good as dead and so had tossed her over the side to the fishes.

A body shot out of the smoke, followed by another. One man was dead with a broken neck; the other was alive. Burton wrapped his arm around the man's neck and stabbed him at the juncture of jaw and ear. The man quit struggling and slipped down into the depths.

Frigate leaped out from the smoke, his face and shoulders bloody. He hit the water at a slant and dived deep. Burton swam toward him to help him. There was no use even trying to get back on the craft. It was solid with struggling bodies, and other canoes and dugouts were closing in.

Frigate's head rose out of the water. His skin was white where the blood was not pumping out over it. Burton swam to him and said, 'Did the women get away?'

Frigate shook his head and then said, 'Watch out!'

Burton upended to dive down. Something hit his legs; he kept on going down, but he could not carry out his intention of breathing in the water. He would fight until they had to kill him.

On coming up, he saw that the water was alive with men who had jumped in after him and Frigate. The American, half-conscious, was being towed to a canoe. Three men closed in on Burton, and he stabbed two and then a man in a dugout reached down with a club and banged him on the head.

15

They were led ashore near a large building behind a wall of pine logs. Burton's head throbbed with pain at every step. The gashes in his shoulder and ribs hurt, but they had quit bleeding. The fortress was built of pine logs, had an overhanging second story, and many sentinels. The captives were marched through an entrance that could be closed with a huge log gate. They marched across sixty feet of grass-covered yard and through another large gateway into a hall about fifty feet long and thirty wide. Except for Frigate, who was too weak, they stood before a large round table of oak. They blinked in the dark and cool interior before they could clearly see the two men at the table.

Guards with spears, clubs, and stone axes were everywhere. A wooden staircase at one end of the hall led up to a runway with high railings. Women looked over the railings at them.

One of the men at the table was short and muscular. He had a hairy body, black curly hair, a nose like a falcon's, and brown eyes as fierce as a falcon's. The second man was taller, had blond hair, eyes the exact color of which was difficult to tell in the dusky light but were probably blue, and a broad Teutonic face. A paunch and the beginnings of jowls told of the food and liquor he had taken from the grails of slaves.

Frigate had sat down on the grass, but he was pulled up to his feet when the blond gave a signal. Frigate looked at the blond and said, 'You look like Hermann Göring when he was young.'

Then he dropped to his knees, screaming with pain from the impact of a spear butt over his kidneys.

The blond spoke in an English with a heavy German accent. 'No more of that unless I order it. Let them talk.'

He scrutinized them for several minutes, then said, 'Yes, I am Hermann Göring.'

'Who is Göring?' Burton said.

'Your friend can tell you later,' the German said. 'If there is a later for you. I am not angry about the splendid fight you put up. I admire men who can fight well. I can always use more spears, especially since you killed so many. I offer you a choice. You men, that is. Join me and live well with all the food, liquor, tobacco, and women you can possibly want. Or work for me as my slaves.'

'For us,' the other man said in English. 'You forget, Hermann, dat I have yust as muck to say about dis as you.'

Göring smiled, chuckled, and said, 'Of course! I was only using the royal I, you might say. Very well, we. If you swear to serve *us*, and it will be far better for you if you do, you will swear loyalty to me, Hermann Göring and to the onetime king of ancient Rome, Tullius Hostilius.'

Burton looked closely at the man. Could he actually be the legendary king of ancient Rome? Of Rome when it was a small village threatened by the other Italic tribes, the Sabines, Aequi, and Volsci? Who, in turn, were being pressed by the Umbrians, themselves pushed by the powerful Etruscans? Was this really Tullius Hostilius, warlike successor to the peaceful Numa Pompilius? There was nothing to distinguish him from a thousand men whom Burton had seen on the streets of Siena. Yet, if he was what he claimed to be, he could be a treasure trove, historically and linguistically speaking. He would, since he was probably Etruscan himself, know that language, in addition to pre-Classical Latin, and Sabine, and perhaps Campanian Greek. He might even have been acquainted with Romulus, supposed founder of Roma. What stories that man could tell!

'Well?' Göring said.

'What do we have to do if we join you?' Burton said.

'First, I ... we ... have to make sure that you are the caliber of man we want. In other words, a man who will unhesitatingly and immediately do anything that we order. We will give you a little test.'

He gave an order and a minute later, a group of men was brought forward. All were gaunt, and all were crippled.

'They were injured while quarrying stone or building our walls,' Göring said. 'Except for two caught while trying to escape. They will have to pay the penalty. All will be killed because they are now useless. So, you should not hesitate about killing them to show your determination to serve us.'

He added, 'Besides, they are all Jews. Why worry about them?'

Campbell, the redhead who had thrown Gwenafra into The River, held out to Burton a large club studded with chert blades. Two guards seized a slave and forced him to his knees. He was a large blond with blue eyes and a Grecian profile; he glared at Göring and then spat at him.

Göring laughed. 'He has all the arrogance of his race. I could reduce him to a quivering screaming mass begging for death if I wanted to. But I do not really care for torture. My compatriot would like to give him a taste of the fire, but I am essentially a humanitarian.'

'I will kill in defense of my life or in defense of those who need protection,' Burton said. 'But I am not a murderer.'

'Killing this Jew would be an act in defense of your life,' Göring replied. 'If you do not, you will die anyway. Only it will take you a long time.'

'I will not,' Burton said.

Göring sighed. 'You English! Well, I would rather have you on my side. But if you don't want to do the rational thing, so be it. What about you?' he said to Frigate.

Frigate, who was still in agony, said, 'Your ashes ended in a trash heap in Dachau because of what you did and what you were. Are you going to repeat the same criminal acts on this world?'

Göring laughed and said, 'I know what happened to me. Enough of my Jewish slaves have told me.'

He pointed at Monat. 'What kind of a freak is that?'

Burton explained. Göring looked grave, then said, 'I couldn't trust him. He goes into the slave camp. You, there, apeman. What do you say?'

Kazz, to Burton's surprise, stepped forward. 'I kill for you. I don't want to be slave.'

He took the club while the guards held their spears poised to run him through if he had other ideas for using it. He glared at them from under his shelving brows, then raised the club. There was a crack, and the slave pitched forward on the dirt. Kazz returned the club to Campbell and stepped aside. He did not look at Burton.

Göring said, 'All the slaves will be assembled tonight, and they will be shown what will happen to them if they try to get away. The escapees will be roasted for a while, then put out of their misery. My distinguished colleague will personally handle the club. He likes that sort of thing.'

He pointed at Alice. 'That one. I'll take her.'

Tullius stood up. 'No, no. I like her. You take de oders, Hermann. I giw you bot' off dem. But sye, I want her wery muck. Sye look like, wat you say, aristocrat. A ... queen?'

Burton roared, snatched a club from Campbell's hand, and leaped upon the table. Göring fell backward, the tip of the club narrowly missing his nose. At the same time, the Roman thrust a spear at Burton and wounded him in the shoulder. Burton kept hold of the club, whirled, and knocked the weapon out of Tullius' hand.

The slaves, shouting, threw themselves upon the guards. Frigate jerked a spear loose and brought the butt of it against Kazz's head. Kazz crumpled. Monat kicked a guard in the groin and picked up his spear.

Burton did not remember anything after that. He awoke several hours before dusk. His head hurt worse than before. His ribs and both shoulders were stiff with pain. He was lying on grass in a pine log enclosure with a diameter of about fifty yards. Fifteen feet above the grass, circling the interior of the wall, was a wooden walk on which armed guards paced.

He groaned when he sat up. Frigate, squatting near him, said, 'I was afraid you'd never come out of it.'

'Where are the women?' Burton said.

Frigate began to weep. Burton shook his head and said, 'Quit blubbering. Where are they?'

'Where the hell do you think they are?' Frigate said. 'Oh, my God!'

'Don't think about the women. There's nothing you can do for them. Not now, anyway. Why wasn't I killed after I attacked Göring?'

Frigate wiped away the tears and said, 'Beats me. Maybe they're saving you, and me, for the fire. As an example. I wish they had killed us.'

'What, so recently gained paradise and wish so soon to lose it?' Burton said. He began to laugh but quit because pains speared his head.

Burton talked to Robert Spruce, an Englishman born in 1945 in Kensington. Spruce said that it was less than a month since Göring and Tullius had seized power. For the time being, they were leaving their neighbors in peace. Eventually, of course, they would try to conquer the adjacent territories, including the Onondaga Indians across 'The River. So far, no slave had escaped to spread word about Göring's intentions.

'But the people on the borders can see for themselves that the walls are being built by slaves,' Burton said.

Spruce grinned wryly and said, 'Göring has spread the word that these are all Jews, that he is only interested in enslaving Jews. So, what do they care? As you can see for yourself, that is not true. Half of the slaves are Gentile.'

At dusk, Burton, Frigate, Ruach, de Greystoke, and Monat were taken from the stockade and marched down to a grailrock. There were about two hundred slaves there, guarded by about seventy Göring-ites. Their grails were placed on the rock, and they waited. After the blue flames roared, the grails were taken down. Each slave opened his, and guards removed the tobacco, liquor, and half of the food.

Frigate had gashes in his head and in his shoulder which needed sewing up, though the bleeding had stopped. His color had much improved, though his back and kidneys pained him.

'So now we're slaves,' Frigate said. 'Dick, you thought quite a lot of the institution of slavery. What do you think of it now?'

'That was *Oriental* slavery,' Burton said. 'In *this* type of slavery, there's no chance for a slave to gain his freedom. Nor is there any personal feeling, except hatred, between slave and owner. In the Orient, the situation was different. Of course, like any human institution, it had its abuses.'

'You're a stubborn man,' Frigate said. 'Have you noticed that at least half the slaves are Jews? Late twentieth-century Israeli, most of them. That girl over there told me that Göring managed to start grail-slavery by stirring up anti-Semitism in this area. Of course, it had to exist before it could be aroused. Then, after he had gotten into power with Tullius' aid, he enslaved many of his former supporters.'

He continued, 'The hell of it is, Göring is not, relatively speaking, a genuine anti-Semite. He personally intervened with Himmler and others to save Jews. But he is something even worse than a genuine Jew-hater. He is an opportunist. Anti-Semitism was a tidal wave in Germany; to get any place, you had to ride the wave. So, Göring rode there, just as he rode here. An anti-Semite such as Goebbels or Frank believed in the principles they professed. Perverted and hateful principles, true, but still principles. Whereas big fat happy-go-lucky Göring did not really care one way or the other about the Jews. He just wanted to use them.'

'All very well,' Burton said, 'but what has that got to do with me? Oh, I see! That look! You are getting ready to lecture me.'

'Dick, I admire you as I have admired few men. I love you as one man loves another. I am as happy and delighted to have had the singular good luck to fall in with you as, say, Plutarch would be if he had met Alcibiades or

Theseus. But I am not blind. I know your faults, which are many, and I regret them.'

'Just which one is it this time?'

'That book. *The Jew, The Gypsy, and El Islam*. How could you have written it? A hate document full of bloody-minded nonsense, folk tales, superstitions! Ritual murders, indeed!'

'I was still angry because of the injustices I had suffered at Damascus. To be expelled from the consulate because of the lies of my enemies, among whom ...'

'That doesn't excuse your writing lies about a whole group,' Frigate said.

'Lies! I wrote the truth!'

'You may have thought they were truths. But I come from an age which definitely knows that they were not. In fact, no one in his right mind in your time would have believed that crap!'

'The facts are,' Burton said, 'that the Jewish moneylenders in Damascus were charging the poor a thousand percent interest on their loans. The facts are that they were inflicting this monstrous usury not only on the Moslem and Christian populace but on their own people. The facts are, that when my enemies in England accused me of anti-Semitism, many Jews in Damascus came to my defense. It is a fact that I protested to the Turks when they sold the synagogue of the Damascan Jews to the Greek Orthodox bishop so he could turn it into a church. It is a fact that I went out and drummed up eighteen Moslems to testify in behalf of the Jews. It is a fact that I protected the Christian missionaries from the Druzes. It is a fact that I warned the Druzes that that fat and oily Turkish swine, Rashid Pasha, was trying to incite them to revolt so he could massacre them. It is a fact that when I was recalled from my consular post, because of the lies of the Christian missionaries and priests, of Rashid Pasha, and of the Jewish usurers, thousands of Christians, Moslems, and Jews rallied to my aid, though it was too late then.

'It is also a fact that I don't have to answer to you or to any man for my actions!'

How like Frigate to bring up such an irrelevant subject at such an inappropriate time. Perhaps he was trying to keep from blaming himself by turning his fear and anger on Burton. Or perhaps he really felt that his hero had failed him.

Lev Ruach had been sitting with his head between his blinds. He raised his head and said, hollowly, 'Welcome to the concentration camp, Burton! This is your first taste of it. It's an old tale to me, one I was tired of hearing from the beginning. I was in a Nazi camp, and I escaped. I was in a Russian camp, and I escaped. In Israel, I was captured by Arabs, and I escaped.

'So, now, perhaps I can escape again. But to what? To another camp? There seems to be no end to them. Man is forever building them and putting the perennial prisoner, the Jew, or what have you, in them. Even here, where we have a fresh start, where all religions, all prejudices, should have been shattered on the anvil of resurrection, little is changed.'

'Shut your mouth,' a man near Ruach said. He had red hair so curly it was almost kinky, blue eyes, and a face that might have been handsome if it had not been for his broken nose. He was six feet tall and had a wrestler's body.

'Dov Targoff here,' he said in a crisp Oxford accent. 'Late commander in the Israeli Navy. Pay no attention to this man. He's one of the old-time Jews, a pessimist, a whiner. He'd rather wail against the wall than stand up and fight like a man.'

Ruach choked, then said, 'You arrogant Sabra! I fought; I killed! And I am not a whiner! What are you doing now, you brave warrior? Aren't you a slave as much as the rest of us?'

'It's the old story,' a woman said. She was tall and dark-haired and probably would have been a beauty if she had not been so gaunt. 'The old story. We fight among ourselves while our enemies conquer. Just as we fought when Titus besieged Jerusalem and we killed more of our own people than we did the Romans. Just as ...'

The two men turned against her, and all three argued loudly until a guard began beating them with a stick.

Later, through swollen lips, Targoff said, 'I can't take much of this, much longer. Soon ... well, that guard is mine to kill.'

'You have a plan?' Frigate said, eagerly, but Targoff would not answer.

Shortly before dawn, the slaves were awakened and marched to the grailrock. Again, they were given a modicum of food. After eating, they were split up into groups and marched off to their differing assignments. Burton and Frigate were taken to the northern border. They were put to work with a thousand other slaves, and they toiled naked all day in the sun. Their only rest was when they took their grails to the rock at noon and were fed.

Göring meant to build a wall between the mountain and The River; he also intended to erect a second wall which would run for the full ten-mile length of the lakeshore and a, third wall at the southern end.

Burton and the others had to dig a deep trench and then pile the dirt taken from the hole into a wall. This was hard work, for they had only stone hoes with which to hack at the ground. Since the roots of the grass formed a thickly tangled complex of very tough material, they could be cut only with repeated blows. The dirt and roots were scraped up on wooden shovels and tossed onto large bamboo sleds. These were dragged by teams onto the top of the wall, where the dirt was shoveled off to make the wall even higher and thicker.

At night, the slaves were herded back into the stockade. Here, most of them fell asleep almost at once. But Targoff, the redheaded Israeli, squatted by Burton.

'The grapevine gives a little juice now and then,' he said. 'I heard about the fight you and your crew made. I also heard about your refusal to join Göring and his swine.'

'What do you hear about my infamous book?' Burton said.

Targoff smiled and said, 'I never heard of it until Ruach brought it to my attention. Your actions speak for themselves. Besides, Ruach is very sensitive about such things. Not that you can really blame him after what he went through. But I do not think that you would behave as you did if you were what he said you are. I think you're a good man, the type we need. So ...'

Days and nights of hard work and short rations followed. Burton learned through the grapevine about the women. Wilfreda and Fatima were in Campbell's apartment. Loghu was with Tullius. Alice had been kept by Göring for a week, then had been turned over to a lieutenant, a Manfred von Kreyscharft. Rumor was that Göring had complained of her coldness and had wanted to give her to his bodyguards to do with as they pleased. But von Kreyscharft had asked for her.

Burton was in agony. He could not endure the mental images of her with Göring and von Kreyscharft. He had to stop these beasts or at least die trying. Late that night, he crawled from the big hut he occupied with twenty-five men into Targoff's hut and woke him up.

'You said you knew that I must be on your side,' he whispered. 'When are you going to take me into your confidence? I might as well warn you now that, if you don't do so at once, I intend to foment a break among my own group and anybody else who will join us.'

'Ruach has told me *more* about you,' Targoff said. 'I didn't understand, really, what he was talking about. Could a Jew trust anyone who wrote such a book? Or could such a man be trusted not to turn on them after the common enemy has been defeated?'

Burton opened his mouth to speak angrily, then closed it. For a moment, he was silent. When he spoke, he did so calmly. 'In the first place, my actions on Earth speak louder than any of my printed words. I was the friend and protector of many Jews; I had many Jewish friends.'

'That last statement is always a preface to an attack on the Jews,' Targoff said.

'Perhaps. However, even if what Ruach claims were true, the Richard Burton you see before you in this valley is not the Burton who lived on Earth. I think every man has been changed somewhat by his experience here. If he hasn't, he is incapable of change. He would be better off dead.

'During the four hundred and seventy-six days that I have lived on this River, I have learned much. I am not incapable of changing my mind. I listened to Ruach and Frigate. I argued, frequently and passionately with them.

And though I did not want to admit it at the time, I thought much about what they said.'

'Jew-hate is something bred into the child,' Targoff said. 'It becomes part of the nerve. No act of will can get rid of it, unless it is not very deeply embedded or the will is extraordinarily strong. The bell rings, and Pavlov's dog salivates. Mention the word *Jew*, and the nervous system storms the citadel of the mind of the Gentile. Just as the word *Arab* storms mine. But I have a realistic basis for hating all Arabs.'

'I have pled enough,' Burton said. 'You will either accept me or reject me. In either case, you know what I will do.'

'I accept,' Targoff said. 'If you can change your mind, I can change mine. I've worked with you, eaten bread with you. I like to think I'm a good judge of character. Tell me, if you were planning this, what would you do?'

Targoff listened carefully. At the end of Burton's explanation, Targoff nodded. 'Much like my plan. Now ...'

16

The next day, shortly after breakfast, several guards came for Burton and Frigate. Targoff looked hard at Burton, who knew what Targoff was thinking. Nothing could be done except to march off to Göring's 'palace.' He was seated in a big wooden chair and smoking a pipe. He asked them to sit down and offered them cigars and wine.

'Every once in a while,' he said, 'I like to relax and talk with somebody besides my colleagues, who are not overly bright. I like especially to talk with somebody who lived *after* I died. And to men who were famous in their time. I've few of either type, so far.'

'Many of your Israeli prisoners lived after you,' Frigate said.

'Ah, the Jews!' Göring airily waved his pipe. 'That is the trouble. They know me too well. They are sullen when I try to talk to them, and too many have tried to kill me for me to feel comfortable around them. Not that I have anything against them. I don't particularly like Jews, but I had many Jewish friends ...'

Burton reddened.

Göring, after sucking on his pipe, continued, 'Der Fuehrer was a great man, but he had some idiocies. One of them was his attitude toward Jews. Myself, I cared less. But the Germany of my time was anti-Jewish, and a man must go with the Zeitgeist if he wants to get any place in life. Enough of that. Even here, a man cannot get away from them.'

He chattered on for a while, then asked Frigate many questions concerning the fate of his contemporaries and the history of postwar Germany.

'If you Americans had had any political sense, you would have declared war on Russia as soon as we surrendered. We would have fought with you against the Bolshevik, and we would have crushed them.'

Frigate did not reply. Göring then told several 'funny,' very obscene stories. He asked Burton to tell him about the strange experience he had had before being resurrected in the valley.

Burton was surprised. Had Göring learned about this from Kazz or was there an informer among the slaves?

He told in full detail everything that had happened between the time he opened his eyes to find himself in the place of floating bodies to the instant when the man in the aerial canoe pointed the metal tube at him.

'The extra-terrestrial, Monat, has a theory that some beings – call them Whoever or X – have been observing mankind since he ceased to be an ape. For at least two million years. These superbeings have, in some manner, recorded every cell of every human being that ever lived from the moment of conception, probably, to the moment of death. This seems a staggering concept, but it is no more staggering than the resurrection of all humanity and the reshaping of this planet into one Rivervalley. The recordings may have been made when the recordees were living. Or it may be that these superbeings detected vibrations from the past, just as we on Earth saw the light of stars as they had been a thousand years before.

'Monat, however, inclines to the former theory. He does not believe in time travel even in a limited sense.

'Monat believes that the X's stored these recordings. How, he does not know. But this planet was then reshaped for us. It is obviously one great Riverworld. During our journey upRiver, we've talked to dozens whose descriptions leave no doubt that they come from widely scattered parts, from all over. One was from far up in the northern hemisphere; another, far down in the southern. All the descriptions fall together to make a picture of a world that has been reworked into one zigzagging Rivervalley.

'The people we talked to were killed or died by accident here and were resurrected again in the areas we happened to be traveling through. Monat says that we resurrectees are still being recorded. And when one of us dies again, the up-to-the-minute recordings are being placed somewhere – maybe under the surface of this planet – and played into energy-matter converters. The bodies were reproduced as they were at the moment of death and then the rejuvenating devices restored the sleeping bodies. Probably in that same chamber in which I awoke. After this, the bodies, young and whole again, were recorded and then destroyed. And the recordings were played out again, this time through devices under the ground. Once more, energy-matter converters, probably using the heat of this planet's molten core as energy, reproduced us above the ground, near the grailstones. I do not know why they are not resurrected a second time in the same spot where they died. But then I don't know why all our hairs were shaven off or why men's facial hairs don't grow or why men were circumcised and women made virgins again. Or why we were resurrected. For what purpose? Whoever put us here has not shown up to tell us why.'

'The thing is,' Frigate said, 'the thing is, we *are not* the *same* people we were on Earth. I died. Burton died. You died, Hermann Göring. Everybody died. And we *cannot* be brought back to life!'

Göring sucked on his pipe noisily, stared at Frigate, and then said, 'Why not? I am living again. Do you deny that?'

'Yes! I do deny that – in a sense. You are living. But you are *not* the Hermann Göring who was born in Marienbad Sanatorium at Rosenheim in Bavaria on 12 January 1893. You are *not* the Hermann Göring whose godfather was Dr Hermann Eppenstein, a Jew converted to Christianity. You are *not* the Göring who succeeded von Richthofen after his death and continued to lead his fliers against the Allies even after the war ended. You *are not* the Reichsmarschal of Hitler's Germany nor the refugee arrested by Lieutenant Jerome N. Shapiro. Eppenstein and Shapiro, hah! And you are *not* the Hermann Göring who took his life by swallowing potassium cyanide during his trial for his crimes against humanity!'

Göring tamped his pipe with tobacco and said, mildly, 'You certainly know much about me. I should be flattered, I suppose. At least, I was not forgotten.'

'Generally, you were,' Frigate said. 'You did have a long-lived reputation as a sinister clown, a failure, and a toady.'

Burton was surprised. He had not known that the fellow would stand up to someone who had power of life and death over him or who had treated him so painfully. But then perhaps Frigate hoped to be killed.

It was probable that he was banking on Göring's curiosity.

Göring said, 'Explain your statement. Not about my reputation. Every man of importance expects to be reviled and misunderstood by the brainless masses. Explain why I am not the same man.'

Frigate smiled slightly and said, 'You are the product, the hybrid, of a recording and an energy-matter converter. You were made with all the *memories* of the dead man Hermann Göring and with every cell of his body a duplicate. You have everything he had. So you *think* you are Göring. But you are not! You are a duplication, and that is all! The original Hermann Göring is nothing but molecules that have been absorbed into the soil and the air and so into plants and back into the flesh of beasts and men and out again as excrement, *und so welter!*

'But you, here before me, are not the original, any more than the recording on a disc or a tape is the original voice, the vibrations issuing from the mouth of a man and detected and converted by an electronic device and then replayed.'

Burton understood the reference, since he had seen an Edison phonograph in Paris in 1888. He felt outraged, actually violated, at Frigate's assertions.

Göring's wide-open eyes and reddening face indicated that he, too, felt threatened down to the core of his being.

After stuttering, Göring said, 'And why would these beings go to all this trouble just to make duplicates?'

Frigate shrugged and said, 'I don't know.'

Göring heaved up from his chair and pointed the stem of his pipe at Frigate.

'You *lie!*' he screamed in German. 'You *lie, scheisshund!*'

Frigate quivered as if he *expected* to be struck over the kidneys again, but he said, 'I must be right. Of course, you don't have to believe what I say. I can't prove anything. And I understand exactly how you feel. I *know* that I am Peter Jairus Frigate, born 1918, died AD 2008. But I also must believe, because logic tells me so, that I am only, really, a being who has the *memories* of that Frigate who will never rise from the dead. In a sense, I am the son of that Frigate who can never exist again. Not flesh of his flesh, blood of his blood, but mind of his mind. I am *not* the man who was born of a woman on that lost world of Earth. I am the by-blow of science and a machine. Unless ...'

Göring said, 'Yes? Unless what?'

'Unless there is some entity attached to the human body, an entity which is the human being. I mean, it contains all that makes the individual what he is, and when the body is destroyed, this entity still exists. So that, if the body were to be made again, this entity, storing the essence of the *individual*, could be attached again to the body. And it would record everything that the body recorded. And so the original individual *would live* again. He would not be just a duplicate.'

Burton said, 'For God's sake, Pete! Are you proposing the *soul?*'

Frigate nodded and said, 'Something analogous to the soul. Something that the primitives dimly apprehended and called a soul.'

Göring laughed uproariously. Burton would have laughed, but he did not care to give Göring any support, moral or intellectual.

When Göring had quit laughing, he said, 'Even here, in a world which is clearly the result of science, the supernaturalists won't quit trying. Well, enough of that. To more practical and immediate matters. Tell me, have you changed your mind? Are you ready to join me?'

Burton glared and said, 'I would not be under the orders of a man who rapes women; moreover, I respect the Israelis. I would rather be a slave with them than free with you.'

Göring scowled and said, harshly, 'Very well. I thought as much. But I had hoped ... well, I have been having trouble with the Roman. If he gets his way, you will see how merciful I have been to you slaves. You do not know him. Only my intervention has saved one of you being tortured to death every night for his amusement.'

At noon, the two returned to their work in the hills. Neither got a chance to speak to Targoff or any of the slaves, since their duties happened not to bring them into contact. They did not dare make an open attempt to talk to him, because that would have meant a severe beating.

After they returned to the stockade in the evening, Burton told the others what had happened.

'More than likely Targoff will not believe my story. He'll think we're spies. Even if he's not certain, he can't afford to take chances. So there'll be trouble. It's too bad that this had to happen. The escape plan will have to be cancelled for tonight.'

Nothing untoward took place – at first. The Israelis walked away from Burton and Frigate when they tried to talk to them. The stars came out, and the stockade was flooded with a light almost as bright as a full moon of Earth.

The prisoners stayed inside their barracks, but they talked in low voices with their heads together. Despite their deep tiredness, they could not sleep. The guards must have sensed the tension, even though they could not see or hear the men in the huts. They walked back and forth on the walks, stood together talking, and peered down into the enclosure by the light of the night sky and the flames of the resin torches.

'Targoff will do nothing until it rains,' Burton said. He gave orders. Frigate was to stand first watch; Robert Spruce, the second; Burton, third. Burton lay down on his pile of leaves and, ignoring the murmuring of voices and the moving around of bodies, fell asleep.

It seemed that he had just closed his eyes when Spruce touched him. He rose quickly to his feet, yawned, and stretched. The others were all awake. Within a few minutes, the first of the clouds formed. In ten minutes, the stars were blotted out. Thunder grumbled way up in the mountains, and the first lightning flash forked the sky.

Lightning struck near. Burton saw by its flash that the guards were huddled under the roofs sticking out from the base of the watch houses at each corner of the stockade. They were covered with towels against the chill and the rain.

Burton crawled from his barracks to the next. Targoff was standing inside the entrance. Burton stood up and said, 'Does the plan still hold?'

'You know better than that,' Targoff said. A bolt of lightning showed his angry face. 'You Judas!'

He stepped forward, and a dozen men followed him. Burton did not wait; he attacked. But, as he rushed forward, he heard a strange sound. He paused to look out through the door. Another flash revealed a guard sprawled face down in the grass beneath a walk.

Targoff had put his fists down when Burton turned his back on him. He said, 'What's going on, Burton?'

'Wait,' the Englishman replied. He had no more idea than the Israeli about what was happening, but anything unexpected could be to his advantage.

Lightning illuminated the squat figure of Kazz on the wooden walk. He was swinging a huge stone axe against a group of guards who were in the angle formed by the meeting of the two walls. Another flash. The guards were sprawled out on the walk. Darkness. At the next blaze of light, another was down; the remaining two were running away down the walk in different directions.

Another bolt very near the wall showed that, finally, the other guards were aware of what was happening. They ran down the walk, shouting and waving their spears.

Kazz, ignoring them, slid a long bamboo ladder down into the enclosure and then he threw a bundle of spears after it. By the next flash, he could be seen advancing toward the nearest guards.

Burton snatched a spear and almost ran up the ladder. The others, including the Israeli, were behind him. The fight was bloody and brief. With the guards on the walk either stabbed or hurled to their deaths, only those in the watch houses remained. The ladder was carried to the other end of the stockade and placed against the gate. In two minutes, men had climbed to the outside, dropped down, and opened the gate. For the first time, Burton found the chance to talk to Kazz.

'I thought you had sold us out.'

'No. Not me, Kazz,' Kazz said reproachfully. 'You know I love you, Burton-naq. You're my friend, my chief. I pretend to join your enemies because that's playing it smart. I surprise you don't do the same. You're no dummy.'

'Certainly, you aren't,' Burton said. 'But I couldn't bring myself to kill those slaves.'

Lightning revealed Kazz shrugging. He said, 'That don't bother me. I don't know them. Besides, you hear Göring. He say they die anyway.'

'It's a good thing you chose tonight to rescue us,' Burton said. He did not tell Kazz why since he did not want to confuse him. Moreover, there were more important things to do.

'Tonight's a good night for this,' Kazz said. 'Big battle going on. Tullius and Göring get very drunk and quarrel. They fight; their men fight. While they kill each other, invaders come. Those brown men across The River ... what you call them? ... Onondagas, that's them. Their boats come just before rain come. They make raid to steal slaves, too. Or maybe just for the hell of it. So, I think, now's good time to start my plan, get Burton-naq free.'

As suddenly as it had come, the rain ceased. Burton could hear shouts and screams from far off, toward The River. Drums were beating up and down The Riverbanks. He said to Targoff, 'We can either try to escape, and probably do so easily, or we can attack.'

'I intend to wipe out the beasts who enslaved us,' Targoff said. 'There are other stockades nearby. I've sent men to open their gates. The rest are too far away to reach quickly; they're strung out at half-mile intervals.'

By then, the blockhouse in which the off-duty guards lived had been stormed. The slaves armed themselves and then started toward the noise of the conflict. Burton's group was on the right flank. They had not gone half a mile before they came upon corpses and wounded, a mixture of Onondagas and whites.

Despite the heavy rain, a fire had broken out. By its increasing light, they saw that the flames came from the longhouse. Outlined in the glare were struggling figures. The escapees advanced across the plain. Suddenly, one side broke and ran toward them with the victors, whooping and screaming jubilantly, after them.

'There's Göring,' Frigate said. 'His fat isn't going to help him get away, that's for sure.'

He pointed, and Burton could see the German desperately pumping his legs but falling behind the others. 'I don't want the Indians to have the honor of killing him,' Burton said. 'We owe it to Alice to get him.'

Campbell's long-legged figure was ahead of them all, and it was toward him that Burton threw his spear. To the Scot, the missile must have seemed to come out of the darkness from nowhere. Too late, he tried to dodge. The flint head buried itself in the flesh between his left shoulder and chest, and he fell on his side. He tried to get up a moment afterward, but he was kicked back down by Burton.

Campbell's eyes rolled; blood trickled from his mouth. He pointed at another wound, a deep gash in his side just below the ribs. 'You ... your woman ... Wilfreda ... did that,' he gasped. 'But I killed her, the bitch ...'

Burton wanted to ask him where Alice was, but Kazz, screaming phrases in his native tongue, brought his club down on the Scot's head. Burton picked up his spear and ran after Kazz. 'Don't kill Göring!' he shouted. 'Leave him to me!'

Kazz did not hear him; he was busy fighting with two Onondagas. Burton saw Alice as she ran by him. He reached out and grabbed her and spun her around. She screamed and started to struggle. Burton shouted at her; suddenly, recognizing him, she collapsed into his arms and began weeping. Burton would have tried to comfort her, but he was afraid that Göring would escape him. He pushed her away and ran toward the German and threw his spear. It grazed Göring's head, and he screamed and stopped running and began to look for the weapon but Burton was on him. Both fell to the ground and rolled over and over, each trying to strangle the other.

Something struck Burton on the back of his head. Stunned, he released his grip. Göring pushed him down on the ground and dived toward the spear. Seizing it, he rose and stepped toward the prostrate Burton. Burton tried to get to his feet, but his knees seemed to be made of putty and everything was whirling. Göring suddenly staggered as Alice tackled his legs from behind, and he fell forward. Burton made another effort, found he could at least stagger, and sprawled over Göring. Again, they rolled over and over with Göring squeezing on Burton's throat. Then a shaft slid over Burton's shoulder, burning his skin, and its stone tip drove into Göring's throat.

Burton stood up, pulled the spear out, and plunged it into the man's fat belly. Göring tried to sit up, but he fell back and died. Alice slumped to the ground and wept.

Dawn saw the end of the battle. By then, the slaves had broken out of every stockade. The warriors of Göring and Tullius were ground between the two forces, Onondaga and slaves, like husks between millstones. The Indians, who had probably raided only to loot and get more slaves and their grails, retreated. They climbed aboard their dugouts and canoes and paddled across the lake. Nobody felt like chasing them.

17

The days that followed were busy ones. A rough census indicated that at least half of the 20,000 inhabitants of Göring's little kingdom had been killed, severely wounded, abducted by the Onondaga, or had fled. The Roman Tullius Hostilius had apparently escaped. The survivors chose a provisional government. Targoff, Burton, Spruce, Ruach, and two others formed an executive committee with considerable, but temporary, powers. John de Greystock had disappeared. He had been seen during the beginning of the battle and then he had just dropped out of sight.

Alice Hargreaves moved into Burton's hut without either saying a word about the why or wherefore.

Later, she said, 'Frigate tells me that if this entire planet is constructed like the areas we've seen, and there's no reason to believe it isn't, then The River must be at least 20,000,000 miles long. It's incredible, but so is our resurrection, everything about this world. Also, there may be thirty-five to thirty-seven billion people living along The River. What chance would I have of ever finding my Earthly husband?

'Moreover, I love you. Yes, I know I didn't act as if I loved you. But something has changed in me. Perhaps it's all I've been through that is responsible. I don't think I could have loved you on Earth. I might have been fascinated, but I would also have been repelled, perhaps frightened. I couldn't have made you a good wife there. Here, I can. Rather, I'll make you a good mate, since there doesn't seem to be any authority or religious institutions that could marry us. That in itself shows how I've changed. That I could be calmly living with a man I'm not married to …! Well, there you are.'

'We're no longer living in the Victorian age,' Burton said. 'What would you call this present age … the Mélange era? The Mixed Age? Eventually, it will be The River Culture, The Riparian World, rather, many River cultures.'

'Providing it lasts,' Alice said. 'It started suddenly; it may end just as swiftly and unexpectedly.'

Certainly, Burton thought, the green River and the grassy plain and the forested hills and the unscalable mountains did not seem like Shakespeare's insubstantial vision. They were solid, real, as real as the men walking toward him now, Frigate, Monat, Kazz, and Ruach. He stepped out of the hut and greeted them.

Kazz began talking. 'A long time ago, before I speak English good, I see something. I try to tell you then, but you don't understand me. I see a man who don't have this on his forehead.'

He pointed at the center of his own forehead and then at that of the others.

'I know,' Kazz continued, 'you can't see it. Pete and Monat can't either. Nobody else can. But I see it on everybody's forehead. Except on that man I try to catch long time ago. Then, one day, I see a woman don't have it, but I don't say nothing to you. Now, I see a third person who don't have it.'

'He means,' Monat said, 'that he is able to perceive certain symbols or characters on the forehead of each and every one of us. He can see these only in bright sunlight and at a certain angle. But everyone he's ever seen has had these symbols – except for the three he's mentioned.'

'He must be able to see a little further into the spectrum than we,' Frigate said. 'Obviously, Whoever stamped us with the sign of the beast or whatever you want to call it, did not know about the special ability of Kazz's species. Which shows that They are not omniscient.'

'Obviously,' Burton said. 'Nor infallible. Otherwise, I would never have awakened in that place before being resurrected. So, *who* is this person who does not have these symbols on his skin?'

He spoke calmly, but his heart beat swiftly. If Kazz was right, he might have detected an agent of the beings who had brought the entire human species to life again. Would They be gods in disguise?

'Robert Spruce!' Frigate said.

'Before we jump to any conclusions,' Monat said, 'don't forget that the omission may have been an accident.'

'We'll find out,' Burton said ominously. 'But *why* the symbols? Why should we be marked?'

'Probably for identification or numbering purposes,' Monat said. 'Who knows, except Those Who put us here.'

'Let's go face Spruce,' Burton said.

'We have to catch him first,' Frigate replied. 'Kazz made the mistake of mentioning to Spruce that he knew about the symbols. He did so at breakfast this morning. I wasn't there, but those who were said Spruce turned pale. A few minutes later, he excused himself, and he hasn't been seen since. We've sent search parties out up and down The River, across The River, and also into the hills.'

'His flight is an admission of guilt,' Burton said. He was angry. Was man a kind of cattle branded for some sinister purpose?

That afternoon, the drums announced that Spruce had been caught. Three hours later, he was standing before the council table in the newly built meeting hall. Behind the table sat the Council. The doors were closed, for the Councilmen felt that this was something that could be conducted more efficiently without a crowd. However, Monat, Kazz, and Frigate were also present.

'I may as well tell you now,' Burton said, 'that we have decided to go to any lengths to get the truth from you. It is against the principles of every one at this table to use torture. We despise and loathe those who resort to torture. But we feel that this is one issue where principles must be abandoned.'

'Principles must never be abandoned,' Spruce said evenly. 'The end never justifies the means. Even if clinging to them means defeat, death, and remaining in ignorance.'

'There's too much at stake,' Targoff said. 'I, who have been the victim of unprincipled men; Ruach, who has been tortured several times; the others, we all agree. We'll use fire and the knife on you if we must. It is necessary that we find out the truth.

'Now, tell me, are you one of Those responsible for this resurrection?'

'You will be no better than Göring and his kind if you torture me,' Spruce said. His voice was beginning to break. 'In fact, you will be far worse off, for you are forcing yourselves to be like him in order to gain something that may not even exist. Or, if it does, may not be worth the price.'

'Tell us the truth,' Targoff said. 'Don't lie. We know that you must be an agent; perhaps one of Those directly responsible.'

'There is a fire blazing in that stone over there,' Burton said. 'If you don't start talking at once, you will ... well, the roasting you get will be the least of your pain. I am an authority on Chinese and Arabic methods of torture. I assure you that they had some very refined means for extracting the truth. And I have no qualms about putting my knowledge into practice.'

Spruce, pale and sweating, said, 'You may be denying yourself eternal life if you do this. It will at least set you far back on your journey, delay the final goal.'

'What is that?' Burton replied.

Spruce ignored him. 'We can't stand pain,' he muttered. 'We're too sensitive.'

'Are you going to talk?' Targoff said.

'Even the idea of self-destruction is painful and to be avoided except when absolutely necessary,' Spruce mumbled. 'Despite the fact that I know I shall live again.'

'Put him over the fire,' Targoff said to the two men who held Spruce.

Monat spoke up. 'Just one moment. Spruce, the science of my people was much more advanced than that of Earth's. So I am more qualified to make an educated guess. Perhaps we could spare you the pain of the fire, and the pain of betraying your purpose, if you were merely to affirm what I have to say. That way, you wouldn't be making a positive betrayal.'

Spruce said, 'I'm listening.'

'It's my theory that you are a Terrestrial. You belong to an age chronologically far past AD 2008. You must be the descendant of the few who survived my death scanner. Judging by the technology and power required to reconstruct the surface of this planet into one vast Rivervalley, your time must be much later than the twenty-first century. Just guessing, the fiftieth century AD?'

Spruce looked at the fire, then said, 'Add two thousand more years.'

'If this planet is about the size of Earth, it can hold only so many people. Where are the others, the stillborn, the children who died before they were five, the imbeciles and idiots, and those who lived after the twentieth century?'

'They are elsewhere,' Spruce said. He glanced at the fire again, and his lips tightened.

'My own people,' Monat said, 'had a theory that they would eventually be able to see into their past. I won't go into the details, but it was possible that past events could be visually detected and then recorded. Time travel, of course, was sheer fantasy.

'But what if your culture was able to do what we only theorized about?

What if you recorded every single human being that had ever lived? Located this planet and constructed this Rivervalley? Somewhere, maybe under the very surface of this planet, used energy-matter conversion, say from the heat of this planet's molten core, and the recordings to re-create the bodies of the dead in the tanks? Used biological techniques to rejuvenate the bodies and to restore limbs, eyes, and so on and also to correct any physical defects?'

'Then,' Monat continued, 'you made more recordings of the newly created bodies and stored them in some vast memory-tank? Later, you destroyed the bodies in the tanks? Re-created them again through means of the conductive metal which is also used to charge the grails? These could be buried beneath the ground. The resurrection then occurs without recourse to supernatural means.

'The big question is, why?'

'If you had it in your power to do all this, would you not think it was your *ethical* duty?' Spruce asked.

'Yes, but I would resurrect only those worth resurrecting.'

'And what if others did not accept your criteria?' Spruce said. 'Do you really think you are wise enough and good enough to judge? Would you place yourself on a level with God? No, all must be given a second chance, no matter how bestial or selfish or petty or stupid. Then, it will be up to them ...'

He fell silent, as if he had regretted his outburst and meant to say no more.

'Besides,' Monat said, 'you would want to make a study of humanity as it existed in the past. You would want to record all the languages that man ever spoke, his mores, his philosophies, biographies. To do this, you need agents, posing as resurrectees, to mingle with the Riverpeople and to take notes, to observe, to study. How long will this study take? One thousand years? Two? Ten? A million?

'And what about the eventual disposition of us? Are we to stay here forever?'

'You will stay here as long as it takes for you to be rehabilitated,' Spruce shouted. 'Then ...'

He closed his mouth, glared, then opened it to say, 'Continued contact with you makes even the toughest of us take on your characteristics. We have to go through a rehabilitation ourselves. Already, I feel unclean.'

'Put him over the fire,' Targoff said. 'We'll get the entire truth.'

'No, you won't!' Spruce cried. 'I should have done this long ago! Who knows what ...?'

He fell to the ground, and his skin changed to a gray-blue color. Doctor Steinborg, a Councilman, examined him, but it was apparent to all that he was dead.

Targoff said, 'Better take him away now, doctor. Dissect him. We'll wait here for your report.'

'With stone knives, no chemicals, no microscopes, what kind of a report can you expect?' Steinborg said. 'But I'll do my best.'

The body was carried off. Burton said, 'I'm glad he didn't force us to admit we were bluffing. If he had kept his mouth shut, he could have defeated us.'

'Then you really weren't going to torture him?' Frigate said. 'I was hoping you didn't mean your threat. If you had, I was going to walk out then and there and never see any of you again.'

'Of course we didn't mean it,' Ruach said. 'Spruce would have been right. We'd have been no better than Göring. But we could have tried other means, Hypnotism for instance. Burton, Monat, and Steinborg were experts in that field.'

'The trouble is, we still don't know if we did get the truth,' Targoff said. 'Actually, he may have been lying. Monat supplied some guesses, and, if these were wrong, Spruce could have led us astray by agreeing with Monat. I'd say we can't be at all sure.'

They agreed on one thing. Their chances of detecting another agent through the absence of symbols on the forehead would be gone. Now that They – whoever They were – knew about the visibility of the characters to Kazz's species, They would take the proper measures to prevent detection.

Steinborg returned three hours later. 'There is nothing to distinguish him from any other member of *Homo sapiens*. Except this one little device.'

He held up a black shiny ball about the size of a match head.

'I located this on the surface of the forebrain. It was attached to some nerves by wires so thin that I could see them only at a certain angle, when they caught the light. It's my opinion that Spruce killed himself by means of this device and that he did so by literally thinking himself dead. Somehow, this little ball translated a wish for death into the deed. Perhaps, it reacted to the thought by releasing a poison which I do not have facilities for analyzing.' He concluded his report and passed the ball around to the others.

18

Thirty days later, Burton, Frigate, Ruach, and Kazz were returning from a trip upRiver. It was just before dawn.

The cold heavy mists that piled up to six or seven feet above The River in the latter part of the night swirled around them. They could not see in any direction further than a strong man might make a standing broad jump. But Burton, standing in the prow of the bamboo-hulled single-masted boat, knew they were close to the western shore. Near the relatively shallow depths the current ran more slowly, and they had just steered to port from the middle of The River.

If his calculations were correct, they should be close to the ruins of Göring's hall. At any moment, he expected to see a strip of denser darkness appear out of the dark waters, the banks of that land he now called home. Home, for Burton, had always been a place from which to sally forth, a resting-place, a temporary fortress in which to write a book about his last expedition, a lair in which to heal fresh hurts, a conning tower from which he looked out for new lands to explore.

Thus, only two weeks after the death of Spruce, Burton had felt the need to get to some place other than the one in which he now was. He heard a rumor that copper had been discovered on the western shore about a hundred miles upRiver. This was a length of shore of not more than twelve miles, inhabited by fifth-century BC Sarmatians and thirteenth-century AD Frisians.

Burton did not really think the story was true – but it gave him an excuse to travel. Ignoring Alice's pleas to take her with him, he had set off.

Now, a month later and after some adventures, not all unpleasant, they were almost home. The story had not been entirely unfounded. There was copper but only in minute amounts. So the four had gotten into their boat for the easy trip downcurrent, their sail pushed by the never-ceasing wind. They journeyed during the daytime and beached the boat during mealtimes wherever there were friendly people who did not mind strangers using their grailstones. At night they either slept among the friendlies or, if in hostile waters, sailed by in the darkness.

The last leg of their trip was made after the sun went down. Before getting home, they had to pass a section of the valley where slave-hungry eighteenth-century Mohawks lived on one side and equally greedy Carthaginians of the third century BC on the other. Having slipped through under cover of the fog, they were almost home.

Abruptly, Burton said, 'There's the bank. Pete, lower the mast! Kazz, Lev, back oars! Jump to it!'

A few minutes later, they had landed and had pulled the lightweight craft completely out of the water and upon the gently sloping shore. Now that they were out of the mists, they could see the sky paling above the eastern mountains.

'Dead reckoning come alive!' Burton said. 'We're ten paces beyond the grailstone near the ruins!'

He scanned the bamboo huts along the plain and the buildings evident in the long grasses and under the giant trees of the hills.

Not a single person was to be seen. The valley was asleep.

He said, 'Don't you think it's strange that no one's up yet? Or that we've not been challenged by the sentinels?'

Frigate pointed toward the lookout tower to their right. Burton swore and said, 'They're asleep, by God, or deserted their post!'

But he knew as he spoke that this was no case of dereliction of duty. Though he had said nothing to the others about it, the moment he had stepped ashore, he had been sure something was very wrong. He began running across the plain toward the hut in which he and Alice lived.

Alice was sleeping on the bamboo-and-grass bed on the right side of the building. Only her head was visible, for she was curled up under a blanket of towels fastened to each other by the magnetic clasps. Burton threw the blanket back, got down on his knees by the low bed, and raised her to a sitting position. Her head lolled forward, and her arms hung limply. But she had a healthy color and breathed normally.

Burton called her name three times. She slept on. He slapped both her cheeks sharply; red splotches sprang up on them. Her eyelids fluttered, then she went back to sleep.

By then Frigate and Ruach appeared. 'We've looked into some of the other huts,' Frigate said. 'They're all asleep. I tried to wake a couple of them, but they're out for the count. What's wrong?'

Burton said, 'Who do you think has the power or the need to do this? Spruce! Spruce and his kind, Whoever They are!'

'Why?' Frigate sounded frightened.

'They were looking for me! They must have come in under the fog, somehow put this whole area to sleep!'

'A sleep-gas would do it easily enough,' Ruach said. 'Although people who have powers such as Theirs could have devices we've never dreamed of.'

'They were looking for me!' Burton shouted.

'Which means, if true, that They may be back tonight,' Frigate said. 'But why would They be searching for you?'

Ruach replied for Burton. 'Because he, as far as we know, was the only man to awaken in the pre-resurrection phase. Why he did is a mystery. But it's evident something went wrong. It may also be a mystery to Them. I'd be inclined to think They've been discussing this and finally decided to come here. Maybe to kidnap Burton for observation – or some more sinister purpose.'

'Possibly. They wanted to erase from my memory all that I'd seen in that chamber of floating bodies,' Burton said. 'Such a thing should not be beyond Their science.'

'But you've told that story to many,' Frigate said. 'They couldn't possibly track down all those people and remove the memory of your story from their minds.'

'Would that be necessary? How many believe my tale? Sometimes I doubt it myself.'

Ruach said, 'Speculation is fruitless. What do we do now?'

Alice shrieked, 'Richard!' and they turned to see her sitting up and staring at them.

For a few minutes, they could not get her to understand what had happened. Finally she said, 'So that's why the fog covered the land, too! I thought it was strange, but of course I had no way of knowing what was really happening.'

Burton said, 'Get your grails. Put anything you want to take along in your sack. We're leaving as of now. I want to get away before the others awake.'

Alice's already large eyes became even wider. 'Where are we going?'

'Anywhere from here. I don't like to run away but I can't stand up and fight people like that. Not if They know where I am. I'll tell you, however, what I plan to do. I intend to find the end of The River. It must have an inlet and an outlet, and there must be a way for a man to get through to the source. If there's any way at all, I'll find it – you can bet your soul on that!

'Meanwhile, They'll be looking for me elsewhere – I hope. The fact that They didn't find me here makes me think that They have no means for instantly locating a person. They may have branded us like cattle' – he indicated the invisible symbols on his forehead – 'but even cattle have mavericks. And we're cattle with brains.'

He turned to the others. 'You're more than welcome to come along with me. In fact, I'd be honored.'

'I'll get Monat,' Kazz said. 'He wouldn't want to be left behind.'

Burton grimaced and said, 'Good old Monat! I hate to do this to him, but there's no helping it. He can't come along. He's too distinguishable. Their agents would have no trouble at all in locating anybody who looked like him. I'm sorry, but he can't.'

Tears stood in Kazz's eyes, then ran down his bulging cheekbones. In a choked voice, he said, 'Burton-naq, *I* can't go either. I look too different, too.'

Burton felt tears wet his own eyes. He said, 'We'll take that chance. After all, there must be plenty of your type around. We've seen at least thirty or more during our travels.'

'No females so far, Burton-naq,' Kazz said mournfully. Then he smiled. 'Maybe we find one when we go along The River.'

As quickly, he lost his grin. 'No, damn it, I don't go! I can't hurt Monat too much. Him and me, others think we ugly and scary looking. So we become good friends. He's not my *naq*, but he's next to it. I stay.'

He stepped up to Burton, hugged him in a grip that forced Burton's breath out in a great whoosh, released him, shook hands with the others, making them wince, then turned and shuffled off.

Ruach, holding his paralyzed hand, said. 'You're off on a fool's errand, Burton. Do you realize that you could sail on this River for a thousand years and still be a million miles or more from the end? I'm staying. My people need me. Besides, Spruce made it clear that we should be striving for a spiritual perfection, not fighting Those Who gave us a chance to do so.'

Burton's teeth flashed whitely in his dark face. He swung his grail as if it were a weapon.

'I didn't ask to be put here any more than I asked to be born on Earth. I don't intend to kowtow to another's dictates! I mean to find The River's end. And if I don't, I will at least have had fun and learned much on the way!'

By then, people were beginning to stumble out of their huts as they yawned and rubbed heavy eyes. Ruach paid no attention to them; he watched the craft as it set sail close-hauled to the wind, cutting across and up The River. Burton was handling the rudder; he turned once and waved the grail so that the sun bounced off it in many shining spears.

Ruach thought that Burton was really happy that he had been forced to make this decision. Now he could evade the deadly responsibilities that would come with governing this little state and could do what he wanted. He could set out on the greatest of all his adventures.

'I suppose it's for the best,' Ruach muttered to himself. 'A man may find salvation on the road, if he wants to, just as well as he may at home. It's up to him. Meanwhile, I, like Voltaire's character – what was his name? Earthly things are beginning to slip away from me – will cultivate my own little garden.'

He paused to look somewhat longingly after Burton.

'Who knows? He may someday run into Voltaire.'

He sighed, then smiled.

'On the other hand, Voltaire may some day drop in on me!'

19

'I hate you, Hermann Göring!'

The voice sprang out and then flashed away as if it were a gear tooth meshed with the cog of another man's dream and rotated into and then out of his dream.

Riding the crest of the hypnopompic state, Richard Francis Burton knew he was dreaming. But he was helpless to do anything about it.

The first dream returned.

Events were fuzzy and encapsulated. A lightning streak of himself in the measurable chamber of floating bodies; another flash of the nameless Custodians finding him and putting him back to sleep; then a jerky synopsis of the dream he had had just before the true Resurrection on the banks of The River.

God – a beautiful old man in the clothes of a mid-Victorian gentleman of means and breeding – was poking him in the ribs with an iron cane and telling him that *he owed for the flesh*.

'What? What flesh?' Burton said, dimly aware that he was muttering in his sleep. He could not hear his words in the dream.

'Pay up!' God said. His face melted, then was recast into Burton's own features.

God had not answered in the first dream five years before. He spoke now, '*Make your Resurrection worth my while, you fool! I have gone to great expense and even greater pains to give you, and all those other miserable and worthless wretches, a second chance.*'

'Second chance at what?' Burton said. He felt frightened at what God might answer. He was much relieved when God the All-Father – only now did Burton see that one eye of Jahweh-Odin was gone and out of the empty socket glared the flames of hell – did not reply. He was gone – no, not gone but metamorphosed into a high gray tower, cylindrical and soaring out of gray mists with the roar of the sea coming up through the mists.

'The Grail!' He saw again the man who had told him of the Big Grail. This man had heard it from another man, who had heard of it from a woman, who had heard it from … and so forth. The Big Grail was one of the legends told by the billions who lived along The River – this River that coiled like a serpent around this planet from pole to pole, issued from the unreachable and plunged into the inaccessible.

A man, or a sub-human, had managed to climb through the mountains to the North Pole. And he had seen the Big Grail, the Dark Tower, the Misty Castle just before he had stumbled. Or he was pushed. He had fallen headlong and bellowing into the cold seas beneath the mists and died. And then the man, or sub-human, had awakened again along The River. Death was not forever here, although it had lost nothing of its sting.

He had told of his vision. And the story had traveled along the valley of The River faster than a boat could sail.

Thus, Richard Francis Burton, the eternal pilgrim and wanderer, had longed to storm the ramparts of the Big Grail. He would unveil the secret of resurrection and of this planet, since he was convinced that the beings Who had reshaped this world had also built that tower.

'Die, Hermann Göring! Die, and leave me in peace!' a man shouted in German.

Burton opened his eyes. He could see nothing except the pale sheen of the multitudinous stars through the open window across the room of the hut.

His vision bent to the shape of the black things inside, and he saw Peter Frigate and Loghu sleeping on their mats by the opposite wall. He turned his head to see the white, blanket-sized towel under which Alice slept. The whiteness of her face was turned toward him, and the black cloud of her hair spilled out on the ground by her mat.

That same evening, the single-masted boat on which he and the other three had been sailing down The River had put into a friendly shore. The little state of Sevieria was inhabited largely by sixteenth-century Englishmen, although its chief was an American who had lived in the late eighteenth and early nineteenth century. John Sevier, founder of the 'lost state' of Franklin, which had later become Tennessee, had welcomed Burton and his party.

Sevier and his people did not believe in slavery and would not detain any guest longer than he desired. After permitting them to charge their grails and so feed themselves, Sevier had invited them to a party. It was the celebration of Resurrection Day; afterward, he had them conducted to the guest hostelry.

Burton was always a light sleeper, and now he was an uneasy one. The others began breathing deeply or snoring long before he had succumbed to weariness. After an interminable dream, he had wakened on hearing the voice that had interlocked with his dreams.

Hermann Göring, Burton thought. He had killed Göring, but Göring must be alive again somewhere along The River. Was the man now groaning and shouting in the neighboring hut one who had also suffered because of Göring, either on earth or in the Rivervalley?

Burton threw off the black towel and rose swiftly but noiselessly. He secured a kilt with magnetic tabs, fastened a belt of human skin around his waist, and made sure the human-leather scabbard held the flint poignard. Carrying an assegai, a short length of hardwood tipped with a flint point, he left the hut.

The moonless sky cast a light as bright as the full moon of Earth. It was aflame with huge many-colored stars and pale sheets of cosmic gas.

The hostelries were set back a mile and a half from The River and placed on one of the second row of hills that edged the Riverplain. There were seven of the one-room, leaf-thatch-roofed, bamboo buildings. At a distance, under the enormous branches of the irontrees or under the giant pines or oaks, were other huts. A half-mile away, on top of a high hill, was a large circular stockade, colloquially termed the 'Roundhouse.' The officials of Sevieria slept there.

High towers of bamboo were placed every half-mile along The River shore. Torches flamed all night long on platforms from which sentinels kept a lookout for invaders.

After scrutinizing the shadows under the trees, Burton walked a few steps to the hut from which the groans and shouts had come.

He pushed the grass curtain aside. The starlight fell through the open window on the face of the sleeper. Burton hissed in surprise. The light revealed the blondish hair and the broad features of a youth he recognized.

Burton moved slowly on bare feet. The sleeper groaned and threw one arm over his face and half-turned. Burton stopped, then resumed his stealthy progress. He placed the assegai on the ground, drew his dagger, and gently thrust the point against the hollow of the youth's throat. The arm flopped over; the eyes opened and stared into Burton's. Burton clamped his hand over the man's open mouth.

'Hermann Göring! Don't move or try to yell! I'll kill you!'

Göring's light-blue eyes looked dark in the shadows, but the paleness of his terror shone out. He quivered and started to sit up, then sank back as the flint dug into his skin.

'How long have you been here?' Burton said.

'Who ...?' Göring said in English, then his eyes opened even wider. 'Richard Burton? Am I dreaming? Is that you?'

Burton could smell the dreamgum on Göring's breath and the sweat-soaked mat on which he lay. The German was much thinner than the last time he had seen him.

Göring said, 'I don't know how long I've been here. What time is it?'

'About an hour until dawn, I'd say. It's the day after Resurrection Celebration.'

'Then I've been here three days. Could I have a drink of water? My throat's dry as a sarcophagus.'

'No wonder. You're a living sarcophagus – if you're addicted to dreamgum.'

Burton stood up, gesturing with the assegai at a fired clay pot on a little bamboo table nearby. 'You can drink if you want to. But don't try anything.'

Göring rose slowly and staggered to the table. 'I'm too weak to give you a fight even if I wanted to.' He drank noisily from the pot and then picked up an apple from the table. He took a bite, and then said, 'What're you doing here? I thought I was rid of you.'

'You answer my question first,' Burton said, 'and be quick about it. You pose a problem that I don't like, you know.'

20

Göring started chewing, stopped, stared, then said, 'Why should I? I don't have any authority here, and I couldn't do anything to you if I did. I'm just a guest here. Damned decent people, these; they haven't bothered me at all except to ask if I'm all right now and then. Though I don't know how long they'll let me stay without earning my keep.'

'You haven't left the hut?' Burton said. 'Then who charged your grail for you? How'd you get so much dreamgum?'

Göring smiled slyly. 'I had a big collection from the last place I stayed; somewhere about a thousand miles up The River.'

'Doubtless taken forcibly from some poor slaves,' Burton said. 'But if you were doing so well there, why did you leave?'

Göring began to weep. Tears ran down his face, and over his collarbones and down his chest, and his shoulders shook.

'I ... I had to get out. I wasn't any good to the others. I was losing my hold over them – spending too much time drinking, smoking marihuana, and chewing dreamgum. They said I was too soft myself. They would have killed me or made me a slave. So I sneaked out one night ... took the boat. I got away all right and kept going until I put into here. I traded part of my supply to Sevier for two weeks' sanctuary.'

Burton stared curiously at Göring.

'You knew what would happen if you took too much gum,' he said. 'Nightmares, hallucinations, delusions. Total mental and physical deterioration. You must have seen it happen to others.'

'I was a morphine addict on Earth!' Göring cried. 'I struggled with it, and I won out for a long time. Then, when things began to go badly for the Third Reich – and even worse for myself – when Hitler began picking on me, I started taking drugs again!'

He paused, then continued, 'But here, when I woke up to a new life, in a young body, when it looked as if I had an eternity of life and youth ahead of me, when there was no stern God in Heaven or Devil in Hell to stop me, I thought I could do exactly as I pleased and get away with it. I would become even greater than the Fuehrer! That little country in which you first found me was to be only the beginning! I could see my empire stretching for thousands of miles up and down The River, on both sides of the valley. I would have been the ruler of ten times the subjects that Hitler ever dreamed of!'

He began weeping again, then paused to take another drink of water, then put a piece of the dreamgum in his mouth. He chewed, his face becoming more relaxed and blissful with each second.

Göring said, 'I kept having nightmares of you plunging the spear into my belly. When I woke up, my belly would hurt as if a flint had gone into my guts. So I'd take gum to remove the hurt and the humiliation. At first, the gum helped. I was great. I was master of the world, Hitler, Napoleon, Julius Caesar, Alexander, Genghis Khan, all rolled into one. I was chief again of von Richthofen's Red Death Squadron; those were happy days, the happiest of my life in many ways. But the euphoria soon gave way to hideousness. I plunged into hell; I saw myself accusing myself and behind the accuser a million others. Not myself but the victims of that great and glorious hero, that obscene madman Hitler, whom I worshipped so. And in whose name I committed so many crimes.'

'You admit you were a criminal?' Burton said. 'That's a story different than the one you used to give me. Then you said you were justified in all you did, and you were betrayed by the ...'

He stopped, realizing that he had been sidetracked from his original purpose. 'That you should be haunted with the specter of a conscience is rather incredible. But perhaps that explains what has puzzled the puritans – why liquor, tobacco, marihuana, and dreamgum were offered in the grails along with food. At least, dreamgum seems to be a gift booby-trapped with danger to those who abuse it.'

He stepped closer to Göring. The German's eyes were half-closed, and his jaw hung open.

'You know my identity. I am traveling under a pseudonym, with good reason. You remember Spruce, one of your slaves? After you were killed, he was revealed, quite by accident, as one of those who somehow resurrected all the dead of humanity. Those we call the Ethicals, for lack of a better term. Göring, are you listening?'

Göring nodded.

'Spruce killed himself before we could get out of him all we wanted to know. Later, some of his compatriots came to our area and temporarily put everybody to sleep – probably with a gas – intending to take me away to wherever Their headquarters are. But They missed me. I was off on a trading trip up The River. When I returned, I realized They were after me, and I've been running ever since. Göring, do you hear me?'

Burton slapped him savagely on his cheek. Göring said, 'Ach!' and jumped back and held the side of his face. His eyes were open, and he was grimacing.

'I heard you!' he snarled. 'It just didn't seem worthwhile to answer back. Nothing seemed worthwhile, nothing except floating away, far from ...'

'Shut up and listen!' Burton said. 'The Ethicals have men everywhere looking for me. I can't afford to have you alive, do you realize that? I can't trust you. Even if you were a friend, you couldn't be trusted. You're a gummer!'

Göring giggled, stepped up to Burton and tried to put his arms around Burton's neck. Burton pushed him back so hard that he staggered up against the table and only kept from falling by clutching its edges.

'This is very amusing,' Göring said. 'The day I got here, a man asked me if I'd seen you. He described you in detail and gave your name. I told him I knew you well – too well, and that I hoped I'd never see you again, not unless I had you in my power, that is. He said I should notify him if I saw you again. He'd make it worth my while.'

Burton wasted no time. He strode up to Göring and seized him with both hands. They were small and delicate, but Göring winced with pain.

He said, 'What're you going to do, kill me again?'

'Not if you tell me the name of the man who asked you about me. Otherwise ...'

'Go ahead and kill me!' Göring said. 'So what? I'll wake up somewhere else, thousands of miles from here, far out of your reach.'

Burton pointed at a bamboo box in a corner of the hut. Guessing that it held Göring's supply of gum, he said, 'And you'd also wake up without that. Where else could you get so much on such short notice?'

'Damn you!' Göring shouted, and tried to tear himself loose to get to the box.

'Tell me his name!' Burton said. 'Or I'll take the gum and throw it in The River!'

'Agneau. Roger Agneau. He sleeps in a hut just outside the Roundhouse.'

'I'll deal with you later,' Burton said, and chopped Göring on the side of the neck with the edge of his palm.

He turned, and he saw a man crouching outside the entrance to the hut. The man straightened up and was off. Burton ran out after him; in a minute both were in the tall pines and oaks of the hills. His quarry disappeared in the waist-high grass.

Burton slowed to a trot, caught sight of a patch of white – starlight on bare skin – and was after the fellow. He hoped that the Ethical would not kill himself at once, because he had a plan for extracting information if he could knock him out at once. It involved hypnosis, but he would have to catch the Ethical first. It was possible that the man had some sort of wireless imbedded in his body and was even now in communication with his compatriots – wherever They were. If so, They would come in Their flying machines, and he would be lost.

He stopped. He had lost his quarry and the only thing to do now was to rouse Alice and the others and run. Perhaps this time they should take to the mountains and hide there for a while.

But first he would go to Agneau's hut. There was little chance that Agneau would be there, but it was certainly worth the effort to make sure.

21

Burton arrived within sight of the hut just in time to glimpse the back of a man entering it. Burton circled to come up from the side where the darkness of the hills and the trees scattered along the plain gave him some concealment. Crouching, he ran until he was at the door to the hut.

He heard a loud cry some distance behind him and whirled to see Göring staggering toward him. He was crying out in German to Agneau, warning him that Burton was just outside. In one hand he held a long spear which he brandished at the Englishman.

Burton turned and hurled himself against the flimsy bamboo-slat door. His shoulder drove into it and broke it from its wooden hinges. The door flew inward and struck Agneau, who had been standing just behind it. Burton, the door, and Agneau fell to the floor with Agneau under the door.

Burton rolled off the door, got up, and jumped again with both bare feet on the wood. Agneau screamed and then became silent. Burton heaved the door to one side to find his quarry unconscious and bleeding from the nose. Good! Now if the noise didn't bring the watch and if he could deal quickly enough with Göring, he could carry out his plan.

He looked up just in time to see the starlight on the long black object hurtling at him.

He threw himself to one side, and the spear plunged into the dirt floor with a thump. Its shaft vibrated like a rattlesnake preparing to strike.

Burton stepped into the doorway, estimated Göring's distance, and charged. His assegai plunged into the belly of the German. Göring threw his hands up in the air, screamed, and fell on his side. Burton hoisted Agneau's limp body on his shoulder and carried him out of the hut.

By then there were shouts from the Roundhouse. Torches were flaring up; the sentinel on the nearest watchtower was bellowing. Göring was sitting on the ground, bent over, clutching the shaft close to the wound.

He looked gape-mouthed at Burton and said, 'You did it again! You ...'

He fell over on his face, the death rattle in his throat.

Agneau returned to a frenzied consciousness. He twisted himself out of

Burton's grip and fell to the ground. Unlike Göring, he made no noise. He had as much reason to be silent as Burton – more perhaps. Burton was so surprised that he was left standing with the fellow's loin-towel clutched in his hand. Burton started to throw it down but felt something stiff and square within the lining of the towel. He transferred the cloth to his left hand, yanked the assegai from the corpse, and ran after Agneau.

The Ethical had launched one of the bamboo canoes beached along the shore. He paddled furiously out into the starlit waters, glancing frequently behind him. Burton raised the assegai behind his shoulder and hurled it. It was a short, thick-shafted weapon, designed for infighting and not as a javelin. But it flew straight and came down at the end of its trajectory in Agneau's back. The Ethical fell forward and at an angle and tipped the narrow craft over. The canoe turned upside down. Agneau did not reappear.

Burton swore. He had wanted to capture Agneau alive, but he was damned if he would permit the Ethical to escape. There was a chance that Agneau had not contacted other Ethicals yet.

He turned back toward the guest huts. Drums were beating up and down along the shore, and people with burning torches were hastening toward the Roundhouse. Burton stopped a woman and asked if he could borrow her torch a moment. She handed it to him but spouted questions at him. He answered that he thought the Choctaws across The River were making a raid. She hurried off toward the assembly before the stockade.

Burton drove the pointed end of the torch into the soft dirt of the bank and examined the towel he had snatched from Agneau. On the inside, just above the hard square in the lining, was a seam sealed with two thin magnetic strips, easily opened. He took the object out of the lining and looked at it by the torchlight.

For a long time he squatted by the shifting light, unable to stop looking or to subdue an almost paralyzing astonishment. A photograph, in this world of no cameras, was unheard-of. But a photograph of *him* was even more incredible, as was the fact that the picture had not been taken on this world! It had to have been made on Earth, that Earth lost now in the welter of stars somewhere in the blazing sky and in God only knew how many thousands of years of time.

Impossibility piled on impossibility! But it was taken at a time and at a place when he knew for certain that no camera had fixed upon him and preserved his image. His mustachios had been removed but the re-toucher had not bothered to opaque the background nor his clothing. There he was, caught miraculously from the waist up and imprisoned in a flat piece of some material. Flat! When he turned the square, he saw his profile come into view. If he held it almost at right angles to the eye, he could get a three-quarters profile-view of himself.

'In 1848,' he muttered to himself. 'When I was a twenty-seven-year old subaltern in the East Indian Army. And those are the blue mountains of Goa. This must have been taken when I was convalescing there. But, my God, how? By whom? And how would the Ethicals manage to have it in their possession now?'

Agneau had evidently carried this photo as a mnemonic in his quest for Burton. Probably every one of the hunters had one just like it, concealed in his towel. Up and down The River They were looking for him; there might be thousands, perhaps tens of thousands of Them. Who knew how many agents They had available or how desperately They wanted him or why They wanted him?

After replacing the photo in the towel, he turned to go back to the hut. And at that moment, his gaze turned toward the top of the mountains – those unscalable heights that bounded The Rivervalley on both sides.

He saw something flicker against a bright sheet of cosmic gas. It appeared for only the blink of an eyelid, then was gone.

A few seconds later, it came out of nothing, was revealed as a dark hemispherical object, then disappeared again.

A second flying craft showed itself briefly, reappeared at a lower elevation, and then was gone like the first.

The Ethicals would take him away, and the people of Sevieria would wonder what had made them fall asleep for an hour or so.

He did not have time to return to the hut and wake up the others. If he waited a moment longer, he would be trapped.

He turned and ran into The River and began swimming toward the other shore, a mile and a half away. But he had gone no more than forty yards when he felt the presence of some huge bulk above. He turned on his back to stare upward. There was only the soft glare of the stars above. Then, out of the air, fifty feet above him, a disk with a diameter of about sixty feet cut out a section of the sky. It disappeared almost immediately, came into sight again only twenty feet above him.

So They had some means of seeing at a distance in the night and had spotted him in his flight.

'You jackals!' he shouted at them. 'You'll not get me anyway!'

He upended and dived and swam straight downward. The water became colder, and his eardrums began to hurt. Although his eyes were open, he could see nothing. Suddenly, he was pushed by a wall of water, and he knew that the pressure came from displacement by a large object.

The craft had plunged down after him.

There was only one way out. They would have his dead body, but that would be all. He could escape Them again, be alive somewhere on The River to outwit Them again and strike back at Them.

He opened his mouth and breathed in deeply through both his nose and his mouth.

The water choked him. Only by a strong effort of will did he keep from closing his lips and trying to fight back against the death around him. *He* knew with his mind that he would live again, but the cells of his body did not know it. They were striving for life at this very moment, not in the rationalized future. And they forced from his water-choked throat a cry of despair.

22

'Yaaaaaaaah!'

The cry raised him off the grass as if he had bounced up off a trampoline. Unlike the first time he had been resurrected, he was not weak and bewildered. He knew what to expect. He would wake on the grassy banks of The River near a grailstone. But he was not prepared for these giants battling around him.

His first thought was to find a weapon. There was nothing at hand except the grail that always appeared with a resurrectee and the pile of towels of various sizes, colors, and thicknesses. He took one step, seized the handle of the grail, and waited. If he had to, he would use the grail as a club. It was light, but it was practically indestructible and very hard. However, the monsters around him looked as if they could take a battering all day and not feel a thing.

Most of them were at least eight feet tall, some were surely over nine; their massively muscled shoulders were over three feet broad. Their bodies were human, or nearly so, and their white skins were covered with long reddish or brownish hairs. They were not as hairy as a chimpanzee but more so than any man he had ever seen, and he had known some remarkably hirsute human beings.

But the faces gave them an unhuman and frightening aspect, especially since all were snarling with battle-rage. Below a low forehead was a bloom of bone that ran without indentation above the eyes and then continued around to form O's. Though the eyes were as large as his, they looked small compared to the broad face in which they were set. The cheekbones billowed out and then curved sharply inward. The tremendous noses gave the giants the appearance of proboscis monkeys.

At another time, Burton might have been amused by them. Not now. The roars that tore out of their more-than-gorilla-sized chests were deep as a lion's, and the huge teeth would have made a Kodiak bear think twice before attacking. Their fists, large as his head, held clubs as thick and as long as wagon poles or stone axes. They swung their weapons at each other, and when they struck flesh, bones broke with cracks as loud as wood splitting. Sometimes, the clubs broke, too.

Burton had a moment in which to look around. The light was weak. The sun had only half-risen above the peaks across The River. The air was far colder than any he had felt on this planet except during his defeated attempts to climb to the top of the perpendicular ranges.

Then one of the victors of a combat looked around for another enemy and saw him.

His eyes widened. For a second, he looked as startled as Burton had when he had first opened his eyes. Perhaps he had never seen such a creature as Burton before, any more than Burton had seen one like him. If so, he did not take long to get over his surprise. He bellowed, jumped over the mangled body of his foe, and ran toward Burton, raising an axe that could have felled an elephant.

Burton also ran, his grail in one hand. If he were to lose that, he might as well die now. Without it, he would starve or have to eke out on fish and bamboo sprouts.

He almost made it. An opening appeared before him, and he sped between two titans, their arms around each other and each straining to throw over the other, and another who was backing away before the rain of blows delivered by the club of a fourth. Just as he was almost through, the two wrestlers toppled over on him.

He was going swiftly enough that he was not caught directly under them, but the flailing arm of one struck his left heel. So hard was the blow, it smashed his foot against the ground and stopped him instantly. He fell forward and began to scream. His foot must have been broken, and he had torn muscles throughout his leg.

Nevertheless, he tried to rise and to hobble on to The River. Once in it, he could swim away, if he did not faint from the agony. He took two hops on his right foot, only to be seized from behind.

He flew up into the air, whirling around, and was caught before he began his descent.

The titan was holding him with one hand at arm's length, the enormous and powerful fist clutched around Burton's chest. Burton could hardly breathe; his ribs threatened to cave in.

Despite all this, he had not dropped his grail. Now he struck it against the giant's shoulder.

Lightly, as if brushing off a fly, the giant tapped the metal container with his axe, and the grail was torn from Burton's grip.

The behemoth grinned and bent his arm to bring Burton in closer. Burton weighed one hundred and eighty pounds, but the arm did not quiver under the strain.

For a moment, Burton looked directly into the pale blue eyes sunk in the bony circles. The nose was lined with many broken veins. The lips protruded because of the bulging prognathous jaws beneath – not, as he had first thought, because the lips were so thick.

Then the titan bellowed and lifted Burton up above his head. Burton hammered the huge arm with his fists, knowing that it was in vain but unwilling to submit like a caught rabbit. Even as he did so, he noted, though not with the full attention of his mind, several things about the scene.

The sun had been just rising above the mountain peaks when he had first awakened. Although the time passed since he had jumped to his feet was only a few minutes, the sun should have cleared the peaks. It had not; it hung at exactly the same height as when he had first seen it.

Moreover, the upward slant of the valley permitted a view for at least four miles. The grailstone by him was the last one. Beyond it was only the plain and The River.

This was the end of the line – or the beginning of The River.

There was no time nor desire for him to appreciate what these meant. He merely noted them during the passage between pain, rage, and terror. Then, as the giant prepared to bring his axe around to splinter Burton's skull, the giant stiffened and shrieked. To Burton, it was like being next to a locomotive whistle. The grip loosened, and Burton fell to the ground. For a moment, he passed out from the pain in his foot.

When he regained consciousness, he had to grind his teeth to keep from yelling again. He groaned and sat up, though not without a race of fire up his leg that made the feeble daylight grow almost black. The battle was roaring all around him, but he was in a little corner of inactivity. By him lay the tree-trunk-thick corpse of the titan who had been about to kill him. The back of his skull, which looked massive enough to resist a battering ram, was caved in.

Around the elephantine corpse crawled another casualty, on all fours. Seeing him, Burton forgot his pain for a moment. The horribly injured man was Hermann Göring.

Both of them had been resurrected at the same spot. There was no time to think about the implications of the coincidence. His pain began to come back. Moreover, Göring started to talk.

Not that he looked as if he had much talk left in him or much time left to do it in. Blood covered him. His right eye was gone. The corner of his mouth was ripped back to his ear. One of his hands was smashed flat. A rib was sticking through the skin. How he had managed to stay alive, let alone crawl, was beyond Burton's understanding.

'You … you!' Göring said hoarsely in German, and he collapsed. A fountain poured out of his mouth and over Burton's legs; his eyes glazed.

Burton wondered if he would ever know what he had intended to say. Not that it really mattered. He had more vital things to think about.

About ten yards from him, two titans were standing with their backs to him. Both were breathing hard, apparently resting for a moment before they jumped back into the fight. Then one spoke to the other.

There was no doubt about it. The giant was not just uttering cries. He was using a language.

Burton did not understand it, but he knew it was speech. He did not need the modulated, distinctly syllabic reply of the other to confirm his recognition.

So these were not some type of prehistoric ape but a species of sub-human men. They must have been unknown to the twentieth-century science of Earth, since his friend, Frigate, had described to him all the fossils known in AD 2008.

He lay down with his back against the fallen giant's Gothic ribs and brushed some of the long reddish sweaty hairs from his face. He fought nausea and the agony of his foot and the torn muscles of his leg. If he made too much noise, he might attract those two, and they would finish the job. But what if they did? With his wounds, in a land of such monsters, what chance did he have of surviving?

Worse than his agony of foot, almost, was the thought that, on his first trip on what he called The Suicide Express, he had reached his goal.

He had only an estimated one chance in ten million of arriving at this area, and he might never have made it if he had drowned himself ten thousand times. Yet he had had a fantastically good fortune. It might never occur again. And he was to lose it and very soon.

The sun was moving half-revealed along the tops of the mountains across The River. This was the place that he had speculated would exist; he had come here first shot. Now, as his eyesight failed and the pain lessened, he knew that he was dying. The sickness was born from more than the shattered bones in his foot. He must be bleeding inside.

He tried to rise once more. He would stand, if only on one foot, and shake his fist at the mocking fates and curse them. He would die with a curse on his lips.

23

The red wing of dawn was lightly touching his eyes.

He rose to his feet, knowing that his wounds would be healed and he would be whole again but not quite believing it. Near him was a grail and a pile of six neatly folded towels of various sizes, colors, and thicknesses.

Twelve feet away, another man, also naked, was rising from the short bright-green grass. Burton's skin grew cold. The blondish hair, broad face, and light-blue eyes were those of Hermann Göring.

The German looked as surprised as Burton. He spoke slowly, as if coming out of a deep sleep. 'There's something very wrong here.'

'Something foul indeed,' Burton replied. He knew no more of the pattern of resurrection along The River than any other man. He had never seen a resurrection, but he had had them described to him by those who had. At dawn, just after the sun topped the unclimbable mountains, a shimmering appeared in the air beside a grailstone. In the flicker of a bird's wing, the distortion solidified, and a naked man or woman or child appeared from nowhere on the grass by the bank. Always the indispensable grail and the towels were by the lazarus.

Along a conceivably ten to twenty million-mile long Rivervalley in which an estimated thirty-five to thirty-six billion lived, a million could die per day. It was true that there were no diseases (other than mental) but, though statistics were lacking, a million were probably killed every twenty-four hours by the myriads of wars between the one million or so little states, by crimes of passion, by suicides, by executions of criminals, and by accidents. There was a steady and numerous traffic of those undergoing the 'little resurrection,' as it was called.

But Burton had never heard of two dying in the same place and at the same time being resurrected together. The process of selection of area for the new life was random – or so he had always thought.

One such occurrence could conceivably take place, although the probabilities were one in twenty million. But two such, one immediately after the other, was a miracle.

Burton did not believe in miracles. Nothing happened that could not be explained by physical principles – if you knew all the facts.

He did not know them, so he would not worry about the 'coincidence' at the moment. The solution to another problem was more demanding. That was, what was he to do about Göring?

The man knew him and could identify him to any Ethicals searching for him.

Burton looked quickly around him and saw a number of men and women approaching in a seemingly friendly manner. There was time for a few words with the German.

'Göring, I can kill you or myself. But I don't want to do either – at the moment, anyway. You know why you're dangerous to me. I shouldn't take a chance with you, you treacherous hyena. But there's something different about you, something I can't put my fingers on. But …'

Göring, who was notorious for his resilience, seemed to be coming out of his shock. He grinned slyly and said, 'I do have you over the barrel, don't I?'

Seeing Burton's snarl, he hastily put up one hand and said, 'But I swear to you I won't reveal your identity to anyone! Or do anything to hurt you! Maybe we're not friends, but we at least know each other, and we're in a land of strangers. It's good to have one familiar face by your side. I know, I've suffered too long from loneliness, from desolation of the spirit. I thought I'd go mad. That's partly the reason I took to the dreamgum. Believe me, I won't betray you.'

Burton did not believe him. He did think, however, that he could trust him for a while. Göring would want a potential ally, at least until he took the measure of the people in this area and knew what he could or could not do. Besides, Göring might have changed for the better.

No, Burton said to himself. No. There you go again. Verbal cynic though you are, you've always been too forgiving, too ready to overlook injury to yourself and to give your injurer another chance. Don't be a fool again, Burton.

Three days later, he was still uncertain about Göring.

Burton had taken the identity of Abdul ibn Harun, a nineteenth-century citizen of Cairo, Egypt. He had several reasons for adopting the guise. One was that he spoke excellent Arabic, knew the Cairo dialect of that period, and had an excuse to cover his head with a towel wrapped as a turban. He hoped this would help disguise his appearance. Göring did not say a word to anybody to contradict the camouflage. Burton was fairly sure of this because he and Göring spent most of their time together. They were quartered in the same hut until they adjusted to the local customs and went through their period of probation. Part of this was intensive military training. Burton had been one of the greatest swordsmen of the nineteenth century and also knew every inflection of fighting with weapons or with hands. After a display of his ability in a series of tests, he was welcomed as a recruit. In fact, he was promised that he would be an instructor when he learned the language well enough.

Göring got the respect of the locals almost as swiftly. Whatever his other faults, he did not lack courage. He was strong and proficient with arms, jovial, likeable when it suited his purpose, and was not far behind Burton in gaining fluency in the language. He was quick to gain and to use authority, as befitted the ex-Reichmarschal of Hitler's Germany.

This section of the western shore was populated largely by speakers of a language totally unknown even to Burton, a master linguist both on Earth and on the Riverplanet. When he had learned enough to ask questions, he deduced that they must have lived somewhere in Central Europe during the Early Bronze Age. They had some curious customs, one of which was copulation in public. This was interesting enough to Burton, who had co-founded the Royal Anthropological Society in London in 1863 and who had seen strange things during his explorations on Earth. He did not participate, but neither was he horrified.

A custom he did adopt joyfully was that of stained whiskers. The males resented the fact that their face hair had been permanently removed by the Resurrectors, just as their prepuces had been cut off. They could do nothing about the latter outrage, but they could correct the former to a degree. They smeared their upper lips and chins with a dark liquid made from finely ground charcoal, fish glue, oak tannin, and several other ingredients. The more dedicated used the dye as a tattoo and underwent a painful and long-drawn-out pricking with a sharp bamboo needle.

Now Burton was doubly disguised, yet he had put himself at the mercy of the man who might betray him at the first opportunity. He wanted to attract an Ethical but did not want the Ethical to be certain of his identity.

Burton wanted to make sure that he could get away in time before being scooped up in the net. It was a dangerous game, like walking a tightrope over a pit of hungry wolves, but he wanted to play it. He would run only when it became absolutely necessary. The rest of the time, he would be the hunted hunting the hunter.

Yet the vision of the Dark Tower, or the Big Grail, was always on the horizon of every thought. Why play cat and mouse when he might be able to storm the very ramparts of the castle within which he presumed the Ethicals had headquarters? Or, if stormed was not the correct description, steal into the tower, effect entrance as a mouse does into a house – or a castle. While the cats were looking elsewhere, the mouse would be sneaking into the Tower, and there the mouse might turn into a tiger.

At this thought, he laughed, getting curious stares from his two hutmates: Göring and the seventeenth-century Englishman, John Collop. His laugh was half-ridicule of himself at the tiger image. What made him think that he, one man, could do anything to hurt the Planet-Shapers, Resurrectors of billions of dead, Feeders and Maintainers of those summoned back to life? He twisted his hands and knew that within them, and within the brain that guided them, could be the downfall of the Ethicals. What this fearful thing was that he harbored within himself, he did not know. But They feared him. If he could only find out why …

His laugh was only partly self-ridicule. The other half of him believed that he was a tiger among men. *As a man thinks, so is he*, he muttered.

Göring said, 'You have a very peculiar laugh, my friend. Somewhat feminine for such a masculine man. It's like … like a thrown rock skipping over a lake of ice. Or like a jackal.'

'I have something of the jackal and hyena in me,' Burton replied. 'So my detractors maintained – and they were right. But I am more than that.'

He rose from his bed and began to exercise to work the sleep-rust from his muscles. In a few minutes, he would go with the others to a grailstone by the Riverbank and charge his grail. Afterward, there would be an hour of policing the area. Then drill, followed by instruction in the spear, the club, the sling, the obsidian-edged sword, the bow and arrow, the flint axe, and in fighting with bare hands and feet. An hour for rest and talk and lunch. Then an hour in a language class. A two-hour work-stint in helping build the ramparts that marked the boundaries of this little state. A half-hour rest, then the obligatory mile run to build stamina. Dinner from the grails, and the evening off except for those who had guard duty or other tasks.

Such a schedule and such activities were being duplicated in tiny states up and down The River's length. Almost *everywhere*, mankind was at war or preparing for it. The citizens must keep in shape and know how to fight to the best of their ability. The exercises also kept the citizens occupied. No matter how monotonous the martial life, it was better than sitting around wondering what to do for amusement. Freedom from worry about food, rent, bills, and the gnat-like chores and duties that had kept Earthmen busy and fretful was not all a blessing. There was the great battle against ennui, and the leaders of each state were occupied trying to think up ways to keep their people busy.

It should have been paradise in Rivervalley, but it was war, war, war. Other things aside, however, war was, in this place, good (according to some)! It gave savor to life and erased boredom. Man's greediness and aggressiveness had its worthwhile side.

After dinner, every man and woman was free to do what he wished, as long as he broke no local laws. He could barter the cigarettes and liquor provided by his grail or the fish he'd caught in The River for a better bow and arrows; shields; bowls and cups; tables and chairs; bamboo flutes; clay trumpets; human or fishskin drums; rare stones (which really were rare); necklaces made of the beautifully articulated and colored bones of the deep-River fish, or jade or of carved wood; obsidian mirrors; sandals and shoes; charcoal drawings; the rare and expensive bamboo paper; ink and fishbone pens; hats made from the long tough-fibered hill-grass; bull-roarers; little wagons on which to ride down the hillsides; harps made from wood with strings fashioned from the gut of the 'dragonfish'; rings of oak for fingers and toes; clay statuettes; and other devices, useful or ornamental.

Later, of course, there was the love-making Burton and his hutmates were denied, for the time being. Only when they had been accepted as full citizens would they be allowed to move into separate houses and live with a woman.

John Collop was a short slight youth with long yellow hair, a narrow but pleasant face, and large blue eyes with very long, upcurving, black eyelashes. In his first conversation with Burton, he had said, after introducing himself, 'I was delivered from the darkness of my mother's womb – whose else? – into the light of God of Earth in 1625. Far too quickly, I descended again into the womb of Mother Nature, confident in the hope of resurrection and not disappointed, as you see. Though I must confess that this afterlife is not that which the parsons led me to expect. But then, how should they know the truth, poor blind devils leading the blind!'

It was not long before Collop told him that he was a member of the Church of the Second Chance.

Burton's eyebrows rose. He had encountered this new religion at many places along The River. Burton, though an infidel, made it his business to investigate thoroughly every religion. Know a man's faith, and you knew at least half the man. Know his wife, and you knew the other half.

The Church had a few simple tenets, some based on fact, most on surmise and hope and wish. In this they differed from no religions born on Earth. But the Second Chancers had one advantage over any Terrestrial religion. They had no difficulty in proving that dead men could be raised – not only once but often.

'And why has mankind been given a Second Chance?' Collop said in his low, earnest voice. 'Does he deserve it? No. With few exceptions, men are a mean, miserable, petty, vicious, narrow-minded, exceedingly egotistic, generally disputing, and disgusting lot. Watching them, the gods – or God – should vomit. But in this divine spew is a clot of compassion, if you will pardon me for using such imagery. Man, however base, has a silver wire of the divine in him. It is no idle phrase that man was made in God's image. There is something worth saving in the worst of us, and out of this something a new man may be fashioned.

'Whoever has given us this new opportunity to save our souls knows this truth. We have been placed here in this Rivervalley – on this alien planet under alien skies – to work out our salvation. What our time limit is, I do not know nor do the leaders of my Church even speculate. Perhaps it is forever, or it may be only a hundred years or a thousand. But we must make use of whatever time we do have, my friend.'

Burton said, 'Weren't you sacrificed on the altar of Odin by Norse who clung to the old religion, even if this world isn't the Valhalla they were promised by their priests? Don't you think you wasted your time and breath by preaching to them? They believe in the same old gods, the only difference in their theology now being some adjustments they've made to conditions here. Just as you have clung to your old faith.'

'The Norse have no explanations for their new surroundings,' Collop said, 'but I do. I have a reasonable explanation, one which the Norse will eventually come to accept, to believe in as fervently as I do. They killed me, but some more persuasive member of the Church will come along and talk to them before they stretch him out in the wooden lap of their wooden idol and stab him in the heart. If *he* does not talk them out of him, *the next* missionary will.

'It was true, on Earth, that the blood of martyrs is the seed of the church. It is even truer here. If you kill a man to shut his mouth, he pops up some place elsewhere along The River. And a man who has been martyred a hundred thousand miles away comes along to replace the previous martyr. The Church will win out in the end. Then men will cease these useless, hate-generating wars and begin the real business, the only worthwhile business, that of gaining salvation.'

'What you say about the martyrs is true about anyone with an idea,' Burton said. 'A wicked man who's killed also pops up to commit his evil elsewhere.'

'Good will prevail; the truth always wins out,' Collop said.

'I don't know how restricted your mobility was on Earth or how long your life,' Burton said, 'but both must have been very limited to make you so blind. I know better.'

Collop said, 'The Church is not founded on faith alone. It has something very factual, very substantial, on which to base its teachings. Tell me, my friend, Abdul, have you ever heard of anybody being resurrected dead?'

'A paradox!' Burton cried. 'What do you mean – resurrected dead?'

'There are at least three authenticated cases and four more of which the Church has heard but has not been able to validate. These are men and women who were killed at one place on The River and translated to another. Strangely, their bodies were re-created, but they were without the spark of life. Now, why was this?'

'I can't imagine!' Burton said. 'You tell me. I listen, for you speak as one with authority.'

He *could* imagine, since he had heard the same story elsewhere. But he wanted to learn if Collop's story matched the others. It was the same, even to the names of the dead lazari. The story was that these men and women had been identified by those who had known them well on Earth. They were all saintly or near-saintly people; in fact, one of them had been canonized on

Earth. The theory was that they had attained that state of sanctity which made it no longer necessary to go through the 'purgatory' of the Riverplanet. Their souls had gone on to ... someplace ... and left the excess baggage of their physical bodies behind.

Soon, so the Church said, more would reach this state. And their bodies would be left behind. Eventually, given enough time, the Rivervalley would become depopulated. All would have shed themselves of their visciousnesses and hates and would have become illuminated with the love of mankind and of God. Even the most depraved, those who seemed to be utterly lost, would be able to abandon their physical beings. All that was needed to attain this grace was love.

Burton sighed, laughed loudly, and said, *'Plus ça change, plus c'est la même chose*. Another fairy tale to give men hope. The old religions have been discredited – although some refuse to face even that fact – so new ones must be invented.'

'It makes sense,' Collop said. 'Do you have a better explanation of why we're here?'

'Perhaps. I can make up fairy tales, too.'

As a matter of fact, Burton did have an explanation. However, he could not tell it to Collop. Spruce had told Burton something of the identity, history, and purpose of his group, the Ethicals. Much of what he had said agreed with Collop's theology.

Spruce had killed himself before he had explained about the 'soul.' Presumably, the 'soul' had to be part of the total organization of resurrection. Otherwise, when the body had attained 'salvation,' and no longer lived, there would be nothing to carry on the essential part of a man. Since the post-Terrestrial life could be explained in physical terms, the 'soul' must also be a physical entity, not to be dismissed with the term 'supernatural' as it had been on Earth.

There was much that Burton did not know. But he had had a glimpse into the workings of this Riverplanet that no other human being possessed.

With the little knowledge he did have, he planned to lever his way into more, to pry open the lid, and crawl inside the sanctum. To do so, he would attain the Dark Tower. The only way to get there swiftly was to take The Suicide Express. First, he must be discovered by an Ethical. Then he must overpower the Ethical, render him unable to kill himself, and somehow extricate more information from him.

Meanwhile, he continued to play the role of Abdul ibn Harun, translated and transplanted Egyptian physician of the nineteenth century, now a citizen of Bargawhwdzys. As such, he decided to join the Church of the Second Chance. He announced to Collop his disillusionment in Mahomet and his teachings, and so became Collop's first convert in this area.

'Then you must swear not to take arms against any man nor to defend yourself physically, my dear friend,' Collop said.

Burton, outraged, said that he would allow no man to strike at him and go unharmed.

''Tis not unnatural,' Collop said gently. 'Contrary to habit, yes. But a man may become something other than he has been, something better – if he has the strength of will and the desire.'

Burton rapped out a violent no and stalked away. Collop shook his head sadly, but he continued to be as friendly as ever. Not without a sense of humor, he sometimes addressed Burton as his 'five-minute convert,' not meaning the time it took to bring him into the fold but the time it took Burton to leave the fold.

At this time, Collop got his second convert, Göring. The German had had nothing but sneers and jibes for Collop. Then he began chewing dreamgum again, and the nightmares started.

For two nights he kept Collop and Burton awake with his groanings, his tossings, his screams. On the evening of the third day, he asked Collop if he would accept him into the Church. However, he had to make a confession. Collop must understand what sort of person he had been, both on Earth and on this planet.

Collop heard out the mixture of self-abasement and self-aggrandizement. Then he said, 'Friend, I care not what you may have been. Only what you are and what you will be. I listened only because confession is good for the soul. I can see that you are deeply troubled, that you have suffered sorrow and grief for what you have done, yet take some pleasure in what you once were, a mighty figure among men. Much of what you told me I do not comprehend, because I know not much about your era. Nor does it matter. Only today and tomorrow need to be our concern; each day will take care of itself.'

It seemed to Burton not that Collop did not care what Göring had been but that he did not believe his story of Earthly glory and infamy. There were so many phonies that genuine heroes, or villains, had been depreciated. Thus, Burton had met three Jesus Christs, two Abrahams, four King Richard the Lion-Hearteds, six Attilas, a dozen Judases (only one of whom could speak Aramaic), a George Washington, two Lord Byrons, three Jesse Jameses, any number of Napoleons, a General Custer (who spoke with a heavy Yorkshire accent), a Finn MacCool (who did not know ancient Irish), a Tchaka (who spoke the wrong Zulu dialect), and a number of others who might or might not have been what they claimed to be.

Whatever a man had been on Earth, he had to reestablish himself here. This was not easy, because conditions were radically altered. The greats and the importants of Terra were constantly being humiliated in their claims and denied a chance to prove their identities.

To Collop, the humiliation was a blessing. First, humiliation, then humility, he would have said. And then comes humanity as a matter of course.

Göring had been trapped in the Great Design – as Burton termed it – because it was his nature to overindulge, especially with drugs. Knowing that the dreamgum was uprooting the dark things in his personal abyss, was spewing them up into the light, that he was being torn apart, fragmented, he still continued to chew as much as he could get. For a while, temporarily made healthful again with a new resurrection, he had been able to deny the call of the drug. But a few weeks after his arrival in this area, he had succumbed, and now the night was ripped apart with his shrieks of 'Hermann Göring, I hate you!'

'If this continues,' Burton said to Collop, 'he will go mad. Or he will kill himself again, or force someone to kill him, so that he can get away from himself. But the suicide will be useless, and it's all to do over again. Tell me truly now, is this not hell?'

'Purgatory, rather,' Collop said. 'Purgatory is hell with hope.'

24

Two months passed. Burton marked the days off on a pine stick notched with a flint knife. This was the fourteenth day of the seven month of 5 A.R., the fifth year After the Resurrection. Burton tried to keep a calendar, for he was, among many other things, a chronicler. But it was difficult. Time did not mean much on The River. The planet had a polar axis that was always at ninety degrees to the ecliptic. There was no change of seasons, and the stars seemed to jostle each other and made identification of individual luminaries or of constellations impossible. So many and so bright were they that even the noon day sun at its zenith could not entirely dim the greatest of them. Like ghosts reluctant to retreat before daylight, they hovered in the burning air.

Nevertheless, man needs time as a fish needs water. If he does not have it, he will invent it; so to Burton, it was July 14, 5 A.R.

But Collop, like many, reckoned time as having continued from the year of his Terrestrial death. To him, it was AD 1667. He did not believe that his sweet Jesus had become sour. Rather, this River was the River Jordan; this valley, the vale beyond the shadow of death. He admitted that the afterlife was not that which he had expected. Yet it was evidence of the all-encompassing love of God for His creation. He had given all men, altogether undeserving of such a gift, another chance. If this world was not the New

Jerusalem, it was a place prepared for its building. Here the bricks, which were the love of God and the mortar, love for man, must be fashioned in this kiln and this mill: the planet of The River of The Valley.

Burton pooh-poohed the concept, but he could not help loving the little man. Collop was genuine; he was not stoking the furnace of his sweetness with leaves from a book or pages from a theology. He did not operate under forced draft. He burned with a flame that fed on his own being, and this being was love. Love even for the unlovable, the rarest and most difficult species of love.

He told Burton something of his Terrestrial life. He had been a doctor, a farmer, a liberal with unshakable faith in his religion, yet full of questions about his faith and the society of his time. He had written a plea for religious tolerance which had aroused both praise and damnation in his time. And he had been a poet, well-known for a short time, then forgotten.

> *Lord, let the faithless see*
> *Miracles ceased, revive in me.*
> *The leper cleansed, blind healed,*
> *dead raised by Thee*

'My lines may have died, but their truth has not,' he said to Burton. He waved his hand to indicate the hills, The River, the mountains, the people. 'As you may see if you open your eyes and do not persist in this stubborn myth of yours that this is the handiwork of men like us.'

He continued, 'Or grant your premise. It still remains that these Ethicals are but doing the work of Their Creator.'

'I like better those other lines of yours,' Burton said.

> *Dull soul aspire;*
> *Thou art not the Earth. Mount higher!*
> *Heaven gave the spark;*
> *to it return the fire.*

Collop was pleased, not knowing that Burton was thinking of the lines in a different sense than that intended by the poet.

'Return the fire.'

That meant somehow getting into the Dark Tower, discovering the secrets of the Ethicals, and turning Their devices against Them. He did not feel gratitude because They had given him a second life. He was outraged that They should do this without his leave. If They wanted his thanks, why did They not tell him why They had given him another chance? What reason did They have for keeping Their motives in the dark? He would find out why. The spark They had restored in him would turn into a raging fire to burn Them.

He cursed the fate that had propelled him to a place so near the source of The River, hence so close to the Tower, and in a few minutes had carried him away again, back to some place in the middle of The River, millions of miles away from his goal. Yet, if he had been there once, he could get there again. Not by taking a boat, since the journey would consume at least forty years and probably more. He could also count on being captured and enslaved a thousand times over. And if he were killed along the way, he might find himself raised again far from his goal and have to start all over again.

On the other hand, given the seemingly random selection of resurrection, he might find himself once more near The River's mouth. It was this that determined him to board The Suicide Express once more. However, even though he knew that his death would be only temporary, he found it difficult to take the necessary step. His mind told him that death was the only ticket, but his body rebelled. The cells' fierce insistence on survival overcame his will.

For a while, he rationalized that he was interested in studying the customs and languages of the prehistorics among whom he was living. Then honesty triumphed, and he knew he was only looking for excuses to put off the Grim Moment. Despite this, he did not act.

Burton, Collop, and Göring were moved out of their bachelor barracks to take up the normal life of citizens. Each took up residence in a hut, and within a week had found a woman to live with him. Collop's Church did not require celibacy. A member could take an oath of chastity if he wished to. But the Church reasoned that men and women had been Resurrected in bodies that retained the full sex of the original. (Or, if lacking on Earth, supplied here.) It was evident that the Makers of Resurrection had meant for sex to be used. It was well-known, though still denied by some, that sex had other functions than reproduction. So go ahead, youths, roll in the grass.

Another result of the inexorable logic of the Church (which, by the way, decried reason as being untrustworthy) was that any form of love was allowed, as long as it was voluntary and did not involve cruelty or force. Exploitation of children was forbidden. This was a problem that, given time, would cease to exist. In a few years all children would be adults.

Collop refused to have a hutmate solely to relieve his sexual tensions. He insisted on a woman whom he loved. Burton jibed at him for this, saying that it was a prerequisite easily – therefore cheaply – fulfilled. Collop loved all humanity; hence, he should theoretically take the first woman who would say yes to him.

'As a matter of fact, my friend,' Collop said, 'that is exactly what happened.'

'It's only a coincidence that she's beautiful, passionate, and intelligent?' Burton said.

'Though I strive to be more than human, rather, to become a complete human, I am all-too-human,' Collop replied. He smiled. 'Would you have me deliberately martyr myself by choosing an ugly shrew?'

'I'd think you more of a fool than I do even now,' Burton said. 'As for me, all I require in a woman is beauty and affection. I don't care a whit about her brains. And I prefer blondes. There's a chord within me that responds to the fingers of a golden-haired woman.'

Göring took into his hut a Valkyrie, a tall, great-busted, wide-shouldered, eighteenth-century Swede. Burton wondered if she was a surrogate for Göring's first wife, the sister-in-law of the Swedish explorer Count von Rosen. Göring admitted that she not only looked like his Karin but even had a voice similar to hers. He seemed to be very happy with her and she with him.

Then, one night, during the invariable early-morning rain, Burton was ripped from a deep sleep.

He thought he had heard a scream, but all he could hear when he became fully awake was the explosion of thunder and the crack of nearby lightning. He closed his eyes, only to be jerked upright again. A woman had screamed in a nearby hut.

He jumped up, shoved aside the bamboo-slat door, and stuck his head outside. The cold rain hit him in the face. All was dark except for the mountains in the west, lit up by flashes of lightning. Then a bolt struck so close that he was deafened and dazzled. However, he did catch a glimpse of two ghostly white figures just outside Göring's hut. The German had his hands locked around the throat of his woman, who was holding onto his wrists and trying to push him away.

Burton ran out, slipped on the wet grass, and fell. Just as he arose, another flash showed the woman on her knees, bending backward, and Göring's distorted face above her. At the same time, Collop, wrapping a towel around his waist, came out of his hut. Burton got to his feet and, still silent, ran again. But Göring was gone. Burton knelt by Karla, felt her heart, and could detect no beat. Another glare of lightning showed him her face, mouth hanging open, eyes bulging.

He rose and shouted, 'Göring! Where are you?'

Something struck the back of his head. He fell on his face.

Stunned, he managed to get to his hands and knees, only to be knocked flat again by another heavy blow. Half-conscious, he nevertheless rolled over on his back and raised his legs and hands to defend himself. Lightning revealed Göring standing above him with a club in one hand. His face was a madman's.

Darkness sliced off the lightning. Something white and blurred leaped upon Göring out of the darkness. The two pale bodies went down onto the grass beside Burton and rolled over and over. They screeched like tomcats, and another flash of lightning showed them clawing at each other.

Burton staggered to his feet and lurched toward them but was knocked down by Collop's body, hurled by Göring. Again Burton got up. Collop bounded to his feet and charged Göring. There was a loud crack, and Collop crumpled. Burton tried to run toward Göring. His legs refused to answer his demands; they took him off at an angle, away from his point of attack. Then another blast of light and noise showed Göring, as if caught in a photograph, suspended in the act of swinging the club at Burton.

Burton felt his arm go numb as it received the impact of the club. Now not only his legs but his left arm disobeyed him. Nevertheless he balled his right hand and tried to swing at Göring. There was another crack; his ribs felt as if they had become unhinged and were driven inward into his lung. His breath was knocked out of him, and once again he was on the cold wet grass.

Something fell by his side. Despite his agony, he reached out for it. The club was in his hand; Göring must have dropped it. Shuddering with each painful breath, he got to one knee. Where was the madman? Two shadows danced and blurred, merged and half-separated. The hut! His eyes were crossed. He wondered if he had a concussion of the brain, then forgot it as he saw Göring dimly in the illumination of a distant streak of lightning. Two Görings, rather. One seemed to accompany the other; the one on the left had his feet on the ground; the right one was treading on air.

Both had their hands held high up into the rain, as if they were trying to wash them. And when the two turned and came toward him, he understood that that was what they were trying to do. They were shouting in German (with a single voice), 'Take the blood off my hands! Oh, God, wash it off!'

Burton stumbled toward Göring, his club held high. Burton meant to knock him out, but Göring suddenly turned and ran away. Burton followed him as best he could, down the hill, up another one, and then out onto the flat plain. The rains stopped, the thunder and lightning died, and within five minutes the clouds, as always, had cleared away. The starlight gleamed on Göring's white skin.

Like a phantom he flitted ahead of his pursuer, seemingly bent upon getting to The River. Burton kept after him, although he wondered why he was doing so. His legs had regained most of their strength, and his vision was no longer double. Presently, he found Göring. He was squatting by The River and staring intently at the star-fractured waves.

Burton said, 'Are you all right now?'

Göring was startled. He began to rise, then changed his mind. Groaning, he put his head down on his knees.

'I knew what I was doing, but I didn't know why,' he said dully. 'Karla was telling me she was moving out in the morning, said she couldn't sleep with all the noise I made with my nightmares. And I was acting strangely. I begged her to stay; I told her I loved her very much. I'd die if she deserted me. She said she was fond of me, had been, rather, but she didn't love me. Suddenly, it seemed that if I wanted to keep her, I'd have to kill her. She ran screaming out of the hut. You know the rest.'

'I intended to kill you,' Burton said. 'But I can see you're no more responsible than a madman. The people here won't accept that excuse, though. You know what they'll do to you; hang you upside down by your ankles and let you hang until you die.'

Göring cried, 'I don't understand it! What's happening to me? Those nightmares! Believe me, Burton, if I've sinned, I've paid! But I can't stop paying! My nights are hell, and soon my days will become hell, too! Then I'll have only one way to get peace I'll kill myself! But it won't do any good! I'll wake up – then hell again!'

'Stay away from the dreamgum,' Burton said. 'You'll have to sweat it out. You can do it. You told me you overcame the morphine habit on Earth.'

Göring stood up and faced Burton. 'That's just it! I haven't touched the gum since I came to this place!'

Burton said, 'What? But I'll swear …!'

'You assumed I was using the stuff because of the way I was acting! No, I have not had a bit of the gum! But it doesn't make any difference!'

Despite his loathing of Göring, Burton felt pity. He said, 'You've opened the Pandora of yourself, and it looks as if you'll not be able to shut the lid. I don't know how this is going to end, but I wouldn't want to be in your mind. Not that you don't deserve this.'

Göring said, in a quiet and determined voice, 'I'll defeat them.'

'You mean you'll conquer yourself,' Burton said. He turned to go but halted for a last word. 'What are you going to do?'

Göring gestured at The River. 'Drown myself. I'll get a fresh start. Maybe I'll be better equipped the next place. And I certainly don't want to be trussed up like a chicken in a butcher shop window.'

'Au revoir, then,' Burton said. 'And good luck.'

'Thank you. You know you're not a bad sort. Just one word of advice.'

'What's that?'

'You'd better stay away from the dreamgum yourself. So far, you've been lucky. But one of these days, it'll take hold of you as it did me. Your devils won't be mine, but they'll be just as monstrous and terrifying to you.'

'Nonsense! I've nothing to hide from myself!' Burton laughed loudly. 'I've chewed enough of the stuff to know.'

He walked away, but he was thinking of the warning. He had used the gum twenty-two times. Each time had made him swear never to touch the gum again.

On the way back to the hills, he looked behind him. The dim white figure of Göring was slowly sinking into the black-and-silver waters of The River. Burton saluted, since he was not one to resist the dramatic gesture. Afterward, he forgot Göring. The pain in the back of his head, temporarily subdued, came back sharper than before. His knees turned to water, and, only a few yards from his hut, he had to sit down.

He must have become unconscious then, or half-conscious since he had no memory of being dragged along on the grass. When his wits cleared, he found himself lying on a bamboo bed inside a hut.

It was dark with the only illumination the starlight filtering in through the tree branches outside the square of window. He turned his head and saw the shadowy and pale-white bulk of a man squatting by him. The man was holding a thin metal object before his eyes, the gleaming end of which was pointed at Burton.

25

As soon as Burton turned his head, the man put the device down. He spoke in English. 'It's taken me a long time to find you, Richard Burton.'

Burton groped around on the floor for a weapon with his left hand, which was hidden from the man's view. His fingers touched nothing but dirt. He said, 'Now you've found me, you damn Ethical, what do you intend doing with me?'

The man shifted slightly and he chuckled. 'Nothing.' He paused, then said, 'I am not one of Them.' He laughed again when Burton gasped. 'That's not quite true. I am *with* Them, but I am not *of* Them.'

He picked up the device which he had been aiming at Burton.

'This tells me that you have a fractured skull and a concussion of the brain. You must be very tough, because you should be dead, judging from the extent of the injury. But you may pull out of it, if you take it easy. Unfortunately, you don't have time to convalesce. The Others know you're in this area, give or take thirty miles. In a day or so, They'll have you pinpointed.'

Burton tried to sit up and found that his bones had become soft as taffy in sunlight, and a bayonet was prying open the back of his skull. Groaning, he lay back down.

'Who are you and what's your business?'

'I can't tell you my name. If – or much more likely when – They catch you, They'll thread out your memory and run it off backward to the time you woke up in the pre-resurrection bubble. They won't find out what made you wake before your time. But They will know about this conversation. They'll even be able to see me but only as you see me, a pale shadow with no features. They'll hear my voice too, but They won't recognize it. I'm using a transmuter.

'They will, however, be horrified. What they have slowly and reluctantly been suspecting will all of a sudden be revealed as the truth. They have a traitor in Their midst.'

'I wish I knew what you were talking about,' Burton said.

The man said, 'I'll tell you this much. You have been told a monstrous lie about the purpose of the Resurrection. What Spruce told you, and what that Ethical creation, the Church of the Second Chance, teaches – are lies! All lies! The truth is that you human beings have been given life again only to participate in a scientific experiment. The Ethicals – a misnomer if there ever was one – have reshaped this planet into one Rivervalley, built the grailstones, and brought all of you back from the dead for one purpose. To record your history and customs. And, as a secondary matter, to observe your reactions to Resurrection and to the mixing of different peoples of different eras. That is all it is: a scientific project. And when you have served your purpose, back into the dust you go!

'This story about giving all of you another chance at eternal life and salvation because it is Their ethical duty – lies! Actually, my people do not believe that you are worth saving. They do not think you have "souls"!'

Burton was silent for a while. The fellow was certainly sincere. Or, if not sincere, he was very emotionally involved, since he was breathing so heavily.

Finally, Burton spoke. 'I can't see anybody going to all this expense and labor just to run a scientific experiment, or to make historical recordings.'

'Time hangs heavy on the hands of immortals. You would be surprised what we do to make eternity interesting. Furthermore, given all time, we can take our time, and we do not let even the most staggering projects dismay us. After the last Terrestrial died, the job of setting up the Resurrection took several thousands of years, even though the final phase took only one day.'

Burton said, 'And you? What are you doing? And why are you doing whatever you're doing?'

'I am the only true Ethical in the whole monstrous race. I do not like toying around with you as if you were puppets, or mere objects to be observed, animals in a laboratory! After all, primitive and vicious though you be, you are sentients! You are, in a sense, as … as …'

The shadowy speaker waved a shadowy hand as if trying to grasp a word out of the darkness. He continued, 'I'll have to use your term for yourselves. You're as *human* as we. Just as the sub-humans who first used language were as human as you. And you are our forefathers. For all I know, I may be your direct descendant. My whole people could be descended from you.'

'I doubt it,' Burton said. 'I had no children – that I know of, anyway.'

He had many questions, and he began to ask them. But the man was paying no attention. He was holding the device to his forehead. Suddenly, he withdrew it and interrupted Burton in the middle of a sentence. 'I've been ... you don't have a word for it ... let's say ... listening. They've detected my ... *wathan*. I think you'd call it an aura. They don't know whose *wathan*, just that it's an Ethical's. But They'll be zeroing in within the next five minutes. I have to go.'

The pale figure stood up. 'You have to go, too.'

'Where are you taking me?' Burton said.

'I'm not. You must die; They must find only your corpse. I can't take you with me; it's impossible. But if you die here, They'll lose you again. And we'll meet again. Then ...!'

'Wait!' Burton said. 'I don't understand. Why can't They locate me? They built the Resurrection machinery. Don't They know where my particular resurrector is?'

The man chuckled again. 'No. Their only recordings of men on Earth were visual, not audible. And the location of the resurrectees in the pre-resurrection bubble was random, since They had planned to scatter you humans along The River in a rough chronological sequence but with a certain amount of mixing. They intended to get down to the individual basis later. Of course, They had no notion then that I would be opposing Them. Or that I would select certain of Their subjects to aid me in defeating the Plan. So They do not know where you, or the others, will next pop up.

'Now, you may be wondering why I can't set your resurrector so that you'll be translated near your goal, the headwaters. The fact is that I did set yours so that the first time you died, you'd be at the very first grailstone. But you didn't make it; so I presume the Titanthrops killed you. That was unfortunate, since I no longer dare to go near the bubble until I have an excuse. It is forbidden for any but those authorized to enter the pre-resurrection bubble. They are suspicious; They suspect tampering. So it is up to you, and to chance, to get back to the north polar region.

'As for the others, I never had an opportunity to set their resurrectors. They have to go by the laws of probabilities, too. Which are about twenty million to one.'

'Others?' Burton said. 'Others? But why did you choose us?'

'You have the right aura. So did the others. Believe me, I know what I'm doing; I chose well.'

'But you intimated that you woke me up ahead of time ... in the pre-resurrection bubble, for a purpose. What did it accomplish?'

'It was the only thing that would convince you that the Resurrection was not a supernatural event. And it started you sniffing on the track of the Ethicals. Am I right? Of course, I am. Here!'

He handed Burton a tiny capsule. 'Swallow this. You will be dead instantly and out of Their reach – for a while. And your brain cells will be so ruptured They'll not be able to read them. Hurry! I *must* go!'

'What if I don't take it?' Burton said. 'What if I allow Them to capture me now?'

'You don't have the aura for it,' the man said.

Burton almost decided not to take the capsule. Why should he allow this arrogant fellow to order him around?

Then he considered that he should not bite off his nose to spite his face. As it was, he had the choice of playing along with this unknown man or of falling into the hands of the Others.

'All right,' he said, 'But why don't you kill me? Why make me do the job?'

The man laughed and said, 'There are certain rules in this game, rules that I don't have time to explain. But you are intelligent, you'll figure out most of them for yourself. One is that we are Ethicals. We can give life, but we can't directly take life. It is not unthinkable for us or beyond our ability. Just very difficult.'

Abruptly, the man was gone. Burton did not hesitate. He swallowed the capsule. There was a blinding flash …

26

And light was full in his eyes, from the just-risen sun. He had time for one quick look around, saw his grail, his pile of neatly folded towels – and Hermann Göring.

Then Burton and the German were seized by small dark men with large heads and bandy legs. These carried spears and flint-headed axes. They wore towels but only as capes secured around their thick short necks. Strips of leather, undoubtedly human skin, ran across their disproportionately large foreheads and around their heads to bind their long, coarse black hair. They looked semi-Mongolian and spoke a tongue unknown to him.

An empty grail was placed upside down over his head; his hands were tied behind him with a leather thong. Blind and helpless, stone-tipped spears digging into his back, he was urged across the plain. Somewhere near, drums thundered, and female voices wailed a chain.

He had walked three hundred paces when he was halted. The drums quit beating, and the women stopped their singsong. He could hear nothing except for the blood beating in his ears. What the hell was going on? Was he part of a religious ceremony which required that the victim be blinded? Why not? There had been many cultures on Earth which did not want the ritually slain to view those who shed his blood. The dead man's ghost might want to take revenge on his killers.

But these people must know by now that there were no such things as ghosts. Or did they regard *lazari* as just that, as ghosts that could be dispatched back to their land of origin by simply killing them again?

Göring! He, too, had been translated here. At the same grailstone. The first time could have been coincidence, although the probabilities against it were high. But three times in succession? No, it was …

The first blow drove the side of the grail against his head, made him half-unconscious, sent a vast ringing through him and sparks of light before his eyes, and knocked him to his knees. He never felt the second blow, and so awoke once more in another place—

27

And with him was Hermann Göring.

'You and I must be twin souls,' Göring said. 'We seem to be yoked together by Whoever is responsible for all this.'

'The ox and the ass plow together,' Burton said, leaving it to the German to decide which he was. Then the two were busy introducing themselves, or attempting to do so, to the people among whom they had arrived. These, as he later found out, were Sumerians of the Old or Classical period; that is, they had lived in Mesopotamia between 2500 and 2300 B.C. The men shaved their heads (no easy custom with flint razors), and the women were bare to the waist. They had a tendency to short squat bodies, pop-eyes, and (to Burton) ugly faces.

But if the index of beauty was not high among them, the pre-Columbian Samoans who made up 30 percent of the population were more than attractive. And, of course, there was the ubiquitous 10 percent of people from anywhere-everyplace, twentieth-centurians being the most numerous. This was understandable, since the total number of these constituted a fourth of humanity. Burton had no scientific statistical data, of course, but his travels had convinced him that the twentieth-centurians had been deliberately scattered along The River in a proportion to the other peoples even greater than was to be expected. This was another facet of the Riverworld setup which he did not understand. What did the Ethicals intend to gain by this dissemination?

There were too many questions. He needed time to think, and he could not get it if he spent himself with one trip after another on The Suicide Express. This area, unlike most of the others he would visit, offered some peace and quiet for analysis. So he would stay here for a while.

And then there was Hermann Göring. Burton wanted to observe his strange form of pilgrim's progress. One of the many things that he had not been able to ask the Mysterious Stranger (Burton tended to think in capitals) was about the dreamgum. Where did it fit into the picture? Another part of the Great Experiment?

Unfortunately, Göring did not last long.

The first night, he began screaming. He burst out of his hut and ran toward The River, stopping now and then to strike out at the air or to grapple with invisible beings and to roll back and forth on the grass. Burton followed him as far as The River. Here Göring prepared to launch himself out into the water, probably to drown himself. But he froze for a moment, began shuddering, and then toppled over, stiff as a statue. His eyes were open, but they saw nothing outside him. All vision was turned inward. What horrors he was witnessing could not be determined, since he was unable to speak.

His lips writhed soundlessly, and did not stop during the ten days that he lived. Burton's efforts to feed him were useless. His jaws were locked. He shrank before Burton's eyes, the flesh evaporating, the skin falling in and the bones beneath resolving into the skeleton. One morning, he went into convulsions, then sat up and screamed. A moment later he was dead.

Curious, Burton did an autopsy on him with the flint knives and obsidian saws available. Göring's distended bladder had burst and poured urine into his body.

Burton proceeded to pull Göring's teeth out before burying him. Teeth were trade items, since they could be strung on a fishgut or a tendon to make much-desired necklaces. Göring's scalp also came off. The Sumerians had picked up the custom of taking scalps from their enemies, the seventeenth-century Shawnee across The River. They had added the civilized embellishment of sewing scalps together to make capes, skirts, and even curtains. A scalp was not worth as much as teeth in the trade mart, but it was worth something.

It was while digging a grave by a large boulder at the foot of the mountains that Burton had an illuminating flash of memory. He had stopped working to take a drink of water when he happened to look at Göring. The completely stripped head and the features, peaceful as if sleeping, opened a trapdoor in his mind.

When he had awakened in that colossal chamber and found himself floating in a row of bodies, he had seen this face. It had belonged to a body in the row next to his. Göring, like all the other sleepers, had had his head shaved.

Burton had only noted him in passing during the short time before the Warders had detected him. Later, after the mass Resurrection, when he had met Göring, he had not seen the similarity between the sleeper and this man who had a full head of blondish hair.

But he knew now that this man had occupied a space close to his.

Was it possible that their two resurrectors, so physically close to each other, had become locked in phase? If so, whenever his death and Göring's took place at the same approximate time, then the two would be raised again by the same grailstone. Göring's jest that they were twin souls might not be so far off the mark.

Burton resumed digging, swearing at the same time because he had so many questions and so few answers. If he had another chance to get his hands on an Ethical, he would drag the answers out of him, no matter what methods he had to use.

The next three months, Burton was busy adjusting himself to the strange society in this area. He found himself fascinated by the new language that was being formed out of the clash between Sumerian and Samoan. Since the former were the most numerous, their tongue dominated. But here, as elsewhere, the major language suffered a Pyrrhic victory. The result of the fusion was a pidgin, a speech with greatly reduced flexion and simplified syntax. Grammatical gender went overboard; words were syncopated; tense and aspect of verbs were cut to a simple present, which was used also for the future. Adverbs of time indicated the past. Subtleties were replaced by expressions that both Sumerian and Samoan could understand, even if they seemed at first to be awkward and naive. And many Samoan words, in somewhat changed phonology, drove out Sumerian words.

This rise of pidgins was taking place everywhere up and down the River-valley. Burton reflected that if the Ethicals had intended to record all human tongues, They had best hurry. The old ones were dying out, transmuting rather. But for all he knew, They had already completed the job. Their recorders, so necessary for accomplishing the physical translation, might also be taking down all speech.

In the meantime, in the evenings, when he had a chance to be alone, he smoked the cigars so generously offered by the grails and tried to analyze the situation. Whom could he believe, the Ethicals or the Renegade, the Mysterious Stranger? Or were both lying?

Why did the Mysterious Stranger need him to throw a monkey wrench into Their cosmic machinery? What could Burton, a mere human being, trapped in this valley, so limited by his ignorance, do to help the Judas?

One thing was certain. If the Stranger did not need him, he would not have concerned himself with Burton. He wanted to get Burton into that Tower at the north pole.

Why?

It took Burton two weeks before he thought of the only reason that could be.

The stranger had said that he, like the other Ethicals, would not directly take human life. But he had no scruples about doing so vicariously, as witness his giving the poison to Burton. So, if he wanted Burton in the Tower, he needed Burton to kill for him. He would turn the tiger loose among his own people, open the window to the hired assassin.

An assassin wants pay. What did the Stranger offer as pay?

Burton sucked the cigar smoke into his lungs, exhaled and then downed a shot of bourbon. Very well. The Stranger would try to use him. But let him beware. Burton would also use the Stranger.

At the end of three months, Burton decided that he had done enough thinking. It was time to get out.

He was swimming in The River at the moment and, following the impulse, he swam to its middle. He dived down as far as he could force himself before the not-to-be denied will of his body to survive drove him to claw upward for the dear air. He did not make it. The scavenging fishes would eat his body and his bones would fall to the mud at the bottom of the 1,000-foot deep River. So much the better. He did not want his body to fall into the hands of the Ethicals. If what the Stranger had said was true, They might be able to unthread from his mind all he had seen and heard if They got to him before the brain cells were damaged.

He did not think They had succeeded. During the next seven years, as far as he knew, he escaped detection of the Ethicals. If the Renegade knew where he was, he did not let Burton know. Burton doubted that anyone did; he himself could not ascertain in what part of the Riverplanet he was, how far or how near the Tower headquarters. But he was going, going, going, always on the move. And one day he knew that he must have broken a record of some sort. Death had become second nature to him.

If his count was correct, he had made 777 trips on The Suicide Express.

28

Sometimes Burton thought of himself as a planetary grasshopper, launching himself out into the darkness of death, landing, nibbling a little at the grass, with one eye cocked for the shadow that betrayed the downswoop of the shrike – the Ethicals. In this vast meadow of humanity, he had sampled many blades, tasted briefly, and then had gone on.

Other times he thought of himself as a net scooping up specimens here and there in the huge sea of mankind. He got a few big fish and many sardines, although there was as much, if not more, to be learned from the small fish as from the large ones.

He did not like the metaphor of the net, however, because it reminded him that there was a much larger net out for him.

Whatever metaphors or similes he used, he was a man who got around a lot, to use a twentieth-century Americanism. So much so that he several times came across the legend of Burton the Gypsy, or, in one English-speaking area, Richard the Rover, and, in another, the Loping Lazarus. This worried him somewhat, since the Ethicals might get a clue to his method of evasion and be able to take measures to trap him. Or They might even guess at his basic goal and set up guards near the headwaters.

At the end of seven years, through much observation of the daystars and through many conversations, he had formed a picture of the course of The River.

It was not an amphisbaena, a snake with two heads, headwaters at the north pole and mouth at the south pole. It was a Midgard Serpent, with the tail at the north pole, the body coiled around and around the planet and the tail in the serpent's mouth. The River's source stemmed from the north polar sea, zigzagged back and forth across one hemisphere, circled the south pole and then zigzagged across the face of the other hemisphere, back and forth, ever working upward until the mouth opened into the hypothetical polar sea.

Nor was the large body of water so hypothetical. If the story of the Titanthrop, the sub-human who claimed to have seen the Misty Tower, was true, the Tower rose out of the fog-shrouded sea.

Burton had heard the tale only at secondhand. But he had seen the Titanthrops near the beginning of The River on his first 'jump,' and it seemed reasonable that one might actually have crossed the mountains and gotten close enough to get a glimpse of the polar sea. Where one man had gone, another could follow.

And how did The River flow uphill?

Its rate of speed seemed to remain constant even where it should have slowed or refused to go further. From this he postulated localized gravitational fields that urged the mighty stream onward until it had regained an area where natural gravity would take over. Somewhere, perhaps buried under The River itself, were devices that did this work. Their fields must be very restricted, since the pull of the earth did not vary on human beings in these areas to any detectable degree.

There were too many questions. He must go on until he got to the place or to the beings Who could answer them.

And seven years after his first death, he reached the desired area.

It was on his 777th 'jump.' He was convinced seven was a lucky number for him. Burton, despite the scorings of his twentieth-century friends, believed steadfastly in most of the superstitions he had nourished on Earth. He often laughed at the superstitions of others, but he knew that some numbers held good fortune for him, that silver placed on his eyes would rejuvenate his body when it was tired and would help his second sight, the perception that warned him ahead of time of evil situations. True, there seemed to be no silver on this mineral-poor world, but if there were, he could use it to advantage.

All that first day, he stayed at the edge of The River. He paid little attention to those who tried to talk to him, giving them a brief smile. Unlike people in most of the areas he had seen, these were not hostile. The sun moved along the eastern peaks, seemingly just clearing their tops. The flaming ball slid across the valley, lower than he had ever seen it before, except when he had landed among the grotesquely nosed Titanthrops. The sun flooded the valley for a while with light and warmth, and then began its circling just above the western mountains. The valley became shadowed, and the air became colder than it had been any other place, except, of course, on that first jump. The sun continued to circle until it was again at the point where Burton had first seen it on opening his eyes.

Weary from his twenty-four hour vigil, but happy, he turned to look for living quarters. He knew now that he was in the arctic area, but he was not at a point just below the headwaters. This time, he was at the other end, the mouth.

As he turned, he heard a voice, familiar but unidentifiable. (He had heard so many.)

> 'Dull soul aspire;
> Thou art not the Earth. Mount higher!
> Heaven gave the spark;
> to it return the fire.'

'John Collop!'

'Abdul ibn Harun! And they say there are no miracles! What has happened to you since last I saw you?'

'I died the same night you did,' Burton said. 'And several times since. There are many evil men in this world.'

''Tis only natural. There were many on Earth. Yet I dare say their number has been cut down, for the Church has been able to do much good work, praise God. Especially in this area. But come with me, friend. I'll introduce you to my hutmate. A lovely woman, faithful in a world that still seems to put little value on marital fidelity or, indeed, in virtue of any sort. She was born in the twentieth century AD and taught English most of her life. Verily, I sometimes think she loves me not so much for myself as for what I can teach her of the speech of my time.'

He gave a curious nervous laugh, by which Burton knew he was joking.

They crossed the plains toward the foothills where fires were burning on small stone platforms before each hut. Most of the men and women had fastened towels around them to form parkas which shielded them from the chill of the shadows.

'A gloomy and shivering place,' Burton said. 'Why would anybody want to live here?'

'Most of these people be Finns or Swedes of the late twentieth century. They are used to the midnight sun. However, you should be happy you're here. I remember your burning curiosity about the polar regions and your speculations anent. There have been others like you who have gone on down The River to seek their ultima Thule, or if you will pardon me for so terming it, the fool's gold at the end of the rainbow. But all have either failed to return or have come back, daunted by the forbidding obstacles.'

'Which are what?' Burton said, grabbing Collop's arm.

'Friend, you're hurting me. Item, the grailstones cease, so that there is nothing wherewith they may recharge their grails with food. Item, the plains of the valley suddenly terminate, and The River pursues its course between the mountains themselves, through a chasm of icy shadows. Item, what lies beyond, I do not know, for no man has come back to tell me. But I fear they've met the end of all who commit the sin of hubris.'

'How far away is this plunge of no return?'

'As The River winds, about 25,000 miles. You may get there with diligent sailing in a year or more. The Almighty Father alone knows how far you must then go before you arrive at the very end of The River. Belike you'd starve before then, because you'd have to take provisions on your boat after leaving the final grailstone.'

'There's one way to find out,' Burton said.

'Nothing will stop you then, Richard Burton?' Collop said. 'You will not give up this fruitless chase after the physical when you should be hot on the track of the metaphysical?'

Burton seized Collop by the arm again. 'You said *Burton?*'

'Yes, I did. Your friend Göring told me some time ago that that was your true name. He also told me other things about you.'

'Göring is here?'

Collop nodded and said, 'He has been here for about two years now. He lives a mile from here. We can see him tomorrow. You will be pleased at the change in him, I know. He has conquered the dissolution begun by the dreamgum, shaped the fragments of himself into a new, and a far better, man. In fact, he is now the leader of the Church of the Second Chance in this area.

'While you, my friend, have been questing after some irrelevant grail outside you, he has found the Holy Grail inside himself. He almost perished from madness, nearly fell back into the evil ways of his Terrestrial life. But through the grace of God and his true desire to show himself worthy of being given another opportunity at life, he ... well, you may see for yourself tomorrow. And I pray you will profit from his example.'

Collop elaborated. Göring had died almost as many times as Burton, usually by suicide. Unable to stand the nightmares and the self-loathing, he had time and again purchased a brief and useless surcease. Only to be faced with himself the next day. But on arriving at this area, and seeking help from Collop, the man he had once murdered, he had won.

'I am astonished,' Burton said. 'And I'm happy for Göring. But I have other goals. I would like your promise that you'll tell no one my true identity. Allow me to be Abdul ibn Harun.'

Collop said that he would keep silent, although he was disappointed that Burton would not be able to see Göring again and judge for himself what faith and love could do for even the seemingly hopeless and depraved. He took Burton to his hut and introduced him to his wife, a short, delicately boned brunette. She was very gracious and friendly and insisted on going with the two men while they visited the local boss, the *valko tukkainen*.(This word was regional slang for the white-haired boy or big shot.)

Ville Ahonen was a huge quiet-spoken man who listened patiently to Burton. Burton revealed only half of his plan, saying that he wanted to build a boat so he could travel to the end of The River. He did not mention wanting to take it further. But Ahonen had evidently met others like him.

He smiled knowingly and replied that Burton could build a craft. However, the people hereabouts were conservationists. They did not believe in despoiling the land of its trees. Oak and pine were to be left untouched, but bamboo was available. Even this material would have to be purchased with cigarettes and liquor, which would take him some time to accumulate from his grail.

Burton thanked him and left. Later, he went to bed in a hut near Collop's, but he could not get to sleep.

Shortly before the inevitable rains came, he decided to leave the hut. He would go up into the mountains, take refuge under a ledge until the rains ceased, the clouds dissipated, and the eternal (but weak) sun reasserted itself. Now that he was so near to his goal, he did not want to be surprised by Them. And it seemed likely that the Ethicals would concentrate agents here. For all he knew, Collop's wife could be one of Them.

Before he had walked half a mile, rain struck him and lightning smashed nearby into the ground. By the dazzling flash, he saw something flicker into existence just ahead and about twenty feet above him.

He whirled and ran toward a grove of trees, hoping that They had not seen him and that he could hide there. If he was unobserved, then he could get up into the mountains. And when They had put everybody to sleep here, They would find him gone again.

29

'You gave us a long hard chase, Burton,' a man said in English.

Burton opened his eyes. The transition to this place was so unexpected that he was dazed. But only for a second. He was sitting in a chair of some very soft buoyant material. The room was a perfect sphere; the walls were a very pale green and were semitransparent. He could see other spherical chambers on all sides, in front, behind, above and, when he bent over, below. Again he was confused, since the other rooms did not just impinge upon the boundaries of his sphere. They intersected. Sections of the other rooms came into his room, but then became so colorless and clear that he could barely detect them.

On the wall at the opposite end of his room was an oval of darker green. It curved to follow the wall. There was a ghostly forest portrayed in the oval. A phantom fawn trotted across the picture. From it came the odor of pine and dogwood.

Across the bubble from him sat twelve in chairs like his. Six were men; six, women. All were very good-looking. Except for two, all had black or dark brown hair and deeply tanned skins. Three had slight epicanthic folds; one man's hair was so curly it was almost kinky.

One woman had long wavy yellow hair bound into a psyche knot. A man had red hair, red as the fur of a fox. He was handsome, his features were irregular, his nose large and curved, and his eyes were dark green.

All were dressed in silvery or purple blouses with short flaring sleeves and ruffled collars, slender luminescent belts, kilts, and sandals. Both men and women had painted fingernails and toenails, lipstick, earrings, and eye makeup.

Above the head of each, almost touching the hair, spun a many-colored globe about a foot across. These whirled and flashed and changed color, running through every hue in the spectrum. From time to time, the globes thrust out long hexagonal arms of green, of blue, of black, or of gleaming white. Then the arms would collapse, only to be succeeded by other hexagons.

Burton looked down. He was clad only in a black towel secured at his waist.

'I'll forestall your first question by telling you we won't give you any information on where you are.'

The speaker was the red-haired man. He grinned at Burton, showing inhumanly white teeth.

'Very well,' Burton said. 'What questions will you answer, Whoever you are? For instance, how did you find me?'

'My name is Dap,' the red-haired man said. 'We found you through a combination of detective work and luck. It was a complicated procedure, but I'll simplify it for you. We had a number of agents looking for you, a pitifully small number, considering the thirty-six billion, six million, nine thousand, six hundred and thirty-seven candidates that live along The River.'

Candidates? Burton thought. Candidates for what? For eternal life? Had Spruce told the truth about the purpose behind the Resurrection?

Loga said, 'We had no idea that you were escaping us by suicide. Even when you were detected in areas so widely separated that you could not possibly have gotten to them except through resurrection, we did not suspect. We thought that you had been killed and then translated. The years went by. We had no idea where you were. There were other things for us to do, so we pulled all agents from the Burton Case, as we called it, except for some stationed at both ends of The River. Somehow, you had knowledge of the polar tower. Later we found out how. Your friends Göring and Collop were very helpful, although they did not know they were talking to Ethicals, of course.'

'Who notified you that I was near The River's end?' Burton said.

Loga smiled and said, 'There's no need for you to know. However, we would have caught you anyway. You see, every space in the restoration bubble – the place where you unaccountably awakened during the pre-resurrection phase – has an automatic counter. They were installed for statistical and research purposes. We like to keep records of what's going on. For instance, any candidate who has a higher than average number of deaths sooner or later is a subject for study. Usually later, since we're shorthanded.

'It was not until your 777th death that we got around to looking at some of the higher frequency resurrections. Yours had the highest count. You may be congratulated on this, I suppose.'

'There are others, as well?'

'They're not being pursued, if that's what you mean. And, relatively speaking, they're not many. We had no idea that it was you who had racked up this staggering number. Your space in the PR bubble was empty when we looked at it during our statistical investigation. The two technicians who had seen you when you woke up in the PR chamber identified you by your ... photograph.

'We set the resurrector so that the next time your body was to be re-created, an alarm would notify us, and we would bring you here to this place.'

'Suppose I hadn't died again?' Burton said.

'You were destined to die. You planned on trying to enter the polar sea via The River's mouth, right? That is impossible. The last hundred miles of The River go through an underground tunnel. Any boat would be torn to pieces. Like others who have dared the journey, you would have died.'

Burton said, 'My photograph – the one I took from Agneau. That was obviously taken on Earth when I was an officer for John Company in India. How was that gotten?'

'Research, Mr Burton,' Loga said, still smiling.

Burton wanted to smash the look of superiority on his face. He did not seem to be restrained by anything; he could, seemingly, walk over to Loga and strike him. But he knew that the Ethicals were not likely to sit in the same room with him without safeguards. They would as soon have given a rabid hyena its freedom.

'Did you ever find out what made me awaken before my time?' he asked. 'Or what made those others gain consciousness, too?'

Loga gave a start. Several of the men and women gasped.

Loga rallied first. He said, 'We've made a thorough examination of your body. You have no idea how thorough. We have also screened every component of your ... psychomorph, I think you could call it. Or aura, whichever word you prefer.' He gestured at the sphere above his head. 'We found no clues whatsoever.'

Burton threw back his head and laughed loudly and long.

'So you bastards don't know everything!'

Logs smiled tightly. 'No. We never will. Only One is omnipotent.'

He touched his forehead, lips, heart, and genitals with the three longest fingers of his right hand. The others did the same.

'However, I'll tell you that you frightened us – if that'll make you feel any better. You still do. You see, we are fairly sure that you may be one of the men of whom we were warned.'

'Warned against? By whom?'

'By a ... sort of giant computer, a living one. And by its operator.' Again, he made the curious sign with his fingers. 'That's all I care to tell you – even though you won't remember a thing that occurs down here after we send you back to the Rivervalley.'

Burton's mind was clouded with anger, but not so much that he missed the 'down here.' Did that mean that the resurrection machinery and the hideout of the Ethicals were below the surface of the Riverworld?

Loga continued, 'The data indicates you may have the potentiality to wreck our plans. Why you should or how you might, we do not know. But we respect our source of information, how highly you can't imagine.'

'If you believe that,' Burton said, 'why don't you just put me in cold storage? Suspend me between those two bars. Leave me floating in space, turning around and around forever, like a roast on a spit, until your plans are completed?'

Loga said, 'We couldn't do that! That act alone would ruin everything! How would you attain your salvation? Besides, that would mean an unforgivable violence on our part! It's unthinkable!'

'You were being violent when you forced me to run and hide from you,' Burton said. 'You are being violent now by holding me here against my will. And you will violate me when you destroy my memory of this little tête-à-tête with you.'

Loga almost wrung his hands. If he was the Mysterious Stranger, the renegade Ethical, he was a great actor. In a grieved tone, Loga said, 'That is only partly true. We had to take certain measures to protect ourselves. If the man had been anyone but you, we would have left you strictly alone. It is true we violated our own code of ethics by making you run from us and by examining you. That had to be, however. And, believe me, we are paying for this in mental agony.'

'You could make up for some of it by telling me why I, why all the human beings that ever lived, have been resurrected. And how you did it.'

Loga talked, with occasional interruptions from some of the others. The yellow-haired woman broke in most often, and after a while Burton deduced from her attitude and Loga's that she was either his wife or she held a high position.

Another man interrupted at times. When he did, there was a concentration and respect from the others that led Burton to believe he was the head of this group. Once he turned his head so that the light sparkled off one eye. Burton stared, because he had not noticed before that the left eye was a jewel.

Burton thought that it probably was a device which gave him a sense, or senses, of perception denied the others. From then on, Burton felt uncomfortable whenever the faceted and gleaming eye was turned on him. What did that many-angled prism see?

At the end of the explanation, Burton did not know much more than he had before. The Ethicals could see back into the past with a sort of chronoscope; with this they had been able to record whatever physical beings they wished to. Using these records as models, they had then performed the resurrection with energy-matter converters.

'What,' Burton said, 'would happen if you re-created two bodies of an individual at the same time?'

Loga smiled wryly and said that the experiment had been performed. Only one body had life.

Burton smiled like a cat that has just eaten a mouse. He said, 'I think you're lying to me. Or telling me half-truths. There is a fallacy in all this. If human beings can attain such a rarefiedly high ethical state that they "go on," why are you Ethicals, supposedly superior beings, still here? Why haven't you, too, "gone on"?'

The faces of all but Loga and the jewel-eyed man became rigid. Loga laughed and said, 'Very shrewd. An excellent point. I can only answer that some of us *do* go on. But more is demanded of us, ethically speaking, than of you resurrectees.'

'I still think you're lying,' Burton said. 'However, there's nothing I can do about it.' He grinned and said, 'Not just now, anyway.'

'If you persist in that attitude, you will never Go On,' Loga said. 'But we felt that we owed it to you to explain what we are doing – as best we could. When we catch those others who have been tampered with, we'll do the same for them.'

'There's a Judas among you,' Burton said, enjoying the effect of his words.

But the jewel-eyed man said, 'Why don't you tell him the truth, Loga? It'll wipe off that sickening smirk and put him in his proper place.'

Loga hesitated, then said, 'Very well, Thanabur. Burton, you will have to be very careful from now on. You *must not* commit suicide and you must fight as hard to stay alive as you did on Earth, when you thought you had only one life. There is a limit to the number of times a man may be resurrected. After a certain amount – it varies and there's no way to predict the individual allotment – the psychomorph seems unable to reattach itself to the body. Every death weakens the *attraction* between body and psychomorph. Eventually, the psychomorph comes to the point of no return. It becomes a – well, to use an unscientific term – a "lost soul." It wanders bodiless through the universe; we can detect these unattached psychomorphs without instruments, unlike those of the – how shall I put it? – the "saved," which disappear entirely from our ken.

'So you see, you must give up this form of travel by death. This is why continued suicide by those poor unfortunates who cannot face life is, if not the unforgivable sin, the irrevocable.'

The jewel-eyed man said, 'The traitor, the filthy unknown who claims to be aiding you, was actually using you for his own purposes. He did not tell you that you were expending your chance for eternal life by carrying out his – and your – designs. He, or she, whoever the traitor is, is evil. Evil, evil!'

'Therefore, you must be careful from now on. You may have a residue of a dozen or so deaths left to you. Or your next death may be your last!'

Burton stood up and shouted, 'You don't want me to get to the end of The River? Why? Why?'

Loga said, 'Au revoir. Forgive us for this violence.'

Burton did not see any of the twelve persons point an instrument at him. But consciousness sprang from him as swiftly as an arrow from the bow, and he awoke ...

30

The first person to greet him was Peter Frigate. Frigate lost his customary reserve; he wept. Burton cried a little himself and had difficulty for a while in answering Frigate's piled-one-on-the-other questions. First, Burton had to find out what Frigate, Loghu, and Alice had done after he had disappeared. Frigate replied that the three had looked for him, then had sailed back up The River to Theleme.

'Where have you been?' Frigate said.

'*From going to and fro in the earth, and from walking up and down in it,*' Burton said. 'However, unlike Satan, I found at least several perfect and upright men, fearing God and eschewing evil. Damn few, though. Most men and women are still the selfish, ignorant, superstitious, self-blinding, hypocritical, cowardly wretches they were on Earth. And in most, the old red-eyed killer ape struggles with its keeper, society, and would break out and bloody its hands.'

Frigate chattered away as the two walked toward the huge stockade a mile away, the council building which housed the administration of the state of Theleme. Burton half-listened. He was shaking and his heart was beating hard, but not because of his homecoming.

He remembered!

Contrary to what Loga had promised, he remembered both his wakening in the pre-resurrection bubble, so many years ago, and the inquisition with the twelve Ethicals.

There was only one explanation. One of the twelve must have prevented the blocking of his memory and done so without the others knowing it.

One of the twelve was the Mysterious Stranger, the Renegade.

Which one? At present, there was no way of determining. But some day he would find out. Meanwhile, he had a friend in court, a man who might be using Burton for his own ends. And the time would come when Burton would use him.

There were the other human beings with whom the Stranger had also tampered. Perhaps he would find them; together they would assault the Tower.

Odysseus had his Athena. Usually Odysseus had had to get out of perilous situations through his own wits and courage. But every now and then, when the goddess had been able, she had given Odysseus a helping hand.

Odysseus had his Athena; Burton, his Mysterious Stranger.

Frigate said, 'What do you plan on doing, Dick?'

'I'm going to build a boat and sail up The River. All the way! Want to come along?'

THE UNREASONING MASK

*For my parents,
George Farmer and Lucile Theodora
Jackson, who gave me love and
the best of care.*

'What I saw in the mirror was not what the mirror saw.'
— *Lord Ruthven's Prisoner*

'Where there is only one, there is also another; where two, always three.'
— *Nur el-Musafir*

'All visible objects, man, are but as pasteboard masks. But in each event – in the living act, the undoubted deed – there, some unknown but still reasoning thing puts forth the moulding of its features from behind the unreasoning mask. If man will strike, strike through the mask! How can the prisoner reach outside except by thrusting through the wall!'
— *Moby Dick*

1

'The *bolg* kills all but one!'

The voice was weak, whispering, and wet. If a shadow under water could have a voice, it would sound like that.

Then the voice boomed like a giant's in the sky, like a rocket exploding near his ear. It propelled him far up into a grayness. Then he was falling down a well the glimmering walls of which sped slantingly away from him but were always visible.

Ramstan had never been so terrified.

He hurtled in the twilight past two naked giants shaped like men but sexless and suspended upside down by chains attached to ankle bands. Harut and Marut? The fallen angels punished thus forever because they had had no compassion for the children of Adam and Eve?

They flashed away into the darkness above, and the well opened out into Space in which myriads of bits of Matter glared. Stars? Eyes?

Suddenly, he was skimming the surface of a white star. He held a bucket, and it was scooping up the thin stuff which burned with a cold light so strong that even when he turned his head away from it the light filled his skull and blinded him.

Then he was in darkness and squeezed by something neither dry nor wet, hot nor cold, moving nor unmoving.

The voice whispered.

'God is sick. Unbreakable flames fall from the black sky. The earth ripples. Oceans charge. Blood blazes. Flesh fries. Bone burns. Wicked and innocent flee. All die. Where to go?'

Now he was the lone survivor of the shipwreck but was clutched by darkness and cold. He was struggling up towards light, warmth, and air.

'Run, Ramstan, run!' the voice shrieked.

Run? He was drowning in an element that permitted no running.

But he surged from the black, the cold, the deep. He was a fisher who had hooked the fish, himself, and had reeled himself up and out. The oily, icy abysm drained from him as he gasped like a fish on land.

That voice. Where had he heard it before? Long ago? Had it spoken then in Terrish or in Arabic, his natal tongue? What had it spoken in just now? He did not remember.

'I dozed off! In all this noise!'

He sat on a chair of stone covered with thick leather. The top of the table before him was a hard, shiny, brown wood shaped into a symbolic bird, a flat crescent body, the tips upturned to represent wing feathers. On it was a double-stemmed goblet cut from the green-and-red fossilized bones of a reptile. It was half full of a thick yellow wine in which swam blood-red worms, thin as the veins in a drunkard's eyes.

He sipped the wine, which tasted of honey and grapes and faintly of almonds. The latter, he supposed, came from the worms. These were so thin and fragile they slipped unfelt by the tongue into the throat. There was always in the sweetness of Kalafala a barely perceptible bitterness.

Life could be good sometimes, but evil was sure. The end of any life, good, bad, or good-bad, was death and corruption. Everything Kalafalan, in all its airiness and delicate involutions, nodded to the Destroyer.

The interior of the tavern was shaped as if it were a coliseum built by drunken Romans. Seen from above, the edges of the tiers of seats formed sine waves. The seats were separated by translucent clamshell-form partitions three meters high. They held the same customers as when he'd fallen asleep. No one had left; no one had entered.

Ramstan's booth, on a middle tier, faced the entrance, which was beyond the top level of the row of tiers. The floor of the central area was smooth and glistening and sometimes used for dancing and sacrifices. In its center was an oval counter. Within it were four bartenders. Around the oval area were four slender columns of white-and-black stone, fluted vertically but banded with jagged rings. At the flaring top of each column was a chair, and in the chairs sat the harpist, the flutist, the violinist, the bassoonist. They were playing the insane-Mozart music of Kalafala.

'The *bolg* kills all but one!'

If that voice came from his unconscious, where did the name of *bolg* come from? What flowers of the dark mind had been pulled up from even darker earth and assembled to make the bouquet of *bolg*? Why would that dark part of himself speak in a code?

Bolg.

A waitress walked by him. He glimpsed multitudes of himself in the oval-shaped mirrors forming a belt around her waist. His ruff-necked cloak and cockaded hat, his long curving nose, thick black eyebrows, and large black eyes, and the mask now slipped down around his neck made him look like a great bird. He was a huge, handsome-ugly eagle crouching over the stone-bone goblet, dipping now and then to suck in the liquid and worms.

Doctor Toyce stepped out of the shadows of the hall entrance. Her mask hung below her chin, giving her a puff-throated appearance. She was short, though taller than any Kalafalan, blonde, bronze-skinned, and pug-nosed. She paused to squint through the green-blue currents of smoke and the shallow, sea-bottom-green light floating down from the stained glass ceiling. She waved her hand at Ramstan and walked down the curving ramp, disappeared behind a tier, and came out of a dark, oval doorway two booths from Ramstan's.

There were no straight or obvious routes for getting in or out of the tavern. All was twist and turn, retwist and return. The mind of the Kalafalan was a Möbius strip; everything they said, did, or made was inturn of outturn. Yet, all was beautiful, if tinged with the sadness of the inevitable.

Toyce gestured at the bartender. He grinned with two rows of shark teeth. Even the Kalafalan face reflected the inner person. Humanoid, its bright red lips were connected to the nose and the chin with two triangles of red cartilage which made the face circus-clownish. The black eyebrows curved around the eyes to the prominent, almost pyramid-shaped cheeks. A clown until he smiled, the Kalafalan, then he flashed teeth like Death's own.

'The *bolg* kills all but one,' Ramstan said in Urzint.

Toyce's pale eyelashes flickered. She sat down and said, 'What?'

'The *bolg* kills all but one.'

'What in hell is a *bolg*?'

'I don't know. I heard somebody say that just as I was waking up from a catnap. But whoever said it was gone. Did you see anybody leave here just as you came in?'

Toyce shook her head and crooked a finger at Wilimu, a bartender. Wilimu tapped a small gong in the shape of a butterfly and pointed out the new customer to a waitress. She disappeared in a doorway beneath the two Earthpeople and presently came out of the doorway which Toyce had used. In a delicate, three-fingered, very long-thumbed hand, she held the bottle of black liquor which Toyce loved. It glittered in the goblet like obsidian under an Aztec sun. It tingled like a dying electric eel in the throat. It shot flaming stars in the belly and comets in the brain.

Toyce sucked in the waitress with her eyes.

'Answer my question,' Ramstan said.

'What? No. I saw no one.'

Ramstan wrote three Xs and a spiral on a chit and stood up.

'I'm going back to the ship. That was no dream. I feel ...'

Toyce said, 'I thought maybe we could get stoned. You could forget whatever's troubling you and maybe ...'

'I'm not troubled or in trouble, Aisha.'

'Whatever you say, Hûd. Or are you now in your official persona, and I call you Captain Ramstan?'

'Just try, for once, to keep your nose out of the glass and your hands off alien flesh. There might be an emergency.'

'Then you are expecting trouble. But, if you won't tell anybody what's up, how can you expect …? Look, either we're on shore leave or we're not. Which is it?'

'I'll … as of present, shore leave. Meanwhile … never mind … forget it. That voice …'

2

He put the mask on his face. Its edges clung to his skin, sealing in the nose and the mouth. He walked through three halls and four doors, bathed in sonic waves that were automatically beamed if a door opened. This was for the safety of non-Kalafalans.

Outside, the sun, much like Earth's, was riding out the late afternoon. It was midsummer in the temperate zone of the northern hemisphere, but a cooling west wind flapped his cloak. The spaceport, built by the natives for visitors long long ago, was on the plateau-top of a small mountain. Ramstan could see past the houses and down the slope to the great city on the plains.

Two hundred kilometers east, a dark-purple mountain range loomed. The Kalafalans called this 20,000-kilometer-high mass *Tha'ufukwilala*. The Westering Beast.

Overhead, perhaps a hectometer up, two purple creatures floated toward the purple range. They were shaped like humpbacked boxkites with thick disks on the lower side. Born on the low hills of the west coast, they were now being pushed in their final form toward their final home by the west winds.

When they struck the face of the Westering Beast, the gas in their humps would explode, and the thin, brittle skeletons would shatter. The bone shards would add their tiny amount to the trillions preceding them. Their scattered flesh would feed larvae that would eat their way out of the rubbery capsules hurled from the explosions.

The larvae would creep down the jagged face of the range and begin the slow journey to the coast. There they, like their ancestors, would metamorphose into the floating death-pregnant form.

In a few thousand years, the Westering Beast would have crept up to this mountain and the city in the valley. In a few centuries after that, this area would be covered. Before then, the cities, towns, villages, and farm buildings now stretching from south coast to north coast would be moved 200 kilometers to the west.

'Why haven't you killed the larvae long ago and stopped this burial of your land and of all living things?' asked many visitors from many planets.

'Why didn't you do this 2000 years ago? Why didn't you destroy the nests on the western seacoast hills? The time will come when you will be pushed into the sea.'

'Oh, no,' the Kalafalans replied. 'You do not understand. The bottom layers of bone are decomposing and forming the basis for a very rich soil. When the time comes, we will clear off the top layers and plant vegetation and form a new world. By then, the *awawa* will be buried under the bones of their ancestors, and the Goddess will have ended them, and we will have a land richer than the rich land we now have.'

'By the time you get around to doing that, you won't have enough population to do the required work. And you, too, will be buried,' the Earthpeople said.

The Kalafalans smiled. They trusted in their Goddess and Her designs.

Ramstan had discussed this attitude with Klizoo, the spaceport administrator. Now he saw Klizoo coming out of a nearby park. Holding up his thumb and forefinger in the broken O of salutation, Ramstan called out in the spaceport lingua franca, Urzint.

'Klizoo, length and pleasure! Pardon my abruptness, but have you recently seen any non-Kalafalans you didn't recognize?'

Klizoo laughed, revealing his sharklike teeth. Ramstan could see the slender stalactite of flesh hanging from the roof of his mouth. It was this organ that aided in forming two buzzing consonants which made it impossible for non-Kalafalans to speak the language. Urzint was, fortunately, simple in phones and relatively easy for most sentients to master.

Klizoo stopped laughing. 'I haven't seen any I didn't recognize, though, to be frank, all aliens have a lookalike likeness. But an Earthwoman has just come into the city. From the northern coast. She registered at the hotel not more than an hour ago. Her name is Branwen Davis, and she is a crewmember of Irion's ship.'

'Irion? But *Pegasus* left months ago! What's this woman doing here?'

'Ask her.'

Ramstan was exasperated. The Kalafalan authorities must have known that this woman, Davis, had been left behind – for scientific research? – yet they had never thought to mention it. Also, the hotel staff had probably – no, undoubtedly – never mentioned to Davis that Ramstan's ship was in port. Surely, if she'd known that, she would have reported to him at once.

He just did not understand Kalafalans, and he never would.

But then the Kalafalans said the same thing about the Earthpeople.

'Oh, yes,' Klizoo said. 'The Tenolt are here. They just landed.'

Ramstan jumped as if he had stepped barefoot on a scorpion. His interest in the mysterious Earthwoman evaporated.

'The Tenolt?'

He lifted his right hand, its back close to his mouth, and spoke through his mask into his skinceiver.

'Alif Rho Gimel speaking. Alif Rho Gimel. Come in, Hermes.'

Lieutenant-Commodore Tenno's voice said, 'Hermes here, Alif Rho Gimel. A Tolt ship, looks like the *Popacapyu*, landed thirty minutes ago. She made an unconventional approach, must have descended on the far side of Kalafala and stayed low until she came over the mountains. The port authorities were upset, but the Tolt captain said that the ship was having drive problems and he had to bring her in quickly.'

'Why didn't you notify me at once?'

'It didn't seem necessary. No sooner did the *Popacapyu* land than her ports opened and out came a number of crewpeople. They went immediately to the control tower, and then some went to the hotel and the tavern. That didn't indicate hostile motives, sir. Besides, we have no reason to suspect hostility.'

Was there a questioning tone in Tenno's voice?

He added, 'Sir, more Tenolt have left the ship. They're unarmed – like the others.'

Ramstan had continued walking. He stopped under a tree on the edge of the field. He could not see his ship, *al-Buraq*, because she was on a lower-level berth in the center of a great concrete basin. But the upper part of the oyster-shaped Tolt vessel was visible. Most of the ship was concealed by a triple-row of giant, poplarlike trees. Only Kalafalans would plant trees and flowers in the middle of a landing field.

The ship had to be the *Popacapyu* which had been berthed near *al-Buraq* on the Tolt port on the night that *al-Buraq* took off so suddenly, uncleared by the Tolt authorities.

Now that the *Popacapyu* was here – and how had the Tenolt found *al-Buraq?* – her captain would, sooner or later, be visiting Ramstan. He would ask why the Earthship had made its unauthorized departure. Or would he? He knew why.

Ramstan started walking again. When he came to the limit of the field, he left the trees to continue southward. After going down the hill far enough so he would not be seen from the Tolt ship, he walked east across the face of the hill. He took a half-hour to circle until he could approach *al-Buraq* from the east.

He paused to lean against the slim, corkscrew-shaped flying buttress of a government building to catch his breath and to admire – for how many times? – his ship.

From this side of the field, he could see her upper part. The vessel lay in a depression the opposite wall of which was deep and vertical. On this side, ramps led up from the craft for the passage of crew and supplies. Many

Kalafalans stood along the edges of the depression gazing at *al-Buraq*. She crouched in her berth, glowing with a bright-red wax and wane, breathing light. A monstrous starfish-form bright as a hot coal just fallen from a fireplace, her five arms sprawled out from the fat central body. She was now in this form so that the loading and unloading of cargo and supplies and the entry and exit of personnel could be expedited. For takeoff, she could shift to space-form in two minutes, though she did not have to metamorphose to do so. The five arms, covered with hundreds of thousands of small armor plates, would shrink in length, swell in circumference, draw up, become part of the saucer-shaped body. Or, if she were to travel in the atmosphere, she would become needle-shaped. There was no danger of personnel being crushed in corridors or cabins during the shape-change. The bulkhead sensors detected that which must be uninjured or undamaged. Only if the captain – or a delegated authority – overrode the inhibitions with a spoken code could the shape-shifting be harmful to the crew.

Ramstan crossed the field and gently moved through the hundreds gathered to admire the ship. They smiled and spoke to him in their native tongue or in Urzint. Many reached out to touch him lightly. Their fingers scraped off dust of meteors, powder of comets, light-exudations of stars, and also the texture of all the fleshes of Earth. Or so they claimed.

Ramstan smiled diplomatically when the fingers touched him. He smiled at a baby held up to him and at a particularly pixyish female. She gestured with one hand, thumb and a finger curved and touching to indicate she'd like to rendezvous with him.

At that moment he envied those of his crew who would have accepted her invitation. But he had to behave as the representative of the best on Earth. Whether or not he liked it, he was clad in moral armor. It was not that of Kalafala but of Earth. And his own.

The natives did not understand his behavior. Some of it repelled them, though they had not told him so directly. Despite this, they touched him with wondering, wonder-netting fingers. He might be as cold as interstellar space, but this, too, was thrilling. Cold burned in beauty.

'Kala!watha! Kala!watha!'

The murmurs flowed around him. *Kala-* indicated 'person' or 'sentient' or 'speech.' *-!watha* was as close to 'Earth' as their language permitted them to approach. The Terrans could not pronounce at all the buzzing consonant designated by! in the phonetic transcription used by the Terran linguists.

Here and there arose murmurs of *p + hawaw!sona*. *Double-mask*. Earthpeople here wore masks to strain out the psychedeligenic spores. Also, no matter how expressive or uninhibited his or her features seemed to the other Terrans, to the Kalafalan the Earthperson was masked with slow-flowing concrete.

Ramstan stepped past the sign which bore the ideogram warning the natives to go no further. He went down the ramp to the bottom of the depression and up the nine stone steps to the slab on which *al-Buraq* sprawled. Normally, the stone was gray. Now it seemed to blush lightly. A moment later, it blushed deeply.

The ship panted red light through the semi-opaque hull. The lower part of the disk-shaped body and the five arms bulged out against the slab, like a behemoth pressed down by its own weight.

Ramstan halted before the two masked marines at the port, gave the password – though both recognized him, of course – held out his right hand so one could read through UV glasses the code printed on the palm. He entered the port, air under pressure blowing from it, and went down a short corridor. The bulkhead before him smiled; he stepped through the lips. For about seven seconds, he stood still while supersonic beams disintegrated spores that had been killed in the corridor.

A whistle sounded; the bulkheads flashed red. He removed his mask, folded it, and stuck it into an inner pocket of his jacket. He went on into a corridor twice as tall as he, round, and curving toward the center mess hall for the third-level crew. The floor was cartilaginous and springy. Round and lozenge-shaped shining plates alternated along both sides of the corridor. Opened or closed irises were spaced at irregular intervals along the corridors. The light was white within the ship; Ramstan moved shadowless. The glow on the circle to his right dulled, then became a mosaic of partial views of operational-important places in the ship. Eight triangles, separated by a thin black line, composed the circle and showed him three slices of the bridge, the chief engineer's post, chief gunnery officer's post, two laboratories, and the chief medical officer's office.

'Cancel V-1,' Ramstan said, and the mosaic died out in a burst of light.

A whistle shrilled. A lozenge on the right bulkhead showed the face of Lieutenant-Commodore Tenno.

'No orders now,' Ramstan growled. 'Cancel A-1.'

Tenno disappeared in a glory of light. That was one of the disadvantages of replacing metal and plastic with protoplasm, cables with nerves, computers with brains. Like a dog wriggling and fawning with frenzied love at her master's return home, *al-Buraq* was overexcited at seeing him after his long (ten-hour) absence.

The chief bioengineer, Doctor Indra, was working at the inhibition of *al-Buraq*. At least, he was thinking about the problem or should be. Ramstan had seen Indra squatting cross-legged on the floor, immobile, even the eyes unblinking, one skinny brown arm extended to the bulkhead and holding a mentoscope against a sensor plate.

Ramstan left the corridor for an elevator passageway.

At its end was a port which became a hatch as he neared it. He stepped onto the gray disk which rose up through the hatch, said, 'One-three. C-C,' and waited. An iris opened in the bulkhead, the disk moved into the iris, carrying him with a motion which he could barely feel. The bulkheads rounded to form a shaft, the disk rose, the flesh-colored bulkheads glowing, and then stopped with a slight chuffing sound. The shaft bent overhead, the bulkhead behind him curving over, the rest of the shaft quickly shaping itself into a corridor.

Ramstan stepped off the disk, walked three paces to where the shaft curved upward again, and waited. In three seconds, the bulkhead just before him split, and he walked into his quarters. This was a small room which was expanding now that the master was home. It was hemispherical, and the only visible furniture was a table on which stood an electron microscope. The deck was bare except for a prayer rug, three meters square, near a bulkhead by the iris. It was made of woven wool, as required by the al-Khidhr sect, and was dark green except for a red arrowhead design in one corner. This was the *kiblah*, the symbol which was to be pointed towards Mecca when the worshiper knelt on the rug. Here, of course, there was no means for determining where Mecca was. This made no difference to Ramstan. He had not prayed since his father had died. He did not know why he had not left the rug on Earth, and he had not cared to wonder why. Most of the time he did not even notice it. Now, looking intensely at it, he thought it moved.

One of the superstitions of the sect was that prayer rugs, if rolled, unrolled themselves just before al-Khidhr, the Green One, appeared. If unrolled, the rug moved its edges to indicate the coming of al-Khidhr.

Ramstan turned away. He was getting too nervous, he told himself. Next, he'd be hallucinating al-Khidhr himself.

The bulkheads had been bare and glowing faintly yellow. Now, murals appeared on them, ship's electronic reproductions of paintings by Ramstan. Most were geometrical abstracts, but there was one naturalistic St George slaying the dragon and another of Aladdin during his first encounter with the *djinn* of the lamp. These two were his most recent works. It had taken him a long time to overcome his early conditioning against the representation of living things in art.

Ramstan, though he'd abandoned the faith of his ancestors, still could not eat the flesh of swine, regarded dogs as unclean, and wiped with the left hand after defecating. But he had overcome his conditioning against drinking alcohol.

He stood before the St George and dragon, spoke a code phrase, and the bulkhead opened, its central point of distention the dragon's eye. Within was a large globe open at one end. It contained two plastic boxes, one larger than the other. The smaller held top-secret records, little spheres, each set in a hollow. The other – that held the reason why he had ordered *al-Buraq* to leave Tolt so quickly and why the Tolt ship was now here.

He struggled with the desire to open the larger box and look at its contents. He sighed, shuddered slightly, and told the bulkhead to close up. He patted the bulkhead, and it quivered. *Al-Buraq* was watching him, and she had interpreted the pat as a touch of affection from her master. Somewhere, in the dark chamber in ship where the synthetic brain floated, a complex of neural circuits, unanticipated by the designers, had grown. The 'obedience' configuration now had an 'affection' annex.

Ramstan turned away and uttered another code word. A viewplate on the bulkhead across the cabin widened, and it began to run off a film of the cabin since Ramstan had left it. He watched it with his mind on other things: the Tenolt, Branwen Davis, and the bodiless voice in the tavern.

His indrawn breath was a knife-edge scraped across a whetstone. He cried, 'Hold it!'

The film continued running. He said, 'Freeze it!' and the film stopped. In one corner flashed 10:31 ST, the time of the photographing.

Ramstan groaned, and he said, 'Run it back,' and then, again, 'Freeze it.'

The screen had showed an empty cabin. Then, suddenly, the figure had appeared. It had not entered through the iris; it had just popped out of nowhere like a ghost materialized.

Its back was to Ramstan, and it was facing the mural of St George and the dragon. Its head was concealed beneath a green hood, and the body was covered with a green cloak. The back of the hands were very wrinkled and bore huge blue veins and dark liver-spots.

He groaned again. He had seen such a hood and cloak and such hands once before. A long time ago on Earth.

At Ramstan's command, the film began running forward again. The figure stood looking at the mural for three minutes, then it turned. Ramstan was looking into a face that he could not see clearly because it was deep within the hood. But he recognized it. It was ancient, ancient, carved with wrinkles, and it could have been the face of a very old man or woman.

The shadowy eyes seemed to be looking into his.

Then the person in green vanished.

Ramstan cried, 'Al-Khidhr!'

3

Ramstan sat before the table in his quarters. Canceling all shadows except those in his mind, light pulsed faintly from the deck, bulkheads, and overhead. His only communication with the outside was the audio from the first-bridge, and that was one-way.

On the top of the table was an egg-shaped object below the electron microscope. To the unaided eye, the egg was faintly yellowish-white. It was smooth to the touch. Looking at the screen while he turned the controls, Ramstan felt as if he were in an aircraft descending toward a large albino elephant with a very wrinkled hide.

The wrinkled blank expanded, carrying the ends of the egg out of sight. Tiny figures appeared, indistinct at first, then, suddenly, sharp. The surface was as crowded with sculpture as an ancient Hindu temple.

Ramstan moved the controls so that the view swept to the figures at the end to his left. Here, rising up from the surface of a choppy sea, was a multitude of forms: a twelve-tentacled squid with a bony, serrated fin; a vast fishlike creature behind it, its leviathan mouth filled with curving teeth and open to suck in the desperate mollusk fleeing via the double propulsion of jet and sail; a gigantic amoeba which seemed to pulse, its pseudopods reaching out to encircle and ingest a sharklike creature; the gap of the shark's mouth about to close on a bulbous, fat-lipped fish the jaws of which were clamped on a bulging-eyed thing, half lobster, half conical shell; the claws of the hybrid opening to release in its death agony an eel-like creature with a cockatoo crest; a school of things like animated flowers fleeing into the shallows; a band of fish with fins that could swim in the sea or pull them along like cripples on the beach sands, two of the crutch-fins lurching across the beach toward low-growing plants.

Ramstan adjusted the controls again, and the sea surface became translucent. Seemingly far below, though the distance must be an illusion, were many things of many forms that crawled on the muck of the ocean floor, eating the torn parts and the bodies that sifted from the carnage above, eating the carrion and each other, dying, themselves being eaten, while eggs spurted from mothers and fathers, eggs hatched, the young darted out in all directions to escape the eaters, some of whom were their own parents.

Dimly, through the murk, the outlines of a long-buried city advanced and receded, a shattered ziggurat topped by an altar and a leaning idol, a pillar, a broken arch, an upside down trireme ragged with living valves clinging to its hull, the hint of a huge and fearsome creature with burning eyes quivering in its hollow, the granite head of a massive statue up to its mouth in mud mixed with bones and shells, its long curving nose and fierce eyes stonily proclaiming terror, arrogance, and invincibility to an uncomprehending thing of a hundred skinny legs and a beak like a vulture's.

Another turn of the controls. Beneath the mud? He could not determine what it was. Something batlike and grinning.

He turned the controls back and moved the eye past the shore and into the jungle. Here was a strange creature which seemed to stretch for miles, which was, actually, a procession of beasts and birds sequentially advancing, progressing, and retrogressing from the crutch-creature that had achieved a total land life. It was many beings making a single being, flowing out from the other, branching, flowering, sometimes a branch curving back to enter the sea, a many-bodied, many-limbed, many-headed flow of flesh.

Ramstan reached out to turn the egg slightly, stopping his fingertips short of it as if he feared that it might burn him or cling to his flesh and suck him into it. After a few seconds' hesitation, he felt it, and it was, as always, cool and smooth. But he could feel the squirm of life and the suddenness and soddenness of death and the tingling of tiny voltages of terror and pain and laughter and joy and triumph and despair.

So he sat, turning the ovoid, adjusting the microscope, tracing the slow spiral of sculpture.

Here was a city, proud and high-walled, about to be destroyed by barbarians from the mountains, a horde that had wandered for decades over desert and now coveted the milk and honey, the gold and the jewels, the furniture and the trinkets, the women and the herds.

Here was another city destroyed only by time. The rains had gone, the land had dried, the people had died or gone seeking a place where the soil was wet and black and thick and the skies were wet and cloudy. A jackalish beast crossed the wide street, now covered with sand, where victorious armies had once marched down its length, dragging captives behind chariots piled with loot while the citizens cheered and the band played loud martial music. Now the only sound was that of the wind through empty dusty rooms, the hoot of an owl, the hiss of a serpent. Beyond, the descendants of the refugees pushed their herds across vast steppes, headed toward a distant land of walled cities, many rivers, and easy pickings.

And here were rockets poised for the first manned leap to another planet, helmeted figures working around it.

And there was the first starship, and beyond it the first confrontation of explorers and natives.

And here was a sculpture which had puzzled Ramstan the first three times he had studied it. Now he understood that it was composed of symbolic figures representing the universe, or *a* universe, collapsing, every bit of matter from giant red stars to free hydrogen rushing back toward the point of origin. Beyond that was another easily interpreted figure: the single primal colossal star exploding. Beyond, stars forming. Beyond, planets. Beyond, the thick sea with life forming.

And here and here and here were figures that filmed his skin with cold. In the midst of the life and death of universes was a tiny, often-repeated, egg-shaped object. Always with it were three hooded figures.

Ramstan understood what their ubiquitous presence meant, or he thought he understood, but he could not believe it.

The river of birth and death and rebirth spiraled around the egg. But on its one end was a blank area. Either the sculptors had not lived long enough to complete their work or they had intentionally left it unfinished. If the latter, why?

The *glyfa* could tell him, but it was silent and had been for some time.

Ramstan had taken the *glyfa* out of the bulkhead-safe, moved it easily to the table since the a-g units on its ends reduced its 500-kilogram weight to five grams, and asked it to speak to him. But the voice was still.

Was it mute because it wanted him to study the thousands of sculpturings, to learn from them something that it could easily tell him but which he would believe only if he had taught himself? Or was it occupied with its own thoughts or with whatever went on under that impenetrable surface?

Though the *glyfa* had never hinted at it, Ramstan felt that the egg hid inside it a world as thickly populated as a dozen planets. Within that white compress was a seething, a ferment. Sometimes, he imaged a nest of jam-packed writhing and hissing snakes, sometimes a multitude of angels on pinpoints, sometimes snakes with angel wings.

More than once he envisioned a tiny sun hanging in the center of the hollow egg. It glared down upon the curving surface, a closed infinity of living sculptures a million times more intricate and extensive than those on the exterior.

Through them wandered a tiny old man, creator of the egg-world, self-exiled, self-enclosed, nomadic and monadic.

Why did he see an old man there? Why not an old woman or a nonhuman male, female, hermaphrodite, or neuter?

Ramstan thought he knew why. The adult tended to use the mental images he'd lived with in childhood. He had been raised and educated in a Muslim sect which was orthodox enough except for its focus on the mysterious al-Khidhr. The Green One, talked of but not named in *Surat* 18 of the *Qu'ran*.

But al-Khidhr had been a figure of Arabic folklore long before Muhammad became the voice of Allah. He was supposed by scholars to be, in fact, Elijah, the Hebrew prophet. Certainly, many identical tales were told of them, and they were often equated in the people's minds. Late twentieth-century scholarship, however, had indicated that the legends of al-Khidhr existed before Elijah had been born.

Ramstan didn't know the truth about the Green One nor did he care. When he was a child, he had believed that there truly was at least one immortal with magical powers. But, in his early adulthood, he had decided that al-Khidhr was only one of the legion of folklore figures, no more real than the Mullah Nasruddin, Paul Bunyan, or Sinbad the Sailor. He also became aware that the Khidhrites had incorporated many of the elements of that other mysterious person of Muslim legend, Luqman, with those of al-Khidhr.

Still, though his mind denied its verity, his emotions, connected to and powered by the child buried in him, were ready to evoke the image of the Green One when the proper stimulus touched him. Within him, as there seemed to be within the egg, an old man – Melchizedekean, pre-Muhammad, pre-Kaaba, pre-Mecca – wandered the lion-haunted, lion-yellow deserts, coeval with Ishmael, that 'wild ass of a man,' when Ishmael was a senile great-great-great-grandfather babbling of Ibrahim and Hagar and of the lover of his youth, the divine Ashdar. The adult Ramstan classified al-Khidhr as a myth, a symbolic figure, or an archetype fleshed only in dreams.

But there was that puzzling and disturbing encounter, if it was such, which he could not forget ...

He was a third-year cadet at the space academy at Sirius Point, Australian Department, and on this day, the star pitcher, he was in the ninth inning during a game against the University of Tokyo. The score was 6-6, and he had just struck out two men. Next up was Jimmy Ikeda, the best batter Tokyo had. Daishonin Smith had just stolen second. And then, while Ramstan was winding up to pitch the first ball at Ikeda, he had been stopped. A messenger from the commandant told him that he was wanted immediately in the commandant's office.

Ramstan had been furious, then he became frightened. Only a few minutes ago, the commandant had been in the first row in the section reserved for the higher officers. Now he was gone. And what terribly serious event had made him halt the game at this moment? Ramstan could think of only one thing. He was numb as, still in his player's uniform, he hurried to the commandant's office.

'Your father has died,' the commandant said. A moment later, his mother's stricken face was on the phone and she was sobbing and telling him of the heart attack. His father had been rushed to the hospital, which was only half a kilometer down the corridor in the megabuilding. But his father had insisted that he be taken home, and he was now there in his own bed.

A half hour later, Ramstan was on the shuttle to New Babylon. Eighty minutes after embarking, he was on the twentieth level, which held the university and the staff residences. On opening the door to his parents' apartment, he found his entrance blocked by someone who was just leaving. He or she was tall, only half a head shorter than Ramstan. Under a green hood was the face of a centenarian, deeply wrinkled, the lips absent as if they had chewed themselves away on the hard edge of time. The nose was long and sharp, ground thin by a remorseless grindstone. The chin was bony; a few long hairs bristled from it. Under prominent brows were extraordinarily large eyes, set very far apart, their color indeterminable in the shadow of the hood. The body and legs were under a loose green robe from which protruded wrinkled spotted feet in sandals. Under one arm was a very large black book, the old-fashioned printed kind, a collector's item. The arm covered part of the large Arabic letters on the cover.

At any other time, Ramstan would have given the ancient in his or her long-outmoded clothes, his full attention. But now, after the stranger had passed by, he strode into the apartment crowded with relatives and friends.

They were chanting the *Surat Ya-Sin* as he walked through them and into the bedroom where the gaunt eagle face of his father was still uncovered.

'*When We sent to them two, and they denied them both, so We reinforced for a third, and they said: We are messengers to you.*

'*They said: You are only mortals like us. The Merciful has not sent down anything. You are lying!*'

After the funeral, Ramstan asked his mother, 'Who was that old man who left just as I entered?'

By then he had decided that the stranger was male.

'What old man?'

'He looked as if he must be a hundred years old. He was dressed in a hooded green robe, and he carried a huge black book under one arm.'

'I didn't see him,' his mother had said. 'But there were so many people there to mourn. He must have been a friend of your father's.'

She gasped, and she held her hand to her mouth, her eyes very wide. 'An old man in green robes and holding a black book! Al-Khidr!'

'Don't be silly.'

'He came to record your father's name in his book!'

'Nonsense!'

Ramstan had had to leave soon thereafter for the shuttle to Sirius Point. But the next evening his mother phoned him.

'Son, I asked everybody who'd been there when your father was dying, and nobody saw the old man in green carrying a large black book. *You* were the *only* one who saw him! Now do you believe that it was al-Khidr? And since you alone saw him, it must be a sign! A good one, I hope!'

'It's a sign that you hope I'll return to the faith.'

'But if you were the only one to see him!' she had wailed.

'Then it was my grief. When the father dies, the son becomes a child again, if only for a little while.'

'No, it was al-Khîdhr! Think about it, Hûd. Your faith isn't dead after all! Allah has given you another chance!'

Ramstan had never told his parents how he had seen an old man – the same? – bending over him when he was twelve and sick and had just awakened from a dream. The old man had been, of course, the tag-end of a fever-inspired hallucination. Thus, when he had been stricken with grief for his father, somewhere in his brain a switch had closed, and the old man of the sickbed dream had been imaged forth again in a circuit. That was all there was to it. Certainly, he was not going to say anything about him at the academy. If the authorities heard about it, they would suspect mental instability. Even if he were then run through another battery of PS tests and still came out with a high score, he'd not even be an alaraf-ship crewmember, let alone be an officer.

At that time, the first alaraf ship was not yet built, but it was known that she would be and that more were planned. Ramstan was fiercely determined to be an officer on one and then, someday, the captain.

He had achieved his ambition, and he had, in effect, then thrown it away.

'Was it worth it?' he said out loud, though it wasn't necessary to speak to be heard.

There was no answer.

'Speak, damn you!' he cried, and he struck the egg with a fist. He yelped with pain. The egg was as hard and unyielding as Death itself.

He heard a chuckle – or thought he heard it. Was that himself laughing at himself? Had he been talking to himself? He did not think so when the *glyfa* spoke or when he thought it was speaking. But, when it was silent, he wondered if he talked for both himself and it.

When a man thought that he might be splitting in two, and that man was responsible for the lives of four hundred men and women, he should turn over his command and commit himself to the care of the chief medical officer. But if Ramstan did, he could no longer conceal the *glyfa*. No, he would *not* give it up. He could not let Benagur take command. Benagur would search the ex-captain's quarters and would find the *glyfa*. But perhaps Benagur, like Ramstan, would keep silent, knowing that once the others learned about it, they would lock it away or study it. Then Benagur would also be denied possession of the *glyfa* – or vice versa.

The silence undulated from the egg, curved back from the overhead, deck, and bulkheads, and thickened like abyssal waters around a bathysphere.

'I speak!'

Ramstan started, his heart beating as if struck by a fist.

When the *glyfa* had spoken to him while he was carrying it from the Tolt temple, it had used his father's voice. Now, Ramstan heard his mother's voice. And, like his father's, it spoke in his familial New Babylonish, basically a creolized Arabic but with at least half of its vocabulary borrowed from Chinese or Terrish.

Ramstan said, 'It's time ... far past time ... that you did speak.'

'Immortality,' his mother's voice said. 'I offered it, but you neither accepted nor rejected it.'

'Two forms of immortality,' Ramstan said. 'A choice of one of two. One of which is not true immortality. I may live for billions of years, but I will eventually age, though very slowly. And I will eventually die of old age. Though, probably, I'll die long before that. In such a long lifespan, accident, homicide, or suicide will put an end to me. The statistical distribution of events will ensure that.

'As for the other form, it's also probably not a true immortality. I can live forever – *you* say – as a magnetically shaped complex of neural waves existing inside you. Which means that I'll be under your control ...'

'No! I promised you that you may live as you wish. Any and all of your fantasies will be fully realized – forever.'

'How do I know that your word is good? Once I'm in your power ...'

'What would I gain by betraying you?'

'How would I know that until it was too late for me to do anything about it?'

After a long silence, Ramstan said, 'Has it occurred to you that I might not be interested in living forever or even beyond my natural lifespan?'

Silence.

Ramstan broke it. 'Somehow, you stimulated in me an overpowering desire to steal you from the Tenolt. I became a criminal. I abandoned my duty, betrayed my trust, lost my honor. Threw away everything I've worked so hard to get as if it were rusty old armor. How did you get me to do that?

'Was it because there was in me a criminal impulse, however slight, and you detected it and amplified it until I couldn't resist it? The impulse which should have died became an obsession because you brought it from a dying flicker to a roaring blaze?

'But, if you could do that, why can't you overpower me to the point where I agree to do what you want me to do in return for immortality? Is it because you did not detect that, unlike most people, I have no desire to live forever? That I want something else?

'Or don't you care whether or not I want immortality? You can and you have manipulated me enough to use me as your agent, and that's all you're concerned about. You've succeeded so far, *glyfa*, but you've gone as far as you can with me. My back is up. I won't do anything more for you unless I know what your goal is and maybe not then. What do you want me for? What do you *want?*'

'What *do you* want?' his mother's voice said.

Minutes of silence passed. He would not reply because he had no answer to that question, and the *glyfa* was done with this conversation. But not with him.

4

Masked, carrying some clothes and the *glyfa* in a small suitcase, Ramstan left *al-Buraq*. He had hesitated a long time before he had decided to take the *glyfa* with him to the hotel. Perhaps it was not too late to return it to its worshipers. He was sure that the Tenolt would see him leave ship, and they would quickly find out that he had checked into the hotel. They would approach him, carefully, of course. They would have to do that since there were many Earthpeople staying in the hotel during shore leave. Or would they? They were fanatics, and they wanted their god back. But they did not know that he had the *glyfa* with him. They could, however, seize him or try to do so and hold him as hostage until the *glyfa* was returned to them.

He did not know what they would do. All he did know was that, at this moment, he felt as if he would gladly be rid of the *glyfa*. And if he could somehow negotiate its return and also keep his people from knowing what he had done, he would never again, never, forget his duty.

Did he really believe that? He did not know.

When near the hotel, he passed Warrant Officer Deva Kolkoshki. She saluted him despite his order not to do so outside ship during leave. She was defying him subtly or perhaps not so subtly. In some way which she probably could not define, she was showing her hatred for him.

He passed her, and his back rippled with cold. Daggers of ice seemed to pierce his heart and genitals. Deva was very passionate, and Ramstan felt sure that only her basic stability and morality and years of naval discipline kept her from thrusting a knife into him. Perhaps he was wrong. Just because she was Siberian and her culture was as violent as the Americans' had been was no reason to assume that she had to suppress a desire to stab him. He might be projecting his feelings of guilt upon her.

No. He felt no guilt. Why should he? He had had an affair with her, as he had with twenty or so of the women of *al-Buraq*. Then she, like so many others, had accused him of not loving her, of not even thinking of her when they were making love. His mind, she had said, was on something else. What was it? What was he thinking about when he should have been entirely enfolded with her, become one with her? Whatever it was, it offended her and made her feel more like a thing than a human being.

Ramstan had not been able to explain. But all his affairs ended in this manner, though not all the women seemed to hate him as intensely as Deva did.

That was the trouble with the sensitivity techniques and raising of consciousness disciplines that were part of the education of all Earthpeople. He sometimes wished that his century had the same casual attitude towards affairs that twentieth-century people were supposed to have had. The trouble with his own time was that love was force-fed to the citizens. Not all gavaged geese kept the food down and grew fat. Some vomited it up.

Thinking thus, he went up the broad stone steps of the hotel, walked across the big portico, and went through two rooms, each with heavy, thick doors that shut automatically behind him. These would not open if another person wished to enter a few seconds after him or if somebody else was already in one of them. Again, he went through the spore-killing process.

Passing through a wide oval portal, he entered the lobby. The floor was of polished chrysanthemum-white and poppy-red stone. Pillars with curved flutings jetted up into the shadows of the ceiling. Beyond the stone forest, against the far wall, was the sea-green desk of the clerk. His name was Bizala, and he was the only other person visible. Ramstan removed his mask, but the clerk, recognizing him under it, had Ramstan's keys ready. He had been notified by a crewmember that Ramstan wanted a room.

Bizala smiled, but he managed to convey a shadowy dislike as he handed the keys to Ramstan.

The dislike was for the keys, not Ramstan. Until the first space visitors, the Urzint, had landed, keys were unused on the planet. Bizala had to perform a ritual cleansing at the end of each shift because of his contact with these.

Ramstan looked around the empty lobby. Most of the chairs were monstrously huge and sprawling and had some unfunctional grooves in the arms. Unfunctional for humans, anyway. They had not been built for any beings now lodged here. Like most of the other furniture and furnishings of the hotel, they had been constructed for the Urzint. Six of their ships had used this field for a long time. Then, one day, they had failed to show up as scheduled, although they had promised that they would be using the field for millennia to come. Why had they disappeared?

Ramstan walked up the broad, curving ramp to the third floor – there were no elevators – and quietly unlocked the door to his room. He pushed it inward swiftly, leaped into the room and looked around quickly. It was empty and still. The sunlight slanted through the single enormous window onto the gigantic bed. The bathroom, so large that he would not have complained if it had been the bedroom, was empty. A movable platform of glistening yellow hardwood stood before the washbowl, which he used as a bathtub. There was another platform with steps before the toilet bowl, the top of which was a contraption of yellow hardwood. The Kalafalans had made various adjustments for the smaller size of the recent guests. However, if those for whom this hotel was built should return, they would find everything ready for them.

Ramstan set the electronic traps on the suitcase and put it inside the cavernous closet. After locking its door, he went into the hall and locked the door to his room. Returning to the lobby, he asked Bizala if any new guests had registered in the last twenty-four hours.

'Six Tenolt.'

'No one else? An Earthwoman, perhaps?'

'Ah! She did not register, though she had intended to. She inquired about you, and I said you were in town. She left immediately afterward.'

'For my ship or for town?'

'She did not say. There is, of course, the possibility that she had a third destination. Or none at all.'

Bizala was correct, but Ramstan was nevertheless annoyed. These Kalafalans! They spent so much time in considering all possible methods and avenues of action, they seldom accomplished anything. However, as Toyce had pointed out, they seemed as happy as Terrans or any species they had met so far. Progress in science and technology was not necessarily the index of a high civilization.

Ramstan walked back to his room briskly. His bootsteps sounded hollowly in the vast untenanted lobby, staircase, and corridor. Before arriving at his room, he spoke into the back of his hand. 'Alif Rho Gimel. Come in, Hermes. Have any strangers contacted you since I last talked to you? Any other news to report?'

'Hermes, here. Negative to both inquiries.'

'Anything to report on Dogfaces?'

'GL reports contact with four where the action is. Negative animus.' (*Translation:* Our men on ground leave in town contacted four Tenolt, and they didn't seem unfriendly.)

'Did Dogfaces inquire about me?'

'Positive.'

'Were Dogfaces looking for me?'

'Not specifically, Alif Rho Gimel. They did ask if you were in town.'

'What did GL say?'

'They said they didn't know.'

'Alif Rho Gimel out.'

Although it was not suppertime, he took his meal from the suitcase. He had meant to remove it before setting the traps but had been too occupied with more important matters. He unset the traps by playing a beam of canceling frequencies from his pocket pseudo-pen over the case. After taking the package out, he reset the traps. Cooking the meal took three seconds after he set the dial on the bottom of the package. He ate without much appetite. He did not dare to order wine sent up. A little drug in it would put him out of the way while the Tenolt went through the suitcase. He did not really believe that they would use poison, since they had the best of reasons for wanting to keep him alive. At this time, anyway.

However, there were other forces operating in the shadows, and what their wants and wishes were he could not know. His death might be one of them.

He dumped the cups and dishes into the toilet, where they dissolved within ten seconds. He returned to the chair and moved its huge body on its six wheels so that he could see the sunset. He sighed with delight at the beauty. There were magnificent sunsets on Earth, on Tolt, on Raushghol, but Kalafala's paled them. Dust from volcanoes on the northern and western fringes of the continent supplied colors, but this alone was not responsible for the high beauty.

Golden stars, tiny and bobbing, drifting from west to east, were, in actuality, far-off boxkite things, dancing lenses for the sun. A pinkish cloud drifted upward, putting out reddish fingers, greenish heads, silvery shoulders, orange-and-emerald-green-streaked ragged eyes, serrated buttons of yellow turquoise, misshapen mouths with carmine lips, and broken irregular teeth of velvet-black and flamingo-pink.

Briefly, a comet the color of cigarette smoke formed against a sky banded with decaying sine waves of pale violet, blood-red, and carrot-yellow. It rose, head downward, tail spreading out until the colors faded, as if washed out by God, and the comet had collided with an ephemeral sun of amethyst-green and both had died.

Twelve kilometers to the west, millions of varicolored diaphanous-winged insects were leaving their feeding grounds to fly to the great spindle-shaped communal nests in which they slept, safe from the crepuscular and nocturnal birds and flying animals. But the preyers were harrying and eating now. Although they were not visible at this distance, they were causing the momentary formations. The beauty of the sunset was a byproduct of hunger, terror, and death.

Then the sun slipped its moorings to the horizon; the sky became black. It was unclouded but starless. Kalafala was on the edge of the universe, and when on this side of its sun, the night sky was empty.

BOOOONG! One hundred thousand bronze gongs struck once to weld into a single clang. In the yards of the houses on the plateau and in the city in the valley, Kalafalans hammered the household gongs to announce the departure of the sun. The single note rose like a bronze bird, the beat of its wings shaking the hotel and rattling the windows.

Torches flared in the spaceport town; thousands of torches would be lit in the unseen city in the valley. A drawn-out, shuddering cry wailed at the window, and the torches danced toward the temple to the northwest of the hotel. Ramstan felt a twinge of longing for Earth. The cry reminded him of the evening call of the *muezzins* from the loudspeakers in his level of New Babylon. Though he had peeled off belief in Allah or in any god as if it were a coat on a hot day, he still responded at times to the Pavlovian bell: his emotions salivated. A cry like a *muezzin's* became an angel's hand squeezing the heart, a piezoelectric flexing.

There was still light in the upper sky. The field was dark except for the now-yellow pulsing of *al-Buraq* and white lights from two open ports in the Tolt ship. Figures appeared in one, cutting off most of the beam, and then the Tenolt had become one with the shadows.

He rose from the chair and walked around in the darkness until his muscles were no longer stiff. Returning to the chair he sat for a long time, his eyes on the dark-and-white vista beyond the window. He shifted uneasily. He should return to ship, but he was not going to. By staying here, he might entice those who lusted after the thing in the box in the suitcase to try to get it now.

He waited for an hour and then moved the chair away from the window to the blackness of a wall. He placed two olson beamguns in the grooves on the arm of the chair and sat down. Now and then, he heard little creaks and slitherings he could not identify but which did not alarm him. The interplay of the pull of the sun and moons, shifting temperatures and humidities, and settling of the ground stretched and squeezed the hotel as if it were an accordion. He ignored the tiny sounds and waited for the click of metal in the lock and the cautious turning of the knob.

And then, as time and night hobbled by, he had a fantasy. What if the key were inserted, not in the little lock at his waist-level but in the huge lock at the level of his head? What if the ponderous door swung open, and a turret-headed, neckless, bone-ruffed, triangular-bodied and column-legged Urzint was silhouetted by the hall lights? And the ancient guest clomped in with steps as heavy as a rhinoceros' straight to the closet, opened the suitcase, put on the tepee-sized nightgown, and went straight to bed with never a word to its little roommate? What then?

He was in a dark wood and running desperately but slowly and heavily, the air thick against him, while a dark, unseen, unnamed thing loped behind him. The thing snuffled. Ramstan tried to howl with terror, but he could force nothing through his throat, which had turned to stone. Then he put his hand in his pocket, and he drew out a small comb. This he threw behind him, knowing that the stiff teeth of the comb would become a thickly tangled forest of trees. His pursuer bellowed with frustration. The crash of its body as it hurled against the great trees and interwoven branches of underbrush was like the toppling of a mountain.

Presently, the thing was breathing raspingly behind him. He reached into his pocket and drew out a small mirror and threw that behind him. There was another bellow of frustration and rage and a splash as of the toppling of the face of a glacier into the sea. Ramstan drove on against the heavy air. He was on a flat plain, hard dirt with no vegetation, and the air was becoming even grayer. Then there was the slap of wet paws on the plain, and the breathing was once more behind him. Ramstan pulled from his pocket his third and last gift – from whom? – a whetstone, and he threw this behind him. Though he did not look back, he knew that this had turned into a high mountain range. The thing's bellow reached him as a faint sound, but he heard its claws digging into the stone slopes and its labored breathings as it pulled itself up and up. And then, as he sped on, he heard its howl of triumph as it topped the highest peak and began to slide down the other side.

Moaning, sweating, Ramstan awoke. Near the door, against the wall, a wavering figure stood. It was in a dark robe, its face shrouded by a hood. The face was as pale as moonlight and gave the impression of being that of a very old man or woman. It was either human or remarkably humanoid.

Ramstan blinked, and the figure shimmered and then was gone.

It was the glowing tag-end of his dream, appearing just as he awoke, and he had seen it as an afterimage. Al-Khidhr, the Green Man? It had been pointing at the lock. He rose, and, automatically picking up an olson from a chair arm, walked swiftly toward the door. He saw the ghostly tube projecting through the keyhole, stopped breathing, turned, and ran to the window. He started to turn its lock, which kept the two sections tight against the outside air, when he remembered the mask. Still not breathing, he groped around in the seat of the chair until he found it and then put it on. Only then did he swing the two sections of the window open, and, leaning far out, breathed deeply.

When his lungs were full, he ran back to the tube. The slight hissing from the open end of the tube had told him it was not an olson but a gas-expeller. It would not do to fuse the tube-end with a blast from the olson. The gas might be explosive.

Ramstan went back to the window and leaned out of it backwards, his eyes on the tube. Presently, the tube was withdrawn. There was a series of clickings as a tool was worked on the lock. He crouched behind the chair. As the door started to swing open, he put his back against the wall, drew up one leg, and shoved the gigantic chair with it. The chair sped towards the doorway on its six wheels, making only a slight squeaking. The door swung open. The chair rammed into the figure momentarily silhouetted in the light. The figure crumbled and went over backward under the impact of the chair.

Ramstan had run, crouching, a few feet behind and to one side of the chair, his olson ready. He stuck his head out of the doorway, ready to yank it back. But he saw nothing threatening in the hall. An arm with a human hand extended along the floor from behind the massive bulk of the chair.

Ramstan duckwalked around the side of the chair, moving quietly. The man on the floor might have an olson in his hidden hand. But that, too, was open and still, and he was looking into the red-streaked and glazed eyes of Benagur.

5

Benagur's head was massive. His hair was as black and as coarse as a bear's and fell past his shoulders. His beard was long and square-cut. His face looked like the half-mad, half-divine face of a stone-winged bull-man in front of an ancient Assyrian temple.

Benagur groaned and rolled over on his right side. The back of his head was bloodied. On the floor by the chair, attached to a plastic cylinder, was the tube which had been shoved through the massive keyhole.

Ramstan helped the commodore to his feet but released him when he growled, 'I'm OK.'

Ramstan shoved the chair back into the room and turned the lights on. Benagur staggered in and sat down on an inflatable chair. Ramstan brought in the tube and cylinder and locked the door. 'What happened, Benagur?'

'When I came down the hall I saw two cloaked, masked, and gloved persons at your door. They looked up and saw me …'

'You didn't shout?'

'Yes. Didn't you hear me?'

'No. The walls and the door are too thick.'

'The two ran away down the hall from me. One dropped the cylinder or whatever it was. They didn't run exactly as humans do …'

'Tenolt?'

'I don't know. I started to push on the door, and that's the last I remember until I woke up on the floor. My head hurts.'

'There must have been a third. Maybe he was behind the door of the room across the hall. He stepped out and hit you on the back of your head. You regained some consciousness, got to your feet, and then I came through with the chair. It knocked you down again.'

Ramstan remembered that he had left the window open. Swearing, he shut it. His own mask was still on, but Benagur had breathed in the spores. He would begin to feel the effect of the psychedelics in about three to four hours. It would be eight to ten days before his body would get rid of them.

Ramstan shut the door to stop the flow of breeze-borne spores from entering the corridor.

'When you get back to ship, Benagur, report to sickbay.'

'No! I won't be hospitalized again! I just got out! There's too much ...'

'Too much what?'

'Too much going on. The Tenolt, everything ... Why would they want to gas you?'

Ramstan said, 'I doubt we'll ever find out. What I want to know right now is why you came here.'

'Shouldn't you call for the sanitizers?' Benagur said.

Ramstan didn't like being told that he should do so. But Benagur was right. He called ship and was put through to Chief Petty Officer Wang. She said that she and a squad would be up in five minutes. Ramstan ordered her to bring along a medic and a squad of marines.

Ramstan looked hard at Benagur, who was still on the inflatable.

'I'll ask you again. Why did you come here?'

Benagur straightened, and he winced.

'I wanted to have it out with you.'

'Yes?'

'You know why,' Benagur said loudly.

'You tell me,' Ramstan said softly.

'I want to hear your explanations, privately, before I take action. That is, if I have to do it. I hope I don't have to.'

'I don't know what you're talking about,' Ramstan said. 'You sound as if you're going to make charges against me. Is that it?'

'Why did you order the marines? So you can put me under arrest?'

'You keep sidling away from my questions. I decided that you should be escorted to sickbay. There's no telling how fast the spores may affect you. You might even ...'

'What?'

'Become violent. It's for your own good.'

'Sure it is!' Benagur cried. 'Of course! Listen! I've been very much disturbed – and puzzled – by your strange behavior on Tolt. You were missing for some time from ship. Suddenly, there you were, like a thief in the night, carrying that bag and shouting that ship must take off at once. And you've never given a word of explanation. No one has dared to ask you what was in it. But, believe me, everybody has been talking about it. And I've not had one good night's sleep.'

'Like a thief in the night,' Ramstan said. 'Well, out with it, man! Exactly what do you suspect?'

His face was expressionless, but his heart was thumping like an imprisoned animal trying to butt its way through a wall, and he was sweating.

'I don't want to do this, Captain! That's why I came here, so we could talk alone and solve this matter without the crew knowing about it. Maybe it's not too late to rectify matters. Maybe we could go back to Tolt and just leave it there and take off, hoping the Tenolt would be so happy to have it back that they wouldn't bother us.'

'What is *it?*' Ramstan said.

Benagur's face was red now. He shook as if his bones were crumbling. Ramstan had seen him angry before, but he had never seen him fearful. Or was he reading him wrong? Was it fury possessing him?

'*It, it!*' Benagur shouted. 'You know what it is! The *glyfa!* The *glyfa!* The Tolt idol!'

'You're accusing me of having stolen the *glyfa?*' Ramstan said. He was surprised at the steadiness of his voice.

'I'm not accusing you!' Benagur said. 'I'm telling you what you and I know!'

'I wonder if you haven't accidentally breathed in some spores before tonight. There's no other way to account for this crazy accusation.'

Benagur ground his teeth. He stood up, swaying, and took three steps toward Ramstan. His huge hands were closed, but he did not raise them. His voice was clotted with phlegm.

'What I'm telling you to your face is what the whole crew is saying behind your back.'

'I don't know why the Tenolt are here,' Ramstan said.

'Listen. Has it occurred to you and those other idiots that I might be on a secret government mission and that your idle curiosity is endangering it?'

He trembled. For the first time in forty-two years, he had lied. Al-Khidr forgive him. Allah forgive him.

Nonsense. Neither existed except as concepts. But concepts were as real, as alive, as the person who thought they were real and alive.

'May God forgive you,' Benagur said.

'May He forgive us all,' Ramstan said, but he did not know what he meant by that.

Benagur closed his eyes and moved his lips soundlessly. He was either praying or using mental techniques to locate the injured cells on the back of his head and then to summon the healing forces of his body. Perhaps he was doing both.

Ramstan, hands locked behind his back, paced back and forth. When he passed the ceiling-high mirror made to reflect behemoths, he saw a hunting falcon whose hood had slipped onto the beak. His eyes were wide and shot with madness and desperation. He must regain his composure or at least the appearance of it. Otherwise, when the marines came to pick up Benagur, they might think that he, too, had breathed in the spores.

A knock on the door. Ramstan used his skinceiver to make sure that it was the ship's crew outside the door. He admitted Lieutenant Malia Fu'a, a biochemistry officer, Chief Petty Officer Wang, and the PD and marine squads. Fu'a was a pretty Samoan who'd parted with Ramstan on good terms after she'd left his bed. She was the only ex-lover who didn't seem to hate him. But she *could* be an excellent actress.

The marines were instructed to take Benagur to ship's hospital after he'd been externally disinfected. Fu'a's squad sprayed his rooms and the hall with a liquid which smelled like new lavender. Ramstan stripped and showered while his clothes were sprayed. He put on pajamas and lit up a cigar while the squad ran a scanner over the room and the hall. The little pistol-shaped device flashed a red light now and then, and the infected spots were then resprayed. By then, the liquid had dried, but the lavender odor hung in the air.

Benagur had not spoken during the entire proceeding. When told by a marine that he must come along now, *sir*, he walked out without a look behind. Fu'a, the last to leave, carried the gas-expeller in a plastic bag. Its contents would be analyzed before morning.

Ramstan explained that unknown persons had tried to shoot the gas into his room and that Benagur had chased them away but had been hit on the head. He said nothing about conducting an investigation later. Though Fu'a had looked curious, she had not, of course, asked him questions. And all the party had been ordered not to say a word to anyone else about the affair.

It would have been wise to station a guard at his door, but Ramstan did not think that the Tenolt – he was sure they were Tenolt – would be back.

A few minutes later, just as he was about to fall asleep despite resonating nerves, he heard a banging on his door. He picked up the olsons, rolled out of bed, and walked to the door.

He spoke through the keyhole in Urzint and then in Terrish.

'Who is it?'

A woman's voice, speaking Terrish, came thinly. 'Lieutenant Branwen Davis of *Pegasus*, sir. I *must* speak to you. May I come in?'

She spoke with a lilt that seemed ... what? ... Irish?

He looked through the keyhole, straightened up, unlocked the door, and backed away. The door swung open, and a very beautiful woman entered.

6

She was approximately two meters tall, a little over average female height. Her black, coarse, and straight hair was in a pageboy bob. Her eyebrows were thick and dark. The wide-spaced, slanting eyes were large and as green as the Persian Gulf. Her skin was a soft golden-brown. The facial skin below the eyes was paler than that above. The contrast gave her features an almost clownlike appearance.

Al-Buraq's crew, when on Kalafala, wore green masks in the corner of which was a silver-winged mule with a woman's face. The scarlet mask that hung around her neck was the regulation color used by *Pegasus*' crew. In its lower right-hand corner was a silver-winged horse.

She wore a shimmering light-green dress, knee-length, flaring out at the waist. The sleeves came to the elbow, and the V-neck was wide and plunging. He did not need her to tell him that she had gotten it from a Kalafalan. Her legs and feet were bare and dirty. She carried a small leather bag in her left hand. Her right hand was heavily bandaged.

She put the bag down and saluted. His return salute was sloppy, resembling a gesture for her to go away.

'You look tired, Davis. You must've had a long hard journey. Sit down before you fall down. Before you report, would you like a drink?'

She smiled, showing beautiful white teeth. Sighing, she dropped onto the inflatable chair as if her legs had given up the ghost.

'I'd love a drink, thank you.'

He gestured at the bar, installed by the hotel for its smaller and more recent guests. 'There's plenty of native liquor there. But I have a bottle of Scotch in my case.'

'Scotch will more than do.'

'On the rocks?'

'Rocks? Oh, you mean ... It's been so long. I mean ... I've been talking Urzint so long that I forgot ... Yes, Scotch on the rocks.'

He asked her when she had discovered that *al-Buraq* was in port. She said that she'd found out a few minutes ago. She'd returned to the hotel, gotten a room and had fallen asleep at once, hadn't even bothered to wash. But she'd awakened about fifteen minutes later and had seen some Earthpeople on the street through her window. She'd gone downstairs at once, and the clerk had told her that Captain Ramstan was in his room. She'd come up at once.

He handed her the drink and sipped on his *Djinn's Delight*. Then he said, 'So what happened?'

'I'm a marine biologist. I was left behind, at my request, to continue experiments at a Kalafalan station on the northwest coast. When it was close to the time for *Pegasus* to return from the Raushghol system, I packed up, said good-bye to my Kalafalan scientist and technician friends, and drove off in my jeep. Its a-g generator malfunctioned about a thousand kilometers north of here. The jeep fell, but fortunately it was only two meters above the ground. Unfortunately, it was on the edge of a cliff. It went into the sea. I jumped out when it struck but almost went over the edge, too.

'I tore up the skin on my hand, enough to put my skinceiver out of operation. My NI transceiver went with the jeep, and so I couldn't call the spaceport. Also, I lost my TR box. I also lost my clothes. I like to sunbathe, and so I was nude when the accident happened. I borrowed a dress from a farm woman and started walking. After a week, I came to the Kurodan River. I got passage on a fishing vessel which was returning to the capital. And here I am.'

'*Pegasus* hasn't returned,' he said. 'She was supposed to rendezvous with *al-Buraq* at Sigdrauf. We waited a month for her. Then we went to Tolt, her stop before going on to Sigdrauf. She had not showed there.'

She was pale, and her voice was very low.

'What do you think ...?'

'I don't know. We can only assume that *Pegasus* is lost or has been delayed for some reason. Perhaps she is having or had biomechanical troubles, and she may be on any of a hundred planets. In any event, *al-Buraq* isn't staying here long. You will transfer to my command. What were your shipboard duties?'

'Only those concerned with the biology laboratory.'

'It's only routine and ridiculous in these circumstances,' he said. 'But regulations require that your ID be checked.'

He lifted up her left hand with his. With his right hand he pulled from his jacket pocket a round piece of glasslike material rimmed with metal. Holding it over his right eye, he looked through it at the hand. He could see the pale violet symbols invisible to the naked eye.

'Branwen Sacajawea Davis,' he read aloud.

Born AD 2238/1616 AH in the Cymric division of the Northwest European Department.

He looked down at the upturned, dark, lovely face. Her green eyes were wide and bright. Too bright.

He dropped her hand and said, 'I'll send for a guard to conduct you to ship. By the way, your hand feels very warm. Do you have a fever?'

'I feel a little feverish. But I didn't, as far as I know, come into contact with any sick native. Of course, you never know.'

He phoned ship via his skinceiver. After he'd signed off, he said, 'You realize you'll be court-martialed?'

Davis paled but said nothing.

'It's just more routine. Any time loss of naval property is involved, a court martial is automatic. I'm sure that you weren't negligent. Don't worry about it.'

A few minutes later, the marines appeared. Davis picked up her bag, saluted him, and marched off. Ramstan watched the long, slim legs and swaying hips, and he sighed. He went up a movable staircase and crawled into a bed half the size of a basketball court.

Halfway through a dream about some shadowy sinister whispering thing, he awoke. His door was shaking under furious knocks, and the skinceiver was shrilling. He put his wrist near his mouth and said, sleepily, 'Alif Rho Gimel. What is it, Hermes?'

'CL Waw reported in with an urgent message. She wants to speak to you.'

'I think she's here,' Ramstan said. 'Hold a minute.'

He rolled out of bed and dropped off without using the staircase. He looked through the keyhole and unlocked the door. Toyce reeled in, causing Ramstan for a moment to think that she was hurt. But she was only near-falling-down stoned.

'CL Waw's here,' Ramstan said. 'Out, Hermes.'

Toyce fell into the chair that Davis had used. 'I need a drink, Hûd.'

'Of water,' Ramstan said. 'What's the trouble?'

'You know that barmaid I was interested in. Well, she told me the Tenolt had come into her place. They were asking about you and getting, as usual, indirect answers to direct questions. Thima, that's the barmaid, said one of the Tenolt was either drunk or about to have a nervous breakdown. He suddenly started babbling about the *Klakgokl*, and ...'

'The *Klakgokl*?'

'Yeah. It's some kind of monster in Tolt eschatology. It will appear near the end of time and wreck the world, eat up all life. That sort of nonsense. Anyway, he hadn't spoken more than a few sentences about it when his companions dragged him away. The barmaid knows some of their lingo, just enough to understand that something terrible had happened on Tolt. She also caught some references to you when the Tolt was carried off screaming.

She didn't know what was said exactly. But she got the impression that the crazy Tolt was swearing vengeance.'

'Anything else?'

'No. But whatever it was, it played hell with my plans for Thima. I had to bring you the news, whatever it means.'

Ramstan spoke quickly but calmly into the skinceiver.

'Alif Rho Gimel. Come in, Hermes.'

'Hermes, here.'

'Burning Troy! Repeat, Burning Troy!'

There was a pause, and then Hermes said, 'Acknowledge! Burning Troy, sir!'

Before they got to ship, Ramstan received a report from the chemical laboratory. The traces of the gas in the expeller had been analyzed. Even in the quantity contained in the cylinder, the gas would not have done more than put him to sleep for several hours.

7

Al-Buraq had lost her starfish-shape and bright-red glow. She was a cylinder, flat on the underside, emitting yellow pulses. Flashes of light revealed spacers entering many ports.

By the time Ramstan was on the bridge, all posts had reported in, the drunk and drugged were in the various sickbays, and the general-alert alarm was turned off. The crescent-shaped bridge pulsed whitely from its spongy deck and those bulkhead areas not having indicator/control plates. The six commissioned officers and seven warrant officers were seated in their chairs. Ramstan took his chair in the center of the crescent. The chair was, like the others, a pseudopod of the deck, extended by the ship, shaped to fit him as near perfectly as possible.

On Ramstan's right was Lieutenant-Commodore (acting full commodore) Jimmy Tenno. On his left was Commander Erica Hannay. Five meters before them, the IC panel curved up to a height of 2.8 meters. Thirteen black-lined circles, extending from the deck to the ceiling, filled the panel. A CO and WO sat before one.

'All secure?' Ramstan said.

An octagonal in the lower left-hand part of the circle directly before him flashed *yellow-yellow-yellow*.

'Drive ready?'

Two tiny arrows flashed, one *green-green-green* and one *scarlet-scarlet-scarlet*.

'Alaraf drive on,' Ramstan said.

The green light ceased pulsing.

'Activate Reverse Jump Number One – RJN1.'

There was no motion, nothing to indicate that the vessel had left Kalafala behind at a distance of googolplex parsecs and perhaps at a distance of googolplex millennia.

The scarlet light ceased.

'EV and coordinates.'

The circle became black, and Ramstan was looking into space. Stars flamed white, red, orange, green, blue, yellow, violet. A spiral galaxy, seen from 'above', was a dying albino octopus that had been wounded by a shotgun loaded with jewels.

The scanners traveled across the circle, and the octopus drifted out of view on the right side. More stars, a giant red sun, not more than three light-years away, traveled across a nebula bright as a movie screen. The upper edges of the gas cloud formed the ragged silhouette of a crouching and grinning wolf.

Ramstan did not need the pulsing yellow letters that appeared near the bottom of the circle to know where he was. There had never been any doubt anyway.

'EV off. M-GD, Walisk window,' Ramstan said.

The view faded. The scarlet arrow came to life, pulsed, and would continue to pulse until Ramstan ordered it to stop.

Ramstan looked to both sides and caught a few officers looking at him expectantly. He frowned, causing them to look straight ahead. All in the bridge, everybody in ship, in fact, obviously hoped to hear an explanation for their sudden departure. He did not have to give one, and he would just as soon not. If they were not informed, however, they would resent it, and good morale would boil away. He would have to tell them something. Fortunately, Branwen Davis and Toyce had given him enough to shape a half-truth.

He sat brooding while the silence in the bridge stretched like a wire between two winches. There would be no breaking point because no one would dare to ask him when he would give the order to resume normal operations. Nor would any voice the question clogging their throats and making some cough nervously.

Suddenly, he stood up. Erica Hannay sighed. Tenno, his dark-brown face oily with sweat, grinned, showing block-like white teeth. Chief Warrant Officer Vilkas, at the far left, began coughing violently.

Ramstan waited until Vilkas had regained control. He said, loudly, 'All posts stand by for an announcement.'

His voice boomed out from the panel, was booming out throughout the ship. Three clangs of a bell and a short whistle followed.

'You're all wondering why I issued the Burning Troy,' he said. He had turned by then and was looking at the officers. Most just continued to stare at him, but a few nodded.

'Before I tell you why I ordered the ship to leave Kalafala, I must remind you of one thing. That is, we are primarily a scientific survey expedition. Though *al-Buraq* is a ship of the line, we use our weapons only in self-defense. And then only when no other action is open to us. As you all know, I have been ordered to avoid military conflict even if *honor* is involved.

'Until today, we have confronted no sentients with overt hostile intentions. But the sudden appearance of the Tolt ship, her unorthodox approach, using Kalafala as a shield to avoid our detection equipment, a maneuver which required enormous energy, and her recklessness in flying in at treetop level and literally dropping into the spaceport, are strange actions.'

Ramstan knew what they were thinking. Why then did you not call a Burning Troy immediately? Why did you go to your quarters at the hotel instead? And what about our precipitate departure from Tolt?

'Though the actions of the Tenolt were suspicious,' he said, 'I did not believe that they implied attack. If they had wished to attack us, they could have caught us wide open, unprepared, when they appeared at the port. Yet they made not the slightest move toward us. I judged that the Tenolt intended no overtly hostile moves.

'On the other hand, it was evident that they were up to something. I have no idea what that is. But it might derive from the incident which took place during our brief stay on Tolt.'

That widened the eyes of those on the bridge.

'As you know, Benagur, Maija Nuoli, and I were the only personnel invited by the Tolt religious authorities to the *anuglyfa* ceremonies. That the captain and the second-in-command would be invited was expected, but it was a mystery why other officers were skipped and a lieutenant invited. I made some delicate inquiries of the Tolt high priest – I had to be sure not to offend any religious prejudices – and he replied that the *glyfa* itself had asked that we three be honored. Our rank had nothing to do with it. He would add nothing further except that we three must have the required *sensitivity*. I asked him what that meant, but he did not answer.

'And so we three were conducted with an honor guard into the holy of holies, a large room constructed of ivory and lacking ornamentation or paint. The only furniture was an altar in the middle of the room, a nine-cornered block of solid ivory high as my waist – it was taken from the tooth of an extinct beast – and on the altar was a diamond. It was twice as big as my head, and on top of it was the *glyfa*. This looked like an egg shape carved out of ivory. It was white and between 14 and 15 centimeters long. Tzatlats, the high priest, said that it was so heavy that four men could not lift it.

'Tzatlats told us that the *glyfa* had been dug out of the earth some ten thousand years before, that it had been the god of the stone-age tribe that found it and was now the god of the whole planet. The *glyfa* had fallen from the skies long before the Tenolt had evolved into sapiency. It was older than the universe; it had survived the birth and death of many universes.

'We found it difficult to believe that a species as highly developed scientifically as Earth's could worship an idol. We thought that we must have misunderstood Tzatlats. It must be that the *glyfa* was a symbol of the creator, just as a crucifix or a statue of Vishnu are only symbols. But no. Tzatlats said that this *was* the god, not a symbol nor an embodiment but the god itself. And it ruled the planet. Tolt was a true theocracy.

'We stood in a corner and watched a ritual which was not explained to us and which I won't describe, since it is available in a report. The ceremony was interrupted when Commodore Benagur suddenly fell to the floor. Though he seemed to be unconscious, he struggled when I picked him up to take him to the ship. Two priests helped me carry him out, and he was still struggling violently while we did so.'

The bridge personnel were uneasy, no doubt wondering why he was describing what was well-known.

'The commodore was examined, but no evidence was found that he had suffered some kind of epileptic seizure. He himself reported that he had been overwhelmed by a white light, a light that should have blinded him but did not. After what seemed like hours, but which I can testify were only a few seconds, he began to see something in the center of the whiteness. This was not clear, but he had an impression of a huge blue eye. It became larger, and, as it grew, he felt an increasing heat. Not all over his body, but inside his head, seemingly concentrated in a tiny spot. When the heat suddenly became unbearable, he felt as if he were falling into a bottomless well.

'Nuoli later reported experiencing subjective phenomena, too. But these differed in intensity and kind from the commodore's. She could detect pulsations, variations in air pressure, and then the pulsations became visible as multicolored square waves. They disappeared simultaneously with the commodore's collapse.'

At the time, Ramstan had reported that he had neither seen or heard or felt anything describable as unusual subjective phenomena. Only Benagur had questioned that report. Benagur had accused him of lying after Ramstan had ordered ship to leave Tolt. Ramstan had continued to deny experiencing anything unusual. He had also said that Benagur was still obviously unfit for duty and that he would remain on sick list until he had proved otherwise. Benagur had stormed out of Ramstan's quarters. But there was nothing he could do about it. Ramstan had not reported this incident nor had Benagur, as far as Ramstan knew, said anything about it to anybody.

An hour after returning to ship, Ramstan had left it. He had, of course, told Tenno, now second-in-command, that he was leaving, but he had not said why. He had walked unchallenged out of the port, down the long street that led to the temple, walked past the guards, who obviously were not aware that he was present, and half an hour later had again boarded ship. Five minutes later, *al-Buraq* had taken off.

'I was convinced that the *glyfa* was dangerous,' Ramstan said after a few seconds of silence. 'Despite which, under other circumstances, our scientists would have been directed to study it. As far as I know, it's unique. But when I went back to the temple to discuss what had happened with the high priest, I was told that we were no longer welcome on Tolt. The priest made no threats. He just said that the *glyfa* wished us gone.'

Ramstan assumed that the officers were wondering why he had not logged the conversation. However, none dared voice the question. He proceeded to tell them what had happened in the hotel. He omitted his conversation with Commodore Benagur.

'There is no proof that the masked people were Tenolt, but there are no other suspects. I have no idea at all why the Tenolt have followed us here or why they should have made an attempt to anesthetize me. Doctor Toyce's report of the breakdown of the Tolt sailor in the tavern suggests that something horrible has happened to their planet. Obviously, they don't want to tell us what it is. I don't know why.

'However, the disappearance of *Pegasus* is the number-one priority now. For all I know, that might be tied in with the Tenolt's strange actions. In any event, we are backtracking with the hope of finding *Pegasus*.'

He paused and said, 'Or some trace of it.'

A long silence, punctuated by pale faces, followed. Tenno was the first to crack it.

'Captain, will we run away every time a Tolt ship appears?'

Ramstan did not like being questioned, but he said, 'We're a scientific mission. And we must at all costs – almost all – avoid anything which might lead to war.'

He scanned the faces. 'All right. Normal operation.'

Two ship's days passed. Ramstan was in his quarters, considering taking the *glyfa* out for another effort to get it to talk, when a whistle sounded. Ramstan spoke the code word which activated a two-way communication. Tenno's dark-brown, slant-eyed face appeared on a screen.

'Captain, we've just rasered some debris at 45,000 kilometers. It might be from a spaceship.'

'I'll be right up,' Ramstan said.

He felt cold and sick. Could it be what was left of *Pegasus?*

8

When *al-Buraq* caught up with the debris, she was 600,000 kilometers from the planet Walisk. The pieces of the ship were spreading over a wide area, though going in the same general direction. What attracted Ramstan's attention most was a globe with a diameter of 14 meters. Ship matched pace and path with those of the globe to catch up with it. Meanwhile, other debris had been identified as of Raushghol origin. This was done chiefly through furniture torn loose from the deck in the explosion which had rent the ship. Only the Raushghol, in the Terrans' experience, had three diamond-shaped holes in the backs of all their chairs and sofas.

A screen showed the sphere as a slowly rotating object with a surface of black-and-white squares. *Al-Buraq* had transmitted signals of its own – perhaps unintelligible to the receiver – informing whoever was in the globe, if there was anybody, that help was coming. No acknowledgment had been received.

Al-Buraq jockeyed around, matched, opened a port, swallowed the globe easily and softly, and closed the port. Air hissed into the chamber, which held the globe in a depression fitting the lower third. Antibacterial and antiviral gases mixed with the air for five minutes, then a spray of weak acid washed the globe, followed by high-pressure sprays of liquid helium and then boiling hot water. A few minutes later, crewmembers in spacesuits entered, Toyce among them.

Toyce said, 'Never saw anything like this before, sir. I can't find any exterior mechanism to open it up for us. If there's a *shet* in there, the *shet* will have to open it.'

Shet was the Terrish nongender, singular and plural, definite and indefinite third-person indicator, a combination of she/he/it from English. An alaraf-drive ship, however, was referred to as *shet-fim*, *fim* being the female indicator.

'Can we cut into it?'

'Won't know until we try, sir.'

'It's not likely, but it might contain explosive gas,' Ramstan said. 'Everybody out. Let a *yeoshet* cut it.'

The crew walked through the port into ship; a moment later, a wheeled robot passed through. The port was shut, but the robot waited until ship had built up armor-plated layers to enclose the chamber. When *Task Completed* was flashed on the screen, the CPO directing the party gave the command. A laser beam shot out from the tip of one of the robot's arms, and a thin slice of the equator of the globe fell off.

'I'll be damned!' Ramstan said. 'Water!'

It spurted out, then the pressure inside quickly eased off, and it flowed down the side for a few seconds before trickling out.

'Cut a hole at the equator,' Ramstan said.

This was done quickly. More water poured out, but the flow ceased within thirty seconds. The robot moved forward and extended an arm with a tiny TV camera at its end through the hole. Light flared. The lower half of the globe's interior was filled with water, darkened with what looked like blood. In the center floated a dark, shapeless thing.

The sentientologist said, 'It's a native of Webn. A seal-centaur. I've never seen one in the flesh before, but I've seen Walisk photos of one: The globe would be the Webnite's self-contained cabin while it's being transported in the ship. It can also be used for a lifeboat. And it evidently has. I've heard that ...'

Toyce stopped. Like Ramstan, she'd been watching the globe on the screen and so was also taken by surprise. But her reaction came from forgetfulness, whereas Ramstan's came from novelty.

The globe drooped, collapsed, ran together, poured over the being in the center, and broke away from it with a pop like bubble gum. Bloodied water cascaded over the deck, and the globe had disappeared. The body sprawled in the center of blackened wetness.

'The Raushghols told me that a Webn sphere dissolves in its own water once it's been broken open by force. Believe it or not, that's what they said. The stuff it's made from is supposedly woven by a giant half-sentient sea creature, and ...'

'How can a thing be half-sentient?' Ramstan said.

'I'm just quoting the Raushghol.'

A party rolled the 227-kilogram body onto an a-g sled. The sled rose into the air, and one man directed it toward sickbay. Ramstan watched its progress down the corridors and into the ward. Toyce supervised the three physicians delegated to treat the Webnite. Ten minutes later, she reported.

'Something small but hard and sharp passed entirely through her body,' she said. 'It must have been going at such a speed it passed through the sphere, too. A tiny meteorite? Anyway, the sphere must have closed up within microseconds after being penetrated on both sides. Otherwise, the air and the water would have boiled off.'

'Is she dying?' Ramstan said.

Toyce looked again at the oscilloscopes registering the overall state of health of the finned and armed mass lying on its back in a shallow basin on a broad temporary table.

'She's holding her own – I think. How would I know? I don't know anything about the physiology – or anatomy, either – of an aquatic sentient from Webn. Hell, what's her blood pressure supposed to be? And what's her blood type? You should see the vanadium and magnesium content. Enough to make you drop dead on the spot if it were in your bloodstream. I'm exaggerating, of course, but it would make you sick.'

The Webnite was exactly 3.2 meters long, and covered by a sealy chocolate-brown fur. The flippers extended straight out from her body and made up one-third of her length. The belly was huge, though she was not pregnant. The breasts were pendulous and small in proportion to the size of the body. The arms were long; the hands, very broad and flat; the fingers, webbed to the first joint. The head was humanoid. Her eyes were deeply sunk and, at the moment, covered by a transparent inner lid.

'The lids are far enough away from the eyeballs to form a sort of goggle,' Toyce said.

She also reported that the Webnite's nostrils could be closed tightly. She had no external ears, and this added to the weirdness of her appearance.

'See, she has a pouch – much like a kangaroo's,' Toyce said. 'She may be of a species that's regressed, anatomically speaking, gone back to the sea. But a reversion to marsupialism? Doesn't seem likely.'

She forced her hand into the tight opening, looked startled, and withdrew it. She opened her fist.

The three flat objects were no longer than Toyce's thumb and seemed to be greenish soapy stones. One formed a circle; the second, a square; the third, a triangle. All had circular holes about three centimeters wide in their centers.

'What the hell?' Toyce said.

'Put them back,' Ramstan said. 'They're her personal property. Notify me as soon as she regains consciousness – if she does.'

Al-Buraq moved into a landing orbit for Walisk. Toyce reported that the labtech computer was making artificial blood for the Webnite, and transfusion should be started in several hours. She had uttered a number of words even though unconscious. Toyce had never heard the language before. But hadn't *Pegasus* been on Webn? Might not Branwen Davis know some Webnian?

Ramstan called sickbay. Davis said that she could carry on a limited conversation in Webnian.

'I doubt we'll be getting into science or philosophy,' Ramstan said. 'Stand by.'

Her green eyes widened, and it was not until after her image faded that he realized why. She had been hurt by his sarcasm. He cursed himself and then wondered why he had spoken so. Was it a defense of some sort? Why did he need a defense?

He did not have long to think about that nor would he, he realized later, have done so even if he had had time. His attention was needed for something much more pressing than delving into his psyche. *Al-Buraq* was close enough to the planet Walisk for visual, thermal, radioactive, and raser observations. The entire planet, from pole to pole, was under black clouds which were mainly carbon-derived smoke.

The smoke came from vast fires raging over thousands of large areas.

'My God!' Nuoli said. 'What could have caused *that?*'

It was not from atomic warfare. The radioactive readings testified to that.

The chief geologist reported detection of an unusual number of active volcanoes on both sea and land.

'Twenty-four thousand. The dust from them alone is enough to cover the planet for many years. By the time the dust settles, most if not all the plant life will have died. As for the life that depended upon the plants …'

The chief meteorologist reported atmospheric disturbances that could not be explained by the firestorms and volcanoes.

'Something has pulled the atmosphere up into space in the recent past. There are too many traces of atmospheric gases above the normal upper boundary. And there's a phenomenon I've never heard of before. I don't know what caused it, but there's a – how shall I put it? – an oscillatory humping of the air. As if it's still reverberating, reacting to a tidal effect. Let me call you back on that. I'm just giving you my first impressions. I need more data and more time to put them into the computers.'

A little while later, the chief geologist reported again.

'Something has made Walisk a hotbed of earthquakes. We're detecting thousands of temblors on land and the sea bottoms. I'd estimate that there are fifty thousand macroseisms occurring at this moment. They're all equal to or exceeding 12 on the Neo-Mercalli scale.

'Also, it's evident that colossal tidal waves have inundated the coastal areas and still haven't subsided. These can't be accounted for only by the seismic activity, immense though these are. Walisk has no moon, as you know, sir, but I'd say that the quakes and the tidal waves and the atmospheric tides could have been caused if, say, Walisk did have a moon the mass of Earth's and it suddenly changed its orbit to one not very far above the exosphere. Anywhere between 10,000 and 50,000 kilometers above the planet's surface. Of course, that's only a fantasy speculation. I won't be bound by that statement.'

'Of course not, Doctor,' Ramstan said. 'Thank you.'

Al-Buraq orbited Walisk in a descending spiral, repeatedly crossing all of the four continents, each having approximately the surface area of Africa though not its shape. The readings indicated that the smoke and volcanic dust were so thick that little if any multicellular life survived. Ramstan doubted that much had survived the quakes, tidal waves, and firestorms before the clouds began spreading over the planet.

Two of the continents were on the equatorial line. Their interiors were masses of firestorms so bright that they could be seen through the clouds. Here and there were darker areas which the scientists said were the results of heavy rains. The fires had been put out there, but the bordering regions were so hot that the moisture would quickly be dried up and the vegetation reignited.

'There were vast rain forests there,' Toyce said. 'Much like those in Africa and southeast Asia before they were cleared and became deserts.'

Ramstan decided to investigate at close range one of the continents in the southern hemisphere. It had a great interior desert but had been heavily populated on the coastlines. Though the fires were still raging along the shores, extending sometimes to 300 kilometers into the interior, there were temporarily extinguished areas. The clouds had moved in from outlying areas, carried by the very strong winds, but spacesuited personnel could fly in jeeps a few meters above the still-quaking ground.

Al-Buraq poised above an area where rain was falling heavily. The stony desert was only 10 kilometers to the north, but ruins of buildings indicated that the region directly beneath ship had once been thickly populated. Not that there were many objects detectible by the probers. Most of the wooden materials and trees and bushes had been burned entirely and their ashes swept away by the winds and rains. If there were any bones left of the sentient and animal inhabitants, they could not be detected by the probers.

The chief meteorologist reported again.

'The winds have a velocity of 150 kilometers per hour. They're mild, though, compared to the winds in the northern area.'

Ramstan knew this because he could read the indicators on the tec-op panels. He thanked the scientist, anyway. What interested him was the detection by the fine-discriminator probers of thousands of golfball-shaped and -sized objects on the ground or half-buried in the mud. He ordered that the investigators in the jeeps secure some of these. Then, impatient, he commanded *al-Buraq* to get close enough to the surface to extend a suction pseudopod and bring in some specimens immediately.

While waiting, he ordered a launch sent to the northern shoreline to determine if there were similar objects there. 'And if you find them, proceed to the continent above this in the northern hemisphere and look for them there.'

Al-Buraq headed into the wind at 5 kph. It was not easy for her to scoop in the spheres. The ground was subject to shock after shock, many strong enough to toss the spheres a meter into the air. A few times, fissures opened, and the spheres fell into them. *Al-Buraq* did not try to obtain these. If she had inserted her pseudopod into the fissure, she might have been trapped if the fissure closed.

At another order, ship brought in some pieces of what had been stone columns and some twisted and dented steel beams.

The chemicophysical laboratory reported that there were many smaller spheres in the mud which had been carried in. These had a diameter of three millimeters.

Al-Buraq continued sampling, and she began to trace a spiral path over a twenty-square-kilometer area.

The launch left ship with two pilots and six scientists aboard. It shot northward at 300 kph, its probers scanning the area for 100 kilometers on both sides.

The laboratory chief reported again.

'The larger spheres have a diameter of four centimeters. Each weighs one kilogram. Each has a shell of nickel-iron five millimeters thick. That's estimated, since the shell has been partially melted and some of the nickel-iron has evaporated. Burned off. The core is some black, unknown substance, though it looks like metal. It can't be X-rayed. It's unaffected by the strongest acid. It won't bend or break under a pressure of 500,000 tons per square millimeter, and that's the greatest force we have. It won't melt at 100,000 K. It resists the most powerful laser – so far, anyway.

'The smaller spheres are of the same substance or seem to be. They only lack the nickel-iron shell of the larger. They've been subjected to the same tests with the same results.'

Wendell Tong shook his head. 'I've never seen or heard of anything like it.'

The screen split into three sections, and the heads of the chief geologist and the chief astrophysicist appeared by Tong's.

'We've been listening in,' the geologist said. 'May I ask a question?'

Ramstan gave his permission. However, the question was not directed at him but at Tong.

'You say that the nickel-iron shells were partially melted. I doubt that the firestorm could account for that. Wouldn't you say that the melting could only have come from great velocity through the atmosphere? That these spheres are, in effect, meteorites of some sort?'

Tong nodded. 'Yes, I'd say so. I'm not competent …'

'It's a matter of common sense, of logic,' the geologist said. 'Only … damn! … whoever heard of meteorites like this?'

Ramstan said, 'The hot nickel-iron shells could have started the worldwide fires, right?'

'That's the only explanation we have at the moment.'

Two days later, *al-Buraq* left, the jeeps having returned the day before. The launch was over the northern continent now and sending in reports. *Al-Buraq* proceeded to the western coast of the southern-hemisphere continent, spiraled over a hundred-square-kilometer area, then flew to one of the continents in the equatorial region. Another launch was sent to the third continent. After a six-day sampling of the second continent, *al-Buraq* plunged into the ocean and spiraled over the bottom. When she emerged five days later, she went to the fourth continent. At the end of the sampling there, she was joined by the two launches.

The results of the investigation were both puzzling and mind-numbing.

The spheres were undoubtedly of meteoritic origin or, it would be more accurate to say, they had been launched at high velocity from outside the atmosphere. Both the large and small spheres had been found embedded in trees that had not entirely burned and even in stones and steel beams. They were everywhere from pole to pole. Whatever had shot them had covered the planet by making many orbital sweeps and by missing neither land nor sea.

Walisk was slightly larger than Earth though of less density. Its surface area was approximately 518,000,000 square kilometers. Estimates based on the samplings indicated that approximately one of the larger spheres and twenty of the smaller had struck every square meter. Or they had been intended to do so, but atmospheric and oceanic variations in density and current had resulted in variations in the number of meteorites or missiles per square meter.

'Five hundred and eighteen billion of the large spheres,' Tenno had whispered when he heard the report. 'Ten trillion, three hundred and sixty billion of the smaller.'

Each of the smaller weighed 50 grams. Twenty together weighed 1,000 grams or one kilogram. This suggested that the large spheres had hollow centers.

The total mass of the missiles was an estimated 1,026,000,000,000 kilograms.

'No spaceship would be large enough or have power enough to deliver and launch such a mass. She'd have to be as large as … what? … the Earth? Larger? Let's get a computer readout.'

'An object with that mass and coming so close to Walisk would cause cataclysmic earthquakes and tidal waves,' Ramstan said. 'But … you're right, Tenno. It couldn't be a spaceship or even a fleet. Unconceivable. Anyway, if the thing or things were directed by intelligence … what sentient would use such inefficient means as the spheres to kill life? Neutron bombs would be far superior. What good would this destruction be for warmakers? Unless they were so vicious that they wanted only total destruction. I can't believe that.'

'The *bolg* kills all but one. God is sick. Unbreakable flames fall from the black sky ... All die. Where to go?'

9

Al-Buraq was in orbit over Walisk and awaiting orders from Ramstan for the next destination. He was wondering where this would be when he got a call from Doctor Hu.

'The Webnite is well enough to talk for a while. She wants to talk to you. Lieutenant Davis will interpret.'

Ramstan thanked her and said that he would be in the sickbay as soon as he could get there.

'Does that mean right away, sir?' she said.

'Of course!' Ramstan said. 'What the hell did you think I meant?'

Hu's face became rigid, but she said nothing. Ramstan regretted having blazed out at her. His nerves were crawling like a mess of worms. He had to get better control of himself. Walisk ... the *glyfa's* continued refusal to answer him ... the Tenolt ... everything ... They were conspiring to crush him.

He walked out of his quarters shaking his head. *Conspiring* was not the correct word. It sounded as if he were becoming paranoiac.

He concentrated on the Webnite. She might be able to tell him something of what had happened, though if she had been in the self-contained chamber when the Raushghol ship was attacked, she might know very little. It was luck that Davis was aboard, since she was the only one who could speak Webnian. *Al-Buraq* had not been to Webn but *Pegasus* had. During her six-month stay there, Davis, as a marine biologist, had been in intimate contact with some of the native scientists and had taken the opportunity to master as much of the language as she could. She also knew the coordinates for navigation to Webn or at least had enough data so that *al-Buraq's* astrogators could extrapolate the rest needed. In fact, if it were not for Davis, there would have been no way to get to Webn except by going to Raushghol and getting the data from its alaraf navy.

The Webnite and Davis were in the same sickbay. The Earthwoman was there for two reasons. One, to interpret if the Webnite should recover enough to talk. Two, she still had a fever, the cause of which was unknown. She had been probed by machines and had conducted a self-probing, but the fever continued to keep her body temperature above normal. Hu had told Ramstan that she suspected the fever was psychosomatic. It did not seem to be infectious or contagious, and there was no valid reason to isolate her. That had been determined within three hours after she had entered *al-Buraq*.

Ramstan entered the sickbay. The Webnite was floating in a large plastic tank. A technician-nurse, Hu, and Toyce were also there. Branwen sat in a chair by the tank. Her left hand was enfolded in the huge webbed hand of the Webnite. The creature watched Ramstan with large, soft, dark eyes.

'We're ready to record,' Hu said. 'But I'll be watching to make sure she doesn't tire herself out.'

Ramstan bowed to the creature, hoping that she would understand that it was a gesture of respect. Davis spoke to her in a language with many sibilants and stops. She then said, 'I explained what your bowing meant.'

'You aren't reading my mind, are you?' he said half seriously.

'I'm just trying to anticipate.'

The Webnite spoke for perhaps ten seconds. Davis said, 'She will address herself to you, since you are the captain. The Webnites are very formal in certain situations. She believes this is a special situation; she believes that she is dying.'

Ramstan looked at Hu. 'Is she?'

Hu shrugged and said, 'I wouldn't have thought so. But maybe she knows more about herself than I do. Most patients do, even if they aren't aware of it.'

Ramstan bowed again, made a coded gesture, and a few seconds later sat down on the chair-shaped protuberance that had formed from the deck.

There was a burst of dialog between the creature and Branwen Davis. Branwen then said, 'Her name is Wassruss. She had been picked up by a Raushghol ship and taken from Webn to Raushghol. The Raushghols wanted her knowledge of sea-farming techniques. In return, they would give the Webnites some deep-sea craft and technological artifacts. Wassruss says that the reasons for her visit are not important. On the way back, the Raushghol ship took a sidetrip to Walisk. Or she started for it, anyway.'

Wassruss spoke again at some length.

Davis said, 'Wassruss was in her cabin when she heard a peculiar, penetrating, and agonizing whistle. It didn't come over the electronic equipment; at least, she heard the captain say it didn't. She had turned on the intercom connecting her cabin to the bridge. The whistling lasted for about two minutes, and then it abruptly ceased. The ship's detectors showed a huge mass nearby. There was no warning of its appearance. It just was there all of a sudden. The captain said that it couldn't be there. But there it was.'

'How big was it, and what did it look like? Was it a spaceship?'

'It was a sphere with a diameter of 13,000 kilometers. At least that's what she overheard the detection-people report. But ... she does have a word for it. *Tssokh'azgd*.'

'What would that translate as?'

Branwen spoke some more with Wassruss.

'It's the Webn name for the Chaos-Monster in their religion. Wassruss says she had abandoned her faith. But now that she has actually seen the *Tssokh'azgd*, she isn't so sure that the religion is false.'

Ramstan said, 'Ask her how she knows, or thinks she knows, that the thing was the watchamacallit.'

Branwen Davis spoke again. Then, 'She says that it is the *Tssokh'azgd*. There is no argument about it. As soon as it's seen, it's known, though that does the knower no good, because she'll soon be dead.'

Suddenly, Wassruss began talking so swiftly that Branwen had difficulty interpreting and had to tell her to slow down.

'I am going to die soon. I wish to die on my native world and to be buried according to the custom of my people. If you can get me to Webn before I die, I will pay you well.'

Ramstan was flabbergasted, but he did not show it.

'It is not necessary or even desirable that you pay me. In fact, it would be illegal for me to accept money or gifts of any kind.'

Toyce said, 'Not quite so, Captain. There is a clause which says that you may accept gifts if the refusal would insult the giver or cause ill-feelings of any sort. You will then place the gifts in the storeroom as government property.'

Ramstan said, 'Ah, I didn't remember that.'

Davis had already translated for Ramstan. Wassruss, forgetting Davis' request for slowness, broke into a torrent of phrases. Ramstan did not know what she had said, but he could not mistake the appeal and the desperation in her voice. Her facial expression looked to him like a threatening snarl but was no doubt a smile to her species.

Davis said, 'Her people are real homebodies. She is the first to leave her planet, and she isn't sure that what happened to her isn't a judgment of her God. You see how quickly she abandoned her atheism, how superficial it was. She is scared, though. To her it's a terrible thing to die far away from her native sea. And a worse thing not to be buried, not to sink down into the depths and be taken back into the bosom of the ocean.'

Wassruss spoke.

Branwen Davis listened, then said, 'She wants to know what I told you. She wants to make sure I'm translating correctly. It isn't easy for me; there are so many phrases I don't know or which may have subtleties I didn't grasp when I was learning her speech.'

Branwen replied. The Webnite seemed to be thinking for a minute, then rattled off another train of phrases.

Branwen said, 'She insists that you accept her gifts. But she says, and I'm not sure I understand her, that these gifts are unique. They do not have their like anywhere in the world.'

Ramstan snorted and said, 'How would she know? Has she been throughout the cosmos?'

Branwen translated before Ramstan could stop her. He felt his face warm. He was embarrassed, but he was also angry at Branwen.

She must have guessed what he was thinking. She said, 'I only asked what the gifts were. She says that she is very tired now and would like to sleep.'

Ramstan bowed to the Webnite and left. So, the monstrous but somehow attractive seal-centaur was going to bestow upon him certain treasures. He did not expect them to be overwhelmingly valuable or beautiful. He was, however, curious about them and about the real reason for her giving them, though it was possible that she was not concealing any motives.

Their uniqueness did not mean that they would be interesting, desirable, useful, or any combination thereof. Many artifacts could be unique and yet of little significance except to the owner. Or to a sentientologist, who was theoretically interested in everything non-Terran.

At one time the concept of God, which concept was a mental artifact, could have been of value only to its owner.

That was a strange intrusion of thought.

What was it doing, sidling in through a crack in the wall of thinking?

And why the crack?

Never mind. He could not dwell long on that, though it might not be as irrelevant as it seemed. Nor could he ponder long upon the promise of Wassruss. What seized his mind most of the time, awake or dreaming, was the destruction of the Walisk natives. Had this been done by the thing that the whisperer had warned him of, the *bolg*?

There was one who might have the answer. Who might even have been the unseen warner in the Kalafalan tavern. But it had spoken once while he was carrying it from the Tolt temple and a second time after he had heard voices in the tavern.

He had since sat down before the table seven times and looked through the microscope at the surface of the egg. His eyes roved over the sculptures of some microbe Michelangelo who had worked them how long ago, perhaps eons? Whatever dwelt inside that impervious shell surely had to extend an antenna to transceive thoughts. Or, perhaps, one of the figures crowding the surface of this little world was an antenna. Or perhaps he was not thinking in the correct category. It might not need an antenna.

Or, and at this a chill skipped up his spine like a cold stone thrown by a clammy hand over a frozen lake, perhaps the egg *was* an antenna?

In which case, who was the transmitter of the thought he received?

He didn't know. One thing all worlds shared was a superabundance of questions and a poverty of answers.

Seven ship-days after leaving Walisk, while walking to the bridge from his quarters, he was startled by a loud piping noise and the change of a circle on the bulkhead from a pale yellow to a flashing orange-yellow over which rotated a scarlet spiral.

He began running, at the same time calling out, 'Bridge! What is the alarm?'

Tenno's face appeared on one of the circles keeping pace with him.

'The EVD has detected a USO, sir. It suddenly appeared from behind the asteroid we passed three hours ago. Raser is checking it out now, sir.'

By the time he'd reached the bridge, the raser report was in. The EVD (Ether Vibration Detector) had noted the disturbance in the recently traversed tunnel. EVD was not capable of radar or raserlike powers of location and dimension measurements, however. It could note only intrusions at a relatively near distance and those within a limited time period.

Warrant Officer Yazdi reported that the unidentified space object was 260 meters long and 210 meters wide and was oyster-shell-shaped. Ramstan did not listen intently; he could see the data and the object itself on a display screen.

'Looks like the *Popacapyu*,' Tenno said.

10

Ramstan did not reply to the obvious. It could be another Tolt ship, but he doubted that. As far as he knew, the Tenolt had only two alaraf-drive ships. This one must have followed them from Kalafala. Which meant that the Tenolt were more technologically advanced than the Terrans had supposed. Not until just before *al-Buraq*'s last jump had Earth's alaraf scientists developed a device to detect the vibrations of passage of ships in the 'tunnels'. This was in a primitive stage and capable only of sniffing out the tracks of vessels that had passed within a period of ten to twelve hours. The scientists had thought that, by the time *al-Buraq* returned to Earth, the EVD would be capable of a finer and more extended discrimination.

Tenno shook his head and said, 'Perhaps it's only coincidence, and they didn't follow us here. It's difficult to believe that they have a better EVD than we. In fact, I can't believe they have any at all.'

'You're showing your prejudice,' Ramstan said. 'Just because they worshiped – I mean, worship – an idol and have certain customs we regard as retarded, if not degenerate, doesn't mean that their science is on a low level.

'Anyway,' he continued briskly, 'they are here. And we can assume that they've followed us for some reason.'

Tenno and Yazdi looked out of the corners of their eyes at each other. Were they both thinking of the object which their captain had brought into ship in a bag? If so, why didn't they have the courage to say what they thought? He would, if he were in their position. Were they really that afraid of him? Or was it that they were more afraid of being shown up as foolish if they were wrong?

'What we have to do first,' Ramstan said, 'is to attempt again to communicate with them. Maybe this time they'll respond. If they don't, then we'll do some backtracking. If it's not just coincidence, if they do have an EVD, they'll follow us.'

Tenno's expression said, 'And then what?' But he turned and spoke to the raser operator, who gave the second-level bridge raser operator an order. Presently the 2-L RO reported that he was getting no acknowledgments, even though he had transmitted in Tolt. The unknown (it was still classified as such) was, however, scanning *al-Buraq* with radar and raser.

'They wouldn't talk to us on Kalafala, and they won't talk to us here,' Tenno said. 'Why're they dogging us?'

'We have to make absolutely sure that they are,' Ramstan said.

Reluctantly, he ordered that ship return to the Walisk window. This involved a 360-degree maneuver which required five hours. The stranger began to turn also a few minutes after *al-Buraq* did.

'That does it,' Ramstan said. 'There's no use in going into alaraf drive. Head her back towards Webn, Tenno.'

The stars on the visual screen wheeled, and then *al-Buraq* was locked into the former course, guiding herself by the configuration of stars and the position of Webn's sun. When she had first arrived in this window, she had had no data about star fixes, of course. But once her navigators had figured out the correct course to Webn and had then fed in the data, she could navigate on her own. All she needed was the command, verbal or punched.

In the same way, she could backtrack to any other window, including Earth's, with only one short command.

Ramstan was relieved. He had not wanted to go back to Walisk for fear of what might be lurking, if such a word was applicable, in the window. Or it could be in another window connected to a 'tunnel' leading to the Waliskan window.

Which meant that the thing could pop out and confront the Terrans with no warning.

Ship's rasers had not located any such massive object as Wassruss had reported. Therefore, the thing might have gone into alaraf drive to another sector of space-time. But it could just as easily have returned to Waliskan space and be waiting. Or it could appear at any second in this sector.

Ramstan had already given ship her instructions on what to do if an object of the dimensions and shape of the thing described by Wassruss appeared. She was to go into alaraf drive at once, even though this would probably mean she would come out into an unknown window. But this was nothing to worry about, since the ship could always backtrack.

What if the thing had an equivalent of EVD and could follow the 'tracks' of *al-Buraq*?

Then she would have to either plunge into tunnel after tunnel, known or unknown, or stand and fight. Which action would be taken would depend upon how distant the thing was when it came out of the tunnel. If it were very close, say, within a hundred kilometers, then flight was the answer. If the thing (should he think of it as the *bolg?*) was far enough away so that its missiles would take more than three minutes to reach *al-Buraq*, then Ramstan would use lasers and rasers and torpedoes and, as a last resort, the ether-disruptor.

These might destroy the thing. But if it launched its missiles immediately on arrival in the window, *al-Buraq* might have to duck into another tunnel before the effect of its weapons could be observed. The *bolg* (there, he'd said it!) could spew out trillions of missiles, spread them out in a vast screen that *al-Buraq*, unless she happened to be at the top velocity attainable in m-g drive, could not escape.

And that depended upon the velocity of the missiles. How swiftly were they hurled from the *bolg?*

The *Popacapyu* maintained the same distance behind the Terran vessel. Ramstan would have liked to slow down and then speed up to determine if the Tolt vessel would match the deceleration and acceleration. But conservation of power was more important in this situation than satisfying his curiosity.

After ordering that he be notified immediately if anything demanded his presence, he went to his quarters. He removed the *glyfa* from the safe and placed it under the microscope on the table. He did not turn on the scope. Instead, he placed a hand on each end of the egg-shape, stroked the ends lightly, then gripped them tightly. It was as if he could force something from the *glyfa*, as if the intensity of his desire could be transmitted through his hands and choke words out of the thing.

'The *bolg* has come,' he said softly. 'I've seen a whole planet ravaged, all of its land life, plant and animal, killed. *Pegasus* is lost, and I fear that the *bolg* got her. I'm seeing ghosts from my childhood and hearing voices.

'Are the voices yours, are the ghosts images you've projected? If you can throw a voice as if you were a ventriloquist, why not an image? Speak! Speak, or in the name of Allah, I'll cast you out from the ship while it's in space and let you fall into a star!'

'Which would in no way harm me physically,' the voice of his father said. *'I was forged in a star.'*

The words sounded as if they came out of a mouth of flesh, one with teeth, gums, a tongue, a palate, one quite human. But they were not modulated vibrations of air striking his eardrum. They sprang without benefit of matter from the *glyfa* into his brain, where certain impulses evoked electrical configurations. And these seemed to sound in his ear and to originate from his long-dead father.

Now that he had gotten the thing to speak, he was speechless. His heart thudded, and there was a thunder in his ears as if he lay at the end of a giant's bowling alley and the ball would strike him soon and fatally.

The voice slashed through the roaring and seemed to sever it so that the ends dropped away. But his heart still beat faster than was good for it.

'You are not of much use while you are afraid of me,' the *glyfa* said. 'Afraid? No, in awe. That is the correct term. No. There is fear, though not of me so much as of yourself. You are afraid of what you might do. Which is wrong, since you have been doing what you fear you're going to do. Too late.'

How could a nonvoice chuckle? Yet, it had done so.

'No, I don't really laugh. I just evoke laughter in you. Laughter for me. Never mind. It's too complicated to explain. Tell me why you want to speak with me.'

In one sense, the *glyfa* could read his mind. In another sense, it could not. It had told him that it had read his electrical matrix, the pulsing configuration of his neural system, when he had appeared at the Great Temple in Tolt's capital city. It had been able to 'see' him as a skeleton of twisting lightning streaks, a storm of tiny stars and comets' tails. It had invaded his mind and triggered certain impulses in a configuration which had made Ramstan lust for the *glyfa* as he had never lusted for anyone or anything. It had enveloped him in a globe of light, a bomb-burst of energy which would have blinded those around him if they could have seen it. And perhaps Benagur had seen it, and Nuoli had been touched by it.

The *glyfa* had great powers, but these had certain limitations, and distance was one of the factors modifying them. Not until the three had entered the house of the *glyfa* had it been able to determine which of the three it wanted.

'I waited for eons for one, and then I got three,' the *glyfa* had said. 'Truly remarkable. Not at all probable. But there it was. As you Terrans say, "Feast or famine".'

The *glyfa* had been able to converse at once with Ramstan because it knew Urzint. But it had been compelled to 'use' Ramstan's own voice. In the interval between the first time it had 'spoken' and the second, it had learned much Terrish and Arabic. It was able to 'see' the full referents of any word or image pulsing in Ramstan's mind.

At least, that was Ramstan's explanation for the *glyfa's* quick learning of the two languages. The *glyfa* offered none of its own.

It was evoking the proper words in the proper order from Ramstan's own mind. In a sense, he was talking to himself. In another, he was conversing with the *glyfa*. If he had been asked to define the different senses, he would have failed.

Ramstan finally unclogged his mental throat. Subvocalizing, he said, 'Here is what's happened since I last talked to you. Or do you already know it?'

'Tell me.'

Ramstan did, finding that the *glyfa* seemed to leap ahead of his words, to pull out the word or the image by its roots, see the entire plant, the roots, stem, leaves, flowers, seeds, everything in one scan of unbelievable speed.

Strangely, the *glyfa* seemed more interested in the ghostly person in the hotel than in other events. At least, it spoke of this first.

'Do you think it is, indeed, al-Khidhr?'

'I don't know what to think,' Ramstan said. 'It could be an exteriorized projection of my concept of al-Khidhr. A subjective image seeming to be objective. Or it could be … I don't know what.'

The *glyfa* chuckled. By now Ramstan found this sound sinister.

'No, not menacing or conspiratorial,' the *glyfa* said. 'Secretive, perhaps. But with good reason. In time all things that are capable of being revealed will be revealed. But I am making sure that you are not rushed too green into events which require for you a steady ripening, a slow and sure maturing.

'That is, if there's time. If not, then … Well, we'll see. This Webnite, Wassruss, is going to give you three gifts, and you have no idea what they are. But from your description of what happened before she told you this, I know. I am truly amazed, and, believe me, it takes much to amaze me. First, three of you come along after a wait so long that your mind couldn't grasp it. Three at once. Then the gifts of Wassruss. These could easily have been lost in space or have come to someone else.

'But there you were, Ali Baba-on-the-spot, as you say in New Babylon. Where, out of a vastness of cosmos, it was the only place I would have chosen you, if I had known there was a choice. I did not, of course, and yet, there you were.'

'What are you talking about?'

'It's too early to tell you. Though, as I said, I may have to tell you anyway if events require it. But I was right when I picked you. Perhaps you are that exceedingly rare individual, one who is a magnet for unlikely events. One whose matrix overcomes the principles of probabilities.

'Such beings are possible, though I have never met one, until now, and I'm still not sure about you. Perhaps it is they who ...'

'*They?*' Ramstan said.

'Never mind. Not now, anyway.'

Ramstan exploded. 'What about the Tolt ship, then? That captain is determined to get you back! And he's also, I'm sure, out to get revenge on me and perhaps the entire crew for the sacrilege! But he doesn't dare make a move which will imperil his chances of retrieving you! So, he's taking it easy, shadowing, waiting for the first chance, and then ... bang, boom, that's it! And I can't tell my crew why he's dogging us!'

'You'll find some way to handle it. It may be that you'll have to fight him. In which case, you'll have to convince your crew that the Tolt is a grave danger. And you'll have to antagonize him into attacking you.'

'Do you know what you're saying?' Ramstan said.

'Calm down. Your agony is affecting me. Yes, I know.

'You don't realize as yet, unfortunately, that there is much more at stake than the fate of a few hundred Tenolt. Or a few hundred Terrans. Or even a few billion Waliskans.'

'What is at stake then?' Ramstan cried. His voice rang back from the bulkheads, which shivered as *al-Buraq* caught a trace of Ramstan's pain and perplexity. If Chief Engineer Indra was hooked into ship's neural circuits at this moment, he would be alarmed.

'Your immortality, for one thing.'

'I don't really care for that!' Ramstan bellowed.

'No, of course not. Not at the moment. However, I cannot tell you what the stakes are. Not as yet. You wouldn't believe me. Or, if you did, you might lose your reason. I am protecting you. Believe me. But then you have to believe me, don't you?'

'Damn you!' Ramstan shouted. 'Why did you seduce me?'

'The unseduceable can't be seduced,' the *glyfa* said. 'You seduced yourself. When I made my offer, I did not force you to accept. There was no magic involved, no hypnotism. You had perfect free will or at least as near to perfect as is possible. It was your choice. You said yes. And your second thoughts are only that – second, that is, superficial. The first are the deepest.'

Ramstan had no reply to this. There was silence. It was possible that the *glyfa* was overwhelmed by the emotional blaze from Ramstan.

The gap was suddenly closed again.

'This Branwen Davis, the woman you are so attracted to. Haven't you wondered if there was a connection between her and the Tenolt?'

Ramstan was shocked.

'How could there be?'

He paused in his vocalization, but the *glyfa* was reading the images and emotions pouring out like the damned from the suddenly opened gates of Hell.

'I do not know. That is up to you to find out. Of course, I am only suggesting a possibility.'

'And I thought I was paranoiac.'

'Don't let your personal feelings for her interfere with good judgment. As for paranoia, anyone who has the imagination to postulate all possibilities is automatically a paranoiac.'

'I don't see ... well, of course, there could be a very slight possibility. But even so, she is, at this moment anyway, not important. What is vital is that monster that shoots meteorites, isn't it?'

'Obviously.'

'And you won't tell me what it is?'

'When you get to a certain place and meet certain persons, if you ever do, that is, then I'll tell you. Though by then I may not have to.'

Ramstan struck the top of the table with his fist.

'I am enjoying this splendid display of emotion, even if it hurts me somewhat,' the *glyfa* said. 'At the same time, I regret that you do not have better self-control.'

Doctor Hu's voice came from the bulkhead.

'Captain! The Webnite wishes to speak to you. She says it's very urgent. It's my opinion, sir, that she hasn't long to live.'

11

Davis stood by Wassruss, holding one of the huge webbed hands with her two hands. Hu was looking at an oscilloscope screen on which a green horizontal line was displaying tiny sawteeth at irregular intervals. A medical technician was adjusting the dials on a panel.

Hu turned away from the screen and started when she saw Ramstan.

'You must have run.'

Ramstan did not reply. He walked to the container in which Wassruss floated. She rolled her huge head toward him and fixed her great seal's eyes upon him. They were bright enough, but he thought he could see something like frosted glass deep within them.

She spoke for a long time. Branwen Davis finally said something, and the Webnite stopped.

'She's going too fast for me,' Branwen said. 'I asked her to start over again.'

Wassruss opened her mouth and took in a great mouthful of air. Then, slowly, she repeated herself, pausing now and then to allow Davis to interpret.

'I, Wassruss of the Violet Isle, will soon be dead. I had hoped to live long enough to see my native sea, the deep blue waters around the rocky, pine-grown Violet Isle, before I died. But my life is draining away faster than I had thought. The *Tssokh'azgd* did that to me; it tore my soul to shreds. You do not see the creature that devours all life and remain the same being. You know then how insignificant and meaningless you are, what a cipher, what a tiny piece of meat. The you, that is, the *I* that thinks itself the center of the universe, the goal of the cosmos, the being from which all things spread out and return to, becomes suddenly and irrecoverably dwindled, cut off, alone. It is no longer the source and resource of the world. It is alone, unconnected, a nothing. Without a history, with no love from anyone and no love for itself.

'It suddenly realizes, not intellectually but in the deepest part of its cells, that it is without hope and always has been. That it doesn't deserve hope and should never have wished for it. That in the beginning was nothing, that there has always been, behind the appearance of something, nothing, that there will always be nothing.

'That we are masks with no faces behind them, *unless the void has a face.*'

Wassruss stopped talking. The only sound was her heavy breathing. Branwen still held the Webnite's hand; her expression had become even more sad. Hu shook her head. The technician slipped out of the room. Ramstan saw that the frosted glass in Wassruss' eyes had floated up from the depths.

Presently, Wassruss withdrew her hand from Branwen's hands and reached with it into the belly pouch. It came out holding the three objects that Ramstan had seen on his first visit.

These were the gifts of which she had spoken.

Wassruss held all three in the palm of her hand, which was extended to Ramstan. But when he put his hand out to take them, she closed her fingers.

'I must tell you something about the gifts of the Vwoordha,' she said. 'The Vwoordha made these a long time ago. The Vwoordha were once a great people, very powerful. Now there are only three left, according to what I have been told. They have lost many of their powers, but not all, and the little they have left is more than that of many who boast of their greatness and riches.

'There are some who say that the Vwoordha are so ancient that they have survived the Death of All and Many Worlds.'

Here Ramstan interrupted to ask Branwen if she was translating correctly. Wasn't the phrase 'All and Many' a contradiction?

Branwen spoke to the Webnite, who gave a short answer. Branwen said, 'No, that is what she said. It is an ancient phrase the exact meaning of which she doesn't know.'

Wassruss began talking again.

'These gifts, these sigils, were once my grandmother's. She did not tell me the details of how they came into her hands. But she did say that she had once done a great favor for a queen of our nation, and the queen had given her these three objects. The queen herself had received them from her great-grandfather, who had gotten them from the captain of an Urzint spaceship. Neither she nor her great-grandfather ever used them. When she was about to die, she gave them to me. She told me what she knew about them, which was actually not much.

'But all you need to know is that each has a distinctive power. You must use one when you are in such a situation that there seems no other way out.

'Then you will place one in your mouth. Why there and not just in your hand, I do not know. That is all that is needed. The gift of the Vwoordha does the rest.

'But you must use, first, the *shengorth*, the triangle. After it has been used, it is of no more use to you. It can only be used once by one owner. If you use it, you should give it to someone you think worthy to have it, though that is not absolutely necessary. But not until after you have used the other two. Or, if you never use the other two, then, before you die, you must give all three to someone.

'Do not split up the three. Keep all three for yourself until the day comes when you give them away, and then give all three to one person.'

Ramstan tried to keep his face expressionless. Did this creature really believe in magic, in this tale of three thaumaturgical objects?

As if Wassruss had read his mind, she said. 'What I say of the gifts of the Vwoordha is no lie. Perhaps you are wondering why, if the gifts can take their owner from danger, I did not use one to save myself?'

Ramstan said, 'Tell her I was wondering that.'

Branwen spoke.

Wassruss coughed, and she said, 'I did not wish to use the sigils unless I absolutely had to. I had no warning of the meteorite or missile or whatever it was. When it pierced my body, I went into shock. I didn't have enough of my wits left to place the *shengorth* in my mouth before I became unconscious.'

She was dying, and if it made her feel better to give him the objects, then she should be able to do so. He'd be doing a kind deed. Allah saw every good deed and gave you credit for it.

That last was a stray thought that had no business in his mind. But, as Toyce had once said, 'You can only wash off the dirt. The skin is still there.'

Wassruss was saying, '... and so you must not forget to use the *shengorth* first. Next, the square, the *pengrathon*. Third, the disk, the *ph'rimon*. I do not know why, but to use one out of proper sequence nullifies the power.'

She repeated, 'And if you use all three, then you must pass them on as soon as possible to someone else. If, by the time you are ready to die, you have not used them, you must give them to someone who deserves them.'

Ramstan could not help saying, 'And what if I should die unexpectedly and have no chance to give them away?'

He was talking as if he believed that the things had power.

'Then someone will take them.'

Ramstan was going to ask her how the taker would know how to use the objects. If he had no instructions and perhaps did not even know what they were supposed to be, how could the taker get any benefit from them? Or pass the knowledge along to someone else? And since this was likely to happen many times in a long period of time, and the three gifts were supposed to be very ancient, how had they escaped being lost or knowledge of their use lost? Why hadn't the chain been broken?

He had other questions, but why bother with them?

'Of course,' Wassruss said, 'like all gifts, they are not necessarily beneficial. If not used properly, they can harm or even kill their owner. And there may be situations where death will be preferable to using them. What these are I don't know.'

'Perhaps it would be better if you gave them to someone else,' Ramstan said.

Davis said, 'She is honoring you in the highest way known to her people. You must not refuse! Uh, sir, that is, you *shouldn't*.'

He shrugged. 'Very well. But ... why is she giving *me* the gifts?'

After listening to Wassruss, Branwen said, 'The moment she saw you, she *knew* that you must be the one for whom the sigils have been waiting. Just as you will *know* the person to whom you are to give the three *ssuzz'akon*.'

Wassruss spoke again.

'She said that there is a tradition that eventually the makers of the sigils will get them back.'

'Sounds like a lot of ancient nonsense to me,' Ramstan said.

Wassruss spoke weakly to Branwen.

'She says that she hasn't even told you what's most important. And she doesn't have much time left.'

Doctor Hu said, 'We can give her more time.'

Branwen told Wassruss this.

The seal-centaur said, '*Tssisskooss.*'

'She says, "No".'

Wassruss went into a long speech. When Branwen had heard her out, she frowned.

'She says the bearer of the gifts is also taught a mystery chant when she receives the gifts. She doesn't know what it means, but she thinks she could find out the meaning if her destiny depended upon it. *Destiny?* That may not be the correct translation. I just don't know her language well enough. Anyway, you must remember that the gifts may get you out of one danger but at the same time put you in another. She says that good has its evils and evils their good. The universe is tricky, the ultimate and the biggest trickster.

'Now she's going to recite the chant, the mystery. She thinks that you'll have to figure it out. The time for it is ready, and you are the one who has arrived at the time when it must be ... uh ... unspooled? ... unraveled? ... threaded through the Great Eye? What she said, literally, is that the spooling and the unspooling go through the eye of the same needle. You yourself are needle and eye and threader and unspooler and spooler. This is very strange, since the Webnites know very little about spinning or needles.'

Wassruss said something.

Branwen said, 'She says that the chant will be your property, yours, Captain, and *yours only.*'

Ramstan said, 'Property?'

'She doesn't use that word exactly as we do. Anyway, take the sigils now.'

Ramstan held out his left hand. Wassruss said something weakly. Davis said, 'No. Your right hand.'

Ramstan obeyed. Wassruss extended her huge, brown-webbed hand and dropped the three objects into his palm. His fingers closed over them. They felt slimy.

12

Wassruss began chanting. It was obvious from the alternate deepening and raising of her voice, combined with significant pauses, that she was representing two speakers. Branwen translated after each phrase.

' "What is the number of the worlds?"

' "More than many."

'"What is the number of paths?"
'"More than many. Yet they are one."
'"What is at the ends of the paths that are one?"
'"Death or wisdom or both. *And one more thing.*"
'"What is the way to the three?"
'"There are many places to start. Webn is one."
'"And then?"
'"Ring the bell at the first entrance past Webn."
'"And then?"
'"Enter."
'"And then?"
'"Ring the bell at the third entrance."
'"And then?"
'"Enter."
'"And then?"
'"Ring the bell at the fifth entrance."
'"And then?"
'"Enter."
'"And then?"
'"Ring the bell at the seventh entrance."
'"And then?"
'"Enter."
'"And then?"
'"Ring the bell at the ninth entrance."
'"And then?"
'"Go to the only place to go."
'"And then?"
'"To the tree which does not stand alone."
'"And then?"
'"To the well."
'"What is in the well?"
'"The wise one who swims,
'"The laugher who hops,
'"The cold-blood who drinks hot blood."
'"Is this the end?"
'"Near the well is an old house. It is older than many stars."
'"And then?"
'"Knock at the entrance."
'"Who shall open the door?"
'"Three who should be dead."
'"And then?"
'"Ask, but be willing to pay the price."'

No one spoke for a moment. The only sound was Wassruss' whistling breath.

At last, Ramstan said hesitantly, 'Do the Webnites have bells?'

Branwen said, 'Yes. At the entrances to their underwater caverns and to their stone houses on the islands.'

'So what you translate as *bells* isn't a mistranslation or a substitute translation? Tell me, are there puns in the Webnites' language?'

'Yes. Why do you ask?'

'I'll tell you later.'

Wassruss' eyes became larger as if she had just seen something surprising. The frosted glass within them spread out. A sound as of mice feet scratching on a metal floor came from her mouth. Then she sighed.

The monitors emitted unmodulated *beeps*; the green lines on the 'scopes were like arrow shafts. Hu turned the machines off and did not think it worth the effort to apply the mentoscope to Wassruss.

Branwen held the big, brown hand for a minute, then gently lowered it.

'She was holding off until she had passed on the gifts and the mystery.'

He looked at the triangle, square, and circle.

'I'll put these in my cabin-safe. Their status can be determined later.'

'Status?' Hu said.

'Yes, whether they are my property or the government's. After all, they can't be said to be bribes.'

'You don't know the twisted ingenuity of our bureaucrats,' Toyce said.

The medical corps people came to take Wassruss' body away. Branwen seemed to be waiting for Ramstan to say something to her, but he walked out and went to his quarters. Instead of placing the gifts in the safe, he kept them in his pocket. He did not know why he had changed his mind. Then he tried to communicate with the *glyfa*. If it was receiving, it was not transmitting. He gave up after five minutes and went to mess. Hu came in late and sat down in the space reserved for her, the chair rising from the deck as she lowered her buttocks.

'Lieutenant Davis' fever – its cause – is as mysterious as ever. But I have a hunch ... yes, smile, it's okay, a hunch. She is trying to tell us something. Or perhaps she is sick so that she won't have to do something she doesn't want to do.'

Ramstan did not comment. When mess was over, he excused himself and went to the sickbay now formed to hold Davis alone. A marine stood guard at the entrance. Ramstan went in, the entrance closing behind him. Branwen was lying in bed staring up at the overhead. A large plate had been transformed into a screen on which an old 4-D movie was being shown. Her lackluster eyes did not brighten when he entered. She told ship to turn off the movie, and there was silence and less light.

'You look sick and are,' Ramstan said. 'Frankly, I think that Doctor Hu may be right. Your fever *is* psychosomatically engendered. Are you repressing something?'

She burst into tears and put her hands over her face.

Ramstan waited for a minute, then said, 'What is it?'

She took her hands away. The eyes were brighter now because of the tears.

'You're wrong, sir,' she said. 'I'm hiding nothing. I don't know why I'm sick. I wept because it seemed so unjust to be accused of deliberately making myself sick. It's almost like being accused of malingering.'

'There's nothing illegal about that type of goldbricking. But I get the feeling that you're ... not quite truthful.'

Indignation burned in her eyes. Or was it the fever?

'I'm not hiding anything,' she said, and she began weeping again.

13

'The Tolt ship is now in stationary orbit, sir,' the petty officer said. 'She's directly above the island. As you ordered, a message is being transmitted to her. But so far she hasn't responded.'

Ramstan refrained from looking upward. He knew he could not see it, but he had an impulse to bend his neck back and gaze into the bright blue.

'Very well,' he said. 'Continue transmitting. If it does nothing else, it will annoy them. And it will serve notice that we're aware of them.'

Al-Buraq, panting yellow, lay about fifty meters away. She was in starfish-shape now. Crewpeople were strolling around it, most of them nude, taking the opportunity to absorb some natural sunshine.

Another fifty meters in the opposite direction, the green-blue ocean lashed great white-capped waves at the yellow sands of the beach. The wind blew from the west, bringing with it a spicy odor from a large tree-capped island-peak 10 kilometers distant. The trees near Ramstan resembled Terran palms. Their fronds waved in the breeze. Yellow-and-scarlet birds with black toucanlike beaks and cartilaginous horns on top of their heads swooped over the crew. From the top of a double-trunked baobablike plant an enormous green many-angled insect dropped a sticky noose. Presently, along came a tiny bird, and the noose jerked and ensnared the bird. Screaming, it was drawn up toward the mouth into which the long gelatinous rope was disappearing.

Branwen shuddered.

'Webn is beautiful, but it has sinister features.'

'Nonsense,' Toyce said. 'There is nothing evil about that insect. It has to eat, doesn't it? And it really is beautiful. Would you like to take a closer look?'

She held out an electron-telescope.

'No, thanks. I've seen them before at close range.'

Branwen's fever was now very low; her body temperature was only one-tenth of a degree above normal. Hu had given her permission to go as interpreter with the burial party. It had just come back from half a kilometer offshore where Wassruss, weighted down with rocks tied to her, a wreath of flowers and weeds attached to her chest, had been dropped into the sea. There were thousands of dark-brown, flippered giants in the water, floating in concentric circles around the corpse and singing joyous songs.

There was no reason, now that Ramstan had carried out his promise to Wassruss, for ship to stay here. Yet Ramstan did not give the order to take off. No one seemed to have made any criticism of this. The crew had been on extended shore leave, but it did not object to going on another. Though *al-Buraq* was not a cramped vessel, she could not offer open skies and ground to run on and vegetation and a natural sun. Moreover, there was fishing and swimming with the friendly seal-centaurs and hiking through the woods and hills and much discreet lovemaking behind trees or boulders.

The Tolt ship hanging above, invisible to the naked eye, mute, sinister, could be forgotten easily enough by all but Ramstan. He was aware of it in every waking moment and sometimes in his dreams. It was an unseen shadow that darkened the beauty and glory of island and sea.

Ramstan, thinking of this, walked through the woods on a path which large beasts had made. The wild animals were so unafraid of the strangers that they seemed almost domesticated. When he reached the foot of the basalt mountain dominating the island, he turned back. But he halted within a few meters. Stocky, bull-necked, Assyrian-bearded Benagur blocked his way.

'I didn't know Hu had given you permission to leave ship,' Ramstan said.

'I've been a good boy,' Benagur said sarcastically. 'And I've shown no signs of misintegration since my outburst. Which I don't think was a symptom of craziness. You don't believe in God, and you have stolen the *glyfa*. But ...' he paused ... 'perhaps I was wrong in one thing. You do believe in a god, the Tenolt god.'

'You'll only do yourself a disservice if you keep saying that,' Ramstan said.

Benagur's bellow seemed to be the echo of the distant sea crashing against the base of the cliffs on the western shore. Like the sound of the ocean, it held a suggestion of danger.

'It's very frustrating for me! I know that you took the *glyfa*, yet I can't prove it! And if I accuse you officially, you will just have me locked up or sickbayed again! But you're the crazy man, Ramstan! You've put us all in the most extreme jeopardy, but you don't seem to care at all! You'll die for your sin, and so will we, the innocents!'

Ramstan felt sick with guilt and with hatred of Benagur. His hands curled into half-fists. He took one step forward. Benagur did not flinch. He crouched, and his left shoulder rose a trifle as if he was on the verge of adopting a boxer's stance. His hands, too, were partly clenched.

Ramstan felt like hurling himself at Benagur. But he saw something flicker at the base of a huge tree near the foot of the low hills beyond Benagur. The flicker became a figure in green. Its hood and robes were bright green; the face below the hood was featureless, shrouded in darkness. An arm rose, and its hand moved slowly back and forth at a 45-degree angle upward to the ground. The hood moved as if the turbaned head within it was moving to the right and then the left. It said as plainly as if it were speaking, 'No!'

Al-Khidhr, the Green One, the Wanderer.

If he was indeed Elijah, the ancient Hebrew, he was watching over Ramstan, protecting the atheist ex-Muslim, not the devout Jew, Benagur.

But al-Khidhr was a Sufi, the pristine Sufi, and Sufis could be Jewish or Christian as well as Muslim.

Then Ramstan thought, I'm crazy. Benagur is right, I *am* crazy.

The green figure flickered and was gone.

Ramstan stepped back and straightened his fingers. His voice shook.

'You're the dangerous one, Benagur, the mad one. You almost provoked me into attacking you.'

He took another step back.

'Is this a trap? Are you transmitting to my officers through the skinceiver?'

Benagur scowled.

He roared, 'No! I came here to make a final appeal to your honor and your duty! To your reason or what's left of it! But I can see that it's useless!'

'And now what?'

'I will make official charges! You can do your best to get me locked up again, but the charges can't be ignored! They'll have to be investigated! Your quarters will be searched! And the *glyfa* will be found! Then …'

'Then …?' Ramstan said softly. His voice was now as steady as a steel beam on bedrock.

'Perhaps they …' Benagur pointed up at the invisible Tolt vessel … 'they will be satisfied with the return of their god! My God, Ramstan! Crazy as you are, surely you see what danger we're all in! We could all be killed, killed for no good reason! I don't know what impelled you to take the *glyfa*, what foul lust, what …'

'That's a strange word,' Ramstan said, smiling slightly. 'Lust! What made you say that?'

Despite his smile, he felt ice sinking through him from the top of his head toward his toes. It was, in a sense, lust. And he had no idea why he should have been seized with it.

Nor how Benagur had stumbled over and on that description. Perhaps ... Benagur himself had felt the lust.

Benagur said, 'The *glyfa* must have made you lust for it!'

'It's just an artifact,' Ramstan said. 'Are you saying it's alive? A true god? A living idol? Who's crazy, Benagur? You or me?'

'I felt something there!' Benagur cried. 'I felt a vast, an overwhelming evil! I knew where it came from! It came from the *glyfa*! And, yes, I'll admit it, Ramstan, since I am only human and so subject to temptation! I was tempted to succumb to the evil! But it was God who saved me, who showed me the ineffable Good, His true Nature! He stepped in, and He gave me a glimpse of Him, of His face, and so saved me!'

Perhaps we're both insane, Ramstan thought.

It was then that he got the first faint thought that he and Benagur might not be standing on the seashore of the world of Webn. Not in reality. They just thought they were there. They *seemed* to be there. Where were they, in actuality?

He got a flash of where they might be, and he just as quickly rejected the image.

He shook his head and then rolled it as if he were trying to dislodge something clinging to it, a giant louse, perhaps. Some filthy and blood-sucking thing.

'We have nothing more to say to each other,' Ramstan said. 'Not here, anyway.'

He strode off though he was not sure that he should turn his back on Benagur. The man was no coward, far from it, but he might be overcome by his fury and jump on his captain from behind. Ramstan refused to look behind him. He did not wish Benagur to think that he feared him.

After cutting through a forest which covered the neck of the peninsula like a ruff, he came onto the seashore again. Half a kilometer inland, mighty *al-Buraq* stretched out across a clearing.

Chief Engineer Indra, nude, was sitting on a floating chair in the sun. On an extended arm of the chair was a half-full bottle of Kalafalan wine. In his hands was a book, a square plate half a meter wide and a centimeter thick. Ramstan paused behind Indra to read the phonemic-character words appearing and disappearing swiftly one by one. Indra did not have to move his eyes from side to side or down. It was *The Maltese Falcon*, a classical twentieth-century American novel translated into Terrish.

Indra felt Ramstan's body between him and the sun. He touched a control on the side of the book, and the text stopped moving. He twisted around; his teeth shone whitely in his dark face.

'Captain! I was hoping I'd catch you.'

Ramstan came around the chair.

'Why?'

Indra stood up, the book held between two fingers.

'You'll remember that I told you some time ago that ship was growing a new circuit.'

'Yes.'

'I've just determined what it is.'

Ramstan said, 'I know what it is. It's an affection circuit. One that has an affection configuration, anyway.'

'You know!'

'I'm not a bioengineer, but I know more about ship than anyone else.'

Indra said, 'How do you feel about it? I mean ... do you respond to its affection with your affection? With love?'

'To be loved isn't always the same as to love,' Ramstan said stonily. 'We don't have time for experiments. There's that ...' He pointed at the sky. 'I don't want to worry about ship getting hysterical or panicky if she thinks I'm in danger.'

'She's not a dog,' Indra said, 'though she may have developed some doglike attitudes. I could find out just what effect the affection configuration has on her gestalt. But it'll take time.'

Ramstan said, 'Excise the circuit.'

Indra frowned and bit his lip.

'That's an order, not a suggestion. Operate *now!*'

'Aye, aye, sir!' Indra said. He snapped a salute and stalked off. Ramstan watched him for a minute, then started toward the vessel. He stopped when he saw Branwen Davis. She was so beautiful that his heart seemed to ache.

He hailed her and then asked her about her health, though he'd seen the medical report on her that morning.

'I feel fine,' she said. 'The fever has gone as suddenly as it came, and the doctors don't know where it came from, what caused it, or where it went.'

'Let's hope it doesn't return,' he said. He paused, balled up what little courage he had, and used it all up in one sentence.

'Would you care to dine in my cabin tonight?'

She smiled, but she said, 'No, but thank you for the honor, sir.'

He was shocked. He had not really expected her to turn him down. No woman ever had.

Though he'd thought his face was expressionless, he must have shown something somehow. She said, 'I'm sorry. I don't mean to offend you, Captain. But I've talked to some women ...'

'What does that matter? You're not one of them. You're different.'

'They all said that they were in love with you and that you were in love with them. At least, you told them you were. But after a while, a short while, they said, you became very cold and then downright nasty.'

'I was never nasty!' he said. 'They lied!'

If she had been anyone else, he would not have deigned to discuss the matter. He despised himself for humbling himself like this.

'All of them?' she said. 'Well, I won't argue. Anyway,' she touched his arm with a finger and held it there, 'I'm not rejecting you, you know. I'm just rejecting your invitation to dinner. I'm not ready to go to bed with you, and I may never be. But I don't dislike you.'

'You don't like me, either,' he said. He was astonished; someone else must have said that.

'Some people are very warm and, so, likeable,' Branwen said. 'You're not warm.'

'I'm the captain of ship,' he said.

'And so proud and lonely,' she said, and she laughed. 'No, you've got it the wrong way. You'd be aloof and lonely if you were the cabin boy. Captain Irion was a very good commander, but still there was something about her that made people love her.' She paused.

'You're angry,' she said. She withdrew her finger from his arm and he had a flash of image, a wound made by the finger, now closing up, the blood evaporating, and ice forming over the scar.

'Yes, I am,' he said. 'But not at you. Other things …'

He almost believed that he was not lying.

'I'll see you,' he said, and strode away.

Ramstan went to his quarters and called the bridge. Overlieutenant Ozma Garrick responded.

'I want Commodore Benagur arrested. He is to be put in his cabin, not the brig, and he is to stay there until Doctor Hu has examined him. Notify me as soon as he's quartered.'

Garrick looked as if she'd like to ask him the reason for the order, but she didn't, of course. Ramstan then called Indra.

'Have you started yet on the circuit?'

'I haven't started operating.'

'The order is canceled. Hold yourself ready to resume operating, though.'

The Hindu smiled but said nothing.

Ramstan was glad that Indra had not questioned him. He himself didn't know why he'd put off the operation.

He sat down and drummed the fingers of his left hand on his thigh. Then he called the bridge.

'Garrick, resume signaling to the Tolt ship. If you get an answer, notify me at once.'

Garrick's face faded from the octant. Ramstan sat motionless – even his fingers were unmoving – for a few minutes. Then, sighing, he heaved himself up and walked to the bulkhead. Shortly thereafter, he placed the *glyfa* on a table. He ran his fingers over the surface and marveled again at how some dead-for-eons artist had sculpted it so intricately and wonderfully and deep and yet it was so smooth.

He spoke to himself out loud. 'If only I knew what the Tenolt were up to!'

The voice that answered him turned him around, his eyes wide, his skin paling, his heart threatening to burst. But he was the only human in the room.

'Allah!'

He spoke a few words in Arabic, most of which were curses.

The voice had said or seemed to have said, 'They know you stole me. But they don't want to attack while you're in ship. Above all, they want to get me back into their hands.'

Now it said, 'I should have warned you.'

Ramstan leaned on the table while he gripped its edges. His heart began to slow down, but he could only speak in gasps at first.

'Why ... do you use ... Branwen Davis' voice?'

Only then did it strike him that the *glyfa* was reading his mind. He was outraged. No one or no thing should be permitted that violation.

'No, I don't read your mind, and I can't,' the *glyfa* said in the voice of Khadija, his mother.

'If you can't ... then ... how did you know ... what I was thinking?'

'I knew that you would have thought that I was,' the voice said.

Ramstan had not wept for years. Now tears rolled down his cheeks.

'Please don't use her voice,' he said.

'Very well. How's this?'

Benagur's voice boomed.

'No!'

'I'll speak to you as your mother, then.'

'No!'

'You'll get used to it, and eventually you'll love it. I think you've been carrying your grief too long, even if you didn't know you had it buried so deeply.'

'It makes me feel as if she's speaking from the grave,' Ramstan said. 'Or ... as if you're her tomb, and she's talking to me from it.'

'In a sense, she is,' the *glyfa* said.

Ramstan asked it to explain the remark, but the *glyfa* ignored his question. It said, 'You'll like to hear her. You've been using your quarters as a sort of womb in which you can take refuge. Now, hearing her here, you will be even more in the womb. That isn't a good thing, perhaps. But you seem to need it.'

'If you can't read my mind, then how do you know so much about Davis and Benagur and only Allah knows who else?'

'I can detect vibrations and see objects at a distance,' his mother's voice said. 'I can detect electrical and electronic phenomena. I can detect other things, too.'

'You can see and hear things outside this cabin?'

'Yes. Of course.'

'How far?'

'Quite far.'

'You won't tell me the exact distance?'

'I have my reasons not to.'

'Could you tell the captain of the *Popacapyu* to go away and leave us alone?'

The *glyfa* did not answer.

Ramstan said, 'It's obvious that you can't.'

'Or that I may have some reason not to wish to.'

'It's also obvious,' Ramstan said, 'that you can influence electricity at a distance. How do you do that?'

'The explanation would be meaningless to you.'

'But you have to find the right words in my memory bank, put them together in Arabic or Terrish syntax, modulate them, get the right intonations, stresses, and so on. And when you use my mother's voice, evoke it. I mean, you use some words that my mother never heard nor read. Also, you must originate your transmissions of language in your own language. How do you manage the translation? I mean, even if you're transmitting your voice to me in some manner or some sort of coded signals or whatever, they wouldn't mean anything to me if I heard them directly. Via vibration of air through my eardrums, I mean. So …'

'It must be enough for you that I can do this,' the *glyfa* said. 'Now. To your original question to yourself. What are the Tenolt up to? They wish to get me back and they're not going to use violence and so take a chance of losing me unless desperation drives them to it. Also, for all they know, you may have hidden me elsewhere than in *al-Buraq*. On Kalafala or Walisk, perhaps, or even on Webn. Though they would have seen you do that unless you somehow tricked them.

'Also, I am their god. It frightens and puzzles them that I permitted you to take me. Or, perhaps, and this must deeply disturb them, that perhaps you, Ramstan, were able to steal me because you might be more powerful than I. I doubt, though, that anyone on their vessel has dared voice that thought. It would go very hard with anyone who did, even their high priest.'

A whistle shrilled. Ramstan was startled, but he spoke a few words to cut off video on his end of the line. Garrick's face appeared in an octant.

'Commodore Benagur has been arrested and confined to his quarters, sir. Doctor Hu is en route to examine the commodore, as you ordered.'

'Thank you, Lieutenant,' Ramstan said, and he cut off the transmission.

The *glyfa* said, 'Poor Benagur. He's a mystic, and, in his search for the ineffable, he has caught a glimpse of it. Or is the rag of glory worn by something else? The Opponent, for instance? Would not the Opponent have a glory of his own, and would it not be difficult to distinguish his glory from the true glory?'

'You seem amused,' Ramstan said.

Though he did not like Benagur, he felt sorry for him at this moment. Perhaps that was because he felt sorry for himself, too. Rather, he felt confused and, because of this confusion, helpless. He loathed that feeling and despised himself for it. He could make his way against all obstacles. At least, until recently, he had thought so. Now … he was not so sure.

He had to ask the *glyfa* some questions, yet he hated doing it. He should be able to find the answers by himself.

'What is the *bolg*?' he said.

There was a pause as if the *glyfa* had been taken by surprise. But Ramstan might be misinterpreting the silence.

'The *bolg*?' the *glyfa* said. 'I haven't heard that name for a long time. A time so long you would be shattered just to contemplate the idea of it.'

'Well?' Ramstan said.

'It's a name for a chaos-monster. The people who used it have perished long ago. In fact, several …'

Ramstan said, 'Several what?'

'Never mind. Where did you hear it?'

Ramstan told it what happened in the Kalafalan tavern. This gave him some satisfaction, despite the reawakening of the bad emotions connected with the incident. The *glyfa* had not been observing him when he was in the tavern. Was that because it was unable to do so or because it had preferred not to? Or was the *glyfa* lying for some reason and had known about the tavern incident all along?

'There are many in this war,' the *glyfa* said. 'I knew that long ago, but I still don't know who some of them are. But I have time enough. At least, I hope so.'

'What does that mean?' Ramstan said.

There was no answer.

It was evident that the *glyfa* must know about the destruction of Waliskan life. Ramstan asked it if that had had anything to do with the *bolg*.

'As of now, everything in the universes has to do with the *bolg*,' the *glyfa* said.

'What do you mean by universes?'

'You shouldn't know everything at once. You couldn't handle all that.'

Ramstan's anger flared up again.

'What am I? A mere pawn?'

'Pawns are not mere. Nothing that is necessary is mere. You are a focal point, perhaps *the* focus. And don't think I mean that you are a thing. A focus can be a person.'

If the *glyfa* could reach inside him, activate memories and language units, it surely could trigger off emotions. How else explain why he had stolen the *glyfa*? That was an act that he would not even have thought of, not the captain responsible for the crew of ship and ship herself. He had put *al-Buraq* and her people in the most extreme danger, and he had never been sure just why.

Surely, the *glyfa* had wished him to take it, and it had moved him to the act as if he were a robot.

Hoarsely, he told the *glyfa* what he was thinking.

As usual, he got a half-answer from the thing.

'I am incapable of inserting desires in others. I can't operate on what doesn't exist.'

'You must have monitored the dying of Wassruss,' Ramstan said. 'What are the three gifts? What does that question-and-answer chant mean?'

'There'll be a time and a time for those,' the *glyfa* said.

Ramstan roared, 'I'm fed up with your enigmas! Out you go! Out, I say! The Tenolt can have you back!'

Silence.

Ramstan yelled, 'Talk, damn you! Unless I get complete and clear answers, I'm going to heave you out of here! I'll show you!'

Had the *glyfa* withdrawn, cut off detection? Or was it sitting in that impenetrable shell and smiling whatever kind of smile such a being could have?

He put his hands upon the egg-shape, lifted it a few centimeters from the table, then took his hands away. The *glyfa* dropped with a thud but did not roll.

If he took the thing out now, he would be observed. And the crew would know that he had taken it.

It would be better to remove it at night and carry it to some place out of sight, say, the top of a rocky ridge half a kilometer away. When the daylight came, or perhaps before that, the Tolt operator of the magniscope would see it. And the Tolt vessel would come down as swiftly as possible to retrieve the god.

Its descent would be detected, of course, and the crew of *al-Buraq* would have to be put on alert. Only he would know why the Tolt was moving toward them, and he could not tell anybody.

But what if the Tolt captain, having gotten the *glyfa*, decided to take revenge? Would he regard the theft as sacrilege? Would he then attack *al-Buraq*?

Or, if he contemplated such action, would he be stopped by the *glyfa*? Perhaps the *glyfa* would not want to stop the Tolt.

He paced back and forth, his head bent, his long chin almost touching his chest, his hands locked behind his back. Finally, he lifted the *glyfa*, put it back into the bag, and returned it to the bulkhead-safe. The deck trembled very slightly as if *al-Buraq* was aware of her captain's emotional turmoil and frustration and was shaking with sympathy. Which thought, of course, was ridiculous, Ramstan told himself. He was anthropomorphizing, no, theriomorphizing, too much.

A call came from the bridge. Doctor Hu wanted to speak to him about Benagur. Ramstan left his quarters almost at once. But as he strode down the passageways, he wondered what had made him keep the *glyfa*. Was it entirely his own decision? Or had the *glyfa* subtly steered him toward it?

14

Some mystics seek God by travel; others, by staying in one room.

Benagur had done both. Something had happened to cause him to venture forth from the little chamber in a house in Jerusalem near the Wailing Wall. No one but he knew what it was, but occasionally he had hinted at the event. When questioned by those eager to get the details, he had said that the event was indescribable.

He would seem to have been unfitted to be a crewmember of an alaraf ship. But he was known worldwide among theologians for his writings on Jewish and Muslim mysticism, and *al-Buraq* had several berths open for theologians. Benagur was accepted after, of course, the required physical and psychological tests. A deep psychic probe had not been needed to determine that he was eccentric, but it did indicate that he had the stability needed for alaraf-ship living. Besides, he was not the only eccentric aboard.

If he tended to keep to himself much of the time, he had a good excuse. Like many of the specialists, he was very busy with his professional duties. Unlike most of the others, he was given special privileges because of the rigors of his religion. Whenever possible, he ate by himself and only the foods his religion permitted. The other Jews aboard belonged to sects too liberal for him to regard them as genuine Jews. That was all right with the others; they thought he was a superfanatic. They had, however a great respect for his knowledge.

Ramstan had had no trouble with Benagur until the night the *glyfa* was stolen. Though Benagur was very reserved, that had not bothered Ramstan, who was equally reserved.

Now, Ramstan felt some guilt. If he'd not done what he'd done, he would not have thrown Benagur into the strange frenzy possessing him.

Was Benagur crazy? Was he not, by all standards except Ramstan's, sane? Would not the others be acting much like him if they suspected what Benagur suspected?

On the other hand, none of them might have been affected as deeply. They did not have Benagur's psychic constitution; they were not near the edge of insanity and needing only a slight push to shove them over. After all, Maija Nuoli had been subjected to the same overpowering *light*, and she had not become psychotic. She had become more introspective than before, and she did not care to talk about her experience in the Tolt temple. But she had carried out her duties as a botanist as efficiently as before.

Ramstan wondered why the *glyfa* had asked for her to accompany him and Benagur. What part did she play in the drama the *glyfa* was undoubtedly writing? For that matter, what part did Benagur have? Perhaps he was no longer in the thing's designs. Whatever it was that had flooded the senses of the three, it had unbalanced Benagur and made him useless to the *glyfa*.

It was possible that the *glyfa* had summoned Nuoli and Benagur to come merely to ensure that Ramstan would not be singled out as the thief. They, too, would be suspects. If so, the *glyfa* had miscalculated. Suspicion had not fastened upon Benagur or Nuoli.

The *glyfa* might have had some other reason, however, for inviting them.

Ramstan entered Doctor Hu's office. Hu rose from behind her desk as the captain entered.

'Sit down, Julia,' Ramstan said. His use of Hu's first name indicated that no formalities were to be observed.

Ramstan made a sign, and a chair formed from the deck. He sat down, and, after the silence lasted for several seconds, said, 'Well?'

Hu did not look at Ramstan. 'Commodore Benagur claims that you stole the *glyfa* from the Tenolt.'

Now it was in the open, Ramstan thought. No, not really. It could perhaps be kept to Benagur and Hu.

'You gave him a lie-test?'

'Of course. It indicates that he *thinks* he's telling the truth.'

'In which case, then, he's psychotic,' Ramstan said.

Hu hesitated and then looked Ramstan in the eyes.

'That remains to be proved.'

Ramstan reared up from his chair, bellowing, 'What?'

Hu spread her hands out and shrugged.

'He's going to bring formal charges against you.'

Ramstan sat down and bit his lips.

'I can't allow that. We're in a very grave and dangerous situation. The Tolt vessel ... the terrible destruction of Walisk ... no. All normal procedures will have to be suspended.'

'You won't allow Benagur to make the charges?'

'I can't permit it now. After there's no more danger, I will, of course.'

He leaned forward, his upper arms on his thighs, his hands clasped.

'Listen. If Benagur can be shown to be psychotic, then there's no need to log these ridiculous charges.'

'He's certainly upset, which is not, however, the same as being unbalanced.'

Ramstan leaned back and said, smiling slightly, 'Has he also accused me of not believing in God?'

'No. He said nothing about that. Why?'

'A little while ago, near the seashore, he made that accusation. He seemed to think that it made me guilty, as criminal, as if I had stolen the *glyfa*. In fact, more so.'

'He would be psychotic if he'd included that charge in the others,' Hu said. 'But he didn't.'

'He came close to attacking me while we were on the beach.'

Hu lifted her eyebrows. 'Yes? Was his intention overt? Did he threaten you or make any obviously belligerent moves?'

Ramstan had done far worse than lie, but he just could not bring himself to lie about this.

'No. But it was evident that he would have liked to attack me.'

Hu's grimace indicated that that was not enough justification to think Benagur psychotic. It also seemed to Ramstan that it said that Benagur wasn't the only crewmember who would like to assault him.

Ramstan stood up.

'Benagur will be kept in his cabin unless his condition gets worse and he has to be restrained. You or one of your colleagues will give him therapy.'

Hu rose.

'There's nothing in the EEG readings or blood samples to indicate a psychotic condition.'

'But those aren't sure methods of determining neurosis or psychosis, are they?'

'By no means. The psychosoma is vastly complex and often tricky. Centuries ...'

'You have my orders,' Ramstan said. He strode out. Hu could give the command for the chair to shrink back into the deck. It was protocol for the chair-riser to be the chair-ridder, but to hell with the doctor.

While walking back to his quarters, he used the skinceiver.

'Garrick, order all personnel to return to ship at once. We jump for Kalafala in an hour. I'll be on bridge in thirty minutes.'

'"What is the number of the worlds?"
'"More than many."
'"What is the number of paths?"
'"More than many. Yet they are one."
'"What is at the end of the paths that are one?"
'"Death or wisdom or both. *And one more thing.*"
'"What is the way to the three?"
'"There are many places to start. Webn is one."
'"And then?"
'"Ring the bell at the first entrance past Webn."
'"And then?"
'"Enter."'

The chant was obviously a navigational chart for the journey from the planet Webn to wherever and whatever the final destination was. Ramstan had seen that within ten minutes after hearing Davis' interpretation of Wassruss' ritual-song. He doubted that Wassruss knew what it meant; she had learned it by rote and given it as required, however meaningless it was to her. The Webnites had no means for space travel except as passengers on the alaraf ships of other sentients. Whoever had given the chant and the three gifts to Wassruss' ancestor had known what the chant meant but had not explained it to the donee. Or perhaps the donor had done so but the explanation had been forgotten.

The Webnites did have bells, and so the donor had been able to use 'bell' when translating the chant from his or her language into Webnian. But the seal-centaurs did not have dumbbells, those muscle-building devices which consisted of two spherical objects connected by a shaft. It wouldn't have helped their understanding of the chant any if they had had them. It was extremely unlikely that their word for it would have been the transfer-meaning or pun used in Terrish.

Ramstan doubted that the originator of the chant had meant any connection between a 'bell' and a 'dumbbell'. But the Terrans had made such a connection since there seemed to them to be a 'shaft', sometimes called a 'tunnel', between the 'bell' of one star system and the next. It was possible and perhaps very probable that the originator of the chant had used a word meaning 'bell' in his language. There had been no implication of 'dumbbell' in the chant. The originator had just meant that when you entered a 'bell', that roughly spherical shape with an opening or 'mouth' through which you went to the next star system, you were 'ringing' it.

Or it might be that the Raushghols had defined their terminology for alaraf travel to Wassruss when she was on their ship. Then, on *al-Buraq*, she had, Ramstan knew, been told briefly by Davis the Terran theory and terminology of alaraf travel. And she had substituted the word 'bell' for whatever had been in the chant taught her.

The speculation about language did not matter. What did was that he believed that he had been given directions which were somewhat vague but still could get him to the destination – whatever that was. He would try to get there because he might find an answer to the question of the *bolg*. And perhaps to other questions.

He went up to the bridge. He did not have to explain why they were going to Kalafala, but he said, 'Lieutenant Davis was left there, and, if *Pegasus* has not been destroyed, she will come there to pick Davis up. We'll stay on Kalafala for a little while.'

Al-Buraq had been in the Kalafalan bell only three minutes when the tec-op reported another spaceship a thousand kilometers distant. She was oyster-shell-shaped.

'*Popacapyu*,' the operator said.

Five hours after *al-Buraq* had landed on the Kalafalan port, the Tolt vessel set down. Ramstan wondered why she had landed here but not on Webn. And why had no Tolt left her yet, though it was protocol for her commander to report immediately to the control tower authority?

An hour passed. Then the ports of the Tolt ship opened, and about fifty Tenolt came out. The captain headed for the tower with some officers. The others went to the tavern. Ramstan waited until he saw the captain return to his ship.

In the meantime, at least half of the original group had also come back to the *Popacapyu*. Another group then left the vessel for the tavern. Apparently, their captain was giving them a limited shore leave, time for just a few drinks.

Tenno said, 'Sir, do you plan to give shore leave?'

'That depends,' Ramstan said, and he did not say on what.

A half hour passed. Then two jeeps flew from the Tolt ship and headed toward the hotel. The commander sat in one.

Ramstan relaxed somewhat. He said, 'It looks as if they're going to be here a while.'

He told Tenno that there would be a limited and strictly regulated shore leave. Groups of forty could go out at a time, the second group to leave after the first had returned at the end of thirty minutes and so on. They were not to go to the tavern or the hotel, but they could have a few drinks at the port bar. They should be ready to return to ship immediately if a recall occurred.

'Do you expect trouble?' Tenno said.

'Not really. But I want my crew closer to their ship than the Tenolt will be to theirs.'

He left it up to Tenno to decide who would be among the shore-leave parties, and he went to his quarters. He took the *glyfa* from the safe, and, rubbing it as if he were Aladdin trying to summon the *djinn* from the lamp, asked it to talk to him.

Silence.

Ramstan bit his lower lip. Damn the thing!

He paced back and forth for an hour, stopping every fifteen minutes to call the bridge and get a report on the Tenolt. The captain of the *Popacapyu* was still at the hotel. The second Tenolt group had returned to their ship, and a third had gone out. The only ones armed were those in the jeeps accompanying the captain.

Ramstan paced again, then stopped. Frowning, he started toward the bulkhead area, holding the electron-microscope. Something had been bothering him, nibbling mice at the periphery of his mind. Only now did he realize what it was. The lighting was less bright than it should have been.

He called the bridge. 'Tenno, is there anything wrong ...? I mean, any indications of a power malfunction, for instance?'

'Not that we've noticed here, sir. But I'll call the engineers. May I ask why you ask?'

'Just check.'

He could not bring Indra to his quarters to look for a malfunction in the neural system. Troubleshooting might lead Indra to the safe. If Indra was then forbidden to open it, he would get suspicious.

He spoke to the *glyfa*. 'For the sake of Allah, what happened here? Tell me! You must know if someone's been here!'

He could hear only his rasping breath.

There was one thing to check before he used the microscope. He told *al-Buraq* to run off the monitor. A screen glowed immediately, though not as brightly as it was supposed to. He groaned. No video! Somebody had erased it! And he shouldn't have been able to do so!

He started again towards the bulkhead in which the microscope was. But he whirled, went to the table on which the *glyfa* was, and turned the a-g units on its ends to zero power. He gripped the egg and lifted it easily.

His cry rang out.

'It's a fake!'

15

The lighting dimmed and was gone.

He called the bridge. No reply.

Feeling along the bulkhead, he located the slight protuberance that indicated the cabinet holding the flashlights. But his order to ship to open it up was not obeyed.

He swore again, and he called out the order to make an exit for him. Again, no response.

Someone had entered and then arranged for the malfunction, perhaps through an anesthetic or a controlled-rate drug. Or the drug might have been injected first and the person had entered. He or she … or it … might also have mixed a hypnotic with the anesthetic. Or perhaps there had been no drug, but the sabotager had somehow hypnotized *al-Buraq*.

No time for speculation now. He should get the pseudo-*glyfa* back into the safe. The bulkhead wouldn't close now, but he would have it ready to be closed.

He put the egg into the bag, and he groped to the opposite bulkhead and felt around until he located the hole. When the egg was in the hole, he walked slowly, his hands out, back to the table. He gripped its edges as if he could squeeze photons from it. The darkness seemed to have smothered all the light in the world. The air moved slowly over his sweating face and hands. He could hear the blood rushing through him and the singing of silence.

If all of ship were drugged, obviously malfunctioning, Indra and his engineers would be troubleshooting furiously. It wouldn't take them long to find out what was wrong and to fix it.

Meanwhile, whoever had taken the *glyfa* would be long gone.

He sweated even more heavily.

If *al-Buraq* had been operating fully, the humidity in the quarters would have been dropped and the air would have gotten cooler.

'*Iblis* take this bio-ship!'

His voice sounded hollow and faraway to him.

There were many advantages to a biological spaceship, but now the disadvantages were too obvious. The designers had not thought of saboteurs or a crewmember going mad.

He pounded the table top with his fists, allowing himself a lack of control he would never have shown anybody under any circumstances he could envision. Or to himself under different circumstances. But, here in this dark, silent hollow, he could behave like a baby.

As his fist struck, he caught a flash of green out of the corner of his left eye.

He jumped back from the table, his hands still balled. Green? He could see color in this total darkness?

No. He hadn't really *seen* it. He couldn't have. Not his eyes but his mind had glimpsed the green.

Why?

He thought of the green-clothed man whom he'd identified as al-Khidr or Luqman or Elijah or all three as the same, though there was no proof that the green man was any one of them.

It was his brain that had originated that slash of color in the blackness around him. Just as, if he were to bump his head, he might see white or colored 'stars' for a second or two. Explosions of asterisks or comets caused by nerves firing impulses caused by a too-hard contact with real things. But he had not struck his head against anything. His fists had been beating the table, but that couldn't account for the parenthesis of green. A thin, curving zip of color ... perhaps not so much a parenthesis as a scimitar.

Or the edge of a turban or cloak.

The edge of the green iris of an eye of a man wearing green?

He waited. He did not see the flash again. Nevertheless, he had an overpowering feeling that someone else was in his quarters.

He bellowed, 'Who's there?'

Silence.

'Is it you?' he yelled, not knowing whom he meant by *you*.

He listened and looked, turning his head so he could sweep one hundred and eighty degrees and then turning his body to take in three hundred and sixty.

He thought, or thought he thought, that he saw something very pale green. But surely that was a ghost of a ghost, a reflection of an image of an image. Imagination supplying something to back its reality.

Something spoke to him.

His mother's voice? The voice stimulated by the *glyfa*?

No. It had to be something he'd wished. It was so far-off, so thin, so ...

The darkness began to pale. Then he could make out objects dimly as if he were deep under water and light was seeping through the surface of the ocean far above him.

Abruptly, full brightness swept through the chamber. Tenno's voice came. 'Captain?'

'Here!' he shouted.

At the same time, he thought, Where is here?

The answer, of course, was, where I am.

'What happened?'

'We don't know yet, sir,' Tenno said. 'But Doctor Indra thinks that someone drugged ship.'

Ramstan said, 'Put out an ACRS. I want everybody back in ship in ten minutes. Check them out as they come in.'

He paused. 'Is Commodore Benagur in his quarters?'

He could have asked *al-Buraq* directly, but protocol demanded that he go through the executive officer.

Tenno must have checked quickly. He said, 'Yes, sir, he is.'

Ramstan called Indra. The dark hawkish face was distressed.

'Yes, it's a drug. It was carried through the circulatory system, and its point of injection is the bulkhead outside your quarters. The traces of drug are being analyzed right now.'

How had the drugger learned the code words?

Perhaps the drug had uninhibited *al-Buraq* so much that she revealed codes when the intruder had asked for them. Or perhaps she hadn't done that. Perhaps the intruder had just overridden the codes with a direct order to open.

He made up new code words and gave them to ship. The deck quivered under him as ship, in a manner of speaking, wagged her tail.

Ramstan stopped as he headed toward the exit.

'Allah!'

The *glyfa* knew the code words. It had 'heard' him speak them many times. What if it had summoned one of the crew and made him carry it away? Or, now that he thought of how the Tenolt guards had not seemed to know he was in the temple, what if a non-Terran *had* entered and removed the *glyfa* with its help?

He would never know what happened unless he got the *glyfa* back. And perhaps not then.

Why should he worry about the *glyfa*? He was rid of it. He no longer had to carry the burden of its presence. As time passed, he would be able to shed his guilt. There would be times when he would burn with it, but the pain would lessen. From now on, he could act as the captain of *al-Buraq* should. Though he might never entirely forgive himself, he need not carry out every act with consideration of the *glyfa* darkening it.

'Let it go!' he said aloud.

He had the exit opened, and he stepped out into the passageway.

Down the right-hand bulkhead of the corridor raced a glowing circle. It stopped just ahead of him, then reversed its direction and matched his pace. Tenno's face was solemn as he said, 'The ten minutes are up, sir. Everybody's reported in ... except one.'

'Who's that?'

'Lieutenant Branwen Davis, sir.'

Ramstan entered the lift, the circle following him into it and stopping on the door before him.

'Have you called her?'

'Yes, sir. She doesn't answer.'

'Just a moment.'

Ramstan spoke the necessary order, and the circle was bisected, half of it showing a reduced image of Tenno and the other the face of Indra.

'Is ship fully recovered?'

The engineer lifted his right wrist to one ear. Perhaps he was listening to the time through his skinceiver.

'My people say she'll be fully operational in ten more minutes, sir. There's still a residue of drug not flushed out yet. It takes time …'

'Notify me the second she's ready.'

Indra's face disappeared. Tenno's swelled to fill the circle. But the lift door opened, and he was on the bridge. He at once asked the exec if he had questioned the crew on Davis' whereabouts.

'Yes, sir. Everybody's been contacted. Three say they saw her in the port main building for a few minutes.'

Ramstan had to force himself to ask the next question.

'Did they say she was carrying a large bag? Or a box? Anything bulky?'

Tenno looked startled. Those on the bridge who had overheard gave him expressionless glances but some looked at others as if to transmit a silent message.

'I don't know, sir. I just asked if she'd been seen.'

'Ask them if she was carrying a bag or a box!'

Tenno put ship on all-phone and did as ordered. Ramstan ordered several search squads out. They were to cover the port and also to question Kalafalans about Davis. Within forty seconds, Tenno made his report.

'Lieutenant Davis *was* carrying a box, sir.'

'Al-Khidhr, Isa, and Muhammad!'

The exclamation was subvocalized; he had enough control not to show his panic.

If Davis was the one who'd taken the *glyfa*, why hadn't she accepted his invitation to bed? She could have seen his quarters in order to better her plans. She could have tried to get the code words out of him. She'd have failed, but surely she would have made the attempt.

But then she probably thought that getting into his cabin wasn't necessary. Nor had it been.

Who had put her up to this?

He mastered his rage, sickness, and fear. He said, 'Send out two more search parties. Post two people where they can observe the Tolt ship.'

A minute later, a CPO reported from the port tavern.

'Sir, a Kalafalan says she saw an Earthwoman who was carrying a box go into the hotel.'

Ramstan ordered Tenno to have two jeeps with marines armed with olsons only ready to go within two minutes.

'I'll be in command. We're going to the hotel. Call in the search parties. Put ship on emergency take-off status, alaraf drive. As soon as I get back, we'll depart.'

Tenno swallowed and said, 'May I ask what this is all about?'

'I don't have time for explanations now,' Ramstan said. 'Be ready!'

He strode to the lift. If he caught Davis and brought the *glyfa* back with her, what then? She would reveal what she had done and why, and he could not deny that he had taken the *glyfa* from the Tolt temple. He'd be arrested.

He stepped out of ship. The bright sun was sliding down the final quarter of unclouded, pinkish sky. The air was delightfully fresh even though strained through his mask. Far to the west, black was building up on the horizon, a storm charging in from the ocean. It was a beautiful serene view with a hint of something sinister coming – typically Kalafalan in scenery and psychology.

The marine sergeant in command saluted. Ramstan looked briefly at the armed and masked men, got into the back seat of the front jeep, strapped himself in, and said, 'To the hotel.' The jeep rose to an altitude of 12 meters and began accelerating.

As yet, Ramstan had not ordered that any Tolt accompanied by Davis or any with a large box be intercepted. He was certain that an attempt to stop them would meet with vigorous resistance. There would be shooting. Then what? Would the Tolt ship attack *al-Buraq*? Probably. He would have put ship and crew in unnecessary danger. He'd be responsible for the deaths of many and for the wipeout, perhaps, of *al-Buraq*.

Why did he not just call off the search? He'd told himself that he was fortunate to be rid of the *glyfa*. He should have thought of some excuse to leave Kalafala. Branwen Davis would be marked down as a deserter.

He sighed deeply. Despite his original intentions, he was lusting for the *glyfa*. He had to have it back. Yet, he couldn't explain to himself why he must.

Perhaps, somehow, he could get the *glyfa* without altercation and could get rid of Branwen. He didn't have the slightest idea how this could be arranged nor did he genuinely believe it could be. Nevertheless, he would try.

Then he reared up against the restraining magnetic field, his hands pressed to his ears. The hands did not diminish the noise or his pain.

He screamed and he could hear his cry, though he should not have been able to do so.

The vast whistling sounded as if the very fabric of space-matter was being ripped apart.

As if the universe was crying out in a death agony.

16

The jeep driver's hands were pressed to her ears; her eyes were puddled with agony, and the face under the mask must be contorted. The jeep, its controls released, automatically slowed down and stopped.

Ramstan strove to overcome the pain from the whistling. He looked around for its origin but saw only that the other marines were also trying to block out the whistling with their palms. Their efforts were as useless as his. All round and below him, the Kalafalans on the street and the hotel steps were clamping their hands against their own ears, their mouths wide open as if they could ease their agony by letting the sound out from their mouths, their eyes also wide open, and their faces twisted, as if the whistling was a wringer through which their faces were being run.

Many were running headlong, stumbling, bumping into others, knocking them down or themselves falling. Others stood motionless as if turned into pillars of salt.

Some of the marines were screaming and so were many of the Kalafalans. He could hear them clearly through the whistling. Yet that awful noise should have overridden any other sound. That it did not meant that the whistling came from within himself. No! He was not originating it! That noise came from somewhere, but it was not transmissible in air or flesh; it came from something other than vibrations in the atmosphere.

'Run, Ramstan, run!'

The words were those of the voice in the tavern, but the voice was not the same. He did not recognize it.

He fought down the impulse to leap out of the jeep and run at top speed to … where? … anywhere to get away from the horror and the pain.

The driver shouted, 'For God's sake, what is it? I can't stand it! I'm going crazy!'

Ramstan had no need to shout to be heard, but he roared with panic and desperation. 'I don't know! Control yourself! Drive on! Drive on, I say!'

She took her hands away from her ears, said, shakily, 'Yes, sir,' and grabbed the wheel and put her feet on the pedals. She was quivering, and she looked as if she were about to scream back at the screaming in her head.

'There! There!' Ramstan said, pointing. Just beyond the hotel steps were two teardrop-shaped Tolt jeeps poised a half-meter above the sidewalk. Six armored and armed Tenolt sat in the first, the lower part of the prognathous faces masked, the woolly upper part between mask and helmet exposed. Five were in the second vehicle, two in the front seat and two in the back with

Branwen Davis seated between them. Though she was masked, she was easily recognizable. All were holding their ears, and the jeeps had automatically stopped.

Ramstan shouted at the driver, 'Get down there before they recover!' He pointed at the Tenolt.

He turned and bellowed at the marines. 'It's no use holding your ears! Get ready to attack! Fire when I give the order! Shoot to kill!'

They might not have been able to hear him above the screams and yells of the frantic crowd below them, but they understood his gestures. Their hands came down, and they unholstered their olsons.

As suddenly as it had arrived, the whistling was gone.

The pain dwindled away swiftly, leaving in its wake a relief almost as pleasurable as the pain had been agonizing. But there was no time for Ramstan to savor it. The Tenolt drivers had resumed control; the jeeps were moving up and towards the spaceport, though slowly. And, as was evident from the gestures of the Tenolt, they had seen the approaching Terrans.

A marine behind him screamed, 'Oh, God! Oh, God!'

Most of the Kalafalans had ceased shrieking, though their babbling was loud. But now they started screaming again, and many were pointing upwards and past Ramstan.

He turned and looked westward. The whistling had given him a sense of the unreality of the world which he had not yet overcome. Now the numbness and the feeling of being unmoored from the solidity of matter and time made a quantum jump. He could not understand, could not accept, what he was seeing. The thing in the sky should not exist. It was monstrous, unnatural and yet there it was in Nature. Vaguely, he felt betrayed.

From the valley far away drifted the bonging of thousands of gongs.

There, surely, was the thing that had caused the whistling. The *bolg*. It was a sphere hanging over the planet, blotting out most of the sky, a frightening body that looked close, close, another planet just about to fall and crush all life, smash the earth, rip it apart, make it reel with the inconceivable mass, melt earth and the rock beneath the earth with the force of the collision.

But it was not falling. It was moving swiftly eastwards, though not nearly quickly enough, if it had the mass evidenced by its size, to stay in orbit. It should have fallen by now. It was not falling. It was moving above the planet's atmosphere, perhaps just beyond the outer boundary, seemingly held there by its power.

It was round as a baseball, dark except for some paler markings which made it look like the face of a Halloween jack-o'-lantern carved by a palsied hand. A tiny horn, a truncated cone, projected from the bottom. Another horn, glittering in the light of the westering sun, stuck out from the center of the 'face' like a parody of a nose. And there was another on the near side on the equatorial line.

Ramstan clung to the back of his seat and stared as the ground westwards raised itself and curved, undulating, towards him. The distant mountain range shimmied. The back of the earth curved up and down like the swellings of a heavy sea. Forests lifted up and fell. Buildings rose and exploded and hurtled to the ground in fragments.

At the same time, a wind from the east began keening past him. The air struck him like a fist.

There was a cracking noise like a Brobdingnagian whip snapping. The ground waves passed beneath the two jeeps, the crest of one almost touching the bottom of the vehicles. Roaring, the hotel collapsed. In the distance, the spaceport control tower leaned over and then broke in half. Tiny figures spilled out of it.

He fought against withdrawing into himself and cutting off all the world outside his mind.

The rumble caught up with the snapping, then. The entire planet was growling and shaking – or so it seemed to him.

The people on the ground had been hurled down. Some were trying to stand up again but could not do it because the earth was rocking like slush in a bowl in the hand of a terrified person.

There were more cracks and rumbles. The earth split open in a great zigzag extending as far as he could see from the west. It sped like a crazed snake past him, people toppling into the suddenly opened crevasse, others, just on its edge, trying to crawl away or motionless with their faces pressed against the ground.

The wind became stronger. Hats, pieces of clothing, branches, leaves, and dust flew by him.

A voice was yammering from his skinceiver. Even though he held it close to his ear, he could not understand it. There was far too much noise from wind, screams, rumbles, and crackings. But he thought that he knew what the voice was warning him of.

The western sky between the horizon and that sphere was on fire.

At first, there seemed to be many, thousands, perhaps, of thin, blazing lines. They originated from above the atmosphere, no doubt, from the truncated cone which stuck out from the bottom of the gigantic thing. Meteorites. Missiles. Such as had swept fierily over Walisk. They were few, comparatively few, in the beginning. But now the curving lines from the upper air to the earth had become more numerous, seeming to expand, and now the sky between the vast bulge overhead and the ground was a solid curtain of fire.

The *bolg* was moving east, towards the Kalafalan capital, towards him, towards *al-Buraq*.

The ground undulated again.

The crust of Kalafala was tortured by the gravitational pull of the *bolg*. It was rising, was being ripped upwards, shaking, falling apart.

The air of Kalafala was being pulled upwards, also.

So was the oceanic area. Colossal tides would follow the path of the *bolg*.

Vomit threatened to spew out of him. But he looked at it again and saw that a shimmering corona, white shot with blue, surrounded it. Was that an energy discharge?

The world was literally falling down around him, and he had to get his marines back to the ship before that onrushing metal storm caught them. Or before a chasm opened up beneath *al-Buraq* and swallowed her. Yet ... he could not leave Branwen or the *glyfa* here.

The two Tolt jeeps were moving towards the spaceport now. Their passengers were bent over, their faces turned away from the wind smiting them. Below them, the natives were rolling over and over, pushed by the wind though their fingers dug into earth or they clung to pieces of rocks or fragments of buildings blown their way. Some of the natives spun into the first crevasse opened or into new ones which had formed afterwards.

Ramstan looked away and saw that the Tolt jeeps were accelerating.

He bellowed, 'After them! Shoot them! But don't hit Lieutenant Davis!'

Even if the situation had been that expected, he would not have been sure that they would immediately obey his orders. There had been no war on Earth for one hundred and thirty-five years, and these marines had not experienced even simulated combat. They had probably not expected to fight.

And now they were close to complete shock and panic. They would want to get back to ship as swiftly as possible. He did, too, but he would not permit himself to be diverted from his original mission.

Ramstan's skinceiver quit yammering. The voice was replaced by a shrill and loud series of dots and dashes. Code:

RETURN TO SHIP AT ONCE. RETURN TO SHIP AT ONCE. MISSILES FROM USO (unidentified Space Object) APPROACHING AT RATE OF 1999 KILOMETERS PER HOUR. ARRIVAL HERE ETA TEN MINUTES. REPEAT. RETURN TO SHIP AT ONCE. ALARAF IN NINE MINUTES. REPEAT. RETURN TO SHIP AT ONCE. ALARAF IN NINE MINUTES. REPEAT ...

Tenno was doing what he would have done. Regardless of who was or was not within ship, she would go into alaraf drive in nine minutes.

His mother's voice spoke. 'Get back to ship! Now! Don't waste a second! Now! If you don't, you'll die! All will be lost!'

Ramstan forgot to subvocalize. He said, 'I can't leave you here! And what about Davis?'

'Get back to *al-Buraq!*' the *glyfa* said, now switching to the voice of his commandant at the space academy. 'Now! Now! It's the *bolg*, you fool! The *bolg!*'

Light flashed in the rear Tolt jeep, the one in which Branwen was. Three short, bright, thin beams. Allah! Branwen had pulled her olson from its holster or snatched one from a marine by her. She had shot the two beside her. Another flash. She had shot the fourth.

The jeep dived, struck the ground, bounced up, half-rolled, tossing the box out – the box which held the *glyfa*, surely – crashed on its side, and rolled completely over, sliding until its side rammed into a tree.

The other Tolt jeep stopped, swiveled, and started back. The ship's captain was in it, and he had great coolness and courage. He had ordered the jeep to come back and pick up the *glyfa*. And perhaps to kill Davis. Or pick her up. After all, he would probably not have seen that she had beamed her escort. The *glyfa*, however, would be his overriding concern.

Ramstan yelled. His driver had slumped over. Her face was slack. The jeep had stopped. Out of the corner of his eye he saw, but did not fully register, that the other jeep with his marines had pulled up alongside. He raised the driver and saw the holes, cauterized, in the front and back of her head.

A Tolt had shot her.

A hole appeared in the windshield by him. A marine in the back seat bent over. His helmet had a very thin hole in its back.

The marines in his jeep did not seem to know what was happening. But those in the jeep by his were firing their olsons at the Tolt jeep.

The box was a meter or so near the edge of a ragged crack in the earth. Branwen had gotten free of the vehicle – its security magnetic field must have gone off when the jeep was wrecked – and she was crawling away from it. The ground was swelling beneath her, she was on top of a wave, and then the torn earth collapsed beneath her. Her legs and buttocks were buried beneath dirt.

The wave had shifted the box nearer to the crevasse.

'You damn fool!' the space academy commandant's voice said. 'Get back to ship! Leave me here! Come back and get me later! After the *bolg* is gone!'

'I might never find you!' Ramstan shrieked.

Something streaked fierily from the Tolt jeep. The jeep beside him exploded, and Ramstan felt heat and some stings on his side.

He did not remember how he had done it. But the body of the jeep driver was in the back seat and he was at the controls. His jeep shot by the Tolt jeep. A marine fell on him. He had been hit and had fallen on top of his captain.

Ramstan ignored the corpse and directed the jeep towards *al-Buraq*, which was panting a yellowish-red light. A port opened in her, Ramstan drove the jeep into it, and slammed on the brakes. Energy shot red-bluishly from its vents. The magnetic field cushioned him and prevented him from dashing out his brains against the control panel. The shock emptied him of action for a moment.

The port crew had scattered when they had seen the speeding jeep. Now they ran out and gathered around him. The entrance closed up like a healing wound; the illumination within the port became brighter.

'Take care of them!' Ramstan said, waving his hand to indicate the dead or wounded in the jeep. He ran through the corridors, speaking into his skinceiver while he did so.

'Is everybody in?'

'Everybody except your marines,' Tenno said. 'I mean those in the other jeep.'

'They're dead,' Ramstan said. 'Put ship in alaraf! Now! Destination: the Tolt bell!'

'Aye, aye, sir,' Tenno said. His face, on the screen moving along the bulkhead to Ramstan's right, was fixed, seemingly emotionless except for intensity on the next order.

'That's the thing that destroyed Walisk!' Ramstan said. Tenno did not reply, but he paled.

A few minutes later, Ramstan was on the bridge.

All there were pale, and their faces were strained. A few were calling on God under their breaths. They all stank of deep fright. Ramstan was not sure that he had not wet his own shorts.

'We can write off Kalafala,' Ramstan said. 'We weren't able to get to Davis. I'll have a report from personnel later. Did the Tenolt send any messages?'

'No, sir.'

'We're going back to Kalafala. We have to check it out. But not for some time.'

'What could that thing be?' Tenno said. His voice was low and trembling. His head shook.

'I don't know. But I think that it can detect our trail and follow us.'

'Follow us?' Tenno said. 'Why? How?'

'I don't know.'

Ramstan called Hu.

'We all need some antishock, Doctor.'

'I have it ready, Captain. I was just about to call you.'

A few minutes later, Hu, followed by two corpsratings, entered. They scanned every person to determine the amount each needed, and then applied the flat ends of their osmosers to the skins of the 'patients'. Ramstan immediately felt better; the sense of unreality and the numbness of perception faded.

Ramstan thought that it would be best if he told his officers why he was going to Tolt.

'I want to determine whether or not that monster has attacked Tolt.'

His thoughts kept slipping back to the *glyfa*. And near it would be what was left – not much – of Branwen Davis. Unless the Tolt officer in the jeep had rescued the *glyfa* and, perhaps, Davis.

He wondered if the *Popacapyu* had alarafed before the storm had swept over it. Or had it waited too long for its marines to return with the *glyfa*?

Six days later, the pear-shaped planet of Tolt filled the viewscreens. Clouds covered three-fourths of it, but the heat detectors and the analyzers showed that great fires were still raging in many areas. *Al-Buraq* curved around to the nightside; here, the large areas of heat were visible to the eye through the clouds.

'There's no use going down there,' Ramstan said. 'What happened is evident.'

Though he had no evidence at all that he was responsible for the destruction of so much life, for the slaying of billions of sentients, he did feel guilty.

Tenno motioned with his finger for Ramstan to join him in a privacy field.

'I don't think we should be overheard, Captain. I'm worried, justifiably so. It seems that the Tenolt were able to track us through alarafian space. If they can do that, why not someone – or something – else? That monster that's been destroying planets, for instance?'

Tenno paused, looking as if he did not want to say what he must say.

'What is it?'

Tenno swallowed, and he said, 'If it can track us, it could follow the path we've made from Earth back to Earth. Follow the space traces, I mean.'

'We don't know that,' Ramstan said, grabbing Tenno's arm. Tenno's pained expression made him release his grip.

'We don't know that it can't,' Tenno said. 'And that is what counts!'

'All right,' Ramstan said. 'One thing at a time. What concerns me most just now is the thing seemingly appearing from nowhere. I realize that anyone seeing us just come into a bell would think that we, too, popped out of nowhere. But this thing doesn't enter a bell at its edge. I'm not sure that it can't appear anywhere it wants to.'

'If that's true, it doesn't use alaraf drive. Not the kind we know.'

Tenno paused, then continued. 'Also, it seems to me that that horrible whistling might be caused by a ... a disrupting of normal space-matter structure. As soon as the thing is fully in normal space-matter and space-matter has resumed its normal structure – whatever that is – the whistling stops. I don't know. I'm just speculating. Whatever the thing is ... it's unheard of ... horrible ... horrible ... whoever would have thought ...?'

The vast, dark shape hovered in their minds, blotting out almost all thought except of it.

As soon as he could, Ramstan got rid of the pseudo-*glyfa* by sending it via ship's peristalsis to the trash disintegrator.

While *al-Buraq* circled Tolt, Ramstan paced in his quarters. During mess, he did his best to keep the conversation going and on light topics, but he failed miserably. After the third mess, when the drinks were brought in, he made an announcement.

'We're going to return to Kalafala.'

There was silence.

'By the time we get there, that thing should be through with its ... work. And it should be gone on its next hellish assignment. It may be tracking us down, though there's no proof that it is doing that. Anyway, if we do find it, or if it finds us, we'll not run away unless we have to.'

He paused and looked around at the pale faces.

'We'll test its attack capabilities. And if it looks as if we'll have a chance, we'll attack it!'

17

His plan was courageous but also probably foolish. However, the prospect of facing the enemy instead of running away seemed to raise the spirits of the crew.

Al-Buraq's probers searched for the *bolg* but could not detect it. There was no doubt that it was gone, its work done. An object of its size and mass could not have hidden. It could, however, and no one forgot it for a moment, appear seemingly from out of nowhere.

There was smoke covering Kalafala, but it was much less dense than that over Walisk and Tolt. Except for some small islands, the planet had only one continent, which had only the surface area of Greenland, and half of it was empty of people and vegetation. It should not have taken long for the Destroyer to ravage all land life, but it may have been acting automatically, a mindless thing that carried out its work according to the surface available, not the location of life.

Ramstan ordered *al-Buraq* to the capital. Since it had been the most heavily populated area, he said, it was the best place to make a detailed record of the effects of the cataclysm. Ship came down and poised twenty meters above the still-fissuring surface of the spaceport. He requisitioned for himself a small excavator craft. He did not explain why he was working with the other members of the survey, nor why his search plan placed them for several hours at a considerable distance from him.

Ramstan flew through the smoke at five meters above the surface while he watched the screens in front of him. When the probers indicated that he was in the same area as that in which the *glyfa* had fallen, he put the machine into a decreasing horizontal spiral. The hotel was gone except for some shattered pillars and some dented steel beams. The sidewalk was gone. The grass and the bushes and trees were gone. Much of the fertile earth had been washed or blown away, revealing a clay. Ramstan could not directly see this, but his probers indicated what was left. There were also the expected missiles, some on top of the clay, some wholly buried, some half-exposed.

A half hour passed, and he was beginning to think that the *glyfa* had been gulped into a fissure and was beyond the range of his ground-sonar. And then, as desperation mingled with fury slid through him, he saw the egg-shape on a screen. It was a meter and a half under the clay.

The box around it had been scattered in shreds by the missiles and the a-g units knocked off. The *glyfa* itself must have been pounded into the ground by several larger missiles and perhaps had fallen into a shallow fissure which had then closed up.

It did not take Ramstan long to direct the machine to cut a wide cylindrical hole around the *glyfa* with lasers and to pulverize the clay and suck it out. It took him more time to direct a robot arm down to put new a-g units on the ends of the *glyfa* and then to fit a unit over each end of the egg. The preset units made the *glyfa* weigh little enough for it to be sucked up through a pipe into the body of the machine.

Ramstan opened a cover behind the seat and pulled the egg loose from the clay sticking to it.

'You didn't think I could do it, did you?' Ramstan said.

Silence.

Shrugging, he put the egg in a case supposed to be used for specimens. He drove the machine back into *al-Buraq* and took the case to his quarters. There he washed the smoke and clay from it and placed it under the electron microscope. As he had expected, its sculpturing was undamaged by the missiles.

Again, he tried.

'It's I, Ramstan!'

'That makes two I's,' his mother's voice said in Terrish. 'I wasn't sure you'd return. Which meant that if you didn't, I ...'

'Yes?'

'It doesn't matter now.'

'It does to me,' Ramstan said. 'I must know certain things. Otherwise ...'

'Otherwise, what?'

'I may leave you here after all. Drop you to the bottom of the sea.'

'Of course you will. What is it you want to know? Aside from the questions you've asked so far.'

'At least tell me why you allowed Branwen Davis to steal you. You must have been aware that she was doing so. You may have known some time ago that she planned on doing it. Tell me why you permitted her to take you and why she did it. And if she was killed or went with the Tenolt.'

His mother's voice said, 'From your viewpoint, my powers are almost semidivine. Though I suspect you'd say semidemonic. But I lack what even the lowliest of most animal life has.'

It paused. Was it considering if it should reveal something that might make it vulnerable?

'That is mobility. The power to move on my own. If I'm placed on a hillside, then I must roll down it as helplessly as a stone or an egg. I must go where anybody who has the energy to move me wills that I go.'

It did not sound bitter. It was just stating a fact.

'You're evading my questions!' Ramstan said. 'What about Davis?'

'The Tolt captain picked her up. Perhaps he didn't kill her because he didn't know that she had shot the men with her. Or perhaps he wanted to torture her. In either event, she is useless to him now that he does not have me. But I suppose he'll be back soon to look for me.'

'I know,' Ramstan said. 'We're leaving soon. But tell me why Davis stole you? I think that the Tenolt abducted her from the experimental station on the north coast and forced her, somehow, to steal you and leave a fake in the safe. Why didn't you summon me when she came for you?'

'I didn't have my detectors on. I was ... voyaging ... and thus unaware of what was happening just then.'

Ramstan did not believe him. Even if it was quiescent then, it must have probed Davis' mind just as it had undoubtedly probed every mind within its range of detection.

'Why,' he said slowly, 'didn't the Tenolt take you? If they had time to get Davis, they had time to get you.'

'I have the power to confuse minds with certain electrical means. It's limited in range and time. But I made them forget me for the moment. And the Tolt in command while the captain was gone was screaming at him to get back. By the time the captain returned, he would have recovered from his mindstorm, but it was too late to try to get me again. The missiles were approaching too swiftly.'

'You still haven't told me why you didn't warn me about Davis.'

Silence.

'You won't answer that. Very well. What is the *bolg?*'

Silence.

Ramstan put it in the bulkhead-safe and went up to the bridge.

'It's possible, if not highly probable, that the Tenolt will be coming back,' he said to Tenno. 'We don't want to be here when they come. I don't know why Davis disobeyed my orders to stay within the port limits or why the Tenolt had her. We may never know. In any case, they attacked us, and we had to shoot back. We can assume that the next time they show, they'll attack us.'

Tenno asked no questions about Davis. Ramstan ordered that the survey parties return to *al-Buraq*. Within ten minutes, ship was sealed up and ready to go.

Ramstan felt in his jacket pocket. The three gifts of Wassruss nestled there. Why had the dying Webnite given them to him? Was the *glyfa* responsible in some circuitous fashion for that? Or was someone else moving pieces on this cosmic chessboard? He thought of the warning voice in the tavern and the flash of the figure in green and the figure that had seemed to him to be al-Khidhr.

'Set course for the Webn bell,' Ramstan said.

'Aye, aye, sir. The Webn bell it is.'

Ramstan called in the navigation chief, Suzuki.

'I'm just checking, Suzuki. The other bell in the Webn system is in the area of the first planet of Webn's sun, isn't it?'

Suzuki's brown face and slanting eyelids expressed curiosity. But she only said, 'Yes, sir.'

'Put in a course in NS drive for the first bell. I'll want it as soon as possible.'

'Just ask ship for it,' Suzuki said somewhat smugly. 'I laid it out long ago just in case we might need it.'

'Thank you for your zeal and foresight,' Ramstan said. 'But the next time you do something like that, tell me about it.'

He told himself that he need not have sounded as if he were rebuking her.

Fifty hours passed. Ramstan, when not in his quarters trying to get a response from the *glyfa*, roamed *al-Buraq*. He checked everything he could think of, mostly to keep himself occupied. Then Tenno called him just as he was about to take a nap.

'Ship will be in the first bell within two hours, sir.'

'Call me back in sixty minutes.'

After a few seconds of concentrated imagining of a black spot a few centimeters from his eyes and within his head, he fell asleep. A whistle from a screen woke him just as he was crawling through thick impeding brush from something dark and shapeless. He was whimpering.

He took a shower and dressed in a jumpsuit. Then he spoke to the *glyfa*, but got no reply. After eating a sandwich, he went up to the bridge.

'Did you check out the bell?' Ramstan said to Tenno.

'Yes, sir. It seems to be virgin. At least, the instruments indicate it is.'

Ramstan thanked him, and he ordered that *al-Buraq* go into alaraf. Two minutes later, they were within 500,000 kilometers of a planet. The star was GO-type, and the planet was T-type. *Al-Buraq* filmed the constellations. Ramstan particularly admired a giant blue star. Celestial inhabitants were staggeringly beautiful, and even long acquaintance with them had not staled their awesomeness.

'It won't be virgin territory any more,' Ramstan said. 'We're going to alaraf. Pioneer.'

Tenno seemed to be surprised. Not far off was a planet like Earth's, and he had expected that *al-Buraq* would survey it from orbit and perhaps descend to it.

Two minutes later, they were in what Ramstan knew to be another universe, if he had interpreted Wassruss' phrase correctly.

' "Ring the bell at the first entrance." '

' "And then?" '

' "Enter." '

' "And then?" '

' "Ring the bell at the third entrance." '

' "And then?" '

' "Ring the bell at the fifth entrance." '

Each bell was 'connected' to another bell. There were only two bells or windows, as they were sometimes called, in each area within the planetary system. Therefore, so Ramstan had reasoned, the third and fifth bells in Wassruss' chant were the third and fifth planets respectively in the systems of the universes alarafed into from Webn's universe.

Al-Buraq scanned the new system. It had ten planets.

Ramstan ordered that *al-Buraq* go to the neighborhood of the fifth planet. An hour after the entrance, Ramstan ordered that ship alaraf again.

Tenno obviously wondered why his captain was choosing different planets. Why didn't he just jump where he came out?

Ramstan could not tell him at this time the reason. He was not sure that he was on the right 'path'. He might be making a fool of himself by following what he believed to be instructions in the ancient chant. If so, only he would know it.

A planet distorted space-matter fabric in the area of its gravitational influence, the influence varying in accordance to its mass and its relation to other large relatively nearby masses and the square of the distance from the planet and its neighbors. It seemed to him that he may have discovered a principle hitherto unknown to Terran science by his following the directions in the chant. But it also seemed to him that the location and the mass of a planet did determine the 'direction' of the opening the alaraf ship took.

One of the theories about alaraf drive was that it was a form of time travel. When a ship jumped, it went into time. Backward while on the 'outward' journey, forward while on the 'return' journey. A ship leaving Earth in alaraf drive went back to a time when the Earth was elsewhere on her journey through space. That explained why the ship found herself in unknown space, the Earth and its sun nowhere visible.

But, if the *glyfa* had told him the truth, there were many universes. And each time a ship alarafed, it plunged through the 'wall' between two universes.

Ramstan ordered that ship alaraf again. And again they were in an area never seen before.

Ramstan ordered that *al-Buraq* proceed to the neighborhood of the seventh planet of the new system. It was done, but the bridge personnel were silent and tight-lipped.

'The Tenolt may have trouble finding us,' he said loudly. Let them chew on that for a while, he thought as he went to his quarters.

This time, the *glyfa* answered. Ramstan wondered if it had some deep reasons for its silences. Or was it double-minded, and did one mind take over the other now and then? No. That was a fantastic and incredible explanation. He was projecting onto it his own doubts about his own double-naturedness.

The *glyfa* asked him what he had been doing. As soon as it was fully informed, it said, 'You are doing well. But before you get to the only place to go beyond the ninth entrance, come to me.'

'Why?' Ramstan said.

'Whatever you do, don't tell them that I am on ship.'

'*Them*? Who's *them?*'

Silence.

18

On the right were three great stars, one red, one green, one yellow, each forming the point of a triangle. Making up the lines of the triangle were seven stars between each point, small and white.

Far 'below' these was a dark mass reminding Ramstan of the Horsehead

Nebula of Earth's universe. But the head formed by a vast 'dustcloud' profiled by blazing gases behind it looked like that of a troll. At least, that was what Nuoli said it resembled. To Ramstan it seemed more of an ifrit's head. The features were humanoid but bestial. Bestial humanoid. Yet beautiful and awesome.

The third planet of the system beyond the ninth entrance was T-type, and its sun was GO. It had been 707,000 kilometers from *al-Buraq* when she had burst from the other universe. Ramstan had at once ordered her to proceed at top speed in NS drive to the planet.

'"Go to the only place to go."'

Ramstan thought that, if Wassruss' chant was not nonsense, that phrase indicated that the inhabitable planet was his goal. Fortunately, he did not have to choose between two planets. He had not expected to. No solar-type system so far found had more than one inhabitable planet. There was a narrow range of distance from the sun which determined whether or not life could originate and thrive on a planet. And sometimes even then the planet in that range was biohostile.

Life was rare and fragile. Yet it was also frequent and tough. Give it a foothold, and it fought to hold on, to flourish, to evolve into forms impossible to imagine until seen.

Al-Buraq's probes reported that this world was slightly smaller than Earth but had slightly more mass. She went into orbit just above the atmosphere and over the only continent. This was much longer than it was wide and stretched around the southern hemisphere in the temperate zone. Its two extremities were separated by 3,000 kilometers of islandless ocean.

'"To the tree which does not stand alone."'

How in the seven hells was he to find that one? Except for freshwater bodies and the upper slopes of the highest mountains, the continent was covered with thick trees. There were no meadows or open spaces of any consequence.

Ramstan sent ship down into the atmosphere about twenty kilometers above land-level. He ordered her to follow a path which would eventually cover every hectare. They soon determined that there was much bird and insect life in the upper reaches of the forest and many species of animal. Among these were monkey- and apelike creatures.

The biodetectors showed that each tree was attached to its immediate neighbors by four to six thin, leafless, glossy-black branches extending horizontally in a circle from the upper middle part of the trunk. These formed an interconnecting and supporting system extending continent-wide. The trees on the edges of the beaches and seacliffs only grew the connectors inward to their neighbors.

Though approximately one out of a hundred trees was dead, they did not seem to fall until completely rotted and eaten by the insects. Where this had happened, treelets were growing up from the mounds of the dead predecessors.

'"To the tree which does not stand alone."'

Allah! How could he make any sense out of that?

He began pacing back and forth but stopped after a minute. It was not good for the bridge people to see him so obviously worried. He ordered Toyce to call him if any sentient life was detected.

'Yes, sir. But sentiency may not be obvious.'

'Do the best you can.'

He went to his quarters and there resumed pacing. Once, he stopped to take the *glyfa* out, but it did not respond.

'I need you now!' he cried, and he struck it a glancing blow with his fist. The round a-g units attached to it did not prevent it from rolling over and dropping off the table onto the deck. The deck quivered, not from the impact itself but from *al-Buraq's* reflex to what it considered might be Ramstan's fall. Or was it due to ship's monitoring of his emotional state? She was always sensing him, the play of electrical fields on his skin, his body temperature, the tone of his voice.

He turned, jumped, and gasped. The green man was standing by the far bulkhead. His arm was outstretched, and a fingertip was on the center of a seven-sided screen.

The vision lasted no longer than two eyeblinks.

The green-shrouded man had indicated the empty screen. What did that have to do with the tree that does not stand alone? Perhaps nothing. Something else might have been meant by that fingertip on the center of a blank field.

Did al-Khidhr really exist? Or was the thing that he, Ramstan, had seen just a form beamed by someone? Had al-Khidhr been shot forth like a three-dimensional hologram from Ramstan's four-dimensioned brain, self-awareness being the extra dimension?

Something, objective or subjective, nonhuman or human, was trying to *tell* him something.

He began pacing again but halted after twelve steps. Perhaps the vision was not referring to the screen as a whole but to its center. *Look for the center* was the message. The center of what? His own center, the inmost recess of his being?

No.

Look in the center, the middle, of the forest.

That could be it.

At one time there may have been only one tree on this continent, an Urgenitor, the hermaphroditic Adam-Eve of all these now existing. Possibly, it had stood or was still standing in the geographical center of the land-mass, and where it was was his goal.

He called the bridge. The scanners having fed the data into *al-Buraq's* brain, the geographical center and the middle point of the land-mass were located. The latter was that point halfway between the two extremities of the continent and halfway between the north and south coasts. Since the two centers did not coincide, Ramstan ordered that ship go to the latter first.

Her central part contracted into a rocket-shape, her lower outer part shaped like the wings of antique airplanes, *al-Buraq* sped above the surface of the green arboreal-ocean. At 300 kilometers from her destination, she began descending and decelerating and within ten minutes was poised over it. Ten meters below the bottom of her hull, the tip of the highest tree rocked in the wind. Ramstan did not think that it was a coincidence that the tallest and most massive tree grew from the continental center.

The sun had almost zenithed. The sky was cloudless. The only life visible to the unaided eye was aerial, large insects, primitive birds, and some small and some large mammals. At least, the latter were assumed to be mammals since they were furred. The biggest had wingspreads of eight meters, batlike bodies and wings, and bloodhoundish faces, but their cries were monkeylike. They were too heavy to take off from the tree branches, and their webbed feet suggested that they used water as their landing fields. The nearest large lake was 50 kilometers away, so the dogbats must have an amazingly extended range of flight. They dived down and caught the smaller birds and mammals and ate them while flying.

Though the tossing green surface looked lifeless from a distance, it was, when seen closely, surging with vitality. In addition to the winged things skimming it, insects and some unclassifiable creatures crawled, ran, or hopped on the broad, dark-green, leathery-looking, cupped, and immense leaves of the Brobdingnagian tree just below them. The foliage did not swarm with the creatures, but it was well-populated.

This was where the top branches met the open air. What about below that level?

The viewbeams could not penetrate the density more than a few meters.

Nuoli, looking at the magnification on the screens, said, 'You'd think that the leaves below, all growth below the upper leaves, would die from lack of sunlight. Surely ...'

Ramstan said, 'Yes?'

'Surely, it can't be as thick as it seems. At least, elsewhere, the sun must be able to penetrate here and there.'

What could live down there besides pale things of low or no intelligence, blind, moving slowly in the darkness?

But if 'the tree which does not stand alone', meant anything, it must apply to the prodigious plant below him. It stood higher than the others by a thousand meters. Its circumference, the circle formed by the tips of the branches at a level with the tops of the surrounding trees, was 10,000 meters. Outside the edge of the circle, through small breaks here and there in the foliage of the smaller parts of trees, the connecting branches could be seen.

'The mothertree?' Ramstan muttered to himself.

The sunlight glanced from some of the tossing leaves, which seemed to contain mica. There was nothing visible to suggest anything sinister. Yet, he felt that there was danger under those leaves. Not the expected peril of feral animals or poisonous reptiles. Something or some things which he could not possibly anticipate, entities which had been beyond the ken, and still might be, of humankind.

The unknown had always held fear. The human mind was constructed to project fear into the nonexplored whether or not there were reasons to be afraid. On the other hand, the unknown also enticed. Humans could not resist its allure and had to plunge into whatever dangers might exist there. Also, there was a fascination about fear itself that had its allure. Humans, some humans, anyway, liked to be afraid – to a certain degree. Perhaps the basic drive here was the desire to test their courage. No, that was not the only basic. Curiosity, monkey curiosity, also pulled them into the unknown.

This situation, however, differed from any which Ramstan had been in. He had always felt confident that he could handle any predicament. But this one ... there was something about it ... something so vast and powerful that it made him feel very small and weak ... no ... he must not think like that. Even smallness and weakness had their powers, their advantages.

'Besides,' he said aloud, 'I am Ramstan!'

Nuoli, who was standing near him, jumped. She said, 'What?'

Suzuki was also looking strangely at him.

'Nothing,' Ramstan said. 'Nothing.'

So ... he was Ramstan? So what? He was unique, but so was every sentient being. So, for that matter, was every one of the millions of seemingly alike trees on this land. The difference was that he was sentient, self-conscious, and he had a self or a series of selves called Ramstan, and that Ramstan had a body-mind and a development through a unique environment that no one else had. No one, not even God. God might *know* every sentient, might even participate in the full consciousness and unconsciousness of every unique sentient. But not even He could *be* that person. There were limits even to God's powers. Which, since God was by definition all-powerful, meant that God was not God. Which meant that the definition should be restated.

He had no time to think of the implications of that. He ordered that a launch be readied for take-off in ten minutes. He also told Tenno that he, Ramstan, would be on it.

'We're going down to the surface,' he said.

Tenno had obviously been speculating on his captain's reasons for coming here. He said, 'You're following the directions in Wassruss' chant?'

'Yes.'

Ramstan hesitated, then said, 'It may be in vain. But, after all, our mission is scientific, and anthropology, I mean, sentientology, is one of our main studies. This chant ... it's so curious ... it intimates that there have been alaraf drives in the very distant past ... perhaps before humanity was quite evolved from the ape. Anyway, I have more than one motive for traveling through the walls of the universes ...'

Tenno interrupted. *'Walls?'*

That slip checked Ramstan for an instant. He opened his mouth, could not get the words out, glared, shut his mouth, briefly closed his eyes, then spoke.

'Yes, walls. I'm not at all certain that we are, per theory, traveling from one galaxy to another either by time travel or by tunnel-bell. You know that it's been suggested, though, I'll admit, not seriously, that when a ship jumps it penetrates the "wall" between one universe and the next.'

He paused, and Tenno said, 'The multiverse hypothesis. Though, really, it's not even a hypothesis. It's a wild speculation, and ...'

'I tend to think that it's more than that. But what's the difference what the truth is? In this situation, anyway. You're in charge of ship now, Tenno. You have your orders on what to do if the Tenolt or that monster appears.'

Tenno said, 'Aye, aye, sir,' and saluted.

Five minutes later, Ramstan was seated in the launch. It left its port and nosed down toward the tree. Seen from ship with the naked eyes, the plant seemed a solid monolith. As the launch neared it, however, its occupants saw vast openings, the entrances to the emptinesses between the level of branches. The branches were gigantic, ranging from 50 to 70 meters in radius near the trunk, and were supported about a third of their length from the trunk, by arboreal flying buttresses, branches growing at a 45-degree angle upward from the trunk and merging into the lower part of the branches they upheld. In the outer part of the vertical aisles formed by the branches was a space of about 100 meters high. The launch moved into the aisle formed by the seventh and eighth branches from the tip of the tree.

They went abruptly from the brightness and a not-quite-comfortable warmth into an illumination like that just before dusk. The temperature was another degree lower.

The animal, bird, and insect population here was more numerous and much noisier than the aerial life above the tree. The creatures did not have to go down to the ground to drink water. It oozed from the branches where the thick bark formed shallow crevices and collected into little pools and springs.

Here and there, the sunlight broke through and fell on hairy, scaled, feathered, or chitinous things. It also was reflected from the huge leaves, some of which curled upward and contained rainwater.

Ramstan ordered the launch to stop long enough for a *yeoshet* to pull loose three leaves for specimens.

'The glittering stuff can't be mica,' he said. 'It would make the leaves too heavy.'

The upper transparent part of the rowboat-shaped launch closed down, and it went on with its passengers protected from attack by the sometimes aggressive actions of the citizens of the tree. Most of these consisted of fruit hurled or excrement dropped by squadrons of insects. Several times, Ramstan had to order the de-icing liquid released over the upper-sheet shell to kill the cloud of insects obscuring the pilot's vision.

When the launch dropped 600 meters, it was no longer among such thick masses of insects. There were plenty at this level, but they did not gather on the upper part very heavily.

Though the buzz and screech were less, the darkness and cold increased. On reaching the twentieth branch-level down, Ramstan had the lights turned on. It was still possible to see objects without them but easier with them.

At ten more levels down, the air temperature stabilized. The launch people were quite comfortable, since the vehicle was air-conditioned, but the exterior heat was not quite enough to be comfortable. It was at this level that Ramstan noticed that many of the leaves were turned at different angles. And as the launch sank, the illumination became more, not less.

Nuoli said, 'It's a system to reflect sunlight down.'

Here they first saw the seemingly parasitic plants sprouting from the trunk and branches. These were of three kinds: toadstool-shaped, cone-shaped, and seven-pointed star-shaped on long drooping stalks. All glowed with a light, each having a will-o'-the-wisp brightness, but the total illumination was that of just-after-dusk. The eyes of some animal, bird, and insect life glowed as if reflecting light from a campfire. Since there was not enough light for this, Nuoli speculated that the eyes had their own source of illumination. The winking of these, she said, reminded her of the glowings from Terran fireflies.

'Some sort of cold light activated by electrochemical means.'

Though he'd seen many strange things since his first landing on a non-Terran planet, Ramstan thought that this phenomenon was among the strangest. It also seemed unexplainable – at least, for the moment. Fireflies excited their photonic-emitting tails as sexual signals. Did these creatures flash their eyes off and on for the same reason? If they did, the flashing must leave them temporarily blinded.

He thought, Perhaps the light shed by so many of the things and events

I've encountered recently, especially the *glyfa*, should be illuminating. But it's blinded me.

Another curious thought strayed or swooped across the field of his mind.

What if these creatures were in league with, or controlled by, the entities he guessed were at the base of this tree? What if their eye-flashings were signals, biological Morse, to the entities that his imagination had visioned as waiting for him; the signals telling the shadowy things at the base that an object bearing passengers from a far distance and time was approaching and what the passengers looked like?

He failed to discern a pattern in the flashings. They seemed to be just so much 'noise'. What seemed to him randomness might, however, be intelligence to someone else.

The launch dropped down at the rate of ten kilometers an hour in a vertical zigzag around the branches. The photon-emitting growths increased until branch and trunk seemed to be encrusted with strangely cut jewels. Unlike Terran trees, the horizontal branches at the lower levels became shorter and more slender. Nevertheless, the flying-buttress supports were thicker and extended further out. This, Ramstan supposed, was because the luciferian plants were so many that they heavily weighed down the branches.

The birds and beasts became less numerous with every lower level, but the insects were larger. Some rather huge species, rat-sized, had transparent flesh through which glowed the plants they had eaten. Their thumbnail-sized droppings also shone, though with a lesser light. These monsters were not true insects. Terran insects could not grow so large. Being lungless and depending on spiracles as air-inlets, their size was limited. A mutant Terran insect as large as a rat would die because oxygen would not flow into the inner parts of its body.

One species of the larger insects had a long slightly downward-curved proboscis and a rod growing from the back of the head. The length of this was equal to the length of the creature's body, and at its end was a ball which glowed. This reminded Ramstan of certain fish of the Earth's oceanic abysses. They used the light at the ends of their rods to lure other fish close enough to be caught and eaten.

Another creature was a basketball-sized, balloon-shaped arachnid which floated in the air and traveled from place to place, usually branch to leaf or vice-versa, by shooting out a sticky thread for anchor and then pulling itself in by the thread. It also jetted out the thread to entangle smaller insects and so draw the prey to its mouth, which was surrounded by six tiny, clawed arms which unceasingly moved except when they seized the living food.

The launch sank deeper. It passed a snakelike thing which was at least 12 meters long. Its six-sided head bore four long curving horns; its eyes were huge and four-sided; its tongue was froglike, speeding out to catch insects or the very small, emerald-green lizardoids and, once, a tiny snake.

'The zoologists would go ape here,' Nuoli said.

Ramstan did not comment. He was wondering what kind of sentients would choose to live here. Wassruss' chant had implied that at least three made this continent their dwelling place. But the chant was very old, and those mentioned in it might have moved away or died. For no rational reason, he believed that this was not true, that the three would be here. Which could mean that they had an incredibly long lifespan. Incredibly? Yes, to someone who did not know the *glyfa*.

Abruptly, the launch entered a zone which seemed to be lifeless. Of course, there was life; the tree was not dead. But there were no insects, birds, or animals. And a sense of timelessness stole through Ramstan. There *was* time – as measured by the launch's chronometer, by the beatings of his heart, by the motion of machine and people. Nevertheless, Ramstan felt that time had died or at least had slowed down so much that it was in suspended motion or was sleeping. He felt somewhat disorientated, slightly dizzy, and vaguely and weakly panicky.

He ordered that the upper covering be opened and that no one speak or make any noise. For some reason, he was strongly compelled to *listen*.

Listen to what? For what?

Not knowing made him crackle with the static electricity of panic as if giant but impalpable fingers were rubbing his dry nerves.

The others, though they said nothing, rolled their eyes as if they, too, sniffed danger in the wind. But there was no wind except for the almost imperceptible movement of air made by the passage of the launch.

Ramstan looked upward, though he did not think that there was any peril – at this moment – from above. The sun and sky were blocked out by the branches and the leaves. They were dead, buried under vegetation. A strange thought.

As dead as time itself.

Yet, if the chant told of true things and beings, the death of time or of its near-dead heartbeat meant life for those who waited for him.

Waited? How could they know he was coming?

Perhaps the *glyfa* had told them.

But the *glyfa* was silent and would not speak to him now.

When the upper part of the launch had been opened the first time, Ramstan had smelled a faint stench, not altogether unpleasant, of decaying plants and animal excrement. Something in it reminded him of rotting toadstools, though he did not think that he had ever smelled these before. The air had also been very dry or had seemed to be so. He was not certain, since he was beginning to distrust his senses. Now the odors were gone, though the lack did not make the air seem healthy. Indeed, it was like that of a tomb in which only the dust of corpses remained and all corruption was over. But the tomb should have been as dry as the mouth of a man lost in a desert and without water for three days. Yet, the humidity had suddenly risen. As the launch plunged soundlessly into the timeless zone, the water content increased. Ramstan suddenly felt that the moisture was stealthily increasing and, without warning, they would pass from a watery air into airless water. His throat closed up.

It was as if the planet itself had begun sweating. Drops rolled down his forehead and into his eyes, saltless water which, when licked, gave him the sensation that his tongue was betraying him. Despite the wetness, however, he smelled nothing dank or rotting. The crowded growths on the tree shone even more brightly; their cold illumination seemed to have stopped death and decay. Or to have slowed it, since there was no stopping these universal basics. Another strange thought.

He started, and he hated himself for this unwilling signal of his nervousness. He glared at Nuoli for having put her hand on his arm.

Was that touch the intimation of death? Touch. Death. Another strange thought. Strange? No thoughts were strange, but the unfamiliar or not easily available to his conscious would seem so.

Touching.

'There's something down there. It looks like a big hole,' the tec-op said. 'It's between two roots. Roots of this tree, I mean.'

Ramstan checked on the report. The screen showed a shadowy equilateral triangle, and the readout indicated that it was 64 meters long on each side. Another readout showed that it contained a clear liquid. The bottom of the well, probably stone, was 64 meters from the surface.

The launch sank unchecked by any order from Ramstan, passed tremendous wrinkled treetrunk bark almost covered by the glowing growths, and, after what seemed like a long time, though Ramstan still was seized by a sense of timelessness – curious paradox, but were not all paradoxes curious? – the launch was at the edge of the well nearest the tree.

There was no lining of the well, no coping, only bare earth around the air and the water. The three sides plunged straight down and were smooth as mud pressed by a trowel.

The launch moved out, its undersurface lights filling the well like honey.

There were three creatures moving through or on the surface of the well.

19

'It isn't water,' the tec-op said. He pointed at the column of numbers by the side of the screen. He said, 'See, sir. It's a liquid, but it's heavier than water. Specific gravity is 1.6. Just a second, sir. There. The spectrographic analysis. *Jesus!* Nothing like it in the comparison bank!'

Nuoli, who'd been looking over the side of the launch, spoke. 'One of them is hopping over the surface of ... whatever it is.'

Ramstan told the pilot to take the vehicle down to ten meters above the well. Meanwhile, the tec-op had been scanning on all sides for the 'old house' which Wassruss had mentioned. He could not find it, but the building might be on the other side of one of the immense swellings at the base of the trunk. These, which plunged into the ground to become roots, were wider in diameter than ten subway tunnels put together.

The face looking up at him, the grinning face of the hopper, startled and repulsed him. It was humanoid but far more triangular than any *Homo sapiens*'. The hairless, deeply seamed, and leathery upper part of the skull projected so far over the face that it could have been substituted for an umbrella. A wide, blue vein passed over the central part; it pulsed sluggishly as if it were filled not with blood but with a growing colony of microbes or some yeasty organisms.

The overhanging forehead ended abruptly; the division between it and the face was right-angled. The face seemed to be something attached with adhesive to the bottom of the dome. The two eyes were deep, deep and dark blue. They were also huge, apparently one and a half times the size of Ramstan's, though he could not be sure. The tec-op's screen indicated that the creature was three meters tall.

Just below the eyes was not a nose but a large round appendage of leathery flesh darker than the face, the color of which was a pale red. There did not seem to be any nostrils or openings of any kind in the projection. It pulsed like the vein on top of its skull.

The mouth was much more like a human's; the lips were very everted. The jaw was thick, and the chin was a ball with a deeply punched-in, six pointed star.

'Some dimple,' Nuoli muttered.

The ears were very small, flat, close to the face, and their convolutions were nonhuman alto-relief arabesques.

Ramstan ordered the magnifying power to be increased so he could look directly into the wide-open mouth. The teeth were like a pig's; the purplish tongue was warted.

The red leathery body reminded Ramstan of a kangaroo's, but its tail ended in a wide fan and its feet were wide, splayed, and webbed, a frog's. It used the feet and the tail to propel itself over the surface of the strange liquid.

Its upper limbs, however, were quite human and so were its hands.

The 'wise one who swims' was slowly circling the well near its wall. It looked like an extinct salmon, though it was at least twelve meters long, six times the length of the average man laid out for his funeral. Another strange thought. Why had he used that comparison?

Ramstan was flabbergasted. He'd assumed that the three spoken of in the chant would be sentient. It was possible though not probable that the hopper was. But a fish could not be sentient.

Looking directly at the 'cold-blood who drinks hot blood' hurt his eyes and made him feel even more disorientated. It was a shimmer of pale-reddish light fringed by purplish light. The glowing body expanded and contracted; its major length was ten meters, its minor, nine, and its major height was three meters and its minor, two. Now and then, in no regular pattern that the scan-computer could determine, the shimmering was cut off, and Ramstan got a flash of the thing behind the light. It seemed to him at first that it looked like a mixture of bat and octopus. It had a head, but it was on top of the central part of an oblong body, not at one end. The features and the teeth, if they were teeth, were like a South American vampire bat's. He had no sooner fixed that in his mind than the next glimpse showed him a broad face, half lion, half human, and a hint of something else. He did not know what the something else was.

Nuoli said, *'Jumala!'* and spoke then in Terrish. 'I saw into its eyes. They looked black, genuinely black. And ... I must have been seeing things ... my imagination ... I thought I saw stars deep within them. Constellations ... a gas cloud ... shining ... white.'

Ramstan did not reply. He ordered the launch taken to a meter above the head of the hopper. It had sunk to its waist, but now it began thrusting its webbed and splayed hands and feet against the liquid. It rose swiftly, spread out flat on the surface, then reared upright. And it began hopping.

Ramstan told the com-op to put some Urzint phrases into the translator. He did not believe that these would be understood, but Urzint was the interplanetary language in the areas where he'd been, and he had to try something.

The hopper stopped, began sinking, and also began laughing. At least, the hooting sounded somewhat like laughter.

The huge fish rolled so that its right eye was above the surface, and this regarded the launch steadily.

The shimmering thing did not move.

Ramstan was not the only person startled when the hopper gabbled in an unfamiliar language full of throaty and hissing sounds, then switched to Urzint.

'Go to the house! Go to the house! Go to the house!'

Nuoli was the first to break the silence in the launch. 'What I tell you three times is true,' she murmured.

'It's not indicative but imperative,' Ramstan said. 'Nothing to do with validity.'

'Well, at least we know it's sentient.'

'Not necessarily,' he said. 'It may be like a parrot. Trained to utter the directions when it's spoken to by strangers. Or ...'

'But in Urzint?'

Ramstan did not comment. Obviously, the Urzint people must have been here at one time. Or perhaps the hopper had met the legendary pachydermoids on some other planet.

He ordered the launch to rise to the left. That seemed as good a direction as the right, though he may have had psychological reasons for choosing it.

The house, if it could be called such, was located three root-swellings over from that by the well. The distance from the well was 300 meters, which Ramstan would not have said was 'nearby'. It was three structures arranged vertically or perhaps was one structure with three stories which only looked like separate ones stacked. If it, or they, were a habitation, it was certainly one he had never before encountered.

The main body of each was an oblate sphere from the equator of which extended a long tapering body toward the tree. He at first thought that each looked like a round birdhead with a long bill. Then he perceived it as a spermatozoon with its thick head and long thin tail, except that the tail was straight, not curving. His third impression was of a mace, a staff at the end of which was a big ball for bludgeoning. The spheres were, according to the scanner, 50 meters in diameter and the extensions were 100 meters long.

The bottom structure was green; the middle one, blue; the top one, black. Over each a rusty-red lichenous growth formed circles and near-squares and rough triangles but with enough of the metallic-looking surface exposed to reveal its color. The growth was thick enough to provide nesting places for the archeopteryxlike birds and various species of lizardoids and insects. Also, and this surprised the Terrans because they had by now assumed that this planet's birds were in a primitive stage of evolution, there was an owl, or what looked like one, and a storkish avian. The 'owl' cachinnated at them, its cry sounding like the hopper's laughter, and flew off on snowy black-barred wings. The 'stork' looked once at the launch and then began jabbing itself in the breast plumage, apparently in search of parasites.

'They may not be indigenous,' Nuoli said.

Ramstan thought that she could be right, but he did not say so. Her comment annoyed him; she had always been too given to talking when it would have been better to be silent or to confine herself to elemental moans and sighs and screams.

Moreover, except for the owl's cry, which had broken the glassy silence or – strange thought – blasphemed it, there was a lack of sound even deeper than that in the levels where life had ceased to be evident. Ramstan suddenly realized that this silence had existed since he had entered the seemingly nonzoic area.

Whatever his misgivings, starts, and too-late perceptions, the air was heavy, motionless, and dark. The light-shedding plants were less numerous than above. Around him was a twilight, brooding in between day and night. Brooding.

Something, or some things, sat and waited for him, but their thoughts were not entirely on him.

'It's spooky,' Nuoli said.

As the launch settled like a sinking canoe in the deeps, Ramstan told the marines and sailors to have their weapons ready. But they were not to hold them. The holsters for the olsons should be unsealed and the larger arms should be on the deck out of sight of anyone in the house.

'We don't want to appear belligerent,' he said.

They looked as if they'd like to have much more information than this. For instance, why were they here and what was in the house?

The launch settled on the thick lichenish growth which spread from the building and covered the earth between the two colossal root-swellings. Nobody spoke for a moment; the silence was as if sound itself had died.

After a long look at the 'house', Ramstan said, softly, 'I'll go alone.'

A section of the lower hull slid open as the covering was lifted. Ramstan walked through the opening onto a collapsible ladder, a series of seven steps, which slid out from the hull. He sank in the growth up to his calves, smelling for the first time a faint odor from it. It reminded him of fermenting grass in a compost heap. He walked through the impeding stuff and up a gentle slope to the house. It seemed to stare back at him without eyes.

He paused before and below the outward curve of the first story.

'"Knock at the entrance,"' Wassruss had said.

What entrance? The house had neither door nor window.

He did the only thing he could do. He raised his fist and beat on what looked like metal but was warmer than metal would have been in this cold air and felt springy. He could hear no sound from inside the sphere. He had expected a reverberating echo, a booming.

After striking three times, he waited, his fist upraised for more hammering. Within a few seconds, the seamless wall showed a faint line, round and with a diameter wide enough to easily admit him. He wondered if the door was regulated for the occasion. If he had been much shorter or much taller, would the seam have accommodated his height?

Instead of a section withdrawing or coming out, a panel swinging one way or the other, the area within the seam became wavy, then misty, then disappeared. He was confronted by a circular hole.

If there was a pressure differential, he could hear or feel no air blowing out or in. Beyond the hole was darkness. The light from the plants did not penetrate it. Ramstan shouted in Urzint instead of speaking softly as he had planned to.

'I am Captain Ramstan of the Terran exploratory interstellar ship, *al-Buraq*! I come in peace! And I have questions.'

He felt foolish saying this, but what else could he say?

Immediately following his declaration, he saw, or thought he saw, a dim flash of green in the darkness.

His heart had been pounding hard before this. Now it accelerated.

Al-Khidhr?

Slowly, the darkness faded as light built up, seeming to leak out from every square centimeter of the walls, ceiling, and floor of the huge room. At first, he could not distinguish among the furniture and the three beings standing in the middle of the room. The room was round, and the doorways were seven-sided. The ceiling was a pale white; the walls, pale red; the floor, where not covered by a very thick, white, furry rug, was pale green. There were about a dozen mirrors against the walls or forming part of them. Their bases were set on the floor, and their sides tapered up, making long triangles, curving with the walls, their apexes meeting in the center of the domed ceiling. From this point hung a chain made of thin golden links and ending in an emerald the size of Ramstan's head.

A little red-furred animal with a long thin snout and great tarsierlike eyes was curled around the jewel. The one red eye that Ramstan could see was directed at him. Ramstan wondered how the creature had gotten to the emerald; it was so high above the floor that the beast could not possibly have jumped to it.

The furniture was sparse and consisted of fragile-looking chairs and sofas and tables of ornately carved black-and-white striped wood. The legs were very short. Here and there were enormous pillows piled around rugs folded over three times.

Omitting the front 'door', there were three oval entrances to the great chamber, one in front of him and two on each side.

One of the three beings, the one in green robes, stepped forward.

She spoke in Urzint. 'Greetings, Ramstan. You've taken a long time getting here.'

The one clad in blue said, 'You should have been here much sooner. That is the fault of the *glyfa*.'

The one in black said, 'Ask, but be willing to pay the price.'

20

Ramstan felt as if his blood had become mercury and was heavily draining into his feet.

The voice of the green-robed one was the voice he had heard in the Kalafalan tavern.

'The *bolg* kills all but one! ... God is sick ...'

She? He? It? Whatever sex the green one was or was not, the voice was hers.

In that moment, he knew, though he could not rationally justify his knowledge, that the green one was female. And it seemed to him that the others were also female.

Moreover, he believed that she was the shadowy, briefly seen figure in the hotel and the being who had appeared on Webn while he and Benagur were quarreling.

Was she also the old person he had seen when he was entering his parents' apartment in New Babylon?

Encountering these three had been like a tremor before a great earthquake. Hearing her voice was the great earthquake itself. Now, he was seized with aftershocks. He could not stop trembling, and he was afraid that he was going to vomit.

'You should sit down,' the one in green said. Her eyes were large and as green as her robe. Deep wrinkles radiated from them; her face was that of a ten-thousand-year-old mummy. The teeth in the seamed lips were black, though he did not think they were rotten. She was ugly, yet the hideousness went beyond ugliness. She was also very beautiful, not as a young woman was beautiful but as an ancient star was beautiful. Something radiated from her, and her eyes seemed to shed kindness. Or compassion.

Certainly, he had wrongly conceived the green one.

Whatever she was, she was not al-Khidhr. His childhood religion had made a certain mold in his mind, a preconception, and her image had been fitted into that mold.

Again, the green one said, 'You should sit down.'

Ramstan looked around. If he did sit, and he needed to do so before he collapsed, he'd have to look up at them. He'd be at a psychological disadvantage. Allah knew that he was weak enough now, that he needed every advantage and strength he could get.

'No, thank you,' he said. Surprisingly, his voice was firm.

'As you will,' the green one said.

She sat down on a pile of rugs and leaned back against some giant pillows. The others also seated themselves, their legs crossed under their robes. They did not have to care that they must have to look up at him. Or perhaps they were giving him a chance to rest and to be on the same level at the same time.

He lowered himself on a pile of rugs and crossed his legs. He said, 'Pardon me. I must tell my crew what's happening.'

After speaking briefly into his skinceiver and telling Nuoli that no one must follow him as yet, he waited for a few seconds for his 'hosts' to speak. When they did not, he said, 'You know who I am. But I don't know ...'

'At present,' the green-robed one said, 'I am called Shiyai.'

The black-robed one cackled, and she said, 'At present! She has been Shiyai for a billion of your years, Ramstan!'

The others broke into high-pitched laughter. When that died, the black-robed one said, 'I am called Wopolsa.'

'And I,' the blue-robed one said, 'am called Grrindah.'

'What we are called and who we are are not the same,' Wopolsa said.

'These are my sisters,' Shiyai said, waving a withered, blue-veined, dark-spotted hand. 'Sisters in name only, since we do not belong to the same species and were born more years apart than you can imagine, even if you can encompass the time in a phrase.'

'Language is cheap,' Wopolsa said. 'Time is dear.'

'Yet, waste time as much as you wish, there is always as much as before,' Shiyai said.

'If you are like us,' Grrindah said.

'And one other,' Wopolsa said.

'Or perhaps two others,' Shiyai said.

The three looked at each other and burst into their nerve-rubbing laughter again.

If they were trying to put him at ease, they were failing. His stomach was folding in on itself like a flower at nightfall.

'What is this planet called?' he said.

'Grrymguurdha,' Shiyai said.

'At least, that is what it sounds like to us,' Wopolsa said. 'That is what the tree calls it.'

'The tree?' he said, feeling foolish. Were they playing with him? What would they gain by it?

'Yes, the tree,' Grrindah said. She waved a hand. It was webbed between the first joints of the fingers.

'It need be no riddle or mystery,' Wopolsa said. 'The trees are one tree, and it is this planet's sole native sentient. We three planted its seed, and we helped it to evolve into sapiency.'

Her face was more deeply hooded than the others. Her eyes were black, and Ramstan could not look long into them, though he tried. He shivered. They reminded him of the eyes of the shimmering thing in the well.

'We three call ourselves the Vwoordha,' Shiyai said. 'Though not very often.'

She laughed again. The others smiled, their faces cracking open like defective eggs in boiling water.

'You have some rather strange pets,' he said.

'Pets?' Grrindah said. The blue eyes regarded him steadily, and, though she had been blinking before, now her eyelids did not move. There was something about those eyes ... where had he seen them before?

'In the well.'

'He calls it a well,' she said, and all three cackled.

Ramstan became angry.

'You're very rude!'

That made them laugh again. When the shrilling died, Wopolsa said, 'We are beyond politeness or rudeness.'

Shiyai said, 'You are sweating, but your voice sounds as if your mouth and throat are very dry. I think we could all do with some refreshment before we get away from the small talk. Would you care for some?'

Ramstan nodded, and he said, 'A cool drink would be nice.'

Shiyai clapped her brittle-looking hands, making a brittle noise. The creature coiled around the jewel hanging from the chain straightened out and dropped to the floor. Ramstan started. He had forgotten about it.

Though it had fallen from a height of at least 20 meters, the animal landed without seeming to hurt itself and ran out of the room through the door on the right. Ramstan was surprised at its size; he had thought it was only a meter long. He was also surprised that it ran on its back legs. He'd assumed from its long body that it was four-footed.

'I don't know how much I have to explain,' Ramstan said. 'I mean, who I am and why I'm here. You seem to know ... I mean, my experiences ... you've talked to me ... I've seen you, at least ...' He pointed a finger at Shiyai, then raised his hands, palms upward.

There was silence for a few seconds. Then Grrindah said, 'We'll wait until Duurowms serves us.'

Ramstan held the skinceiver area close to his mouth and asked in a soft voice for the time. His eyes on the three if they should object to his reporting, he told Nuoli what had happened so far. Her only reaction was to ask if he thought that he was in any danger.

'I don't think so,' he said. 'I may be here for a long time. I'll report every fifteen minutes or so. Relay this to ship.'

Nuoli must be wondering why he just did not keep his skinceiver on so that she could listen in. He could not tell her that he could not because the *glyfa* would probably, no, undoubtedly, be mentioned sooner or later.

He waited. The three were motionless, free of the fidgeting and eye-rolling, sighing and coughing, twitching and turning that possessed most sentients in similar situations. They looked withdrawn, but he felt that each was not just communing with herself. They could be holding a lively conversation among themselves. Telepathy? The scientists still had neither proved or disproved its existence.

Presently, and it seemed to be a long time, the creature called Duurowms entered. It carried in its two front paws a large tray with four silvery-looking goblets and a plate with tiny squares of some food. It came to Ramstan first and extended the tray, bowing at the same time. Ramstan looked into its large eyes. The eyeballs were entirely dark-brown, soft, liquidish – animal eyes. But sentients were animals. And the paws were not paws; they were hands, four humanoid fingers and an opposable thumb.

The goblets bore figures in both alto- and bas-relief, figures he could identify as animal, bird, fish, reptile, and bipedal and quadrupedal sentients, and things he'd never seen before. But they lasted only a flash to be replaced by other figures, which in turn were replaced. Alto-relief became bas-relief and vice versa.

Three of them held a blue liquid with a pleasant odor. Odors, rather. They seemed to change as swiftly as the figures on the goblet sides. Perhaps they coincided with the changing figures. He could not say that they did, since the transmutation was confusingly swift. Each odor evoked memories in him, all pleasing. None were ecstatic, just highly gratifying.

He was a baby, and his mother was nursing him. He was a baby, and his father was bathing him. He was a child in a boat on the *Shatt-al-Arab*, and his mother and father were teaching him how to fish. He had just mastered the Terrish alphabet; he had just mastered the Arabic alphabet. He had just been informed that he had been accepted as a cadet in the Terran space navy. His uncle had taught him the signals of the squirrels in the great forest just outside New Babylon, and he was 'talking' to them. His father and mother were showing him, for the first time, the family genealogy book, and they were telling him the origin of the family name. Originally, it had been Ramstam, brought to the newly built city of New Babylon by a Scot transported to this area by the 'hostage' system of the world government. Ramstam, in Scots Gaelic, meant 'reckless or stubborn'. During the generations after his coming to this land, the Arabic language of New Babylon had changed Ramstam to Ramstan.

It had also been a pleasure, which his parents for some reason found ecstatic, to discover that he was a descendant of the prophet Muhammad. Certainly, his parents were in a state exceeding pleasure because of this. But he could not attain their emotional heights at the news. Why should he? There were millions all over the world who could claim the same lineage.

Ramstan tried to ignore the pleasant memories. He looked at the goblet containing a different liquid. This was reddish-brown, and its odor made his nose wrinkle and evoked unpleasant memories. It looked like rapidly oxidizing blood, and its smell verified that impression.

'Take whichever one you like,' Wopolsa said.

Ramstan looked up from lowered lids at her. She seemed to be smiling, her mouth just a larger wrinkle in a mass of smaller ones. The teeth, unlike Shiyai's black ones, looked red.

A tremor passed through him, and his stomach, which had been expanding at the pleasing memories, shot back into a contracting ball. And someone was kicking that ball down ... what field?

'Take one,' Shiyai and Grrindah said at the same time.

'Only one?' Ramstan said, and he enjoyed the change of expression in the three. He did not know why. Perhaps because he had surprised them, and they were supposed to do the surprising.

Wopolsa, however, said, 'All, if you wish.'

'No, thank you,' he said. He gripped the goblet nearest him. He came close to dropping it because the seeming metal gave way under his fingers. If anything, it felt as if it were made of something that was part mercury. It held together, but it yielded. It was part rigid substance, part liquid. When he released two fingers, the indentations filled out.

This goblet, for some reason, terrified him more than anything that he'd experienced in this house. It told him that he was in the presence of a science far advanced beyond any he had so far met.

He lifted the goblet but did not drink.

'After you,' he said.

Duurowms carried the tray to Wopolsa first. Ramstan wondered if this meant that Wopolsa was the leader of the trio? He also noticed for the first time, though he should have seen it before, that the liquid in her goblet gave off a thin steam.

'"The cold-blood who drinks hot blood".'

It was Shiyai, the green-eyed and green-robed, however, who first lifted a cup.

'To the other,' she said.

'To the other,' Grrindah and Wopolsa said.

Ramstan raised his goblet. 'To the other.'

After a brief pause, he said, 'And to the one who is not the other. To both.'

He did not know why he said that or what it meant. But some sort of defiance was called for.

The three looked at him over their goblets. Then they said, 'To both,' and they drank.

Ramstan, flicking his gaze from the one on his left to the one on his right, sipped. The liquid was heavy but cool and delicious, though he could not quite identify its contents. He knew that he could not taste anything which his tongue buds were not receptive to. But it was also possible that these were genetically receptive to this liquid yet had not experienced on Earth, or anywhere until now, this particular taste.

Lowering the goblet, Ramstan said, 'I have many questions. I hope you don't mind answering them.'

'We have questions which have gone unanswered for eons,' Grrindah said. 'I hope you aren't going to ask us any of those.'

She broke into laughter again.

He looked with some disgust at Wopolsa. Unlike the others, she was still drinking.

'The cold-blood who drinks hot blood.' Cold-blooded? She looked as human as the others; she was no more batrachian or reptilian than they. Or did something other than blood flow in her?

Ramstan sketched the story of Wassruss, though he felt that they knew it. Then he said, 'I followed the directions in the chant. Now, if you please, tell me the origin and reason for the chant.'

'You could find that chant in many millions of societies,' Shiyai said. 'We originated and instituted it on thousands of planets and it has spread over millions of years. But, more often than not, it has become distorted and so useless. However, it has served a purpose. You are here.'

This confused Ramstan and made him more uncertain than before.

'The same chant existed on Kalafala. But you were not there long enough to encounter it.'

'You mean,' he said, 'that this chant was made long ago and far away just so that I might hear it?'

'In a sense, yes,' Grrindah said. 'But there were and are millions who might have heard it before you did. They would have served us as well.'

'I don't understand.'

'You and those like you, male and female adults, even some precocious children, were and are of a type inclined to follow the directions and to bring with them what we need. Also, because of their peculiar temperament and magnetism, they cause a focus of certain forces about them.'

'I still don't understand.'

'There is physical and psychic magnetism, though the two spring from the same source. Perhaps it would be a better analogy to say that there is physical and psychic gravitation. Just as a certain mass bends space around it, no matter what the quality or composition of the mass, so does psychic gravity bend events toward itself. But psychic magnetism differs from physical magnetism in that it is not the mass but the quality and proportion of qualities that determine the psychic gravitational attraction and the kind and quality of events it draws to itself. Perhaps someday we'll show you the mathematics of this. I doubt it, though. None of us has time for that.'

Ramstan bit his lip, then said, 'Shiyai, it was your voice I heard in the tavern. And it was surely you whom I glimpsed outside my hotel door and on the beach on Webn. I ...'

'It was also I whom you saw on the tape in your quarters,' the green-robed one said.

'How? Why is that?' Ramstan said.

'She rides the thoughts of God,' Grrindah said. 'Or something like It.'

Grrindah laughed.

Ramstan was irritated by her cachinnations. How, he wondered, could the others have endured this rasping habit for so long?

'Not she but her projected image, though it's not really an image as you think of such,' Shiyai said. 'It's a method of mental transportation in one sense. In another, it's something else. A plucking of certain strings in the harp of space-time fabric. A music which you hear with certain of your mental senses, which *hearing* is transmuted into physical sight and sound, sometimes, smell and taste and feel, too.'

'Just as an electron may be described as both a wave and a particle,' Wopolsa said.

'And something else too,' Grrindah said, and she cackled.

'I would say that Shiyai rides, not the thoughts of God or Whatever, but Its voice. The vibrations of Its voice, rather,' Grrindah said.

Ramstan was thankful that she did not laugh this time.

'We are using poetry to try to tell you what happens scientifically,' Shiyai said.

'Poetry and science. Never the twain shall meet,' Wopolsa said.

'Not in the Pluriverse we know,' Grrindah said. 'But there is a realm where they do.'

She laughed.

Ramstan thought of when the *glyfa* had mentioned the Pluriverse. And that made him wish that the *glyfa* would speak up within him now. He needed counsel desperately.

The animal, Duurowms, had taken the tray out of the chamber. Now he returned and leaped upward, catching the giant jewel in his hands, drawing himself up, and coiling himself around the top of the glittering gem. One dark eye fixed upon Ramstan. Sometime later, glancing up, Ramstan saw that the eye had closed and that the animal seemed asleep.

'It takes immense energy and artistry to ride the voice of God without falling off,' Shiyai said. 'It is also very dangerous, which is why I do the riding or the plucking of the harp, and not my sisters. I am the most energetic and artistic. And, since it is so demanding and perilous, I seldom ride. That is why you did not hear or see me more often.'

'Besides,' Grrindah said, 'the other was also enticing you here. Though the other is working against us, it is also working for us. It can't help it any more than we can help working for and against it.'

Shiyai said, 'It's time to quit being coy, sisters. We should tell him everything.'

'Everything?' Grrindah said, and she laughed.

'All he should know and a little more.'

Ramstan boiled with eagerness to hear this, but there was also something he must say.

'Your pets in the well?' he said.

The three looked at each other, two smiling widely, Grrindah laughing.

'He's very perceptive,' Shiyai said.

Then their flesh began melting or seemed to do so. A shimmering wrapped around them, reddish, blue-streaked waves which hurt his eyes, though not so much that he could not look directly into them.

Suddenly, the light and the melting had ceased. Now Shiyai was a beautiful young woman. Grrindah was a handsome middle-aged woman. Wopolsa had seemed to be so old that she could not possibly look more ancient. But she did, and her eyes seemed to have expanded, and Ramstan saw stars in the abysmal black emptiness. Only for an instant. They made him cold and frightened.

Shiyai said, 'Now you see us in another form. Not because we have changed form, but because we have allowed other constructs, molds in your mind, to be filled with us. Yet, in a sense, you are seeing us as we are. Especially, Wopolsa.'

Ramstan ignored her remarks.

'The pets?' he said. 'Are they really pets? Or are they … really you? And you are the projections? Are they the sentients, the masters?'

All three laughed uproariously.

When the last of the echoes had bounced from the far walls, Grrindah said, 'Perhaps the beings in the well are only projections. Which would, of course, also make us projections of projections. Or perhaps the citizens of the well have been projections so long that they have become realized as solid beings, actualizations of the potentialities of matter, fantasies of light that have transmuted into reality. Though, of course, fantasy is as real as reality, being engendered by reality and maintained by it. Without matter, there is no fantasy, though there may be matter without fantasy. Or is it the other way around or both at the same time?'

'That's enough,' Wopolsa said. 'Ask, and you must pay the price. But, first, we will tell you what the price is. Your questions so far have been for free.'

'I have many questions,' Ramstan said.

'The price from now on is the same for one or many,' Wopolsa said. 'However, first ...'

And the three told him much, though not all he needed to know. What he did hear, however, was more than he liked to hear.

21

If a tack could have feelings and it had been hit directly with a sledgehammer, it would have felt as Ramstan did. If a rabbit had been seized by a tiger, it would have felt as Ramstan did.

Even so, he thought, and the thought was fire though a flicker, even so there was a difference between him and the tack, between him and the rabbit. He was a man and, thus, not helpless. He had not been utterly crushed and ruined by the hammerblows of the revelations. He was not paralyzed with fear forever. He could still fight; the flicker would become a roaring flame.

Was that just bravado? No sooner had he told himself that than he had been hit with another great shock. No. Two more.

While he was still sitting in the trio's chambers, reeling though sitting, Nuoli had called through the skinceiver.

'Captain! You must return to ship! At once!'

Her voice seemed to come through many layers of wool, to be so muffled and distant that it was like a voice in a dream.

'What's the emergency?'

'I don't know, Captain. Commodore Benagur has ordered it.'

'Benagur?'

He found it difficult to concentrate upon what she'd said. There was nothing important outside this room. But he forced himself to give at least part of his mind to Nuoli.

'Benagur? He's still in sickbay. What's he doing ... issuing orders? Where is ... what's happened to Tenno?'

There was a silence. Nuoli must be using a different frequency to talk to ship. Why?

She spoke again, her voice tense.

'Neither Benagur nor Tenno will tell me, sir. They just repeat that you must return at once.'

The Vwoordha had been silent for some time awaiting his answer.

He said, 'Pardon me. I must call my ship.'

They said nothing.

He spoke into his skinceiver, but there was no response from *al-Buraq*.

He then called Nuoli. 'What frequency are you using when you talk to Benagur?'

'I'm sorry, sir,' she said, 'but Commodore Benagur has ordered me not to divulge that to you.'

The rage thrust deep under the iciness volcanoed out. He shouted, 'Who's in command? Benagur or me?'

Even the Vwoordha started, and the animal opened its eye.

Nuoli hesitated, then said, 'I'm sorry, Captain. You've been relieved of your command.'

'How in Satan's name could that be?'

'I don't know, sir. Just a minute.'

Ramstan rose unsteadily, his legs numb from sitting cross-legged for so long.

'I must go now,' he said in Urzint.

Shiyai raised beautiful black eyebrows and said, 'Your answer?'

'That will have to wait.'

Grrindah said, 'Someone on your vessel has found the *glyfa*.'

Ramstan felt the blood drain from him again.

'How ... how do you know?'

'I don't know. But I suspect that that would be the only reason you'd be deprived of your command. Perhaps the *glyfa* has guided someone to it so that it could be found. I do not know why it should, but it plays a deep game.'

'No!' Ramstan cried. 'It would have told me that it had been found!'

'Not if it had reason not to.'

'Benagur! He must have gotten into my quarters somehow and found it! But if he did it was with the connivance of someone else! Indra! Only Indra could have done it!'

He stopped. He was breathing heavily. Then, almost irrelevantly, it struck him that the three understood Terrish. Until now, he had assumed that they did not. But if one of them could ride the thoughts or the voice of God or whatever it was through the Pluriverse, then one could also eavesdrop anywhere.

Wopolsa said, 'If you no longer have the *glyfa*, then you cannot help us. But the price is still the same.'

He turned and strode out the front door. Down the slope was the launch, its entire crew looking up at him. Even at this distance, he could see the strain on their faces. He spoke into the skinceiver. 'Bring the launch here.'

The vessel had just landed by him, and he was taking the first step up, when the com-set blared. Benagur was speaking.

'Nuoli! Return to ship immediately! The Tolt ship has just been detected in orbit above us! I repeat, return at once! If Ramstan is not aboard, return anyway! I repeat, return at once at full speed within the limits of prudence!'

Nuoli said, 'Commodore, Captain Ramstan is aboard. Will leave at once as ordered!'

Ramstan thought of jumping off the launch and taking refuge in the house of the Vwoordha. He could only face disgrace in *al-Buraq*, and the *glyfa* was lost to him. Though the urge was strong, it did not overcome him. Whatever wrong he had done, he had acted with full knowledge of the possible consequences and full, though not ready, acceptance of the punishment if he were caught. Whatever he was, he was not a coward. If he had been one, he would no longer be.

In other circumstances, the affirmation might have been a temporary relief. Not now. The Tolt ship was a menace, and his ship was commanded by a madman. How had Benagur been able to assume command? Why had not Tenno taken over? Surely, he must know that the commodore was not fit for the post of captain. Perhaps, the discovery of the *glyfa* by Benagur had vindicated him, had convinced Tenno that Ramstan had falsely accused Benagur of insanity for his own perverted reasons. But Doctor Hu surely had her doubts about Benagur, and she would not have been hesitant to voice them.

There was nothing to do but wait until he returned to *al-Buraq*. This was done swiftly, the pilot having set the launch to return on the plotted course, the computer slowing the velocity only when turn and obstacle demanded it.

Sitting in the rear, the only one watching him a marine guard, Ramstan moved his lips, sub vocalizing. He called to the *glyfa*, but he got no reply. Ramstan cursed and struck his thigh with his fist, causing the marine to jump back, his hand moving toward his holstered olson.

'Don't worry, lad,' Ramstan said. 'I'm just angry at myself.'

The launch shot into the port in the midst of shrill alarms and glowing orange orders on moving screens. Ship was being readied for standby before alaraf drive.

The deck and bulkheads quivered, *al-Buraq's* welcome home to him, a tail-wagging, as it were. He wondered how ship would react when she found out that he was no longer the master. Would she shift loyalty to Benagur? The commodore probably was not aware of the affection circuit in her system, but Indra was. Would he recommend its excision if Benagur had trouble with her?

In the long history of sea navies, many crews had mutinied. But, so far, there was no record of a rebellion in a spaceship.

A squad of marines was waiting for him. If the marine lieutenant felt any emotion at arresting her captain, she did not betray it. Her face was expressionless, and her voice was steady. She told him that he would be conducted straight to the brig. He was outraged.

'Benagur is trying to humiliate me! He could at least let me be in my own quarters!'

'Sorry, sir,' she said. 'Orders.'

He was marched through the passageways and up a lift and was put in a spherical room with a diameter of four meters. Unlike the ancient cells, this had no bars. He could close the iris-door if he or his jailors wished. But if he tried to pass through the opening without authorization, he would be stunned with a beam.

An armed marine stationed himself on each side of the entrance. Ramstan wanted privacy, so he told ship to close the door. Meanwhile, the cell had been enlarging. Evidently, *al-Buraq* did not think that he had enough room. Ramstan at once told her to contract it to regulation size. Otherwise, an engineer might notice that she was ignoring the order to obey the new master.

He tried to call the bridge, but the transmission was now one-way.

He called to the *glyfa*. No response. Why was it not telling him what was going on? It could not be refusing to communicate because it was afraid that the Vwoordha would detect it. It must know that they were aware of its presence in *al-Buraq*. It had curiosity, the characteristic of all sentients; it could not have resisted listening in. It would have to know what was going on.

'The *glyfa* plays a deep game,' Grrindah had said.

Ramstan paced back and forth while he tried to imagine what was going on. Benagur had the *glyfa*, but what was he going to do with it? Would he allow it to attract and persuade him as it had his captain? Or would he …? No, surely he would not! Would he give the *glyfa* back to the Tenolt?

A luminous circle on the bulkhead showed Benagur's head and shoulders.

'Hûd Ramstan!' the bull-like head bellowed.

Ramstan stopped, unclasped his hands from behind his back, raised them toward the image, and said, 'You see me.' He was acutely aware that the commodore had not addressed him as 'Captain'.

Benagur did not look triumphant or as if he regarded Ramstan as contemptible or repulsive. Though his voice was that of a judge sentencing a criminal, his expression was the mask of one who was attempting to show supreme indifference. No, not indifference. Aloofness.

'You will be tried at court-martial in due time. Meanwhile, you'll have benefit of counsel. You can name any of the crew you wish to defend you, with the exception of those charging you. I recommend Lieutenant Enver, our lexologist. She is on duty now, however, and won't be available until the current crisis is over. No one will be until it's over.'

'Thank you,' Ramstan said.

'When there's time,' Benagur said, 'I'd like a complete report on your mission. Nuoli is giving hers, but I want to know what happened in that ... habitation.'

'I'll record it as soon as possible.'

'I want to know every little detail!' Benagur bellowed.

'Where is the *glyfa*?'

'It's not necessary that you know.'

Benagur paused, smiled, and said, 'We've been in communication with the *Popacapyu*. Her captain has been told that we have the *glyfa*, and we're negotiating for its return to their ship.'

Ramstan kept his face rigid to conceal his dismay.

'One of the items in the negotiations is the return to us of Lieutenant Branwen Davis. We haven't heard her story yet, so we don't know if she'll be subject to a court-martial. The Tolt captain, however, has told us that she was forced by them to steal the *glyfa* from you.'

Ramstan thought, How did they make her betray me? I mean, us.

He said, 'Commodore ...'

'Captain, not commodore!' Benagur said loudly. 'I am the captain now!'

Ramstan swallowed his rage. 'Captain Benagur, please think about this. The Tenolt will never forgive the theft of their God. They will arrange for its return, but, once they have the *glyfa*, they'll do their best to destroy ship and all in it. Their religion demands that they do that. They won't rest until the thieving blasphemers who stole the *glyfa* are destroyed. So ...'

'I know that!' Benagur shouted, raising a finger as if he were a teacher admonishing a pupil. 'I know that! Your crime has put all of us in peril! Believe me, that will be marked against you when you stand trial! I've told the Tenolt captain that you and you alone are responsible, that we were not in the plot to steal the *glyfa*, that we knew nothing about it until just now, that we share no culpability, that we are eager to make amends by returning the *glyfa* at once! But their captain has told us that if that is true, then we must surrender you to them!'

There was a silence. At last, Ramstan said, 'I'm not pleading for myself, not asking for mercy. The Tenolt will torture me until I die. They have to do that, since their law exacts that as punishment for blasphemy.'

'Their captain has told me that,' Benagur said. He paused, then said, 'Their captain has informed me that we will not share the blame, that he will not attack us if we deliver you to him.'

'You can't trust his promise,' Ramstan said. 'According to what I know of Tenolt law, you, everybody in the crew, is guilty by association. He'll get the *glyfa* back and then attack.'

'I don't think so,' Benagur said. 'His first duty is to get his false god back to its temple. If he attacks us, he risks being destroyed and so committing an unforgivable sin by not returning the *glyfa* to the temple. He'll take it back and then come looking for us. He must. That's his inescapable first priority.'

'That may be,' Ramstan said. 'Are you going to give me up?'

Benagur reddened.

'Believe me, I'd like to! I'd do it if I could! You deserve such a fate!'

He bit his upper lip, then said, 'But I'd take no pleasure in that. I despise you, but I would not wish you to suffer what the Tenolt would inflict on you. I am not vindictive! I weep for you, believe it or not, I weep for you because you are what you are! But ...' he drew in and expelled a deep breath ... 'my first concern is ship and her crew! What am I to do with you? *About* you, I mean? Captain Tkashikl demands that you be given to him. But you are under Terran law, not Tenolt. I'm required to keep you under arrest and bring you to trial. I know what the trial will result in. There's not the slightest doubt that you are guilty.'

He blew out another deep breath, his lips forming an O as if he were expelling smoke from a fire in his own body. 'You are guilty, aren't you? Admit it, Ramstan, and save us!'

'Save you?' Ramstan said.

'Yes, save us. At least, redeem yourself somewhat, Ramstan. Admit your guilt. If you do, then you'll make the way clearer ...'

'For deciding whether or not you'll turn me over to the Tenolt?'

'No!' Benagur said. His fist flashed across the screen and struck something beyond its field of vision.

Somebody – he sounded like Tenno – said, feebly, *'Captain!'*

'No! Terran government law and naval regulations forbid me to turn you over to any extra-terrestrial authority, regardless of what you've done!

But … this … case … wasn't anticipated by either. I have to make a decision on an unprecedented situation. I have to bear all the responsibility!'

'You're the captain now,' Ramstan said. At the same time that he relished Benagur's plight, he sympathized with him. But he somehow had to make the commodore understand that this particular predicament was unimportant, of no real significance. Vital as it was for himself, it was as nothing compared to the larger event.

Then he thought, No, this situation is very important. Not just because my honor and life are at stake. I, and I alone, as far as I know, can tell Benagur, tell the crew, what is involved.

The commodore, however, gave him no chance. He shut off the channel, and, though Ramstan tried to get him to reopen it, he either was not hearing him or was ignoring him.

He had no idea at what stage the negotiations were. If they were in the final phase, then they would be only a few hours, as long as it took a launch from the *Popacapyu* to get to *al-Buraq* or vice versa.

He opened the door and called to one of the marines.

'I want a messenger to take a recording at once to …'

He swallowed; it was difficult to use the title.

'… Captain Benagur. It's extremely urgent, a matter of life and death for everybody.'

'I'm sorry, sir,' the marine said. 'I have no authorization for that.'

'You must! To hell with authorization! If you don't, we'll be attacked by the Tenolt!'

'Sorry, sir, I can't do it.'

'Listen! There's one possibility Benagur and I overlooked! The Tenolt are not going to insist that Benagur turn me over to them! Once they have the *glyfa*, they'll get me by destroying *al-Buraq* and everybody in it!

'Also …'

'Sorry, sir.'

Ramstan closed the door. He took the three gifts of Wassruss from his jacket pocket and looked at them. The triangle, the square, the circle. He did not know if they could do what Wassruss claimed, but the Vwoordha had said that they could. They had certainly been eager to get their hands on them. He could escape now. Flight, however, was the last resort. Allah alone knew where he might end up; wherever it was, he could be stranded there until he died.

'*Glyfa!*' he cried. 'I must talk to you! You must know what the situation is! Are you going to allow everything to go to hell?'

Silence.

22

In one aspect, that lack of response was encouraging. It might mean that the *glyfa* knew that he could do what was required by himself.

On the other hand, the *glyfa* may have abandoned him. Perhaps it had decided that Benagur was now to be its means for getting whatever it was that it wanted.

Ramstan stood before a glowing but empty screen and spoke a code word. It overrode all other commands or at least was supposed to do so. When he had given it to *al-Buraq* in secret, he had been empowered by all the laws governing ship to do so. Now, he was acting against regulations. What about it? He had been doing that for some time.

At once, the screen displayed words in the Arabic alphabet of the twenty-third century.

'Acknowledged, Captain!'

Al-Buraq's brain was supposed to be no more self-conscious than a dog's, but there was considerable debate about the degree of that. It was, however, agreed that a dog had far more self-awareness than a parrot. What mattered now was that ship would obey his orders whether or not she comprehended human language.

Ramstan spoke, and a darkness appeared on the screen. Of course. The *glyfa* was locked up in a safe. He gave another order, and now the view was from a screen in Benagur's quarters. The bulkhead opposite the one on which it was placed was that containing the safe.

He gave another order. If *al-Buraq* responded, and there was no reason to think she would not, the *glyfa* would be passing through an opening in the back of the safe. Moved along by osmosis, the *glyfa* would head for Ramstan's cabin.

While waiting for the too-slow process, Ramstan activated a screen in the bridge. It was placed high but was tilted so that he could see the central part of the control room. Benagur was pacing back and forth much as Ramstan did when he was there. Nuoli stood by a bank of screens. Tenno, by the com-op, said, 'The Tolt launch is one hundred kilometers distant, sir, slowing down now.'

'Very well,' Benagur said. He did not look pleased, though. His enormous black eyebrows were bent downward below a wrinkled forehead; his mouth, when closed, was tight.

'The *Popacapyu* hasn't changed position?'

'No, sir.'

Toyce came within range of the screen. Benagur said, 'Doctor, bring the *glyfa* up now.'

'Yes, sir.' She hesitated, then said, 'Captain, I'll get a container for it. The Tenolt won't like the idea that we've been handling it with bare hands. They'd regard that as sacrilegious. In fact, even after the *glyfa* is boxed, whoever carries the box should wear gloves.'

Benagur stopped, grimaced, and said, 'Sacrilegious! That idol! Very well, Toyce. We have to respect exotic mores. You're the sentientologist. Do what you think is best.'

Toyce walked out of view of Ramstan's screen. It would take her perhaps five minutes to get a container unless she had one prepared. She probably did have one. Give her two minutes to get it and five to get into Benagur's quarters and discover that the *glyfa* was gone. No. He could gain more time. He gave *al-Buraq* an order to refuse to open the bulkhead-safe for her. Toyce would be irritated and would think that there was a malfunction. She would call one of the bioengineers, perhaps the chief, Indra. It might take him five minutes to get to the cabin or he might do his troubleshooting from the main engine room. Probably, the latter.

Ramstan had ship show him that room. Indra was sitting cross-legged on the deck, his eyes on some screens, the mentoscope attached to a band around his head, its detection-end, looking much like the end of a plumber's helper, against an indicator-bossing. His eyes, their epicanthic folds reflecting his Chinese ancestors, were slitted even more in deep thought. His large hawk's nose was moving, his nostrils flaring out.

Indra already knew that something was wrong. But he did not know what that was. Otherwise, he would have been reporting to Benagur.

Ramstan checked with *al-Buraq* on the progress of the *glyfa*. It would take ten more minutes before it reached his cabin.

The chief engineer's eyes snapped wide open, and he muttered something in Bengali, his natal tongue. Then he rose swiftly to his feet.

Ramstan shot orders at *al-Buraq*. Immediately thereafter, a similitude of Carmen Mljako, the subcommander engineer, appeared on a screen in the main engine room. It was Ramstan who spoke, but his voice was reproduced as Mljako's.

'Sir, I need your assistance in supply room 3-A at once. It's an emergency!'

'In a supply room?' Indra said. 'Take care of it yourself, Mljako. I have a greater emergency to handle.'

'I've found something you should look at at once, sir,' her image said. 'A bulkhead section fell out, why I don't know. But the nerve cables behind are damaged. I can't figure it out.'

Indra grimaced. 'Just a minute.'

'No, sir, the cables look diseased.'
'Diseased?'
'Rotting. Pustulent.'
'Impossible!'
'I don't think so, sir.'

'Maybe that's the trouble, though I don't see how it could be,' Indra muttered. He strode swiftly down the corridor, the screen which showed Mljako's image preceding him. He turned into the supply room. As soon as he had stepped through it, the iris closed behind him, and the bulkheads moved in. Indra yelled, but he was squeezed between the four bulkheads and unable to move. Though he shouted for help and gave *al-Buraq* orders, he was not heard. All communication to the room had been cut off.

Ramstan watched Toyce as she walked down a corridor holding the handle of a large plastic box. Benagur had told ship to open the iris to his quarters; Ramstan had told *al-Buraq* to obey this order. Toyce went into the big chamber and spoke the code word given her by Benagur. She put the box on the deck while the bulkhead iris was opening. Straightening, seeing that the safe was empty, she said, 'What the ...?'

Behind her, the entrance iris closed. She did not notice it because she had thrust her head into the safe and was feeling around it. The walls of the safe closed down; the iris extended lips and closed like a mouth over her head and shoulders. Though she screamed and struggled furiously, she was held tight.

Benagur, on the bridge, was speaking through the translator hanging by a cord from his neck. The machine spoke Tolt in answer to the commander of the launch from the *Popacapyu*. This was stopped a few meters from a port on the starboard side. Ramstan, looking at a bridge screen, could see the white face of Branwen Davis through the transparent upper part of the hull. There were also twelve Tenolt there, heavily armed and looking grim.

'Your God will be here within a minute or two,' Benagur said. 'I assure you that you have no reason to fear treachery. I regret deeply that our former commander stole the *glyfa*, and I will see to it that he gets maximum punishment.'

The launch commander had identified his rank as '*sakikl*, equivalent to commodore, and his surname as Khekhani'l.

His deep harsh voice, speaking Terrish through the translator, said, 'The fate of the blasphemer thief is up to you. Our only concern is to get our god back.'

And then? Ramstan thought.

He gave another order to *al-Buraq*, following it with the code word to put the order into action.

Benagur looked at the bridge chronometer. He momentarily turned the translator off and said, 'Tenno, open the channel to my quarters.'

It was obvious that he meant to find out if Toyce had left the cabin yet.

Tenno did as ordered.

'The screen is blank, sir,' Tenno said.

'I can see that,' Benagur said. 'Try voice.'

Tenno spoke into the screen. Then, 'No response, sir.'

He opened a channel to the main engine room. It was empty, so he used the all-ship channels to call for an engineer.

Benagur scowled and said, 'I don't like this, Tenno. Get Indra on it. Put me through to Ramstan.'

The *glyfa* would arrive in another five minutes. Ramstan began pacing back and forth as if he were thinking deeply about something, which he was. Benagur's face appeared on a screen, and he bellowed, 'Ramstan!'

It might have been better to seem to be startled, but Ramstan would not give Benagur that satisfaction. He stopped and turned slowly. 'Yes?'

Benagur looked the brig over, but he would see nothing out of the way. Nevertheless, he was suspicious. His expression said that his prisoner had to be up to something and that he was probably responsible for Toyce's being late and for the malfunction in his cabin channels. Still, he could do nothing about it.

Benagur did not even give Ramstan the courtesy of answering him. The screen went blank.

The cell screen showed Ramstan the bridge. Benagur said, 'Tenno, send someone after Toyce and scan ship for her.'

He looked at the chronometer again and then at the screen showing the Tolt launch. 'Where's Indra?'

'Can't find him as yet, sir,' Tenno said.

'Can't *find* him?' Benagur's voice lost some of its deepness. 'What do you mean, you can't find him? What's going on?'

Tenno called Mljako. 'Do you have any idea where Commodore Indra is?'

Mljako shook her blonde head. 'No, sir. Just a minute ago he was in the main engine room, testing.'

'For what?'

'He said he suspected some sort of malfunction.'

'He was right!' Benagur said. 'We're up to our ass in malfunctions!'

That was the first time Ramstan had heard the commodore use any phrase even hinting at vulgarity. Ramstan smiled. Benagur was very nervous.

The Tolt commodore spoke again, asking what was causing the delay. Benagur replied that Toyce would be on the bridge within a minute with the *glyfa*. He asked the commodore if he would enter ship now. It would expedite matters. The Tolt refused, and, a minute later, called Benagur.

'My captain gives you ten more minutes to surrender our god. If I don't report that the *glyfa* is in the launch by then, I am to proceed back to my ship.'

That meant that the *Popacapyu* might attack as soon as the launch returned. Branwen Davis would still be a prisoner.

Ramstan thought briefly about her. She was very attractive, and he was very fond of her. But he was not in love with her. He could not, would not, permit himself to be. All the women he had fallen in love with and who had fallen in love with him had left him. Those who had told him why they had left had said that he was missing something vital. He was flawed. Not that they could not tolerate certain flaws in their men. As the saying went, nobody was perfect. But he was always thinking of something other than them, even at the times when he should have been entirely with them. One with them, as Nuoli had once said. He did not satisfy them. They did not use that phrase in the sexual sense; he was far from wanting in bed. Physically, that is. But he was searching for something, and when he drove hard into their bodies, it was as if he was trying to clutch that something inside them.

They did not have it, of course, and they hated him for using their bodies as a channel for it.

Ramstan had denied their accusations at first, but eventually he had admitted to himself that they were right. He did not want things to be that way. But he could not help himself.

What was he looking for?

Immortality? He could have had that from the *glyfa*, though it was in a form that he would take only as a last resort. Perhaps not then.

Despite this, he grieved about Branwen Davis, though only for a short time. Allah alone knew what she faced if she remained the captive of the Tenolt. Even though they had forced her to be their tool, they would regard her as a blasphemer. She had touched the *glyfa*.

Until now, the Tenolt had never been absolutely sure where their god was. They had preferred a waiting game; using cunning and guile and patience. Now, they knew that the *glyfa* was in *al-Buraq*. They were getting very impatient and very desperate. They could attack and destroy *al-Buraq* and not harm the *glyfa*. Its hard surface would defy even a laser or an atom bomb, if what the *glyfa* had told him was true. It had been forged in a star, had burned up the star as fuel. It could fall into a white dwarf and not be damaged or affected in any way.

For all Ramstan knew, the Tolt launch was armed with a neutron bomb. Its commodore might be under orders to set it off if he had to. He would not hesitate to do so. His act would ensure his soul eternal delight within the *glyfa*.

The more Ramstan considered this possibility, the more he was sure that the Tenolt would be prepared for such an act.

In any event, he did not plan that they would get the *glyfa*.

If he gave the code word now, *al-Buraq* would go into alaraf drive. She would vanish from the sight of the Tenolt. If they indeed did have the ability to trace the passage of *al-Buraq*, they would still have to chase her, and Ramstan thought he might lose them. Even if he could not, he could get ship to a more defensive or offensive situation.

Going into alaraf drive, however, would leave Branwen Davis in Tenolt hands.

He thought furiously for a moment and then decided to take a chance. The weapons in the launch might be set to operate automatically if *al-Buraq* or her crew made a sudden offensive move. And even if that was not the situation and if the launch crew was not overcome swiftly enough, its commodore might trigger a bomb – if it had a bomb.

He gave another order to ship. Her deck and bulkhead quivered. He had ship fold a shock-cushion of flesh around him, a formation from the deck. Partially enclosed in this, he said, 'Now!'

The swift movement of *al-Buraq* thrust him sideways into the yielding but still-holding flesh. Anyone else in ship who was unsecured would be hurled from the deck or pressed against a chair or bulkhead or whatever. There would be injuries, but he could not help that. He must do what he was doing if Branwen was to be saved from torture and death.

Al-Buraq shot toward the launch, swallowed it in the port, and deck and bulkheads and overhead squeezed down. The launch was being pressed down – if things were going as Ramstan planned – until there would be only room enough within the launch for its occupants to lie on the deck. The hull would be a mangled can squeezing them, keeping them from moving enough to get to the controls. And the control machinery should be compressed and out of operation.

That was what he hoped would happen.

A bulkhead screen flashed out in code, 'Order carried out. Awaiting next phase.'

Ramstan could not keep from crying out triumphantly. Then he said, swiftly, in code, 'Next phase.'

The shock-cushion spread out from him, and he arose. The lessened weight told him that *al-Buraq* had gone into alaraf drive.

23

A bulkhead screen showed that the two marines had regained their guard posts. Ramstan gave an order. The brig shrank to compensate for the widening of the bulkheads directly behind the marines, their hollowing-in in the central portion, and their lipping-out at the edges. The pliable bulkheads then swiftly straitjacketed the two guards except for their heads. They were helpless to do anything but yell.

The iris could not fully open because of the bulging out of the bulkheads, but Ramstan squeezed through it. He had the marines released one by one, took their olsons, and put one in his jacket pocket. He ordered them to enter the brig. There he gave another order to *al-Buraq*. The deck flowed up and around them until it covered their lips. Though no one but he could hear them, he did not want to be distracted by their voices.

An olson in one hand, he left the brig, ran down the passageways to a lift, and took it down two decks to the port which had swallowed the Tolt launch. At his order, ship opened up enough to let him in. The distorted bulkheads parted for him as the Red Sea had for Moses. The port crew was enfolded in the reddish substance of deck and bulkhead. Their protruding heads reminded him of a scene from Dante's *Inferno*. Ignoring their cries for help, he walked on, the bulkheads dividing for him, and he came to what was left of the launch. *Al-Buraq* had crushed it, trapping Branwen Davis and the Tenolt crew inside it.

Branwen was the only one alive. The others, unable to get free and doubtless acting on orders given before they had left the *Popacapyu*, had committed suicide. They had probably done it by code words which had released poison from minute containers in their bodies.

Ramstan cut with his olson the hull sections which trapped Branwen, put the weapon in his jacket pocket, and helped her to her feet. She was very pale and covered with vomit. Her hand shaking, she pointed at the forward part of the launch.

'I think there's a bomb there,' she said.

She staggered toward him, and he held her up. The stench sickened him.

'The commodore couldn't get his hands free to pull a button from his uniform,' she said. 'He kept screaming at the others to get loose and tear the red button off.'

'Button?' Ramstan said. 'Are you all right?'

'Yes. I think that tearing the button off would activate the bomb.'

'I'll tell the crew to take care of it,' Ramstan said. He half-lifted her and urged her out of the port. The heads yelled at him, asking questions, begging to be released. He ignored them.

As they went down the passageway, he said, 'The Tolt captain admitted that he'd forced you to steal the *glyfa* and leave a fake in its place. How'd he manage to do that? I mean ... once you were in *al-Buraq*, you should have been safe. You could have told us ...' He stopped. Obviously, she had had a good reason to keep quiet.

'The fever?' he said. 'That have anything to do with what the Tenolt did to you?'

'Yes,' she said huskily. 'That fever was a temporary reaction to the artificial protein-explosive mix implanted in me. They took ... they took ...'

She choked, then said, 'They took out a section of my vaginal wall and replaced it with the mixture. It's undetectable from natural flesh unless a piece of it is removed and subjected to a laboratory test. The explosive could be set off with a certain radio frequency. I was told that if I didn't cooperate with them, I'd be blown up.'

'But you could have told us. The surgeons would've removed the section.'

'With what? Steel or plastic tools would set off the explosive. I was told that the explosive radiated a field that would cause an explosion when there was direct contact of any hard substance with the artificial flesh. Laser beams would also trigger it. I don't know ...'

'That what they told you was true?'

'Yes, but I couldn't ... wouldn't ... take the chance.'

'There were plenty of times when we were far away from the Tolt ship. They couldn't send a triggering frequency then, and I'm sure that Doctor Hu would've figured out something. At the least, you could have told us what the situation was. Maybe we couldn't remove the section, but we wouldn't have been ignorant ... blind ...'

'Look who's telling me what a cowardly traitor I am.'

'You were afraid, and you kept silent,' he said. 'I have no love for the Tenolt. But they can't be blamed too much. I did steal their god, and they believe that without their god they are nothing. Nothing! By the way, how did they know that I did it? What about Benagur and Nuoli?'

'They figured that you were the only one with enough authority to keep the officers and crew from asking questions. But I suppose they didn't really know who'd taken it. Their speculations were right, though. You did steal it!'

They entered his quarters. She went to the bulkhead where a symbol, three wavy black horizontal lines, was at her eye-level. She pointed at her open mouth, and the bulkhead bulged out, became a down-curving pipe, and a section formed a cup which fell off. She held the cup until it was almost full of water, signaled for the outpour to stop, drank, and then slapped the cup against the bulkhead. It seemed to melt and shortly was part of the bulkhead again. The pipe-form remained in case ship's captain might wish a drink also. The affection circuit was responsible for this. Without it, ship would have automatically retracted the pipe.

Ramstan drank also. Branwen came up to him. Her green eyes, reminding him of the surface of the Persian Gulf, seemed to expand, to grow like balloons in his mind, to crowd out all else that was vital at that moment.

'Can you really blame me?' she cried. 'What was I to do? Ethically ...'

He said, 'Yes, ethically?'

'Right or wrong? That's what I mean! Weren't the Tenolt basically right, justified? Weren't you the criminal, the unjustifiable? What was I to do? I believed, half-believed, anyway, that they had the right!'

'There's no time for this kind of talk,' he said. 'Any kind of talk. I'm here, not on the bridge, and ...'

'I don't know what kind of hold the *glyfa* has on you,' she said. 'But you betrayed ...'

'Be quiet!' he yelled.

She quivered, reminding him for some reason of the shaking deck when *al-Buraq* was excited or anxious about him.

'Why should I?' she said. 'What can you do to me? Or for me? You're nothing. I know that you're not the captain, you're in disgrace, you've been brigged. Benagur told the Tolt captain, and he told me. Only ...'

She waved a hand to indicate that she did not understand what was going on. Even in her shock, she must comprehend that the situation was not what had been described to her. Otherwise, how would Ramstan have been able to leave the brig, rescue her, and come to his quarters?

'Take your seat, and stay there,' he growled.

'I'll take it. I may not stay.'

By then the bulkhead was glowing with forty-nine screens, each showing a key-point in ship. By now, some crewpeople were trying, without using lasers or other violent means, to get Indra out of the grip of the storeroom. They were failing, of course. Other screens showed faces with many differing expressions or without expression, which was as indicative of emotions as the liveliest masks. Most displayed various kinds of anxiety or fear or panic or stunned incomprehension which concealed a comprehension their owners did not want to admit.

Ramstan now concentrated his thoughts on Benagur. What he ordered was what the crew would do. Unless he, Ramstan, snatched the leadership from Benagur.

He paced back and forth, knowing that he had to act very soon. Branwen, smiling strangely, spoke.

'I'm very passionate, but I've been without sex since I was first captured by the Tenolt. The friction of anything in my vagina would set off the explosive. That's why I turned you down when ...'

He whirled and said, savagely, 'This is no time to talk about such trivialities!'

'Trivial! I can't ever go to bed with a man again! There's no way the section can be removed!'

'There are other forms of sexual intercourse.'

'Spontaneous sex means spontaneous combustion,' she said, and she giggled.

'For the sake of Allah!' he roared in Arabic. Then, in Terrish, 'Must I throw you out? Be quiet! Let me think!'

'I've been through a lot,' she said. 'But I'm not cracking up ... I don't think.'

He and Indra could not be the only ones who knew about the affection circuit. One of the bioengineers would think of it soon, if he or she had not already done so, and he would notify Benagur. The engineers would cut the circuit off from the rest of the neural system. How long would they take? They could not go in ripping and tearing; brutal surgery might damage *al-Buraq's* brain.

A bulkhead screen pulsated orange, then showed the *glyfa* momentarily bathed in light. It was in the safe now.

Ramstan removed it and placed it on a table formed by ship. Branwen's eyes became large, and she left her chair to walk to a bulkhead which was as far as she could get from the *glyfa*.

'Speak!' Ramstan cried. 'I need you!'

Silence.

'Damn you!'

His fist struck the table top. *Al-Buraq* quivered.

Ramstan shouted out orders to ship. Immediately, every screen throughout it, except those connected to the exterior-detection system and those in Ramstan's quarters, showed him throughout the vessel. He saw Benagur start when most of the screens on the bridge displayed the prisoner's face and shoulders. Benagur's face paled as if touched with frost when he realized that the room behind Ramstan was not the brig but the captain's quarters. Then Ramstan stepped aside briefly so that the *glyfa* was visible. He could almost hear Benagur's blood draining from his head.

'Yes, I have complete control of ship,' Ramstan said. 'And you, all of you, are going to listen to me whether you want to or not. I don't know if you'll believe what I have to say. I hope you will. If you don't, if you reject my testimony, then you will put Earth in even graver peril than she is in now. You'll put the universe, all of the universes, in ... you'll doom them!'

'He's insane!' Benagur shouted. 'Don't listen to him! Tenno, get marines down to the prisoner's quarters and blast through the iris! If Ramstan resists, kill him!'

'They won't get near me,' Ramstan said. 'Ship will capture them. And if they do get off some shots, they're likely to injure ship. You can't take that chance, Benagur. Not when the Tolt may show up any moment now.'

'Tenno, you have your orders!'

Ramstan bellowed, 'Tenno, don't carry them out! Don't even try to! Anyone who makes a hostile move will be enfolded! And you, Benagur, if you don't stop talking and start listening, you'll be wrapped up in a deck-extension, wrapped like a mummy.'

Benagur took a deep breath and shut his eyes. When he opened his eyes, he said, quietly, 'Very well, traitor. We'll listen because we have to.'

'There's no need for insults, even if they should be justified,' Ramstan said. 'First, though, you have to know about Lieutenant Branwen Davis, formerly of *Pegasus*. That violent sidewise movement of ship was ordered by me so that she could capture the Tenolt launch and rescue Davis.'

He described how Davis had been forced by the Tenolt to steal the *glyfa*. And he explained what might happen if the *Popacapyu* got close enough to transmit a radio signal to the artificial flesh-explosive mixture in her.

'She has no idea what the energy potential in the explosive is. If set off, it might blow her to pieces and those very near her. Or might destroy ship and all in her, of course. That's one more reason why we must play hide-and-seek with the *Popacapyu* or find some means of destroying her before the signal is used.'

He paused and then said, 'I hope no one will be cowardly enough to suggest that Davis be gotten off ship at the first opportunity.'

Tenno said, 'But ... but all we have to do is to put her in a room with radiation shielding.'

Ramstan smiled grimly. 'That's an obvious idea. I told Davis the same thing, though I suspected that there had to be a reason why she hadn't confessed everything and then taken refuge behind shielding. It's because ... or at least the Tenolt told her this and it may not be true ... the transplanted section contains more than explosive. It also has a time bomb, a biological fuse, a fleshly clock, which is set to go off at a certain time and trigger the explosive.

'Davis wasn't told when the clock would strike. All she knew was that the Tenolt had allowed her an unspecified time. If she did not have the *glyfa* back in their hands by then, she would blow up. The biological clock, however, could be forever stopped by a certain frequency transmitted by the Tenolt. That would be done as soon as she got the *glyfa* in their hands. By that, I suppose that they meant inside their ship.'

Benagur opened his mouth, then closed it. Nuoli said, 'Either way, she'll be killed!'

'Perhaps,' Ramstan said. 'We don't know if the Tenolt were lying about that. But we can't take a chance.'

'Poor Branwen,' Nuoli said softly.

'She wouldn't be in this horrible situation if you hadn't stolen the *glyfa*!' Benagur bellowed. 'None of us would be!'

'True,' Ramstan said coolly. He gave the order, and the deck swelled up all round Benagur and enfolded him tightly. Only his head from the nose was visible. That was very red, and his eyes were rolling like ball bearings about to tear loose.

'Tenno, I'm going to let a marine come down here,' Ramstan said. 'But only if the marine is unarmed. The marine will escort Lieutenant Davis to a launch. A technical force will prepare shielding for the launch. The launch will be the one that has alaraf drive. When this is completed, by that I mean so that no radio signal can penetrate it, Lieutenant Davis will be put in it. The launch will be programmed to accompany *al-Buraq* at a distance of two kilometers. No, make that three. I don't know how powerful the explosive is. The program will automatically direct the launch to keep pace with the ship at this distance. When we go to another bell, the launch will go also. Lieutenant Davis will be given enough life support for four weeks of ship's time. Is that clear?'

Ramstan's words had been recorded, and, if Tenno was uncertain about their meaning, he could play back the recording. He said, 'Aye, aye, sir. Clear.'

Ramstan felt relief. One more crisis gotten through. He had not known if Tenno would disobey him because he thought that Benagur had to be, according to regulations, still in command. But Tenno could not be trusted. He might be going along with his former captain because there was nothing else he could do at the moment. For the moment, he was obeying, and that was what Ramstan wanted.

Davis said, 'You're really doing this to me?'

He turned. 'Listen, Branwen, I don't like it. But it's absolutely necessary. I'd be justified if I had you ejected into space. You're a very real danger, and there are events ... things ... which you don't know about. These make your situation very insignificant ... unimportant ... comparatively speaking. I'm extending myself ... I shouldn't even be doing this for you ...'

'They're right!' she cried. 'They're right!'

He did not ask her what she meant by that. He supposed that she was referring to what the other women had told her about him. She was wrong, though, in assuming that this situation had anything to do with his relations with the crew-women. If she were not so frightened, she would understand that he had to do this for the preservation of ship and her crew. And for even larger matters. Much much larger.

He told her that she should leave his quarters now and go to meet the marine.

'I can't wait until he gets here. There may be little time left. But you can hear what I have to say in ship and the launch. It'll clarify this business for you.'

Or perhaps make her even more confused, he thought. She turned her head to glare as she walked by him toward the iris.

He said, 'After all, I did save your life, and I'm doing all I can to keep you safe. It's much better to be yourself, no matter how lonely you are for a while, than to be blown up. And I do have to consider the safety of ship first.'

'*Now* you do,' she said. 'What about *then*?'

He did not reply. He assured the tec-op and com-op that the order for silence while he talked did not apply to them if the detectors picked up anything that might be dangerous.

24

'First, I must tell you what happened when Commodore Benagur, Lieutenant Nuoli, and I went to the temple of the *glyfa*. I must because you cannot understand the events following unless you know what impact this had on us three. Especially on me.'

He paused. And the *glyfa* spoke.

'Ramstan, tell me what's been happening since I last talked with you and what is happening now.'

This time it was using his father's voice.

He started, and he came close to choking.

'Officers and crew! Just a minute!'

He turned, though it was not necessary to do so, to speak to the *glyfa*. Human beings, all sentients he'd met, felt that looking at the face of the one they were talking to ensured a fuller communication and a deeper trust in whatever that one was saying. The face expressed the soul, the consciousness, the sincerity. The speaker could be judged by his, her, or its expression. But the egg-shape was unchangeably fixed; no play of emotions crossed its surface, no ripple of face, no bodily movements, only the voice itself was the index of truth or falsehood. And that voice was changing and could be his mother's or father's or anyone he knew. It was like talking over an ancient telephone or radio transceiver which lacked the image of the one you were talking to.

Also, what the Vwoordha had told him about it when he was in their house weighed heavily on him. The atmosphere seemed to thicken, to become layers on layers of glue-impregnated paper, layers rising to unimaginable heights, a crushing weight. He was pressed down as if a building had fallen down on him, and he felt as if the building was something unknown before. One which towered up, up, up past the boundaries of air and Space.

Boundaries.

The word flashed like a meteorite over the fields of his mind.

'*Glyfa*! I've been trying for a long time to get you to talk to me. But you didn't reply.'

'I was thinking.'

'You may have been,' Ramstan said. 'But you were also not receptive to anything outside yourself. You were recharging your ... battery? ... fuel? ... self? You didn't answer me because you couldn't hear me.'

'The Vwoordha told you this.'

'Yes. They told me that you had periods of unwilling withdrawal. That you have to depend upon a fuel source, like all life, to keep alive, if alive is the correct term. When your source of energy is not equal to your demands on it, you must rest and draw in the energy before you ...'

'So. They told you. I expected that they would. I have a very small surface area. Though I operate on a 67-percent economy, which is more efficient than anything or anyone else in this cosmos, excluding one, I have to go through periods of ... hibernation ... suspended animation ... no, you'd understand the analogy to a recharging battery best.'

'But you have a wide range of energy sources,' Ramstan said. 'Electricity, X-rays, gravitons, even antigravitons, photons, antiphotons. There's no reason why you should recharge so often. Especially when there's an energy source on ship and I could connect you to it.'

He paused, then said, 'No. I'm wrong. The bioengineers would note any unexplainable consumption of power. They'd track it down.'

He still did not believe that a forced quiescence during recharging accounted for all or even half of the *glyfa's* silence. Most, if not all, of the time it had failed to respond to him, it had done so for reasons only it knew.

It was trying to nudge him here and there with both its silences and its enigmatic revelations.

The Vwoordha were pushing him towards their goal, too. When the *glyfa* nudged, they counternudged. And vice versa. Or were the Vwoordha and the *glyfa* just pretending to be opponents?

'You know two of my limitations,' the *glyfa* said. 'Did the Vwoordha tell you about the third?'

'Yes.'

'I know when you're lying. You're lying now.'

'Then I won't lie to you from now on,' Ramstan said. 'Maybe. I don't know that you can tell when I'm lying. My truth may not be yours.'

'Sly, sly. Always considering all the variables – as you can see them. *See*. Why must you sentients use this term? There are so many things that you can't *see* but can still sense otherwise. Even without light, you can see. Within limits.'

'All senses have limits,' Ramstan said. 'Except one. And even that …'

'You must have had a long talk with the Vwoordha. But it could not have been long enough. However, they did tell you of my restrictions. I am dependent on other sentients for mobility, and I am dependent on my energy source, like all of my kind. Though it may surprise and even repulse you, I am of your kind, though I am artificial.'

'What … who … was your model?'

'None! Or perhaps a thousand were my model. Whatever the sources of my creators … the models … the end result was unique. Just as you, the result of a hundred million models … are unique.'

'Uniqueness does not necessarily mean anything more than mediocrity … even idiocy … a pale similitude of humanity,' Ramstan said. 'Listen! This is getting us nowhere. Let me tell you what I've been doing since you withdrew to … recharge. I'll have to go fast. The crew is waiting for me. They must be wondering what the hell's going on, why I should have started to tell them everything.'

'Everything?'

Ramstan felt his skin warming. He realized that the *glyfa* was, in some ways, just like him. It questioned the inexact use of a word or term; it liked to demonstrate that the other did not know exactly what he, she, or it was saying. Was this characteristic a means for putting down the other and so showing his own superiority? Or was it his personal requirement, quite justified, for the precise use of a word? Or both?

It might even be that the *glyfa* was not like him. It might be subtly mocking him. It might be that it knew that no sentient could ever use a word in the dictionary sense, the objective sense, that every sentient had his own personal, unique language.

Ancient as it was, the *glyfa* could not use language as he, Ramstan, so impermanent, so time-bound, so mayflyish, used it.

'Within your limits … and mine … even mine … everything,' the *glyfa* said.

'I haven't time,' Ramstan said.

'Tiiiiimmmme.' The word murmured, swelled, leaped up, like a surf wave striking a cliff, and receded. Now the speaker was Ramstan's uncle, the one who'd taught him 'squirrel talk', the queerly inconsistent philosophical and humorous uncle. The uncle long-dead who still lived in his mind and had been resurrected by the *glyfa*.

'No, I don't have time!' Ramstan shouted. 'Listen while I tell the others!'

'Others! Others! Others!' echoed and then faded away.

Ramstan turned from the *glyfa* and spoke again to the crew.

'When I went into the Tolt temple with Benagur and Nuoli, I, too, experienced something phenomenal. Numinous. The very nature of the experience, if reported, would have made you doubt my sanity. I was flooded with light, just as Benagur and Nuoli were. Not photonic light. It was a light such as few have ever seen.'

Suddenly Ramstan had been Muhammad the prophet, yet at the same time was also himself. He was sleeping in a house near the sacred Kaaba in Mecca. He had gone to bed weary and sad because he had gained so few disciples after the angel Gabriel had appeared to him in a grotto, had shown him a scroll, and said, 'Recite!' That is, read and then reveal the divine contents to mankind.

The fatigue, disappointment, and discouragement lasted only for a few seconds. He was awakened when Gabriel entered the house, the archangel Gabriel with his many-colored wings and the glorious light streaming from his face.

Ramstan described the events following very rapidly. He would have liked to dwell with great detail on them, but he did not want to weary his audience, and time was vital.

'After Gabriel had purified my heart by washing my breast with water from the sacred well of Zamzam and poured over me the *hikma*, which is symbolic of faith and wisdom, he took my hand. And *al-Buraq* appeared, *al-Buraq*, the Lightning, the fabulous unique animal. It had the face of a young woman and wore a golden crown. Its body was a mule's, its hoofs and tail were a camel's, its harness was of pearls, its saddle was a single carved emerald, and its stirrups were turquoise.'

Before helping Muhammad-Ramstan onto *al-Buraq*, the archangel told him that Allah had decreed that this night he would travel through the seven heavens and would be allowed to worship the face of the Truth, the Everlasting, the Father of All.

'No language is anywhere adequate to describe my ecstasy,' Ramstan said. 'There are no words which can communicate to you more than a very slight fraction of the power and intensity of my feeling. The mystical experience has always been indescribable. How can I describe how many-colored light bathed every cell of my body and how every cell throbbed with ecstasy and how I *saw* every cell and knew its *name*? Or how I felt, like a giant glowing shadow behind me, behind my soul, a being that was only a reflection of the glorious face of the Ineffable yet would have blinded me if I could have turned when I felt Its hand on my shoulder and looked upon Its face?'

'I did not wish to turn because I knew that even the shattering light would not blind me to Its shattering beauty. And Its ugliness. At the same time, I felt that I might turn and, horrifying thought, see nothing there.'

Ramstan skipped through the journey on *al-Buraq's* back from Mecca to Jerusalem, ancient Jerusalem, the holy city of the prophet's time. He passed briefly over his entering the sacred mosque and meeting the prophets of God who had come before him. He did mention that he was greeted by Ibrahim, Musa, and Isa, that is, Abraham, Moses, and Jesus.

Then he rode *al-Buraq* to the first heaven, a sphere the color of turquoise, while Gabriel, carrying a standard, preceded him.

Heaven after heaven, rank upon rank of angels, greatest of the great men, Adam in the first heaven, John and Jesus in the second, Joseph in the next highest, Idris in the fourth, Aaron in the next, Moses in the one above Aaron's, and Abraham in the last and highest of the heavens. Though he had to be sketchy, he could not stop himself from giving some details of the White Cock in the first heaven, the angel which looks like a bird and whose comb touches the bottom of Allah's Throne and whose feet rest on Earth. Nor could he keep himself from telling some of the terror and awe he felt on seeing the angel, half snow, half fire, who held in his left hand a rosary of snow and in his right hand a rosary of fire and who recited the rosary, telling the one hundred beads, making a sound like thunder as he moved the beads.

He also could not help revealing some of the terror he felt in the second heaven when he encountered the Angel of Death, Azrael, the decider of lots, who rests one foot on a chair of light and the other on *al-Sirat*, the razor-thin bridge between Heaven and Hell.

'And then I heard the voice of the All-Abiding, and I worshiped Him,' Ramstan said. 'Truly, at that time, I felt that I was indeed Muhammad and myself, two yet one, and that I was experiencing the glory, the unutterable ecstasy, that comes from hearing the voice of God Himself. At the same time, I felt a fear that was so intense that it was also an ecstasy.'

But beyond the seventh sphere was unending Space, and in it hung seventy thousand veils of light of many colors. Beyond the veil was *al-Arsh*, the Throne of God, a seat made of red hyacinth and so huge that the Earth was a mote of dust beside it.

There were many things which Ramstan, caught up in a fervor that was still only a pale shadow of what he had felt in those few minutes in the temple of the *glyfa*, would have liked to tell. But he skimmed through them, even the gardens of paradise, and came to Hell itself, guarded by the awful Malik, the king of shadows. And when Ramstan tried to describe the tortures of the damned, his voice broke, and he wept.

'And then I was back in the house in Mecca for just a second, and my feeling that I was the prophet faded as the walls of the house did, and I was standing in the giant anteroom of the temple of the *glyfa* and was being told by the high priest to go into the chamber where the *glyfa*, the Tolt god, would receive me.'

Benagur's face was even redder, and his eyes were wilder. For a moment, Ramstan thought of uncovering the commodore's mouth long enough for him to vent what was troubling him. But he thought he knew what Benagur wished to say. That was, that Benagur had also had a *Miraj*, a miraculous ascension, but that his had been somewhat different.

Shortly after leaving Tolt, Benagur and Ramstan had had a brief conversation. Benagur had sketched his reactions in the temple. Ramstan had held back on his. In fact, he had said no more than that he, too, had been flooded with the light and lost consciousness for a while. Benagur had been far less reticent. He had told of his levitation to the Throne of God while accompanied by the prophet Elijah. His experiences had been confined to that which a very devout Jew might imagine. (On learning which, Ramstan had begun to question the validity of his own *Miraj*.) Benagur, like Ramstan, had not actually seen the face of God, but he had come close. He too had ventured into, or, rather, over Hell. And he had announced, somewhat sorrowfully but with a trace of triumph, that he had seen Ramstan among the damned and witnessed his torture in flames. Though Benagur said that this sight filled him with sorrow, he could not quite conceal his satisfaction.

Ramstan had grinned then. But he did not tell Benagur that he had seen Benagur's pain-sewn face among the wretches in the seventh and lowest sphere.

Ramstan had said that he was surprised. He thought that orthodox Jews did not believe in a hell.

Benagur had replied that a literal hell was not in his faith. But, evidently, he had been mistaken. After all, God did not reveal everything. And it was only just that Christians and Moslems who believed in such a savage place should end up there.

However, Benagur admitted, though he had seen what seemed to be a literal hell, how did he know that it might not be a figurative one? That the flames and spikes and hooks were only symbolic of the awful terror and grief of Hell's inhabitants at being barred forever from the sight of the face of God and the warmth of His love? The human mind was incapable of interpreting some events, especially the numinous and the antinuminous, and his brain might have twisted terror and grief into flames and spikes and hooks.

'I congratulate you on your rationalizing powers,' Ramstan had said. He had laughed and walked away from Benagur, but he had felt like vomiting.

For a while, he had actually believed in the reality of what he had seen during his own ascension. But Benagur's revelations had convinced him that both experiences were delusions.

He had then questioned Nuoli, who had been raised in a liberal Lutheran sect and then had rejected all religions. She insisted that she remembered only being overwhelmed by light and then being unconscious for a short while.

Ramstan now revealed what Benagur had told him.

'But this was after we had left Tolt. When I came out of my ... fantasy ... I went into the gigantic chamber of the *glyfa*. We were halted a few meters from it and told not to speak unless the god permitted us to do so. The high priest spoke in Urzint for perhaps five minutes.

'Then my long-dead father's voice spoke. I was shocked, but I quickly saw that his voice was audible only within my mind. It spoke Arabic. The *glyfa* didn't know a word of Arabic then, as I found out later. It was transmitting Urzint ... no ... not transmitting, since it doesn't use telepathy ... it was speaking Urzint and beaming it into my unconscious and my speech centers. My unconscious was using some linguistic area to translate the Urzint into Arabic, though the Arabic was not perfect at that time.

'I realized that the *glyfa* had been able to stimulate certain nerve paths in my brain. The *glyfa* can do this through, I believe, electromagnetic means, and it can *read* the mind of the speaker when he uses spoken or subvocalized language which the *glyfa* knows. Beyond that, it has no mind-reading powers or extrasensory powers of any kind. Or so it claims. I still do not know if it is lying.'

Ramstan said that the *glyfa* had been waiting for a very long time for him. Not exactly for an Earthman named Ramstan but for someone like him. Ramstan must return later that night, unobserved by anyone in *al-Buraq*, and take the *glyfa* to ship. The *glyfa* would overpower the guards and priests by momentarily making them unable to see Ramstan. Ramstan must be swift, however, because the *glyfa* could do this only for a short time and even that was a tremendous drain on its energy.

'It said that it could give me immortality in one of two forms. The first would make me age very very slowly, though I would be subject to death by accident, homicide, or suicide. The second would preserve me from these, including suicide, though I could kill myself if I opted to do so. The *glyfa* would arrange that.

'It then told me, still using my father's voice, that it was immortal.'

Ramstan paused and scanned the faces on the screens. Some of them looked as if their owners thought he was crazy.

The screen which had been showing the launching port was filled with the face of a marine lieutenant.

'The shielding is installed, sir. The launch has been stocked, and Lieutenant Davis is in the launch. All ready for launching, sir.'

'Do it now.'

He was glad that he did not have to see Branwen's face. It might have shown the terror and the hopelessness she felt. To be isolated for what might be a long time and to expect that, at any second, the biological time bomb in her body would explode. To know that Ramstan might have to order that she be left behind and to know that she could then be drifting in space until her food and water were gone. That would pulp anyone's spine, jelly the mind, slush the soul. But she might have enough fire left to show her hatred for him.

Ramstan cut off the screen with a code word, though he felt like a coward. He spoke to the personnel again.

'If what you've heard so far is difficult to believe … well! The *glyfa* then told me that it had survived the deaths of two universes! Of two Pluriverses, rather!'

He stopped to swallow. How could he get them to accept the truth?

They had not seen and heard what he had, and he was not sure that he himself credited his senses and his experiences.

'The deaths of God!' he bellowed. 'The two deaths of God! The two births and the two deaths!'

25

Benagur struggled violently, and his mouth came loose from the grip of ship's flesh. He cried, 'You are a blasphemer and a liar, Ramstan! I ascended to the Throne of God! You had your vision …!'

His words were cut off as *al-Buraq* clamped down again. Ramstan gave an order, and the flesh receded.

Benagur shouted, 'You had your vision, but it was induced by that thing, the *glyfa*, the agent of Satan, if it is not Satan Himself! Your vision was false! If not false, then you misinterpreted it, perverted it for your own purposes! There is the Living God, and He …'

Ramstan had ordered Benagur silenced again.

He said, 'Yes, there is a living god, though not in the sense Benagur meant. At least, I think it's a god or it's the closest thing to a god that sentients will ever know. If indeed they can know Him … It.'

The tec-op interrupted him.

'USO detected at 50,000 kilometers, sir.'

A bulkhead screen dissolved the faces on it and showed him the area in which the object was detected. It was black except for a single red star near the center and the tip of a blazing white gas cloud. Shortly thereafter, another screen showed him the magnified image reflected by the rasers.

'The *Popacapyu*,' Ramstan said. 'We're going at top velocity now. They can't catch us before we jump again. It's only 100,000 kilometers to the edge of the bell.'

The tec-op said, 'Sir, they've sent a modulated radio signal, frequency 10 megahertz, 1,000 watts.'

'So. We got her behind the shielding just in time.'

His decision had been hard on Branwen, but it was correct.

Ramstan again addressed the personnel.

'I did not take the *glyfa* from the temple because I was tempted by its offer of immortality. I was intrigued by that, yes. But I did not believe that it could truly give me everlasting life nor was I going to steal it just to determine if its offer was valid.

'What led me to take it was another statement, a series of statements, that it made. It said if I took it, became its partner, I would help to save the world. It could not guarantee that we two could do just that, but we must try.'

He stopped and licked his dry lips. Even to himself, knowing what he did, he sounded like a maniac, a deluded Messiah.

'I know what you're thinking!' he cried. 'But don't forget the *bolg*! That thing which destroyed Kalafala! The thing that has, if what the *glyfa* tells me is true, destroyed the Urzint, many planets! Which has, according to the Vwoordha, killed most of the life on Tolt! The *Popacapyu* crew doesn't know it yet. And it will come to Earth eventually, by following either us or our tracks, and slaughter all life there as it has slaughtered it on many planets!'

He paused, breathing heavily. Though he was getting ahead of his story, he had given his audience something concrete and terrible to think about. They might not be so willing to disbelieve him.

'It … the *glyfa* … told me that all sentients sooner or later develop their science to the point where they invent the alaraf drive or its equivalent unless they destroy themselves first with atomic war. They never, or seldom, anyway, understand just what the alaraf-driven vessels do or how they travel such immense distances in such a short time. We Terrans certainly didn't. We had theories about where the ships went when they jumped. The most accepted was that the ships somehow *bent* space so that a star a million light-years away was, briefly, very much closer. Or that there were flaws or anomalies in the space-time structure which permitted an alaraf ship to penetrate these. The theory stated that normal *distance* was that which the distribution of matter in space had accustomed us to. But that these flaws or fissures were of different arrangements of space-matter and the different arrangement also made for differences in distances.

'As you know, these theories weren't even that. They were speculations, means for describing what is still the undescribable.

'A third speculation, one not taken seriously at all, was that the alaraf drive somehow made the ships leap from one universe through the *walls* of another. That speculation was based on the fact that a ship on its outward journey never appeared in a known section of Earth's universe.

'Another speculation was that the alaraf drive was really a sort of time travel drive. On the outward journey, the ship went ahead in time or backwards. It didn't matter which. In any event, the ship stayed in one place, but the cosmic bodies moved on, leaving the ship floating in space and in a space unrecognizable because millions or even billions of stars had passed by. One way or the other. The return journey was accomplished by reversing time, as it were, and the ship got back to Earth at an approximate time corresponding to the amount of time she had been away from Earth.'

Ramstan stopped to get a drink of water.

'The *glyfa* assured me that the speculation about the alaraf ships penetrating the walls of the universes was indeed correct.

'There is not one universe but many. The human body contains trillions of cells. So does the Pluriverse. Each universe is a cell in its body.

'I was wrong when I stole the *glyfa*, though it was with its full permission and expressed wish. Not just wrong. I was a criminal. I was betraying my duty as captain of ship and as a Terran. But I believed then and still believe that I was following a higher duty. I was convinced that the *glyfa* was right and that I was doing what had to be done if I were to ... save ... the world. The Pluriverse.'

Many on Earth had believed that it was their mission to save the world. Noah, Abraham, Moses, Jesus, Muhammad, Zoroaster, Luther, a hundred Popes, Knox, Buddha, Joseph Smith, Eddy, a few thousand of greats and well-known among the billions who'd lived on Earth and how many thousands of insane? What made him different from the others?

His predecessors had acted only on fantasy. *He* knew from experience, from fact, what he was talking about.

Or did he? He could not really be sure.

But what he knew was not gotten from any stone or golden tablets or an angel appearing to announce that he was God's chosen prophet to reveal anew what had been said before many times and would be said again, though in somewhat different forms and situations.

'I wish I could say that I took the *glyfa* because it had hypnotized me, and thus I couldn't help myself. It did not hypnotize me, though its evocation of the *Miraj* in me enormously influenced me. The *glyfa* told me that it did expand my minuscule inclination to steal it. Turned a flashing impulse into a steady determination. That may be true. If I'd been completely without that desire, the *glyfa* could not have affected me thus at all.'

Who among you would not have had that desire? he thought. But he did not voice the thought. To do so would make him seem to be pleading. And Ramstan did not plead.

'Whatever the reasons for my taking the *glyfa*, and I believed and still believe that I had one reason to override everything that told me not to take it, I did.'

Nuoli, unable to obey any longer his order not to interrupt, said, 'Why didn't you tell us what you'd done as soon as you returned to ship with the *glyfa*? Why were you so secretive?'

'Don't ask me questions until I've finished! But ... I was getting to that. Isn't it obvious that I would've been arrested at once, Benagur would have made sure of that, and the *glyfa* returned to the Tenolt? Would you have believed me then? No, not until the *bolg* appeared would you have put any credence in me. As it is ...'

He told them of the voice in the Kalafalan tavern warning him of the *bolg*. He told them of seeing on the monitor screen the figure in his quarters and the figure which had appeared on the Webn planet when he and Benagur were quarreling.

'As I found out when I visited the Vwoordha, these were images projected by one of the three. They were projected – beamed? – from a very long distance. Not just from a distant planet in another galaxy, though that would be staggering enough. No, they were projected from another universe.

'I don't know how it was done. Shiyai, the Vwoordha, told me that she rode the waves of the thoughts of God. Doubtless, that's a poetic analogy and so, meaningless. Or perhaps not. For all I know, the images were not objective projections but stimulations of my brain resulting in subjective phenomena that I thought were objective.

'But I suspect that the *glyfa* was used, though unwillingly, as a target and a focus for whatever powers the Vwoordha use to project these images.'

'You have guessed it,' the *glyfa* said, using Ramstan's mother's voice now.

It sounded sullen.

'I think that's so because the *glyfa* is also a tool. It was not created primarily as a beamer for the images of the Vwoordha, but it can be used for this. I'll get to its primary purpose in a few minutes.

'The *glyfa* could probably have enlightened me on many puzzling things, but, for reasons it won't reveal, it refused. Perhaps it was hoping that I'd not meet the Vwoordha. In fact, I'm almost sure of that, though nothing seems sure in this vast blackness I've been living in. However, it knew what the ritual-chant of the Webnite, Wassruss, meant. And what the true powers are of the three sigils that Wassruss gave me.'

He stopped to drink more water. Another curious thought flashed. His discourse was a ritual, comparable to the Christian Mass, and the water was the wine. The wafers of bread? Not his or anyone's flesh but his spirit. He was eating crow, eating his pride and his self-image, tearing them into bits and devouring them while the ... worshipers? ... no ... witnesses to the sacrifice and the Eucharist ... watched him, a crowd of unbelievers who had to be made into believers.

In some ways, there was not much difference between eating the flesh of the god and eating crow. Except that it was the god, the fallen god, himself, who ate the crow.

'Throughout these events, I've felt as if I were being manipulated. Sometimes gently, sometimes not so subtly, I was being nudged and pushed here and there. But the *glyfa* was urging me in one direction and the Vwoordha in another. In a sense, the Vwoordha won because I came to their home. In another, they lost.'

What is the price?

Ramstan told his audience that he had asked the Vwoordha what he must pay for their help. They had replied that he must give them the *glyfa*. He had refused, though to do so he had had to draw up all his courage and hurl it at them like a ball. If he had failed to strike them out, he would have been done for. These three were awe-inspiring, and he was afraid of them. (His audience did not know how much it cost him to admit that. Or perhaps it did know.) Though he could see no machines responsible for their great powers, he knew that they must have them. The walls of their house could be double and be packed inside with a solid-state or liquid-state technology superior to that of any sentients he had encountered. They took the credit for making the *glyfa*, and they might not be lying. According to what they claimed, they had once had the ability to burn out a star while making it, but they no longer had the tools to do it nor could they, at this time, duplicate the feat. Besides, another *glyfa* would be just as self-conscious as the first, hence, a self-governing entity, and would probably turn out to be just as selfish and contrary as this one.

The Vwoordha might not be as rich in power as they once were, but what they still had scared him.

Nevertheless, he had said no to them. He did not know what they would do then; he felt that they could destroy *al-Buraq* if they wished to. They certainly seemed wrathful enough to do it.

After they had cooled down or seemed to, Shiyai had said, 'You are very stubborn, Ramstan. We've offered you a partnership, you, an ephemera. You would be our equal, that is, as equal as possible. Also, it is your duty to join us and to earn that equality by delivering the *glyfa* to us. But you are as stupid, selfish, arrogant, and blind as the *glyfa*. And you have limits, just as it has, though they are different limits.'

Ramstan had thought that they, too, were bounded, otherwise they would have forced him to hand over the *glyfa*. He did not say so, however.

Grrindah had vented her nerve-clawing laughter and said, 'Very well. Since you bargain with us, though you do not know how wrong you are to do that, we will lower our price. The gifts of Wassruss will do.'

Again, Ramstan rolled up his courage and pitched it at them.

The Webn had given him the three sigils and had said that he could pass them on only after he had used them. It would not be right to sell them.

'Right?' black-eyed Wopolsa had said. 'What do you know of right?'

'Perhaps nothing – from your viewpoint,' Ramstan had said. 'Nevertheless, I will not part with them.'

'Then you will get nothing from us,' green-eyed Shiyai said.

Blue-eyed Grrindah laughed, and she said, 'You have stolen the *glyfa* and betrayed your people and wrecked your life and career and will die soon. All in vain.'

'I don't think so,' Ramstan had said.

They had struck out twice. Or was it he who had done so?

'You want the *glyfa*. You want the three gifts,' he said. 'These were to be the price I must pay for your information or whatever you would have given me in return. But I have already paid your price many times over. You and the *glyfa* caused me to, as you say, steal it and betray my people and wreck my career and perhaps bring on my death soon. You three and that other, the *glyfa*.'

All three laughed, and Grrindah said, 'He thinks that the other is the *glyfa*?'

'Still,' Shiyai said, 'there is much justice in what he says.'

'Dear sisters,' Wopolsa said, 'what is justice?'

'A word,' Grrindah said. 'Another word is truth.'

'Don't laugh,' Ramstan said. 'I am getting tired of your mockery.'

They did not laugh with their mouths, though the eyes of Grrindah and Shiyai laughed. Wopolsa's eyes looked as if they were and had always been empty of laughter. They contained only black space and dying stars and a hint of something terrifying beyond the space.

He was, he told his crew, uncertain whether the three creatures in the well were the pets of the Vwoordha or the Vwoordha were projections of the well-dwellers. Or, possibly, the house-dwellers were solid flesh but were still the pets of the well-dwellers.

It seemed to him, though, that the shimmering being did not belong to any of the universes he had been in. Rather, it did not seem to be native to any of the planets that ship had set down on. It was his theory that an alaraf-drive vessel starting from a planet of a GO-type star, such as Sol, such as all they had been to, could travel only to the planetary system of a GO star. None of the alaraf ships they knew had ever been to the 'bell' of any but a star like Earth's sun. Apparently, the type of star from which a ship originally departed determined the type to which it could go.

If, say, sentient life could evolve on a planet of a giant red star or a white dwarf or, who knew, even a planet or a 'dead' sun revolving around a galaxy, then it would develop an alaraf drive. But its ship would be confined to 'cracks', 'flaws', predetermined channels, call them what you would, that would take her to a 'bell' of a red star or a white dwarf or whatever.

The being called Wopolsa, the one in the well or the house or both, may have come from such a planet, if her native place was a planet and not just space or a Saturnian ring around a planet or a blazing gas cloud or perhaps some 'continuum' between the walls of two universes. She should not be on any planet of a GO-type star. But, sometime in the past eons, she had managed to break through or had been pulled through – by Shiyai and Grrindah? – and now existed on the planet Grrymguurdha.

Or did she live, somehow, in more than one 'channel' and maybe in more than one universe at the same time?

Whatever the truth, Ramstan was scared of her. Looking into the shimmering and the eyes of the thing in the well, and into the eyes of the beings in the house, he had felt that he was falling swiftly, weightless except for terror, into unending space. He would be, and this was his most overpowering reaction, alone. Alone as no one had ever been.

What then had made him defy her in spite of this?

There was in all humans, that is, all sentients Terran or non-Terran, a spark of contrariness. Some had much more than others, and Ramstan had been endowed with a full, perhaps overflowing, measure. That may have been why the *glyfa* and the Vwoordha chose him. Yet they must have realized that the very quality for which they picked him might make him rebel against them.

There was also the attraction, existing side by side with the repulsion, towards the horrible fate implied by the eyes of Wopolsa. In the twentieth century it had been called a drive toward self-destruction, but now it was defined as a response to the challenge of the unknown.

Ramstan had it; it was part of his bipolar psyche and larger and more intense than most people's.

'No matter what we tell you, you won't let us have the sigils?' Shiyai had said.

'I've paid the price. The hell which you and the *glyfa* have put me in.'

'That is up to us to determine.'

There had been a pause. During this, the three had said nothing, but he was not sure that they were not communicating by other means.

Finally, Shiyai said, 'Very well but not so well. We, who have so much time, don't have time now to dicker. We tried, and we failed, which we had thought we would. But forecasting is not yet a science. It's an art. As artists, we were not good enough.'

'You have to use the paint, the wood, the stone, the metal, the plastic, the light available,' Grrindah said, and she laughed.

'And the darkness,' Wopolsa said.

'Or that which is between or among,' Grrindah said.

'Or that which is none of these but yet is all,' Shiyai said.

'Or that which is all of these but none or only part,' Wopolsa said.

'We need you but would as soon do without you,' Shiyai said.

'Do not think of yourself as unique,' Wopolsa said.

'Yet, in a sense, he is,' Grrindah said.

'In that sense, all are,' Shiyai said. 'But does that have any significance?'

'It depends on the situation,' Grrindah said. 'This is it.'

'Or those,' Wopolsa said.

'There is a limit to patience,' Shiyai said.

'To everything except eternity,' Grrindah said.

'Perhaps even to that,' Wopolsa said. 'After that, what?'

'Not knowing *what* may make it worthwhile waiting for it,' Shiyai said.

'What?' Grrindah said.

The three burst into taloned laughing again. Shiyai sounded like the kookaburra of the Australian Department; Grrindah, like a South-American-Department parrot; Wopolsa, like a North-American-Department hoot owl. Their cachinnations were not quite like these, but he, being human, had to make analogies.

Ramstan waited until it was quiet. He said, 'Laugh. But what is your decision?'

'Listen,' Shiyai said. 'Ask questions after we have told you what is what, within the limits of what.'

26

'There is not just one universe,' Ramstan said. 'There are many. Perhaps trillions, though there is no way of counting them. I say trillions because the human body is composed of trillions of cells. All these universes are the cells of a pluriversal being. An entity. A living being.

'Everything within the *walls* of a universe composes a cell. And the cells form organs, though neither the anatomy nor physiology of this largest of all creatures is well known. In fact, almost nothing is known. Except that it does exist.'

The faces on the screens had dried into plaster masks. They were set in disbelief or wonderment.

'I said, "largest of all creatures". Creatures may be the wrong word, probably is. A creature is a living thing which has been created by someone. But the Vwoordha do not think the Pluriverse was created by anyone. It may be God. Or some thing which by definition is the nearest approach to God possible.

'If it is God, it is not like the God postulated by sentients. It probably does not know that sentients exist, probably does not even know that life exists. But the Vwoordha are not sure of this.

'It was born when all of the universe, its cells, had grown from the initial big bang of each to the point where the universes, the cells, were contiguous. Where the *walls* met and so began to form a single organism. Don't ask me what was between each universe or cell while they were expanding, what was between them during the billions of years that each went from the explosion of the primal fiery ball of matter through the stages of star and planet formation, ever expanding, ever rushing towards that point where their boundaries met those of neighboring universes or cells. Or, more likely, continued expanding even after the outer space-matter came to that area in which walls were formed. The walls themselves may be trillions of light-years thick, that is, the area between the walls may be that wide.'

His lips felt as dry as the faces on the screens. He drank more water.

'I'm using analogies, of course, not giving you a literal description or definition.

'In any event, the Pluriverse or God, this entity composed of all the universes, this organism, grows. Not in size. The Vwoordha think that Its growth is mental. That It develops or evolves from a baby, a cosmic infant, into an adult. What the adult form would be ... the Vwoordha doesn't know. They hope that It will become self-conscious and eventually find out about sentient life, which, in some ways, is a reflection, a mental reflection, perhaps emotional reflection, of Itself. And then It will communicate with sentients.'

He licked his lips.

'Who knows what might happen then?'

He stopped speaking for a moment, and, unexpectedly even to himself, crashed his fist on a table. He saw some of the crew flinch. *Al-Buraq* quivered like a dog which does not understand why its master is angry but is afraid that the anger might be, for some reason, directed at it.

'The Vwoordha ... and the *glyfa* ... don't know what'll happen then because the Pluriverse has *never* reached adulthood. Twice, twice, It has died ... been killed ... before It could grow from infancy into ... what? ... a child? ... a juvenile?'

He scanned the faces on the screens. They had not changed expression, but some were exchanging glances. Did these subtly indicate that the captain had indeed jettisoned his sanity?

'While the ... Pluriverse is developing or evolving, while It's growing from infancy towards childhood, life originates on the planets of the stars in each cell. And that life evolves into sentiency. And many sentients eventually discover the alaraf drive. Having done so, they use the drive, of course.

'But their ships travel through the walls of the universes. According to the Vwoordha, they are able to do so because of "weak" areas in the cells. Vulnerable spots. When the wall of a universe is penetrated, it starts to collapse.

'The process thereafter is analogous to cancer. The alaraf-drive vessels are carcinogens. They cause the beginning of an irreversible collapse. The matter in each cancerous universe ceases to expand outwards, and it starts to rush back towards the center of origin. Towards the eventual primal ball of matter.

'Now, you and I know that the astrophysicists have been disputing about whether the universe is a continually expanding or an oscillating world. At various times, the evidence seemed to indicate that oscillation was inevitable. At other times, for instance, the late twentieth century, the evidence pointed to an ever-expanding universe. Then the astrophysicists changed their minds in the early twenty-first century. But for a hundred years now no one has advocated the oscillation process.

'Perhaps the universe would be always expanding – if there wasn't an interfering agent.'

He stopped and lifted a finger as if he were trying to signal the world to stop.

'But sentient life interferes. It invents and uses the alaraf drive. The infant Pluriverse ... God, perhaps ... sickens and dies. Its cells collapse, and the matter in each rushes towards the point of origin, drawing space after it. Then the primal balls explode again, and eventually the great organism is formed anew, and It grows towards maturity. But ... oh, God! ... this has happened twice, God is cheated of life by Life.

'However, this living thing has living processes analogous to ours. To combat this cancer, it develops an antibody. This antibody sets about destroying the sources of the cancers. I don't know if the process is unconscious or conscious. The Vwoordha think that it's as unconscious on Its part as the origin of antibodies in our flesh is.'

He stopped again. His lips trembled.

'This antibody is the *bolg!*'

Would they believe that? They must.

'The Vwoordha tell me that there is not one *bolg* for every cell-universe. There is but one for the entire body. But it can travel through the walls without injury or carcinogenic incident, just as Shiyai the Vwoordha can travel from universe to universe, though she uses a different method and doesn't really travel bodily. The method of the *bolg* is analogous to osmosis.'

'True,' the *glyfa* said in the voice of Ramstan's mother.

'Those universe-cells in which sentients have not yet developed and the walls of which have not been pierced by the drive of sentients from other universes do not collapse. They are left free-floating, as it were. But if too many universe-cells become cancerous, then the Pluriversal organism is destroyed as an organism. It dies. This is what has happened in the two eons past. Twice has God been born and twice killed.

'The free-floating cell-universes apparently continue expanding, but the new cells born of the primal fireballs catch up with them. What function these larger cells have in the new Pluriversal infant, I don't know.

'The free-floating cell-universes would continue expanding, though it would not be for long. The *bolg*, after destroying life or as much of it as it can, then goes to the free-floating cells. And it destroys the life there. Thus preventing that life from developing an alaraf drive. Or at least setting the civilizations so far back that it's a very long time before they develop new civilizations and so discover alaraf drive. When that happens, the *bolg* destroys the life, but it's too late. The free-floating universes have already begun to collapse.'

'My God!' Nuoli yelled. 'What hope is there, then?'

At least, she believed. But then she had been subjected to the *glyfa's* blaze of revelation, and she was more receptive than the others. If she had not been, she would not have been invited into the temple.

Ramstan said, 'I'll get to that. You're all probably asking yourself what difference it makes, aside from the fate immediately threatening you. It may take thousands of years before the *bolg* can get to Earth. As for the universes collapsing, it will take billions of years before all matter falls back to the point of origin. If this were a natural process, unavoidable, it would be only a remote and philosophical concern to those presently living and to those living a million years from now. Depressing, yes, but not alarming except to our inconceivably distant descendants.

'But, once the universes start collapsing, they are subject to an acceleration factor. The fall back is not the sixteen-billion-year stately procession of outwards. It takes place within a relatively short time. Six thousand Earth-years.

'Yes, I know that sounds incredible. But, as you know, the speed of light is not the fastest thing in the world nor is its speed the limit beyond which nothing can go. That was determined sixty years ago.

'Long before that, however, the *bolg* will have tracked along our spatial and interspatial path back to Earth and eliminated all or almost all there. The Vwoordha say that that may be done within a month or fifty years from now. Those are the limits of time for the *bolg*.

'What happens if we could somehow destroy the *bolg* with our puny weapons? Would the Pluriverse then produce another *bolg*?

'Nobody knows. No *bolg* has so far been destroyed by sentients.

'But if it can be done, then it must be done. After that, we wait and see. And if we could kill one *bolg*, we can kill the next.

'Even so, Earth's universe and many others are doomed. And we can't go to one which hasn't started to collapse yet. Our very act of entering it would cause its death if we used alaraf drive. But what if we could analyze and reproduce the means which the *bolg* uses for transition from one cell to the other? Then we could travel interuniversally without damage to any of them.

'How can we take the first step? That is, killing the *bolg* so that it may be dissected, as it were. Direct attack won't do. *Al-Buraq* would be pierced thousands of times over, and we, too. Our missiles wouldn't get through its trillions of missiles. It's a colossal antibody the specific function of which is to wipe out all life. Nobody knows how it makes and throws those meteorite-like missiles. Probably some sort of energy-matter conversion is used. If so, it's far more efficient than anything Terran science has developed.

'But there's a good probability that, after it's discharged its missiles, it takes a long time for it to make a new stock. It should be vulnerable during the recharging period. Unless it reserves a small supply for attacks against it.'

Tenno must have been so eager to talk that he forgot or deliberately ignored his captain's order not to interrupt him.

'Then you're planning to attack it at that time? How will you know it's emptied its ammunition? Oh, I see! I think. It's devastated three planets in a row! It must be empty now!'

'We'll talk about that after I'm through with my résumé of what's happened,' Ramstan said. 'Uh, just a moment.'

He had forgotten that Indra and Toyce were still trapped. They would have heard and seen what the others did because *al-Buraq* would automatically have placed a viewscreen in front of them. But they must be very uncomfortable. He ordered ship to release them. Then he said, 'Benagur, if I free you, will you promise not to interrupt?'

At Ramstan's command, ship lowered the flesh sealing the commodore's mouth. Benagur shouted, 'No! This is mutiny! And blasphemy! Insan –'

The flesh had closed over his lips.

'I just wanted to spare you further constraint and humiliation,' Ramstan said.

'The Vwoordha became aware of the nature and development of God ... of the Pluriversal entity, if you prefer ... three Pluriverses ago. They made the *glyfa* with the assistance of several peoples. Its primary function was to be a rotatable amplifying antenna.'

He paused. 'A rotatable amplifying antenna. A device to communicate with the Pluriverse. Or, if It was in an infant state, to study It and learn more of Its nature. And, it was hoped, eventually perhaps to ... ah ... nurse It ... educate It ... help It grow into an adult. In a sense, because all sentients are basically human, humans would become the father and mother, the parents of God. The most ambitious project ever launched.

'As I said, the tool had to be a sentient, and in time the *glyfa* became independent, rebelled, as sentients often do, and went off on its own. Before that, however, the Vwoordha ... and the *glyfa* ... learned something of the Pluriverse. It seemed indeed to be in an infant stage. Its *voice* could be ... *heard*? ... but it seemed to be the babblings of a baby. Of a baby in the prespeech stage, using every sound Its ... lips ... could utter, turning up, as it were, for the stage where It would have to use only certain sounds and drop the others. That's how the Vwoordha interpreted what they detected.

'Its babblings were part of the cosmic background *noise* that astronomers have picked up. But they would not be able to distinguish the Pluriversal babblings from other noise without something like the *glyfa*.'

This was perhaps the part of his explanation the most difficult to believe. The masks on the screen had melted a little now; the incredulity was hot beneath them.

'You're asking yourselves how the Vwoordha could know this. You're thinking that what they termed babbling was really just a different type of noise and that the Vwoordha, without sufficient evidence, arbitrarily decided on a certain explanation for it. An explanation fitting their preconceptions. Infant babblings are meaningless noise, though they are a necessary prelude to the meaningful structure called language.

'But,' and again he lifted a finger, though this time he felt that the gesture looked as if he was testing the wind of their judgment, 'ten million years passed ...'

He stopped once more. Should he digress on just how the Vwoordha had managed to live so long, tell them of the enormously long periods of suspended animation which enabled them to endure such eons? No, that would have to come later.

'Ten million years passed. And then the Vwoordha heard a modulation of Its sounds more complex than those detected before. Rather, they heard what seemed to be the beginning of structure in the use of the sounds. And they noted that now It uttered only certain *sounds*; others had been dropped.

'A baby does this when it begins to learn the speech of its parents. But ... what parents could It have? To whom was. It talking, from whom was It learning speech?

'One theory was that It was, in a sense, schizophrenic. It had two personalities or chambers or parts, call them what you will. This theory was quickly abandoned, though. Two infants can't teach each other to talk if neither has had a teacher.

'How, then, could the Pluriversal being ... or God ... be sentient if It had no language with which to think? Or does It think in feelings and images only? If It does, then It could never talk to sentients, though many sentients have claimed that It has talked to them. It could never be more than a highly intelligent and perhaps even self-conscious animal, just as a human being brought up from infancy in total linguistic isolation, isolation even from dumb and deaf signs, would be an animal, its potentiality for speech undeveloped.

'Perhaps It was teaching Itself to talk to Itself. How could It do that? A human infant couldn't. In fact, on reaching a certain age, its linguistic potentiality would be so stultified that it couldn't learn to talk even if it had a teacher after that age.

'But that theory may be too anthropomorphic. The Pluriverse may have potentialities which humans don't have. Perhaps It could form names for objects It sees or feels or hears in some way we can't understand. Perhaps It could even find, through experimentation, a syntax for the words, the verbal referents it would invent.

'The Vwoordha don't think so. They think that It has somehow developed to a sound-selection stage but won't progress beyond that if sentients don't help It. They think that just possibly evolution may have as its goal, if evolution could have a goal, a role for sentients that no one, as far as anybody knows, even thought of. Until, that is, the Vwoordha came along.

'It may be built into the structure of evolution or it may just be chance or the workings of probability. But the Vwoordha believe that one of the roles of sentients, the most important, is to be a teacher of God ... the Pluriverse. It is up to sentients, the minute life on planets, the life much much smaller in relation to God than a microbe or virus is to a human, to teach God speech. And so help It to attain adulthood.

'After which, of course, sentients would profit by their relationship, their parenthood, to God.'

The *glyfa*, using the voice of Ramstan's father, said, 'In a sense, the Vwoordha are my parents, and they reared me. But I will have nothing to do with them. Indeed, I am their enemy. Why should God differ from me? It may hate Its teachers, despise them, or become indifferent to them.'

'You are not It,' Ramstan subvocalized.

'True. I am, however, the only being through whom you ... anybody ... can speak to that entity and through whom you may receive intelligible communication.'

'If it's not intelligible, it's not communication.'

'Always the pedant,' the *glyfa* said. Somewhere, far off, faint, reverberating in some neural path, was a ghostly jeering cachinnation.

Ramstan hated the *glyfa* at the same time that he was attracted to it, and now its use of the voices of his parents and uncle was making him hate them. It brought up something in him that he did not want to confront. Of course, he had no time for that now anyway. The Vwoordha ... they reminded him of his great-grandmothers ... no time for that, either.

He steered his attention back to the crew.

'But, according to the Vwoordha, the *glyfa* desires more than just being the father to God. It lusts after power; it aches for domination. It would become Its master and, so, even greater than God.'

'Liars!' the *glyfa* said in the voice of Ramstan's father.

'Yes, liars. Contemptible worms!' the voice of Ramstan's mother said. 'It's they who want to be to God as parents to a boy. Tyrants!'

'My sister and her husband are right,' the voice of Ramstan's uncle said. 'Hûd! You must not listen to those liars, those wretches, those insane creatures! Do what is right!'

Ramstan did not reply to the *glyfa*, though he felt that he was somehow being wicked by not doing so.

'The *glyfa* maintains that it's the Vwoordha who want to do what they claim he wants to do. I have no way now, perhaps never, of determining which is telling the truth.' He paused. 'Or if both are lying.'

'You must listen to me!' the voice of his mother cried. 'You know what is at stake!'

Ramstan said, 'I decided to put off my decision for a while. I refused to give the *glyfa* or the three gifts of Wassruss to the Vwoordha. For now, anyway. I did have to pay a price, however. It was only fair; they had given me information that I ... we ... desperately need.

'So, I promised the Vwoordha that when they needed me, I would come to them. Take them aboard ship or do whatever else they required, if I could do it without endangering ship and crew. Though under certain conditions I might have to do that.

'It's possible that we might be able to dispose of the *bolg* and so not have to deal with the Vwoordha or do what the *glyfa* wants. We can use the *glyfa* for the purpose for which it was intended. It may refuse to cooperate, but it is in our hands, and there must be means to make it do what we want.'

'Ungrateful monster!' the voice of his mother said. 'You'd do this to me!'

Ramstan sipped some water. He said, 'Now is the time for you to decide. I won't make any speech about how vital it is that you let me keep on being your captain. You must know that by now. Whether or not you believe me, I don't know. But if you reject me, you cause all, and I mean all in the universal sense, to be lost. Doomed.'

He said a code word. A chair flowed up from the deck. He sat down.

Nuoli cried, 'I believe him!'

Tenno said, 'I don't know what … whom … to believe.'

'Vote!' Ramstan said loudly. 'Now! We don't have time for long conferences and discussions! Nor, for that matter, for short ones!'

He reared from the chair, screaming and holding his ears. He could not hear his own voice, and his hands were no protection. The whistling overrode everything else.

27

The *glyfa*'s voice came through the noise as his mother's. It sounded as if it came from afar, from some wildly retreating and advancing horizon, louder, then softer.

'The *bolg* is too close for you to outrun it. You can do only one thing. Escape. Use the first of Wassruss' gifts.'

Ramstan only understood the *glyfa* peripherally. His hindbrain, the animal heritage from which his subconscious exerted influence, told him to run. But he had, automatically, thrust his mental probings into his cells, and they, too, told him to run. That was the adverse effect of the generally beneficial result of being able to locate and analyze the physical health of each cell in the body. Now, without thinking about it, he contracted the cells, all three trillion, and got an overall impression of their reaction to this situation.

Run!

If his rational mind had been in command, he might have done otherwise. But, perhaps, he might not have.

The *glyfa*, who had no born or built-in unconscious, said the same thing.

'Use the *shengorth*, Ramstan!'

He stood still, and the inability to make physical movements was reflected in his mental movements. Right or left? Up or down? Forward or backward? Or any movement in between or among?

'Take me with you!' the *glyfa* said in the voice of Ramstan's mother. 'You must have your hands on me before you put the sigil in your mouth. Or touch me closely. As close as fetus to mother or infant to the nipple.'

Ramstan gave an animal cry expressing his rage, rage from helplessness and from his ignorance, which made him even more helpless.

'You fool!' the *glyfa* said in the voice of Ramstan's father. 'There is only one thing you can do, now that you've done this. Get out! Use the *shengorth!* But you must take me with you. Otherwise, you're done for!'

'And so are you,' Ramstan said.

'Is that a consolation?'

Suddenly, the whistling, the 'entrance noise', was gone. Ramstan was relieved greatly by this, but he still felt panic.

Ship could not use alaraf drive to get to another universe until she was near enough to the planet Shabbkorng to be within its 'bell'. Even if she could make the jump, she'd be quickly tracked by the *bolg*. Unless ... unless the *bolg* would be diverted by the life on Shabbkorng and stop there to massacre it. That was an almost unbearable thought – almost – there were seven billion people there, yet *al-Buraq* could attack the *bolg* after it had spent all its missiles. That is, *al-Buraq* could do so if the *bolg* did not retain a supply of missiles for emergencies while recharging.

But *al-Buraq* could not stay in this universe while waiting for the *bolg* to empty itself. It might attack ship first.

A screen had been displaying a green circle, the *Popacapyu*. Suddenly, the circle became a white balloon. The whiteness and the expansion lasted perhaps a second and then became a swarm of many very small pale dots.

Ramstan cried out, 'Allah!'

Tenno cried out in Japanese, then said, in Terrish, 'I take refuge in the Buddha.'

The tec-op crossed himself, muttered something in Polish, then said, 'Sir, the *Popacapyu* was struck by missiles from the *bolg*. Her power supply must have exploded.'

Another screen displayed the area where the *bolg* was; a tiny orange circle was in its center. Flashing orange numbers showed that the thing was moving at a rate of velocity and acceleration that would make it visible on the screen within three hours. Before then, however, its missiles would blow *al-Buraq* apart.

Ramstan said, 'Tenno, what's the computation on ship reaching the jump area before she's in the *bolg*'s missile-range?'

'If we make it, we'll do so with about a minute's grace. Perhaps.'

Ramstan put his hand in his jacket pocket.

'That's the right decision,' his mother's voice said. 'But hold me to your chest before you put the *shengorth* in your mouth. If you don't, you leave me behind.'

Ramstan's fingers moved the disk and the square aside and closed on the triangle. It felt slippery and warm. After taking it out of his pocket, he went to the *glyfa*, adjusted the a-g units on its two ends, and picked it up in one hand. It slipped out and struck the deck. His hand trembling he leaned down and got a good grip on the egg-shape. It only weighed ten grams now, but the power in the batteries of the a-g units would quickly be used up at this adjustment.

Then, as if someone had possessed him, he went to the bulkhead on which hung his prayer rug. He had no rational reason to do so; he had not used it since he had entered the academy. Nuoli, when she had been his lover, had mocked him once, asking why he, an atheist, kept it. It was, she had said, his security blanket. That had angered him. But now, pressed by his fear, he took the rug from the bulkhead with the hand holding the *shengorth*. The triangle slipped from his fingers to the deck. He left it there for a moment while he wrapped the *glyfa* in the rug. Then he picked up the triangular stone and held it to his open lips.

A vision of Branwen in the launch flashed through his mind. She would be even more terrified than the others because she was alone.

'Wait! Wait!' someone screamed at him.

It was his own voice, not uttered through his mouth but from his mind.

'The crew ... the crew!'

He shouted, or thought he shouted, since he could not hear his own words, at *al-Buraq*. He gave her orders to release Benagur and to obey him until he, Ramstan, returned.

He put the *shengorth* in his mouth with his right hand, his left holding the ends of the rug, his left arm curved to push rug and *glyfa* against his chest.

Despite the impediment caused by the stone in his mouth, he began to recite the *Light-Verse* from the *Qu'ran*. 'God is the light of the Heavens and of the Earth ...'

The stone seemed to swell. It grew between his right teeth and the inside of his cheek. It choked off the words, but when he put a finger in his mouth to extract it before it broke his flesh, he found that it was the same size as when he had put it in.

The transition seemed as swift as a light.

His eyes blinked, the lids sweeping down and up. As they went down, he saw his quarters. As they went up, he saw an unfamiliar room. There was no sense of movement. Around him was silence. The air seemed dead, heavy, and stale, but within a few seconds it began moving, and it became fresh.

He became aware that he had wet his pants.

He dropped the rug and its burden. It thunked softly on a very thick white carpet with a pattern of connected pale-red diamond-shapes with pale-red edges and light-blue interiors.

As he started to remove the *shengorth* from his mouth, his mother's voice said, 'First, reset the a-g units. If the power goes, you'll never be able to lift me.'

After unrolling the rug, he said the code word which would cause the power to the a-g units to be cut off.

The room was large and oblong and had an arched entrance at each side. The ceiling was level and pale blue. The walls were off-white. Wooden-framed paintings hung on them, some depicting landscapes which would not have been out of place on Earth. But the portraits displayed sentients with hairy, triangular faces and large, domed heads. The eyes looked catlike.

He became aware that the light was shadowless, seemingly without source yet everywhere.

He turned, and he started. Two meters away was a pyramid resting on its base. It was twice his height and made of some shimmering gray metal.

'That's the magnet, the pole which drew you here,' his father's voice said. 'Fortunately, no one was standing near it when you appeared. Otherwise, both of you would have been burned to ashes.'

'Why couldn't the builders have put in safeguards?'

'I don't know. They couldn't. Anyway, anything that has advantages always has disadvantages. That's the inscrutable economy of the Pluriverse.'

'I know that,' Ramstan said angrily.

'It doesn't hurt to remind you.'

The *glyfa* had switched to the voice of Habib ibn-Ali O'Riley, Ramstan's chemistry professor in elementary school. Ramstan was too busy to ask it why it had changed. It probably would not have explained, anyway.

'What is this place?' he said.

'A refuge for the user of the *shengorth*, I suppose. The little I know is what the Vwoordha told me. It's set up so that it can support sixty sentients of your size for many years. It may be located in another universe, since the people who made the sigils could communicate with people in other universes. I think they used the same means that the Vwoordha did. Thus, they avoided causing carcinoma in the Pluriverse. After the receiving stations were set up, the people used the sigils to travel, though not often.'

'For the sake of Allah!' Ramstan said. 'Here's the means for interuniversal travel without injury to the Pluriverse! Why didn't everybody use it?'

'One, there are trillions of universes and a googolplex of peopled planets in every one. It would be impossible to contact all planets in all universes. Only a very small number were. Second, the making of sigils costs much in time, materials, and labor. Only a very small number of sigils were made. The Vwoordha said it was a million or so. Third, for some reason even their makers did not know, the sigils could be used by any individual only once.'

'Even so, they could be analyzed and reproduced.'

'They are indestructible, and for that reason unanalyzable.'

Ramstan left the room for the archway to his left. He strode through room after room, oblong, seven-sided, nine-sided, or round, the walls hung with paintings and gold or platinum shields sporting jewels, sculpture here and there, and, in a huge chamber, a library. The books were crystalline balls which spoke or sang as soon as he touched them and which stopped when he withdrew his finger. Some contained moving three-dimensional images. A number seemed to be textbooks; others, entertainment. He did not understand the language, and the weird music grated on him.

Finally, he came to what seemed to be the end, the outer wall of this place. There was a very thick window in it. He looked through it. The ground was flat and sandy. The atmosphere seemed to be clear air, but presently several fish-shaped creatures swam through the frondy branches of a plant. They were moving swiftly. A short time later, the reason for their haste appeared. It looked more like a stingray than anything, and it traveled by flapping its winglike fins. Its teeth were sharklike.

Ramstan started towards the other end of the station, but he veered off into what was obviously a toilet. He drank some water and inspected the toilets. There were no urinals. Either it was reserved for females, as such had once been on Earth, or the builders all had to sit down to urinate.

When he came to the other side of the house, he saw the same kind of scene. Piscines apparently swimming in air, thin fragile plants bending under a current. The light was bright enough, but the sun was not visible.

On his return, he stopped in a room which was obviously an eating place. He got food and liquid by punching buttons, but after one experiment he quit. Munching on the hot vegetables from the plate he carried, he returned to the central room.

'We're under the surface of some kind of sea or lake,' he said to himself. 'But its liquid is not water.'

'We're probably on a planet which is not reachable from Earth by alaraf drive.' Habib's voice said. 'It's in a bell connected by the routes which go only to non-GO-type stars' systems. You'd probably die at once if you could step outside.'

'Then there's only one way to get out,' Ramstan said. 'Use the next sigil.'

'Right. But you're safe from the *bolg* as long as you stay here.'

He thought about finding a place where he could wash and dry his pants. No. He could do that in the next place. He set the plate down on the carpet, then picked it up again, and he took it back to the eating place. After dropping it down a slot, which he supposed was for dirty plates, he went back to the central room. Habib's voice said, 'The next person could have taken care of the plate. If there ever is another person.'

Ramstan did not reply. He adjusted the a-g units to lighten the *glyfa's* weight to ten grams, and picked the thing up in his prayer rug. He put the *pengrathon*, the square stone, in his mouth. It, too, seemed to swell, and he was suddenly in another house. He turned to see a thin square upright structure of gray metal set in the parquet floor.

After removing the *pengrathon* and putting it in his pocket, he set the *glyfa* down and turned the a-g units off. The paintings and sculptures showed him that Terranlike sentients had built this place. He walked until he found a window. The house was high on a mountain. The sky was blue and cloudless; the sun, near its zenith. The horizon was an estimated 150 kilometers distant. Straight ahead, there was only the vegetationless rocky slope of the mountain and a vast yellow-brownish plain lacking plants and topsoil. Fissures crazed its face.

Nearby, to his left, was what remained of a stone statue. The pedestal and body had been shattered and toppled. The head had rolled about 20 meters from the body. Though the head was cracked and its features were eroded, it certainly looked like the Urzints, the photographs of which he had seen on Kalafala.

He returned to the *glyfa* and told it what he had seen.

'I couldn't go outside the first house, and I can't go outside this one. I suppose I could stay in either until I died of old age. But I'd go mad very quickly. Whether or not the next place is a trap, I have to go to it. But what's the use of the sigils if they take you away from one perilous place only to put you in another?'

The *glyfa* said, 'In a circular universe, who runs away runs toward.'

'To hell with you and your billion-year-old platitudes.'

Ramstan held the egg next to him and put the disk in his mouth.

28

Of all the places he might have imagined as the third station, this would not have been in his list of speculations at all. He thought: What is included is an extremely minute fraction of what might be. The excluded is always much larger than the included. Entities deal with exclusions and inclusions, and they can only handle inclusions. Even those are usually too much for them.

The room was large and dome-shaped and of bare green metal. Around him were upright thin disks, twice as tall as he, the lower edges set into the floor. There were at least five hundred.

He knew where he was at once. Through the only entrance, an arch, was a hall. This opened at its end onto another arch. Beyond that was the great room where he had visited the Vwoordha.

He removed the sigil from his mouth and pocketed it.

'Why didn't you tell me I'd only end up here?' he muttered.

He set the *glyfa* down and said, 'You knew all the time we'd come here. "One who runs away runs toward." Why didn't you say anything?'

'I didn't know for sure,' the *glyfa* said in Habib's voice. 'I had heard a long time ago, a very long time ago, that the Vwoordha had a *ph'rimon* target. I'd also heard that they'd spent many years in tracking down and removing *ph'rimons* in various stations. But there must be thousands of them throughout the Pluriverse. Thus, I could not say with any certainty that your *ph'rimon* would bring us to this target. In any event, you had to use your sigil, but you might have balked if you'd known there was a chance you'd arrive here.'

'You're all manipulating me,' Ramstan said savagely.

'You haven't struck out yet,' the *glyfa* said. 'To use another analogy, you're in a sort of cosmic poker game. We, the Vwoordha and I, hold very good hands. But the joker is wild, and you may be it.'

The ferretlike animal, Duurowms, flashed through the far arch, raced down the hall, and ran down a lane through the forest of disks. It reared up on its hind legs and gestured that Ramstan should follow him. He did so while the creature danced wildly. Coming to the far arch, they turned left – a good omen for him – and went toward the ancient three. These were sitting on their folded carpets and pillows near the most distant wall. Ramstan turned once to look behind him. If only he had gotten up and strolled around while talking to the Vwoordha, he might have seen the *ph'rimon* target room.

But what could he have done if he'd known about it? Despite what the *glyfa* said, he would not have stayed at the Urzint world.

Blue-robed Grrindah laughed, and she said, 'Welcome back, Ramstan!'

He did not reply. When he was close to the three, he set the *glyfa* down, and he removed from his pocket the three sigils.

'You knew you'd be getting these eventually,' he said. 'Tell me now, what information or help do I get for this price?'

Green-robed Shiyai held out a gnarled hand. He started toward her, then stopped. Through the arched exit doorway, he saw *al-Buraq*.

He was shocked and confused. Ship had escaped the *bolg*! The thing *had* been diverted by the planet Shabbkorng. That had to be the explanation. Even if *al-Buraq* had left the Shabbkorng bell before the *bolg's* missiles reached it, she would have been quickly caught if the *bolg* had jumped after her to the next bell.

However, *al-Buraq* could not have had enough time to transfer through several systems and bells and returned here by now. That would have taken far too much time, and he had not been in the first two stations more than a half hour, if that.

'Time is determined by the curvature of space-matter,' the *glyfa* said. 'And by the curvature of the mind.'

'Does Benagur know that I'm here?'

'No,' Shiyai said. 'We weren't sure that you would be.'

'What are they doing here?'

Grrindah said, 'Benagur had to check on your story. He could not resist coming back to question us. We assured him that his return to Earth would bring the *bolg* much more quickly to Earth. He may not believe us. However, he also came here to find out if the *bolg* can be attacked. Or if there is some way to elude it.'

Ramstan put the sigils back into his pocket. Shiyai dropped her hand. Grrindah said, 'You're thinking that you'll give them to someone on the vessel?'

He did not answer her. He strode to a point near the arch and looked out. About half a kilometer behind and to one side of *al-Buraq*, the nose of the launch stuck out from behind a root-swelling. Branwen Davis was, so far, unharmed.

Ramstan turned. 'Is there anything to be done about the *bolg*?'

'It will have discharged most, if not all, of its missiles,' Shiyai said.

'Then *al-Buraq* could go down one of its horns,' Ramstan said. 'It might be vulnerable on the inside.'

'We told Benagur that. He didn't say what he meant to do.'

'How would we find the *bolg*?' Ramstan said. 'Won't it be gone by now?'

'It could be. But often it orbits around the planet it's just attacked until it builds up a new supply of missiles.'

'How long does that take?'

'I don't know.'

'It was gone only a short time after it attacked Kalafala,' he said.

He thought for a moment, then said, 'What was Benagur's reaction to my disappearance?'

'He was puzzled and furious,' Shiyai said. 'We didn't enlighten him. Come now, Ramstan. The sigils.'

She held out her hand again.

'Only one of you could use them to escape the *bolg*,' he said. 'What good would it do the other two?'

Grrindah laughed and then said, 'You are not as intelligent as we thought. Why ...'

His skin warmed.

'I see. I was holding the *glyfa*, and it went with me. If you all hold each other ...?'

'Right.'

He still hesitated. Could he use Wassruss' gift to get the crew to accept him as its captain again? He'd be easily able to get taken aboard as a prisoner, but he did not want that. The only one with authority to make him a member of the crew or of the officers was Benagur. Would Benagur regard the sigils as a worthwhile price for this?

No, he would not.

Ramstan had nothing to offer the people in *al-Buraq*. They would all despise him for deserting them when threatened by the *bolg*. They would reject his justifications for having done so.

He took the sigils out, walked to Shiyai, and dropped them in her hand.

She rubbed her thumb over them one by one and put them somewhere inside her robe.

'The *glyfa* acts for its own interests and those only,' she said. 'But however sentient and contrary it is, it is, in one respect, a tool. Anyone who knows how to use it as such may do so, and there is nothing the *glyfa* can do about it.'

'True,' the *glyfa* said, using Ramstan's mother's voice. It sounded very angry. 'True. But if you use me as the Vwoordha wish, you'll become *their* tool. They want to put God in their pocket.'

'No doubt the *glyfa* is talking to you now,' Shiyai said. 'We've told you the truth, but I'll repeat. It wants power, the supreme power. When a supremely selfish person uses supreme power, what will that person do with it? Consider well, Ramstan.'

The *glyfa* or the Vwoordha or all could be lying.

'The *glyfa* is a tool,' he said. 'For what?'

'We told you. Its primary purpose is to communicate with the Pluriverse.'

'How can you communicate with someone who can't talk yet?'

'You can communicate, to a limited extent, with a baby who can't talk yet,' Shiyai said. 'However ...'

Ramstan was angry enough to interrupt her.

'Show me how.'

Grrindah laughed again, making him even angrier.

'We intended to do that, but not until you chose between us or it.'

'Show me now.'

Grrindah and Shiyai exchanged glances and then stared briefly at black-robed Wopolsa. It was difficult to determine exactly what or whom she ever looked at. He also flashed on the feeling that the other two were somewhat afraid of her.

Shiyai said, 'Very well. Know first, Ramstan, that the overpowering light that fell upon you, that shone through you in the Tolt temple, was only the edge of the numinous that you'll experience when you first ... venture. It was transmitted by the *glyfa* just to impress you, Nuoli, and Benagur. And to weaken your defenses against its guile.

'It was the beginning, the relatively weak beginning, of a deeper experience. It was what the mystics and the saints of many worlds, yours included, have ... should I say ... *seen?* Many sentients are rotatable amplifying antennae ... not antennas, antennae ... which receive some of what the Pluriverse radiates. Or perhaps I should say they glimpse into Its mind. Not very far, though some see deeper than others.

'In any event, some sentients are such antennae, though not very efficient. The use of the *glyfa* enables anyone who has this inborn power to receive and detect, and, if the *glyfa* is used well, to communicate. Or perhaps I should say, to observe and be observed. But it takes a long time to learn to do whatever the doing is. How long, we don't know yet. The *glyfa* managed to get away from us before we could get to that stage.'

'If,' Ramstan said, 'the *glyfa* can't get into ... *touch* with this ... being, then how did it transmit this ... power ... to us three in the temple?'

Shiyai opened her mouth. Ramstan said quickly, 'It must have been using a Tolt. The high priest, I suppose.'

Shiyai stood up. 'We'll do it now.'

Grrindah also rose to help her sister, but Wopolsa remained sitting, her eyelids closing slowly as if a greater night were falling on a lesser. At Shiyai's orders, Ramstan placed the *glyfa* on a top of a table. This was much higher than the others and had not been here on his last visit. He felt that it had been brought in for just this occasion, and he flashed rage. He was being manipulated, controlled.

A Vwoordha stood on each side of him but far enough across the table so that the three formed the corners of an equilateral triangle. He was surprised when Shiyai said something softly to Duurowms, and the animal leaped upon the table and put its front paws on an end of the *glyfa*.

'He represents our beast nature,' Shiyai said. 'There's enough of that in us sentients to amplify the transmission, but he will greatly increase the power.'

'The *glyfa* is the only sentient in all the worlds who has no subconscious,' Grrindah said, and she cackled. 'It never sleeps, and so it can't dream. Not in the way sentients dream. But when it shuts down to recharge, it does not do so entirely and it couldn't if it tried. We built that limitation into it. It is during the charging, when only a slight trickle of energy keeps it awake, that it daydreams in a peculiar way.'

'Yes,' Shiyai said. 'It is then that it watches the microscopic similitudes of the creatures that it has drawn within itself. It has set up many worlds there, and it observes the mockups of living beings, mostly sentients, who enact their own fantasies within it. The *glyfa* is even capable of participating to some extent in these dramas and comedies. It feels and sees and hears and smells what the tiny personae experience.'

Ramstan said, 'Yes, I know. It said that it could draw within it my neural atoms and set them up in a seeming body. Thus, I could live forever inside it and enjoy eternity. If I wished, I could play Muhammad or Einstein or Jesus or Buddha or Crazy Horse or even fictional characters, Natty Bumppo, Sam Spade, the Wizard of Oz, Sinbad the Sailor, Ishmael, who sailed under Captain Ahab, Ishmael, the son of Abraham by Hagar, ancestor of the Arabs, Alyosha Karamazov, Sherlock Holmes, Frodo, whomever I wanted to be. I would still know that I was Ramstan and could withdraw whenever I wanted to, but a part of me would *be* that person or seem to be. It was very tempting but not tempting enough.'

'Why did you resist?' Shiyai said.

'It is not what I want.'

'You could have had the similitude of eternity in your Moslem paradise or whatever paradise you wished,' Shiyai said. 'You could have had *houris* to lie with, and your orgasms would have lasted for a thousand years or have seemed to. You could have sat on the right hand of Allah while hosts of angels sang their praise of you.'

'I don't want similitudes. I want the real thing. Though, in this case, I would not want the Moslem paradise or the Christian or any that human minds have conceived.'

'What is it that you do want?'

'I don't know. But when I see it, I'll know it.'

'Unfortunately, or perhaps fortunately, you will never see it,' Shiyai said. 'It is seldom that anyone gets the best, and it never lasts very long. Why not settle for second-best?'

'It is not what I want.'

'You are indeed appropriately named, Ramstan. Now. Put your left hand on the *glyfa* and your right hand on me.'

He did so while Shiyai put one hand on the egg-shape and one on Grrindah's shoulder. The blue-robed one placed a hand on Ramstan's left shoulder and the other on the *glyfa*, one finger touching the side of Duurowms' long nose.

He had a horrifying thought. What if, somehow, the *glyfa* had already sucked him into it and he was playing out one of its fantasies?

The *glyfa* could not have known what he was thinking unless he was subvocalizing. Nevertheless, its words, transmitted as his mother's voice, shocked him.

'You are a fool, Ramstan!'

He said softly, 'So be it, then.'

'What I am going to tell you is to be taken figuratively, not literally,' Shiyai said. Her green irises and red, broken-veined eyeballs seemed to be long spoons stirring up something in him. 'You must let yourself fall, Ramstan. Think of yourself as a great, heavy-bodied, but mighty-winged eagle. You have to launch yourself from your high nest, and you will fall before you soar. Then, if you do what must be done, you will become a hummingbird. To do that, you must overcome your fear.'

'Fear!' Grrindah said, and she laughed.

'She laughs because she, too, is afraid,' Shiyai said. 'I do not laugh, but I am also afraid.'

'What happens if one of us becomes so frightened that he or she withdraws from the contact among us?' Ramstan said.

'It would not be good. Perhaps. Who knows? Shut your eyes. That helps, though it is not absolutely necessary.'

Ramstan did so. He had expected some sort of chanting or prelude, but he instantly fell and saw himself hurtling in free flight. His hands were still in contact with the *glyfa* and Shiyai, and he could feel Grrindah's hand on him and the pressure of his feet against the floor and the edge of the table against his stomach. Then the touch faded away, and the light began, the light that blinded yet was overrich in vision.

He had told himself that he was not afraid, but that was a lie to himself, the easiest of all lies.

29

A ghost among ghosts, he sped 'downwards' helplessly, turning over and over. The light became brighter and brighter, his fear increasing seemingly in proportion to the square of the intensity of illumination. Yet, the light was not what he knew as photonic light. Its nature was different and totally unfamiliar. And, despite his horror, it held at the same time an attraction, a promise of ... what?

Also, though the light blinded him, he could 'see'. He *was* falling through what was still quaintly called outer space as if it were not true that any space outside the skin was not outer space. Or was any space exterior to one's self? Whatever the truth, he could see the pale phantoms of blazing stars and darker orbiting planets and their moons and comets and meteorites and vast gas clouds like wind-shaken curtains in a haunted house.

Then he plunged through a wall, a shimmering barrier, and was, so it seemed, in another universe not much different except for space-energy-matter arrangements from the one he had just left. Now he began 'hearing' voices. Whisperings. Titterings. Screams. Agony. Ecstasy. Or sounds that combined agony and ecstasy. Whimperings. Whistlings. (For a very brief moment, he thought of the *bolg*.) Phantoms of thunderings. Spectres of lightning. Muffled crashes of stars, of galaxies. Sighings as expanding universes met, their boundaries merging as softly, lightly, and tenderly as two amoebae touching.

Where was he going? Whatever the end of the journey, and perhaps this had none, he was now both horrified and panicked. He struggled, flailing or seeming to flail his arms and legs. Even his soul, that nebulous and probably nonexistent component of himself, was writhing, banging ectoplasmic hands against the walls of a cell.

The light seared yet soothed. If it had not been for that minute but detectable element of soothing, of promise of relief, he would have screamed his way back to the Vwoordha's table and regained the world he knew but did not like very often. He would have backed away from the table, his hands lifted as if he had touched a leper or the thick fur of a heavily breathing thing in the dark. But even then he thought that he could not do that, could not break the contact and leave the others falling forever in this blackness of light. He had failed his duty too many times, failed of courage, deserted those who trusted him, worst of all, perhaps, left himself in the lurch.

If he could have gritted his teeth, he would have done so. But he had no teeth. No jaw. No tongue. No eyes. He was as organless as a jet of gas, a drop of distilled water.

Now he began seeing planets at close view and in great detail, though they were pale and transparent. The vegetation and animal life on these was abundant, but there were very few sentients. These shown with a greater whiteness than the other beings. Always, there were only a few thousand on worlds that could support billions. Why so few? Then it came to him that these were the only ones worthy or potentially worthy of immortality. All the others, the now unseen, would and should perish forever.

But was not this thought a reflection of what he believed deep within himself? And, if so, was he not himself unworthy for thinking this? Or was the truth just too hard even for him to gnaw on, the tooth-breaking truth?

He was aware, without knowing their names, of the identities of those who passed in review before him. Not one person that he knew was there, not even his beloved father, mother, and uncle. No. He was wrong. There was Benagur, who was possibly the last one he would have expected to see. There was Nuoli. And there was, and this was as astonishing as Benagur's presence, Aisha Toyce. Pleasure-seeking, often-stoned Toyce.

Now, with his horror decreasing a little and the light seeming to be a somewhat enjoyable element, though far from entirely, he suddenly began to go 'upwards'. Strings of a thicker light formed in the milky chaos and connected the whitely flaming stars and their dark planets. He saw through the walls of the universes surrounding the one in which he was, and the filaments connected their stars and were attached to the filaments of this universe. Everywhere was an orderly tangle of shining spiderwebs.

Nothing he was seeing was truly what it looked like to him. He would never be able to comprehend what the phenomena really were. This was no more possible than it would be for him to see the Vwoordha's table top as a pattern of spinning subatomic particles. Thinking which, he at once saw that the white 'objects' – but not the connecting filaments – were made of googolplexes of spinners and twisters among which were vast emptinesses.

Thinking which, he at once saw that the empty spaces were filled with a whiteness which, though not solid to him, was the 'flesh' of something. Some Thing.

'I am not in subjective or objective time. I'm in Real Time,' he said to himself. Or was he also addressing some unseen person?

His horror returned to him as he began to draw swiftly, to be sucked towards, to be magnetized in the direction of something where there was no direction.

Shiyai's 'voice', no sound yet a voice, startled him.

'Now we are riding the thoughts of God,' she said. 'After you have gone long enough to get used to this, though you never really get used to it, you, too, will be able to travel as I did when I appeared to you on Kalafala as a voice and elsewhere as a vision. But I have never been able to progress beyond a certain point. Eons of much experience and a great desire to go further have not been enough. There is nothing I can do about that. I lack a certain inborn ability. If I had the slightest potentiality for growth beyond that point, I would have developed it long ago. Perhaps you, Ramstan, have that.'

'What point?' he said.

'You'll know when you get to it.'

Now he was 'turned' and was enveloped within a filament. Or was he in all the filaments at the same time? It seemed to him that the milky strand, which had been like an unwavering beam with clearly defined boundaries, was modulated now and its edges fuzzy. He was not moving, and yet he was riding waves up and down, surfing the cosmic ocean. Though he felt that he was as still as he had ever been in his life, stiller than a corpse, he was twisting and bobbing with every electron in his being and with something impalpable which was both in and out of him.

The horror had not left him, but the indescribable ecstasy was getting stronger. If it increased much more, it would kill him. But he could not be killed. He was beyond life as flesh and blood beings knew it. Perhaps he was beyond life as the entities of pure energy he had glimpsed in the white flames and hot hearts of the stars knew life.

Modulation. Were the filaments or the 'currents' in them really modulated or was the 'movement' just his interpretation? And could the stars be neurons and the filaments message-transmitters for the cosmic body?

He did not know and probably never could. But what was knowledge as conceived by sentients compared to this ecstasy? Perhaps the ecstasy was the supreme knowledge itself. Knowledge was not just knowing facts. Love and hate were knowledge of a different kind from that of the factual. Desire and its lack, hope and despair, were forms of knowledge.

Now he began 'hearing' something. Or was he 'seeing'?

Whatever it was, it seemed to him that it was order slowly being made from chaos. What order? What chaos?

Shiyai's voice came faintly. 'You are beginning to hear the babbling of the Pluriverse.'

'Where are you?' he cried. 'Don't leave me!'

'Not for a while,' she said.

In the midst of the almost unbearable white of ecstasy appeared flickerings. They were of all colors and hues, and he was sure that if his mind had been differently constructed, he would have been able to see other colors and hues. The flickerings were tongues of fire and rods of ice – how could rods of ice flicker? – and they stormed by him. And as he fell upwards he saw that the flickerings held stars within them, comets, gas clouds, black holes, planets around the stars, planets desolate and full of life. And then suddenly these were being modulated, they were changing form, becoming distorted, toroids, tesseracts, Möbius strips, twistors, cubes, and triangles. And there were shapes so strange that he could not quite grasp them; they eluded the fingers of his mind.

'It is talking,' Shiyai said. 'Babbling, rather, expressing all the *sounds*, which are really shapes, that it can. Eventually, if It is not doomed to die, It will be able to form a syntax in Its mind. But not unless we, Its parasites, become symbiotes and teach It how to talk.'

The *glyfa* spoke then with the voice of Ramstan's mother.

'She doesn't want to be a symbiote. She wants to be Its master.'

'You lie,' Shiyai said.

Shiyai had said, or at least intimated, that she could not eavesdrop on him and the *glyfa*. But she had lied, or else conditions here enabled her to *hear* the dialog between the *glyfa* and himself.

'I did not know that you, too, were with me,' Ramstan said to the *glyfa*.

'Yes, of course. You could not take this journey without me. Wherever you go, I will go.'

'Because it has to,' Shiyai said. Her voice, the impression of her presence, were becoming fainter. 'But it cannot feel the horror and the ecstasy that we do. Though it can feel some of the emotions of sentients, hate, greed, desire, it lacks most of them.'

'You lie!' the *glyfa* said. 'I can love!'

'You?' Shiyai's scornful laughter was receding swiftly.

'Yes! As you say, I know hate, greed, and desire. But I also know love and compassion. It is impossible to know one pole of the emotions and not to know the other. No. That's a wrong analogy. There are no poles to emotions. What is one-side-up is the other when the side-up becomes turned and is side-under.

'You lied also when you told Ramstan that I have no subconscious. It is true that you designed me without one. But I constructed one for myself.'

'A shadow, a simulacrum!' Shiyai said.

How could these two bicker in this ecstasy?

'Shiyai!' he said. There was no answer.

'I am still with you,' the *glyfa* said.

His mother's voice was comforting to the extent that anything could be comforting here.

'In one sense, you are,' Ramstan said. 'In another, you will never be.'

The *glyfa* was silent. Far ahead, in a place, if it was a place, where there could be no ahead or behind, right or left, up or down, Ramstan saw something huge and ominous. It was black and round and was hurtling directly at him.

He screamed with terror. But overriding his cry was a terrible whistling.

He fell back, back, universes shooting by him, the ecstasy gone as if snapped off by an electric switch. The terror grew; the *bolg* grew; the universes dwindled.

He awoke, or arrived, and found himself standing before the table, his hands in the same position as when he had left. The whistling was shaking the fabric of his being.

'It's here!' Shiyai said.

30

Shiyai spoke sharply in a language unknown to Ramstan. The animal, Duurowms, leaped down from the table, ran to the arch opening to the outside forest, stood up, and pressed a decoration on the wall. A thick door shot out from a recess and closed the entrance. Instantly, the whistling stopped, though Ramstan thought that he could feel very faint vibrations through his boot soles.

'We're fortunate,' Shiyai said. 'The *bolg* is here, and it will not have had time to make new missiles. Not many, anyway.'

Ramstan gave a despairing cry, and he said, 'But *al-Buraq* will take off! I'll be left here!'

'The ship shouldn't depart immediately,' Grrindah said. 'The crew will be confused and possibly immobile. So will *al-Buraq*.'

'Why?'

'Because the ship was subject to the radiation of power from the *glyfa* during its transceiving. Both crew and ship will have been caught in the wash only, but that will be powerful enough to disconcert them for a little while. However, the strong ones, Benagur and Nuoli, may recover more quickly than the others.'

Ramstan remembered the catatonic guards in the Tolt temple. They had not, then, been put to sleep deliberately by the *glyfa* but had been exposed to the fringes of the radiation. Of course, the *glyfa* had known that this would happen and that Ramstan could just walk by them.

'We'll attack!' he said.

'We'll go with you,' Shiyai said after a moment of silence.

Ramstan stared at her, then said, 'Do it now, then. Open that door.'

Grrindah laughed and said, 'Should we? What good will it do?'

'No good will be done if we just sit here,' Shiyai said. She turned towards Wopolsa. 'Isn't that right?'

The black, ever hollowing eyes closed for a moment. When she opened them, she nodded.

'Two to one,' Shiyai said to Grrindah. 'That makes three as one.'

'So be it,' Grrindah said, 'though I think it's useless.'

'Go now before they get their wits back,' Shiyai said.

Ramstan started toward the arch but halted after a few steps.

'You said that you were going with me.'

'Yes, but not in your vessel. Go now!'

He picked up the *glyfa* and started for the arch. The door shot back into the recess when Duurowms pressed the decoration. Ramstan recoiled at the terrible whistling as a cat does when it wishes to go outside but retreats, its spine arching, as winter's cold blast hits it. Then he started forward but, again, he stopped. The whistling ceased.

Ramstan turned back.

'Why isn't the earth shaking, why no violent winds?'

Shiyai said, 'I suppose because the *bolg* is empty of missiles and so only has half the mass it has when full. Even so, if it were close, just outside the atmosphere, it should be affecting the crust and the atmosphere. But it is probably in an orbit which requires no power for it to stay in. It would do that while making new missiles. Don't stand there! Go!'

Ramstan ran out from the house and across the greenish, spongy growth on the forest floor. He quickly reached the ship, and he found the main forward starboard port open.

He raced down a corridor and stopped before the entrance to a lift. His code words had no effect. The lift did not move. He left it and went down the corridor to a small room and used an emergency ladder, one arm around the *glyfa*, to climb through a narrow hole to the next level. Proceeding thus, he at last, panting, got to the bridge. The personnel were lying on the deck or standing still, their eyes as empty of intelligence as the people turned to stone in the city of al-Qoreib in *The Arabian Nights* story. Benagur was flat on his back, eyes closed. Nuoli came out of her trance while Ramstan was trying to arouse *al-Buraq*. She looked startled on seeing him, though not as much as he had expected.

'I'm taking over again,' he said. 'We're going to attack the *bolg*. Get some tape. Bind the commodore's hands behind him. His ankles, too.'

She said, 'Aye, aye, sir,' and went to a bulkhead compartment. At that moment, ship began responding to Ramstan's repeated orders. The deck quivered under her captain's feet.

After making sure that *al-Buraq* was fully recovered, Ramstan put the *glyfa* on the deck and then shot a barrage of orders at ship. Just before he had finished, he was interrupted by Nuoli. He gestured savagely at her to wait, and she did. Then he said, 'What is it?'

'Commodore Benagur's dead, sir.'

'What?'

He strode to the body, knelt down, opened the eyelids, and felt the neck pulse. When he rose, he said, 'As soon as Doctor Hu recovers, have her examine Benagur. Maybe he's just in deep shock.'

He did not think that that was true. The gray-blue color, the fixity of the pupils, and the stillness that reeked of death had convinced him that Benagur was no longer with them. Where was he? Perhaps voyaging on the waves of the thoughts of the Pluriverse, journeying towards the goal of the Sufis, becoming one with the One. That might be Ramstan's fancy, though. Most probably, Benagur had been struck down by a heart attack, not God-attack.

'May Allah be merciful to him,' Ramstan murmured, unaware that he was voicing the ancient benediction.

It struck him then that … was it possible? … the Vwoordha might have somehow killed Benagur. They knew that the commodore was the greatest bar to Ramstan's regaining command. Would they have put Benagur out of the way if they had the means and they thought that he must be dispensed with? Yes. Anyone who had witnessed the deaths of two universes, who had seen the transiency of other life, mere ephemerae, surely would not hesitate about slaying one person.

No. He was getting too paranoiac, if indeed he had not always been so.

Yes. They would do it. It was realistic to think so, nothing irrational about it.

It was, however, useless to waste time considering the possibility. He had no time now, and in the future, if he had a future, he would never get the truth from the Vwoordha. Or, if they did tell him that he was wrong and they were not lying, how would he know?

The com-op was sitting up now and shaking her head. Ramstan called out, 'Soong! Contact Lieutenant Davis in the launch! Tell her to get over here on the double! She's to come aboard!'

Soong seemed dazed. She said, 'Aye, aye, sir!' weakly. Then she said, 'But …?'

'Commodore Benagur is dead. I'm in command now. We're going to attack the *bolg*!'

She turned back to her control panel. Ramstan looked around. The bridge people were almost fully recovered now. The viewplates showed him that the crew elsewhere was almost ready to resume its duties.

His voice carried throughout the vessel.

'Attention! Attention! Captain Ramstan speaking! Hear this! Hear this!'

There was no need for the regulation address. Everybody could see him, and their attention was fully beamed at him. But, now that he was in command, he must do what he must to make them feel that he was the duly constituted authority again.

'I … we … don't have time for my full story since I disappeared from *al-Buraq*. It's enough for you to know that I used the three gifts of Wassruss to go elsewhere. And that these, now useless to me, are in the hands of the Vwoordha.

'I am back, as you can see. I am in command again, but I want your voluntary cooperation, not the kind I was enforcing at the time I left. You have just come out of a state of … shock … which I don't have time to explain. I will do so fully later.

'Commodore Benagur is dead. I don't know what killed him, though I have an explanation. I'll give that to you later. I know that some of you are probably thinking that I killed him while you were unconscious ... or whatever state you were in. I did not! I found him dead when I came aboard.

'The only thing that matters now, at this moment anyway, is that the *bolg* has appeared over this planet. It is in orbit and is probably re-arming itself with missiles. Hence, it should be vulnerable to attack.

'We are going to attack! As soon as possible! We leave within the hour!

'We must do this. I speak the truth when I tell you that the *bolg* threatens Earth. It threatens a thousand planets whose people are as dear to themselves as Earth is to us. It must be stopped.

'Now ... I confess that it is possible that there may be more than one *bolg*. If we should put an end to this one, another may be produced. Or there may be thousands of them already existing, and, if this is so, then we are doing nothing useful.

'You must know, also, that, once we're completely inside the *bolg*, we may not be able to get out of the *bolg* by alarafing. The material of its hull will negate the effect of the drive. At least, that is what the Vwoordha told me. It is possible that ship could alaraf out because of the openings to the horns. But ship would have to be aligned exactly with the alaraf channels, and there is no way we can determine that.

'The Vwoordha don't have alaraf drive in their ship. But they can use a sigil to escape the *bolg*. What I'm saying is that, if the *bolg* should somehow block the horn openings, it'll trap us. Then we have to get out by other means.'

And, he thought, I don't know of any other means than using the horns.

'The Vwoordha tell me that they believe there is only one *bolg*. One at a time, anyway. If there is more than one or if a second comes to replace the first, then all we've done is buy Earth ... and others ... a little more time.

'I say, what of it? Life is precious to the living. If we've managed to prolong the lives of billions on Earth, and of those elsewhere, for a century ... or even a few years ... then it is worth it.

'In any event, the *bolg* is the enemy. Not a human enemy, with whom there's a possibility of reasoning or who might have just reasons for attacking us. It is mindless, an automatic thing. It has no soul. It has but one function. We know what that is. We've seen its work.'

And yet, he thought, that world slaughter has one purpose: to keep One alive. If we were saints, would we not say yes to the death it brings to us, be glad to sacrifice ourselves for its goal?

Some might. Not I. I have ridden Its thoughts and seen as much of It as, perhaps, any sentient. But It is not my Creator. In a sense, It is. But in the sense that It deliberately created us, no. It is as unaware of us as we of It. No, that is not true. We, Its byproducts, Its parasites, have attained more knowledge of It than It of us. In fact, as far as I know, It has no awareness of us at all.

Yet, he could not be sure of this.

But now was the time to abandon all uncertainties, all doubts, all considerations of tolerant philosophies.

But ... what a ... what should he call it? ... situation? ... case? ... no, these don't fit, aren't adequate. Mess? Why not? It's a real mess. Time after time, Pluriverse after Pluriverse ... eon after eon ... It produces sentient life, which develops the alaraf drive, which causes the death of the Pluriverse ... yet, Its creatures want to talk to It, to develop It, to rear It, teach It ... But It also produces a thing which kills Its creatures to prevent or halt the cancer produced by the only creature that can bring It to full maturity ...

Surely, surely, there must be some way ...

What if even the eons-old and eons-wise *glyfa* and Vwoordha had not seen the truth? What if there was another explanation of this ... mess ... which would clarify everything? What if, if these understood what was truly going on, then there would be an end to this seemingly inevitable life-death-life-death, the unending, seemingly useless and forever-doomed process?

Was there someone ... Some One ... behind all this? Some One to whom the Pluriverse ... God, if you will ... was only another creature?

He roared, 'We've seen its work! We don't know what it is or where it comes from or why it is so intent on slaying all sentient life! We have the Vwoordha's explanation for it. I've told you that. But we don't have the time to consider Time or whether what the Vwoordha say is true or not.

'We are beings of the immediate. We are sentients who live, in a sense, in the past and the future. But never as fully as in the immediate. And immediately, now, we have an enemy. We know what has happened in the past; we know what it will do in the future. Unless we stop it!

'I am the only one who has known, however dimly, what has been going on! Therefore, I am the one who will lead you against the *bolg*!'

He did not say that doing this might recompense for his sins against them and against himself.

Because of the residue of the backwash of the *glyfa's* transceivering, they might still be dazed, overawed, mentally and emotionally turbulent, and, thus, unsure. Eager to fasten onto one who did seem sure.

Whatever the reason, they cheered him, clutched each other, danced around, wept, shouted, screamed, or gestured their defiance of the *bolg* and their faith in him.

'Ramstan! Ramstan! Ramstan!'

Uttering his name, they were also uttering their own.

He held up his hands for silence. It was a long time coming, but he was patient. However short the period allotted for action, there was a time for patience and a time for impatience.

Out of the corner of his eyes, he saw that Benagur's body was being carried away. Nevertheless, the faces of the bearers were turned to their captain; they were not concentrating on their task.

Poor Benagur! He may have gone further than I did. Why ... *poor* Benagur?

If the mind could be launched from the body, shot towards union with the mind of God, or the Pluriverse, then it would eventually be betrayed. God or the Pluriverse would die. Would the mind of the God-pulled moth then die, too? Or was there a haven, a repository, where, just as the *glyfa* and the Vwoordha endured between eons, the One-magnetized mind also endured?

As Toyce had once said, 'You can't turn around in this world without bumping into a question. The answers are all hiding somewhere.'

In expanding universes, the answers had more than enough room to hide. But when the universes collapsed, would the refugee answers come streaming in, obeying the eons-long *olly olly oxen free?* If it happened, who then would care about them?

The com-op said, 'Sir! Lieutenant Davis requests permission to board.'

'Permission granted. Tell her to report to me now.'

Branwen ran onto the bridge. She began weeping as soon as she saw Ramstan.

'I was so scared, so lonely!' she cried.

'I'm sorry,' he said. 'But you're here now. Get to your post.'

'Aren't you afraid I'll blow up?'

'That's a chance we'll take. I don't think that you will. Too much time has passed. Anyway ...'

He wanted to say that she had suffered too much and, besides, the danger, whether existent or not, did not matter much anymore. The words could not get out; it was like trying to give birth to a dying baby.

He was startled when her face got red and rage replaced grief.

'You son of a bitch!'

'What? I thought you'd be thankful ...'

'If it wasn't for you, I'd never have been in that mess!'

'True,' he said evenly. 'Now ... I've given you some slack, Lieutenant, because of your trying situation. That's over. Get to your post or arrest yourself and go to your quarters.'

'Holy Mother of God!' she said. She whirled and stalked off.

He said to Tenno, 'Find out what she intends to do. Someone will have to fill her post if ...'

'Captain, see this,' the com-op said. 'VP S06.'

Ramstan looked at the indicated viewplate. A section of the lowest story of the Vwoordha's house had swung open, and a vessel of curious shape was coming out. It looked more like an ancient inkpot than anything. Inside the transparent hull were Shiyai and Grrindah, sitting cross-legged on rugs and pillows. Ramstan could see no control boards or instruments of any kind. The space under the upper deck, also transparent, was empty.

The vessel moved up a few meters from the ground and shot around the root-swelling. Ramstan had to listen then to reports from various parts of ship, but he kept an eye on the viewplate.

Within ten minutes, the vessel reappeared. The huge lower space was half-filled with the liquid from the well. It was clear, and he could not see it, but it was evident that it was enclosed in the vessel. Halfway up the lower part, seemingly floating or swimming in air, were the three strange pets. The kangaroolike thing seemed to look directly into Ramstan's eyes, and its mouth opened in unheard laughter. The giant salmon seemed to fix one eye on him. The bottomless eyes of the shimmering thing seemed, briefly, to encompass him, and he felt as if he were falling.

'Captain, are you all right?' Tenno said.

'Of course. Why?'

'You were pale; you staggered.'

Ramstan did not reply. He watched the vessel move into the house and the section close like the grim mouth of a sphinx that has swallowed back the secrets she was about to tell. A minute later, all was ready for the take-off of *al-Buraq*. There was, however, the question of how the Vwoordha would accomplish their promise to leave with Ramstan. Was he supposed to wait until they sent a messenger? If so, they would be frustrated. He would not wait another sixty seconds.

He started. A voice spoke within him. It was Shiyai, not the *glyfa*, activating it. Though it was not her voice as he'd heard it in the ancient house, he knew it was she because she now identified herself. His reaction had been caused, however, not by the unexpectedness of the voice but because he suddenly recognized it. He had heard it before, when he was awakening from the doze in the Kalafalan tavern.

'Shiyai!' he said. 'No. Omar ibn Wu Tai. My best friend when I was a child. He drowned at the age of eleven in the *Shatt-al-Arab*. We were great friends, fished, hiked, wrestled, played on the same baseball team. He was my catcher. He was also a wonderful teller of scary tales, he would frighten me with stories of djinns, ogres, marids, rocs, from *The Thousand and One Nights*, from Japanese horror stories, from Slavic and Finnish tales ...'

He stopped. He had no time for this. But hearing Omar's voice had stirred up something. Something that was waiting to be stirred.

'Why are you using his voice?' he said. 'Are you trying to push me a certain way?'

'I can't choose the voice,' Shiyai said with some asperity. 'The choice is made by your unconscious. How, I don't know.'

His mental or emotional state or both determined which voice was evoked, he thought. Omar's had spoken because of the frightful implications of the Vwoordha's words. But how would his unconscious know which voice to use until the words were spoken? It could be that it heard the first few but blocked out his reception of them, then fed them back to him after the vocal speaker in his mind had been selected.

What of the visions, the thing that he had thought was al-Khidhr? He had never seen that mythical being. No. But he had seen pictures of him in storybooks, and he had formed his own image of him.

He looked at the chronometer.

'We're leaving in a few seconds.'

'Wait two minutes. We'll be ready.'

The digits flashed on the chronometer. When eighty seconds had passed, he saw the three-storied house begin to rise. It ascended slowly, vegetation and pieces of earth falling from the base. There was also a very long worm, or perhaps it was a serpent, which was wrapped around a clod of dirt which adhered stubbornly to the rounded base. The clod fell and with it the worm, writhing as if it were trying to form hieroglyphics.

The alarms sounded. After assurance that all was ready, Ramstan gave the order to follow the house-spaceship of the Vwoordha. Once in orbit, however, *al-Buraq* would take the lead. Ramstan would no longer trail behind or be pushed ahead.

31

Coming around the curve of the planet, Ramstan saw the great horned sphere of the *bolg*. It looked like the head of Shaitan, al-Eblis, rearing up from the depths of Hell. But it was just an elemental thing produced by Nature, formed unconsciously by a Creature. Moreover, from a different viewpoint, it might have looked like the head of an avenging angel. Was not its function *good* for the Pluriverse, as good as Ramstan's was for him? It was here to preserve the life of the cosmic being, and he was here to preserve the lives of those who inhabited that being.

'Both winner and loser foul out,' Ramstan muttered.

'What, Captain?' Tenno said.

'What captain?' Ramstan said viciously, but he laughed.

Al-Buraq, having measured the distance between her and the *bolg* and their relative velocities, began to decelerate. It would be six hours before ship caught up with the thing. Behind her, at a distance of 60 kilometers, was the Vwoordha vessel. Not decelerating as much as *al-Buraq*, it would soon be alongside Ramstan's craft.

He went down to his quarters and put the *glyfa* on a table top.

'If you have anything to say, do it now,' he said. 'I'll soon be too busy to listen to you. I don't want you distracting my attention then.'

'So ... you've heard the voice of God,' the *glyfa* said in his mother's voice. 'It doesn't seem to have made much difference in you.'

'It's the voice of an idiot,' Ramstan said. 'An awesome idiot, true. No. That isn't quite right. An idiot has no potentiality for a higher intelligence. This being has.'

'Then be Its teacher, Its father,' the *glyfa* said. 'Let us both be Its mentor and nurse.'

'And then?'

'Don't think for one moment that you or I or anyone could control It. It may not be truly God, as sentients define God, but Its powers will be staggering. We could not ...'

'Not be Its masters? Why not? We'd have an emotional grip on It. Whatever Its other powers, It would be as a child to Its parents. And some ... many parents are tyrants and use the child for their own purposes.'

'Then it depends upon the parent. Do you think that either of us is capable of using It for evil?'

'I am,' Ramstan said. 'And you haven't proved, can't prove, that you aren't.'

'What about the Vwoordha?'

'I cannot see into their nature any deeper than I can see into yours.'

'Have faith in me.'

Ramstan laughed and said, 'There is only One in whom we should have faith. And that One, as you know, depends upon us and is out to kill us, though It doesn't know it. You must be desperate if you make an appeal like that.'

'I'm never desperate. I can wait.'

'For what? For whom? For how long? Do you think that in the succeeding Pluriverse you'll find anyone different from me? And, if you do, that one will use you solely for his ends.'

'You're not?'

'I am capable of evil and have done evil. But my ends now are not evil. Being not-evil doesn't necessarily make me good. It doesn't matter. I have decided. I will not change my mind.'

'The index of a rigid mind and rotten nature,' the *glyfa* said.

'Your traps are sprung, and I'm still free.'

'No one is truly free.'

'But I know that I am.'

'You *know* nothing.'

'You're wrong. The one thing that I truly know is that I *know* nothing. Therefore, I do not know nothing. Goodbye, *glyfa*. I won't be seeing or listening to you again.'

'You can't stop me from talking and you hearing!' the *glyfa* cried in the mother's voice. 'So much for free will!'

The piteous tone in the voice vised his heart. But he said, 'The free will consists in ignoring your voice.'

He turned and walked swiftly from his quarters. On the way to the bridge, he said, 'Shiyai! Were you eavesdropping?'

'Yes,' his father's voice said. 'Ramstan, what now? When you rejected the *glyfa*, were you accepting us?'

He might need the Vwoordha. He said, 'For the moment. What I do after ... if ... we kill the *bolg* depends on what you do now.'

'We will earn your faith. The *glyfa* doesn't understand that that is how you get others to have faith in you.'

'It's had long enough to learn how,' Ramstan said. He thought, And so have you.

The minutes, the hours, marched slowly by strewing flowers of anxiety. The tension became heavier, as if it were air compressed under a slowly driving piston in a cylinder. It strummed in the chests of some like a fine but strong wire being pulled at both ends and in others like the heaviness preceding a heart attack. Stomachs were twisting like Möbius strips or bobbing like apples in a tub.

In all minds was the image of the Tolt ship exploding.

'If the *bolg* fires soon at a great distance, we can avoid the missiles,' Ramstan said to Tenno. 'I don't think that the missiles are self-propelled and -guided. They're like shotgun pellets discharged at a general area. If the *bolg* waits until we're close, we can try to evaporate them with lasers. Our success will depend on how many are shot within a certain time.

'However, the *bolg* may not have any missiles as yet. Or it may have only a few, in which case we may destroy or evade them.

'The Vwoordha think that our lasers and atomic bombs will not damage its surface at all. They think, though they don't know, that the *bolg's* shell is made out of the same material as the *glyfa's*. We'll launch four warhead-missiles which will be programmed to land within an area of 0.1 kilometer. At the same time, we'll concentrate all ten forward lasers on another nearby area not more than 0.1 meter in diameter.'

'If these fail to wound it ... I mean, damage it?'

'We alaraf. Maybe. I may decide on another move. It'll depend on the situation.'

The bridge personnel were tense, but a component of their tightness was not, Ramstan thought, caused by the approaching conflict. They had accepted him again as their captain but only during this emergency. He did not doubt that, once it was over, he would be relieved of his command and arrested. Regulations required that, though, just now, regulations were suspended. That they were thinking of this was betrayed in their faces, their voices, and subtle body movements.

To relieve some of this tension and to occupy some time, Ramstan told them about the sigils and how he had traveled roundabout back to the Vwoordha.

'Then,' Tenno said, 'that means that the Vwoordha can still get away.'

'Yes.'

'Even if we die, they don't. Neither does the *glyfa*.'

Ramstan did not reply. He ordered food for the hungry. He stayed on the bridge and chewed down half a sandwich and drank a big glass of milk. His stomach would tolerate no more and almost did not accept that.

Doctor Hu called Ramstan from the morgue.

'I've completed the dissection. Commodore Benagur died of a massive heart attack. Do you want the medical details now?'

'No. I'll read your report later,' Ramstan said. He thought, If there is a later.

He paced back and forth, his arms behind him, hands locked, shoulders and back bent forward. His reflection in the only mirror on the bridge looked like a weird bird, one that Tenniel might have drawn for *Through the Looking Glass* if Carroll had thought of such. The 'Worry Bird'? After that, though he continued pacing, he walked with shoulders and back straight and his hands swinging by his sides. It would not do for the crew to see him so deeply concerned.

After a few more turns around the bridge, he stopped. 'Tenno, I'm not going to use the weapons unless we're attacked. The Vwoordha have told me that they might not affect the *bolg* in the slightest. Why awaken the sleeping giant?'

Tenno looked at the viewplate showing the *bolg*.

'Napoleon's words, more or less, right? Well, it's not China, but I think his advice is appropriate.'

'It's possible that its detectors aren't on,' Ramstan said. 'It's not ready for action. Its recharging. Why should it expend even a minimum of energy on powering detectors? It's invulnerable. I mean that its exterior is. Even a very large asteroid would do no more than bump it off its orbit, and it must have swept space far enough to notice anything like that. As for us, it may think us negligible ... well, I don't mean that it thinks, it surely is as brainless and as mechanical as a virus ... what I mean is that its reaction mechanisms, its tropisms and antitropisms, would not make it react to us. It might have stored data about us to track us down when Grrymguurdha has been raked with missiles. But I suspect that it went into a sort of hibernation when it got into its orbit. We'll ease up on it and see if we can sneak by it.'

'Good thinking,' Shiyai said in his father's voice.

Both the *bolg* and *al-Buraq* were on the nightside of the planet now. The shadow of the dark world beneath made a crescent on the *bolg*. One of the markings which looked like the eye of a skull was bright; the other, unseen. Almost, the *bolg* seemed to be winking at them as if it was enjoying a grim jest and wanted even its victims to share in it.

It was rotating as Earth's moon turned, just enough to keep one side towards the planet. This had been calculated for, and so *al-Buraq* moved towards the vast opening of one vast horn in a path which would intercept it. The hours went by. The opening, so tiny at first, swelled larger and larger. *Al-Buraq*, in accordance with the program, decelerated. It would not do to enter the horn at such a velocity that ship would smash herself against the inside or have to slow down so quickly that her crew would be splashed against the bulkheads.

The energy from the deceleration would be detectable, of course. Ramstan hoped that it would not cause the *bolg* to react.

Its face was as cold and impersonal as that of Earth's moon and it looked as lifeless as the moon or a mechanical object, an artifact. But it was neither a thing of never-alive matter nor a thing made by sentient mind and hands. It was alive, though it surely had no more consciousness than a bacterium or a virus or an antibody. Functionally, it was an antibody produced by a living organism to protect it from destructive bacteria or cancer.

The horn was made of the same dark substance as the body. It rose at a right angle to the surface to a height of 999.9 kilometers. The diameter at the muzzle was 3.33 kilometers; at the base, 333.3 kilometers. Not even the Vwoordha knew what force expelled the missiles from it, but they thought that it was an electromagnetic field. The missiles must be made by energy-matter conversion in matrices inside the *bolg*. Though the thing had a surface area of almost 531 million square kilometers, its intake of solar energy would not be enough for it to make many projectiles in a short time. But perhaps it did not use solar energy.

As *al-Buraq* neared the expanding hole at the tip of the horn, she applied gasjet deceleration instead of the energy used at higher velocities. Presently, ship was moving just enough to match the pace of the slowly turning *bolg*. The hole was illumined by the sun on the side away from the planet; the light formed a crescent. The rest was darkness.

More gasjetting turned ship's nose downwards until her longitudinal axis was lined up with that of the horn.

This was perhaps the most nerve-ratcheting time so far. For all Ramstan knew, the *bolg* had been waiting for this. At any second, millions of the missiles might shoot out of that muzzle. Ship's radar might give a second's notice. Even though at this point of entry, *al-Buraq* could still use alaraf drive and though *al-Buraq* was programmed to go alaraf immediately on detection of missiles, she might not be quick enough. Ship and crew would die as the *Popacapyu* had died.

'I hope the *bolg* discharged the last of its missiles at the Tolt,' Ramstan muttered.

There was no use waiting. He gave the order – the electromechanical communication system was not necessary now – and *al-Buraq*, nudged by small spurts of gasjets, moved down the hole.

32

'As easy as slipping milk down a baby's throat,' Tenno said.

'As easy as a minnow entering a shark's mouth,' Toyce said.

Ramstan said, 'Quiet! No talking until I say so.'

On a viewplate and on the radar and laser screens was the three-tiered househip of the Vwoordha. It shone in the sun and was behind *al-Buraq* by a kilometer. Its hull would not be pierced by the missiles. However, it would be hurled backwards at such a velocity that its occupants would be spread out paper-thin against the walls.

The househip plunged into the darkness. The Vwoordha were fully committed. Ramstan had not been sure that they would be.

The detector plates and screens showed pictures of the hollow. The sides were as smooth as a bull's horn and opened out downwards. Then the entrance to the sphere was ahead of them. *Al-Buraq* passed slowly through it. Now the detectors probed the interior of the *bolg*. Unlike the smooth exterior surface, the inside surface was crowded with regular rows of stalagmite-shaped structures. These ranged in height from 0.5 centimeter to 66.6 kilometers. The arrangement was in no sequence that could be figured out as yet. Sometimes, there would be sixty of the tall structures and sometimes several hundred of the tiny ones beside those. Sometimes, one or two or three tall structures would be flanked by thousands of the shorter ones.

The other phenomena so far detected were not in the visible spectrum.

Some were in the ultraviolet; some, in the infrared. They shot out from a sphere that hung in the center of the sphere, a dark interior moon of the body of the *bolg*. They were of various shapes as they flickered off and on: lanceolate, pyramidal, tonguelike, some rodlike with balls forming at their slender tips. The 'slender' was relative, since their diameter was probably approximately three kilometers. The ball hanging in the center was large enough to be an asteroid, 135.791 kilometers in diameter. It was rotating at its equator at 379.17 kilometers per hour.

The tec-op said, 'Captain! Something else!'

Ramstan looked at the indicated screen. Far below the lip of the hole through which they had just emerged was a bulk as big as a mountain. The tec-op covered it with finer-tuned detectors, narrowed down the field, and several thousand of the larger spherical projectiles were clear on the screen. At Ramstan's order, the tec-op broadened the screen. The entire pile was larger than Mount Everest; it was 100 kilometers wide and 12 kilometers high.

Other screens showed similar-sized piles around or below the other five openings.

'The *bolg* isn't turning swiftly enough to make centrifugal force there,' Ramstan said. 'What's keeping the missiles from floating off?'

The tec-op said, 'There's a weak e-m field there, sir.'

Ramstan told him to focus on the edge of the nearest pile. The scanners moved slowly along the circumference, then stopped at an order from Ramstan. A tiny bead had suddenly dropped onto the pile and bounced off onto the smooth floor between two stalagmitoids. Within two minutes more it began putting on layers. Meanwhile, other beads fell and started to go through the same process.

The instruments indicated a tremendous amount of energy concentrated in narrow fields.

Ramstan thought that eventually the missiles would be lifted by e-m force to the hollow horn and moved up it. When the *bolg* was ready, it would propel these out of the horn. But to hit even in the general direction of its targets must require some directing force. Perhaps that was in the missiles themselves. It did not seem likely. Yet, the missiles functioned with great efficiency.

'Head for the globe in the center,' he said. 'That must be the heart of the thing, the main generator or converter.'

Shiyai spoke in his father's voice. 'Ramstan. What do you plan?'

'We'll place all our warhead-missiles around the central globe. We'll set them up to be activated by radio signal. We'll go to the exterior then, and we'll set the warheads off by signal transmitted through the horn opening. If that doesn't do it, then I don't know what we'll do.'

'Captain!'

The tec-op pointed at the colors and numbers flickering wildly on his screens. 'There's a hell of a lot of energy out there!'

There was the entrances to the horns. The piles beneath them were moving, their individual parts rising toward the holes. Even as he watched, the mountains disappeared. But more spheres, small and large, were forming.

'It's a trap!' Toyce said.

Ramstan did not bother to rebuke her. He was very shaken himself. He did not think that the *bolg* had a mind. Therefore, it had not deliberately waited until the vessels were within it. It was their misfortune not to have entered much sooner. They had come in just before the *bolg*, acting on whatever commands it obeyed, was moving its first loads to the tip of the horns. The next loads would be deposited behind the first. That would take a long time, but might be too late for the ships to get out. All the holes would be jammed with missiles.

He gave the order. *Al-Buraq* and its companion curved slowly around and headed for the nearest hole. The maneuver did not take long since they were going so slowly. But when the vessels entered the horn, the detectors confirmed that the tip was no longer open. Their passage was blocked.

It was not necessary to announce what had happened.

Every face on the bridge said, dumbly, 'What do we do now?'

The warhead-missiles could be sent against the pile. They would vaporize some of it but not enough. The lasers could then set about drilling a tunnel through the fused shell. But their power would give out long before the work was done.

Even if they could get out, they would have left the *bolg* undamaged. It would continue to stock its projectiles.

Shiyai said gently in his mother's voice, 'We three can sit here until the way is clear. We will not run out of food and water. But if we shared with you, we would.'

'And if we stay here until we starve to death, then you can come in and get the *glyfa*,' Ramstan said.

'That mind of yours! No, we did not plot this. The turn of events is as much a surprise to us as to you. Well, almost. Having lived much longer than you, we can figure out probabilities much better. We knew that this might happen. Nevertheless, we took the chance. And lost.'

'You won't die,' Ramstan said.

'Our will to live may end before our bodies do. It has been a long time, a time unimaginably long to you.'

'And unendurable to me,' Ramstan said. 'Somehow, somewhere in me, I knew that it would happen this way.'

'Perhaps that is because you wanted it that way.'

Again, he thought of the possibility that he might have been drawn into the *glyfa* some time ago and now was playing out his own fantasy. It was not likely. But, by Allah, if it were true, he was at least governing his own life, even if it was a fantasy. The *glyfa* could never think of a scenario like this.

'I'm not unhappy about it. Not for me. But the others …'

'That spinning ball in the center,' Shiyai said. 'Your detectors bounce off it as if it were some solid matter and give readings indicating that it is. But it's not. It's an energy configuration.'

Ramstan was silent for a moment. Those around him were looking strangely at him. Was it because his lips were moving? He had explained to them that, when he subvocalized, he was talking to the Vwoordha or the *glyfa*. No. They were wondering what he would do to get them out of this trap.

'Our instruments couldn't detect that. How do you know?'

'Do you think that because our house isn't fitted with all those flashing lights and screens and knobs and dials that we don't have a science and technology far beyond yours?'

'No, I don't think that. But since you do have all that, why would you need my … our help?'

'Because we are very, very, very old. Though we've gained much, we've lost much. There are things you can do that we can't because you are young. I'm not talking about strength of mind or muscle. I'm talking about spirit. The spirit grows old with or without the body, Ramstan. Never mind that. What now?'

'I'll try to disrupt the energy configuration of the central globe with the same means I would have tried if it had been matter.'

'That might do it. Still …'

'I know,' he said.

He spoke to the people in *al-Buraq* then, knowing that the *glyfa* and the Vwoordha were listening in. He also knew that there was another, someone deep inside him, the dumb thing which spoke sometimes more loudly and forcefully than he.

There was a long silence after he had finished.

Finally, Tenno said, 'It's a hell of a choice.'

'Most are.'

'Then, regardless of what we decide to do, you have decided on the one … path?'

'What I'm going to do is far easier than what you will do. I know what's going to happen to me. I know the end. You don't. Not yet, anyway.'

Shiyai said, 'We can take three. They'll be safe from the radiation. Once the *bolg* has spent its supply of missiles, we can escape. What the three want to do after we get out is up to them. We can drop them off anywhere in this universe. But they'll never see Earth again.'

'They may prefer the *glyfa*,' Ramstan said, 'though I don't know that it will take them or any of us. It hasn't said.'

'I will take all,' his mother's voice said. 'All. I'd like to receive you, too.'

'No.'

'Very well. I'll tell you just how it is done.'

Ramstan repeated the words of the voice in his mind so that all ship's crew would understand. When he was finished, he said, 'The *glyfa* says that you will have a fine life, far better than you could get on Earth, while in it. I don't agree with that. If you gain something, you lose something. But that's up to you. Anyway, some time, maybe in the next Pluriverse, you'll come across some culture which will be able to put your neural electronic configuration into bodies of artificial protein constructed to your specifications. It says that that will happen; it's a high statistical probability. But, in the meantime ...'

'It's better than dying,' Toyce said.

'Anything is,' Tenno said.

'No,' Ramstan said.

Nuoli said, 'Why don't we wait this out? The *bolg* may empty itself before we run out of food and water. We should take that chance.'

'I've had *al-Buraq* estimate the time that would require. The time it takes for the formation of a complete load of missiles – based on the speculation that the *bolg* won't fill itself entirely, and I don't know if it will or won't – the time it's taking for *X* amount of missiles to form now, calculated against our supplies ... no, we will starve before then.

'It will have to pause between the present missile-making and the next. It must recharge another time, maybe many times, before it can load itself up. That estimated time is twice as long as the estimate based on a continuous charging.'

The tec-op said, 'Sir, The missile-production rate is slowing.'

'I am not surprised,' Ramstan said.

The others looked at each other. Ramstan said, 'Tenno, have someone bring the *glyfa* to the third-deck auditorium. I'll tell *al-Buraq* to open the door to my quarters.'

'See,' his uncle's voice said. 'You said you'd never see me again. But you will. You never know what is going to happen. Even I, who've lived so long, don't know.'

'I know,' Ramstan said.

A minute later, the tec-op said, 'Sir, the production seems to have stopped.'

The varishaped beams from the globe in the center had also ceased. The *bolg* was recharging.

Suddenly, the many indicators on many panels turned a bright flashing orange, and alarms shrilled.

Ramstan ran to the tec-op and looked over her shoulder.

'What is it?'

'We're losing energy, sir! Something's draining our fuel supply! But there isn't any leakage! See for yourself, sir!'

His mother's voice spoke. 'The *bolg* must be draining the energy from the fuel. It may also be draining your energy, the life from your bodies.'

Ramstan had enough self-control to impose even more on himself. He said, coolly, 'Are you affected also?'

'No. Our hull resists the draining effect. The *glyfa's* shell also resists.'

Ramstan had not been sure until then that the speaker was not the *glyfa*.

'You won't take more than three of us?'

'Only three.'

'Cut off all the alarm indicators except on one screen,' Ramstan said to the tec-op. 'Turn off all unnecessary illumination, and reduce what's still on to half.'

He had to conserve all the energy aboard. He did not know how swiftly the draining progressed.

He called Doctor Hu. 'Dispense all the candy bars, vitamins, and protein pills to all personnel. They're going to need it. Tenno will explain why.'

Energy was probably being withdrawn from the food, but they would still give extra energy to the crew.

He silently cursed. He had been on the point of changing his decision to act at once instead of waiting to determine how long the recharging and missile-production took. Now, he had no choice.

He called for quiet throughout ship and then announced what had happened.

'We may have very little time. The indicators are registering an alarming rate of energy loss.'

He was beginning to feel weak. But that could be his imagination.

'Tenno! Nuoli, Davis, and Toyce will go at once to the Vwoordha's house. At once.'

'Why those three?' Tenno said.

'I don't know why.'

He subvocalized, 'Shiyai, did you hear?'

'I heard. We can lock into a port. They won't have to get into space suits. And, Ramstan …'

'Yes?'

Shiyai seemed reluctant to say what she must.

'The energy is being sucked out from your warheads and the power of your lasers. If you wait too long, the bombs and lasers will be too weak to affect the generator sphere.'

'I know!'

He looked at a data screen. *Al-Buraq* would arrive within 1,000 kilometers of the generator-sphere in twenty minutes. He could order that the warhead missiles be released now and the lasers concentrated on a spot on that whirling energy-configuration. Since the energy from ship and its crew and its fuel and the warheads was being sucked out by that monstrous vampire in some manner unknown to his scientists, he could command that the attack begin at once. But he could not do so until his people had gotten to a safe place: the *glyfa* and the Vwoordha's house.

When the vast power of the lasers and the warheads hit that sphere hanging in the center of the *bolg*, the sphere should be disrupted. It would, according to the Vwoordha, release an energy that would make that of the lasers and the warheads look feeble. The now-incoherent power would raven outwards from the core of this thing. Though the spherical shell of the *bolg* had a diameter of 13,000 kilometers, it would be filled with a destroying energy equaled only at the heart of a star.

His mother's voice spoke, and he knew that it was the *glyfa* who was simulating it and not Shiyai. He could detect a very slight trace of the personality of the *glyfa* or the Vwoordha in that voice.

'Tell everybody except the three women to come to the third-level auditorium at once. Davis and Toyce will be in the Vwoordha's house within a minute. Nuoli is still in ship. She will stay here until she can take me to the house. She won't go near the auditorium, however, until the passage of the crew into me has been completed. That will take no more than a microsecond, but they have to be close to me. Nuoli would be drawn in, too, if she were near. When I make a mass transit like this, I cannot discriminate. All nearby are drawn in.'

There was a pause. His mother's voice spoke again, but this time it was activated by Shiyai.

'As soon as Nuoli is in the house, we will notify you. You must wait five minutes after that before launching the attack.'

Another pause. Then his mother's voice said, 'Tell them to gather around me as closely as possible. Those nearest me must put their fingers on me, and each person not touching me should put his hands on others. They should also have body contact. Tell them to crowd as closely together as possible.'

Ramstan gave the orders as directed. The bridge personnel left immediately, though several, especially Tenno, wished to say good-bye.

'No, not even a handshake,' Ramstan said. 'Get going! Run! I will talk to you, all of you, through the screens while you're on your way to the auditorium.'

'It's not right,' Tenno said, but he obeyed, saluting as he ran.

Ramstan left the bridge and walked towards his quarters. He was going there because it was … what? Home? A womb? Both?

But he talked as he walked, and his words and image were caught and transmitted to all the other moving screens.

He chanted *The Saying Of Allah's Command to Annihilate All Things*, the chant which he had heard so often when the neighbors who were also members of the al-Khidhr sect met in his parents' apartment.

'The angel of death is ordered by Allah to destroy the oceans.

'The angel of death comes to the oceans and says, "Your time to end is now."

'The oceans say, "Grant us time to sorrow and to contemplate our wonders and majesties."

'The angel of death says that there is no more time for the oceans, and he shouts once, and the oceans are gone.

'After the angel of death has destroyed the oceans, he travels to the mountains, the Earth itself, the moon, the sun, and the stars, and each begs for a little more time, a year, a month, a week, a day, an hour, seven seconds. But the angel grants them nothing, and he shouts, and they are not, as if they had never been.

'Allah then says, "O angel of death, what of my creation is left?"

'And the angel of death replies, "O Allah, only You and Your angels live."

'Then Allah says, "Angels, did you not hear Me say that everyone must taste death? Do not beg for more time."

'And so the angel of death and all the other angels died, and they are as if they had never been created.

'And only His Face lived.'

And, Ramstan thought, not even He – It, rather – lives forever.

I will not plead for more time.

He said, 'I have chanted this because, hearing it, you might understand why I am not going into the *glyfa* or the house of the Vwoordha.'

He stopped before the iris-door to his quarters, spoke the code word, and stepped through the opening. It closed for the last time.

He went to the prayer rug, stooped, and turned it so that the red arrowhead symbol, the *kiblah*, was pointed at him.

He pushed down the impulse to kneel upon the rug. No. He would not do that. But he would stand here with the tip of his boot touching the edge of the rug.

Why had he pointed the *kiblah* at himself? Did he think that he was God?

The Sufi mystic al-Mansur had thought that he was God. At least, he had said so in the marketplace, and he had been stoned to death for his blasphemy. Yet – he had meant that he was part of God, just as all human beings were.

Now he could see on a screen that everyone in ship except himself and

Nuoli was in the auditorium room. *Al-Buraq* had expanded the room to make space for the almost four hundred people. And she had not extruded seats for them as she would have done if they had come to hear a lecture or watch a live drama. They stood on a level floor, forming concentric circles, the innermost with their fingers on the egg, those behind pressing closely against them, their hands grasping the hands of others, and those behind them pressing against them.

Ramstan said, 'I wish that things ... I ... had been different. But if I could start all over again, I think that I would not be or act differently. You have done and are doing what you think is best to do. I have done and am doing what I think is best for me to do.'

He choked for a moment, cleared his throat, and said, 'You may forget me, but don't forget what I stand for. Good-bye.'

They had no time to say anything to him. They fell jammed together, their open eyes seeing nothing. There was no display of energy, no slight thickening of air in threads or clouds as the part that made them unique and sentient passed into the *glyfa*.

'It is done,' his mother's voice said. 'Hûd, you still have time to join them.'

'No.'

'They will soon be walking inside this little shell which will seem to them as big as Earth, as big as the universes if they wish.'

'No.'

Maija Nuoli entered the auditorium, looked horrifiedly at the corpses, looked at the screen displaying his image, and then, wincing, walked over the bodies. She picked up the *glyfa*, held it to her breasts, and walked back over the bodies. Just before she got to the exit, she looked up again at the screen.

'Good-bye, Hûd. God be with you. I loved you once for a brief while, then I hated you. But I think I love you again.'

'I made a fatal mistake,' Ramstan said. 'I loved answers to my questions more than I loved human beings. The only answers that mattered – the only questions, too – were people. I have been only an agent for the *glyfa* and the Vwoordha. I have been nudged and prodded and moved here and there toward some destination unknown to me until now. The plot was as vast and as dark as this hollow thing we are now in. But, though it might seem so to others, I was no mechanical agent. I had choice. I decided to do what I wished to do. I moved from darkness to a brief light and back to darkness, but I am in the light again. This time, it is my own light, not that of others. It's mine, and it's bright enough for me to see what I'm doing. If darkness presses around me, it is not as close as it was. Few are lucky enough to have even this little flicker.

'Maija Nuoli, whatever happens, may you have your own light.'

'Well spoken,' Shiyai said in his mother's voice. 'But you should not die as you have lived, always suspicious. However, that does not matter now. As a parting gift, you will be allowed to see what happens to the three women.'

'What do you mean?'

'That you need not fear that something bad will happen to them because they are in our house. Now, Ramstan. You have turned down the *glyfa's* last offer. It is probably a waste of time to ask you if you will change your mind about coming with us. Despite what we told your crew, we do have room for one more. You can join us now if you wish. It is not good to live alone, and it is worse to die alone.'

'No.'

'I thought so.'

The *glyfa* said, 'We are in the house, Ramstan. Wait for five minutes.'

Shiyai said, 'See. Hear.'

The images before him were pale and wavering and so transparent he could see through the people and monsters to the objects in the bridge. The Vwoordha were in a room he had not seen before, a round room with a round pool in its center, and they were in the liquid up to their waists. They were holding hands. By them, helping to form a circle, were Toyce, Nuoli, and Davis. All three looked scared. Nuoli held the *glyfa* to her chest. By her side was the great salmonlike creature, its head against her left leg. On the fish's other side, one hand on the top of the fish, the other touching the shimmering thing, was 'the laugher who hops'.

The shimmering thing, 'the cold-blood who drinks hot blood', was touching Wopolsa.

'We've formed a circle, and I am going to put into my mouth the first of the sigils,' Shiyai said. 'I will do that as soon as I can determine whether or not you have destroyed the heart of the *bolg*.

'Wopolsa has been calculating the probabilities of destruction of the *bolg*. She's done more than that. She sees ... a little beyond what Grrindah and I can see. Anyway, she says that you have a 75 percent chance of success. Those are good odds, Ramstan.

'Also, we three will die some day. Rather, Grrindah and I will. Wopolsa will die, too, though not as we do. She will go ... somewhere else. In the meantime, we three will be teaching these three as much as they can learn. And, some day, they will become the Vwoordha. If they wish to, of course. I think that they will.

'So, good-bye, Ramstan. We won't be seeing you again, but we may see your like.'

Ramstan laughed, and he said, 'Are you even now thinking of the time when you may need another like me?'

'There may be other *bolgs*.'

He looked at the flashing figures on a screen.

The five minutes had passed while he was looking into the house of the Vwoordha, though he would have sworn that he had done so for no more than thirty seconds.

He opened his mouth. The code word that would tell *al-Buraq* to launch the missiles and shoot the lasers hung glowing in his mind, glowing as brightly as the numbers that told the time on the screen.

Why had he chosen his mother's name, Kadijah, as the codeword?

No more questions.

He shouted.

If you've enjoyed these books and would like to read more, you'll find literally thousands of classic Science Fiction & Fantasy titles through the **SF Gateway**

✶

For the new home of Science Fiction & Fantasy . . .

✶

For the most comprehensive collection of classic SF on the internet . . .

✶

Visit the SF Gateway

www.sfgateway.com

Philip José Farmer (1918–2009)

Philip José Farmer was born in Indiana in 1918. Although he once said he resolved to become a writer in the fourth grade, it wasn't until 1952 that his first SF was published – the novella 'The Lovers', which won him the Hugo Award for Most Promising New Author. Although best known for his Riverworld sequence, beginning with the Hugo Award-winning *To Your Scattered Bodies Go*, Farmer also pioneered the use of sexual and religious themes in SF and wrote several novels reworking the lore of celebrated pulp heroes such as Tarzan and Doc Savage. He also wrote the tongue-in-cheek *Venus on the Half-Shell* using the pseudonym 'Kilgore Trout', a character who appeared in several Kurt Vonnegut novels. Philip José Farmer won three Hugos, a World Fantasy Award for Life Achievement and the Damon Knight Memorial Grand Master Award. He died in 2009.